SHE WAS AS INTOXICATING AS A DRUG . . .

Yana was half relieved and half disappointed that he was departing without attempting to seduce her. She longed to feel his arms about her, to taste his lips, to join her body with his. She walked him to the door, but he turned before he pressed the open button.

Dagan gazed into her rich blue eyes and scanned her faint blue skin and blond hair with the same blue tinge. "You're a beautiful and desirable woman, Yana; I hope we'll see a lot of each other before you're gone."

"That would please me," she responded. But that was not totally true. Not as Yana, anyway.

JANELLE TAYLOR

MOONBEAMS AND MAGIC

PINNACLE BOOKS
KENSINGTON PUBLISHING CORP.

PINNACLE BOOKS are published by

Kensington Publishing Corp.
850 Third Avenue
New York, NY 10022

Pinnacle and the P logo Reg. U.S. Pat. & TM Off.

First Printing: October, 1995

Printed in the United States of America

One

"Moig . . . we have a complication down here," Starla reported to her teammate on the transporter's upper deck via a wrist communicator. Winded from a struggle with a tall and muscular man moments ago, she explained between gasps for air, "There was an intruder in the last bay. He's human . . . still stoked from his fierce glare . . . but I have him subdued. Do I leave him unconscious or take him with us?"

"No, Vedris, kill him!"

To prevent a surprise attack, Starla Vedris remained on alert at a safe distance, a laser weapon aimed at the center of the auslander's broad chest. She was dismayed by her companion's swift and deadly response, as they tried to avoid trouble during their criminal raids on other spaceships. Her heart pounded in dread and from physical exertions, though she kept her expression impassive. She gazed at the man on his knees, his palms resting on sleek thighs and still breathing hard. A look of astonishment in his dark-blue eyes at being bested in a fight by a female who now had him groveling before her changed to one of anger as he overheard the icy extermination order. She lifted her left arm and spoke into her communication device. "Moig, did you say, 'kill him'?"

"Yes, we can't leave behind an open mouth to speak into the wrong ears about us. He's seen your face and knows our names, so get rid of him. We were told only one android would be aboard this vessel, but our talker was wrong. Somebody's going to catch *Karlee* for this mistake."

"Should we make this crucial decision on our own? You know the penalty for life-taking during a theft: disintegration in an annihilator unit."

"Do it, Vedris, or I'll come send him into oblivion myself! If I have to do your job for you, that'll prove you aren't as brave and loyal as our leader thinks and you'll be out of his hire. Blast him to *Karlee* or he could be the death of us later. Don't forget, I'm in charge. Zap him, Vedris, now!"

Starla took a deep breath and scowled. "Don't zone out, Moig. I'll get rid of him, but this is the only time I'm taking such an order from anybody. I didn't agree to have life-taking charges added to my record, which is already too long and grim for comfort."

"It's for self-defense, woman, to save all of our skins!"

"I said I would do it. Vedris out," she told Moig, ending their talk. She said to her android, who was aboard her ship nearby, "Cypher-T, I'm fine. Thanks for the warning and keep alert for more trouble. No reply needed."

The man stared at the armed and beautiful space pirate who was clad in a snug bronze jumpsuit that covered a shapely figure from slender neck to small wrists and black-booted feet. Long and lustrous brown tresses tumbled over her shoulders in thick waves. Green eyes examined him with what appeared to be a mixture of professional and personal interest. Her tawny complexion was flawless and glowed with good health. Her features were perfect, exquisite, arousing even now in this vexing situation. Her stance and posture exhibited confidence, and implied a dash of arrogance. The way she held her weapon told him she knew how to use it. She had proven she was skilled in hand-to-hand combat. He was amazed—under those grim circumstances and following an embarrassing defeat—that he noticed so much about her, but his perceptions came easily and from an instinct borne of necessity. Was she, he mused, a hazard, even if her lovely features were set in resignation of obedience? Yes, he decided, but he had gotten out of worse predicaments in the past, so he watched for an opening.

Starla knew if she refused to kill him Moig would do so without remorse, and she would be ejected from Tochar's band. She realized there was only one thing she could do to protect herself and her plans. She gave a loud sigh and shrugged. "Sorry, handsome, but you're in the wrong place at the wrong time. You've made your last error in this time phase."

As he started to rise and argue, Starla warned, "Don't be reckless; this weapon isn't set on stun. I can put you down forever before you get to your feet, much less reach me. You may be the best-looking specimen I've ever seen, but I still have my wits and orders. You won't suffer."

"You don't want to do this, Vedris. If you obey him, you'll be in deep trouble. Killing me isn't worth a visit to a disintegration unit or permanent habitation on a penal colony on some barren planetoid. That's no place for a beautiful young woman. If you'll spare my life, I'll—"

"Silence!" she ordered as he fingered his mussed black hair. *Don't let him distract or sway you.* "To fail my leader offers more of a threat than your words coming true. If I betrayed him, there would be no place for me to hide in the entire Microcosm. Too bad, handsome; you would've made a valuable captive on the slave market if I had time to be troubled with you. With your looks and spirit, I bet you'd be an excellent breeder, highly skilled on a *sleeper*." Time was limited. Starla's finger pressed a button on her weapon to fire a beam into his broad chest before the grinning male could respond. A buzzing sound filled the area and a dazzling shaft of light illuminated it. The stranger fell backward and didn't move again.

She lifted her left arm and said, "It's done, Moig. Let's

get this cargo loaded and blast off before any parsec jumpers show their unwanted faces. I'm not in a mood to challenge an *I-GAF*er." The last thing she needed was to be confronted by anyone from the Inter-Galactic Alliance Force! Each of those space rangers was extremely hazardous, and facing more than one meant certain capture or death to *villites!* She knew that *I-GAF*ers—often called "parsec jumpers"—were almost a law unto themselves, elite agents who roamed the five united galaxies of the *UFG* investigating and solving multijurisdictional crimes. No, she didn't want to be thrust into conflict with men of such awesome power and authority; that would ruin or imperil everything she had worked for since leaving her world of Maffei. Thankfully, the Free-Zone was beyond *I-GAF*er reach so its members couldn't interfere with the completion of her crucial goal—if she could make it back there alive. Starla frowned, as the auslander's intrusion struck her as being a bad omen.

"Do you need any help down there?" Moig asked.

"No, I'll be up in a *preon;* I'm finished here. Vedris out," she said, using her alleged last name as was Moig's unusual custom.

Starla switched off the communication link to Moig to complete her task in a hurry, but the one with Cypher—her android—always remained open. She took a last look at the attractive male, then grabbed a tan sack of thin material, dumped its contents, and covered his face before giving him a necessary injection from a phial in her belt holder. She gathered the items she had been sent after and headed for the passageway.

Before she reached the exit, the door swished open and Moig entered the vessel's smallest compartment. "Why did you come down?" Starla asked. "I said I was on my way up. I took care of the problem, and I have the sunbursts. We need to shove off fast; we've taken too long. Even if

*I-GAF*ers aren't in this quadrant, *Sekis* might be; this is Kalfan space."

"This won't delay us much, and your android will warn us if any space rangers appear on his sensors." Moig walked past his vexed companion to where the male was lying as he must have fallen, almost on his stomach. He noticed the sack on the man's head and assumed she hadn't wanted to look her victim in the eye while slaying him. Wisely, he did not tease her about that action. Moig squatted and placed several fingers on the man's jugular vein, waited a few moments, then pressed his ear to the center of the man's back; he felt no pulse and heard no heartbeat and was pleased.

"Your actions say you don't trust me," Starla accused in a chilly tone.

Moig looked at the brown-haired beauty with the annoyed gleam in her green eyes and he grinned. "Just being sure you didn't make a mistake that could endanger us later. You're tougher and stronger than I imagined. Good work, Vedris. Tochar will be pleased with your obedience and with these weapons. We're in for a nice cut of this deal. Let's finish loading our haul and blast off. I'm ready to spend a lot of time at the drinker."

The sooner we get out of here the better, you reality-impaired Icarian! her mind fumed. "Let's do it," she concurred aloud.

As the last crate of weapons was passed through the *jerri* hatch connection to Starla's ship and the two pirates went aboard, Moig asked, "Why are you so stoked? Your jaw is clenched and your eyes are stormy."

The woman stood after securing the hatch and looked at the man with small dark eyes and a short golden beard, as all Icarians had various shades of blond hair and black eyes. "Blast it all, Moig! I'm tired of being tested! Surely by now, you and Tochar and the others know I can be trusted without me having to prove myself again and again. I'm beginning to think I shouldn't close my eyes or turn my back if I ever make a mistake. That puts me on edge."

"We trust you, Vedris, or you wouldn't be working with us."

"If that's true, why am I never told where we're heading or when we'll depart until the last *preon*? Our destination is kept secret until we take off, and so is our target until after we reach its location. Since we use my ship part of the time, I need those facts to make certain I have enough energy for my warp drive and enough supplies for the trek. I need to plan the best and easiest way to reach our destination, and plot several escape paths in case of trouble. If I'm trustworthy, why that secrecy?"

"Tochar doesn't trust anybody with such facts except me, Auken, and Sach. That way, there's no problem with loose lips."

Starla knew the names of Tochar's other top hirelings and friends, Icarians like himself. "I've never suffered from that condition, by accident or intention. I'm loyal to whomever hires me. My record speaks for itself, and Tochar checked me out in every way, including the use of truth serum."

"Be patient, Vedris, and you'll eventually enter the upper ranks with us. Now, let's blast off. I won't relax until we're on the other side of that stargate, out of this parsec, and back in Tochara."

"Cypher-T knows to get us under way as soon as the *jerri* hatch is sealed. By now, he's already disengaged our connection, cloaked the *Liska,* and we're leaving this vector before another ship can reach it. You did set the transporter's auto-pilot to take it in the opposite direction?"

"Yes," Moig confirmed, "but I don't want to be near that vessel when it's sighted, boarded, and checked, and the body is found. I wonder who he was?"

"Since he was hiding below, probably a free-rider on the run. I didn't ask him any questions and he didn't volunteer any information."

"You don't think he was a *Seki* or cargo protector or ranger, do you?"

"No, his hand didn't bear any of those authority symbols and he wasn't in a uniform, just an ordinary jumpsuit. He didn't seem to be there to trap any possible raiders. He wasn't even armed. I doubt he realized he was traveling on a ship transporting weapons or he would have broken into one of those crates earlier and been able to defend himself against me."

"That's impaired-reality after being aboard for so long."

"Not if he was on the run," Starla explained. "Any tampering with those crates would have exposed him to the android pilot/guard when it patrolled the ship."

Moig continued to dissect the situation. "He could have disabled the robot if he got his hands on a weapon."

"Then, who would have piloted the vessel to its next port?" she countered. "If he lacked the skill to take over, he would have drifted in space until he died or the ship was tracked and boarded and he was captured." She saw Moig shrug and frown for not reasoning out those points himself.

"How did you overpower such a big and strong male?" This fascinated him.

Since her ship was cloaked and was en route to their base, they both could relax, and in the process she might learn something valuable. "Since the transporter is piloted by an android, there probably isn't any food or drink aboard, so he could have been weakened from a lack of them," Starla suggested. "And, like most men, he no doubt assumed a mere female wasn't a serious threat or any real competition in a hand-to-hand fight; I tricked him and, as you noticed, won."

Moig chuckled and stroked his fuzzy beard. "Perhaps Tochar should keep a sharp eye and ear on you; with your skills and intelligence, you could replace him as our leader if you had a mind to challenge him."

"I have no interest in becoming a leader. Serving Tochar suits me just fine, so he doesn't have to worry about a challenge from me, as if a takeover were possible by anyone!"

"Good, because Auken and Sach would slay anybody who harmed him."

"Do *you* envy or covet Tochar's rank?" Starla queried in a calm tone.

"No, he's my friend and he pays me well, pays all of us well."

"True. I'm tense after my struggle with that intruder, so I'm going to refresh myself; then I'll join you and Cypher-T on the bridge." She did not have to worry about Moig following her to her quarters and trying to seduce her; though she perceived his lust for her, the alien lacked the courage to do anything to displease Tochar or to provoke his leader's wrath. She detested the man and his presence on her ship, her home when away from her galaxy, but she had to pretend to like and accept him.

"You talk to and about your android as if he's alive," Moig teased.

"To me, he is. He's my best friend, my family. We've been together for *yings*. He's saved my life and gotten me out of danger countless times."

"Is that why you keep communications open to him when we use your ship, so he can warn you and protect you?"

"Yes, and that's why I'm sometimes nervous when we're using Auken's ship and Cypher-T isn't around to guard me or alert me to danger. I don't understand why we can't use my ship during every raid; it's faster, better equipped, and my cloaking device is newer. Some forces have the capability of penetrating Auken's old style, so we could be detected and attacked."

"Auken won't raid using any ship except his. If you're worried about our safety, loan him your cloaking unit until they learn how to attach one of those *Destructoids* to his ship like Tochar uses to protect Tochara. Of course, after his *Adika* is armed with one of those new beamers, we can attack and destroy any vessel and location; they'll be helpless against us."

Moig had spoken a horrifying fact she and her superiors realized all too well, as the *villites* had stolen the only three *Destructoids* in existence, weapons with formidable capabilities and impossible to replace. "Auken's ship lacks the power to operate and the means to install my type of cloaker," she explained. "We've been fortunate to come and go undetected, Moig, but our luck could jettison any *preon* with galactic leaders weary of our costly raids, especially the Kalfans and Serians. I don't even want to imagine what would happen to us if *Sekis* or *I-GAF*ers got their eager hands on us."

"Tochar agrees to Auken's wishes, so we have to obey their orders. Don't worry, Vedris," Moig soothed, "we won't get caught; Tochar knows many secrets."

There must be a special reason for using Auken's ship when we raid for moonbeams, our most dangerous and profitable treks. If not, we'd use mine. "I know, but if the *Adika*'s cloak is penetrated, we'll be tracked to Noy; and Tochar tries to appear innocent of our daring raids."

"Wouldn't matter if we're tracked; Noy's in the Free-Zone. It's closer to the Thracian and Ceyxan galaxies than to the Federation. The *UFG*'s *I-GAF*ers and Kalfan rangers don't have any authority beyond the boundary. Besides, nobody can invade Tochara, not with our defense system."

Starla knew that the Thracian—of which Icaria was a planet—and the Ceyxan galaxies had tolerated the *villite* strongholds on Noy and several other small planets in the Free-Zone because the pirates provided them with things they wanted and because the *villites* wisely did not operate in their sectors. Yet, if those empires changed their minds, the stronghold of Tochara was impregnable, even by starships. But *I-GAF* teams from the United Federation of Gal-

axies—made up of Maffei, Seri, Kalfa, Androas, and Pyropea—could decide to challenge the *nefariants* who preyed
on their solar systems. A bold course of action could not
be undertaken, however, until matching weapons were built,
which could not happen until white crystals of the same
size and power were found either in Seri or Kalfa. "For
now, we seem to be safe, but who can say what the future
holds?"

"Tochar's too smart to endanger himself, his stronghold,
and men." Moig's strong tone reflected his confidence in
the leader.

*Not his hirelings, you brain-lacking yema; he sends us
into great peril on every raid!* "That's why I hired on with
him: he's the most powerful leader beyond the *UFG* boundary."

Four days later as Starla and Moig sat chatting while
eating, she received a message from her android on the
bridge. "What is it, Cypher-T?"

"We are approaching the stargate portal. We will enter
the Free-Zone in twenty *preons*. No interceptor is registering on our rear sensors. There are no instrument malfunctions. There are no obstacles in forward view."

"That's good news, Cypher-T; continue on course. We'll
join you soon." Starla looked at her repulsive companion.
"Well, Moig, we'll reach Noy in three *deegas* and complete
another successful trek."

Starla remained quiet and alert as she listened to Moig's
report to their leader, an attractive male with nape-length
blond hair and piercing black eyes. Tochar was four *hapax*
taller than Starla's own height of sixty-nine *hapaxs*. His
lean, sleek body and commanding aura implied virility and
power, but an evil and avaricious air exuded the alien male.

She knew it was dangerous to cross or challenge him, as some men had learned the hard way before their painful deaths, but she was willing to take that risk in order to defeat him. With his band of thirty Enforcers, he ruled and controlled this settlement. It was one of several on the planet, but none other had his impenetrable defense system. He existed in luxury in a large and magnificent abode on the side of a low mountain; yet, despite his power and wealth, he could not live or travel where he willed because of his past criminal activities. He was forced to habitate in the Free-Zone, a man who sat atop the worst pile of *villite* debris in the universe. Starla had a healthy fear of him, but she would work for him until she achieved her goal for coming to Tochara and hiring on to his nefarious band

Tochar smiled and said, "A superior job as usual, Starla. You continue to impress and please me. I was smart to take a chance on you."

Starla forced a smile in return. "Thank you, Tochar, but I would like to settle one matter now: no more killing unless our lives are in jeopardy."

"Leaving a witness behind does place us in jeopardy, Starla. You and Moig acted wisely to eliminate any possible threat to us. As a reward for your extra task, please select any four weapons you desire from those you delivered to me. This," he said, as he handed her payment for her job, "should be an ample cut for your services this time."

Starla accepted the bag of *crozes* and thanked him again. It wasn't necessary to count or examine the gems, as they were spendable anywhere she traveled. "You are most generous, Tochar, and I appreciate your faith in me. If that's all for now, I'll take my leave and get needed rest."

"I will summon you when your services are required again. It will be soon, Starla, and at that time your cut will be even larger."

"I stay ready to comply." Starla nodded farewell and, after selecting the four weapons she wanted from several open crates nearby, departed.

She stepped from the *trans-to* at the base of the high ridge and headed toward the grid where her shuttlecraft had landed—a ten-*preon* walk away—leaving a landrover for Moig's use for transportation into the settlement. En route, Starla scanned the area below her still-elevated position where Tochara stretched out for a long distance in the canyon.

Since her arrival, she had learned that Noy was a world of semi-desert to arid desert terrain in various shades of red. Nature had sculpted many rocks, cliffs, ridges, and knobs into rugged and unusual formations. The oppressive red cloak was rent only by an occasional splotch of light or dark gray rock, so hard it rarely crumbled enough to add its shade to the fiery-colored soil whose dust was a nuisance. According to the weather or the time of *deega,* even the sky was a pale to vivid red. In every direction, mountain ranges—whose odd configurations seemed to have ruptured the ground almost violently during an upheaval eons ago—provided boundary markers. Thick-walled structures with formidable defense weapons sat on two flat-topped bluffs. Starla glanced at those sites with a feeling of hopelessness before returning her thoughts once again to a study of the locale.

Due to a lack of fertile soil in this wilderness, some food plants and fruit bushes were grown in containers inside enclosed domes and were watered by a crude system of pipes and pumps from sources owned and controlled by Tochar. However, the majority of supplies was imported, usually after being stolen by bands of *nefariants* who either lived or traded there, which created a steady flux of space traffic. Caves found inside three ridges possessed springs and pools of fresh water; they were guarded and their valuable resources dispensed by Tochar's thirty Enforcers, as were the two defense sites. Though rains were infrequent, when a deluge came, it sent torrents of water gushing down the upheavals and washes, and was absorbed by dried mudflats and hardy red plants.

Tochara was one of many colonies on the secluded planet and, from what she had been told, was the best and safest place in the notorious Free-Zone; it was a vivid contrast to the mutant-roaming wastelands and other crude villages and harsh landscape where even the plants and animals were hazardous. Though noisy, the area was unlike the profound and eerie silence beyond it where only the wind was heard.

The story was that Tochar had arrived with his large band of *villites* two *yings* ago and conquered the lesser armed and unskilled inhabitants who had created the colony after fleeing oppression in an alien world. The original occupants who were not slain were sold into slavery on other planets which still allowed the barbaric practice.

Starla was glad there were no children here, as birth control with *liex* was an easy task and these were not family people. There were few pets and none were permitted to roam free. Abode builders were wealthy because materials had to be imported and were expensive. Still, in many areas where the unkempt and less successful raiders dwelled, it was smelly and dirty and cluttered. They lived in huts and shacks made of such usable scrap materials as metal and discarded wood. Lacking advanced technology, fuel for cooking sent gray and pungent smoke drifting upward where it was devoured quickly by a hungry red atmosphere, as were the fumes from generator-created electricity from stolen fuel.

Most of the inhabitants were rough and lawless men—dregs of the universe, people from many planets and galaxies, pirates, smugglers, traitors, adventurers, *bijonis,* and those males and females who earned their subsistence by satisfying the *villites'*s needs. Most clustered and worked in groups for defense and profit during raiding treks, though all were ruled and levied by Tochar and kept regulated by his mighty band of Enforcers. The inhabitants' goals appeared to be eating, drinking, partaking in risky deeds, fulfilling sexual desires, and having a safe haven. All facets of life and the inhabitants here were primitive and coarse when compared to the people and places Starla loved and missed. Yet, a strange camaraderie flourished among them—an odd respect, affection, and loyalty to each other, and unflinchingly to their leader. That same type of bonding was true even for the carnivorous desert mutants—*Skalds*—and for colony fringe scavengers.

While waiting for the shuttle door to open and the steps to extend, she glanced at Tochar's abode, which overlooked the leader's domain. The rectangular, bilevel structure had been built on a wide rock shelf and nestled against a lofty peak high off the ground for defense and for observing his stronghold. Most of its many chambers had views of three directions through floor-to-ceiling *transascreens* made from a material visually impenetrable from the exterior, even when the interior was illuminated at night. A generator-operated *trans-to* carried the owner and his visitors to and from the remarkable location.

As she loaded the weapons and closed the door, Starla recalled other things she had learned. One alien slave and several robots tended to Tochar's dwelling and needs. A well-endowed and sultry female named Palesa sated his carnal cravings. A forceful and wicked alien from the planet of Icaria in the Thracian Empire, Tochar fed his lusts on riches and power, and within Palesa's sensuous body. He seemed to care nothing for politics elsewhere or conquest of any planet, but Starla feared that *deega* would come. His sole deprivation lay in being unable to enjoy freedom and safety anywhere he yearned to travel, at least until he obtained the capability of mounting a moonbeam laser weapon on his ship. She knew from the *fiendal*'s record and from her observations that Tochar was clever, careful, greedy, and dangerous. He stayed in Tochara—beyond any galaxy's boundary and authority and attack ability—while his small band of *spacekis* foraged the nearest sectors for goods he sold at high prices. He remained safe—his life and possessions protected—and seemingly innocent of those raids.

Discovering Tochar was indeed her target was a quick and simple task; but uncovering his distant partners and capturing him or luring him away and into a trap seemed difficult but heady challenges.

Starla prepared the shuttle for lift-off to return to her ship. She hated Tochara and those who lived there; she could hardly wait to be gone from them. At least she had her ship—clean, safe, comfortable; she didn't want to imagine having to quarter herself in the crude settlement and was relieved the head *fiendal* had not insisted she do so.

She landed the shuttle in the docking bay of the *Liska* and joined her companion on the ship's bridge. She ordered a drink from a *servo* unit and sat near the control panel. She looked at Cypher and took a deep breath.

"You are tired and your spirits are low, Bree-Kayah," the android noted, having been programmed to communicate as a person. "Explain."

"After spending three *malees* under Tochar's probing gaze, I know he's responsible for the pirating of moonbeams we were sent to investigate, but I still don't know how he obtains facts about their transport schedules and routes. Having hirelings or partners in Seri and Kalfa is the only way he could know when and where to strike at those secret cargoes. Only men in power have access to those facts and to untraceable communications, yet, no one in either of those locations has fallen under suspicion or been caught sending word to him. Until I earn these *villites'* complete trust and acceptance and gather those facts, we can't finish our mission and leave."

The young woman almost leapt to her feet to pace the deck, an unusual action for her, and one the android grasped and evaluated.

She continued. "This assignment is crucial, Cypher; moonbeams are too powerful to fall into enemy hands; their uses in weapons, medicine, and defense are awesome. Researchers find more uses for them during every *malee* that passes. No wonder the Thracians and Ceyxans and other galaxies will pay or do anything to get their hands on as many as possible. Once those crystals' full potential is known and put to use by those who aren't in the *UFG,* the balance of power between the galaxies will be destroyed and our worlds will be threatened by conquest or destruction, or subjected to brutal raids. We can't fail Maffei or our allies. At least Tochar doesn't suspect a female agent is working against him. If he's on the alert for a spy, he shouldn't even glance in my direction. Correct?"

The android observed, recorded, and analyzed her words and mood. "He trusts you because you passed his truth serum test. He does not realize you are immune to it; all Elite Squad members have been rendered immune to it. The false identity and record you were given cannot be disproven. He believes you are a rough and tough loner who seeks wealth, adventure, and survival, and have committed many daring and illegal deeds to obtain them. Bree-Kayah Saar of Maffei is unknown to him, to those in Kalfa, and to all in Seri except their supreme ruler; that is why *Raz* Yakir and your Supreme Commander selected you for this mission."

"This is the first time I've been loaned to a neighboring galaxy—a member of the United Federation—to carry out a mission, one which will also threaten our world if we fail." Starla went over the facts with Cypher. It was vital to success that only a few people knew of her assignment and location: Yakir, the Serian ruler; her superior in the Elite Squad; her family—the Saars—in Maffei; and her unique android. As far as everyone else was aware, Bree-Kayah Saar was on extended leave to rest following a series of difficult and exhausting missions.

"Do not forget: you infiltrated Tochar's band and earned their trust with skill and speed; if that is an inaccurate conclusion, Tochar would not allow you to go on raids on your ship and with only one man as a teammate."

"But he doesn't permit me to use my ship to go after moonbeams, and secrets of those treks are withheld from me until the last *preon,*" Starla reminded the android. "Isn't that suspicious, proof he doesn't fully believe me?"

"Tochar takes those actions because he is careful. The possibility of him learning the truth about you is minuscule. If he does, we have the means to dupe him and escape. I am your guardian and I monitor you at all times; you are safe from peril. Even if I were captured, he cannot extract information from me; my program is inaccessible to everyone except you."

"You've snatched me out of danger many times, Cypher, but no plan is totally foolproof and no person is totally unreachable by evil forces. If I'm exposed and his reaction time is swifter than ours, he could signal his attack stations to blast my shuttle or our ship into oblivion before I could reach it, cloak the *Liska,* vanish from their sensors, and flee."

"Do not fear, Bree-Kayah, I will not fail you or the Federation."

"I know, my friend, and I'm fortunate to have you."

As she sipped a cool drink, Starla thought how lucky she was indeed to have this particular android, the most advanced model available anywhere, one with a male appearance both in facial features and body build. His flesh and features displayed realistic human colorings, including his synthetic silver hair. The only giveaways he was nonhuman were his expressionless eyes and lack of sexual organs beneath his blue jumpsuit. His seventy-six *hapax* frame was strong and agile, made of a metal indestructible, thus far, until a moonbeam was discovered that could cut through most known metals. She did not want to imagine any *villite* slicing him apart to reach his chips and circuits, as that would initiate a self-destruct sequence and he would be lost to her forever. She did not want to think about an existence without him. She knew she would do anything to protect him from harm, would kill to save him from evil, and Cypher was cognizant of that fact.

She was glad he had the capability to analyze any situation and to make decisions on his own when necessary. His flesh-colored face and silver eyes revealed no presence of feelings, but he had been given an emotions chip to help him understand her and other humans. With it, he could be amusing and even vexing at times, as if he possessed a real personality. She loved, respected, and trusted him as if he were human. When others were present, she called him "Cypher-T" to alert the android to a caution/duplicity mode. As part of a test program, the technologically advanced unit had become her partner during her second mission for the undercover Elite Squad of the Maffei Galaxy, her world. The pairing had worked so well that they had been left as a team. If he had been with her during her first assignment, she thought, perhaps Antarus would be alive and perhaps they would be lovers; and that auslander wouldn't have been so tempting, unforgettable. *Don't think about him; he's gone forever.*

Starla looked at Cypher and asked, "What if something goes wrong?"

"Relax, Bree-Kayah; you will succeed in your duty and mission; I will prevent failure and your destruction. It is unlike you to experience such doubts."

"I know, but this time it's different because so much is at risk, more than my life and the lives of those of my world. If only Tochar didn't have those incredible weapons on two ridges and atop his dwelling, Serian and Kalfan forces could attack and obliterate him. He was lucky his first crystal raid included them. Powered by such large white moonbeams, they can disable a fleet of starships, even with their deflective shields engaged. Those crystals don't require any maintenance or other driving force and will last for *yings*. They can fire upward and in all four directions by fast manual movement. He also has smaller laser guns on all four sides aimed landward to thwart any ground attack. When I witnessed their capabilities, I was astounded and frightened. Those structures are impregnable, Cypher, so there's no way we can reach and disable the *Destructoids*. Tochar doesn't allow anyone inside those sites except his Enforcer guards and his closest friends. The same is true for the smaller version atop his dwelling."

A weary Starla flopped down in a seat and continued talking to the android. "I doubt I would be part of his band if his other unit hadn't been terminated during that first raid and he needed to form a new one. Auken, Sach, and Moig were the only ones to escape that fierce battle, but—fortunately for Tochar and horrible for our side—the weapons and crystals were on Auken's ship."

"You also have a powerful and secret weapon to aid you," Cypher reminded. "Yakir was intelligent to select you and to supply you with it."

Starla grasped his meaning. "It feels so strange when I become another woman in looks, but it's also exciting."

"It is good that shapeshifting does not cause pain."

"What's also good is that Yakir allowed me to have that Serian secret to use, as few know of its existence. Perhaps as Yana I can learn things Starla Vedris can't. We make a good team, Cypher; I'm glad you're with me. My world and family are so far away and no contact with them is possible. They must be terribly worried about me, but they realize I had to come. I would be more afraid if I were here alone and doing all the work myself."

Cypher could not smile, but his emotions chip sent a good sensation through his circuits, one his unique program understood and appreciated. "Yes, Bree-Kayah Saar, we are a good team."

"I learned on the last crystal raid that no matter what precautions the Serians and Kalfans take, Tochar learns their plans. I'm sure our band's raids are connected with some crucial matter for always having to use Auken's ship. Every time you cloak and follow us, nothing shows up on our sensors. We must look harder and closer, my friend, a clue is there somewhere."

"We will find it. Tochar is clever, but we are smarter."

Starla laughed and teased, "Is that conceit and boasting I hear?"

"I speak only the truth to you as my program insists."

"Did I act wisely during that raid with Moig?" she asked her trusted android. "I was ordered to do whatever was necessary to obtain victory, but don't I have limits in some areas? What if that action returns to trouble me?"

Cypher scanned that incident file in his advanced system. "You did as you must. Delete it from your memory cells."

"I'm afraid I don't have an erase switch or command. He shouldn't have been aboard. I don't know who he was or why he was there, but if you hadn't warned me and I hadn't dealt with him as I did, Moig would have slain him, and Tochar would have kicked me out of his special unit."

"You must not do anything to expose your identity or to endanger yourself; disobedience would have provoked both." Cypher probed a matter he needed to understand. "Why did your vital signs register strange signals when you met and dealt with the intruder?"

Starla gazed at him. "What do you mean?"

"Your heart and pulse rates became fast and erratic. Your body temperature fluctuated. Your chemical balance and brain wave pattern altered. Your muscles quivered. I have not picked up that mixture of signals before, and the sensors did not malfunction. Explain."

"I don't know what happened to me in that storage bay. He took me by surprise and we fought quite a battle, but he underestimated me because I'm a woman and didn't fight at his best. He was a magnificent specimen, Cypher, and he affected me in a strange manner. There was something about him that made me warm all over."

"It is physical attraction, the desire to mate."

Even as Starla envisioned the handsome male with black hair and dark blue eyes and knew Cypher's conclusion was correct, she laughed and scoffed, "Don't be ridiculous. He was a stranger, a peril; and I handled him in the only way open to me, with one of my little phials."

"I analyzed your reactions; my conclusion and program are accurate. You always speak the truth to me, Bree-Kayah; why is this time different?"

"Guilty of deceit, my friend, and I'm sorry. I just didn't want to confess my foolishness and don't want your deduction to be true. I admit he was handsome and virile and arousing, but . . ." *Stars afire. Just thinking and talking about him is stimulating!*

"Continue."

"I would never mate even with an appealing stranger, and certainly not with a *villite*. Since he was hiding on that vessel, he must be a criminal on the run. Be sure to notify the Kalfans of his presence aboard so he can be taken prisoner by their *Sekis*. Under the circumstances, there was no way I could apprehend him, but he's captive aboard that transporter. He's gone, so I'm safe from temptation. Whatever it was, let's drop the subject."

"Why? Do you not want to understand or experience such emotions and pleasures? Are they not normal biological functions for your species?"

"Yes, but I haven't felt such emotions since that incident with Antarus before his death. Even then, my heart and will were barely involved since I was delirious," Starla answered, aware Cypher would grasp the reference to her first sexual experience, since he knew everything about her. She had no secrets from the trusted android; it was necessary for him to know how she would react under all circumstances.

She also spent most of her time with him during missions, so many long and candid talks had taken place over the *yings*. "He made me uneasy, Cypher, and I don't like control and focus losses. I need only to think about Tochar and my mission. The sooner we finish it, the sooner we can go home. I miss my family and friends, and I hate this awful place and these horrible people. After I bathe and eat, we'll play a game of *resi* before I retire. You're in charge of the ship now. See you later."

Four days had passed when Starla was summoned to Tochar's dwelling. She entered his oblong work chamber in the elevated structure and approached him, noticing that someone was with him, his back to her. Black hair told her it wasn't Moig, Auken, or Sach, who were light-haired like all Icarians. For a strange reason, she tensed, but managed to keep her expression pleasant and calm.

Tochar stood, smiled, and motioned her forward. "There is someone I want you to meet, Starla. Dagan Latu, this is Starla Vedris, one of my best pilots and raiders, and also a beautiful and fearless woman."

As the male also stood, then turned, Starla's heart skipped several beats before pounding rapidly. As she faced the man Moig had ordered her to kill eleven *deegas* ago, she knew Cypher must be concerned over her erratic vital signs—reactions carried to him via her wrist device which always kept her in contact with him. Surely the android was deciding if her sudden distress indicated she was in terrible danger and he should teleport her to safety, though she had not signaled him to do so.

Questions filled her mind in a rush: Who was he? How had he gotten there? Had she been exposed and walked into a trap? Was he one of Tochar's men, one she hadn't met until now? Had he been aboard the ship to test her loyalty and reflexes? No, she reasoned, or he would be dead if she had carried out Moig's order. Somehow the cunning stranger had escaped and would soon place her and her mission in jeopardy. *Well. Bree-Kayah Saar, how are you going to get out of this threatening predicament?*

Two

Starla was trained to think and react quickly to unexpected and hazardous circumstances. She cautioned herself not to panic and flee, as that would terminate her crucial mission and become her first failure during an assignment. Yet, she remained alert and prepared to signal Cypher to rescue her if the situation worsened. Though she was quite uncertain, she tried to calm herself so the android would realize she had matters under control. Since the man had not spoken, Cypher would have no clue as to why she was unsettled. No doubt the android was running his name through their computer bank at this moment, which would reveal Dagan's identity but not the reason behind her distress. The instant he spoke, however, Cypher would recognize his voice pattern and understand.

Even if he's told Tochar about the transporter incident, stay and bluff your way out. Starla moved forward and said, "It's a pleasure to meet any friend of Tochar's." She extended her hand and they clasped wrists in the usual manner of greeting. The stranger's grasp seemed too snug and lasted too long. She had seen surprise register in his blue eyes before one of amusement mingled with intrigue replaced it. She was relieved his back was to Tochar, so the leader missed Dagan's reaction. Her green gaze locked with his blue one for a few moments as if in challenge. She pulled her arm from his grip as it loosened, seemingly without his awareness or intent; his touch, face, his presence, were dis-

turbing, arousing, irritating. As if he detected her reaction
to him, he looked pleased and cocky. She shifted her gaze
to Tochar and smiled. The leader grinned as if he assumed
they had been evaluating each other and saw the sparks of
physical attraction between them. She decided that was an
advantage, as it would mask any departure from her normal
behavior.

The leader laughed and corrected, "Dagan is not a friend,
but I am hoping he will become one and hire on to serve
me as superbly as you do. I must tell you, Starla, his reputation spreads far, and is a colorful one. It will be good to
have another brave and bold person working for me, if he
accepts. According to his record, he will prove an excellent
member of our group. I am sure you two would work remarkably and profitably together."

Good, he's a stranger to you. "I'll work with any man
or woman you select, Tochar; you are our leader, a generous
and superior one," she replied in a smooth and professional
tone, though she surmised the *fiendal* was using her to
tempt Dagan Latu into becoming one of his hirelings.

Tochar chuckled. "I am the only potentate you have ever
served." He glanced at Dagan. "Like you, Starla has always
been a loner, a success on her own. But I persuaded her to
work for me and to enjoy the sanctuary and rewards I have
to offer. I hope you will do the same."

"The offer you made sounds appealing," Dagan said, "especially the refuge and hefty payments, both of which I am
in dire need of at present. As to Starla Vedris, she must be
skilled in many ways to be thought and spoken of so highly
by you. She is indeed beautiful, and a pleasure to meet.
I'm certain I'll enjoy working with her at every available
chance." He was fascinated by the desirable space pirate
who appeared just as intrigued by and drawn to him, as he
was to her.

"Starla is exquisite, but I must caution you, Dagan, to
use care and respect with her. She is one of my best raiders,

so I cannot allow anyone to provoke her into leaving me by offending her with an unwanted pursuit. Of course, she is free to select her own companions and diversions."

"I catch your meaning, Tochar, and I'll honor your caution."

"Excellent, because you and Starla will make a fine pair for some of my most important treks. With you two as a unit and Auken, Sach, and Moig as another, I will have two superior teams to handle crucial raids. Sit and relax, you two. Starla, would you care for a refreshment?"

She took the *seata* nearest Dagan's to prove to both men she was not afraid of the newcomer. "*Mumfresia* will be fine." She watched Tochar press a button on his control panel; the female slave appeared with haste, as if she feared a delay would anger her master and provoke punishment. Starla had seen bruises on Zarafa's yellow skin that implied abuse. She detested any male who used brutality on a helpless victim of any age or sex. Yet, she was not in a position to defend or rescue the alien slave. When she completed her mission, she would endeavor to do so.

"*Mumfresia* for Starla, and refills for me and Dagan."

She noticed the kindly behavior the cunning Tochar exhibited toward the slave to make a good impression on Dagan. She knew that the leader and this settlement had no automatic *servo* units to provide refreshments and meals by request using coded metallic cards and advanced technology, just as it lacked other features to make work easier and life more enjoyable. Most of the living conditions and amenities were like those in her world more than a hundred *yings* ago, as it was not a place which attracted scientists and technicians to build, operate, and repair them. Yet, the primitive lifestyle suited the type of people who populated Tochara. After the woman's departure, Starla asked Tochar, "Will we be going out again soon? I get itchy sitting around too long."

"You see, Dagan, Starla is as eager to get rich as you

are, but for different reasons. Yes, my lovely creature, your next departure is in two *deegas*. It is another risky and profitable venture for you. Auken will give you the schedule; you will be using his ship this time."

That news told her their target was another cargo of moonbeams, but it didn't reveal the crystals departure point: Seri or Kalfa. She would ponder the matter later. For now, she needed to stay alert for trouble from the handsome male nearby, who kept glancing at her and who probably was surprised to see her again. She could not guess so soon if he was going to expose her with the hope of gaining his new leader's gratitude and favor. Perhaps the appealing *villite* wanted her to sweat for a time out of revenge for defeating him, or perhaps he was repaying her for sparing his life. Or perhaps he assumed extorting her would be more profitable than revealing her defiance to Tochar, especially if she found a cunning way to excuse it. She also tried not to think about the audacious remarks she made to Dagan before she allegedly killed him, words he no doubt found amusing and enticing from his expressions.

As the slave returned and served them, Dagan pretended to listen to Starla and Tochar chat, but his mind kept drifting to the incident on the transporter and her provocative words. He couldn't surmise why she hadn't slain him, but he was grateful enough to conceal news of her defiance, no matter if revealing it would score him big points. She didn't seem worried, so her partner that *deega* must not have seen him, as she had covered his face with a sack. But if Moig recognized him, they were both in trouble for keeping secrets. Maybe he shouldn't take that risk; maybe he should expose her while he had time to joke it off. If he waited and Moig fingered him, Tochar would be suspicious of why he held silent and would send him on his way.

But, Dagan deduced, he might get Starla Vedris killed or punished for no reason, if Moig was ignorant. For certain, Tochar wasn't a man to dupe without an excellent motive, especially while sitting in his stronghold. He had noticed the discolored spots on the slave's face and arms and the terror in the poor creature's eyes. Any man, Dagan felt, who could do such despicable acts was an unpredictable and untrustworthy lowlife. If this job wasn't imperative, he would be gone on the next ship out. As to Starla, she was a mystery; he had never heard of her and her exploits. He wondered how and when and why she had linked up with Tochar and how she felt about the man. He needed to learn her secrets fast or she could be trouble for him if his guard rebelliously relaxed around her. It didn't sit well that he was so attracted to her, that he might jeopardize his wants and needs to save her life and skin.

Starla was looking down at the three powerful crystals lying on his desk. "Those are exquisite moonbeams, Tochar, but rather small ones," she remarked. "They would be breathtaking if they were gems and were studded into a gold neck ring. Of course, they're too valuable and useful for mere adornment."

The leader fingered them almost erotically. "Dagan just sold them to me. He won them in a *resi* game from a cunning thief."

Dagan grinned. "If I had known those gems were so precious, I wouldn't have held on to them for so long. They're about the only thing I rescued after my little problem with those *Sekis*. Too bad my ship wouldn't fit in my pocket like they did. If I could get my hands on more of those, I'd be rich very soon with what you're willing to pay for them."

Tochar lifted one moonbeam, held it toward the light, and admired its color. These are the last ones you will be able to win in any game. No worker can sneak them out of the mines anymore because of security inspections, and markets for them are rare and buyers are dangerous to seek."

"Ships transporting them would make perfect targets," Dagan hinted.

"Do not attempt to raid one unless you are ready to die

or you know for certain it is safe to attack," Tochar warned. "The Serians and Kalfans are very protective of these beauties, very secretive about them. At least they tried to keep news of their discovery from general knowledge, but word always filters out about something so unique and potent."

"What's so special about them? Why the secrecy?" Dagan inquired as he leaned forward to inspect the small crystals again.

"They have many uses. Research is being done to determine their full potential. But let us talk of other things, get better acquainted."

Starla deduced Tochar's reason for changing the subject: he didn't want Dagan—or anyone—to become fully aware of the moonbeams' enormous power and value. The two yellow ones could be ground into minute particles, then placed inside a tumor by surgery or injection to destroy it without damaging healthy cells or tissues and without side effects; yet, scientists did not know how the crystal differentiated between healthy and abnormal cells. The same was true for viral destruction when the moonbeams were ingested with liquid. It could repair broken bones in a few *horas* when inserted into their location. The blue crystal could be used on a scalpel to make thin incisions which instantly sealed vessels and capillaries to prevent bleeding. The cut would then heal within a *deega* after the operation and never became infected or leave a scar. Other moonbeams, according to their sizes and colors, created powerful weapons and sources of heat and light that were long-lasting and safe. With such awesome capabilities, it was no wonder why the crystals were so valuable and craved, or a target for *villites* like Tochar. She wanted to know how Dagan had come across those three. She wondered if Tochar suspected the newcomer of being deceitful; if so, it was not revealed in the leader's expression or tone. If Dagan Latu *was* a liar or threat, that fact would be exposed as soon as Tochar used truth serum on him. She could only hope that Dagan wasn't asked any questions about her while under that revealing drug's control. *Don't worry, Bree-Kayah, if Tochar puts you under again, with your immunity, you can lie your way out of trouble. As for you, Dagan, if you're being deceitful, you're a dead man.*

"How long have you been on Noy?" she asked him. She was amazed that he or any man would enter Tochar's domain coated with red dust, his garment torn and rumpled, his hair uncombed, and his skin unwashed.

"Two *deegas*. I landed at another settlement, but decided I would like this one better. It isn't a secret that Tochar's is the best, and I was hoping he would be willing to hire me until I earn enough for a new ship."

That information told Starla he had left the transporter and headed there as soon as he awakened from the temporary cryogenic drug she had given him, a rare chemical from Yakir that had decreased his vital signs to the point Moig could not detect them. But how, she mused, had he gotten off the vessel, and what had become of it, and why land elsewhere if Tochara was his destination? "How did you cross the wasteland?" she began her probe. "From which direction? Did you have any trouble with the flesh-eating mutants who roam it?"

Dagan was stunned that she would ask any questions about his travels. He glanced down at his sorry appearance and answered, "I stole a landrover but, it malfunctioned before I reached Tochara, so I walked the rest of the way. I was lucky that one of Tochar's patrols sighted me and brought me to him. I didn't run into any mutants. I guess I was lucky I survived my little misadventure."

Starla was eager to return to the *Liska* and learn about Dagan Latu, as Cypher would have a report ready for her, but she must not appear nervous or in a rush to depart. "Yes, you were very lucky," she remarked casually. "I'm sure you're grateful to whatever force saved your life. What happened to your old ship?"

"Depletion of power forced me to abandon her, but I escaped from a *Seki* before he could take me in to be sent to a penal colony. I caught a lift on a supply transporter to the Keezian colony. After I landed and examined the place, I came here for rest, sanctuary, and work. What about—"

Auken, Sach, and Moig joined them and interrupted Dagan's query. As the three Icarians greeted their leader with respect and affection, Starla and Dagan sipped their drinks and listened.

The golden-haired Auken reported, "We'll get everything prepared tomorrow and leave the following *deega*. We should reach our target, grab its cargo, and return quickly. We'll take Starla with us."

She exchanged smiles with Auken when he glanced at her.

Tochar introduced the newcomer to his men, "This is the infamous Dagan Latu, my friends: adventurer, *bijoni*, raider, and rogue. He barely escaped capture numerous times for some of his cunning and daring deeds. The *Sekis* would give a small fortune for his capture and destruction. If his reputation is accurate, he lives for pleasure, wealth, challenges, and excitement, as we do. Dagan will be going with you on the next trek. If he proves worthy, he will become a regular member of your special team."

Dagan clasped wrists with each of the men. He realized Tochar had checked his criminal record earlier when he was out of the chamber for a while, as this was his first time on Noy. "Where will we be heading?"

Tochar replied for his best friend, "Auken will tell you all you need to know after you are under way. Why do you ask?"

Dagan chuckled. "Considering my recent brush with capture, I just wanted to make sure I wasn't sticking my nose out too close to those Kalfans again; I kind of like it, so I don't want their *Sekis* to laser it off."

Tochar also chuckled. "The danger and risks are small,

and no space rangers will be in that sector. Starla, you work with Dagan and teach him how we operate. Make sure nothing happens to him during his first raid for me. I would like to keep him around for a long time."

Starla set aside her empty glass. "As you wish, Tochar."

Moig ventured with a grin, "Don't worry, Dagan, Vedris will watch out for you and get you back here in one piece. She was with me on my last raid; she tricked a robot pilot into letting her come aboard his transporter and she disabled him as fast as a shooting star. Vedris isn't afraid of anybody or anything. She obeys orders and does her job well."

Dagan surmised from Moig's behavior that their secret was safe, and, oddly, it felt arousing to share it with the exquisite pirate. "I'll trust her to take excellent care of me and to be sure I don't make any mistakes."

"If there is nothing else to discuss, you are dismissed," Tochar said. "If you are in need of . . . diversion, Dagan, the Skull's Den is the best place to look. Radu, its owner, can find you a clean and quiet chamber to rent. If you need anything, ask Radu, and tell him you work for me. I will meet with all of you upon your successful return, except for you, Dagan. I want to see you here again tomorrow on the tenth *hora*."

Dagan nodded, then spoke with Moig, Auken, and Sach for a few *preons*. Starla made her exit and was out of sight when he stepped from the *trans-to* with the other men. He wondered how she vanished so quickly.

Auken chuckled. "She returned to her ship, the *Liska;* she lives on it in orbit. She doesn't share a *sleeper* with any of the men here."

Dagan laughed. "My interest in her is that obvious?"

Sach nodded. "She's beautiful but special," he told him, "so be careful with her. She's one of us, so we protect her from annoyances."

"What if I'm not an irritant to her?" Dagan asked.

"That's for Starla to decide," Auken answered.

"Any of you pursuing her? I wouldn't want to intrude."

"We're just friends. Starla comes, goes, and does as she pleases. The inhabitants know she works for Tochar, so they leave her alone. Only an outsider would dare to approach her in an offensive way."

"And then only one time." Moig chortled. "Vedris fights and shoots better than most men, so she can take care of herself. If not, that android of hers would lay a threat low."

Dagan was surprised by that news. "Android?"

"She has one she treats like a real person. Who knows? Maybe that's why she doesn't need a man; maybe old Cypher takes care of her in all ways."

Sach scowled. "Careful, Moig, you know that isn't true."

Dagan noticed how the shortest man defended Starla, and how the golden-haired Auken nodded agreement with Sach.

"I was only teasing. Everybody knows androids aren't equipped like that, only certain cyborgs."

"We don't have any cyborgs here," Auken said, "we don't allow them; they can't be trusted."

"Let's head for the drinker; I'm thirsty and I need a juicy female."

Sach concurred with Moig, "I'm ready for a few pleasures myself. I heard Radu has hired two females with real special skills I'd like to try."

"What I need is a bath and clean garment," Dagan said.

Auken told the newcomer that Radu would take care of his needs, then reminded him not to forget his meeting with Tochar the following day.

"I'll be there," Dagan replied, wondering about the reason for it.

Starla rushed to the bridge of the *Liska* and took a seat next to Cypher. Her computer system had a memory bank and certain programs that no one could enter except the two of them and members of the Maffei Elite Squad; they didn't even show up on the screen unless a particular command was given. The advanced system—along with her security clearance level and her android's skills—had the capability and access codes for tapping in to numerous *UFG* and other sources without being traced back to her unit. She took a deep breath and murmured, "We came close to exposure, but he held silent about our first meeting for some reason. Who is Dagan Latu? I'm certain Tochar or his contacts have already checked his file, and the *fiendal* seemed impressed by what he learned. That doesn't bode well for my impression of him and gives us an unneeded complication."

The intelligent android pressed a key to display the intruder's record and image on the screen. "Name: Dagan Latu. Age: twenty-eight *yings*. Height: seventy-five *hapaxs*. Weight: two-twenty *pedis*. Hair: black. Eyes: blue. Origin: Gavas, capital planet of the Kalfa Galaxy. Mate status: none. Family status: all deceased. Current location: unknown, recently escaped from a Kalfan *Seki* after a fuel raid and his capture on Gavas."

The news he had no mate strangely pleased Starla, whose eyes were locked on the magnificent male's image as it was shown from all sides. *"Sekis* are well trained, my friend, so Dagan must be cunning to perform such a feat. Few men have done so." She listened as Cypher spoke in the humanistic manner of his program, one which made him seem real to her.

"His criminal record is long, but the most serious parts consist of strong allegations and suspicions."

As she read the list and remarks, Starla realized why she had never heard of him in the past because he operated outside of her sectors. Language had not provided an enlightening clue, as all people had translator chips implanted in their ears at birth so that any tongue spoken to them was understandable. Too, an intergalactic form of visual language—*WEV*—was used in multiculture settings so that anyone could read names, signs, and messages. She was relieved only *WEV* was used in Tochara where people from many planets lived and worked, though she was skilled in the written and visual forms of several languages.

"If this record is only half accurate, Cypher, he's clever, careful, fearless, and intelligent; those traits are proven by his escape from one of the most sophisticated and highly trained law-enforcement units in Kalfa and in his ability to avoid detection and capture. It says he normally travels and works alone, but it's believed he occasionally hires on to bands of smugglers, raiders, adventurers, and *bijonis*. His goals appear to be wealth, pleasure, excitement, challenges, and retaining freedom."

For a wild moment, she wondered what Dagan would say if she offered to pay him more than Tochar if he worked with her on her current assignment. She could provide more challenges and adventures than Tochar. As a man, he could get closer, faster, to the other band members and might gather facts she needed to complete her mission and fly home. Working together, perhaps they could find a way to disable the *fiendal*'s defense system, which would have to take place simultaneously at the two sites; then, the Serians could attack. It was too risky for her and Cypher to make that attempt, as it would leave no one aboard her ship to rescue them if things went wrong. She was determined to win, but she was not foolish and reckless. *Villites* had crazy codes of honor and loyalty toward the men who hired them, she was aware, even for short spans of time and despite all perils involved. Perhaps a full pardon would ensure Dagan's assistance, as a matter of such grave importance surely justified the rewarding of one.

The only way she could determine his real character was to get close to him, but not as Starla, whom he surely would be watching closely after her defiance. Yet, a sensuous and seductive Yana might be able to entice facts from him if he was a boaster trying to impress her and lure her to a *sleeper* beneath him. Besides, he might not live past Tochar's truth serum test in the morning. That thought distressed her more than she cared to admit or consider.

"So, he has been a *bijoni* as Tochar said, a fighter for hire in matters which meant nothing to him except payment and stimulating risks. That fact strikes me as surprising and peculiar for the kind of man he seems to be, self-contained and self-reliant. What is his loyalty record?"

"He has not betrayed any superior from his past; nor have they exposed him," Cypher revealed. "Since leaving their hire, all are victims of annihilator units, captives on penal colonies, or are hiding in other galaxies. Use caution on him, Bree-Kayah. His physical effect on you could be perilous and distracting. I can detect every time your thoughts drift and you think about him; you did so before speaking again. Is that not accurate?"

Starla laughed. "Perhaps I should remove my wrist device when I'm with him so you can't read my mind and worry about me."

Cypher's silver visual sensors focused on the young woman whom he loved, if that was possible in his nonhuman state. At a height of seventy-six *hapaxs,* seven *hapaxs* taller than his companion, she had to look upward to meet his unreadable gaze. The expression in her eyes troubled him, as did the unknown factor who evoked it. "There is conflict within you concerning him. Do not forget who and what you are and why you are here. Do not forget he is an adversary, the same as Tochar and his space pirates."

"I know, my friend, and I'm grateful for your concern and affection; I'm glad your program allows you to experience such perceptions. I promise to be careful around Dagan, if he lives past tomorrow. Tochar will be giving him *Thorin* to test his credibility, and he might fail that examination. Wouldn't it be wonderful if I could infuse Tochar with a dose, question him, and finalize this mission? I doubt the *fiendal* has had access to *Rendelar* to make him immune; that chemical and process are guarded too well and only a skilled scientist like my mother can use them properly and safely. Besides, Tochar never allows anyone to get that close to him except Auken, Sach, Moig, and Palesa, who aren't threats to him. I wish his dwelling was penetrable by our probing devices so we could hear what is said at all times; he would have no secrets then to keep us here. Even with the needed coordinates recorded in our system, I can't transport into his chamber to search it, since we can't scan it for anyone's presence. I'm not worried about his session with Dagan tomorrow; I can elude any disclosure problems. But for some crazy reason I can't explain, I want him to survive it."

She changed the subject to her assignment. "We have one important advantage: from what I overheard between Auken and Sach, Tochar is storing the moonbeams we've stolen so far. When he has an ample supply of the five types of crystals, he plans to summon buyers from Ceyx and from his Thracian world. At least the crystals haven't fallen into enemy hands. If we can discover where they're hidden, perhaps we can destroy them before a deal takes place. Since we can't recover them, that was *Raz* Yakir's order if the opportunity arose. To avoid suspicion, I haven't asked any questions about the moonbeams. If I can earn their complete trust, perhaps I will be told or shown where they are being kept."

"With the Latu complication, it is good Tochar lacks the scientific ability and source to check for the detection of *Rendelar* in your body."

"If that were possible, he would know I can overpower *Thorin* and dupe him. But it would require one of the most intelligent and skilled scientists alive, secret formulas, and highly specialized equipment to do such a complicated test: things that *fiendal* doesn't have, thank the stars. It's also good that *Raz* Yakir wanted a female for this task; I believe, as he and my Elite Squad superior do, that a woman is less suspicious. This is a critical assignment, Cypher; we are lucky to be chosen to carry it out for them. I hope we succeed, and soon. I miss my parents, my brother and sister, and their families. This is the longest time and distance I've been away from them."

Cypher placed his hand on her shoulder, knowing that action was used to supply comfort and encouragement. "It will be over soon. I will cloak the *Liska* and follow the *Adika* on its next trek. I will search for clues to solve this mystery. I will guard you from harm."

Starla smiled, reached for his hand, and clasped it between hers. "Thank you for being here with me. Now," she added as she released her grip and stood, "it's time for Yana to go to work for us."

Starla went to her quarters and stripped off her green jumpsuit. She opened the hidden compartment, retrieved a phial of unknown chemicals, and drank its contents. She stiffened as strange sensations assailed her body, flesh quivered and altered, colorings changed, and the shapeshifting transformation took place. It was an uncomfortable and weird feeling, but not painful. *Raz* Yakir had given her the supply to use as needed, a secret and powerful discovery a Serian scientist had developed. While the chemicals completed their task, she selected her garment and accessories.

She entered the bathing unit and remained for a short time, then exited clean and refreshed. A familiar and yet totally different image greeted her gaze in the mirror as she completed her grooming and dressed. She placed a heady fragrance—Yana's scent—on her neck, wrists, and between her breasts, a bosom larger than her own. She strapped a *lazette* to her right thigh, a small weapon in a holder, to ward off trouble. The only time she was disarmed was when she entered Tochar's chamber and when she was aboard her ship. She made certain she had the chemical—contained in what appeared to be a belt decoration—to return her normal image if needed before the transmutation's time span—twelve *horas*—elapsed.

After finishing her tasks, she joined Cypher at the transporter unit. "Is the women's private chamber at the Skull's Den unoccupied?" she asked the android.

"The coordinates are entered. Scanners register no presence there. It is safe to travel. Step onto the pad when you are ready to leave."

As Starla Vedris, she had gathered those coordinates earlier so she could beam in and out without being seen or followed. Since many ships came and went and orbited Noy, Yana's comings and goings could be explained without suspicion. To help protect her other identity, she had rented an abode from Radu where Yana supposedly lived, one which Cypher kept in order and stocked in case Yana had a visitor who needed to be duped. But she had given Radu a false story as to why privacy about her whereabouts was needed. Since others often came to Tochara to conceal themselves for a while, her story and behavior were not suspicious. "How do I look?" she asked, turning for inspection.

"As Yana, you are perfect. The human saying is: you are a woman to evoke uncontrollable desire in most men and envy in other females."

Starla smiled and laughed. "Good, that's Yana's purpose. *Raz* Yakir certainly chose an alluring facade for me to assume. Bree-Kayah could not dress and behave as she does. I even sound different with the changes in my nose, mouth, and throat. No one could see through this cunning disguise, not even Tochar with his wicked gaze." She closed her eyes and repeated, "I'm Yana, I'm Yana, I'm Yana" to get herself into that identity's character. She opened her eyes, took a deep breath, stepped onto the sensor pad, and told Cypher she was ready to depart. "Wish me luck."

The android did just before her presence shimmered and vanished. He checked the scanners to make certain she reached her destination without discovery. He remained in the transporter room to be ready to retrieve her in a hurry if necessary, monitoring her words via a device in a neck ring of *plantinien* and fake jewels. He did not like to depend upon the wrist and neck devices to stay in contact with and to monitor her, since they could be removed or broken. Until this mission, a tiny unit had been implanted under the skin of her right forearm, one which had to be removed because of the shapeshifting process. It was at times like this that his emotions chip was a disadvantage, because it permitted him to experience worry.

In her Yana form, Starla left the women's chamber and strolled into the large dome, the exterior of which, with its strange shape and many openings, resembled a skull. It was filled with people from many worlds and reverberated with a variety of noises: voices, laughter, music, and the clatter of glasses. She walked to the long bar and ordered a drink.

The owner smiled. "Haven't seen you for a while, Yana. It's good to have you back; you give this place a glow with your beauty."

"Your tongue is smooth and your words are pleasing to hear, Radu. I have been in my abode; I was in need for a few *deegas'* rest and quiet."

As he drew her drink from one of the large kegs in a row on the wall, he said, "I was afraid you had started visiting another location."

Yana's gaze drifted over the rotund alien with gray hair and eyes, a Ceyxan of at least sixty *yings*. His rippled forehead and the countless solid gray circles on his pale skin, were traits of those of his race of a certain age. He was always genial to her and to most of his customers. One of a few men who did not have a criminal past, she could not imagine why he would want to live in Tochara and serve such evil. "There is no place in the settlement as nice as yours, Radu. The others are too rough and crowded for a gentle woman of my tastes. The Skull's Den is clean and safe and serves the best quality drinks and refreshments."

Radu pushed the *plantinien* chip back to her. "Those words and your adornment of my place earned you a free drink."

"You are a kind and generous man, a good friend. Thank you."

After the owner excused himself to serve others, Yana turned and glanced around the location that was separated into three areas. In one, games of various types were being played and enjoyed. In another, a few pairs danced, some of them doing little more than rubbing their bodies together in time to the music. Men outnumbered women; and most females present were either visitors to Tochara, or were mates or lovers of *villites* who lived in the settlement. When Pleasure Givers were not sating men's desires—which was rare—they served drinks for Radu. But most customers had to go to the bar for their needs, where two men assisted the owner. The third area was for drinkers and talkers, her location.

Yana recognized familiar faces, whether or not she knew their names and foul deeds. Many of them sold stolen goods to Tochar and paid him a yearly fee for the privilege of existing in this rugged haven; others were buyers of those goods or had stopped by for rest and diversions. She didn't see any of the leader's thirty Enforcers and assumed they were on guard at the defense sites and water sources or patrolling the settlement. Nor did she see Auken, Sach, or Moig and surmised they were secluded with Pleasure Givers on the next level. She had learned that a few of those desire-saters were males who dressed and looked like females, as some men preferred that type of erotic satisfaction. Also on the upper level were small chambers where patrons could indulge in various drugs, alone or with a partner. Virtual reality devices were located there in private cubicles; some, she had heard, offered sexual games which evoked incredible sensations when enhanced by drugs, but she had never been tempted to try them. She had a virtual reality unit on her ship for diversion and for practice sessions with assignments, one which could be programed with any image and scene she desired and which allowed her to either control the action or allow the situation to travel where it willed.

Yana's roaming gaze paused and drifted over Dagan Latu who sat alone at a table with a drink before him and his eyes focused on her. She complimented herself for seizing his attention so quickly—even though her Yana facade and manner were responsible—and before she got close enough for her special fragrance to ensnare him. One of the few unoccupied tables was beside his position, so she walked in that direction with a subtle sway to her hips.

Dagan observed the voluptuous creature with eyes as blue as a Kalfan sky in summer and features that were flawless in shape and size. Her hair was thick and long, with little curl, and as golden as the midnight sun that orbited his world. Her figure and movements were perfection. She was clad in a multicolored jumpsuit with flesh-revealing circles along the lengths of her arms and legs, and with matching cutouts at her abdomen and back. He noted a wide gold ring around her slender neck. It was her sole adornment, as no jewelry graced her ears, wrists, or fingers. A *lazette* was secured to one sleek thigh just above the knee, the fake jewels of its holder catching light and sparkling as she moved. There was a sultriness and allure about her that was arousing, especially since it had been a long time since he had enjoyed sex, a fact he had been reminded of during his two encounters with Starla. He had hoped Starla would appear this evening, but that seemed unlikely now; perhaps that denial was fortunate since he seemed to be susceptible to the enchanting pirate.

As the striking creature neared, Dagan smiled and stood to seat her, assuming from her thorough scan of his person

MOONBEAMS AND MAGIC   49

that she was joining him. He was amused and bewildered
when she broke their visual bond with nonchalance and
claimed the next table, putting her back to him. Almost
feeling foolish, he sat down. He realized she was from the
Asisa Galaxy, as the faint blue tinge to her hair, skin, and
sclera of her eyes were traits of that alien race. He couldn't
help but wonder what she was doing in a rough and crude
settlement like Tochara. He ruled out the position of a Pleasure Giver, as she would be occupied on the next level of
the Skull's Den. He doubted she was anyone's steady companion, as no intelligent man would allow her to come there
alone. A lack of a marriage band on her wrist told him she
was mateless. She must be a regular customer, since Radu
appeared well acquainted with her. For certain, she was not
Tochar's lover; he had seen that redhead earlier and knew
she was *Binixe,* an hermaphroditic race from a planet in the
Thracian Galaxy.

Dagan leaned back in his seat, sipped his drink, and tried
to ignore her. He was about as successful as the other men
present, who were almost drooling over the beauty. He decided that either she was off limits or had scorned them in
the past because none approached her, which increased his
curiosity. Her heady fragrance filled his nose, despite competition from the many other smells in the area. It was as
if she exuded a powerful pheromone which stimulated his
sex glands and enticed him as potently as Starla Vedris did.
He looked at her tresses flowing over the chair and halting
near a slim waist. Vain and a teaser, he concluded. He
wasn't in the mood for games, and conceit always cooled
his physical interest in a female, no matter her beauty, or
how badly he needed sexual release.

Yana sensed his potent gaze. She was not surprised he
didn't approach her after a seeming rebuff on her part. In
fact, she was glad he did not pour himself over her in an
attempt to lure her into a casual sexual encounter, though
he must be fighting a fierce battle to resist her Kalfan mat-

ing scent. Cypher had prepared the pheromone and mixed it with an exotic floral aroma, and she had applied it sparingly for this first encounter. Four men who were regular patrons asked her to dance or to join them, and she told them she was waiting for a companion to arrive. After a fifth, a stranger to Tochara, proved difficult to discourage for a while, she turned and asked Dagan, "Would you mind sitting with me while I have my drink so I can enjoy it without being bothered again?"

Dagan was taken off-guard by the request, spoken in a soft and polite tone. "I'm comfortable here, but you can join me if you wish. I assure you you'll be safe and untroubled at my table. Conversation is by your choice."

Yana took the seat across from him and smiled. "Thank you for the assistance. May I buy you a drink out of gratitude?"

"Later, if you're here when I finish this one. Name's Dagan Latu."

"I'm Yana. Have you just arrived? I don't recall seeing you before."

Dagan lowered his glass, and his gaze met hers. Mysteries intrigued and challenged him, so he would play along with her ruse, because he was convinced she had intended to join him from the *preon* she had arrived. Perhaps she worked for Tochar and he was being studied. "That means you must be a regular in here during stopovers or you live in Tochara." It was a statement on his part, not a question.

"Both. Is this a visit for you or a move here?"

"I'll be around for a long time. I just hired on to work for Tochar."

Yana lifted her light-brown brows and widened her gaze to indicate surprise. "Every man in the settlement craves such an elite position, so you must possess many skills to catch Tochar's eye. He hires only the best."

He changed the subject abruptly. "I thought I caught your eye for a while there, but I guess I was mistaken."

That was not the response she expected, but her wits did not scatter for more than a few moments. She lowered her long lashes and smiled before meeting his gaze again. "You did, but I don't approach strangers and normally do not accept their invitations to join them."

"Unless you require one's assistance or protection." He watched her eyes brighten and her lips give way to another radiant smile as she nodded.

"I don't like to cause noisy scenes and Radu doesn't tolerate trouble. In a settlement where men vastly outnumber women, it is difficult to be left alone when I only want to relax and have a drink."

"Even if females outnumbered males, you would have that problem. What do you do in Tochara?" he asked, wording his query with care.

"Very little. I'm only staying for a short time longer. There was a situation I had to escape and decided this was the last place anyone would search for me. I didn't realize Tochara was so . . . primitive. Fortunately, I know how to protect myself and to survive even under crude conditions." She laughed when he sent her a doubtful grin. "I meant, defend myself during perilous situations. Men like those five are nothing more than nuisances who need to be sent away quickly and quietly to avoid drawing unwanted attention and embarrassment to myself. Or to them, since men do not take such predicaments well. As soon as matters are settled and it's safe, I'll return to where I came from."

Dagan leaned forward, propped his arms on the table, and ventured, "Which is the Asisia Galaxy."

She feigned a look of dismay to lure him into her spell. She reasoned that a man like him would be drawn to a woman in danger, snared by a challenging mystery, not to mention highly responsive to the sensuous image Yakir had given her, and weakened by the captivating fragrance. "You know me? Were you sent to locate and retrieve me? I rarely talk with anyone, and when I do, it's to the wrong man. Your vile task will not be easy; I have sanctuary here."

Dagan grasped her hand and kept her from rising to depart, noting how soft and warm her skin was. He was intrigued by her distress and hints, as he hadn't heard anything about a political upheaval in that location. No *bijonis* had been summoned, and its ruler had no daughters. That left him with the conclusion that the matter was a personal dilemma. "Don't panic, Yana; I'm not here because of you. I guessed from your colorings."

Her gaze seemingly searched his as she asked, "Is that the truth?"

He nodded and smiled. "You're still safe, so relax. Is it something you want to talk about with me? Can I help in some way? I'll guard your secret."

"Perhaps you would, but I'll keep it for now." As she finished her drink, she realized either he would be dead tomorrow or he would become one of her targets as Tochar's hireling. Both thoughts were unsettling, and it was more strenuous than she had imagined to spend time with the appealing and disturbing man while on constant alert against slips. She had made the initial contact and seized his interest; that was sufficient for now.

"Would you like to have another drink to calm you?" he offered.

"Thank you, but no. It's late and I need to leave."

"Will I see you again?" he asked, suspecting he would.

"If you're alone when I return next time, I'll join you and stay longer, or you can join me if I arrive first."

"Can I walk you to your dwelling?"

"It isn't necessary. Perhaps next time, after I know you better."

Dagan was unsure how to interpret her meaning. "If you need me for anything, *anything,* Yana, Radu knows where to find me."

She nodded acceptance of his offer, whatever it entailed.

She stood and said, "Thank you for the rescue and I look forward to seeing you again."

"Any time, Yana." He watched her enter the women's private chamber. Radu approached and blocked his view as he was deciding whether or not to follow her to see where she lived and check if she met with anyone.

The owner of the Skull's Den interrupted his thoughts. "Your abode is cleaned and ready to habitate," Radu said. "Drose will guide you there at your signal."

"Thank you. Tochar will be pleased by the good service I've received. I needed the bath, food, and fresh garment." He looked the owner deep in the eyes. "Tell me, Radu, do you know who Yana is and why she is in Tochara?"

The stocky man knew, but felt it was Yana's right and place to reveal those facts if she chose to do so. "My mouth does not travel across other's space. She visits here on occasion, but keeps to herself. You're a lucky man to have shared a drink with her; that's a rare event for Yana. I can tell you no more. Summon Drose when you're ready to leave."

Dagan realized the man knew more than he had revealed, but was glad Radu wasn't a loose talker. He watched for Yana to reappear, and finally decided she had left while his view was obstructed. A woman that beautiful and alluring, he reasoned, couldn't be hard to locate if he decided to do so another time. Too restless for sleep, and the hour too early, he purchased another drink and settled back in his chair to observe some more. It remained to be seen if signing on with Tochar would be profitable, but it surely would be challenging, and he had no choice under the circumstances in any case.

Only an *hora* passed before Starla Vedris arrived, glanced around, and locked gazes with him. He lifted his hand and motioned for her to join him. From her expression and stroll to the bar, it appeared as if this wasn't his night to succeed with any woman. He realized he was wrong again as he

watched her purchase a drink, then walk toward him. His
lagging energy was renewed and thoughts of Yana vanished
just by looking at the beautiful and mysterious *spaceki*. His
keen wits went on alert and he prepared to see what he
could learn about the lovely space pirate and his other teammates.

Three

Dagan watched Starla approach in a green jumpsuit that matched her eyes. Long brown tresses tumbled over her shoulders. Her movements were fluid and graceful, confident. Her aura was feminine, despite the laser weapon strapped to her waist. She sat down and sipped her drink as they studied each other. "It's late. I had given up on seeing you tonight," he told her.

"We didn't have plans to meet."

"I know, Starla, but I was hoping you'd come."

"Why?"

"So you could tell me about Tochara and working for Tochar."

"You'll learn all you need to know later, after your meeting with Tochar; that's when you'll be told if he accepts you or not."

Dagan leaned forward and propped his arms on the table, catching a whiff of her fragrance, which was so different from Yana's heavier scent. "I was under the impression he had hired me and assigned you as my teacher."

"Not until he has a lengthy and private talk with you."

"About what?" he asked, and took a long drink from his glass.

"That's between you and Tochar. I can't tell you anything until you're an insider and we're certain you can be trusted."

Though the crowd had lessened at the Skull's Den, Dagan leaned closer and murmured in a low voice, "You should know I can be trusted, since I didn't betray you. What's my continued silence worth?"

Starla walked her gaze over his grinning face with deliberate leisure. "Since I didn't take your life, that should be ample payment."

"Weren't you just a little nervous and surprised when you saw me?"

"No more than you were when you saw me."

"Aren't you afraid I'll change my mind and expose you?"

Starla leaned forward and whispered, "No, but do it and I'll kill you for certain next time because you wouldn't deserve this second chance."

Dagan scrutinized her frosty gaze and heard her cold tone, but felt they were faked. She had been scared and tense during their earlier meeting, but she had concealed her feelings with skill and practice. Her full mouth was tempting and he wanted to taste it. He wanted to know everything about her, but not succumb to her many charms. He chuckled. "I believe you would attempt to kill me, so I'll try hard not to rub you wrong or be caught off guard again. Why exactly did you let me live?"

Starla felt her rebellious body and emotions responding to him and ordered them to cease. "I don't want to have life-taking charges placed on my record, and I don't kill unless my life is in jeopardy. I presumed you wouldn't be a future threat because you'd be long gone from this sector; I figured you must have been free-riding for a good reason. I was partly right."

"I assume, since you covered my head, Moig didn't see me."

They were keeping their voices low and could not be overheard. "That's right," she admitted. "But even if you tell Tochar who you are, I doubt it will get me exiled; I'm too valuable to him. He'll consider it a weakness but not a fatal flaw. Don't forget, Tochar knows and trusts me."

"Will he, after learning you lied to him and Moig about

my death? From my experiences, disobedience is more acceptable than deceit."

"I'll deal with that problem if it comes up. Besides, you also deceived him and could be exposed. Why did you hold silent about me?"

"I doubt Tochar would hire any man who was recently disabled by a woman, or by another man for that matter. That would tarnish my prowess, right? Surely you didn't expect me to admit you tricked me and stung my ego. Besides, I felt I owed you for sparing my life. If our positions had been reversed that *deega,* I would've taken your same course of action. Despite what we are, taking lives unnecessarily is dangerous and costly. What you did doesn't make me doubt your loyalty to Tochar, so why report it? Besides, Moig made that decision and gave my extermination order."

"But Tochar agreed with it after our return and even rewarded me for killing you. Now, tell me. How did you really get here?"

"After I came to, hardly able to breathe thanks to you and that sack, I piloted the vessel close enough to use the escape pod, then sent it on its way out of this sector. I came down in the wasteland, out of their sensor range, and walked here. Tochar's patrol found me and took me to him. I'm sure he's already checked me out thoroughly."

That's what you think, Dagan, but you're in for a surprise tomorrow. "So, you were heading for Tochara all along?"

"It sounded like the best way to earn plenty in a short time and in a safe haven. I was planning to take over that transporter that evening, but you intruded. Since we're going to be working together, it would be nice to be friends. We already have a bond of protective secrecy."

"Let's keep it like that. Did you get a good price for those crystals?"

"I doubt it, because I didn't know their value. Tochar does, so I assume they're targets during raids, despite his warning. I saw the way he looked at them and touched them, and he told me large ones supply the power for his defense system. What do you know about them?"

"If you join our team tomorrow, I'll tell you about the crystals and our raids."

As she took a swallow of the purple liquid, he asked, "Why do you keep saying 'if'?" He watched her tongue collect a droplet from her upper lip and felt his loins quicken and flame at the enticing action.

"You're a clever man so you must realize Tochar wouldn't hire anyone on first sight. He'll want to question you further, in detail, in private."

"No problem; I'll tell him whatever he wants to know."

For certain and without control, my ignorant auslander. I wish you would stop looking at me like that. What is it about you that's so irresistible? His black hair seemingly begged her to hide her fingers in its depths. His full lips called to her to kiss them, as did his handsome face and throat. His dark-blue eyes were as potent and mesmerizing as a swirling vortex, drawing her ever toward it. But he was a criminal, one of her targets soon, so she must not lose herself in him.

"What's on your mind, Starla? You look puzzled, worried."

"Somehow you don't strike me as a man who works for others."

"I rarely do, but I have no choice if I want to purchase a new ship. I heard Tochar pays well and gives unreachable sanctuary to his men. Of course, if I could get my hands on a load of those crystals, I'd be rich."

"If you could find a buyer without being captured and terminated."

"They're that important?"

"You'll see if you're around the next time Tochar tests his weapons or gives a display of power and warning to would-be attackers. It's formidable; not even a fully armed fleet of starships could attack here. Those beams are so powerful they can penetrate force shields. They also have other abilities."

"That means rich buyers are needed, and it's a risky venture to steal them. Why do you take such chances for him?"

"For the payment and excitement, and I have nothing else to occupy me at this time. As you know, it requires a lot of money to keep a ship supplied and fueled, and there are only certain kinds of raids one can pull off alone. Tochara is the best place to rest and hide."

"Hide from what? From whom?"

"Anybody who's after me."

"Such as?"

"Lots of people, maybe some of the same ones who are seeking you." She was enflamed by his sexy grin and rich chuckle after her response. He certainly made it difficult to keep her mind where it should be!

"That's possible, since we're so much alike. Auken told me you have a ship and live on it, and Tochar said you're one of the best pilots he's seen."

"All true, and I'm not boasting."

"I believe you. How long have you been on Tochara?"

Starla shrugged. "Who keeps track of time without a reason?"

"How long do you intend to live and work here?"

"I'll stay until I'm bored, since I doubt I'll get a better offer."

He noticed a tiny smile that time, but it didn't soften her steady gaze, so he decided it wasn't a natural one. "Where are you from?"

"All over, many places."

"I meant, what's your origin point?"

"It doesn't matter. I left it long ago and won't be returning."

Noting her sad expression, Dagan probed, "Any particular reason?"

"Several."

"Such as?"

"Nothing worth telling you. Besides, it's in the past, long gone."

Dagan realized he wasn't getting much information from her. She was as tight-lipped as a Kalfan leech, and was on tense alert. He wondered why he was making her so nervous, since she wasn't worried about him betraying her to Tochar. He finished his drink. "Any family?"

"No, all dead. What about you?"

"The same. My ship was my home and I miss her; she's probably been destroyed by now."

"That's too bad; our ships become like a part of us. It's certainly impossible to come and go freely without one."

"Where and when did you learn to pilot a ship?" he asked.

"Long ago and by somebody special to me." *My father and brother.*

"How long have you been living and traveling alone?"

"Apparently not long enough, since I'm still doing it."

"Doesn't it get lonely and scary for a woman in space by herself?"

"Is that how it affects you, why you're willing to be a lander?"

Dagan surmised she was amazingly quick and clever, an expert at this sort of get-nowhere conversation. He was more impressed and intrigued by the *preon.* "It happens on occasion to the best of us, doesn't it?"

"If you say so. But I'm not alone; I have an android for company."

"I know; Moig told me. But a robot isn't the same as a real person."

"Cypher is. He's the only companion I need, that I trust fully."

"You're a strange and beautiful woman, Starla Vedris, but a captivating mystery. Are you always so distant and secretive with everyone?"

"I prefer it that way; work and diversion never mix well."
*They definitely would not mingle safely and wisely with you,
Dagan Latu.*

"Are you speaking from experience?"

"Let's just say I'm convinced of that conclusion."

Dagan saw her green gaze widen and her enticing mouth
part in surprise when he asked, "Are you interested in Tochar as a man?"

"Tochar has a lover; Palesa. Beautiful and . . . feminine.
I'm certain Palesa is very talented at servicing his needs."
Cravings for both sexes would be his only reason for having
a *Binixe* lover. At least his carnal preference had prevented
any sexual overtures toward her. She had been ready to allege
she was a lesbian if such an offensive predicament arose.

Dagan leaned closer to her from across the small table.
His gaze meshed with hers. "You didn't reply to my query.
Are you afraid to answer?"

Starla decided that if she were compelled to get closer
to Dagan for any reason, she mustn't allow him to think
she was chasing after or was involved with their leader. "In
the sense you mean, I'm not attracted to or bound to any
man, including Tochar, and even if Palesa didn't exist. My
sole interest here is my work. Why would you ask such a
personal question?"

"Are you displeased you'll have to work with me?"

"Why should it bother me? One partner is as good as
another, if he has the skills to be my equal and backup. If
not, he doesn't work with me. So, why did you ask if I had
any interest in Tochar or any other man?"

"What if a teammate finds you lacking in some vital
area?"

"That hasn't happened so far. Now, reply to my previous
query or our conversation is over."

Obviously she didn't fear his answer or she would stop
pressing for it. Was she hoping he would admit to an interest

in her? If so, he mused, why? "Just curious. I'd like to see your ship. Any chance for a visit?"

"You will, if you join our unit, because we use it sometimes. We were on the *Liksa* that *deega* we met. Tochar often pairs me with Moig."

"From your look and tone, you would prefer Auken or Sach; right?"

"Yes; they have more skills and prowess and personality. Moig seems to enjoy harassing me under the guise of silly jokes. I find that annoying."

"I promise to make you an excellent partner when we travel as a team, which I hope is very soon. How old are you?"

Stars afire, go trekking alone with you! "Twenty-two *yings,* why?"

"Just curious. Would you like another drink? Your glass is empty."

"No thanks. I'll be leaving now." She needed to put distance between them after two lengthy and trying encounters in the same night. He was far too appealing to suit her, and she could not bear the stress any longer.

"Can I see you tomorrow night to get better acquainted as a team?" Dagan asked. "We'll be leaving on our first raid in two *deegas* and I have much to learn."

A bold idea entered her mind. "What if someone else joins you first?"

Dagan noticed instant, but rapidly concealed, vexation with herself after that query slipped from her mouth. "Were you here earlier?"

She had not made a rash slip, but pretended she had. She reasoned that if he didn't want to risk offending Starla, suspecting her interest would keep him from making a premature move on Yana, as sexual overtures to Yana would force her into making a decision about how far she was willing to go for the success of her crucial mission. Too, Yana might not be able to extract clues if she didn't surrender to him.

She also hoped that hearing she had sighted him with the sultry temptress would stress the point they were different women. A little encouragement might also pull him toward Starla in case he proved worthy of being trusted and asked to work with her on her assignment. Since he was a man who loved challenges, winning over a reluctant Starla should be enticing to him. If not, Yana would have to use him. "I'll see you around, Dagan Latu, if you stay past tomorrow," she said in parting.

Dagan grasped her hand, forcing her to stay seated. Realizing he had done the same thing with Yana gave him an eerie feeling. Her hands were a little larger than the golden-haired beauty's, but Starla's were cool and just as soft. Her green eyes glittered in warning, a contrast to Yana's alluring blue ones. Her complexion was darker, but flawless and supple. Her figure, as perfect as Yana's. Comparing the two women was like trying to parallel night and day. Yana was desirable and provocative, but the space pirate had intoxicating spirit and vitality. Starla was strong; yet, still feminine. Yana was the type of female perfect for enjoyable company and pleasure, but Starla Vedris was of value at any time and place. "You don't like being attracted to me, do you?"

She leaned so far forward that she knew he could smell the heady beverage on her breath and the fragrance she had applied after washing off Yana's scent. There was only a forearm's distance between their faces, and their challenging gazes were locked as she murmured, "Let's get one thing straight, Dagan: work is all we'll do together, and only if Tochar teams us up after your meeting with him; so keep your feelings and thoughts to yourself. Better still, find a woman who will be responsive to them. I'm not."

Dagan did not release his grip when she tugged to get loose. He sensed her increase in tension and saw the way her gaze engulfed him. Surely he wasn't mistaken about the desire glowing in her eyes. "If you're referring to Yana, we met by accident. She needed rescuing from nuisances."

"I'm sure she did, and you were only too eager to help her. Let's drop this topic because you two aren't of interest to me."

"As you can see, Starla, I'm still here and she's gone."

"I doubt that was your idea, so don't try to mislead or charm me. I've met men like you before, so don't think you can blast off with me."

"You're wrong, Starla, you've never met anyone like me, so don't be afraid to get to know me; I'll behave myself during that process." As if to prove his words, he released her hand and leaned back in his chair.

"If you give me trouble, Dagan, Tochar will have to choose between us. If you behave, we'll work together just fine. Good night."

"Good night, Starla, and thanks again for saving my life."

"Just don't make me regret it," she quipped.

Starla passed Sach as she was departing for the landing grid. She halted to talk with him for a few *preons*. Afterward, while en route to her shuttle, she pondered her crazy feelings for Dagan Latu. Perhaps her strong attraction to him resulted from having his life in her hands and being able to save it, when she had been helpless to do the same for Antarus Hoy following the crash of their spacer three *yings* ago during an Elite Squad mission. Both injured and their supplies depleted and on the brink of death, she had surrendered to his need for her. Except for anguish over being unable to protect her and fearing she wouldn't survive, he had died a happy man, believing she loved him as much as he loved her. The mission had been a success and she had been rescued, but she had lost her first and only teammate. Then she had been paired with Cypher, an arrangement which suited her just fine and had proven successful.

Since Antarus's death, she had enjoyed evenings with

other men, but none had affected her as Dagan Latu did. What, she mused, was his special and potent appeal if not for her hand in his fate? Perhaps she had spared his life only to be forced to take it on a future *deega* if it came to a life-or-death battle for escape, or be forced to endure his loss to a annihilator unit or exile to a penal colony after his capture, dependent upon which of his past charges were true and what he did while in Tochar's hire. She must not allow herself to become emotionally involved and ensnared by him. She must keep reminding herself he was a *villite*, a man out of her reach.

But what if you could turn him away from his nefarious ways? What if he could be persuaded to help you defeat Tochar? What if he could obtain a pardon for— Don't think such foolish things. Bree-Kayah, that's flying on a dangerous course for you and the entire UFG.

She reached her shuttle, prepared for lift-off, and went to her ship.

Sach joined Dagan. "You look better than you did earlier," he jested.

Dagan leaned back in his seat and smiled. "I feel better, too; trekking through that wasteland was rough. I'm lucky I didn't encounter any of those *Skalds;* from what I've been told, human flesh is a treat for them."

"At least those mutants stay in the desert and don't trouble us, not since Tochar scared them away from the fringes with a taste of his weapons. You'll be safe here, because nobody challenges him and those beamers."

"That's good news, since there are more than a few people who would like to get their greedy hands on me, and I'm grounded. I don't like feeling vulnerable to them. I'm eager to fill my pockets and get me a new ship; it feels strange not having a deck beneath my boots and warp drive at my fingertips. With what Tochar pays, that shouldn't take more than a *ying* or two, depending on what type I purchase next time. It will definitely have a cloaking device and lots of speed. That run-in at Gavas with a *Seki* is the closest I've come to getting caught, and it didn't flow over me well. That's the only time the old girl failed me and it wasn't her fault. I think I'm going to enjoy Tochara. It has plenty to offer; so does Tochar. I'd like to keep working for him and living in this haven even after I get a new ship, if that suits him. How long have you been with Tochar?"

"Tochar, Auken, and I have been a team since we were young. We've raided all over the Cosmos. Moig joined us about five *yings* ago, long before we settled here." Sach tossed down his drink and purchased another one.

"What about Starla Vedris? She and I were just talking, but she isn't very communicative. Or maybe it's me she doesn't like," Dagan chuckled and downed the remainder of his drink.

Sach also chuckled. He wasn't worried about chatting with Dagan, as the man would be silenced the following day if he didn't prove trustworthy. "She'll open up more after you get to know her. She was quiet and private when we met. She's been on her own for so long and staying just a few leaps ahead of capture that she's wary and used to keeping to herself, careful about who she gets close to and trusts. The good thing is that Tochar likes and wants you. He says you're perfect for our special unit."

"What is the 'special unit' and who's in it?" Dagan asked.

Sach explained about his leader's Enforcers and how everyone who lived or traded in the colony paid Tochar for that privilege, for water, and for protection. "Only our team raids for him alone. There were four of us until you came along: me, Auken, Moig, and Starla. You'll learn more tomorrow and during our first raid."

Only four space pirates in the band . . . "Since there are so few of you going on raids, that speaks highly of the unit's skills. It's comforting to learn I'll be working with people who know how to take care of themselves and back up their teammates." Dagan watched Sach smile in pleasure at his compliment. "I've never met a female pirate before Starla. I've seen women traveling and working with men, but never alone. What's her story?"

"She's grabbed your interest fast and hard, eh?"

Dagan grinned. "She's a beautiful, fascinating, and unique woman."

"You're right, but don't treat her as an easy conquest; she still flies by herself where men are concerned."

"Is there a reason why?"

"Auken thinks it's because she was either hurt by a man or lost one she loved. Probably doesn't want to get close to anybody she could lose again, and we do lead dangerous lives. Or could be she's just very selective. She doesn't talk much, if any, about her past. Seems to live for the *deega*."

Dagan noticed that Sach was becoming more and more relaxed, perhaps due to the many drinks he was consuming. He continued his questioning. "How long has she been here?"

"About three *malees*. She was trying to escape a Serian patrol after raiding an orbiting supply station for food, water, and fuel. They chased her across the entire sector, determined to capture her or blast her to pieces. We were on Auken's ship, returning from a raid, when they shot through the stargate, just missed hitting the *Adika*, and zoomed past us like speeding comets. You should have seen her evading their blasts; she's the best pilot I've ever encountered. We watched and listened to their exchanges. They ordered her to stop and surrender, but she told them they had no authority across the boundary. They said she wasn't escaping them if they had to chase her across three galaxies. When she realized that patrol wasn't going to give up, she turned her ship and went straight at them, firing away. Blasted them into bits of debris. We contacted her and told her to head for Noy. It took a while to convince her she would be safe here, but she took a chance."

"She actually destroyed a patrol ship and crew?"

"She had no choice if she wanted to survive, and the fools were in the Free-Zone. She probably confused them by turning and fighting; they didn't think a woman would respond that way. She was lucky to be on this side of the stargate when she destroyed them; that put them out of communication with their force, so life-taking charges didn't go on her record. All the Serians know is that one of their patrol ships vanished while in pursuit of a pirate. Starla's been real careful about working on the sly to keep her record short in case she's ever captured. She's tough, but she doesn't like to kill unless it can't be avoided."

"But she does have an incriminating record?"

Sach nodded. "Mostly made up of things like that Serian raid, enough to get her sent to a penal colony for life. She planned to leave us as soon as she rested, but Tochar convinced her staying would be safe and profitable."

"How long was she operating in Seri?" Dagan asked after Radu served them another drink.

"That was her third raid; she picked up weapons on one and a part for her cloaking device on the other. That's why she couldn't cloak and elude them, no time to install it. Since she's been here, Cypher repaired it."

"I'm curious. Where did she get the android?"

"It was being delivered to her father, a scientist on a skyball when the entire floating city was destroyed by a reactor malfunction. She was born and raised there, but she had gone with her brother to get the unit, the first time she had been off her world since birth. The android was ready for programing, so she ordered him to serve her. I don't know much about robots and computers and such, but that Cypher talks and acts so like a human sometimes that it's eerie. That's probably why Starla treats him as if he is alive. After that skyball exploded, she traveled with her brother for a couple of *yings*. He became a smuggler, but wasn't very successful. He taught her to fly, fight, and use weapons. After he and his men were killed by one of his buyers, she took off in his ship with Cypher as her crew."

"I haven't heard of her before; where was she operating before Seri?"

"Pyropea, Androas, Maffei, and other places. When it got hot for her in one sector, she left for another. She isn't rash or impulsive, but she had no choice about that last raid; she needed supplies and fuel to vanish for a while. Tochar was impressed by her; he said we could use a pilot with a fast ship and somebody with courage, wits, and skills like hers. He offered her sanctuary and asked her to join us. She hasn't failed or disappointed him. The rest of us enjoy working with her; she's good, real good."

Dagan was learning a lot about Starla. He wanted to learn more, so he continued questioning Sach. "Was all of her family killed except her brother?"

Sach nodded. "She's lucky she was gone when its reactor went critical because there was no time for evacuation. The few ships that took flight were caught up in the blast; it must have been a huge explosion."

"That's a real shame. Those incidents must have been tough for her, being a female and one so young."

Sach nodded again and downed his drink. "Starla's educated, intelligent, and well bred; her family was rich and powerful. I guess it's hard for a woman to lose everything and not change a lot."

"I understand how she feels. After those *Sekis* terminated my father and brother for alleged crimes, all I wanted to do was pay them back."

"It sounds like you've given them trouble for a long time. They don't take defeat and humiliation good, and you've given them plenty of both."

"That's part of the excitement and challenge: to bite and run, have them pursue, then elude them and leave them with singed pride. Do you think Starla's a permanent inhabitant here?"

"I don't know. If she ever gets tired of being a pirate, she could have her looks changed and live elsewhere. I'm sure Tochara doesn't have much to offer a woman like her; that's why she lives on her ship. But after Tochar makes his improvements here, she might stay for good." Sach grinned and jested, "Unless you lure her away when you leave, if you do. You may want to stay here after Tochara becomes a real city. All it needs is more time, wealth, and power, and some of those magic crystals. Best empty many glasses tonight and tomorrow, Dagan, because no drinking is allowed during raids."

"That's a wise precaution. Tell me, why does Moig call her Vedris?"

Sach laughed heartily. "To keep him from thinking of her as a woman. Moig didn't stand a flick of a chance with her; he's finally accepted the fact he isn't her type."

"Am I?"

Sach chuckled as he toyed with his empty glass. "Don't know. As I said, she keeps to herself about men. About the only one here who could match her is Tochar, and he's involved with Palesa."

"That's good news; he would be a tough competitor for her."

"You're lucky he doesn't desire Starla or she would belong to him. If all you need is a woman for your *sleeper,* there are plenty of Pleasure Givers here."

"That isn't why Starla appeals to me." *Give it to him good, Dagan; nothing like supposedly sharing a secret to dupe a person into believing you like him and trust him.* "To be truthful, Sach, I don't know why she gets to me and how she did it so fast. She has some kind of powerful magic and pull. I've never been tempted to go after a woman for serious reasons. Maybe that's a warning to avoid her before I'm snared in a crazy trap."

"Just take it slow and easy until you decide. Don't hurt her."

"I'll take that good advice. I guess I better turn in; it's late and I have to meet with Tochar in the morning. Been enjoyable talking with you."

"Same here, Dagan, and good luck."

"With my meeting or with Starla?"

"You'll need plenty of it to succeed with both."

After Sach stood and left, Dagan pondered the Icarian's parting words. He had a suspicion he was in for a huge surprise tomorrow.

It had been three *horas* since Starla took a seat in the Skull's Den to await news about Dagan. She didn't know if she wanted him to pass Tochar's *Thorin* test or not. If he failed, that meant he wasn't evil like the other *villites* or—even if he was proven to be just as wicked—wouldn't truly subject himself to the head *fiendal*. But failure meant his extermination. Yet, if he passed the truth and loyalty queries, he would become one of her targets to defeat and destroy, and would prove he was no different from them, prove her favorable impressions of him were wrong. By passing, he would be alive and in close proximity, until and if her mission succeeded. She felt trapped between two black holes in space, floating in peril, wondering if or when she would be sucked in and crushed by either one.

She knew from experience that the drug-induced interrogation and full recovery lasted for *horas:* thirty *preons* to be dazed completely, several *horas* of lengthy and detailed questions to learn his full history and motives, and one *hora* to return to complete awareness, plus travel time to and from the *fiendal*'s abode. According to that schedule he should have been finished five *horas* ago. Even if he had been taken on a tour of the defense sites and colony after he passed scrutiny, she reasoned, he should have appeared by now, if for nothing more than to have a drink and relax following his ordeal and perhaps to see if she and/or Yana awaited him. He wasn't with her Yana identity, but he could be celebrating on the second level with a Pleasure Giver. She attempted to quell the rash sparks of jealousy and anger that troubled her. It was a fact that most men believed they must have sex on a regular basis and, often, the face and name of the woman beneath them did not matter. Those carnal drives were strong in Tochara, where men lived and thrived on sating physical needs and thought only of the present.

She had played two games of *resi* with an off-duty Enforcer. She had eaten a rather tasty meal with the slowness of a *yema*'s pace to stall for time. She was on her second drink, the weakest type Radu stocked, as it seemed appropriate behavior for her Starla Vedris character to imbibe a little, and it gave her a plausible reason to remain in the place for a long period.

When she saw him enter the dome, her heart leapt with relief and happiness, uncontrollable reactions to learning he was alive. Of their own volition, her green gaze softened and almost misted; her heart beat faster; her lips parted. He was clad in a sleeveless top with a V neck in the front, the same shade as his blue eyes, a garment which displayed his muscled arms and shoulders and sun-darkened flesh. It fit him like a second skin, so his broad chest and flat abdomen were noticeable. His pants were snug, black like his boots and windblown hair, and hinted at sleek and strong legs beneath them. A weapon's belt was secured around his waist and hung low on the left side where a laser gun rested in a holster secured to his thigh. A sheathed knife was attached to the belt's right side. He was the epitome of a virile and handsome man, a pinnacle of strength and courage.

As Dagan's roving gaze found her and he smiled, Starla returned the gesture without awareness, her wits scattering.

Without taking his eyes from hers, she watched the Kalfan head toward her with an agile and confident stride. She stood entranced by his very presence, until Radu halted him for a brief word. As soon as their visual bond was severed and other thoughts invaded her mind, the strong and magical spell was broken and she became clearheaded. She scolded herself for being susceptible to Dagan's abundant charms. From now on, she reminded herself, he was one of her enemies; he must be viewed and treated as such, used in any way necessary to ensure the success of her mission. She took a swallow of her drink and did not look in his direction again.

Dagan sat down adjacent to her instead of across the small table. He was cognizant of her change in mood. There was no doubt in his mind that Starla had been excited and pleased to see him but had withdrawn into herself when Radu intruded on their spiritual connection. Now that he was acquainted with her troubled history, that reaction was understandable. He glanced up and thanked Radu for a drink the man delivered, compliments of Tochar, as was anything Dagan ordered tonight on either level of the Skull's Den. He ignored the beverage to ask, "How long have you been here?"

Starla was alert and calm by that time; yet, strange sensations of sadness and weariness plagued her. "For a while."

"Were you worried about me?"

Starla leaned back and toward the right side of her chair to put more distance between them. "No, why would I be?" She watched him grin.

"Because you knew what I was facing. Too bad you couldn't warn me."

"Was a warning needed? Would it have changed anything?"

He chuckled. "If I wasn't who and what I claimed to be,

I could have gotten out of Tochara before I was exposed and slain."

"There's no place you can hide from Tochar's reach and wrath."

"You didn't think I would pass scrutiny, did you?"

She looked him straight in the eye and admitted, "No."

Dagan was pleased by her honesty and her skepticism about his bad character, despite a criminal record and shady reputation. Yet, he sensed disappointment that her assessment of him had been proven wrong. "Why not? You passed interrogation when *Thorin* flowed in your veins."

Unlike with you, his truth serum had no effect on me. "You struck me as being your own man, a loner, self-reliant, a leader, not a follower."

"Do taking orders from Tochar and being loyal to the man who hires me prevent me from having those traits?"

"Does it?"

"Not in your case, nor in mine; we're still independent and self-reliant loners, but we bend and bond when we must. Under the grim circumstances, I have to work for him to get what I want and need." Dagan grinned to release their tensions and teased in a husky voice, "Unless you want to lure me away with a better offer."

Starla did not smile. "How would I accomplish that enormous feat?"

"You have the *Liska;* we could travel as partners, keep all we steal." *Access to your ship would give me a means of quick escape if needed and would provide the opportunity for private communication out of the Free-Zone. But that could imperil you if I used them, used you for my needs, which might become necessary if matters change.*

Starla wondered why Dagan was studying her so strangely. "Why would I forfeit Tochar's generosity and sanctuary to take risks with you? Besides, he would track us and slay us for committing such treachery. As with me, since you're alive, that means you told the truth about being loyal to him, so you're only teasing me. It also means you're part of our special unit."

Stars afire, woman, you're quick, clever, and captivating! To throw her off balance, he grinned and murmured, "Was I teasing?" Starla didn't smile or reply, so he hinted, "No congratulations? No welcome aboard? No glad you survived?"

Once more, Starla had the impression that Dagan Latu was a cunning and complex male. If she didn't know any better, she would think he had deluded Tochar. It worried her that she could not depend upon her normally keen instincts and gift for good judgment with him. She took a swallow of her drink and eyed him over the glass's rim before she lowered it and responded, "Welcome to the special unit, Dagan. Since we're going to be working together in dangerous situations, becoming friends would be wise. I wouldn't want an enemy at my back."

"Being your enemy is the last thing I want, Starla, and becoming friends will do for a start."

"What more do you want and expect from me?"

"Right to the point, a bold and direct woman. I like that."

"I'm pleased you think I have admirable qualities and traits."

"I made that discovery the first time we met; you're an amazing woman. In case you're worried," he began in a near whisper, though no one was nearby, "Tochar didn't ask any questions about that incident, or about how I allegedly got to Noy, or about you. Except," he added and saw her tense, "he did ask if I knew you or anybody else here before I came. It was easy to be honest because I didn't know you prior to my arrival."

She stared at him. Was it possible he was immune to *Thorin,* that he had tricked Tochar, that her initial appraisal of him was indeed accurate? And why tell her—one of Tochar's *Spacekis*—such a hazardous secret? "How could you know what he asked while you were under that drug?"

If you're wrong about her, Dagan, you could be entrapping yourself. When she arrived here, she was truthful about her record and history and about giving fealty to Tochar or she would be dead now, but hopefully she's attracted enough to you to hold silent. "I had a recorder concealed in my boot and I listened to my session afterward." He witnessed a look of astonishment in Starla's eyes, as well as something he decided was dismay.

Four

The Kalfan's revelation took Starla by surprise and she responded before thinking, "That was taking a big risk, Dagan; Tochar isn't a fool, nor a man to deceive if you want to stay alive and work for him."

Her spontaneous reaction pleased Dagan, as it implied she cared about him and his survival. "If he was a dimwit, he wouldn't have control of this settlement and I wouldn't be interested in him. Besides, I had to be sure I didn't say anything disadvantageous or hazardous to me."

Starla regained her self-control. "Either you're daring and clever and fearless, or you're reckless and savor living on the edge." She saw him grin as if she had described him with accurate insight.

"I always try never to be reckless or impulsive." *But with you, woman, that's difficult; you're much too tempting and disarming. Maybe I should be worried that my interest in you equates with the one in Tochar, and that isn't smart; it could complicate and jeopardize the situation; Tochar has what Phaedrig wants, and I vowed to get it for him, any way necessary.*

Starla placed her glass on the table, unsettled by his mental study of her. "Do you use your little hidden unit very much? Is it on now?"

"Neither, and I destroyed that tape. Does he do more than one test?"

"Not to my knowledge. Afraid you'll change your mind,

allow that independent streak to break through, and ruin future results?" She listened to his rich chuckles. She wished it wasn't such a fierce struggle to keep from staring at him and so strenuous a task to remain alert in his distracting presence.

"I just like to know what I'm up against. I don't like flying through a storm without sensors to guide me. I can use a friend while I'm grounded and a trusted co-pilot when we take flight, so I'm glad you aren't being defensive and distant with me anymore. I imagine you have your reasons for being that way, especially with strangers."

"I do. As a woman in my type of work, I have to be stronger, braver, smarter, and tougher than even the weakest of men to be accepted and respected. Or at least be a skilled pretender to dupe them into thinking I am. If I let down my guard, many try to take advantage of me or forget I have just as much prowess as they do and—in some cases— more."

He realized she wasn't bragging or exaggerating. Yet, he sensed her hard exterior was a protective shield for a unique and tender woman. Still, she was too enchanting and disarming to suit him. "I'm convinced you possess those traits; you took me down quick and easy on that ship. It was quite a shock and enlightenment. I remember every detail about our misadventure."

Starla didn't want to discuss their first meeting because of provocative things she had said to him, expecting never to confront him again and surely not as his teammate. "It's getting late, so I'll see you again at departure time."

"I hoped we could talk longer. You are supposed to edify me." He yearned to stretch out his fingers to fluff the tousled fringe of hair across her forehead. He wanted to touch and kiss her full lips and flawless skin, each exquisite feature on her face. He hungered to caress soft but firm flesh beneath a white jumpsuit which was a vivid contrast to dark-brown tresses that covered straight shoulders. Her green eyes enticed him to dive into their depths and search for the truth about her, to locate and claim the real woman. Even the weapon she wore heightened his desire for the mysterious and complex creature from a distant origin.

Starla knew it was futile to order herself to stop being attracted to him. "Don't you think you've seen and heard and done enough for one *deega?*" she asked in an attempt to control those intrusive emotions. "You were shown the defense sites and settlement, correct?"

"I got a tour. Those *Destructoids* are amazing. All it takes is removal of a cap to fire a formidable beam. I'm amazed such powers exist. Do you realize how mighty and invincible that makes Tochar and this colony?"

"That's why it's considered the safest haven for *villites* like us. Did they tell you the caps are the original encasements for those white crystals?" She waited for him to nod. "Whatever that rock is made of, it's the only thing that imprisons its laser force. Crystals are round or oblong in their natural state. A ray can be created only after a white one is given a pointed end, and only a blue one can spall other moonbeams." She related medical facets of the yellow crystals like the ones he sold to Tochar. "Imagine how handy it would be to have that powder in your pocket during a crash or accident. That blue one you had can be made into a scalpel with almost magical traits; it's the only color that can be cut by manmade instruments." After revealing its abilities, she said, "Nature is amazing; only one kind of crystal can give access to the powers and secrets of the others, and those capabilities depend upon their sizes and types."

"You know a lot about moonbeams. That *is* what they're called?"

"Yes, because their beams reminded discoverers of rays of moonlight, and their scientific name is long and hard to pronounce. You'll learn more during our raids; they're one of our targets. Despite their value and many uses, Tochar doesn't sell them or offer their magical powers here; to do so would cause a flood of buyers to come and attract too much attention, and it would provoke others to steal them and become competition. I learned all of this by keeping my eyes and ears open. It's good to gather any fact that might prove useful to me one *deega*. His most trusted men—his three closest friends—do make tiny slips on occasion, especially during raids."

"Auken, Sach, and Moig?"

"That's correct, so don't challenge them in any way or you're gone."

"Thanks for the warning; I suspected as much. If what you said about those crystals is accurate, if Tochar gets his hands on enough of them, he could rule the Universe, or enable his buyers to do so. One *ying* we could all be working for him or be under his subjection."

"If he has aspirations of conquest, I haven't heard them. His buyers would obtain the capability of preying on other worlds if he sells them the right type of crystals. I can't imagine him allowing anyone to gain such power; that slip could imperil him and his stronghold. As for me, I like the Universe as it is. Imagine how our existences would change if Tochar did become a conqueror, or if he enabled others to destroy the current balance of power between the galaxies. We would have no say in our fates."

"Sounds repulsive to me, almost a return to barbaric slavery."

"That's why the Serians and Kalfans tried so hard to protect that secret, but it slipped out, as most secrets do when profit is concerned. It hasn't been long since the crystals were discovered and mining began, and finding large specimens—especially those white hunks—is rare. Of course, without blue ones, the others are worthless. They make me think of colored ice."

"Why would either galaxy risk transporting them off their planets?"

"Shipments of them are small, but research and testing have to be done on secluded planetoids for safety and secrecy because their power is great and their potential not fully known. Tochar was fortunate that his first moonbeam raid resulted in acquiring those three awesome weapons."

"How did he accomplish such a feat?"

"The planetoid's force shield was disengaged during their transfer to a vessel for shipment to Ulux, Seri's head planet. Tochar's two units attacked them while they were vulnerable. His crafts were cloaked, so the androids and scientists didn't detect their presence until it was too late. Help was summoned, but the patrol's late arrival gave Tochar's band time to disable the androids and steal the cargo. One team and part of Auken's were trapped aboard the other vessel and wiped out during a battle and their craft destroyed, but the *Azoulay* cloaked and escaped with the *Destructoids;* that's what Tochar named his new weapons and it describes their power perfectly. Auken, Sach, and Moig were the only survivors. Tochar is rebuilding his special team; that's why he hired us. His Enforcers never go on raids; they remain here to protect him and Tochara."

"I'm surprised they told you such things when you joined up with them. Seems they would have kept quiet about such a disaster and the perilous risks you'd face; they didn't expose that information to me."

"When Sach is on Tochara, he likes to drink, drink heavily at times; that loosens his tongue to someone he trusts. But drinking is forbidden during treks. Sometimes all three get so accustomed to me being around that they forget I'm there and forget they aren't supposed to talk about such things in front of me, so they make slips. A dull-witted Sach once bragged about those being the only *Destructoids* in existence because large white crystals are rare. Tochar never lets them leave his colony; that would make him vulnerable to attack. If he ever gets his hands on another one, he'll mount it on an attack ship; then no target will be unobtainable to him. I also keep my eyes and ears open without notice."

"I will, too. I thought Auken's ship was named the *Adika.*"

"It is, but they were using Tochar's that *deega;* it's faster, and has a better cloaking device and force shield. The *Azoulay* is useless until we steal a part needed for his energy system. It has only enough power left to stay in orbit and sustain life-support for a small crew. The parts he located are inaccessible and hazardous for a four-member team to go after. As we know from past experiences, power units or fuel can't be obtained without the proper papers and approval, and space stations are dangerous to raid."

"You're right, and I'm paying for that reality. Those moonbeams intrigue me, especially since I virtually gave away three out of ignorance. I'm curious. Why isn't their transportation guarded by huge forces?"

"How do you know they aren't?"

His answer came quickly. "Because four pirates couldn't attack a vessel or a planetoid and escape with any crystals if they were confronted by a large and well-armed force."

"You're very astute," Starla complimented. "The shipments are carried out in assumed secrecy, usually with only one or two androids aboard to prevent drawing attention to them or giving the impression of a vessel worthwhile to attack."

"Then how does Tochar know when and where to raid?" His questions flowed swiftly and fluently. "How do we get those android pilots to halt and lower their force shields? How does Tochar market something so secretive and dangerous?"

Starla noted how intelligent and educated he seemed, in particular for a space pirate, and how inquisitive. "Obviously he has contacts in Seri and Kalfa, important men in the know. You'll soon learn we have various ways of assaulting our targets. As to his buyers, I don't know anything

about them, or if he's even sold any to date. I wouldn't
advise asking questions about moonbeams or his sources;
Tochar only shares that information with his three friends.
Even I'm not told our destination and target until we reach
them. I'm sure it will be the same with you."

"So, we're trusted, but we aren't. We're tested and accepted, but kept blinded. Interesting. . . . I've never hired
on with anybody who withheld information and didn't allow
me to help plan our strategy. That makes me a little wary
and edgy. How about you?" He saw Starla nod. "We can
be of great help and protection to each other if we stick
together."

Starla fused her gaze with his. "That's a tempting offer;
just prove it's an honest one, and keep all I've told you to
yourself, or we're both in deep trouble."

"I will, trust me."

"Give it time and patience. Good night, Dagan."

Starla looked at Cypher. "I wonder why he disclosed such
perilous things, if they're true. He doesn't seem the type to
do anything without a good reason, one in his favor. If he
thinks I'm so naive that allegedly sharing secrets will ensnare and bind me to him, he's wrong. I suspect he was
trying to draw me toward him for a purpose I haven't
grasped yet. Perhaps Tochar is suspicious of me and he's
hired Dagan to get close enough to expose me. It's possible
Dagan lost that struggle during the last raid by intention.
On the other hand, Tochar knows I don't do life-taking,
though he believes I killed the crew chasing me when I was
attempting to make my initial contact with him, and that
ruse worked. What he doesn't know is those were advanced
androids similar to you who only looked and sounded human. It's that traitor—or traitors—in Seri who have me concerned. *Raz* Yakir is supposed to be the only one who knows
of my assignment and identity, but what if he let them slip

to the wrong person, the one supplying Tochar with information about moonbeams and their shipments? Or maybe I said or did something to cause him to doubt me."

Cypher had not intruded on her rush of questions and remarks; he comprehended she was reasoning out matters aloud to clarify them in her mind, a trait of hers, and a means of letting him know her thoughts. "I require more data to classify Dagan Latu's character, motives, and goals. It is improbable Tochar doubts you; analysis of voice patterns do not indicate suspicion in him or the others. It is illogical for *Raz* Yakir to expose you to anyone, even those close to him, because one is a traitor."

The android's words were reassuring. "If Dagan didn't know about the truth serum test, why would he take a recorder with him? And if he did know, why would he subject himself to uncontrollable scrutiny unless he was certain he would pass it?"

"He could have suspected *Thorin* would be used."

Before Cypher could continue, Starla's gaze widened and she asked, "Do you suppose Dagan was sent here by an enemy of Tochar's to check out his defenses and activities, to look for any weaknesses? Perhaps to search for a way to disable Tochar's weapons so an attack could take place?"

"Tochar has many enemies. Those would be logical steps for a challenger to take if an attack is being planned. It is not known everywhere that Tochar has *Destructoids*."

"You're right. That means Dagan could have been sent by a rival to study Tochar's strength. Do you think he's trying to lure me to his side?"

"He revealed suspicious things to you. Perhaps it is a strong attraction to you that loosened his tongue and dazed his wits. If he is working for a rival, obtaining an ally or source of information would be of value to him."

Starla did not like the idea of being used by Dagan or anyone, but Cypher's second sentence did warm her from head to feet. "If he's an enemy or working for one, how could he dupe *Thorin?*"

"Many galaxies have secrets from the others. He asked about future retesting; that could mean his immunity is limited by time and induced by a temporary blocker."

"We've never heard of such a chemical or treatment."

"That does not mean one does not exist elsewhere. He is of Kalfan origin, but his loyalties could be to another, for hire or another reason. He is a *villite* in his world and his record reveals he becomes a *bijoni* at times."

"Perhaps revenge for something Tochar did in the past is his motive."

"That is a possibility."

Starla realized that an immunity to *Thorin* meant Dagan could have deceived Tochar and might not be as wicked as he alleged. . . . But her speculations, and Cypher's, could be farfetched—and Dagan was in reality as bad as his record claimed.

"Why did you reveal so much about moonbeams?" Cypher asked.

Starla's answer came easily. "So Dagan would realize the enormous dangers involved in his new position and weigh the risks and his payments against Tochar's profits and safety; I'm hoping he'll decide they do not equate to suit him. If he leaves, that's one less *villite* to defeat." *And the removal of a disarming temptation.* "If he stays, it might cause dissension and disloyalty. Even a man like Dagan wouldn't want anybody to become so invincible that he could never break free and any resemblance to life as he knows it would vanish. He knows Tochar took advantage of his ignorance about moonbeams when the *fiendal* purchased them from him. No leader of honor would trick one of his men, and Tochar was hiring him. I doubt Dagan won the crystals in a *resi* game. Either he lucked out on a shipment and stole them, or one of Tochar's contacts is double-dealing. If he believes I trust him—or I'm irresistibly attracted to him—maybe he'll open up to me. If so, there might be a way to exploit it to aid our mission. I must confess, Cypher, no matter what Dagan Latu claims to be or how his record reads, my instincts tell me he can be trusted in a dark *hora;* but I promise I won't act on that impression until I am assured of its accuracy. If he is working for a rival, maybe they will destroy each other and complete this mission for us."

"If that is a fact, be careful you do not get caught between adversaries in a violent takeover."

"I'll be careful, and I have you to monitor and protect me. What does Dagan's voice pattern reveal to you?"

"An analysis is impossible without a base line of truth with which to compare his words and inflections for honesty."

Starla pondered that matter for a *preon.* "Is there any type of device I can press against him so you can obtain readings?"

"That is impossible. Without a foundation line for comparison, I could not differentiate between what is fact and what is prevarication."

"That means I just have to go on my instincts and training."

"They have never failed you in the past."

"Hope and pray they don't desert me this time."

Dagan completed a scan of his chamber for listening and observing mechanisms and found none. Afterward, he retrieved a cryptographic message awaiting him on the communications device concealed in his knife handle, the most advanced and smallest unit in existence. It told him that two perusals of his criminal record had been made, both from untraceable sources who had access codes to the same mass memory computer network into which he and his friend could tap. He was certain the first probe was Tochar's, but the second was a mystery. He deduced it was carried out by one of Tochar's cohorts from either Seri or Kalfa, contacts Starla had mentioned. Those men must have supplied the data base password to the Icarian and may have double-checked Dagan Latu's identity and discovered he had a lengthy file, confirming his claims. He had expected to be examined thoroughly, but thanks to precautions, Tochar knew only what he wanted the man to learn.

Dagan pressed a button on the device to block detection of his out-going signal and transmitted a message to the man who had sent him there, though he also had a personal reason for wanting to see Tochar slain. Before he could see to that, he had to earn the trust of the leader and his band; that was the only way he could get close enough with a weapon to carry out that daring feat.

Dagan didn't need to ask for information about Tochar; he was well acquainted with the man's history and now, thanks to a beautiful pirate, abreast of his present. He requested information on Starla Vedris and Yana of Asisa, as either or both could become complications for him. With the aid of his secret contact and the man's access to the *I-GAF* computer network, all he needed were their fingerprints to learn everything about them that use of their names didn't provide. Of course, obtaining those prints could be difficult and entertaining, but he was looking forward to it. Until he received replies on the females, Dagan decided, he would study and deceive both women to determine which, if either, unknowingly could help him achieve his goal.

Eight *deegas* later as Dagan and Starla awaited the impending raid in the *Adika's* meeting compartment, Dagan glanced at their attire and down at their hands. "Why were we told to wear *I-GAF* uniforms and imprint these fake badges on the backs of our hands?" he wondered. "Though I admit, they do look convincing. Even if false markings were put on Auken's ship, our target shouldn't halt or allow us to board her without the correct hailing frequency and watchword."

From the corner's of her eyes, Starla had noticed how appealing Dagan Latu was in that deep-blue uniform which matched the color and potency of his gaze. The snug garment, all-powerful badge, and illustrious image of an Inter-Galactic Alliance Force officer suited him perfectly. She found herself aroused and wishing the implication was true; then, he would be someone worthy of taking home to meet her family, someone within reach as a mate, someone she could team up with to defeat Tochar. He wasn't, so she cast those foolish fantasies aside and ventured an answer to his query, "Probably because Tochar knows them; he has ways of acquiring even the most secret and guarded information."

Dagan sensed her keen study of him, but he couldn't think about how tempting she looked or how he affected her. He had to quell his hunger for her and concentrate on his goal, so he continued questioning. "How? From whom?"

Starla shrugged. "I have no idea; they don't reveal such things to me."

"Why were we ordered to stay in here while we approach our target?"

"I suppose because there are things Tochar doesn't want us to see or hear. Perhaps he's afraid if we learn his secrets, we won't need him."

"That's logical and wise, but I don't like being kept in the shadows and maybe mistrusted when my life and payment are on the line. It makes me uneasy."

"Me, too, but if you want to stay in Tochar's hire, don't complain about or question his orders. You were given that advice, correct?"

He nodded. "How long does it take to be trusted and accepted fully?"

"I've been with them for over three *malees,* but I'm sitting here as ignorant as you, so wouldn't you agree I'm still being tested? For certain, if they promote a newcomer to the inner circle before me when I've earned that rank, I'm gone from Tochara." *That should convince you of my alleged identity and my motive for joining and staying in that* fiendal's *band.*

Before Dagan could express an opinion, the door slid open and Auken instructed them to go to the transporter room. In the passageway, he asked, "You mean our target halted and will allow us to board her?"

The golden-haired man laughed and boasted, "Our disguises and ruse worked perfectly. Her engine is shut down and she's in a communications blackout as ordered. Let's hurry before somebody wonders why and sends a patrol to check out the problem. So far, nothing hazardous is registering on our sensors and no patrols are supposed to be in this sector for the next three *horas;* that's plenty of time to get what we came after and be gone. Starla, you and Sach will disable the androids while Dagan and I collect our prize and search the ship. We don't want another free-rider to intrude on this raid like that one did with you and Moig; we don't want any warnings sent or complications to arise."

Starla refused to let memories of that last raid cloud her mind. "Do you want us to delete their communication with us and record of our presence and put the vessel on automatic pilot as usual?" she asked.

"That won't be necessary this time; she'll be obliterated after our departure." Auken continued after he entered the transporter room. "Sach will handle that precaution; you assist him."

"Understood," she replied, shocked by his destructive intention. Yet, there was nothing she could do to save the vessel and the androids, unless she revealed herself and took the *villites* prisoner. She was a skilled, highly trained, experienced fighter and authorized law enforcer, but to attempt to incapacitate four men with stun beams was too risky. Even if she succeeded, that would terminate her crucial mission. She knew Cypher was nearby in the cloaked *Liska,* protecting her and recording this incident as usual, but there was nothing he could do either or his presence would be exposed. The moment Auken divulged his plan, she slyly had pressed a button on her wrist device to signal Cypher to noninterference of the last statement.

Auken, Sach, Starla, and Dagan stepped onto the sensor pads so Moig could transfer them to the other ship, as he was to remain aboard to monitor their safety and operate the transportation unit.

It did not take long for Starla and Sach to disable the androids. Afterward, they headed to the engine room so the Icarian could set an explosive charge which would leave nothing behind except space debris. Then, the rugged man carried out an unexpected task. Starla watched as he used a laser tool, powered by a small white moonbeam, to open a recently installed and concealed flight recorder box. He poured Myozenic Acid inside to dissolve its contents and beacon, eliminating any clues about the incident and obliterating its tracking signal.

Sach contacted Auken by transmitter. "All tasks are done," he announced. "How long do you need before I switch on the timing device?"

"We're finished and ready to leave," Auken answered. "Arm the charge and meet us in the transporter room. Let's get out of here."

Within five *preons,* the raid was completed and the group was sitting on the *Adika*'s bridge with Auken and Sach at the controls. While en route, they observed the distant explosion on the cloaked ship's viewing screen.

"That was too easy," Auken jested. "No challenge at all."

"I like easy and quick to protect my skin," Moig revealed. "That's a pretty view, bright colors and pieces flying in all directions, no evidence to point at us or Tochar. *Karlee* fire, those androids are stupid to be so smart; I love those glitches in their programs so we can bypass their orders."

Karlee was exactly where Starla wanted the evil *villites* to go one *deega,* as a hellish existence and punishment were what she felt they deserved. She made a mental note to report Tochar's knowledge of the investigative apparatus, a secret measure only certain people in Seri should be aware of, one that perhaps would provide the mistake needed to unmask its traitor. She would tell Cypher to add that discovery to their file on this mission.

Dagan leaned back in his seat. "Auken's right; there were no challenges to stimulate the blood and test our skills. But I wouldn't mind keeping this uniform and marker; might come in handy for future use."

"You planning on leaving us?" Auken queried, glancing back at him.

"No time soon, not until I earn enough to buy a new ship; it will take a *ying* or two for the kind I want. Who knows, maybe I'll stay and hire on as a private raider for Tochar. I do like his generosity and sanctuary. He's smart, so he should be open to that suggestion; having several teams working for him would bring in more profits. You think he would allow me to use the *Azoulay* if I can get her repaired?"

After checking his sensors and adjusting his course to head for the stargate, Auken asked, "How would you do that?"

"There's an old space station orbiting Gavas in the Kalfa system. I've made a few stops at Sion in the past. It's rarely used anymore because the others are newer, better equipped, and more advanced. The parts storage bay might have what Tochar needs to get her going again. Sion was still well stocked the last time I was there, but it could be empty and abandoned by now. If not, only a skeleton crew would be manning it; they shouldn't give us any problems we can't overcome. If Tochar has trusted contacts in Kalfa, he could check out that possibility; if it's safe and the part he needs is there, we could get one for him. I'm sure I remember my way around that station, so we could be in and out in a hurry. We could use these disguises to obtain permission for docking."

Starla was dismayed by Dagan's suggestion, as it might endanger the lives of any humans assigned to Sion. If they were divided into teams, she could be given Moig as a partner and assigned raids that didn't include those for moonbeams, which would hinder her investigation and imperil her mission. If she and Moig used her ship while the others used the repaired *Azoulay,* which was superior to the *Adika,* that also would prevent Cypher's stealthy trackings. She mustn't allow that obstacle to thwart her.

"I'm pleased by your idea and offer of help, Dagan," Auken said, "but Tochar doesn't permit anybody to go anywhere in the *Azoulay* unless he's aboard. But he would be grateful to you for getting him that part."

Dagan grinned and shrugged as if in acceptance of the Icarian's words. He hoped Tochar would permit him to repair the ship and that the leader would be tempted to take a trek in it for diversion or testing, as that would get Tochar away from his formidable defenses and make him vulnerable to attack. "That's reason enough to do him a favor. That idea came to me after you mentioned the *Azoulay*'s troubles last night."

Starla was relieved to hear that news, as she feared Auken would ask how Dagan had learned about the *Azoulay*'s problem and might wonder why she had mentioned that fact to the auslander. She suspected Dagan had made that statement to enlighten her. "If our job is completed," she said to Auken, "I'm going to change out of this uniform and scrub off this fake tattoo. It makes me nervous to be this close to them. I don't even want to imagine what an *I-GAF*er would do to us for impersonating one of their units. That ranks as one of the gravest offenses we could commit."

Auken increased their pace to starburst speed. "You're right, Starla, but who's going to find out with the evidence destroyed?"

Her gaze settled on Auken's light hair. "No secret or security is totally impregnable, my friend; somebody—somehow, someway—always finds a means to penetrate them. Our success on this trek proves that's a fact."

"You aren't losing your courage, are you, Vedris?"

She looked at the shorter man who was stroking his golden beard. "No, Moig, but it's good to be cautious, and healthy fear is wise. That's what keeps one from making fatal mistakes."

"She's right, Moig," Sach said, "so don't tease her or laugh. I would be nervous and worried too if I didn't know for certain our secret is safe. Starla doesn't have the same knowledge and advantage we do."

"It stokes her to be ignorant," Moig disclosed, "she told me so."

"Wouldn't being kept in the dark bother *you* when your life is at risk? If I were nothing more than a simple hireling, I wouldn't expect to be told things, but I'm a member of this team and been with it for a long time. I just don't understand why I'm not fully trusted and enlightened."

"Don't worry, Starla; that won't be true for much longer."

"Thank you, Auken; you're a good friend and teammate."

The Icarian smiled. "Thanks, so are you."

"I'm going to freshen up and change garments. I'll return soon."

"You can relax and rest back there if you want. It's four *deegas* to the boundary and three to Tochara. Nothing much to do until we reach base."

"That's a good idea, Auken. Signal me if there's trouble." Starla left the bridge for privacy as they headed toward the boundary which separated the Free-Zone from Kalfa. The Zone had a small sun but only a few planets and planetoids orbited it every six *malees,* all close enough to the solar body to make their climates and landscapes extremely dry, but not uninhabitable. The Zone was surrounded by Kalfa, Seri, Thracia, and Ceyx; with stargates in each direction to provide fast and easy access from it to those galaxies, especially with certain planetary alignments and their various speeds: sublight, starlight, and starburst. Soon, she fretted, she'd reach Noy again.

After the journey was over and she was back aboard her ship, Cypher summoned Starla from her sleeping quarters to respond to an undetectable communication link with Thaine Sanger, Star Fleet Commander and head of Maffei's undercover Elite Squad, and son of her parents' best friends.

She addressed her superior who had assigned her to this mission, "Lieutenant Bree-Kayah Saar responding, sir."

"Bree-Kayah, I wanted to warn you that somebody scanned Starla Vedris's record and requested data on Yana of Asisa. That cue I inserted in the program alerted me to the probes. The origin point was untraceable, so whoever did it has inside knowledge and sophisticated equipment. Do you have any speculations about the intruder's identity and motive?"

"No, sir. I doubt it was Dagan Latu because he doesn't have access to communications. Too, I'm sure he was searched by Tochar after his arrival, so he couldn't have brought a device with him." She assumed he had gotten the recorder from one of the traders who was selling stolen goods in the colony. "The only explanation that comes to mind is that Tochar is doing a second scrutiny because he saw the two of us with Dagan. Perhaps Tochar wanted to make certain there were no connections between us."

"You've already used your Yana identity to approach Latu?"

"I was hoping she might learn things Starla couldn't, but

I didn't extract any useful information during my first attempt."

"Anything else to report?"

She told him about the recent raid and how it was accomplished using *I-GAF*er disguises and knowledge of Seri's secret communications frequency and watchword. She told him about the concealed flight recorder's fate and about a possible raid on the Sion space station.

"I'll warn *Raz* Yakir to change his communications frequency and code word. I'll suggest he make a list of people who knew about the installation of that recorder and beacon, and to watch them carefully for clues of guilt. As to the Sion raid, I hope that succeeds; if Tochar gets his ship repaired, he might be tempted to take a voyage in her. If he does, we could lay a trap for him. You couldn't warn us about his trek if he takes you along, but Cypher can while he's cloaked and tracking you. If we got our hands on that *fiendal,* we could replace him with a lookalike cyborg and take control of Tochara's defense system and finalize this mission fast. I wish I could contact *Autorie* Zeev of Kalfa or the head of *I-GAF* to make certain a raid on Sion would work, but I can't risk them learning we have an agent inside Tochar's band because we don't know who or where the traitors are."

"I hadn't thought about entrapping Tochar away from Noy, but that seems a good plan. I'll keep you informed on that angle. Who knows, maybe Dagan Latu will help us without knowing it? I agree with not telling the Kalfan ruler about my presence; we know Tochar has at least one contact there, somebody important and trusted." She revealed everything else she had learned since their last talk, observations and facts that would be disclosed to Yakir. "The mission is progressing, but slowly."

"Don't get discouraged or take any risks," Thaine Sanger coaxed, "you're doing fine. At least we know more about Tochar and his settlement than we did before your arrival.

You're getting closer to them and victory every *weg*. Be wary of Latu; he's cunning and dangerous, and obviously out to stick himself snugly to Tochar for profit and sanctuary."

"I'll be careful," Starla promised, "if you learn anything else about him, send it to me. I don't want any unknown factors thwarting me. Now, tell me, how is my family?"

"Doing fine, just worried about you. I'll assure them you're safe and doing a superb job. I'm very proud of you, Bree-Kayah."

"Thank you. Anything important happening there?"

"Not at the present. But I don't want to imagine the troubles we'll face if Tochar continues to get his hands on moonbeams. As with every galaxy in existence, Maffei would be utterly helpless to repel his attacks and to protect itself. Yakir wishes he had never allowed those weapons to be invented and constructed, and he's distressed about them falling into enemy hands. He had no intention of ever using them against anyone; he just wanted to know the crystals full potential so he could guard against something like this happening."

"I like and respect *Raz* Yakir; he's a good man and superior ruler. The Tri-Galaxy Alliance was fortunate when Seri and Kalfa decided to unite with Maffei, Androas, and Pyropea. It would be frightening to know those two galaxies possess such formidable crystals if we weren't allies. It must be a terrible burden for him and *Autorie* Zeev to be responsible for controlling such awesome power, to have the Microcosm's fate in their hands."

"There have been times in the past when the fates of Maffei and the Tri-Galaxy rested in our fathers' hands, and in your mother's during that viral sabotage. I haven't forgotten the things your sister and her mate and Galen's mate did to save Maffei from our enemies' treacheries, and how our fathers saved your mother's home planet from destruction. Many of Star Fleet's best officers have come from your family and bloodline, including our past ruler. No *kadim* can ever be as wise and revered as your great-grandfather was. I hope Galen and I are as skilled and worthy of our ranks as our fathers were, as *you* are, Bree-Kayah. Well, we'd better sign off. The longer we stay in touch, the riskier it is for some unknown type of technology to detect our signal."

Thaine's reflections made Starla homesick for her family and friends, but sent a flood of pride in their accomplishments flowing through her. Her superior and her brother had been best friends since childhood and had carried out many crucial missions together. She had known Thaine and his family since her birth, twenty-six *yings* after her twin siblings were born to Supreme Commander Varian Saar of Maffei and scientist Jana Greyson Saar of Earth. "Tell Father and Mother and the others I love them and miss them. I promise, Thaine, I'll do everything I can to defeat Tochar and to recover or destroy the moonbeams in his possession. Bree-Kayah out."

"Watch your back, Bree," the close friend in him advised. "I want to bring you home alive and safe. Supreme Commander Sanger out."

As Starla deliberated the conversation and discussed matters with Cypher, another communication was received. This time, it was from Tochar, an astonishing message to which she would react tomorrow.

Five

After finishing her talk with Tochar, Starla asked Cypher's input on the special and secret task Tochar wanted her to help the others carry out the next day. "Why would he signal me so late?" she questioned the android, "If we're not going on another raid or leaving Noy, what could it be?"

"There is insufficient data to theorize the possibilities."

"I'll have to come up with a program to teach you to use gut instincts for making guesses," she teased. "Of course, intuition can be wrong, so perhaps it's best to base decisions on facts."

"It is rare for your perceptions to be wrong; in all instances when you made an error, it was not a serious or incorrectable one."

If only Antarus had listened to me that fated deega, *he would be alive now. At least our mission was achieved and he was awarded a posthumous commendation. If he had survived, would I have fallen in love with him and become his mate? I think not.* She took a deep breath and exhaled.

"Where do your thoughts and feelings travel, Bree-Kayah?"

She looked at Cypher. "Into the distant past with Antarus where they do not belong. Thank you for your confidence in me and my abilities. I would be lost without you at my side, dear friend."

"Even if I were not programed to serve and guard you, you have earned trust and loyalty."

"What a wonderful thing to say, Cypher. Now, back to our mystery: I think Tochar's plan has something to do with buyers for the moonbeams we've stolen so far, at least for part of them. Obviously he doesn't want to involve his Enforcers and wants to keep them unaware of the crystals' power and value, so he needs his special team either to go with him or to carry out the sale and delivery. He wouldn't meet with them in Tochara and risk being seen together by the wrong person. That indicates a probable rendezvous point in the desert. Do you have the device ready that *Raz* Yakir told you how to construct?"

"I completed it before I summoned you to speak with your superior." He lifted the tiny square and said, "I assembled it with the frequency *Raz* Yakir supplied. His theory of destablatory electromagnetic pulsations is rational, but there are no means by which to test the unit's prime function."

Starla was glad Cypher had many scientific and technological chips within his advanced system and had access to numerous others in several computer networks' data bases. "If it works as Yakir's inventors say it will, all I have to do is get close enough to those moonbeam crates to attach it without getting caught. Do you believe the sound waves it emits can agitate the crystals' internal power source and cause them to shatter into particles too minute to be of use to Tochar? I don't understand the full concept, but it sounds as if it's some type of implosive sequence." Starla was glad Cypher always tried to explain things to her in a comprehensible way.

"That is what *Raz* Yakir's report said it would do."

"But I thought moonbeams were infrangible."

"Nothing is indestructible. For every force in nature, there exists a counterforce if it can be found and mastered by thought and action." His control center told him to clarify his meaning in simple language. "Only a blue crystal can be cut by manmade instruments and only a blue crystal can penetrate the other crystals' surfaces, but all crystals appear to have the same internal structure and power source, *heart,* as you humans would say. The color of its covering, its skin, alters or decides its capability. Their entire complexities, composition, and potentials are still unknown."

"Perhaps the Serians and Kalfans have stumbled upon the portal to doom's *deega* and unleashed the evil beyond it, because an intergalactic war with such awesome weapons would be catastrophic."

"If such a doorway exists, we will close and seal it again."

"How does one halt a solar storm after it begins and recall a laser's beam once it has been fired? It is the same with the crystals' power. It has been revealed and loosened upon a weaker mankind."

The android analyzed her words and grasped her meaning. "One who is intelligent, strong, brave, and agile can evade both forces. We will find a way to defeat your enemies and destroy their threat."

"If that device works, Cypher, why can't they create a larger unit with the same frequency band and aim it at those *Destructoids?*"

"Distance between the apparatus and its target would prevent success. *Raz* Yakir's communication stated it must be within a certain range to work."

"If I were allowed inside the defense sites, I could plant units there, but Tochar is too careful to imperil his treasures. As long as those weapons guard Tochara, an attack by our forces is impossible. Yet, the more raids we make, the more I help him to get stronger. Why can't the Serians and Kalfans halt shipment of those blasted crystals until Tochar is defeated, or at least increase their security and protection?"

"It is too late for research to be halted and it must be done in isolation," the android explained patiently. "To use a show of force would draw attention to the transportation vessels and a valuable cargo; that would provoke bolder attacks by larger pirate bands. If raids are prevented, no clues are released and gathered; the identities of the traitors could not be discovered. Tochar would wait in safety on Noy until shipments were resumed. If Tochar is prevented access to all crystals, he could be tempted to attack to obtain them; if accomplished, there would be no defense against it."

Those were frustrating points Starla knew well, but reasoning aloud with an analytical Cypher often helped elicit new ideas which might prove helpful. "Your list of reasons is grim but accurate." She took a deep breath. "It's a shame the Serians and Kalfans can't construct large devices and shatter the crystals in their possessions to prevent enemies from obtaining them, and seal those mines forever. That would prevent a threat like this from ever occurring again."

"Is it logical to destroy the good to destroy the bad? Remember what the other crystals will do to help mankind."

"You're right; if mining continues, they can't control what types and sizes of moonbeams they locate. Still, the hazards of having such powers are enormous. Besides, if the mines were sealed, only Tochar would own *Destructoids*. Now, others must be built for a balance of power, if more large white crystals are found. Let's pray that little device works and slows Tochar's evil."

"I did as you ordered. I attached an adhesive circle for concealing it underneath a crate and disguised it as a metallic disk for your belt. It is ready for use."

"I'll take it with me tomorrow in case my speculation is accurate. This might be the only chance I have to get close to those crystals. Attach it to my belt while I'm sleeping, if I can sleep tonight."

"Take a *Calmer* if necessary; rest and renewed energy are needed."

"Don't follow us tomorrow, but keep us monitored and record the incident. We don't want to take more risks than necessary with our trick when you leave orbit to shadow me. I'm afraid somebody might discover we're using a hologram and fake signal and your absence would be revealed. If its auto-pilot or image maker malfunctioned, we would be exposed."

"I am programed to protect and assist you," Cypher reminded her. "I can not accomplish that order from a great distance."

"I know, and I'll be extra careful. Even if it seems I am in danger, do not interfere unless I signal you to help or rescue me. I don't want Tochar or the others to grasp the full extent of your capabilities or your constant observations. Victory is contingent upon duping them."

"Take no risks, Bree-Kayah; do not expose or endanger yourself."

"I promise, I won't attach or switch on the device unless it's safe. Don't worry, we may only be going on a weapons' or supply sale or buy."

"You can not deceive me to prevent concern. Tochar handles such business in his abode."

Starla's eyes brightened. "What if he's going to meet with one of his contacts? If that's true, I can discover his identity and report it."

"Do not break contact with me to prevent concern."

"You've covered all the warning angles, so relax and trust me. An Elite Squad member of Star Fleet would not jeopardize herself or her mission." She reminded for a final time, "Do not react in any way unless I signal you."

"What if you are unable to signal me?"

"Unless I'm dying or in chains, do not rescue me. Make certain they cannot handle the peril before revealing yourself to them. Even if the situation looks grim, wait until the last *preon* to take action. Understood?"

"Your meaning is explicit; I will obey your order."

"Good. Now, I'll get some sleep while you finish your task."

Two landrovers with rear cargo holders headed to a secluded location beyond the busy colony. Tochar, Auken, and Sach traveled in one; Moig, Dagan, and Starla rode in another to their left.

From her seat behind the two men, Starla made a quick and furtive study of Dagan Latu. He wore a thin and billowy white shirt with full long sleeves and corded ties below his throat. Earlier she had noticed those lacings had been left hanging free and loose, displaying a triangular expanse of hard chest covered with wispy dark hairs. His black pants were snug, their bottoms tucked inside matching boots. A weapons belt was secured around his waist and held a laser pistol and sheathed knife, a large one with a jagged edge on one side. His dark wind-tossed hair grazed broad shoulders, shorter from a recent cutting. He had shaved recently, as well, and his strong jawline was smooth and free of stubble. Though he seemed to laze on the seat, she sensed he was prepared to react in a flash if trouble threatened, and knew he possessed the skills and agility to do so. He was such a magnificent and virile male that his mere presence aroused her to forbidden desire. She was all too aware of the fact that if something went wrong later, this could be the last time she saw him, if they survived.

After they halted, red dust created by their movements wafted past them or settled on their bodies and garments and on the transportation vehicles which lacked bubble covers. The arid canyon was desolate and hot, but the temperature cooled after sunset, which was imminent. The mostly flat terrain of semi-desert topography was altered in that area by clusters of burnt red rock formations and barren cliffs to their right and left, both revealing hollows in various sizes and shapes. Slashes of mountains could be seen in the distance and the ridges on two sides of Tochara. In a few spots, gnarled scrubs and bunches of wiry grass grew low to the ground and close to the odd configurations, as if cuddled against them for protection from these harsh conditions. The sky was a hazy red and no clouds were in view, indicating that no refreshing rain was forthcoming in the near future.

"Koteas and Terin are uneasy about this buy, so they will not land in their shuttle until the crates are in view and no one is near them except me," Tochar revealed to Auken and Sach. "Unload the rovers and move back to an acceptable distance," he instructed. "Stay alert, you two, but I do not anticipate any trouble or problems. I will not allow the crystals to be touched until I am paid and standing with you."

As she stepped from the vehicle, Starla overheard Tochar's words but pretended she was not listening as she glanced at the rugged setting with its forbidding aura and drab colors. She recognized the names of Koteas and Terin of Icaria—which also was the origin point for the *fiendal* and his three best friends, and was the capital planet of the Thracian Empire, the neighboring galaxy. The leaders of Thracia had refused to join the United Federation of Galaxies, claiming their solar system—beyond the Free-Zone—was too far away and separated from the others for uniting with the *UFG* to be of any benefit to their worlds and people. She, as other *UFG* members, believed that was a devious excuse so the Thracians could continue doing as they pleased—such as continuing their barbaric slavery practice and militaristic government—without interference and observation.

Auken passed along Tochar's orders, and the group obeyed them.

Though she knew she appeared calm, Starla's heart pounded fast and hard. A sudden heightening of tension plagued her as the moment for action arrived. While the others were collecting more crates and Tochar was distracted, in a hasty and unseen motion, she removed the buttonlike disk from her belt and attached it beneath one of the moonbeam containers. That sly task was accomplished during her second delivery to a mounting stack that also included a large supply of a new pleasure-evoking drug from a past raid. She had pressed the start button as she applied the device, but knew she had a safety interval of thirty *preons* to get out of danger's range. Thanks to the Icarians' demand for privacy, that seemed possible. By detonation time, since Tochar was in a rush to finish before dark, perhaps the *fiendals* would be standing near the crates when the crystals' internal pressure increased to a destructive level. She hoped the device's inaudible frequency transmission was undetectable except by a certain instrument and no one would know to use it. She worried that Tochar's Serian spy might have learned of the device's existence and warned the pirate leader about it. She shoved that horrible thought from her mind. If she were injured or slain, she could be replaced, but she must not allow moonbeams to get into Thracian hands.

Starla grouped with the others beside the empty landrovers, aware the *preons* were clicking off on an imaginary timer inside her head.

"That's all of them," Sach said. "Where do you want us to stand guard?"

Tochar glanced at the hovering shuttle before he pointed to a cluster of contoured rocks with odd-looking apertures in their red surfaces. "Move over there and stay alert. Weapons at the ready. I will join you after I make my deal. They will land as soon as I am alone with the crates."

The five obeyed their leader's words as the last rays of sunshine vanished, allowing enough light for visibility for another *hora*.

With the others, Starla watched the shuttle touch down, blowing about sand as it did so. Two men exited and approached Tochar, who was spanking debris from his gar-

ments. As with the *fiendal* and his friends, the other two
Icarians had various shades of golden hair and black eyes,
genetic traits of their race. As the three *villites* talked, she
observed with fingers grazing the butt of her laser weapon.
She wished she could draw it and put an end to the crimes
in progress, but chances of defeating seven armed enemies
were slim to none. She knew Cypher was positioned in the
Liska to witness and record this secret meeting as evidence
and for clues. She was glad no one nearby was speaking,
as that might intrude on her android's ability to pick up the
nefariants' conversation via her wrist communicator. After
it was recorded, all other sounds deleted, and those three
voices were amplified, she and Cypher and their superiors
could listen to the talk.

Dagan was intrigued by Starla's intense concentration on
the scene, just as he was intrigued by the woman herself.
She was not clad in her usual jumpsuit. She wore a bronze
top that covered her torso from armpit to waist and bared
her shoulders front and back. The band was fitted to her
figure so no straps were necessary for holding the garment
in place. Her hips were covered by a matching short skirt
with many pointed ends at the hem; underneath it was a
pair of flesh-colored leggings covering long and sleek
limbs. The top and skirt were decorated with dull *plantinien*
disks at their borders. Her feet were encased in knee-high
bronze boots; her slender waist, with a wide and studded
belt with weapons attached. He assumed she had secured
her brown hair into one plait which dangled down her back
to prevent strands from blowing into her eyes and for keeping her cool in the arid location.

Dagan knew his body heat was rising steadily, but not
because of the weather; it was Starla's effect on him. Her
skin looked soft and he saw nothing to mar its smooth surface, not even the dirty red smudges where she had wiped
away grime and salt-tinged perspiration. She was the most
beautiful, desirable, and fascinating female he had met in

all of his travels. He enjoyed her company, even when she
was being aloof or wary or falsely spurning him. She had
a smile, voice, and manner that summoned enormous cravings within him, emotions and sensations that were unfamiliar and close to alarming. She would be a prize for any
man who was lucky enough to win her heart and loyalty,
but that couldn't be him, wouldn't be him . . . It was as if
she didn't know he was alive and standing beside her, so
focused were her attention and green eyes on the meeting
beyond their hearing range. But there was something unusual, contradictory, about the beauty that he couldn't put
his finger on . . .

"I'm thirsty and my throat is dry," Starla remarked, praying her voice didn't expose the tension she felt, results both
of Dagan's keen examination and the impending blast. Did
the Kalfan not realize that his gaze was so potent that she
sensed it? She was concerned because his interest seemed
to be more than a casual or merely sexual one. Perhaps he
wasn't duped by her Starla identity. She forced her thoughts
back to her bodily discomfort. "I wish we had brought
along something to drink."

"I didn't think about it," Auken admitted with a wry grin.

"Neither did I, so you aren't to blame," she replied and
smiled.

Auken grinned again. "This business won't take much
longer. It's getting dark. You'll be soothing that dry mouth
soon."

"At least a breeze is stirring now and cooling me off,
but it's kicking up more dust. I feel as if I'm covered in it.
A bath will be wonderful," she said as she received two
vibration signals from Cypher on her wrist unit. *One* meant
danger at a distance and *two* meant peril was close by. It
told her that his sensors had detected something unusual.
She heightened her alert and glanced around as she tried
to discover the hazard. It sounded like movements and whispers were coming from inside the cavities in the rocks.

Dagan also had heard the eerie noise, become vigilant, and caught a glimpse of something in the shadowy recess before it vanished into the darkness. He warned the others they weren't alone, be it man or beast.

The five backed away from the formations and eyed them as they drew their weapons to prepare for trouble and self-defense. Suddenly, numerous unkempt men in filthy and ragged garments leapt from the closest orifices as they sent forth strange clickings with their tongues. The horrible-looking creatures brandished clubs and spears in hands covered with new and old sores. Mutants also poured into the large clearing from hollows on the other side of the canyon and from others on the space pirates' side, continuously flowing from the dark holes like the yellowy fluid oozing from their pustules.

"Skalds!" Auken shouted in alarm, his black gaze widening.

"Tochar! Take cover! We're under attack!" Starla shouted to dupe the startled leader with feigned loyalty and affection as she took refuge with her companions between the land-rovers, and signaled Cypher not to panic.

The team ducked and dodged the rocks that were thrown at them as they fired at the mutants running toward their leader. Koteas and Terin, cut off from their shuttle, raced toward the armed pirates with Tochar. The *Skalds* darted about with such speed and nimbleness that even skilled shooters like Auken, Sach, and Moig had trouble hitting their targets; but Starla and Dagan struck down attackers with each blast.

Laser fire buzzed in all directions, but the mutants kept coming at them, almost tripping over the bodies of their fallen companions. Their wild eyes and scabby faces exposed fierce determination to capture and devour them. Their arms and tattered clothing were beyond dirty. Their feet were bare, but the sand had cooled allowing comfort to their strides. Beneath the layers of grime, it was impossible to tell their skins were pale, as were their ghostly eyes. Nocturnal beings who could not take the blazing sun, they had waited and watched their chosen victims until the safety of dusk appeared.

"They've never come this close before or tried to attack our fringes or patrols," Auken exclaimed. "They usually prey on less guarded colonies."

"This will be the last time they attack us!" the leader vowed.

Tochar used a communicator to order *Destructoid* beams from his mountaintop defense sites to slay and repel the flesh-eating *Skalds,* and for Enforcers to come rescue them. When he saw mutants going after the crates of crystals and drugs, his black gaze narrowed in fury. "Aim near the crates!" he shouted to the men controlling the *Destructoids.* "They're trying to steal my delivery! Stop them! Kill them all!"

Bursts from the *Destructoids* chewed into the dirt near the stack of containers as the team fired in rapid succession at howling mutants closing in on their location. Then a loud explosion occurred that terrified the *Skalds,* killing those in the blast's vicinity and causing the others to flee for the rocks. The air was filled with minute debris from shattered crystals and scattered drugs, small pieces of the containers, and red sand.

Tochar gaped at the costly destruction and cursed his losses. "We will be lucky if we can find even a few of those crystals. Probably all of them are buried in the sand or concealed in crevices, and those drugs are history. As soon as it is light tomorrow, I want a large, well-armed unit out here to search for those crystals; nothing can destroy them, so they still exist."

A suspenseful silence surrounded the group for a few *preons* after the rumble landed and Tochar spoke. With targets gone, the *Destructoids* had ceased firing. Except for the sounds of their mingled breathing, nothing could be heard. Everyone glanced about, but no live enemies were in view.

"Let's take the rovers and get out of here," Auken suggested. "It's almost dark and they might return. We're too outnumbered."

"The Enforcers will be here soon," Tochar said. "Nypeer should have them gathered and en route by now."

"Nypeer better hurry because they're coming again!" Sach shouted.

As *Skalds* crept from the orifices, showing caution and wariness this time, an enraged Tochar ordered more blasts from the *Destructoids* and demanded the rescuers get there fast.

Starla looked at Tochar. "Do you want me to see if I can reach Cypher-T, get him to lock in on my signal, and give us added firepower?" she asked. Before the leader could respond, a sharp pain stabbed through her head and her senses gave way to blackness.

Dagan grabbed her body as it slumped forward. "They hit her with a rock," he told the others as he examined the injury.

Between blasts at attackers, Auken asked Dagan about her condition.

The worried Kalfan replied, "Out and has a head cut, but breathing. We'd better get her back to the colony fast in case she has a concussion."

"We will after my unit arrives and finishes off these ugly creatures," Tochar said. "I see dust rising, so my Enforcers will be here soon."

"Not soon enough if they don't hurry!" Moig yelled. "Those beasts are almost on top of us! *Karlee,* we can't kill them fast enough!"

Dagan positioned himself between Starla and the new threat. "Those carnivorous brutes won't get their hands on you, if I have to die preventing it," he murmured. He twisted and turned as he shot countless targets. When his energy pack was drained, he grabbed another from his belt and shoved it into place. Two *Skalds* almost reached them, but the quick and accurate Dagan terminated those perils. He was amazed that the mutants lived and preyed so near the settlement without being seen—or smelled, as their bodies and breaths reeked of the damp muskiness of underground and foul stench of unwashed bodies, and of rotten meat and unbrushed teeth, too. Before the next rush at him, he glanced at her, stroked her cheek, inhaled her fragrance to clear his nostrils of the creatures' offensive odors, and whispered, "Hang in there, Starla. I promise I'll get you out of here."

Destructoids fired away at the attackers, as did the Enforcers, who arrived before a cloud of red dust and using weapons more powerful than those of their entrapped friends. The sounds of laser beams, shouts, yelps of pain, and shattered rock filled the air. Wind, laser impacts, and rapid movements stirred up more dust. Light was vanishing fast, but the Enforcers were wearing night vision gear.

Within *preons,* all mutants were dead or hiding in their apertures.

Koteas and Terin were eager to leave the dangerous setting, and did so after the shuttle was checked to make certain no *Skalds* were lurking there. The craft lifted off to return to its ship and to head for their planet to await news from Tochar that more crystals and drugs were available.

While the Enforcers stood guard, Tochar and his team climbed into their rovers. Dagan lifted Starla in his arms and carried her to a vehicle, placing her in his lap for the swift and bumpy ride. Darkness engulfed the canyon as the group drove toward the settlement in the next one.

Starla was awakened by the jostlings. While her wits were still dazed, she sighed dreamily and nestled closer to Dagan, whose smell was familiar to her. She liked being held in his strong and possessive embrace. She just wished those intrusive noises, bounces, and ache in her head would go away.

"Starla, are you all right?" Dagan asked. "How does your head feel? You took quite a hard hit on it back there."

Starla realized she was not dreaming or fantasizing. She opened her eyes and stared into Dagan Latu's blue gaze, one filled with concern and desire. She was sitting in his lap, in the landrover. Except for the vehicle's lights, it was dark, night. They were traveling, safe, alive, with Moig. She lifted her hand to check the sore area on the back left side of her head.

Dagan captured her hand and said, "Don't touch it. We'll let a doctor look it over when we reach Tochara. That mutant's rock struck you hard."

Moig glanced over. "Glad you're alive, Vedris. You had us worried good. Those *Skalds* about did us all in."

"What happened?" Starla gathered her wits to ask, "Is everyone safe?"

Dagan related the events that took place after she was rendered unconscious. "Tochar's planning to have those rock formations shattered by *Destructoids* to prevent mutants from having places to live and hide so close to his settlement. It will be done late tomorrow after the area is searched for crystals, though he doubts any can be found. After a blast like that one, they're probably lost in the sand and rocks."

Starla could imagine how angry Tochar was about their loss. If the device worked as Yakir said, there wouldn't be any crystals to recover, and no evidence of the unit to find. "I guess that means we'll be going after more to replace them. At least no one was hurt during the blast and attack."

"Except you," Dagan reminded, and smiled at her.

Starla was aroused by his touch and gaze. She felt safe in his embrace, but that was a perilous place to be. Since there were only two seats in the front of the vehicle, she did not make an attempt to leave his lap and arms, and getting into the backseat while moving was impossible. "I'll be fine by tomorrow. Thanks for taking care of me."

"Despite the grim circumstances, it was an enjoyable task."

The group reached the settlement and halted at the Enforcers' command station. Tochar approached Starla to check on her condition and to suggest she visit the only doctor in the colony, one with a lost license.

"Thanks, but Cypher has a medical program and my ship has a sick bay with equipment so he can check me out and take care of this minor injury. All I want are a bath, clean clothes, a cool drink, and some rest. That was quite an intimidating adventure. We expect to confront dangers and risks during raids, but not in or near our base. We weren't prepared to battle that much trouble. I'm glad everyone else is safe and unharmed."

"That hazard will be destroyed tomorrow, so you must not worry about being safe in Tochara."

She smiled at the leader. "We are all grateful to you for taking such good care of everyone. What happened to cause that explosion?" She saw him frown.

"I do not know. Nypeer vows it was not from *Destructoid* fire."

"Perhaps since it's powered by a crystal, its blasts so close to the others destabilized them. Too, sitting in the hot sun so close together might have created some type of chain reaction. My father was a scientist," Starla alleged, "but I don't know much about those kinds of things or those moonbeams."

"Whatever it was, Starla, they are gone now and my sale is lost."

"Only until we can replace them for you," she responded.

"I was smart to hire you, Starla Vedris. If you need anything tonight or your android cannot handle that injury, contact me."

"I will, and thank you. Can one of the men take me to my shuttle?"

"Dagan, will you see that Starla gets to the landing grid safely?" Tochar requested.

"It will be an honor and a pleasure. I'll see you tomorrow, Tochar."

The leader grinned at Dagan as if to say, you owe me for this favor.

Starla and Dagan left in a rover and traveled toward the landing grid, both holding silent for a time and cognizant of their close proximity.

During the ride, Starla evaluated their surroundings to keep her mind off being alone with Dagan. They passed single and multi-unit dwellings and a variety of businesses, none over two levels. Several nightspots sent forth loud music and most were crowded with customers, obvious from views through large *transascreens*. Small groups of people gathered here and there. She overheard them chatting or discussing sales or relating news of recent raids as the rover moved along slowly to avoid hitting walkers. Old-style signs, some painted and some illuminated, revealed what one could buy or the service one could obtain inside those places. The only ground transportation available was rental landrovers, offered by a company that paid Tochar for that privilege. The streets and walks were made of a hard white material, and were spray-washed frequently to get rid of the red dust accumulation.

"You're mighty quiet, Starla. Are you sure you're all right?"

"I'm fine, thanks. Were you told that if caught stealing here," she began to end the strained silence, "means one's choice of exile into the desert or the loss of a hand? No fights—either with fists or weapons—are allowed, and the penalty is the same. If men disagree to such a strong point, they must leave the colony to settle the matter. The punishment for murder is execution. Cheating another in a deal results in the loss of the defrauder's possessions and subsequent exile. Littering is against Tochar's orders, so the settlement is clean and rather neat except for the outer fringes where the less fortunate live and hardly anyone visits. No one lands on or visits Tochara without our leader's and his Enforcers' permission. It seems as if Tochar has created a safe place for him and his inhabitants to live and for guests to visit, a rough sort of civilization. I was told it isn't the same in the other settlements on Noy where it's every male for himself, so crimes are rampant and conditions are crude in those places."

When Starla paused to catch her breath, Dagan asked, "That's what you were thinking about so hard and long?"

She laughed, but didn't look at him. "That, and how lucky we are to be stranded in Tochara instead of one of the other settlements on this near primitive planet. Unless you've seen them in the past, you have no idea how horrible they are. At least, that's what the others told me."

"Even this colony doesn't seem like the place for a woman like you."

"What is a 'woman like' me?" she asked, warmed by his implication.

"You're civilized, educated, intelligent, well mannered, and gentle-spirited, though you try to hide that last trait."

Starla noted how husky his voice had become, and the sound of it sent tingles over her body. "Where does a woman like me belong?"

"Not in this setting or this type of work, and not with these people."

"That isn't my choice; this is where I have to be." *For now.*

"You could change your appearance and identity and start a new life."

"Until my forged identification papers were exposed?"

"The Microcosm is big, Starla; there's someplace you would be safe, someplace where you could live the kind of life you deserve."

"Are you trying to get me to quit and leave so you can

take my place in Tochar's band?" she jested. "Do you dislike having a female teamer?"

"Not for those reasons. I'd like to see you live longer and happier."

"Who says my life will be short and miserable?"

"What else could it be in this line of work?"

"Is that how you see yourself, Dagan, dying young and unhappy?"

He chuckled as he halted the vehicle. "Yes. Unless I change my ways, or I make another mistake. We can only elude capture so many times."

Starla stepped out and thanked him for his help and escort, dropping the confusing subject. Dagan halted her departure with a question.

"If you're feeling all right after Cypher checks you over, why don't you meet me at the Skull's Den for food and drinks?"

"Thanks, Dagan, but not tonight. I'm tired and tense; that was the closest I've ever come to getting killed." She saw him grimace as if that thought troubled him, but perhaps he was only trying to beguile her.

"What about tomorrow night?" he countered, as there were things he needed to learn from and about her.

"Maybe. If so, I'll see you there about dusk."

"I'll be waiting. Get inside and close the door before I leave."

"Worried about my safety?" she teased.

"Tochar would punish me if I allowed anything to happen to you, and you are supposed to be my teacher."

"From what I've seen, Dagan Latu, there is nothing I could tell or show you that you don't already know or do expertly. Good night." She sealed the shuttle door for take-off. She wanted to get to the *Liska* and Cypher fast because there were important things to do.

Six

"I'm glad you stayed calm when I was hurt or they would have wondered how you knew to come and rescue me," Starla told Cypher.

"The sensors in your wrist monitor indicated your injury was minor; your vital signs remained normal. You ordered me not to expose our contact unless you signaled me for help or your life was in imminent danger. I locked on to your coordinates to transport you to the ship if the *Skalds* reached your location or your condition changed. I moved into position to provide assistance if the threat increased. I must examine your injury."

"After we finish checking out things here; my head's sore but there's no headache or dizziness or blurred vision. That vibrator signal was an excellent idea, Cypher; it's worked for us many times. If Tochar suspects sabotage, he shouldn't look in my direction after my offer of help during the attack and he knows I was never alone with the crates while traveling with Moig and Dagan. Besides, he should doubt I—or any of the others—would risk death or injury to betray him in his stronghold and with his armed men nearby. Let's listen to his talk with Koteas and Terin. Is it ready?"

"It is ready." He pressed a key to start the event's recording.

Starla listened and frowned. "Nothing of help there, no clues about his raids or contacts, but it does give us evidence against him and we learned who two of his potential buyers are."

As Cypher reached his hand forward to switch off the button, she stayed it and said, "Wait, I want to hear what happened after I was knocked out." She murmured as she listened to combined sounds of men's voices, mutants' yells, and laser discharges, "It was a fierce battle, wasn't it?"

"I detected many *Skalds* on my sensors," Cypher revealed, "but rescue was near and the Kalfan was guarding you, so I did not make my presence known. I would have done so the *preon* your life was in peril."

"You acted wisely, Cypher; your analysis program is excellent. I'm glad you're able to make those kinds of decisions."

"Your speculations to Tochar concerning the explosion were clever. The Kalfan affected you strangely again while you were in physical contact with him after the attack and during your ride to the shuttle."

"That doesn't surprise me since I was practically held captive by his body. He's such a unique and complex male; I'm certain there is far more to Dagan Latu than we see on his surface. He may be a *nefariant,* but he has good traits. I wonder if he could be turned around."

"That is possible, but improbable; few men like him change."

Starla was warmed by the things Dagan had said to and about her when he didn't know she would discover them and wasn't trying to charm her for a selfish reason. He had seemed surprised by her garments and appearance. She had purchased the outfit in Tochara from a trader. Though it was sexy and feminine, it looked appropriate for that setting and her alleged identity. Perhaps it had sent the point home to him that she was a woman. Yet, his remarks in the rover still befuddled her. If he found her desirable, why would he attempt to persuade her to leave Noy? Unless it was with him or because he feared for her safety. *Don't be ridiculous,*

*Bree, he isn't the mating kind. He's a carefree loner, and a
villite to be defeated.*

"Let's go to sickbay so you can examine my injury. I
have a hard head, but I don't want any problems with it."

"Your immunity levels are in the upper range, but we do
not want to risk an infection. We are far from base, and
unknown germs or viruses could exist in this sector and in
such primitive conditions."

After Cypher cleaned, sterilized, and sealed the wound
with a *latron* beam, Starla received a communication signal
from the Serian ruler. "Bree-Kayah Saar here, sir," she responded.

"I wanted to make certain you are safe and well and the
mission is progressing. Are the dangers too great for you
to continue working there?" The concern was evident in
Raz Yakir's voice.

"I'm fine, sir. I appreciate your concern and your faith
in me." She told him about the destruction of a few of the
crystals using the device design he had provided. The elderly leader was happy and relieved at the news. "Do not
tell anyone—even your closest friends and advisors—about
Koteas and Terin and our first triumph," she cautioned. "We
don't know who the traitor is, and only Dagan and I were
present besides those *villites,* so Tochar would realize one
of us betrayed him. I'm sure you don't want to believe it's
one of them, but only a man in the know could tell Tochar
the secrets he learns and uses: for example, that flight recording device, and the watchword to convince those androids to let us board the vessel on the last raid. Since the
evidence was destroyed, Tochar assumes it's a mystery as
to how we accomplished our feat and who's responsible for
the theft."

"Your conclusion is logical and must be accurate, though
it pains my old heart to experience such doubts. Iverk is

investigating for leaks, but he has found none, perhaps because I do not share my knowledge with him."

Starla recognized the name of the Serian *Ysolte,* head of Seri's galactic defense and third in line for rulership. "I'm sorry you must keep secrets from Iverk, but he mustn't learn of my existence and mission. He could make a slip or ask the wrong person a revealing question. If that happens and I'm exposed, I'm dead and the mission is destroyed."

"Do not worry, Bree-Kayah," *Raz* Yakir assured. "I will keep my lips sealed to protect you. Supreme Commander Sanger keeps me informed of your reports to him. It is safer for you and our critical task because his conversations appear to be about Federation business or friendly chats. I contacted you this time because I needed to hear your voice to make certain all is well."

"It is, sir, and I'm grateful for your concern. I think I know where Tochar is hiding the moonbeams we steal, but the cave I suspect he's using is guarded and inaccessible; the cavern is in the same ridge as his dwelling, but not within close proximity to it. So far, we've only seen Tochar, Auken, and Sach enter it following every moonbeam raid. If I'm given the opportunity, I'll destroy the remaining crystals. Cypher will have another device ready by tomorrow for me to use if an occasion arises; there is no way I can recover them and return them to you and *Autorie* Zeev."

"The crucial point is to prevent Tochar and others from having them."

"Is there any progress on matching or bettering his firepower?"

"To date, we have not located any white crystals large enough for constructing more weapons like the ones he stole from us."

"They have terrifying capabilities, sir, and there's no way I can get near them to plant destructive devices; they're guarded and off-limits."

"Do not take risks, Bree-Kayah; I want you to remain alive."

"Cypher and I are being careful, sir; we won't be reckless."

"Have you experienced any problems with shapeshifting?"

"None, sir; I've used it several times with success and secrecy. I still have an ample supply of the chemical needed for the alteration process."

"Be sure you keep one phial for an emergency, in the event Starla Vedris must vanish swiftly to escape danger."

"I carry that one with me at all times, sir; and Cypher monitors me every *preon* in case I need assistance or a swift rescue."

"I am glad he is there with you and his intelligence is so advanced."

"So am I, sir."

"I will terminate our transmission now. Farewell and survive, Bree-Kayah Saar of Maffei. I will reward you greatly whether you succeed or not."

"That isn't necessary, sir; my reward is in defeating Tochar and saving the Federation from his threat. Bree-Kayah signing off."

"Raz Yakir signing off."

Starla looked at Cypher and said, "I think I'll get cleaned up and see if I can gather any clues from Dagan."

"You told him you would not return to see him tonight."

Starla grinned. "I'm not; Yana is."

"What clues do you seek to extract from him?"

"I want to know what kind of man he really is."

"How will you discern that fact?"

"By seeing how he reacts to Yana when Starla's back is turned."

Cypher analyzed and grasped that response. "What if your plan fails?"

"How can it fail?"

"If he surrenders to Yana's magic, that action will harm you."

"How so, my friend?"

"It will injure your emotions and perhaps become distracting. You do not want him to unite bodies with Yana, but you will tempt him to do so. That is contradictory and hazardous."

"I know, but it's the only way to study him, because I can't do such things as Starla. If Starla ensnares him, he won't divulge anything to her. But as Yana, many secrets are loosened on a *sleeper;* or so I'm told. Please don't worry," she assured her trusted android. "I haven't made that decision yet, and I won't make it lightly or impulsively or unless it seems imperative to my mission."

"Be careful with the mating scent application; do not use so much that he cannot control his physical responses and actions."

"I'll use it sparingly; I don't want to bring out the carnal beast in him, only enchant him for a while, dull his wits, loosen his tongue."

Yana looked up at light coming through the apertures of the skull-like facade of her destination. She had transported to the rental abode where Yana allegedly lived, and left from there. Music and other sounds of merriment came from speakers in the "skull's ears" to entice regular and new customers inside. She walked between "teeth" columns to enter, and took a deep breath to prepare herself to share time with Dagan if he was present. Even with his back to her, she recognized his black hair and magnificent physique. She strolled to his table. "May I join you?"

Dagan knew that sultry voice and smell. He turned, smiled, and stood to assist her with a chair next to him. "It's nice to see you, Yana."

"It's nice to see you again, Dagan," she echoed. "I was

hoping you would be here. I stay mostly to myself, but I need diversion at times. I hope you don't mind my intrusion, but I feel safe when I'm with you." She watched his blue eyes sparkle and a sexy grin curl up the corners of his full mouth. His teeth were white and straight. His clothes were clean and neat, brown pants and a tan shirt in a material that stretched taut over his muscled torso. He hadn't shaved so dark stubble was visible on his angular jawline, making him appear rakish.

Dagan was aware of her keen study. "That's a stimulating and pleasing compliment, Yana. Why don't I get you a drink? What would you like?"

"Radu knows my favorite drink if it's available. Thank you." She watched the captivating Kalfan almost swagger to the bar and lean against it in a nonchalant posture. He possessed such a commanding aura that no one else in the place could match him in looks or manner, in her opinion.

While Radu fetched a glass and filled it with *Clearian* wine, Dagan's gaze roved Yana's lovely profile and long sunny gold hair, almost the same shade as his own without his Dagan Latu disguise. Even the aqua tone of her bodysuit beneath a multihued flowing garment in a diaphanous material, a garment as ethereal as the stunning creature herself, matched the real color of his eyes before they were chemically dyed for this crucial mission. Yana, he concluded, was created and adorned by some mischievous force to be an intoxicating temptation to men. Her appeal to him was purely physical, though she was a likable female. She was so different from Starla Vedris, a greater and many-faceted temptation. He didn't normally take up time with women during an assignment and he moved around too frequently and rapidly to be ensnared by romance and never by love, not since a terrible tragedy *yings* ago played havoc with his emotions and life.

Yet, Dagan realized, his gut instinct—which rarely failed him—warned him not to trust her, told him she wanted something from him, something he needed to discern, and fast. He suspected she was either a spy for Tochar or was a cunning scout for one of the man's many enemies, perhaps a rival who wanted to take control of this settlement and the *fiendal*'s possessions. If the latter was true, she or her employer could be the person who ran that second check on his Dagan Latu record—an unquestionable one—to see if he was for real or was approachable as an ally against Tochar. Perhaps the Asisan ruler had sent her to check out the weapons and moonbeams, but Yana had been unable to get close to Tochar since the man had a satisfying lover. Perhaps—though he could not imagine how—she had failed to entice Auken or Sach into her clutches and extract needed information, so she had focused on beguiling him. There was an almost irresistible allure about the beauty, but no matter how tantalizing or talented she was, Yana would never extricate his secret identity and goal or sway him from it. With his special immunities, neither could Tochar nor anybody else, even with the aid of torture or their ineffective truth serums.

Yana took the glass he handed to her, smiled, and thanked him again. "What was the commotion about earlier this evening outside the settlement?" Yana asked. "I saw and heard those mountaintop weapons firing into the desert. Did Tochara come under attack?"

"It was just a test of the defense system. Perhaps Tochar should have announced it so people wouldn't worry. I'll point out his oversight to him."

"I'm glad that's all it was. It frightened me. To be honest, I'll be happy when I leave this place. It's much too primitive and rough for me."

"When will you be leaving?"

"In another *malee* or two, or as soon as I receive a certain message. Do you have to leave often for work and remain gone for long periods?"

"I never know my schedule until the last minute. Why?"

She sent him a radiant smile and laughed in a sultry tone. "Because I wouldn't have a trusted escort and bodyguard while you're gone."

Dagan's keen intuition and training told him that wasn't her purpose for signaling him out to receive her attentions. He would not underestimate Yana's cunning and talents, as he had done with Starla on that transporter. As she chatted for a few *preons* with Radu, his mind scoffed that he didn't think any of the other ninety-nine *I-GAF* agents would believe her, either. Officers like him were selected, tested, trained, and skilled at investigating and solving tough and perilous interplanetary and intergalactic crimes; so an *I-GAF*er was hard, if not impossible, to dupe or defeat. They had never failed to succeed in their assignments and he would not fail in this mission to destroy Tochar and those dangerous crystals, destroy the same *fiendal* responsible for his own personal torment *yings* ago, a man he hated and wanted dead, but only after his victory was ensured.

Whatever it required, Dagan resolved, Tochar's reign of terror would be terminated before it reached a critical level. As an *I-GAF* agent, he had the power and authority to do anything necessary to achieve his goal. He reported only to his superior, commander of an awesome force that was almost a law unto itself; his work and methods could not be questioned and reprimanded by anyone else. Only his superior and the other special agents knew who and what he was, since his birth face had been surgically and chemically altered. Though he used a different disguise for every mission, between assignments he worked and lived as Dagan Latu to keep that role well-established and credible. He recalled how that *I-GAF* uniform had felt so familiar, and the anger he had experienced at dishonoring it during the commission of a crime. But Tochar lacked the secret of how to create and conceal an *I-GAF*er hand badge. The symbol was tattooed into the flesh on the back of the right hand with an invisible dye which was made evident as needed by smearing a particular chemical over it and was concealed again with a different one. Those chemicals and dye were unreproducible formulas; for that reason, a pretender was easy to unmask.

As he watched Yana work her charms on Radu, Dagan decided he might have to take steps to beguile her into dropping needed clues. Yet, something intangible about her was making his job difficult and uncomfortable, as it was an unfamiliar struggle to keep his arousal in check. The alien beauty was having a potent effect on him. He could not surmise why his body was battling with his mind. Perhaps Asisan women had a magical pull about which he hadn't heard; perhaps one could exude an irresistible phero-mone to enslave her victim. For certain, the next time he lay on a *sleeper* with a female, he wanted it to be Starla, even if she was one of Tochar's hirelings and his targets.

Dagan spoke with Radu before the man departed. His gaze met hers as he asked, "Who are you, Yana? What or whom are you hiding from?"

Yana went quickly on alert again. "I can't divulge that information."

"So, you only trust me to a certain degree?" he jested.

"I'm sorry, but privacy is a must until a particular matter is resolved."

"You won't leave Noy before saying good-bye, right?"

"I promise, unless you're away when I must depart. When do you take another journey? And how long will you be gone?" she asked to see if Tochar had confided anything of interest to his new hireling.

"I don't know I'm awaiting Tochar's orders."

She laughed. "Impatiently? You appear to love traveling."

He lowered his glass. "What gave you that impression?"

"You always seem a little restless."

"Not when I'm in such entertaining and ravishing com-pany."

She traced her forefinger around the glass's rim as she

fused her gaze to his. "That was a quick and smooth response. Do you charm all of the women you meet so easily and swiftly?"

"Does that mean our attraction is mutual?"

She halted her movement to prevent tipping over the glass when her hand trembled. "Yes, but I think, where relationships are concerned, I move more slowly and carefully than you do."

Dagan chuckled. "Impulsive and reckless I'm not, Yana."

"Neither am I, Dagan. Now, why don't you tell me about yourself and your work."

He downed the last swallow of his drink. "It's getting late and I've had a long and busy *deega*. We can get better acquainted next time. What if I escort you to your dwelling to ensure your safety?"

Is that all you have in mind? "That would be kind of you."

They left the Skull's Den in silence as she led the way to Yana's abode.

"It's located there," she said, pointing to a small dome-shaped pod. At the entrance, she slid a metallic card into a slot and the door swished open. She turned and asked, "Would you like to visit for a while?" She half expected and needed him to refuse, but he did not.

"Only for a few *preons;* it's late, and we're both tired. But I wouldn't mind seeing your surroundings and having a last drink with you."

"There isn't much to see," Yana remarked as they entered the rental unit. "It's plain and serviceable and clean. Radu owns it." As she poured two glasses of *Clearian* wine, she told him, "I was fortunate to arrive when I did because the person who habitated it before me had to leave that *deega.*"

"That was a stroke of good luck," he said, taking the drink from her.

Yana watched him stroll around as if looking for things that would give him clues about her. She sat down, wondering what would happen next. She saw him glance over a waist-high partition into the sleeping and dressing area, then into another where the cooking and eating area was located. He didn't have to ask where the one door went: into the bathing chamber.

Dagan sat beside her on a small but cozy *seata* and sipped his drink. She was right, there wasn't much to see or anything to provide clues about her. That told him she was clever and cautious about her privacy; perhaps she stayed ready to flee at a *preon*'s notice.

"You don't like to talk about yourself, do you?" Yana queried.

Dagan shrugged and grinned. "There isn't much of interest to tell. And you're just as tight-lipped as I am."

"I promised I would tell you everything about me later. In any case, since we'll know each other for such a short time, do facts about me really matter?"

"I suppose not, but I'll decide as we go along." He nodded toward an odd-looking figurine. "That's an interesting piece of sculpture. Is it yours?" he asked.

"No, it's part of the decor."

"May I see it?"

"Of course." She set down her glass and fetched the item.

With her back to him, he switched their glasses, having been careful to keep his liquid even with hers. Dagan examined the object and said, "Looks like an artist's strange interpretation of a Thracian *kilitar.*" He handed it to her as if asking for her opinion. As she made her decision, he pretended to absently toy with a paper casing on the lower part of the glass for capturing moisture and preventing a slippery surface.

"It does slightly resemble that six-legged beast." Immediately after Dagan downed the remainder of his drink, she asked him if he wanted another one.

"No, thanks. I'll be leaving now, but I'll see you again soon." He stood and stretched as if weary, then furtively stuffed the glass's wrap into his pocket, the one with Yana's fingerprints on it, retrievable with a special process he knew. Added to the voice print he had made that evening on his recorder, Yana's identity wouldn't remain a mystery much longer.

She was half relieved and half disappointed that he was departing without attempting to seduce Yana, her. She craved to feel his arms about her, to taste his lips, to join her body with his. She walked him to the door, but he turned before he pressed the open button.

Dagan gazed into her rich blue eyes and scanned her faint blue skin and blond hair with the same blue tinge. "You're a beautiful and desirable woman, Yana; I hope we'll see a lot of each other before you're gone."

"That would please me," she responded, though not totally true, not as Yana.

Without releasing her captive gaze, Dagan cupped her face between his hands, lowered his head, and sealed their lips. He couldn't help but close his eyes and pretend she was Starla, which proved to be a mistake. As his body flamed with fiery cravings and she yielded her mouth to his, he told himself if he didn't leave soon, his control would vanish.

Yana's wits danced freely. The kiss was everything she had imagined and more: tender, delicious, arousing. His manly scent pervaded her senses. His hands were strong yet gentle, as was he. But the kiss was too short to suit her.

Dagan leaned back and smiled. "Good night, Yana. I'll see you soon."

"Good night, Dagan. I enjoyed our brief evening together."

"Perhaps it will last much longer next time," he murmured.

Yana watched him disappear into the shadows, then closed the door and leaned against it as she tried to quell her tremblings of excitement. So, he didn't leap into a *sleeper* with a woman just because she was "beautiful and desirable"; that was good, and it prevented her from making that serious choice tonight in a weakened state.

She communicated with Cypher who had overheard everything via her monitor, "I'll wait here for a while to make certain he doesn't return and wonder where I am or how I departed if he's lurking outside."

"That is unnecessary," the android replied. "I took a body reading and am following it with my sensors. He is returning to his chamber."

"Then, there's no need to remain. Ready for transport."

Starla entered the Skull's Den shortly after dusk the following day, purchased a drink, and took a seat near the dome's outer shell. It was a slow night for business on the first level and in that area, so it was quieter than usual. Even the music from the adjoining section wasn't loud, nor the voices and laughter of the few patrons there. She wondered how long Starla and/or Yana could hold Dagan Latu's attention if one or both of them failed to share a *sleeper* with him. Should she, *could* she, in either form, surrender to such a perilous temptation? Did her sense of duty and the importance of her mission justify using her body to obtain victory? She was so lost in thought that she didn't notice Dagan's arrival until his commanding presence filled her line of vision as he joined her.

"Looks as if you were mentally trekking far away," he murmured as he leaned back in his chair and gazed at her. A strange warmth flowed over him every time he was near her, one that worried him.

"A hazard of our fate-altered lives, wouldn't you agree?"

"I suppose so," he replied, then sipped his drink. He wished he could convince her to leave Tochar and Noy, remove herself as one of his targets. As soon as Tochar was defeated and slain, she would have no leader and this settlement would be destroyed to scatter and weaken the remaining *villites* who used it. Afterward, she would be thrust into space on her own again or be caught up in the whirling vortex which would swallow and crush the wicked elements in Tochara.

In his opinion, Starla couldn't be held totally to blame for her illegal actions; she had gotten entrapped in this dangerous existence while in a vulnerable state, pulled in by her own brother. He hoped Tochar's influence wasn't too strong and she would escape it soon; if not, there would be no way he could ignore her position in the *fiendal*'s band and her participation in its crimes, even though the ravishing pirate enflamed his passions and touched his emotions. Her effect on him evoked a battle of personal feelings vying against professional ones.

"Is your real name Starla Vedris?" he questioned suddenly.

Following his long and intense and arousing study of her, she had not expected that odd question. She stared at him for a moment. "Why, does it really matter? One name is as good as another in our work."

He leaned forward and propped his elbows on the table. "I like you, Starla, so I want to get to know you better."

"That takes time, Dagan, time we might not have in our risky lives."

"Since our fates are uncertain, we should enjoy every *preon* we have."

She wondered if that was a sexual overture. "Only if those diversions don't shorten or worsen our existences. I think it is unwise to live only for the *deega,* as so many do here. Indulgence can be self-destructive."

Dagan locked his blue gaze to her green one. "What kind of future do you want? Any desire for a normal one with a mate and offspring?"

Her heart raced at his odd queries and his desire-igniting expression. She fought to keep the trembling of strong emotion from her voice. "Is that what you want? Do you ask because I'm a woman and you assume that's what all females crave?"

Dagan felt himself heating up beneath her sultry gaze. The fates have mercy, he wanted her badly, and was sure she felt the same. "Why do you always reply to certain queries with a question so you can avoid sharing something personal about yourself?"

Starla laughed to release tension. "You answered your own question."

"I sense that you're a private person and probably have reason to be, but is it just me or everyone you want to keep at a defensive distance?"

"Would you think me vain if I said no man on Noy has interested me in that way since my arrival? Unless I'm wrong about your meaning."

"Your conclusion is accurate. Does 'no man' include me?"

Starla's gaze roamed his face. She found his expression unreadable except for glimmers of fiery desire which matched the flames searing her. "I haven't decided what I think or feel about you, not yet. I try not to make hasty judgments; that can be rash and hazardous."

"Thanks for being honest; and it isn't vain to be discriminating."

Starla thought it was best to change the subject. "I would like to thank you again for being willing to sacrifice your life to save me from those carnivorous brutes."

"I'm sure you would do the same thing for one of your teammates." *But how do you know what I said when you were out cold?* Dagan withdrew his knife and extended it toward Starla. "You should get one of these. It comes in handy if you run out of power packs. It's good for close-range fighting and for throwing a long distance. Has lots of other uses in a bind." He watched her take the knife and examine it, supplying him with her fingerprints. Added to the voice pattern he was recording, soon he would know everything about Starla Vedris or whoever she was, as she would be registered in the *I-GAF* data base, as were all *UFG* citizens.

"If you don't know how to use one, I'll be glad to teach you," he offered.

Starla returned the knife. "Thanks, but I do know how. You might want to change to a curved handle for a better grip."

Her practical idea impressed him. "Has Auken told you we're leaving tomorrow to head for the Sion space station to get that part for Tochar's ship?"

"No, I haven't seen or heard from him. I take it Tochar has checked and knows the part is available and the station is approachable. He amazes me with the number of contacts he has in other places. It seems as if there is little he can't learn, so they must hold high and trusted positions." She laughed, then feigned a jest, "If I had his sources, I wouldn't need to work for him or anyone."

"We take a lot of risks and steal valuable cargoes for such small cuts of the profits. Not that he doesn't pay well, better than most leaders, but he sells those hauls for huge amounts, so our services should be worth more."

"Too bad it's dangerous to leave his employ or we could venture out on our own. He has long arms and a good memory, so any departure has to be agreeable to him. Can you repair his ship after we get that part he needs?" she asked.

"Yes, I checked it over this morning; nothing to it. Being on my own for so long, I have to know a ship from top to bottom. I can't exactly call for help if something malfunctions, and I don't want to drift alone in space until death claims me. You're lucky you have an android for company and assistance."

"I'm very fortunate to have Cypher for many reasons."

After she enumerated a few, she asked, "Did Auken say whether or not I'll be going along on the raid?"

"The entire unit is going. Why?"

"Since we're leaving tomorrow and I haven't been told, I wondered."

"He's probably been busy getting the *Adika* ready to depart."

"I hope that's the only reason; being excluded wouldn't sit well."

Dagan didn't tell her he had hinted to Auken that only three or four of them were needed to carry out the raid, one which would be allowed to succeed with the hope of enticing Tochar away from his stronghold. Though there shouldn't be any risks involved, unless something unforeseen came up, he wanted her kept away from as many dangers and punishable crimes as possible. But Auken was loyal and ignored his words.

"Would you care for a fresh drink?" Dagan asked.

"No, thanks. Since we're leaving tomorrow, I won't even finish this one, and I need to get back to my ship to rest and prepare. Good night, Dagan."

"Good night, Starla; I'll see you at sun-high at the landing grid." He watched her rise and exit, her departure evoking an odd feeling of loneliness. *Stop letting her get to you so fast and easy; she's a* villite, *Curran, despite good traits. Don't forget, she's in the forbidden zone. And get moving before Yana appears; you don't want to deal with her tonight.*

Starla took a seat on the bridge of her ship with Cypher. "I'm relieved Auken sent a message to you about the band leaving tomorrow," she told her trusted android. "I can't allow them to shut me out now that they have Dagan. If necessary, I'll find a way to disable one of the men to prevent it from happening. Don't follow us this time and do something small to make your presence in orbit known while I'm gone, maybe purchase supplies to restock the *servo* and have them delivered by shuttle. Since we aren't going after moonbeams, there won't be any clues dropped for you to collect, so let's not risk using the hologram and beacon. I'm convinced that Tochar has made certain the needed part is there and it's safe to raid that space station, so I'm certain I won't be taking any risks going without you in the shadows."

"Your reasoning is logical," Cypher affirmed. "I will obey. Keep alert for complications."

"I will, so don't worry. And report our imminent trek to my superior."

From the bridge of the *Adika,* Starla watched the docking procedure after they were given permission to stop at Sion. She noted that Auken had the correct hailing frequency and password and wished she knew how Tochar had obtained them. She glanced at Dagan and the others, who were clad as *I-GAF* officers, just as she was. She surmised she and Dagan had been allowed to remain on the bridge because the secret moonbeam codes weren't being used today. She hoped the raid went smoothly and that no humans were inside, as Tochar was told.

"Connection complete and ready to enter the station," Moig announced.

Auken thanked Moig and told him to remain right there and be ready for a swift take-off if needed. "The rest of you, come with me," he commanded. "You know what we're after and where those parts are stored. Let's move fast and get going."

Inside the entry corridor, Starla watched Auken and Sach head in one direction while she and Dagan walked in the other to collect certain items. The tubular hallway was long and dim, with only one series of well-spaced lights illuminated. Their booted steps echoed against the metallic flooring. Their fingers grazed the butts of their laser weapons, ready to battle any unknown threats. The android in the control room wouldn't trouble them, as it was duped.

"The fuel rods we want are down the next corridor and on the left," Dagan informed Starla. "Stay alert in case Tochar's information isn't accurate."

Starla acknowledged his words and kept glancing over her shoulder for any sign of trouble. She followed him into the storage bay and helped him load the rods onto a carrier. She saw him gather other items Tochar wanted for future use or sales.

They returned to the ship and unloaded their haul, then headed down another corridor for a second and last pickup in a bay on the far side.

Shortly after leaving that storage area, Starla tensed as she overheard a shocking message from Moig to Auken via their transmitters. She and Dagan exchanged looks of surprise and displeasure.

"We've got a problem, Auken. I have a *Spacer* on the sensors; it just decloaked and showed itself. The pilot is communicating with a man inside the station somewhere; they're *I-GAF*ers. Sounds like he was dropped off by another craft and this one's picking him up. He's already gotten permission to dock from that android controller and he's coming in. We have five *preons* or less to disengage our connection and get cloaked."

"Starla, Dagan, did you hear that message?" Auken asked.

"We heard," Starla responded, "and we're heading back in a hurry. It'll take a while; we're almost on the other side of the ring."

"Drop everything and move fast, but we won't leave without you two."

After the communication ended, Starla murmured to Dagan, "Do you really think they'll hang around very long with an *I-GAF*er aboard and another one coming? If we don't rush, we'll be stuck here and in big trouble. These uniforms and fake badges won't fool those clever agents."

"Don't worry, we'll bluff our way out if the one here sees us. Just don't act suspicious."

"I won't have to: I'm a woman. There are no female *I-GAF*ers."

"Yes, there are, a few, so behave like you're one. All we need is enough time to disarm them if they approach and challenge us. If Auken deserts us, we'll just have to steal their *Spacer* and escape."

Starla pressed her fingers to his lips and whispered, "Somebody's coming."

"Get down!" Dagan shouted, and pushed her to the floor. Almost in the same sweeping motion, he drew his laser gun and fired at the agent who rounded the corner at the end of the corridor. He knew he had to stun the man before he was seen, recognized, and perhaps exposed.

Starla grabbed her gun and fired in the opposite direction after the second agent came into view, his own weapon drawn. The man got off one blast, which zinged against the metal carrier near Dagan after she had kicked it between him and the shot's angle. Dagan whirled to check out the peril, saw the downed agent, and looked at her oddly. "He's only stunned," Starla announced. "I'm not killing an *I-GAF*er. If you do, you're a fool, Dagan. Tochar couldn't pay me or scare me enough to murder one of them."

"I only stunned mine, too; I don't kill unless necessary." He called Auken and said, "The agents are down, so relax and wait for us. We're bringing our haul; no need to abandon it now."

After the loading and disengaging procedures were carried out, the *Adika* took flight and cloaked. Auken and Sach were at the controls, and the other three were sitting nearby trying to calm themselves.

Moig, his brow sweaty and his face flushed, complained,

"I thought there wasn't going to be any threats in this sector. That was too close."

"Tochar was told there wouldn't be any Kalfan *Sekis,*" Auken said, "but he can't control or learn the actions of the *I-GAF*ers. Did you kill them?" he asked Starla and Dagan.

There was no hesitation in Dagan's response, "No, we stunned them, because they didn't get a chance to see our faces. One docked at the portal nearest us and the other was going to meet him; we were caught between them."

Auken shrugged. "Wouldn't matter if they had seen you."

"As for me, I don't want them eager for my blood," Starla refuted.

"Look at the rearview screen so you'll stop worrying," Auken told her.

Starla's gaze widened as the orbiting space station exploded and sent debris flying in all directions. She reflexively blinked at the bright light and gasped in astonishment. "Why did you do that, Auken? They didn't see us. There will be *karlee* to pay for this reckless deed."

"When that *Spacer* appeared, we lost the time to get to the internal recording system and the android to wipe out the report of our transmission, and our faces and voices; so we had no choice. We can't leave evidence behind."

Starla watched the debris slow and begin to float in endless space. Two Inter-Galactic Alliance Force officers had been murdered to conceal their identities and operation methods. At least, she thought sadly, the men had been unconscious and hadn't suffered.

"I know you don't like life-taking, Starla, but it couldn't be helped. They shouldn't have been there, and I wish they hadn't been."

Starla realized it was foolish to argue with the *villite;* she mustn't let him think she lacked the courage to do whatever was needed to protect the unit and their leader or she could be ousted.

"Do you understand?" Auken asked.

"As you said, we had no choice. At least we got what we came after."

Dagan observed with keen senses and realized how upset she was, which pleased him. He was furious with Auken and Sach, and tempted to slay them on the spot, but he couldn't; too much was at stake. Later, he would take revenge for the two fellow officers, though they were not close friends of his. If Auken had revealed his lethal intention earlier, he would have captured the band and returned to rescue the two agents. He would have turned the prisoners over to them, then headed for Tochara to delude their leader. Or he could have pretended they were all slain, altered his guise, and headed for Noy to become the first member of Tochar's new unit. No matter, it was too late to save their lives. Obviously his superior hadn't warned them to stay clear of Sion or hadn't known they were in the area.

Auken turned to Dagan. "What about you? Any problem with that course of action?"

"Not at all; things happen; they can't be avoided."

Starla noted how Dagan's fingers gripped his kneecap as he replied to Auken's query. She guessed the gesture was indication of Dagan's anger about the two deaths, which relieved her following his disturbing remarks. *Maybe you are different from them. Maybe you can be turned around after all.*

Dagan looked at Starla. "Thanks for saving my butt back there. That was quick thinking. I owe you for my life."

"You're valuable to Tochar and our unit. I'm glad I could help."

"What about being valuable to you?" Dagan jested with a grin.

"Friends and team members are important to me, too."

"I think Dagan wants to be a real close friend, Vedris," Moig teased.

"Don't start me, Moig; I'm too tired and tense for games."

"Speaking of games, how about we play *resi* to help us relax?" Dagan suggested.

"Sounds good to me. I'll get the chips," Starla said to silence Moig. She wasn't looking forward to the lengthy trip back to base: seven *deegas* to the Kalfa/Free-Zone stargate, then four to Noy in their current alignments. She didn't like the tight confinement with the men . . . and especially with Dagan.

After they landed at Tochara, for the first time, Starla was asked to help transport the load to a cave their leader used for storage, one guarded by Tochar's Enforcers. Yet, she and Dagan were allowed only to place the crates in the entry cavern, and the many recesses beyond it weren't visible for inspection. As she worked, she pressed a button on her wrist device so Cypher could lock in on and record the coordinates for future use, as she was positive this was where the crystals were being kept.

When the task was finished, Dagan asked Starla to join him later for the evening meal and drinks. First, he needed to report the two agents' deaths and see what Phaedrig had discovered about Starla and Yana from their fingerprints and voice patterns. He was eager for those facts, but dreaded what he might learn.

Starla politely declined. "Thanks, but I want to rest. Perhaps I'll see you tomorrow around dusk at the Skull's Den. I just need to be alone for a while."

"After being caged with four men for *deegas* and what we went through at that station, I understand. See you tomorrow, I hope."

Starla nodded and left in her shuttle to make a report to Supreme Commander Thaine Sanger about the fatal incident at Sion. She knew that Cypher would be concerned when he heard the bad news, but there wouldn't have been anything he could have done to save those men. By the time Auken exposed his action, it had been too late even for *her* to save them. She yearned to know how that episode was sitting with Dagan, but doubted he would reveal anything to Starla. Yet, perhaps Yana could extract facts and feelings from him about the incident and Tochar, especially if she used an alluring splash of her irresistible fragrance.

Seven

Yana took a deep breath and pressed a button near the door to Dagan's chamber, after making certain no one was nearby to witness her bold visit. He was renting one of four dwellings in a tubular-shaped pod of a heat-resistant material. Its entrance was on the back, facing the ridge, and the passageway to it was deserted at present. Since her Yana abode wasn't far away, she had transported there and slipped to this location without being seen. When Dagan did not respond to her signal within a short span, she assumed he wasn't there and started to leave. As she turned, wondering where he was and if she should seek him out, the door swished open.

"Yana, what are you doing here?" Dagan asked as she faced him.

"I haven't seen you for *wegs*. Have you been gone or evading me?"

"We just returned from a long trek this evening."

"Then you must be tired, so I'll let you rest. Please excuse my intrusion, but I wanted to see you. I've missed you."

What are you up to, woman? You didn't come here dressed like that just to talk. His gaze noticed the visually impenetrable but thin and silky garment in a multicolored pattern. Thick and shiny tresses flowed around her shoulders and framed her beautiful face like liquid sun. The blue smeared on her lids intensified the hue of her eyes and its faint tinge to her flesh and hair. Her lips were full and pink, and parted slightly. He had to detain her to see why she had come. He had made certain all of his secrets were concealed before he answered the summons, so he asked, "Would you like to come inside for a while?"

"If you're alone and it won't intrude on your relaxation schedule."

Dagan grasped her hand and led her into the multi-purpose room. "Have a seat. Would you like something to drink? I have *Clearian* wine."

Yana saw him smile, but the action did not reach his remarkable eyes. She wondered if it was her imagination or if he was displeased to see Yana in his quarters. "That would be nice." She sat down on the only *seata* in the small and sparsely furnished dwelling, which was sectioned off by waist-high partitions, much like her rental pod. She watched him fetch a bottle from a cooling unit, and two glasses. She put her daring wile into motion as she pretended to toy with her neck ring.

As he poured two glasses of purple liquid, Dagan asked, "What have you been doing lately?"

"The usual, nothing, very little."

"Life on Tochara is boring?" he asked as he replaced the bottle.

She laughed and nodded. "There aren't many diversions here."

He joined her. "Not the kind you're accustomed to?"

"Thank you," she said as she accepted the proffered glass. "True, but I can manage for a while longer."

"How much time is that?" he asked, and sipped his drink.

"I don't know; things that affect me are happening very slowly."

You're a talented beguiler, whoever you are. I want to know why your fingerprints were surgically or chemically eradicated and why there's no record of you or your voice pattern. It's strange that both you and Starla have no fin-

gerprints on your lovely hands, but at least there's a file on her, and thankfully it's a nonpriority one. The whorls, arches, and loops on his own fingers had been obliterated to protect his many identities; and that was often the case with *villites.* Perhaps Starla's had been removed to conceal past crimes which were more hazardous than he realized, but he hoped not. "You still don't want to discuss your problems with me?"

"No, not yet, but I hope that situation will change soon."

"So do I; mysteries can be as frustrating as they are intriguing." He chuckled and grinned to disarm her. Yet, a strange feeling assailed him. His body was becoming hot and eager for mating, and his mind told him she was within reach and enticing him. *Control yourself, Curran, and see what you can learn.*

Yana saw his cheeks flush and his eyes brighten. He was trying to appear calm, but she sensed his tension. She watched him lick his lips, shift his position, and twist the glass in his grasp. She knew her ploy was working on him. "Did you have a successful trek? Was it dangerous?"

Right to the point of your motive for coming? Though his race had lost the ability to exude at will their ancient mating pheromone and his nostrils didn't detect any odor other than her heady fragrance, it was as if her skin had been bathed in that titillating chemical, as if the air and his lungs were filled with it, as if that stimulus was gushing through his pulsing body. His erotic need was making it difficult to concentrate on his goal of unmasking her and her ruse. He was troubled by his inability to ignore those irresistible sensations. He wanted to remove her temptation, but couldn't allow himself to be thwarted and overpowered by carnal urgings. He finally summoned his wits to answer, "Both."

"I'm happy you survived whatever perils you confronted. What do you do when you're away from the settlement, if that isn't a secret?"

"Sorry, but it is. Maybe I can tell you about it some *deega.*"

"I doubt we will see each other again after I depart."

Dagan watched her tease soft fingertips over his arm as he battled her potent allure. It was as if every *hapax* of him craved to undress and seduce her. He scolded himself for not casting aside such an absurd weakness. "That means you won't be returning to Tochara after matters are settled?" he asked, trying not to stumble over his words.

"This will be my one and only visit." She put aside her glass.

"Do you have a lover or mate waiting for you somewhere in Asisa?"

Yana placed a hand on his taut thigh and pretended to absently stroke it. "No. Do *you* have someone special in your life?"

"Not yet, but perhaps I will in the distant future." *If Starla doesn't get herself killed, exterminated, or incarcerated on a penal colony. That's it, Curran, think about Starla so you can disregard Yana's eerie magic.*

Yana fastened her gaze to his muscled thigh as she drew finger circles on it. "Do you ever get lonely or dissatisfied with your existence?"

Dagan set his empty glass on a side table. "Do you?"

Yana lifted her hand and moved aside a strayed lock of black hair from his cheek, brushing a finger against his flesh as she did so. "Yes, but you're making my time here pass swifter and easier."

You're one talented temptress, Yana, but two can play at your little game. Let's see how far you're willing to take it to charm me over to your side. He grasped her hand and stroked her thumb with his. "But not enough to entice you to stay longer than planned?"

"This isn't the kind of life I want for myself. What about you?"

Dagan noticed that her chest seemed to rise and fall at

a swifter pace and her breathing pattern altered. Her cheeks flushed and she began to fidget on the seat, seemingly unaware of responding to his trick. Taut points stood out on her breasts, the thin material unable to restrain them. Her fingers tightened around his hand. Her gaze filled with readable desire and glued to his captivating one. So, he mused, she was susceptible to him; it wasn't just an act. "Presently, I'm right where I want and need to be."

Enchanted by the virile and handsome Kalfan, she couldn't help but ask, "What do you want and need most at this *preon?*"

He realized he was snared by his own verbal trap. "I'm not sure," he murmured.

Yana noted his husky tone and the hunger gnawing in his eyes, the same ravenous one which chewed at her wits and will. She—Bree Kayah Saar, Star Fleet officer, Elite Squad member, agent on a crucial mission—wanted this perilous and forbidden prize with every fiber of her being. "You want and need me, isn't that true?"

"Are you sure this is what you want?" *Please say no and leave fast!*

She slipped one leg over his hips and sat across his lap, their bodies touching through the materials of their garments. Her hands cupped his strong jawline and she fused her gaze to his. "Yes," she murmured before she meshed her mouth with his, knowing the scent on her face would fill his nostrils and remove any lingering self-control.

Dagan's senses whirled rapidly and wildly as if he were caught in a spinning vortex. His arms banded her waist and pressed her against him. He spread kisses over her face and the soft column of her throat. As she rubbed herself against his throbbing groin, he lost the battle to resist. His hands grasped the hem of her flowing garment, lifted it over her head, and cast it to the floor. His deft fingers quivered as they released the lacy band around her full breasts before he nestled his face between them. His mouth wandered over each luscious mound and his lips teased at both pinnacles in turn as his hands caressed her sleek back. He had no choice except to possess her or surely he would zone out forever.

Dagan was creating blissful sensations within Yana and exhilarating her with his actions. Her fingers roamed his broad shoulders; they played in his dark mane; they drew his head closer to her taut peaks, encouraging him to ravish them. She moaned and writhed in his lap, aware of the hardness straining against his jumpsuit and pulsing against her private domain. She had planned to ensnare him and loosen his lips with Yana's surrender; but now, only thoughts of seizing great pleasure for herself filled her mind.

They stood in unison and together they peeled off her panties, then his boots, jumpsuit, and briefs in a feverish rush. They kissed and caressed, naked and enflamed. Soon, they sidled as if one entity to his *sleeper* and fell upon it with Dagan atop her, rubbing their ignited bodies together.

He fondled and kissed her in an almost mindless frenzy, results, she knew, of the potent pheromone and her brazen enticements.

So enthralled and tantalized was he, that Dagan could not stop himself from entering her immediately. He sank deep into the core of her until his hardness was surrounded by her delicate folds and soft triangle of bluish-blond hair. He explored that exciting terrain as his hips undulated with haste and greed. Though skilled at giving sensual delights, he could not help but seek his own satisfaction, dazed beyond thinking about sating hers.

It was unnecessary for Dagan to guide Yana to her pinnacle because she was so stimulated that her body responded to his of its own volition. Her eager and supple limbs imprisoned him. Sweet ecstasy coiled steadily within her pleading loins and prepared itself to unwind when she could endure the glorious torment no longer. She matched each thrust he sent into her receptive body and coaxed him with murmurings and movements to continue his pace.

She had just enough presence of mind to realize this experience was nothing like the one she had shared with Antarus *yings* ago. While both were weakened in body and wits and believed death was imminent, she had allowed Antarus to take her so he could die happy. His kisses and caresses had not evoked the potent effect Dagan's did. She had not craved or responded to Antarus in a wild and eager way, nor to any other male. She was glad she didn't have to worry about complications, as Maffeian females were given a time-releasing chemical upon reaching puberty to halt the release of ovums; that measure required the infusion of another chemical after she was bonded to a lifelong mate for restoring reproductive ability or at a selected period when she was ready for children. That action wasn't taken to promote or condone promiscuity, but to prevent unwanted pregnancies either from carelessness or a tragic criminal attack.

Both soon reached the brink of release. They labored as one until they were rewarded with rapturous climaxes. Yana gasped and arched her back as she clung to him. Dagan rode her with fervor until gratification was complete, his enormous craving slaked. For a few *preons,* their mouths and flesh remained united as their senses and bodies returned to normal.

Fulfilled at last, Dagan was astonished and dismayed by his crazed behavior. This wasn't the woman he wanted lying beneath him, not the woman he wanted to share such moments and feelings. He dreaded to imagine the damage this carnal episode could do to his budding relationship with Starla Vedris, if she discovered it. Yet, how could he conceal it from her and others, if Yana started to cling to him in a possessive and intimate manner? On the other hand, how could he learn Yana's secrets if he sent the Asisan on her way? He berated himself for falling into such a perilous and costly trap. If he didn't know better, he would believe his immunities to all known drugs and tricks had failed him. Whatever Yana's allure was, it was potent, and he cautioned himself to be on alert against it in the future.

"You're too quiet and distant, Dagan," Yana observed. "Is something wrong? Did I fail to please you? Do you think badly of me for succumbing to your charms?"

The *I-GAF* officer realized he had no choice now except to take advantage of the unwanted predicament. "I'm just relaxed. You were more than satisfying, Yana, and my opinion of you hasn't changed."

She noted that he didn't relate what that "opinion" was, and sensed he was being careful with his words, perhaps deceitful. "I'm glad, because I want to remain close to you while I'm here, if that's agreeable. But we must be careful about being seen together too often or appearing to be too close."

"Why is that?" he asked, then wished he had agreed immediately.

"If the other men learn we've shared a *sleeper,* they might become sexually overt with me. I also think some might become jealous and angry that you succeeded with me where they failed; that could cause some nasty situations."

"I understand and concur with your logic and precautions. In public, we'll act like nothing more than friends. As to sharing moments like this one, we should wait a while before doing so again. I don't think it's a good idea for either of us to be seen coming and going from private dwellings."

Yana pressed a kiss to his bare shoulder. "Thank you for being understanding. A woman cannot be too careful in a place like Tochara where most men seek only the pleasures of the present. Now, tell me: How long do you plan to remain in the colony and work for Tochar? Where will you go and what will you do after you leave them?"

Hadn't they, he mused, covered those areas before?

Maybe she was making small talk to get past an unsettling moment. Yet, he believed she had enjoyed their sexual encounter, perhaps too much and unexpectedly to suit her. "I'll stay until I get bored and restless," he responded, "or earn enough to replace the ship I lost, whichever comes first, I suppose."

"What if living and working here remains exciting and rewarding, even after you buy your own ship?"

"Tochara will have to improve greatly to keep me here longer than necessary to accomplish my goals."

She continued her probe. "What if Tochar doesn't want you to leave his employ, ever?"

"That isn't his decision."

"What if he made it his decision? I've never heard of any man leaving his force, alive anyway. Wouldn't he fear you revealing the secrets you learn about him? And wouldn't he attempt to prevent you from becoming stiff competition by using his secrets for your own gains?"

"Do you really believe he's that dangerous and unpredictable?" Dagan asked.

"I overhear alarming things on occasion. I don't want you to get hurt."

"I doubt Tochar will live here permanently unless he can make it a nicer settlement. Rich and powerful men prefer better living conditions."

"If he resettled elsewhere, would you go with him?"

"I don't like to deal in unknowns, so I can't say."

"Perhaps if you decide to leave Noy at the same time I do, you can deliver me to my destination. Traveling together would be fun."

"Perhaps, when the time comes for you to leave, if I'm available."

"I hope you're gone by then."

"Why?"

"Because Tochar is gathering many enemies from both

sides of the law. I wouldn't want you caught up in a fierce rivalry or attack."

Who was she thinking of? "Do you have a particular rival in mind?"

"No, but a man like him must be craved by the authorities and men like him must envy his position and possessions."

"That's logical, but it's unlikely anybody will challenge him."

"Why? Because of those weapons he has to guard himself and Tochara?"

"What do you know about his *Destructoids?"*

"I've been here long enough to witness their power several times. It's frightening to realize what he could do with them if he used them elsewhere, such as in my world. Doesn't it worry you to be connected to such a man, a destroyer, an enslaver?"

"Only if Tochar is that kind of person; he hasn't shown me that side."

"Won't it be too late to escape him after he does expose his evil nature? Would you help him conquer and ravage other worlds?"

"Why would I? Do you think I match your dark opinion of him?"

"No, that's why I hate to see you get so entangled with him."

"Are you afraid he'll attack your planet?"

Yana rolled to her back, fluffed her long golden hair, and adjusted her neck ring. "Yes, because we have many things greedy men crave. Despite our strength, we could not defend ourselves against his assault."

Dagan rolled to his side, propped on his elbow, and gazed down at her as he questioned, "Did the Asisan leader send you here to spy on him?"

She stared at him and said, "Of course not; I swear it."

"Did one of those shadowy rivals send you here for study?"

"No, I swear that, too. You must believe me; I came for other reasons."

"Reasons you'll confide in me one *deega?*"

"Yes, when the time is right."

Dagan concluded she sounded honest; that surprised him and increased his intrigue. Was it possible she had told him the truth about everything except her name? Was she only hiding out on Noy for personal reasons? Was she truly drawn to him as a man and had no ulterior stimulus for yielding to him? Could she be falling in love with him? If those speculations were accurate, his association with her could both evoke complications with Starla and endanger Yana's life if he was exposed. If she was what she claimed to be, he didn't want to mislead her about his feelings. As he gazed into her limpid eyes and ravishing face, a searing heat and inexplicable urge to possess her overwhelmed him again. Before he was cognizant of what he was doing, he leaned forward and sealed their mouths. Soon, he was a slave of her sweet lips, roving hands, and ardent surrender. Yet, with his eyes closed, it was an exquisite pirate whom his mind saw and touched.

Yana knew he had not seen her press the added disk on her neck ring to release more of the ancient pheromone. Though Kalfans had lost the ability to produce and release it, he had not acquired an immunity to the chemical stimulus which Cypher had duplicated for her. She had used the trick again to end their conversation, and she needed to have him once more, as she had no idea when they could unite their bodies again. Within moments, she also was lost in the wonder and flames of raging passion with the only man who had stolen her heart and will.

Twice in a short span, Dagan had behaved like a rutting and thoughtless animal for the first time in his life. Yet, he realized—from the flush on Yana's face and chest, her actions, and her gaze—she had received enormous pleasure and gratification. He was certain an unknown force had dazed and provoked him to fulfill this raw and unbridled passion, though he could not surmise what it was. Perhaps Asisan women emitted a mating scent when aroused which affected males in such a manner. His body had been snared, but his heart and mind had not wanted either encounter. With Starla, it was different; he desired her with total clarity and yearned to make love to her. Perhaps he had ruined any chance of that happening.

Relaxed in the golden aftermath of the exquisite experience, Yana cuddled in his embrace and drifted off to sleep.

When Dagan noticed her peaceful slumber, he didn't awaken her, as it was too late for her to return safely to her abode. And, at this *hora,* their presence outside if he escorted her there would be noticed by those still up and around. It would be easier for her to slip out tomorrow morning. He closed his eyes and soon was asleep, exhausted from his confusing exertions.

Aboard the *Liksa,* Cypher was worried and helpless. He knew the shapeshifting chemical's time span was twelve *horas,* and she was asleep. The problem was, with her wearing Yana's one-way neck ring unit instead of Starla's two-way wrist device, he could not send her a vibrating signal or contact her. If Bree-Kayah failed to awaken and escape before transmutation occurred, she would be exposed to Dagan Latu, as her emergency phial could not be used for continuation of her current state. He also was concerned by the fact she had been emotionally involved in her ruse, revealed to him by the physiological readings in his monitoring system. It was his duty to enlighten her to the complications and distractions of such behavior and emotions after her return to the ship.

The android watched the timer until only forty-five *preons* remained to be spent, and Bree-Kayah was still asleep. He analyzed the dilemma, but could not deduce a way in which to warn her to come to her senses. It was illogical for him to transport into Latu's quarters and expose himself to the *villite* when his intelligent partner might find a way to protect their mission even if she were unmasked to him. He also concluded he should not lock on to her coordinates and teleport her out prematurely, as that action would assuredly provoke Dagan's suspicions. Though she was not thinking clearly or acting wisely, he reasoned he must have faith in her and her abilities.

Still, the *preons* continued to vanish from the timer, one by one.

Eight

Dagan's eyes opened shortly after sunup. He turned his head to find Yana still slumbering nearby, her breathing slow and even. His gaze roamed her serene face and naked body, and he was pleased his body did not go wild with another surge of mating lust. To ensure that wouldn't happen this morning, he slipped from the *sleeper* to shower and dress, and to get out of there before she could enspell him again.

Yana only pretended to be asleep when Dagan arose, though it was a struggle to keep her expression calm and breathing controlled. She had seen—via slits in her eyelids—light coming through the overhead *transascreen* and almost panicked. Lying on her side and facing him, her panic had lessened when she saw bluish-blond hair spread on the pillow instead of brown tresses. As she pondered an escape plan, he had risen and entered the privacy chamber. She glanced at the timepiece on a far wall and her gaze widened in renewed alarm; Yana had less than thirty *preons* to get out of there, hopefully without being seen by others or being delayed by Dagan. She heard water running and knew he was using the old-fashioned bathing method in this primitive place that lacked automatic cleansing cubicles.

"I'm awake, Cypher," she whispered. "Lock on to my

coordinates and wait for my signal to transport me out of here."

She yanked on her garments and entered a message for Dagan in the communication system nearby. After pressing a signal button to catch his attention, she whispered to her android, "Get me out of here fast, Cypher."

As soon as she reached her ship, Starla assured him she would never lower her guard that far again. "It was stupid and reckless," she confessed. "I don't know what Dagan would have done if I had changed before his eyes. I'm sure he would have been furious with me for tricking him. I can't imagine what I would have told him to protect myself and our mission. You heard the answers he gave to me after we . . . had sex. I haven't decided if he is trustworthy or not, or worthy of saving. I do have another plan in mind for this evening. I'll relate it to you and tell me what you think about it."

After she finished, Cypher said, "It is dangerous from two angles, but both are clever ideas. If you are cautious and no hazards are present, you can succeed. Your second idea contains the same level of high risk."

"But I will go as Starla this time."

"No matter which identity you use, you are too susceptible to him."

"Dagan caught me off guard last night; I didn't expect him to be so irresistible, didn't realize my attraction to him was so strong. I know my conduct was foolish, and forbidden under these grim circumstances. I'm only human, Cypher, so I lost self-control for a time. I've never faced this kind of situation and challenge before; I'm aware I didn't handle them right. Now that I know how strongly he disarms me, I'll be on alert to thwart my weakness."

"It is not your behavior that was imprudent and prohibited; it is your emotions which war against your intelligence; your heart and body are in intense conflict with your head."

"You're right, Cypher, so I'll have to find a way to halt that struggle."

"Do you love this Kalfan?"

"Pralu, my friend, but the truth is, yes! Is there a drug or treatment you can perform to make me immune to him and these feelings?"

"This is one time I cannot help you resolve a serious problem. It will be propitious if he does not love you. Reciprocation could be detrimental to you and to our mission."

"Even if he told me he loved me, I would not believe him."

"Perhaps it could be true, or he could be convincing."

"Pray that neither of those traps appear."

"I do not possess a religious or spiritual program."

"Then I'll pray hard enough for both of us." *Kahala, save me, if that perilous snare approaches me! Don't forget, Bree, Dagan Latu is an enemy.*

"I'm going to refresh myself and prepare for my tasks later. Take care of your part while I'm gone. And, Cypher, thanks for everything."

Dagan's tension diminished when he found Yana gone after he left the privacy chamber: showered, shaved, and dressed to depart in an alleged hurry. He heard the message unit beeping and checked it. Again, relief filled him after learning she thought it was best they avoid each other for a few *deegas.* He needed time and privacy to decide how to discourage her interest in him. He didn't want Yana to fall in love with him, if that was the case. It was possible she had selected him as a protector and companion if matters failed to be resolved in her world and she could never return there. Even if she was stranded on Noy, she couldn't dock at his bay and latch on to him for security. Yet, after his mission was over and if she was still present and in trouble, he decided he would get Phaedrig to settle her elsewhere. Maybe he did owe Yana something for last night—if she hadn't tricked him—but assistance into another life was as far as he could go to repay her.

Dagan discarded those worries for now, as he was to report to Tochar's ship this morning to begin the repairs on it. He still had not decided if he was going to tamper with other parts, because Tochar had said he would not make an ensuing test run which might place him in harm's way before his vessel was armed with an invincible weapon. Since someone else might be assigned to test the *Azoulay* before Tochar was tempted to go trekking, problems would be suspicious. He must bide his time while making observations and getting closer to the band to cull clues. He couldn't make a move against Tochar or his men until he unmasked the Kalfan traitor who was feeding the *fiendal* secret information and helping him obtain moonbeams from their mines on the planet Orr. Or act against the *villites* until he weakened or destroyed the colony's defense system. But, he vowed, somehow and some way, he would achieve those goals; and he would slay Tochar and his friends for their personal offenses *yings* ago.

Don't get in my way, Starla, or you'll have to go down with them. I hope you'll leave this place before the end arrives, which it will. If I was convinced you would take my side and help me, I would confide in you. After we get to know each other better, I can make that decision.

At dusk, Staria stepped onto a sensor pad and looked at Cypher who was standing at the transporter's control panel and watching her. She took a deep breath and gave her plan one last mental going-over. What she had in mind was risky; she could lose her life and destroy her mission if she failed. "If I don't survive, my friend, cloak and leave for home immediately. Report my fate and our findings and suspicions to Supreme Commander Sanger, and hand over our evidence to him. Only to him, Cypher. There's a message for my parents, my brother, and my sister in the computer; make certain it reaches them if I never return. If I'm captured and we lose contact, cloak and wait three *deegas* for my escape; I'll shapeshift to Yana and hide in her abode, so monitor it for my arrival and rescue."

"What if you cannot escape in three *deegas?*"

"If I haven't freed myself by then, either I'll be dead or flight will be impossible. If that occurs, obey my first order to cloak and leave."

"I am programmed to protect and assist you; I cannot desert you."

"The mission must take precedence over my life and safety if anything goes wrong this evening. We do not have all of the answers to this mystery, but we have things which will be helpful to the agent who takes my place. You are responsible for getting those facts and speculations to Thaine."

"I will obey. Use caution, Bree-Kayah, and return unharmed."

"I'll do my best, Cypher. Always remember our friendship and my love for you. I could not have done all I have in the past without you."

"I will not delete my memory chip of you."

"Let's do it. Ready to go."

Starla watched his image and the location vanish and the cavern appear before her line of vision. She drew her weapon and placed her finger near the button to signal Cypher for rescue if necessary since speaking could be perilous if anyone was nearby. Her gaze scanned the dim recess and she listened for any hint of a threat, but saw and heard nothing to alarm her. She inched her way to the rock corridor, flattened herself against the hard surface, and peered around its edge into the next hollow section. Again, she heard and saw nothing to indicate danger or anyone's presence.

Using caution, she made her way to the targets, recognizing them from their containers during raids. She also saw crates of weapons, the parts they had stolen from the space station, holders with drugs, and other pirated items. Since Tochar had tried to sell crystals to the Thracians, she assumed he would make another attempt soon and she could not allow the moonbeams to fall into enemy or rival hands. She knew Enforcers were standing guard outside the cave's mouth and could enter for a check at any time, so she must hurry with her daring task. If anyone did arrive, she must slay him to avoid exposure and to achieve her goal.

The Elite Squad officer put away her weapon and withdrew the three new devices Cypher had constructed, two extra ones to make certain the job was accomplished. She placed the tiny units underneath the crystals' containers and pressed the initiation buttons to begin their sequences. In one *hora,* if the devices did not malfunction, a massive explosion would occur and everything in the cave would be gone. The only thing left to do was get out of there fast and set up her alibi, with Dagan or some other person.

As she headed to the coordinates for her beaming point, she heard voices and froze. She prayed it wasn't Dagan and they wouldn't stay long in case she had to take drastic measures for escape. She concealed herself, listened, and waited, aware the timers were running and she was trapped within the detonation range. She mustn't signal Cypher to lock on to new coordinates unless she was certain she could not make it back to the original ones, as the light and sound of the transporter would expose someone's presence and treachery. She wanted the explosion to be a mystery, not compel Tochar to look for an enemy or to go on alert.

Starla caught the voices of two of Tochar's Enforcers. She tensed as they paused to chat and joke not far from her hidden location. She willed them to hush and leave, but they didn't get her mental message. She waited in mounting anxiety as her heart pounded and her body trembled.

At last, the men strolled outside to enter a guard shelter. In a rush, she returned to her spot and signaled Cypher to extract her. The moment she was aboard her ship, she yelled, "I have to hurry. See you later or in the morning." She ran down the corridor to a shuttle and piloted it to the landing grid. Fortunately, Auken was leaving the *trans-to* to Tochar's dwelling. She hailed him and received a ride into the settlement, making him a superb witness to her whereabouts if one was needed.

"Would you like to have a drink and play *resi* with me?"

"Thanks, Starla, but I have other plans with a friend. Another time?"

"Of course. I'm sure I can find somebody to lose to me tonight."

Auken laughed at her jest and humorous tone. "I'm sure you can."

They entered the Skull's Den together and parted for Auken to go to the second level where the Pleasure Givers plied their trade.

Starla glanced around the interior and saw Dagan motioning to her to join him. Without halting to purchase a drink at the bar, she walked straight toward him.

"I was afraid you'd forgotten we agreed to meet tonight."

"I think I only said *perhaps* we would."

"Back on alert against me, are you?"

"If so, I didn't realize I was. Are you going to buy me a drink or do you want me to get it myself?" she inquired with a smile.

"What about if I serve you one at my place?"

Starla's gaze met his as she ventured, "Go to your place?"

"We could talk there in private; it's getting busy and noisy in here. I give you my word of honor to behave."

"Behave like what?" she teased.

Dagan warmed to the sparkle in her green eyes and the

sexy curve to her mouth as she smiled again. "You're in a good mood tonight."

"I didn't realize I was always in a bad one. Am I?"

"No, but you seem more relaxed and happier tonight. I hope it's because of the company you're in."

"You did save my life on that space station."

"And you saved mine twice," Dagan reminded.

"That means you owe me one."

"I hope we're never put in the position of you having to collect it."

"I'd rather collect it than suffer the consequences," Starla quipped.

"Well, do we stay or go?" he inquired, wanting to leave in case Yana appeared on the scene. He could only hope the Asisan did not attempt to visit him again tonight.

"We can go if we take food with us; I'm hungry."

He chuckled. "I'll order something from Radu. Any suggestions?"

She licked her lips and said, "Surprise me."

"I hope your likes and dislikes match mine if I'm making the choices."

"You are, so we'll soon find out, won't we?"

"That we will, Starla. I've only taken one swallow from my drink if you'd like to finish it while I get our meals."

"Thanks," she said. Starla lifted the glass and took a sip, passing her tongue over her mouth afterward. "So, you like *paonee* with *arple*. Nice flavor."

"I asked Radu not to make it too strong; I like to keep a clear head."

"So do I. It's a shame we sometimes allow certain things to dull our wits, isn't it?"

"I suppose it's according to what or whom dulls them. I'll return soon." Before Dagan reached the bar, he halted to speak with Sach as the Icarian headed for the second level.

As the men talked, a loud explosion was heard over the

music and voices; then a continuous rumbling noise. The dome shook. Tables and chairs rattled. Glasses and bottles tinkled; several fell over and broke. Light fixtures swayed, and a painting on one wall crashed to the floor.

"What was that?" Dagan exclaimed as he glanced around the room.

"We could be under attack! Let's go see what's happening."

Starla joined Dagan and Sach and asked, "What's wrong?"

"We don't know," Sach muttered, "but we're going to find out."

"I'm coming with you two," Starla said.

They hurried outside and sighted a huge dust cloud near Tochar's dwelling, which appeared unharmed. Rocks still tumbled down the ridge. They looked skyward for signs of enemy vessels and laser fire, but none were present. Other people crowded around and asked questions, some pointing to the fiery-colored dust drifting upward.

"That's where the storage cave is located. Let's see what happened."

Starla and Dagan climbed into the landrover with Sach and rode toward the scene. Within a *preon* Auken came behind them, still adjusting his garment and fingercombing his tousled hair. Enforcers, those on and off duty, gathered at the site, their black uniforms a stark contrast against the reds of the landscape. Tochar was there, his expression filled with fury.

"What's the trouble?" Sach asked his leader and friend.

"There was an explosion in the storage cavern; the entrance is sealed off by a cave-in. Without tunneling equipment and expert technicians, we will never be able to clear that rubble or recover what is inside."

"What caused the blast?" Auken asked.

"I do not know. Perhaps some of those starbursts or crystals were volatile. A check was made of the area not long before this happened, and nothing unusual was detected. No one was inside or had been inside lately except for the two guards."

"So you're ruling out sabotage?" Sach queried.

"I do not see how an enemy could have done this, but I want the area and settlement inspected for any suspicious signs. I also want those two guards to be questioned under *Thorin* to make certain they are loyal to me."

"We'll handle that matter for you tonight."

Tochar nodded agreement to Auken's words.

"Is there anything you need us to do?" Starla offered, feigning a tone of concern.

Tochar shook his head. "Nothing I can think of. Where were all of you? Did you see or hear anything strange before the explosion?"

"Me, Sach, Dagan, and Starla were at the Skull's Den," Auken replied. "I don't know about Moig. We heard the noise and felt the vibrations and came as fast as we could. Anybody have any speculations?"

With cunning, Starla suggested, "Do you think some type of detonation device could have been concealed in one of the crates we brought here? Perhaps one with a delayed timer which was set to explode if not switched off by a certain *hora* or *deega?*"

"It is possible that a device was hidden in one of those shipments. If so, it was done cleverly, as all crates are checked before storage. But that is a good idea, Starla, one we will watch more carefully in the future."

"There's another plausible angle, Tochar," she continued. "What if the crystals require special handling or storage measures to prevent destabilization when kept close together for a long period and out of their rock casings? What if they overload with some type of energy force that must be restrained in a particular manner? Perhaps your contact could investigate that angle, since we know so little about them. If they're dangerous when mishandled, they could explode on the ship before we reach base. Especially if secret devices are being planted in the cargoes."

"I have not been alerted to any new security measures, but it is a possibility I need to study," Tochar stated. "But from here on, all crates will be examined before loading them on the ship, and all crystals will be stored in separate containers, with space between them and preferably in their rock casings. Each cargo must be stored in different locations to prevent such a massive loss again. If another incident occurs, we will know which item and person caused the trouble."

"It would be wise to get a list of the ships in orbit and names of visitors in the settlement," Dagan said, "then we can make sure they're all trustworthy. Was there more than one entrance to the cave?" he asked.

"No, and without the right coordinates, it would be dangerous for anyone to transport into a cavern. He could materialize inside solid rock."

"Somebody might have thought that was a risk worth taking or might have found a way to get the coordinates. The items stored there were of enormous value. On the other hand, perhaps one of the weapons or other containers had a beacon implanted for obtaining the right coordinates."

"That is excellent reasoning, Dagan. Auken, get that list of ships and names for me. But there is no way we can look for trickery this time."

"Which caves will we use in the future?" Sach asked.

"Not those with water; their resources are too precious to imperil."

"Using more than one will spread the Enforcer guards thin."

"That cannot be avoided, Sach; safety measures must be taken."

"At least you didn't store those crates in your dwelling."

"Perhaps that is what an unknown enemy hoped I would

do and that I would be destroyed. I will not take any risks in the future."

"It could have been nothing more than an accident."

"That is possible, Auken, but I want to make certain it was, and it does not happen again."

"What about the *Destructoids?*" Auken hinted. "Do you think they're unstable or will become unstable? If so, we'd be defenseless."

"So far, nothing suspicious has occurred. Examine them tonight."

"But they're kept covered with their rock casings," Starla reminded. "Maybe that controls their energy force. Yet, if transporting crystals out of their casings were dangerous, they would be ensheathed when we steal them. Perhaps it has to do with a certain time span of safety."

"I will check into that matter immediately. Starla, Dagan, you two can leave; there is nothing more to be done here. Auken, Sach, you two handle those other matters for me. Tell Nypeer to put the Enforcers on full alert and watch everybody's comings and goings for a while. Find Moig and see why he did not join us; his absence is strange."

"I saw him enter the Skull's Den earlier and go to the second level," Dagan said.

Auken frowned. "He must be engrossed in one of those virtual-reality games with a drug inducer; he's becoming addicted to them. If he's in one of those cubicles and dazed, he doesn't know what's going on."

"Make certain that is where he is," Tochar ordered.

Dagan and Starla returned to the Skull's Den to purchase meals before entering Dagan's chamber. They sat down at his table to eat and drink.

To lessen any uneasiness she might feel, he remarked, "That was some unexpected excitement, wasn't it?"

Starla finished chewing before she said, "Yes, and Tochar is lucky he didn't have those crystals stored in his abode or he would be dead."

"If the moonbeams were responsible for that blast." Dagan could not divulge that he had not heard of such a possibility. If the Serians knew that secret, they had not shared it with his people. Yet, if Nature was giving them a helping hand, he did not object and was grateful. The first moment of privacy he obtained, he would inform Phaedrig of the strange incident. With the thefts destroyed, that left only the *Destructoids* to handle. He hoped those weapons would self-terminate and make Tochar vulnerable.

Starla was thinking along similar lines, yet, she could not imagine how she could destroy those weapons. If she did find a way, she could finalize her mission soon and be gone. No, there still remained the mystery of who was supplying Tochar with secrets. "I wonder if Tochar knew or suspected the crystals were dangerous," Starla mused. "If so, he didn't tell us and he put our lives at great risk."

Dagan shook his head. "He might endanger us, but I doubt he would imperil his friends. I think those two explosive episodes have him confused and worried. I'm sure he assumed he had lucked out on a valuable, powerful, safe product."

"I wonder if his contacts know the truth, but took a chance they could make a large profit before the crystals' flaws were discovered," Starla said.

As Dagan poured them more *Clearian* wine, he reasoned, "If that were true, they wouldn't have let him get his hands on such powerful weapons, then provoke him to revenge. That would be stupid."

They ate for another short span before Dagan looked up at Starla and suggested, "Maybe you should think about leaving the settlement. If those weapons malfunction, Tochara will be vulnerable to attack. Anybody here when that happens will be slain or captured."

"What about you?" she asked. "Are you thinking of leaving soon?"

"I can't; I have to stay until I earn what I came after.

You have a ship, so you can depart at any time, work or resettle somewhere safer."

Finished with her meal, Starla stood to discard the container. "Is there a safe place for people like us?" she asked.

Dagan rose and tossed away his container as he answered, "You could change your identity and begin a new life, a legal one."

"So could you," Starla retorted with a smile as she took a seat in the adjoining area. "For now, this seems to be the best place to stay."

Dagan sat down and eyed her. "I don't want you to get hurt, Starla."

"That's nice of you to say."

"It has nothing to do with being nice or with you saving my life."

"What does it have to do with?"

"You, as a person, as a woman, as a friend, as a . . ."

"A *what,* Dagan?" she asked, locking her gaze to his.

"Somebody I want to get to know better."

"How can you if I take your suggestion and leave?"

He stroked her cheek under the guise of pushing aside a stray lock. "I'd rather see you live and be happy than to . . ."

"Why do you keep stopping? Than to, what?"

"Than to have a chance to get closer to you."

"How close do you want to get?"

He grasped her hand and held it, noticing its sudden chill. "I want to make love to you; I have since the first *deega* we met."

Starla stared at him, surprised, and yet not, by his words. She no longer needed him as an alibi, so she could escape his temptation. But she needed—wanted—him in another way. How else could she discover what kind of man he truly was unless she stayed with him tonight? "What if it doesn't work between us and complications ensue?"

"How and why would that happen?"

"I don't know. It's hard to think of a good reason with you looking at me like that."

"Like what?" Dagan murmured in a husky tone.

"Like you want to kiss me, devour me."

"I do," he murmured, then slowly leaned toward her. When she did not retreat, he sealed his mouth to hers. He pulled her into his embrace and savored the taste and feel of her.

Starla looped her arms around his neck and guided her fingers into his dark mane, drawing his head closer. She loved his soft, tender kisses. She was both weakened and enflamed as his mouth roved her face and neck. She felt his embrace tighten and his kisses become urgent and deeper after his lips returned to hers. His strong and gentle hands stroked her arms and back, making her aware of every part of her yearning body. When his hand roamed over her shoulder to her breast and cupped it, heat and tingles raced over her flesh. Her nipples grew taut. The core of her being called out for appeasement.

Dagan halted his actions, stood, and extended his hand to her, his message clear and enticing. He hoped she would respond to it because he craved her beyond belief. "You don't need to be afraid of me, Starla; I would do everything within my power never to hurt you in any way."

Starla gazed at his hand, then looked into his beckoning blue eyes. "Your skills and experience in this area far outweigh mine, so you might be disappointed you initiated this encounter." As he shook his head, she placed her hand in his and was helped to her feet, her knees shaky and weak. She let him guide her to his *sleeper,* where he halted to kiss her.

As he had dreamed of doing many times, he peeled off her garments. To lessen the tension he sensed within her and read within her green eyes, he kept his gaze fastened to hers as she lay down and he removed his boots and jumpsuit. As fast and smoothly as possible, he joined her, pulled her into his embrace, and kissed her again.

"Relax, Starla; I do want to devour you, but it will be a painless deed."

The warmth of his breath and huskiness of his voice in her ear caused her to quiver. Somehow she knew his promise of ecstasy would come true.

Together they surrendered to their soaring passions. They yielded to the glorious torment of wanting each other so deeply and strongly they would risk complications with their missions. Fervent needs consumed them as they kissed countless times and fondled scorching bodies. They savored the wonder and rapture of this compelling episode. It seemed right, natural, for them to bond in this physical and emotional manner. Embers of desire were fueled to ignite into a roaring blaze which neither could nor wanted to douse or control.

Starla felt the sleek strands of his black hair as she twirled them around her fingers. She eyed his perfect features, and her fingers and lips trekked them with ardor. She relished his kisses and caresses, which were slow, seductive, and dazing. There was not a spot on her that did not burn or quiver with longing and pleasure. Nestled in his strong embrace, his fingers wandered over her from head to knee— admiring, teasing, enflaming. Her head lolled on the pillow as his deft lips fastened to one breast and tantalized its peak to taut eagerness as his hand kneaded the other mound to anticipation of that same action. She wanted this man with all of her heart and soul. She responded to the signal from his nudging hand to part her thighs so it could drift up and down those sensitive lengths before one tenderly invaded her woman's domain. She sighed in bliss as the peak hardened under his masterful touch. There was a quickening in her stomach and a sweet tension building in her loins. His finger slipped within her, delving, thrusting, moistening her, assailing her very core. She moaned and thrashed and drew every drop of splendor from that new experience and eagerly awaited many more.

Dagan brushed his fingers over her rib cage and traveled the curves and planes of her pliant body. She caressed his shoulders, arms, and back with light but highly arousing gestures. He ached to bury himself inside her, but he did not want to rush this cherished event. First, he wanted to titillate her to great heights. His fingers dove into the shiny, thick waves of her brown hair. Her lips brushed kisses over his neck, throat, and face while he did the same to hers. He loved feeling her naked flesh next to his. Once more his mouth captured her breast and claimed its nipple. He kissed, teethed, and brought it to full attention.

Starla savored the magic of his deft tongue and talented hands. A blast of searing heat stormed her body, one so potent and demanding and swift that it astonished her. She felt the tautness and erotic heat of his protruding desire against her hip. "Take me, Dagan," she coaxed.

He moved atop her, the force of his weight controlled. She wrapped her arms around his back and pressed her fingers near his spine to entice him to unite their bodies and relieve their longings. His mouth melded with hers as their lips tantalized and their tongues teased. He slid the tip of his erection into her, paused a moment to draw a deep and needed breath for renewed restraint, then thrust further past her delicate folds until his arousal was concealed by her soft and damp haven. He was stimulated by the way she captured him between her legs with overlapped ankles.

Starla felt no shame or modesty with the man she loved. Yes, she admitted, *loved*. A flood of suspenseful rapture washed over her, one so powerful that she could deny him nothing he wanted from her. The proof of his matching hunger feasted on and within her. She trailed her fingers over the rippling muscles of his back where no scars marred his flesh. He entered and departed her open body, making many journeys to and from it as their mutual passions soared. It was as if primal urgings trapped within them surfaced and demanded a swift mating. She matched his pace and pattern, clinging to him, refusing to allow him to withdraw for any distance or any length of time.

Dagan's ravenous appetite for her only heightened. When he felt her stiffen and heard her gasp for air, he knew she was in the early thralls of sweet release. He hastened and strengthened his thrusts to give her supreme pleasure; as she writhed and moaned, he knew he had succeeded, and joy suffused him. He was so enraptured by her and their wild bonding, that nothing else could have seized his attention at that moment.

A spinning vortex of exquisite splendor carried them away as they climaxed within minutes of each other, their releases overlapping, then subsiding as one. Their greedy mouths and questing hands continued to send delightful and receptive messages; signals of satisfaction and serenity. They remained cuddled and quiet for a time.

Dagan propped on his side, leaned forward and kissed the tip of her nose. "I was right," he murmured.

Starla eyed his confident expression. "Right about what?"

He caressed her flushed cheek. "Us being a perfect match."

"In what area?"

Dagan trailed his fingertips over her collarbone and grinned. "In every area. Don't you agree?"

Starla captured his hand to halt its distracting motion. "I think it's too soon to make a judgment; we don't know each other that well."

"If your instincts and impressions are as good as mine, I'm right." He pulled their clasped hands to his lips and kissed hers.

His mood and motive confused her. "Have you ever been wrong?"

He chuckled. "Not many times, and they weren't important." *All except one, yings ago, and I'll correct that error very soon . . .*

"What if this—I'm—one of your rare mistakes?"

"Is it? Are you?"

"As I said, I don't know, yet. We're almost strangers."

"Then why is it that I feel as if we've known each other a long time?"

"We have been working together and closely for quite a while."

Dagan noticed she was contradicting her earlier statement, that they were "almost strangers." They had known each other for over seven *wegs*. "Working together doesn't explain our quick and easy rapport."

"Have you forgotten we haven't been friends for very long?"

"There was a spark between us the first time we met, Starla."

"I don't deny I found you attractive, but . . ."

"But, what? Continue. You have my full attention."

"I never expected this to happen between us. In fact, I never expected to see you again after our initial encounter on that vessel."

"Perhaps fate brought us together for a purpose."

"What kind of purpose?" she asked.

"That's something we'll have to wait to learn."

"Perhaps you're reading too much into what just happened."

"Perhaps you're not reading enough into it," he refuted.

"You're confusing me and making me nervous."

"Why, because you don't want to get this close to any man? You're the most fascinating, beautiful, and enchanting woman I've met. I don't want you to slip through my fingers." *Or get hurt by your connection to Tochar.*

Starla was bewildered and alarmed. This was not how he had behaved with Yana, even while dazed by the phero-mone! Was he being honest or was he trying to beguile her for some reason? Either way, she could not fall under his spell and become disarmed. "Don't expect me to become your lover, Dagan; I'm not ready for that kind of commit-ment."

"Maybe your head isn't, but your heart and body are."

As he leaned forward to kiss her, Starla placed her hand on his chest to stay him. "Please, don't do this. I can't begin a relationship with you."

"You already have, Starla, so why run scared now?"

"You don't understand."

"Then, explain what you mean so I can."

"This is . . . too sudden, too . . . unexpected, too . . . frightening."

"I promised not to hurt you, so trust me."

"I can't, not this soon. Give me time, Dagan, or it's over now."

He studied her panicked expression, then took a deep breath. "I won't pressure you, but I will continue to pursue you."

"To what end?" The question leapt from her mouth.

"To become my mate one *deega*." He hadn't meant to go that far, though the words were true; yet, he didn't retreat from his statement.

Starla's gaze widened. "You can't be serious?"

Maybe that was the only reason she would leave Tochar and the colony, so he continued. "Why not? We can't live this kind of life until death."

"You would alter your existence and character to have me?"

"When the time is right, yes." *If I can extricate you from the charges against you, and if you don't make them worse, and if I can get you away from here before the end comes.*

He needed to get a better grasp of her true character, so he challenged, "Would you do the same for me?"

With their gazes locked, Starla deliberated how she should respond, as an answer in either direction seemed hazardous.

Nine

Starla formed a reply slowly. "When and if the time is right," *but I doubt it ever will be with us on opposite sides of the law,* "and if we truly are compatible, perhaps a future together is possible after we retire from our current lifestyle. As for me, it still remains to be proven that we are a good match for such a serious relationship. Many changes would be required, and I can't imagine a man like you settling down and beginning a family, if you could even locate a safe place to do so and find another means of support."

Dagan was cognizant she had responded with caution. "That's sufficient encouragement for now; a slow and easy course makes sense to me. After you get to know me better, you'll probably be surprised by what you learn. I have many unseen facets, Starla, just as you do."

I hope so, Dagan, my love. I truly hope so. "We'll see."

"That we will, my ravishing and irresistible teammate."

Dagan kissed and caressed her, and soon they were making passionate and glorious love again.

In the golden aftermath of their union, they cuddled for a while in silence, sated and content. Yet, each was troubled by what loomed before them: their missions and what victory could cost them.

When Starla left his arms, he tried to coax her not to go. "Stay tonight," he implored.

As she pulled on her garments, she glanced at him and

said, "That wouldn't be wise; someone might see me departing in the morning."

He grinned. "Want to keep our relationship a secret from everybody?"

"Until it is a relationship, yes, I do. Good night, Dagan. I'll see you tomorrow; Tochar has a task for us to do."

"Wait until I dress and I'll escort you to the landing grid."

"That isn't necessary; it isn't that late; and I'm well armed. Almost everyone here knows I work for Tochar, so no one would dare attack me. If anyone tries, I can protect myself."

Dagan chuckled. "I remember your superior skills well from when you battled me, but I would slay anyone who harmed you."

"Thanks, but revenge can be a dangerous and self-destructive task."

Not if one is careful and justice is a must for peace of mind. I'll have it again after Tochar is destroyed, just as I'll find a way to have you. "Good night, Starla, and be careful."

She allowed her gaze to roam his handsome face and virile unclothed body. Every facet of him was enormously appealing; and she was susceptible to him in all ways. *Get moving, Bree, before you weaken and succumb again!* "I will. See you tomorrow."

The next morning, Starla sent *Raz* Yakir a message via Thaine Sanger to warn the Serlan ruler be on alert for an incoming communication from Tochar to his spy on the capital planet of Ulux or crystal mining planet of Kian. Yet, she suspected his signal could not be detected or traced, just as hers couldn't be; she wished the *fiendal* did not possess that technology and instrument so the traitor could be unmasked. She reported to her superior and friend in

Maffei that all moonbeams stolen so far had been destroyed by those secret devices, and to expect imminent raids for more, though she had not been informed as to dates and sites for them.

After that task was finished, Starla looked at Cypher and said, "All we can do now is wait and watch for clues. If only we could discover the leaks in Seri and Kalfa, destroy the weapons protecting Tochara, and prevent more crystal raids, we could complete our mission here and go home. I need to get away from these terrible people and this awful place; I want to see my family." *I need to talk with Mother; she would know what I should do about Dagan. When she and Father met, they were enemies from different worlds, and their relationship appeared doomed. Now, no two people could be more in love or happier. Despite their past dissimilarities and problems, they are matched perfectly and everything was resolved between them.* That also was true for her brother, Galen, and his mate, Rayna; and for her sister, Amaya, and her mate, Jason of Earth. All three couples had overcome seemingly impossible and tormenting obstacles and had been bonded blissfully for *yings. If only it could be that way for me and Dagan.* But, Starla reminded herself, her love was a criminal, a willing hireling of Tochar; and his future seemed grim.

The android analyzed from her expression that she was thinking and reasoning on a dilemma and allowed her time to do so. When she looked at him, he said, "You also want to escape Dagan Latu because you fear him."

"Not him, Cypher, but his powerful effect on me. My uncontrollable feelings for him grow stronger and run deeper every *deega*. It's an inexplicable bond between us, as if we're matched in a strange and potent way. It's more than a physical attraction, at least for me, and he appears to be telling the truth about his feelings. Yet, I can't say for certain if he is falling in love with me or he's only beguiling me for an unknown or selfish reason. Either angle can create trouble and torment for me."

Starla lazed back in her chair and frowned. "He makes it difficult for me to concentrate on my duty and to remember he's one of our targets. I love him and I want him, Cypher, but I know that's wrong for me and perilous for my mission. Soon, I might be forced to betray him. If that happens, he'll hate me and curse the *deega* we met. You can't imagine how tempted I am to warn him to flee while there's still time for escape or to attempt to convince him to side with us, but he could expose me to Tochar. I'm certain he holds no kind feelings for that *fiendal*, but men like him have a strange code of honor to the leaders who hire them. Dagan's record says his father and brother were slain by *Sekis* following a suspicious incident of treachery, and that's when he turned wicked. I wonder if he could be turned around again. Even so, there are many charges and allegations against him; and I'm not certain I could get him a pardon for helping us."

"If you request a pardon and it is denied, then he escapes or you allow him to flee punishment for his crimes, you will come under suspicion and an investigation will ensue. You must not dishonor yourself, your rank, and your family; or breach their faith in you."

"I know; as hard as it will be, I will do my duty. But it torments me to think of him being terminated forever or being confined for life on a barbaric penal colony. I know there is much good in Dagan Latu if he is given the chance to show it."

"You cannot alter his fate, Bree-Kayah; he chose his evil way of life. If there are grim consequences from his choice, he must suffer them."

"My head tells me you are right, but my heart rebels against such bitter reality. If only I could persuade him or trick him into leaving Tochar's hire and settlement, my dilemma would resolve itself. But there isn't enough time left for him to earn enough to purchase a new ship to return to work for himself; but if he stole one from somewhere, he could leave."

"It is only a remote possibility for Tochar to permit him to quit and depart. There is a chance Latu would ask you to leave with him. If he loves you and you refused to go, he would not depart and would remain in Tochar's hire."

"I had not reasoned it out that way. He said I was running scared, and he's accurate; he just doesn't know the correct reason for my contradictory behavior. I should not have become physically involved with him as Starla or as Yana; being so close to him confuses my emotions and dulls my instincts. I must find the strength and wits to resist him, without arousing suspicions in him for my sudden rejection."

"When the time comes for you to make a decision about his fate, you will make the right one."

Starla looked at the intelligent android, her eyes misty, her soul in anguish. "Will I, Cypher? Can I trust my head to overrule my heart when the moment of truth arrives?"

"You are Bree-Kayah Saar; you will do your duty."

"Promise me you'll make certain I do what is right."

"I will prevent you from making an error in judgment."

"Thank you, Cypher." She took a deep breath and wiped the moisture from her eyes. "I'm going to eat and freshen up before it's time to leave to do that futile task for Tochar. You're in control of the ship."

Starla left the bridge to order a meal from the automated *servo* that had been restocked recently by a traveling supply vessel. She dreaded what she must do to Dagan later, but she had no choice.

As he dressed, Dagan pondered the report from his superior early this morning. The two *I-GAF* officers who had been slain on the Sion space station had been there without

Phaedrig's knowledge, en route from a secret assignment, so a warning to stay clear had not been issued to them. As the Kalfan combed his black hair, he mused upon a mystery: Sach had told him Starla had destroyed a Serian patrol ship and its crew three *malees* ago before joining up with Tochar; yet, there was no record of that incident against her in the *I-GAF* files. He could not surmise why the Serians had not reported an intergalactic episode, but was glad that serious charge wasn't registered against her. If murder was committed during the commission of a crime, Starla Vedris was doomed, if he exposed her. Dagan knew it was his duty as an *I-GAF* officer to do so. Yet, he realized what that exposure would cost Starla and himself: her death. With every fiber of his being, he believed she loved him and was a good person, and would change her existence if given the chance. If only, he brooded, he could keep her out of trouble and danger from now until he completed his assignment, one progressing too slowly to suit him. True, the stolen crystals had been destroyed, but not because of him; and he was no closer to solving the mystery of the traitor or to defeating Tochar than when he arrived. The longer he took to finalize this crucial case, the deeper Starla was drawn into it, and the farther she was pushed from his reach. He had to do something and fast to get the situation resolved. But what, he did not know.

Starla, Dagan, Auken, Sach, Moig, and members of the Enforcers searched the area around the demolished cave for clues to the cause of the explosion and for any signs of enemy involvement. None were found, much to their leader's annoyance, as that would explain the mystery. Even so, Tochar ordered his men to remain on full alert and to take extra precautions when storing future stolen goods.

After they were dismissed and left the others, Dagan asked Starla to join him for the evening meal at the Skull's

Den. He was surprised and disappointed when she refused his invitation, and was dismayed by her chilly aura. "What's wrong?" he asked as they reached her shuttle.

"I need time to think about what you said to me and what happened between us. I'm not sure I want the same things you do. If we go into this with different expectations and feelings, it could cause problems."

Dagan became wary. "What kind of problems?"

"Resentment, spitefulness, a lack of concentration and loyalty during raids. That could be dangerous for us and the others, and dissension would irritate Tochar, possibly to the point of getting rid of us."

"I'm confused, Starla; I thought you wanted me as much as I want you. I thought our desires and goals matched perfectly."

"I don't understand or know you, Dagan. One *preon,* you seem like one person and the next, you're totally different. I've never met a man like you before: enigmatic and captivating. You make me . . . think and behave in foreign ways, and that alarms me. Before we see each other again, I want to give you and any future relationship deep and careful study."

"How can you get to know me if you refuse to spend time with me? Besides, we can't avoid each other, since we have to work together."

"I meant, see each other like we did last night. I'm just not ready to get that close to you. And, I get the impression you aren't ready for love and romance, either. I suppose what I'm trying to say is that I'm not into casual sex."

"Neither am I, and that isn't what I want from you. Do you think I'm unworthy of your attention and affections?"

"That isn't what I meant to imply. If I did, I'm sorry. Look at how and where we live, Dagan; we can't change or move, at least not anytime soon. To initiate a serious affair at this time would evoke complications."

"Do I understand you correctly: you aren't jettisoning your feelings for me, only docking them for a while?"

"I suppose you could put it that way."

Maybe, Dagan reasoned, she had a good point. He was in a precarious position and shouldn't drag her into it and endanger her life. He eyed her sad expression and perceived her mixed emotions, things he suspected she did not realize she was revealing. Something had inspired intense conflict within her, but he could not deduce the cause. He took a deep breath and locked gazes with her. "Take the time you need, Starla; I'll be patient; I'm not going anywhere anytime soon. Just let me know when you change your mind." After she nodded, he smiled and left her standing there, aware her gaze was fastened to his back as he walked away.

Starla was relieved when Cypher told her that Dagan had not tried to visit Yana's abode that night or the following one. She had remained on her ship so she would not be tempted to surrender to her lover, but she had been prepared to shapeshift and transport to Yana's dwelling if a signal came that Dagan or another approached it. She had decided that she also must rebuff him in that form, as Yana could not extract any secrets from him, and to unite Yana's body with his was just as precarious to her emotions.

On the following morning, Starla was ordered to attend a meeting at Tochar's. She found the *fiendal* and Moig awaiting her upon her arrival. She took a seat and listened to the surprising news.

"There is a task I want you and Moig to do for me. You will leave in your ship after we complete our talk. Serian patrols have stored a large supply of confiscated drugs on Zumali. Two androids are guarding them. I want you to help Moig get them and bring them to me to replace those I lost during that curious incident with the *Skalds*. Moig has the details and their location, and there should not be any problem stealing them."

"You want us to go alone?" Starla asked.

"Yes, the rest of my team is doing another task for me. They left earlier this morning. You should return within two *deegas* of each other. Is your ship supplied and ready for a flight?"

She nodded. "It was serviced by a supply vessel while I was gone on our last trek; my android handled it for me." Starla knew she could not refuse Tochar's order, and thought it unwise to ask probing and suspicious questions. She would delve for clues with Moig during their journey. She was vexed about the unit being divided and sent on separate raids, as she assumed the other men had gone after more crystals, but she concealed her annoyance. If she didn't learn anything useful from Moig, she would be forced to seek information later from Dagan, and there was only one way to accomplish that feat . . . "We can be ready to depart within the *hora.*"

Tochar smiled. "You never fail to please me, Starla."

She faked a bright smile of gratitude. "Thank you, sir. Moig, are you coming with me now or do you want me to return for you later?"

"I'm ready to go," the bearded man replied.

"Have a safe and successful journey," Tochar said.

"We will," Moig boasted with a grin.

Seven *deegas* later, Starla and Moig transported to a clearing on the snowy surface of Zumali, a small planet on the edge of the Seri Galaxy, far from its solar body. She pointed to the square complex a lengthy distance away, nestled against a white-covered ridge. Gusts of cold wind yanked at their synthetic fur garments, but protective helmets with visors shielded their faces from the weather and exposure of their identity. Cypher reported that no life-forms registered amidst the rocks and hills nearby, so they headed toward their target, trudging slowly and gingerly in ankle-deep snow.

Before they reached the structure and used their faked papers and uniforms to obtain entrance from the android guards, Cypher contacted Starla. "A Serian patrol is approaching; arrival in five *preons*. Abort raid and return to the ship. There is insufficient time to carry out your task and the risks are increasing with haste. Three officers are transporting to the surface; ten *leongs* from the complex entrance. Departure is crucial."

Starla watched the three Serians materialize, spot them, and shout a warning to surrender or they would attack. She could not slay them and must not allow herself to be taken captive and be exposed to Tochar's spy. "Take cover behind that large rock, Moig, fast!" she ordered.

She did the same, then told Cypher, "Lock on to our coordinates and bring us aboard. The *preon* we're safe, cloak, raise the defense shield, and go to starlight speed." She knew the android could handle only one task at a time, and that the cloaker and shield must be lowered to retrieve them, making her ship vulnerable to destruction during that period. Even with Cypher's intelligence and abilities, the series of actions had to be scheduled just right to prevent perils and would take a few moments to set into motion. She knew if an attack came while the ship's defenses were lowered and she was in transport, her life-force would be lost forever.

Laser weapons were fired at their location, striking and spalling rock and tossing about snow and ice. Moig was hit in the arm by a stun-beam as he tried to return their blasts before Starla could halt him. The patrol carried oblong defense shields before them, so the Icarian's fire was deflected as he was knocked unconscious.

The setting vanished as the *Liska*'s transporter beam rescued them just as the protective rock was destroyed. The moment she materialized on the sensor pad on her ship, Starla glanced to her right and saw Moig's frame. "Get us out of here quick, Cypher! Evade them as necessary, but do not fire upon them."

Cypher reported to her as he worked, "Shield up. Cloaker engaged. Patrol firing a broad sweep of beams at our last visible location. Going to starburst speed in one *preon*." A minute later, he said, "Clear of danger. Course laid in for stargate to Noy. Patrol heading in opposite direction."

"Excellent, Cypher. Moig was stunned, so I'll remain with him until he arouses. You know what to do, and thanks for saving my life again."

"What happened?" Moig asked an *hora* later in sickbay.

"The Serian ship was hidden from our monitors by the planet. When it came into view, it was traveling fast; they detected us on their sensors and was told no authorization had been given for a landing. We barely escaped before they shattered that rock we were hiding behind. They attacked my ship, but Cypher got us cloaked and shielded fast. We're on the way to base now; there's no way we can get those drugs with them on alert."

"Tochar will be angry we failed him."

"It wasn't our fault. Somebody gave him incorrect information and it almost got us killed or captured. Surely he wouldn't expect us to hang around and make another attempt with a patrol in the area."

"I guess not, but he'll be riled. He needs those drugs for his buyers. The meeting is already scheduled. He promised them drugs and crystals."

Starla realized Moig was making slips. "He can't blame us; we did our part. I'll play the record of our attack for him so he can grasp our peril and realize we had no choice except to abort the raid. Cypher picked up their communications; they know two people were involved and one was injured, but they couldn't see our faces through our visors. How's the head, Moig? You struck it hard after you were stunned."

"It hurts like *karlee.*"

"I'll give you something for the pain and to prevent infection. As soon as Cypher can leave the bridge, he'll seal the cut with a *latron* beam. He has a medical program and he's repaired me many times."

"Thanks, Vedris, for saving my life."

"You're welcome; that's what partners do for each other."

Starla prepared the injector with a clear liquid and infused it in Moig's arm. She chatted with him while the potent chemical took effect. As soon as the Icarian was dazed by the *Thorin,* she said, "Moig, you will answer my questions with total honesty. Do you understand?"

Controlled by the truth serum, he replied, "Yes."

Starla knew her action was daring and dangerous, but she needed information and this might be the last time she could extract it. With the attack record in her possession to play for Tochar and using another clever ruse to keep Moig disabled, the bearded Icarian could not expose this deed after they reached base. "Where did Auken's team go? What was his target?"

"Moonbeams in Kalfa."

"Are they for Koteas and Terin?"

"Yes."

"When is the meeting with them scheduled?"

"Four *deegas* after our return to Tochara."

"Is it set to take place near the settlement?"

"Yes."

"Do you know the name of Tochar's contact in Seri?"

"No."

"How does Auken know when it's safe to approach a ship carrying moonbeams? Is there a special reason why we use his ship for those raids?"

"Yes. A device is put on the transport vessel. It sends Auken a signal. He has a unit to pick up that signal."

"Is that why no one is allowed on the bridge when we're approaching a target except you, Auken, and Sach?"

"Yes."

"Does Tochar trust Starla Vedris?"

"Yes."

She sighed in relief. "Does Tochar trust Dagan Latu?"

"Yes."

"Do you know the name of Tochar's contact in Kalfa?"

"Yes."

Anticipation and joy flooded her. "What is his name?"

"Syrkin."

Starla gaped at the dazed man. "The officer in charge of crystal mining and shipments?"

"Yes."

"Why would Syrkin help Tochar steal moonbeams?"

"After Tochar is rich and powerful, Syrkin will join him as a partner and will rule Kalfa."

"Does Tochar have contacts or partners in other places besides Kalfa and Seri?"

"Yes, in Maffei."

Astonished and dismayed, she asked, "Who?"

"I do not know."

Starla did not have the time to ponder who from her world could be a traitor or why. She would leave that investigation up to Thaine. "Is there any way to disarm or destroy Tochar's defense weapons?"

"No."

"Do you know that for certain or is that what you were told?"

"That is what I was told, what Tochar was told."

"Why did Tochar divide the team and send us on separate raids?"

"He needed the drugs and crystals fast, soon. The *Adika* and *Liksa* were needed to carry out the two raids."

"Why did Tochar send you with Starla instead of one of the others?"

"He thinks Vedris and Latu are attracted to each other and might be distracted by their feelings during a trek."

"Is he angry they like each other?"

"No, he does not care, if it does not distract them from work."

Starla thought hard to make certain there were no other questions she wanted to ask Moig before she placed him in a chemical coma, one from which he could not arouse until given the antidote; that would not be until after her mission was completed. She knew the doctor on Noy would not be able to detect Moig's true condition or to treat it. With Moig out of the way, she reasoned, Tochar could not divide the band again and exclude her from crystal raids. She had not dared use this tactic sooner because there had been no previous occurrence to explain a coma until this incident provided one.

After Cypher joined her, Starla related what she had done and told him everything Moig had said. "Bandage his head but do not seal the wound," she instructed the android. "I want Tochar and the settlement doctor to see it. They should assume he has a severe concussion and possible brain damage. Connect a feeding tube and vital-sign monitors. One *villite* down and many to go."

"This was a clever move, Bree-Kayah. On the next crystal raid, I will scan for the signal he mentioned and record its frequency."

She smiled at the android. "At long last, my friend, we're making valuable progress. I must report these findings and what I've done to Supreme Commander Sanger. Thaine can have either a Serian or *I-GAF* unit cloaked and standing by to capture Koteas and Terin after they obtain those moonbeams and leave Noy. I dare not risk exploding another load, if Tochar allows anybody to get near them again. Thaine or Yakir will have to either let Syrkin continue his ruse for a while or find a way to remove him without anybody learning how Syrkin's treachery was uncovered. We can't risk the wrong person discovering an agent has infiltrated Tochar's band. At least that nefarious *fiendal* doesn't suspect me. What I can't understand is why Tochar has a contact in Maffei, since we don't have a crystal mine."

"Perhaps the Maffeian supplies him with other data and needs."

"You could be right, but that angle worries me. He'll be harder to unmask than the other two, since his motive isn't obvious. I'm glad Tochar didn't send me with the others; we accomplished far more on our trek."

"It is good to see you smile."

"I feel quite wonderful, Cypher, but I do have another hard task ahead: I might have to dupe Dagan again to see if he learned anything during their trek, and you know there's only one way I can ensnare him. First, I might let Yana give it a try; if she fails, it will be up to Starla."

As they approached Noy, Starla contacted Tochar with her bad news.

"I have been informed of the trouble at Zumali," he responded. "I will have the doctor awaiting your shuttle. We will talk after your arrival."

After she landed, Tochar and the doctor came aboard her craft. "I'm sorry, sir, but we were trapped and attacked," Starla explained. "Cypher and I have done all we can for him." She handed Tochar a disk and said, "This is a recording of the communications between the Serian patrol and the complex, and the patrol and their base. You will hear how and why we failed you."

"A patrol was not supposed to be in that sector, so I do not blame you and Moig for what happened. When I was warned of its presence, it was too late to alert you in your communications blackout. I am glad you were not slain or captured. You did well, Starla, as always."

"Thank you." She turned to the doctor who was examining Moig to ask about his condition, but was told to wait outside. Though the doctor spoke to Tochar in whispers, Starla knew Cypher was picking up their words as the communications switch had been left on in preparation for such an incident. She walked a short distance away so the two men could talk freely, and was stunned when they joined her shortly and reported that Moig had "died from his injury."

"But I got him here as fast as possible and kept him nourished."

"It is sad to lose a longtime friend," Tochar said, "but life makes such demands of us." He motioned for two Enforcers to come forward, then told them to collect Moig's body for burial. "I know you did all you could to keep him alive, but he is gone now," he said to Starla. "When the others return, I will contact you for a meeting. Rest, Starla, this trek was hard on you."

"I'm sorry things went wrong," she said, faking an apology and grief. "I'll be on my ship if you need me for anything."

Starla entered her shuttle and returned to the *Liska*. She hurried to the bridge to join Cypher. "What happened to Moig? His death isn't natural; his injury and condition weren't terminal. What could have happened?"

The android pressed a button to replay the shocking scene.

The doctor's words came first. "His condition is serious, Tochar, and I'm not qualified to treat it. I lack the proper medical facility and means to do anything for him. I do not think he can recover or even live very long, at least not here. Perhaps you could send him to Icaria for treatment. Perhaps they can help him."

"I cannot risk anyone there extracting my secrets," Tochar's words were firm, "and Moig knows most of them. Too, he is delving too deeply into drugs. He is beyond our help and should not be forced to live in this state, so do as I ordered."

"Give him a lethal injection?"

"I have no choice. I cannot allow him to become a threat to me. After it is done, forget it happened. Do you understand me?"

"I understand; I won't tell anyone."

"So," Starla murmured, "they killed Moig to silence him. So much for friendship and loyalty."

"He was a *villite,* Bree-Kayah. If Tochar had sent him to Icaria and he was diagnosed correctly and was given the antidote, Moig could have betrayed and imperiled you. His death serves us well, just as his data will serve us well. You are not responsible for his fate."

Two days later, Starla was summoned to Tochar's elevated dwelling. Dagan, Auken, and Sach had returned and were present. Dagan passed his gaze over her as if making certain she was unharmed, but it was Auken who spoke first.

"Tochar told us about the trouble on your raid, Starla. We're all glad you're alive and uninjured."

"Thank you, Auken; it was scary there for a while. I'm sorry about Moig's loss; I know he was a close friend to you three for *yings.*"

"Tochar said you did all you could to save him."

"Obviously it wasn't enough, Auken, or he wouldn't be dead."

"Don't blame yourself; it was that patrol's fault."

"Thank you, Sach, but we were on my ship, so I feel responsible. I just didn't know what to do to help him; Cypher did all his medical program allowed, but he doesn't have the in-depth knowledge that was required." She needed

We've got your authors!

KENSINGTON CHOICE is the only club where you can find authors like Janelle Taylor, Shannon Drake, Rosanne Bittner, Penelope Neri and Phoebe Conn all in one place…

…and the only service that will deliver their romances direct to your home as soon as they are published—even before they reach the bookstores.

KENSINGTON CHOICE is also the only service that will give you a substantial guaranteed discount off the publisher's prices on every one of those romances.

That's right: Every month, the Editors at Zebra and Pinnacle select four of the newest novels by our bestselling authors and rush them straight to you, usually *before they reach the bookstores.* The publisher's prices for these romances range from $4.99 to $5.99—but they are always yours for the guaranteed low price of just $4.20, up to 30% off the publisher's price!

All books are sent on a 10-day free examination basis, and there is no minimum number of books to buy. (A postage and handling charge of $1.50 is added to each shipment.)

As your introduction to the convenience and value of KENSINGTON CHOICE, we invite you to accept

4 BOOKS FREE

The 4 books, worth up to $23.96, are our welcoming gift. You pay only $1 to help cover postage and handling.

Plus as a regular subscriber….you'll receive our free monthly newsletter, <u>Zebra/Pinnacle Romance News</u> which features author interviews, contests, and more!

To start your subscription to KENSINGTON CHOICE and receive your introductory package of 4 FREE romances, detach and mail the card at right *today.*

We have 4 FREE BOOKS for you
as your introduction to
KENSINGTON CHOICE
To get your FREE BOOKS, worth
up to $23.96, mail the card below.

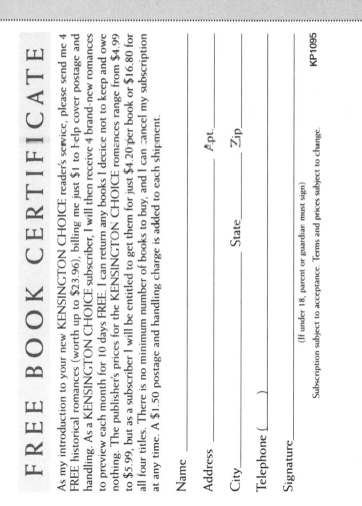

FREE BOOK CERTIFICATE

As my introduction to your new KENSINGTON CHOICE reader's service, please send me 4 FREE historical romances (worth up to $23.96), billing me just $1 to help cover postage and handling. As a KENSINGTON CHOICE subscriber, I will then receive 4 brand-new romances to preview each month for 10 days FREE. I can return any books I decide not to keep and owe nothing. The publisher's prices for the KENSINGTON CHOICE romances range from $4.99 to $5.99, but as a subscriber I will be entitled to get them for just $4.20 per book or $16.80 for all four titles. There is no minimum number of books to buy, and I can cancel my subscription at any time. A $1.50 postage and handling charge is added to each shipment.

KP1095

Name _____

Address _____ Apt. _____

City _____ State _____ Zip _____

Telephone ( ) _____

Signature _____
(If under 18, parent or guardian must sign)

Subscription subject to acceptance. Terms and prices subject to change.

We have
4
FREE
Historical
Romances
for you!

(worth up
to $23.96!)

Details inside!

to change the subject. "Was your raid successful? Did you encounter any trouble?"

Auken grinned and said, "We were in and out like a comet."

"Let us get our business handled," Tochar said, "then all of you can seek rest and diversions, both of which are needed and well deserved. My buyers are arriving in two *deegas* for the crystals. In three *deegas,* you will leave again and bring me another supply of drugs for them. This time, there will not be a patrol in that sector."

"We're going back to Zumali?" Starla inquired.

"I have been assured it will be safe this time. They will not expect you to strike at the same place and so soon; they will be guarding other sites."

"Who will go with me this time?" she asked.

"The entire unit will make the trek together."

Starla nodded understanding and agreement to Tochar.

"Meet for departure at the landing grid on the morning of the third *deega* from this one. Until then, do as you please."

"Don't you need us to guard you for the buyer meeting?" Dagan asked.

"No, I am taking a large and well-armed unit of Enforcers with me. Unless you have other questions, you may leave and enjoy yourselves. Dagan, stay behind for a while; I have more to talk about with you."

Starla left with the others and walked to her shuttle. She was glad she had warned Thaine to prepare a surprise attack on the Thracians who were coming for the crystals, since she would not have an opportunity to destroy them, and doing so again would be reckless. When she returned to her ship, she would send Thaine an update to confirm that delivery schedule and would report Moig's death, as she had waited for this meeting to take place before contacting her superior. She hoped no Serians would be near Zumali during the next drug raid, as she wanted to avoid a lethal battle. She would warn *Raz* Yakir via Thaine, as it would be dangerous for the ruler to give his forces a command to stay clear of the planet since that information could enter the wrong ears. She would ask both men not to act upon that news and risk exposing her to the Serian traitor, and she was certain they would concur with her precaution. So far, Yakir had kept his word about protecting her identity and mission; because she was still alive and free.

She decided against waiting for Dagan to finish his talk with Tochar. She would return to her ship, make her report to Thaine, and change into Yana before seeing him tonight.

Dagan rounded the corner of the structure to head for his chamber and sighted the sultry creature leaning against the wall near his door. She looked up and smiled, then straightened her posture and fingered her long golden hair. *Blast it all, you're the last person I want to encounter tonight! I need to file a report with Phaedrig and try to reach Starla.* "Yana, what are you doing here?" Annoyance dripped from his words.

"I saw Auken and Sach in the Skull's Den, so I knew you had returned. When you didn't appear or answer my signal, I waited for you. It's been a long time since we saw each other. Can we visit tonight?"

"Come inside; we need to talk." Dagan slid the metallic card into a slot and the door swished open. He stepped aside for Yana to enter first, her scent teasing into his nostrils as she did so. He felt his body warm, and he was annoyed by her effect on him. *Keep your distance from her!* He walked to the eating area and fetched himself a cool drink which he downed with haste; he offered her no refreshment. He looked at the sensual woman who took a seat and gazed at him.

"You're angry with me for coming here, aren't you?" she asked.

"Not exactly," he replied, staying where he was, a partition between them. "I don't want to hurt you or mislead you, Yana, but nothing can happen between us again. From here on, let's keep our distance."

Yana widened her fake blue gaze. "Why?" she asked. "What have I done to be rejected like this? We're a good match. I thought you were as attracted to me as I am to you. We enjoyed each other. Am I being too forward and easy? Did I displease you on the *sleeper?*"

"I'm involved with another woman, so I can't see you again."

"Surely a virile male like you can have more than one relationship."

He shook his head. "This one is serious and important to me."

"If you love and want another woman, why did you have sex with me? You cannot tell me you did not find pleasure and satisfaction with me."

As she stood to approach him, he ordered, "Stay where you are!"

Yana halted and stared at him. "What's wrong with you? I am not an enemy; why are you afraid of me?"

"I don't know how you did it, and maybe it was unintentional, but you snared me in some unknown trap. That's the only way to explain what happened with you. Perhaps Asisan females possess some biological magic. It won't happen again. If you're in trouble or danger, I'll try to help you; but that's as far as our relationship can go."

"You think I tricked you into surrendering to me?"

"I didn't want you that night and I don't want you tonight, but there's something you emit that makes you irresistible at close proximity."

"There is a special chemistry between us, Dagan, so why fight it? You affect me in the same way; that is why I came to you both times."

He chilled his tone. "Leave, Yana, and don't return again.

I love and desire another woman. I won't allow you to destroy my chances with her."

Yana was astonished and aroused by his words and expression. It would be wrong of her to use the pheromone on him again, and she was glad she had sprayed it on so lightly he could do battle with it. "You sound determined. True love is rare and valuable, so I will not intrude on your life again. I'm sorry you don't trust me. I will not bother you in the future unless I am in dire need of your help. Good-bye, Dagan."

"Good-bye, Yana, and I'm sorry if your feelings are injured by me."

"I am a survivor, Dagan Latu, so do not worry about me."

He watched Yana leave and hoped she wouldn't cause him trouble with Starla. It seemed she had given up too easily to be trusted. If a problem arose, he told himself, he would handle it. Right now, he had work to do. He checked the security of his chamber, filed his report, and awaited a reply as he thought about Starla and how close she had come to death. Even so, the incident had not frightened or convinced her to terminate her work. How, he worried, could he protect her when they were separated, if that happened again? How could he coax her away from Noy and Tochar?

Dagan was astonished by Phaedrig's response: an *I-GAF* unit was already standing by to prevent Koteas and Terin from returning to Icaria with the crystals they had stolen recently. Phaedrig did not know where the information had come from; it had been entered into their private network from an untraceable source, one using the proper code and password. In case the data was true, Phaedrig had sent a cloaked ship and special team to handle the matter in guarded secrecy.

Dagan could not imagine who had gotten those facts in time to put his superior's plan into motion, when he and the others had been told only less than an *hora* ago. Was it possible there was an agent working in Icaria, he mused, or could Tochar's lover be a traitor to him? Who else could know the *fiendal*'s plans so far in advance except someone close to Tochar or to his buyers? At least he wouldn't have to worry about the crystals being used by the Thracians, but a further mystery had arisen. If another agent was working on this same mission, who was he? Who had hired him and what was his location and why the secrecy from *I-GAF*? He needed to be on alert for clues to the answers to those questions.

Dagan showered and changed, then headed for the Skull's Den to ask Auken or Sach how he could contact Starla on her ship. He hoped Yana had not returned there as he didn't want to confront her again. He was relieved when he sighted Starla sitting alone at a side table.

Dagan joined her and smiled. "I was coming to search for you, woman. I've been zoned out since I heard about your close brush with peril. Are you sure you're all right?"

"I'm fine; I can take care of myself." Starla sipped her drink.

"Still chilly from your visit to Zumali? I was hoping you had changed your mind about us and would soften toward me."

Her gaze met his. "Do you really need two women at one time?"

He tensed. "What do you mean?"

"I was coming to see you earlier, but you were busy, so I left."

"You have it all wrong, Starla; please, let me explain."

She leaned back in her chair. "Then, explain, if you can."

Ten

Dagan glanced around the room which was becoming crowded and noisy. "Not here, in private, at my place or on your ship," he whispered.

"Cypher is on my ship. I know he's an android, but he's like a real person to me, like a brother; so I don't want to go there to talk."

"Will you come to my chamber?"

"What if she returns?" Starla asked, trying to impress upon him they were different entities, even though it was unlikely he would suspect shapeshifting.

"I can promise you she won't, if she leaves me alone as I ordered her to do. I didn't invite Yana there and didn't want to see her; I swear."

Starla pretended to study him for a moment. She needed to learn if he had discovered any clues during his last raid which he might share with her, by accident or volition. She also wanted to draw him closer to her in case his help and protection were needed soon, if he truly loved her and would provide them. "Let's go. I'll hear you out this one time."

They left the Skull's Den and walked the short distance to Dagan's chamber.

Dagan took a position facing her. He rested his right arm along the back of the *seata,* his fingers touching her shoulder. He gazed into her green eyes. "Yana was waiting for me when I returned; I asked her to come inside so I could settle the matter with her. Despite what I am, Starla, I'm not a cruel person. I didn't want to hurt her and didn't mean to mislead her. I told her I'm involved with another woman and made it clear nothing could happen between us. I suppose she's never been rebuffed before, so she looked confused and surprised by my rejection, and maybe her feelings were injured. I told her I loved and desired only you, and I wouldn't allow her to cause trouble between us by making it appear as if I was betraying you in secret." Dagan noticed Starla's controlled expression and reaction. When she didn't respond to his last sentence, he continued with his explanation.

"I don't know who she is or why she's here, but there seems to be a serious problem where she habitates. I got the impression something important must take place before she can return home. She puts on a good facade of being brave, but I think she's afraid and lonely, and that's why she turned to me. I offered to help her if she got into trouble here, but that's all. She said she believed me and wouldn't approach me again unless she was threatened; I hope she was telling the truth. If not, please don't misread any contact between us. In fact, if you see us together, join me and prove to her I'm off-limits, prove to yourself I'm not chasing her." Dagan thought it best not to reveal their sexual encounter and his suspicions about how and why it happened. "I love you, Starla Vedris, and I want you, only you, and forever. I hope you either feel the same way or will some *deega*."

Starla took a deep breath and kept her gaze locked to his blue one. She knew an intimate relationship with him was hazardous, but it seemed necessary. Yet, she felt guilty about deceiving him and worse about using him, and couldn't imagine her torment if she had to betray and arrest him.

"Do you believe me?" Dagan asked, his chest tight with dread.

"Yes, I do." She saw him exhale in relief, then smile. "I

don't understand this fast and potent attraction between us, but it exists. Let's move slowly and carefully and see where it takes us."

Dagan clasped her hand in his as he vowed, "It will guide us to our future if we don't resist its power and magic."

"Our future?" We have none as long as your trajectory is wrong. Recalibrate it, my love; decontaminate yourself, Dagan, so I can have you, if it's not already too late for you to escape your nefarious past.

Her silence and intense study worried him, as did the chilled flesh on her hand. "Yield to me, Starla; bond to me as you have to no other man. Let me love you, protect you, cherish you above all females who have lived or will live. I will do everything in my power to defend you and to keep you at my side forever, this I swear with all my heart and soul."

As she gazed into his blue eyes and listened to his words, she could not convince herself he was being anything other than serious and honest. Yet, the obstacles between them were enormous, seemingly insurmountable. *Why did cruel fate send you here to create havoc with my emotions and mission? Why did I fall in love with a forbidden rogue?* She felt the vibration in her wrist unit as Cypher signaled a warning she was losing control of herself and the situation, a fact the android had deduced from monitoring her physiological reactions. Starla pressed a tiny button to let Cypher know she had gotten his message, the response masked by her rise from the *seata.*

Dagan grasped her arm and entreated, "Don't leave."

"I was heading there," she replied, nodding toward his *sleeper.*

Dagan stood and embraced her. "I feared I had panicked you with my confession and the revelation of my great need for you."

Starla rested her head against his chest and wrapped her arms around his waist. "The only thing I fear at this *preon* is that this mysterious bond between us won't be strong or tight enough to hold us together for the rest of our lives. I don't want to lose you, Dagan, but I'm afraid something or someone will tear us apart; that would evoke terrible anguish."

He hugged her. "We won't allow that to happen, my love."

"There are many forces in the Cosmos stronger than we are, so that choice might not be ours to make."

Dagan lifted her chin and fused their gazes. "If necessary, my ravishing moonbeam, I will battle both *Kahala* and *Karlee* to have you."

"Moonbeam," her troubled mind echoed, the endearment her father used for her golden-haired mother and the crux of her mission: a word with such disparate meanings: love and unity, death and separation. "Whatever happens beyond this night, Dagan, know I love and desire only you."

"I have no doubt you are the perfect woman for me, my destined mate, my partner in all things," Dagan murmured. *I must find a way to keep you, but also do my duty. How, I don't know at this time.*

Dagan's mouth slanted across Starla's in a tender kiss to which she responded with eagerness. Many others followed, the pressure of his lips varying from gentle and soft to firm and demanding. His deft hands roamed her back and his mouth soon journeyed down her neck and over her ears, driving her wild with feverish cravings.

Starla yearned to feel her bare skin making contact with his. She wriggled her fingers between them and removed her top, then his, with Dagan helping her to peel off their garments. Her senses were alive, responsive, enchanted. She pressed her hips to his, bringing their fiery loins into snug and tantalizing proximity.

Dagan's body begged for appeasement. He trembled from need and in a battle for self-control. Her mouth seemed to ravish his with undeniable urgency. His tension increased and he wondered if he could explode just from touching her and being touched by her. No female had aroused him to such great heights of hunger, to such near mindless abandonment of will and wits. His knees felt weak and shaky, so he lifted her and carried her to his *sleeper* where they reclined.

His hands fondled and kneaded her breasts, their buds growing hard beneath his fingers. His mouth joined them to labor lovingly on their points, to circle their mounds, and to delve into the valley between them. Soon, one hand drifted down her rib cage, moving slowly and sensuously over each bone. His palm flattened over her stomach and moved from hipbone to hipbone as he relished the smooth and warm surface, each trip carrying it lower and lower.

Starla quivered in anticipation, then squirmed in delight as his fingers explored the pulsing nub and silky folds surrounding it. She trailed her fingertips over his broad back and shoulders, stroking the soft covering over his hard frame. She wanted him to continue this thrilling sport, but her body begged to have him within her. "Take me, Dagan," she panted. "Make me yours forever; I can wait no longer to bond with you."

His mouth trekked back to hers and melded their lips as he moved atop her. He entered her feminine domain and reveled in the welcome he received. He began to thrust and withdraw as he kissed and caressed her. His desires heightened, his pleasures intensified. When passion threatened to overwhelm him, he paused for a few moments and took several deep breaths, retreating until only the tip of his organ was poised at her rosy portal. But Starla's hands and mouth protested the delay and her hips and legs urged him to resume his previous actions. "Easy, my love;" he chided. "I want you so fiercely I can barely stay within you without losing all control."

Starla murmured in his ear, "There's no need for control or hesitation, my beloved."

Heat and suspense rose in her loins as he slipped within her. Sparks of ecstasy licked over her body, dazed her mind. Those tiny jolts built into powerful ones that staggered her senses and swept her away to a glorious climax. She gave herself totally to him and to the blissful experience.

For a wild minute, Dagan speculated that her responses were oddly and strongly similar to Yana's. Though the sultry Asisan was pleasurable and beautiful in a physical sense, Starla had so much more to offer him. Again, he briefly worried about his love and desire for the space pirate conflicting with his duty. Even so, his wits scattered and his heart pounded as she once more confessed her feelings for him.

"I love you, Dagan Latu, and I've never wanted a man as I desire you. This might be the craziest thing I've ever done, but I can't help myself."

He echoed her fiery sentiments. "I love and desire you, Starla Vedris, more than you can know or imagine." He buried his face in her flowing brown hair and thrust into her until every drop of love's nectar was spent. *This may be the most reality-impaired thing I've done, but I can't help myself, either. Whatever your magic is, my radiant and potent moonbeam, I'm enchanted by it and you.*

Afterward, almost breathless from their exertions but sated to a supreme level, they cuddled in each other's arms, sharing and savoring their closeness and serenity.

"You're mine, Starla, tonight and forever."

"If it's possible one *deega,* I do want a future with you," she said with certainty.

"As soon as I earn enough to buy another ship, we're gone from this perilous place and existence." *What if,* he worried, *she offers you her ship? Clear your head, Curran!* He tried to prevent that predicament by saying, "Call it ego or male pride, but I have to get on my feet again using my own skills. Right now, I have little to offer you except me, but we can't live on love, as delicious as it is. When I'm back in full control of my life, I'll have the means to support and protect you."

Starla was relieved he gave her an excuse not to suggest they depart on her ship, as she had not considered that complication when her last words escaped from her lips. *Uncloud your mind, Bree, and get back to work; that's why you're here tonight!* "I understand and agree with your reasoning and motives. We also have to be cautious, Dagan; we can't flaunt our relationship or it might worry Tochar; he could think it might be distracting for us or may fear we'll pair up and leave him." She faked soft laughter and a jest, "He needs us, so we wouldn't want him to be tempted to harm one of us to keep the other here. Seriously, those recent incidents might have his thinking reality impaired. If he has an enemy or rival working against him, the man is clever and leaves no clues. I'm afraid that if anything else happens, suspicion could fall upon either of us as the newest members of his unit. In view of those two explosions and my thwarted raid on Zumali, Tochar might use that truth serum on us again. If he does, there is no guessing what we would say if our feelings and thoughts have changed since joining up with him and after meeting each other. Too bad there's no way around such a powerful and precarious probing." Starla knew she was immune to *Thorin,* but she could not reveal anything to Dagan that might be extracted by the *fiendal,* which was why she had changed her mind about mentioning a suspicion about Moig's death.

Dagan was thinking much the same; he must not tell Starla anything that Tochar could learn from her during another drug questioning. "Tochar knows I'm working for him only for a limited time, so my eventual departure won't be news to him if he tests us again, and I'm always loyal to whomever hires me."

"Tochar is my first leader, but I would never betray him after I've given him my word of honor," Starla fabricated, "and I try to do everything he expects of me. It wasn't my fault that drug raid failed and Moig died from his injury, so I hope he doesn't blame me or think less of my skills."

Dagan caressed her still-flushed cheek. "There's no way he or the others could blame you. I'm happy you escaped alive and unharmed."

"I'm glad you weren't harmed. In my opinion, it's risky to send small teams on raids, so I hope he doesn't divide us again. Where did your team go? What did you do? Tochar wouldn't give me any details, as usual. I was worried about you facing perils with only two men as back-up."

"I didn't know why you and Moig weren't along until we were heading back after our raid. Then I couldn't get here fast enough to check on you. I suppose Auken didn't reveal that news so I wouldn't be distracted. They kept me in the transporter room during our approach; I don't know why Auken doesn't want me to witness the initial contact with our targets. We made a raid on Orr; we pretended we were there for a secret pick-up of crystals. We had convincing papers, codes, watchword, identification, and uniforms which duped the guards. It was quick and simple, and the crystals were handed to us without trouble. That's terrible security for something so valuable."

"You're right. We've never raided at a mine before; that boldness surprises me. I wonder how and where Tochar gets his information."

"It has to come from somebody in an elite and trusted position."

She nodded agreement. "I would rather be a pirate than a traitor; a betrayer's fate is worse than death if or when he's exposed."

Dagan concurred, then posed a query. "Is there any way I can persuade you to go some place safe until I can join you later? With all these strange incidents occurring, I don't like you taking so many risks."

She trailed her fingers over his collarbone. "How can we

get to know each other and test our feelings if we're separated? It would be a long and lonely time before you could join me. Besides, you need somebody you can trust completely to guard your back, especially if matters worsen. It's naive to believe the Serians and Kalfans and *I-GAF* will continue to allow us to raid them without taking action against us, despite our defense system here."

As she played with dark curls on his chest, she ventured, "In fact, I'm amazed that at least one if not all of those forces hasn't laid traps for us; our goals and tactics must be clear to them. If they have set snares, Tochar is kept informed about how to elude them; that's probably what Auken checks on when we're exiled from the bridge, some unknown measure he doesn't want us to discover."

When Dagan failed to respond to her evocative statements, she said, "There's another angle to consider: Tochar may not allow me to leave or he could send a team of his men after me if I did. With his elite sources, I'm certain he could locate me wherever I went. Until he has the invincible power he wants and I'm no threat to him, he might refuse to release me, refuse to release both of us."

Dagan was impressed by Starla's perceptive wits. "You're right. Be careful you don't do anything to get into trouble with Tochar or to make your record worse. When we leave, we don't want anybody in hot pursuit of us."

"The same applies to you. So far, our records aren't that bad, so let's keep it that way. No life-taking charges against us, agreed? As long as we don't do anything to get us terminated if we're captured, there's always a chance for escape or rescue and being reunited."

He nodded compliance. "That will be our safeguard for survival. You're a smart and intuitive woman, my love."

Starla's yearning for him was enflamed by his endearment. "You're an intelligent and clever man, so perhaps we are a good match as you claimed."

He smiled and murmured, "Trust me, my ravishing delight, we are."

As he kissed and caressed Starla, he planned, *Before our next trek and after I see if Tochar will use Thorin to interrogate you again, I'll set up a meeting place in case we get separated.* Since she had a ship and possessed great prowess, there was a strong possibility she could escape during a crisis or attack, especially if he decided to warn her about one in advance, and if that daring assault came from *I-GAF* teammates. What concerned him was an unexpected intrusion by the mysterious person also working on this mission, one whose name and goal were still unknown to Phaedrig. At least only his superior and other Inter-Galactic Alliance Force members had access to the *I-GAF* computer files which contained their personnel and assignments records, so his identity and mission were safe. Their headquarters—computer/data center, strategy chambers, medical labs, between-missions quarters, armory, recreation and training facilities, and ship storage—were located underground on a barren-appearing planetoid in Kalfa; it was protected and hidden by an impenetrable force shield, and only *I-GAF* members knew the entry code. Even if an enemy learned the password, no one could get beyond the main portal without the proper retinal and digital scans. If only he had a *Spacer* at his disposal, he could stay prepared to thwart trouble, but his was in a storage bay at headquarters until he completed this mission and retrieved it—a swift and sleek craft with advanced cloaking ability to conceal his comings and goings, and a weapons system that could defeat any force except Tochar's.

Dagan couldn't help but wonder if Starla would find Curran Thaiter as appealing as she found Dagan Latu, as their looks and characters were so different. He also wondered if he was deluding himself about her feelings for him and about sharing a future with her. There were many barriers between them and many hurdles to vault. After this mission was over, a difficult talk with her loomed before him; he was certain she would be angry and hurt and would feel betrayed and used. Somehow he must find a way to convince her he had no choice except to do his duty: to destroy Tochar and his threat to the United Federation of Galaxies, and to seek personal revenge against the *fiendal* for a lethal crime against his loved ones. Yet, the joy of having justice within his impending reach was overshadowed by the grim possibility of his victory costing him the woman he loved.

He didn't know how he was going to accomplish the gigantic task, but he was determined to find a way to save Starla from a black fate so she could share a golden one with him. He loved her; he wanted her; he needed her; and with *Kahala*'s help, he would have her at his side forever. *I can't lose you, Starla, but neither can I fail my duty and the UFG. I hope and pray it never comes to a choice between you and them because there's far more at stake than just our lives and our love.*

Dreamily her fingers grazed through the ebony waves on his head, deserting that location only to roam a supple terrain of bronze lean and hard flesh. She adored the smooth and strong body touching hers. Yet, she was painfully aware this could be the last time she enjoyed such a union if anything went wrong during her mission or if it terminated soon. She didn't know how she could exist without him and didn't want to envision that horrible event, not tonight.

Dagan trailed his lips and hands over her face and throat, returning time and time again to her tasty mouth. He had never taken such a perilous risk during a mission but he could not help himself. His kisses became deep, greedy, as were hers. She had become a vital part of him, one he could not excise from his life without slaying his soul. His hand cupped a breast and teased its taut nipple before sliding past her hip to grasp her buttocks to lock her groin snugly and possessively against his. He savored the way her legs imprisoned him and the ardent way she surrendered to him.

Love her? his mind asked. Yes, his heart replied, with all his being.

Starla writhed in exquisite delight, as if it had been *wegs* or *malees* since they had last united their bodies. She could hardly believe such a great hunger had attacked her again. She knew his restraint was stretched tightly, precariously, and she soared with pleasure at his great need of her. She meshed her mouth to his as the sensations mounting within her waxed achingly sweet and potent. Her hands pulled him closer, and Dagan's mouth fastened to hers as their passions burned higher and hotter until they were engulfed in rapturous flames. He felt her tense, arch her back, and cling to him as she moaned a glorious victory. Without delay, he rushed to join her, to conquer the same pinnacle of magic. When the last spasms ceased, he rolled to his back and carried her with him, cradling her in his strong arms.

Spent and sated, neither spoke nor moved for a long while.

Finally, Starla lifted her head and looked at him. Her heart warmed at his glowing smile and tranquil gaze. "I have to leave now; it's late."

"Will I see you tomorrow?"

"Yes, about this same time, and same place," she added, smiling.

Two days later while en route from the landing grid to the settlement, Starla saw Tochar and a group of well-armed Enforcers leave his dwelling to rendezvous with Koteas and Terin near the shattered rock formations where the last thwarted encounter had been held. Since she could not destroy the new supply of crystals, she prayed the *I-GAF* team was standing by to defeat the Thracians and to send the crystals hurling into the vast Cosmos where they would float forever among space debris. She was certain that the *I-GAF* commander must wonder who had gathered that data and how it had been entered into his communication system, one which *Raz* Yakir was privy to with its files and secret code; the leader had performed the task through an untraceable method. By now, the commander must have initiated an investigation into the mystery and possibly changed the password. Even so, she reasoned, a man of that elite rank would be compelled to check out the anonymous lead in case it was authentic. Soon, Duald Phaedrig would be convinced, and one more victory would be obtained for her side. Perhaps at this very moment, a cloaked *I-GAF* ship and team were witnessing the exchange of crystals for payment.

Once Syrkin and the Kalfan mine were eliminated from Tochar's reach, Starla deduced, the *fiendal* would be constrained to lean toward his Serian nexus. When that happened, perhaps a slip would be made by the conspirator. If that source could be eradicated, that left only the indomitable weapons here to be obliterated. Without his *Destructoids* and contacts, Tochar would be vulnerable to a full-scale assault.

Starla wanted her work on Tochara to be finalized fast and soon, but she cautioned herself against reckless action and rash mistakes. She was getting too close to victory to risk a setback or defeat. Success, she was aware, limited her time with Dagan, perhaps limited his existence in the universe. She didn't want to think about that grave complication and shoved it from her mind.

She headed for Dagan's chamber to spend the next few *horas* with him before their scheduled departure for Zumali in the morning. Her lengthy union with him last night had been as wonderful as the two couplings the night before. She didn't know how it was possible, but each fusion of their bodies was more exciting than the last. They had shared new and daring experiences only *horas* ago, seeking and exploring various carnal delights. It was as if she had become insatiable, though every climax was rapturous and satisfying. The way he touched her, kissed her, looked at her drove her wild with desire. There were so many ways to make love and she wanted to enjoy every one of them with him.

She knew Cypher was concerned about her behavior. He had warned her not to trust Dagan completely, as a proud man who felt betrayed and used would not protect her or take her side during a crisis. She did not know how her lover would react if she were exposed and imperiled, but she hoped he would stand by her, would believe she loved him. Even so, she took Cypher's cautions to heart and kept Dagan ignorant of the truth.

At the landing grid the following morning, Tochar told Starla to remove her wrist device and leave it in her shuttle since she was traveling with Auken on the *Adika* and it would not be needed for communication with her android.

Starla concealed her sudden tension. She smiled and shrugged. "I wear it all the time, so I never think to remove it. If it concerns you, I'll leave it behind. Do you want to examine it for a problem?" she asked as she held the wrist monitor/communicator out to him, knowing it would not function without contact with her right forefinger and certain signals.

"That is unnecessary. I just want to prevent any frequency it might emit from being detected by the wrong person and endangering my team."

"Is that what you think happened on Zumali last time? You think that Serian patrol picked up the communication between me and Cypher?"

"I do not know, but it is not worth taking a risk. Correct?"

"Of course, you're right, and I'll comply since it isn't needed this time." Starla entered her shuttle and placed the device in her pilot's seat. As she did so, she whispered to

Cypher, "Don't worry, I'll be fine. Don't follow us; Tochar is in an odd mood and might check on you." Even without a response, she knew the android heard her and would obey.

Starla closed the shuttle door and joined the others to leave in another craft for Auken's ship in stationary orbit over the settlement. After boarding the vessel and as she was settling in to her assigned quarters for the trek, she relaxed by envisioning the lovemaking with Dagan last night. She tried not to fret about Tochar's motive for his odd request and told herself it was nothing more than a precaution following several strange incidents. She hoped the *fiendal* was not suspicious of her or testing her. No matter, she would be on constant alert against a slip; she would be on her own this time without Cypher's guard, but she had Dagan as a back-up if needed.

A *weg* later and beyond the Free-Zone on the snowy surface of Zumali, Auken told the android guards at the complex that they had been sent to transfer the drugs stored there to another location because a second raid would be attempted within a few *deegas*. Using official-looking papers and uniforms and issuing the proper code words, they were given access to the structure and its valuable contents. The minute they were inside, the androids were disabled and their memory chips were dissolved by a highly corrosive acid. The video/audio monitoring system was destroyed in a similar manner to prevent their exposure as the perpetrators.

Auken, Starla, and Dagan gathered the drugs for conveyance to the *Adika* while Sach stayed aboard to watch the sensors for danger and to be prepared to transport them to safety fast if trouble arrived.

During their task, Starla and Dagan were given their first moments of privacy since leaving Noy. "Why was Tochar so interested in your wrist device?" he asked.

Starla noticed his anxious expression. "I don't know, but it was strange and scary. Maybe he's only looking for someone or something to blame for those weird incidents. We'll discuss it later. We don't want Auken to catch us whispering and think we're sharing secrets or conspiring."

"Be careful, love, and I'll watch your back. I won't let them fault you or harm you for what's been happening."

She sent him a radiant smile of gratitude and love.

After the drugs were transferred to the ship, Auken took one final precaution: he placed explosive *sunbursts*—those stolen by Starla and Moig when she met Dagan—around the complex and set their timers to destroy it, to make certain all evidence or clues were eliminated.

"Let's go!" he shouted to Dagan and Starla to his rear. "We want to be far away when this place blows."

As they were leaving, Dagan snagged his shirt on a sharp object and cut his arm. He wrapped his fingers around the area to halt the bleeding.

"Wait," Starla told Auken. "Let me sear this jagged spot to obliterate Dagan's blood or his presence could be exposed if it's found and tested."

"No need," the Icarian told her. "The blast will take care of it."

"Are you sure?" she asked, and Dagan responded to her panic.

"He's right, Starla. Let's hurry before we get trapped here."

Later in the *Adika*'s medical bay, after sterilizing the location, Starla used a *latron* beam to seal her lover's wound: techniques she had learned from her scientist mother and sister.

"Where did you learn to do that?" he asked, impressed by her skill.

"When one is a loner and on the run, one must know

such tricks for survival. Actually, Cypher taught me. At
least, I learned by watching him repair me a few times
following accidents. I also remember my father . . . doing
such a procedure before . . . his death," she was compelled
to lie after Auken entered the bay during Dagan's query. "I
hope I did it correctly. The bleeding has stopped and the
skin color is good. Does it hurt?"

Dagan flexed his fingers. "No, not at all. Thanks. They
taught you well. She's an excellent asset to our team, isn't
she, Auken?"

"That she is; both of you are. Tochar is pleased with
your work and skills. He's hoping you two will remain with
us for a long time."

Dagan grinned. "Considering the amount I need to purchase a ship, I certainly will be. You aren't tired of us and
our adventures, are you, Starla?"

"This team consists of the best and only friends I have,"
she alleged. "Where else would I go and earn such large
payments and have a safe haven? Besides, after Tochar is
rich and powerful, he'll make the settlement a nicer place
to live; or he'll relocate us to a wonderful stronghold. Either
way, I'm with him for as long as he wants me and I please
him."

"That's good news," Auken said. "He'll be happy to hear
it. Why don't we go test our wits and skills with a few
hands of *resi?*"

"That sounds fun to me," Starla responded.

"Me, too," Dagan added, intrigued and concerned by the
easy way Starla had deluded Auken, which he was certain
she had done.

After they reach Noy and the others departed from the
landing grid, Starla told Dagan to freshen up while she did
the same. She would return in her shuttle for him in two
horas, she promised. Then she would treat him to a meal

and a tour aboard her ship, which would give Cypher a chance to observe the man who had stolen her heart. First, she needed to make a report to Thaine and to check with Cypher about any incidents while she was gone.

"Tochar contacted me twice during your absence," the android related. "One *deega* after your departure, he said a *mechano* vessel was in orbit and wanted to know if we required any repairs. I responded in the negative. Three *deegas* later, he said a *servo* vessel was in orbit and asked if we required any supplies or service. I responded in the negative. He has not communicated with me since that *deega*."

"Surely he knows we were serviced recently. Do you think he was checking to see if you followed me or had anything to do with the attack on Koteas and Terin? It did take place, didn't it?"

"The Thracian vessel and all aboard were eliminated on schedule. A communication came from *Raz* Yakir to confirm that action was taken. The destruction was done in a manner to appear an internal problem and accident; no warning to be picked up by other sources was issued."

"They believed our information and observed the Icarians's guilt or they wouldn't have taken lethal and covert action."

"That is a logical assumption. The *I-GAF* network code was changed, but *Raz* Yakir is privy to the new one if it is needed."

"Let's hope it isn't necessary as that will narrow down the possibilities of who's inserting our clues. I'm sure the *I-GAF* commander will investigate everyone with access to the code and computer network, but if Phaedrig sends an agent here to investigate, *Raz* Yakir will warn us."

"That would be a logical conclusion and course of action," Cypher concurred.

"It's a good thing you stayed behind with the ship or we would be exposed by now. Maybe Tochar is only checking out any possibility of an enemy or agent working against him. It would be sensible to start with any newcomers, especially one with a private vessel. Anything else happen?"

"I constructed you a one-way communication device in case Tochar refuses to permit you to wear your wrist monitor again. I will attach it to whatever garment you select to wear; its size and shape will delude them."

"You're so intelligent and foresighted, my friend. Now, I must get ready for our guest. I want you to remain with us until we retire for the night to my quarters; that way, you can observe Dagan and tell me what you think about him later." Starla filled her trusted android in on what happened during the trek, then said, "Inform our superior of our current status and my safe return from Zumali while I freshen up."

Starla headed for her quarters in a mixture of excitement and suspense. Soon, Dagan would view how she lived and they would share a glorious night on her *sleeper*. Yet, worries about Tochar's actions troubled her. Positive she was in for another encounter with his truth serum, she wasn't concerned about passing his test, but she dreaded Dagan's submission to it. Tonight, she cunningly must prepare him for facing that hazard or he could endanger both of them.

Eleven

Dagan was impressed by Starla's spaceship which was a larger and more advanced vessel than he had expected. The four-*ying*-old model was sleek and swift. Its color was an almost perfect match to the gray-blue space encasing it, far above the reddish atmosphere of the planet. He quickly learned the many facets of the *Liska:* its potent power source; superior force shield; phenomenal weapons capability; the best quality in sensors, communications, and instruments; a superb bridge with two pilot seats; a well-fitted medical room; a shuttle bay with a small landing craft, an emergency escape pod, and decontamination unit; and a transporter room. In the personal area he was shown an eating location with automated *servo* and disposal equipment, one sufficiently-sized guest suite, and her femininely decorated quarters with a grooming chamber.

Near her *sleeper* he noticed a control/communications panel and, on the adjacent wall, he saw a viewing monitor and audio system for amusement. There was a short *seata* with a square table beside it. A small *servo* unit was located in a wall nearby for quick access to refreshments. He noted a collection of miniature animals and image disks of an older man, a lovely woman, and younger male on a wall shelf; he decided to study them closer another time since her family was deceased and speaking about them could cause her pain. Yet from a glance, she favored her mother. Variegated tints of ivory, blue, and green were the colors of her quarters, which gave them a light and relaxing aura. He noted a panel above her *sleeper* which covered a *transascreen* for exterior viewing.

All doors and controls were voice activated by either her command or by Cypher's rather than by floor-pressure panels; no doubt, he assumed, because Moig had journeyed on her ship on occasion and she wanted to ensure her privacy. The environmental system was automatically controlled; lights came on and went off when someone entered a room or area, unless their sensors were overridden by voice command, such as for sleeping.

Dagan smiled. "I'm almost speechless, Starla; this ship is a beauty. I can see why you prefer to habitate here instead of in the settlement."

From his reactions, he appeared to believe her ruse. The spacecraft—styled in the manner, marked appropriately, and registered to the obliterated skycity where she allegedly had been born and reared—was decorated to convince anyone who came aboard of her false identity and origin, down to faked family image disks. Everything inside and outside the *Liska* had been skillfully "aged" to four *yings,* the purported date of her survival and the loss of her world. "I feel safer and more comfortable in my own surroundings," Starla admitted, then switched to another subject. "Do you have any questions for Cypher-T? I asked him to accompany us in case you did, since he knows more about the ship and its functions than I do. I learn more every *weg,* but I would be lost without his help and lonely without his companionship. As many times as he's either rescued me or warned me of danger, I would probably be a captive by now if not for his assistance and protection. He can do just about everything, even any maintenance required on himself."

Starla observed Dagan as he walked down the passageway with her android and probed the unit for information about their weapons, force shield, power source, and their speed capability. She was amused when the Kalfan asked the android about himself, and Cypher—intentionally, she surmised—related his abilities in scientific and technological terms to prevent clarity. She assumed Dagan didn't ask Cypher to explain in words he could understand because her lover didn't wish to appear as if he lacked intelligence and comprehension.

They reached the eating area and made their selections from a row of metallic cards which were inserted into an order slot, marked with words or symbols in *WEV,* the universal language for communication. There were four recessed spaces, of which three contained units with smoky doors: the first for dispensing liquids, a second for serving hot foods, and a third for serving cold ones. The last was for disposing of containers which were cleaned and returned to stock for future use. Leftovers and wrappings were disintegrated by an internal device, commands given by a memory chip.

As they ate, Dagan was cognizant of the android's continued presence, as Starla had not dismissed him. Cypher's expressionless silver eyes seemed to remain focused on him as the android stood at attention near the door. Cypher was male in appearance—even his silver hair, body covering, limbs, and features looked real. Dagan had an eerie sensation that the advanced unit was analyzing him as if he were a complex problem to be solved. He also had the weird idea that the android didn't like having him aboard and with Starla, as if the sophisticated automaton actually possessed feelings and they were in conflict with his logical, nonemotional programming. He observed the almost human rapport between his lover and her longtime companion, one who clearly was protective of her. At times, he found himself forgetting the android wasn't alive, so Dagan fully understood why Starla thought of Cypher as a living being. Foolish as it seemed, he was almost jealous of their tight bond and cohabitation arrangement.

Between bites, Dagan said, "I'm surprised Tochar doesn't let us use your ship or his during raids since both are superior to Auken's."

"Even with the *Azoulay* repaired, thanks to you, Tochar wouldn't risk its loss during an attack on us; and mine is too small to carry a crew of five—four now that Moig is gone—and any large amount of stolen cargo."

Dagan finished chewing before he said, "I suppose you're right . . . I must say, this food is delicious, better than the colony's fare."

Starla smiled and thanked him after lowering her liquid container. "You're lucky my supplies were restocked recently. A traveling vessel arrived during our last raid and Cypher handled the task for me."

Dagan glanced at the alert android before he told her, "You're fortunate you have him to take care of the *Liska* while you're gone. No matter how good an automatic pilot system is, they can malfunction and cost you your ship." Before taking another bite, he asked Starla, "Do you think we'll be going on another raid soon?"

"I don't know; Tochar doesn't inform me in advance."

"Why is that?" he asked as he pierced a succulent morsel.

"I suppose he has to wait until his contacts supply him with needed data on our targets. He's a clever and cautious leader."

"Do you think he trusts us?"

Starla swallowed as she eyed him. "I don't see why not; we've given him no reason to doubt us."

"Do *you* trust *him?*" He watched her think, then shrug.

"He hasn't given me a reason to doubt or defy him, or done anything to provoke me to leave his hire. Working for him and living here have many advantages I'm certain I couldn't find elsewhere. As for Auken and Sach, they're excellent teammates. I didn't care for Moig, but that was personal."

"You think and feel much like I do; that's good."

"Yes, it is."

They finished eating in silence, each pleased with their necessary performances. Yet, both experienced qualms of guilt over their deceptions. Afterward, they disposed of their containers and she wiped off the table.

"Cypher-T, you're in control of the bridge. If you need me, we'll be in my quarters. That's all for tonight."

"Affirmative," the android responded and left the room.

Dagan pulled Starla into his arms. "Alone at last," he murmured. "It's been *wegs* since I last held you and kissed you; I've missed those pleasures."

"So have I." As he nuzzled her neck and she laughed at the ticklish sensations, she murmured, "Let's retire to my quarters and get comfortable."

"Sounds wonderful to me," he responded in a husky tone, ready and willing to forget everything and everyone except her for the next few *horas*.

Inside the private haven and as they undressed, Dagan motioned to her wrist device and asked, "Do you need that here? Is he listening to us?" He hadn't thought about the device until Tochar expressed interest in it, but recalled she hadn't taken it off during their previous encounters.

Starla laughed as she removed the unit and put it aside. "I see you're also forgetting he isn't real," she jested.

"Isn't he?" Dagan quipped. "I was beginning to think he wasn't going to give us any privacy. He doesn't have a jealousy chip, does he?"

"Not to my knowledge, but I'm not that educated on androids. He is loyal and he takes excellent care of me; that's how he was programmed."

"Just so he isn't too possessive and doesn't consider me a threat to you. I would hate to battle with him to win you; he's bigger and stronger, and no doubt knows every trick and skill in existence. From the way you fought with me the first time we met, he's taught you most of them."

"I bested you because you didn't take me seriously as an opponent."

"Maybe and maybe not, but I won't underestimate you again, woman."

"And I won't misjudge you. Soon, I want you to tell me everything there is to know about you."

"Craving all of my secrets?"

"Yes."

"You sure they won't change your nice opinion of me?"

"How could they? You did say we're perfectly matched, alike."

Dagan's gaze roamed her unclothed body. "Not alike in all ways, thank goodness. I was referring to our good sides and traits."

Starla leaned her frame against his, the unobstructed contact stirring. "Have you ever done anything that was really horrible?"

Dagan lifted a strand of lustrous brown hair and toyed with it. "In whose opinion? Mine or that of the authorities, or my targets?"

"I'm only interested in yours, for now."

He thought for a minute, shrugged, and said, "I don't think so."

"Good, because I haven't, either."

Dagan recalled her destruction of the Serian patrol ship and crew before she hired on with Tochar. He was tempted to question her about it, but decided this wasn't the right time. Though the incident wasn't listed against her in the *I-GAF* files, he—an *I-GAF* officer—knew about it and it troubled him, as did her apparent lie moments ago. He reasoned she didn't know he had been enlightened and had deceived him to protect her image. Yet, if she could lie to him at this point and look so innocent, perhaps she could—and had—duped him in other areas. No, he had to be understanding and lenient, considering her past tragic history and her love for him.

Dagan backed her to the *sleeper* with a sexy grin on his face. "Now, it's time for my dessert: you, woman."

"That's why I didn't serve you one in the eating room," she jested.

"Then, I suppose I'll have to taste you *hapax* by *hapax* until I find the best treat to sate my empty spot. Get ready, my love, this greedy space pirate is about to go araiding for real treasures."

"I stay ready for you, my beloved, shameless and bold as I am."

Dagan chuckled before he pulled her against him and sealed their mouths with a tender and leisurely kiss. It melded into one that became swift, passionate, and ardent as his hands roamed her bare flesh and he savored her response. She was so disarming and enchanting as she swayed against him that his intense yearnings increased. For a time, duty didn't exist; nothing beyond his rampant desire for this woman. The eternal flame of love had been ignited in his heart and it would burn forever. He felt her tremble with a mutual longing and he knew this bond between them was meant to be.

Starla clasped his handsome face between her hands and almost ravished his lips. He was tantalizing and tempting her beyond reason and reality. Her arms looped his neck and she pressed closer to him. She rubbed her body against his to titillate and pleasure him. She leaned her head back when he trekked down her throat and trailed kisses over her pulse point, then willingly lay on the *sleeper* when he urged her backward and downward to its surface.

Dagan's mouth traveled her body with skill and persistence. He kissed the straining points on her breasts and stroked them with his cheek. He heard her moan with delight. His hand took a sensuous path down her body to the fuzzy triangle between her thighs. His palm flattened over her mons and absorbed its heat before drifting up and down the soft surface from her groin to her knees. He ached for her. Slowly and provocatively, his lips covered the same terrain his hands had just traveled so he could feast upon the fruit of paradise.

As his mouth captured her tiny bud, Starla moaned and writhed. She abandoned herself to his rapturous and daring conquest. Her nails gently raked at his shoulders. Then, she buried her fingers in his dark hair, relishing the way the strands wound around them as if in a possessive embrace. A primitive wildness overtook her when he slipped a finger within her and deftly manipulated it. The core of her womanhood tensed as her need for release mounted, and she opened herself completely to his actions. She encouraged him to do as he pleased with her, because anything he did to her felt glorious. As his fingers and tongue trekked her very essence, she experienced exquisite thrills. She wanted to relax, but she couldn't; his actions wouldn't allow it. Her stomach muscles continued to ever tighten. Soon, she could not help but fall over the precipice she had climbed, the one he had pushed her toward with expertise and generosity.

When every spasm ceased, she grasped his arm and pulled him up beside her. Her hands slowly roved his hard chest, flat belly, and lower abdomen, her fingers finally toying in the dark hair around his manhood. She captured the rigid arousal and placed kisses along its full length. Her tongue danced around the tip. Her mouth enclosed him and she stimulated him with lips and hands until he was groaning and wriggling in pleasure and increased hunger.

Dagan knew that only total fulfillment could be sweeter than this splendid prelude. He reached for her arms and lifted her, his arousal penetrating her fully as he seated her upon it. In a near dazed state, he watched her rock back and forth, every fiber of his being alive and pleading for more. He thrusted in and out as his hips undulated; he sucked on the fingers she had been stroking his lips with, and he kneaded her breasts. He didn't want to stop but knew he must or she would get left behind. "I can't hold out much longer, my love," he admitted in a ragged tone.

"Neither can I, so come with me. Now, Dagan, now."

He rolled them to her back. Their gazes fused as tightly as their loins as their passions soared and hearts pounded. Their mouths meshed and they kissed with urgency. They climaxed in unison this time, their loins throbbing and contracting as they found their gratification.

As they rested and their bodies cooled, they lay nestled together, her fingers stroking his damp chest and his drifting up and down her back.

"You have a magic and allure about you that I can't resist, Starla. I've never been tempted to settle down until I met you. I wish this had happened at a different time and place in our lives because we're stuck here for a while longer. We have to remain loyal to Tochar for many reasons."

"I understand and agree. One *deega* it will change for us, so we must be patient, and careful. Now tell me, my lover, how did you get into this kind of existence?"

Dagan wasn't in the mood to lie to her tonight, not after what they had just shared. "I promise to tell you all about me another time. It's late, so I should return to the settlement. We have that early meeting with Tochar in the morning; we need to be fresh and alert."

"You're right. It slipped my mind; you're much too distracting, Latu," she teased as she sat up and gazed down at him.

"You're the one who's disarming and distracting, my beautiful love. You capture and enspell me as easily as you take a breath."

"I was under the impression you did the chasing and snaring."

"Once we met on that transporter and tangled, I doubt either of us stood a chance of escaping the other's interest."

"It must have been fate, Dagan, so why fight it?"

"My thoughts and feelings exactly. Let's get dressed and moving."

"Yes, sir," she said, and gave him a mock salute. "Your shuttle will be ready and waiting in fifteen *preons,* so you best get off this *sleeper* before I'm tempted to change my mind and hold you prisoner."

The *Spaceki* team—Starla, Dagan, Auken, and Sach— met with Tochar the following morning. As they sat before him, his piercing black eyes passed over each one in turn, then he stared downward for a time. The four sensed a problem and exchanged curious glances.

Starla masked her anxiety, but knew trouble was brewing.

"I have more bad news and it troubles me deeply."

When Tochar fell silent, Auken asked, "What is it, my friend?"

Tochar looked at his lead man and close friend. "Koteas and Terin are dead; their vessel destroyed, one *deega* after your departure."

All four team members stared at their leader in disbelief.

"What happened?" Sach probed. "Were they attacked?"

"I do not know, but the matter is suspicious, highly suspicious. Their vessel was still registering on our sensors when it exploded."

"Did our sensors pick up another ship or a laser blast?"

"No, Auken; that is the mystery. One *preon* it was there; then a fiery detonation; then it was gone, leaving only debris to drift forever." Tochar slapped his hands together, causing all except Dagan to jump in surprise. "Blam, and no more Koteas, Terin, or moonbeams."

"If our sensors didn't detect another ship or weapons' fire, it must have been an accident," Sach surmised.

"That is possible, but coming atop the other strange events, I am unconvinced. Any speculations?" Auken shook his head and so did Sach. "What about you," Tochar asked Starla and Dagan, "any theories?"

Starla knew from Yakir's report to Cypher during her absence that the smaller *I-GAF* ship had been obscured from Noy's sensors by the larger Thracian vessel when it briefly decloaked to fire a destructive beam. "Perhaps the crystals truly are unstable under certain conditions, since similar incidents occurred two previous times. Or perhaps your buyers mishandled them in a hazardous manner. The cave and desert were hot and dry locations which might have affected them. We haven't experienced trouble on the ship while transporting them to you in a location where humidity and temperature are controlled. What if your buyers stored theirs in a compartment without environmental control or their system malfunctioned? In light of three losses, it must have something to do with conditions or how the crystals are handled. Have you questioned your contact? If there's something we're doing wrong, that jeopardizes us during raids, and you and the settlement after delivery."

"And it will make future buyers nervous," Dagan added. "Whatever the trouble is, it needs to be discovered and resolved fast."

"I agree. As to my contact, he vows there is no problem with the crystals destabilizing; nor do they require special handling."

"If that's true or accurate, Tochar, what's causing the explosions?"

"That is what I am determined to learn, Starla. I hope none of you take offense or become provoked to leave me, but I must check my security. To do so, everyone around me—my special unit, my Enforcers, and even my Palesa—must be questioned with truth serum. Does anyone object?"

Starla, Dagan, Auken, and Sach shook their heads almost simultaneously. Tochar smiled and said, "Excellent, because this precaution is necessary for everyone who will continue to work for me. We will begin the tests immediately. Starla, would you go first?"

"That's fine with me, Tochar."

"Dagan, you go next; then, Sach and Auken. It requires thirty *preons* to go under and thirty for questioning; recovery can be done in an antechamber to save time. After I complete your tests, Auken and Sach can assist me with those for the Enforcers. Any tests not completed before your departure in two *deegas* will be carried out by me and Palesa during your absence. The rest of you can await your turns in the recreation chamber so Starla and I can get started and get this annoying but necessary matter behind us. Your cooperation and understanding are appreciated."

Starla exchanged smiles with the other three team members before they left the room. She followed Tochar to a smaller one which contained an oblong padded table, cabinets on one wall, a counter with recording equipment and a tray with an *Airosyringe,* and a tall sitting stool. After the door closed behind them, the man told her to take her place on the table. She obeyed his order and calmed her tension as much as possible.

"I am sorry this must be done, Starla."

As Tochar placed the *Airosyringe* against her right arm and pressed the button to infuse her with *Thorin,* she smiled and said, "I understand. If you were not a smart and cautious man, I would not be working for you."

"I am grateful for your trust in me. Put your arms at your sides. As you recall, these straps are to prevent you from falling off the table while you are drugged. Relax, and I shall return soon."

She nodded as he secured strong bands across her chest, hips, and ankles. She watched him exit, then closed her eyes. She knew the drug required only twenty *preons* to take affect on anyone not made immune via the *Rendelar* chemical and process, as were her world's leaders and all members of the Elite Squad. That chemical and procedure belonged to Maffei and were inventions of her father's deceased half-brother, made in his laboratory on the planetoid of Darkar. Her mother had once owned the powerful and impregnable complex where unreproducible chemicals and formulas were created, but Jana Greyson Triloni Saar had turned it over to the Maffeian government after her marriage to Varian Saar.

Starla was certain that Tochar would give a fortune to own or to be able to raid Trilabs—which also produced other drugs and weapons—but no one could penetrate Darkar's advanced defense system. Unless, she reminded herself, Tochar got his hands on a portable laser cannon powered by a large white moonbeam which could pierce its force shield and blast through the complex's doors. She could not allow that to happen, as Trilabs was too vital to her world's survival and too dangerous in a *villite*'s control.

She had witnessed many interrogations of suspects under *Thorin*'s influence, so she knew how to act and speak to dupe him, as she had done once before. She was not worried about revealing any secrets, but she didn't like feeling so vulnerable and helpless in this imprisoned state. She also fretted over what Dagan might expose to the *fiendal*.

She heard the door swish open and knew Tochar had returned. She was prepared to deceive him, thanks in part to a harmless tablet she had secreted in her belt for this anticipated occasion and had slipped into her mouth without notice while following Tochar to this location. The tiny tablet created a flush on her cheeks and a glazed look in her green eyes. She commanded her body to go limp and her breathing to slow. She saw Tochar when he opened her lids to check her eyes, then allowed them to close again. She heard him approach the counter to turn on the recorder and return to take a seat on the stool beside her.

"What is your name?"

"Starla Vedris," she responded in a slow and soft tone.

"Who is your leader and where does he habitate?"

"Tochar of Tochara on the planet Noy in the Free-Zone."

"Are you completely loyal to him?"

"Yes." She was glad he hadn't told her to open her eyes and to look at him, as concentration on her responses was easier with them closed.

"Do you know anything about the recent explosions and mysterious events, those so-called accidents which have plagued Tochar?"

Starla related only what she was supposed to know about the incidents. When he asked who and what she held responsible for them, she repeated the speculations she had fabricated earlier.

"Do you know if any enemies or rivals are working against Tochar?"

"No."

"Have you ever disobeyed Tochar's orders or been lax during raids?"

"No, I obey and do my best for him."

"What do you know about moonbeams, the crystals?"

She related facts she had overheard by accident or been told by him and his friends. "I fear them because they could be unstable and dangerous; their power is enormous and destructive. I would not approach or handle them if I were not ordered to do so."

"Do you know the identities of Tochar's contacts in Seri and Kalfa?"

"I have not been told their names."

"Do you know Dagan Latu?"

"Yes."

"Can Dagan be trusted?"

"I believe so."

"Do you love Dagan?"

Starla decided she should respond honestly in order to fool Tochar completely. "Yes, but such new and powerful feelings frighten me."

"Why?"

"I have never loved a man in this way. These emotions are strange and confusing, and we have not known each other very long. I lost everyone I loved in the past and I fear that could happen again if I put myself in a vulnerable position. It is hard to explain how I feel."

"Does Dagan love you?"

"He told me he does, but I need more time to fully believe him."

"Do you plan to become his mate and leave Tochar?"

"One *deega* in the future if we remain alive and uncaptured and if he is the man he appears to be, I would like to bond with him."

"If you decide to bond with him, when do you plan to leave Tochara?"

"After Dagan purchases another ship."

"Why do you not depart soon and use your ship?"

"Dagan is a proud man; he must stand alone before accepting me and standing with me. He lost everything before he came to Noy and must raise himself again before he feels worthy to claim me." She heard Tochar chuckle at what he must consider silly romantic notions.

"Do you intend to work against Tochar as a rival after your departure?"

"No; I will settle with Dagan where it is safe and begin a new life, if our relationship is a true and worthy one and withstands the test of time."

"Have you shared a *sleeper* with Dagan?"

Starla didn't want to reveal such a private matter but it was possible Tochar had discovered or suspected the truth, and would learn it when he asked Dagan that same nosy query. "Yes."

"Why do you hide your relationship from Tochar and others?"

"I do not want Tochar to worry about my loyalty and length of stay or distraction during raids, and I want to make certain the relationship is solid before it becomes known by others. It would be humiliating to me if it becomes meaningless. If I parted with Dagan, other men could think me an easy conquest and approach me for sex."

"Would you remain loyal to Tochar even if Dagan turned against him?"

"Yes; Tochar is my leader and friend; he protects and supports me. If Dagan turned against him, Dagan would not be a good and honest man. I could not mate with one who is untrustworthy and wicked."

"Was Moig's death an accident?"

She was glad he had left his previous topic. "Yes and no."

"Explain."

"We were fired upon by a Serian patrol; he fell and struck his head. We were attacked, but he was not slain by laser fire. I rescued him and tended him, but I lacked the knowledge to treat his injury. He died."

"Do you know of any man or woman whom Tochar cannot trust?"

"No."

"If you learned Tochar's secrets, would you steal or reveal them?"

"No, I gave him my word of honor; keeping it is important to me. And he does not confide his secrets in me, only in his friends."

"Why is that?"

"I suppose because I have not yet earned his complete trust."

"Do you deserve Tochar's complete trust?"

"Yes."

"Do you have any feelings for Tochar?"

"I admire and respect him; he is a superior and intelligent leader."

"Do you have any sexual feelings for Tochar?"

That odd query made her nervous. "He is handsome and virile, but my heart belongs to Dagan." She heard Tochar murmur his approval to her response. She waited while the *fiendal* apparently scanned his mind for any remaining questions and was relieved when he seemed to find none. She heard him rise, turn off the recorder, and leave the room.

It wasn't long before Dagan entered with Tochar, unfastened her straps, and carried her to a guest chamber. As her lover placed her on a *sleeper,* she was glad Tochar was with him so Dagan couldn't ask her any questions while she was allegedly under the influence of a truth serum. The two men departed, and she turned to her side to relax until the drug supposedly wore off and she awakened.

As she lay there, Starla fretted over Dagan's answers to some of the same questions Tochar had asked her; she prayed he wouldn't expose anything detrimental to him or anything that might make her appear to have lied, which would be suspicious to Tochar. She cautioned herself to remain ready to signal Cypher for a rescue if necessary.

Twelve

Dagan lay on a *sleeper* in another chamber after his session with Tochar. He was amused and annoyed by the man's probings into his private life. He had admitted to a love and desire for Starla, but claimed he didn't believe he had won her completely as of this time. He also admitted to plans to make her his legal mate in the far future, but wanted time to have more adventures and to earn his own way before he settled down. What vexed him was Tochar's queries about Yana; they had been seen together and the perverted Icarian wanted to know if he had shared sex with the Asisan beauty. Needing to dupe Tochar and to prevent suspicions, he had felt compelled to confess he had done so on one occasion but would not do so again because he didn't want to risk losing Starla.

Tochar had asked the expected questions, probably the same ones he had used on Starla. Dagan hoped she had satisfied the leader's curiosity and assuaged any doubts without revealing any harmful information. He would learn that fact soon enough by Tochar's reactions in the next two *deegas*. If Starla had made slips during her interrogation, there was no way he could extricate her, not when surrounded by Tochar's men; that feeling of helplessness when his love might be imperiled angered him. He cautioned himself to stay alert and to try to come up with an escape plan if one was needed, though escape from Noy seemed unlikely without a ship at his disposal. Should he, Dagan wondered, trust Starla with the truth about himself and his mission in case her ship was required for either or both of them to flee? Would she feel betrayed, accuse him of using her as a cover to obtain information? He could not decide how she would react, so he told himself he should be patient and watchful a while longer.

At least, he reminded himself, Tochar couldn't extract any secrets from him, not with the immunity supplied to him and all *I-GAF* members from Trilabs in Maffei, one of the strongest members of the United Federation of Galaxies. He didn't understand exactly how *Rendelar* worked, but it did, and *Thorin* had no effect on him. If only that were true for his cherished Starla, he wouldn't have to worry about her safety and survival.

Dagan wasn't surprised Tochar was skeptical of recent incidents; so was he. Though he could not venture a guess as to how an enemy or an agent had reached and destroyed them, he didn't believe those crystals had exploded on their own either time. Nor did Phaedrig, but his superior could not ask Syrkin about the possibility of that occurrence since Syrkin was being investigated for alleged complicity with Tochar and to do so would reveal an agent was present on Noy and working against Tochar. If Syrkin was guilty of treachery, he would be arrested and terminated as soon as he made a slip. Somehow Dagan wasn't shocked by Syrkin's probable conspiracy; he had lost trust, admiration, and respect for the man when Syrkin was his *Seki* superior. He realized that a longtime connection between the two men would explain several frustrating episodes in the past when Tochar eluded capture and revenge by Curran Thaiter. It was advantageous to him that Syrkin believed Thaiter was dead and that Syrkin had no idea he was Dagan Latu or an *I-GAF* agent.

If Syrkin was taken down, Tochar would lose the traitor's assistance. That meant the Icarian would be forced to focus his raids on Serian crystals, which should make it easier to discover the second conspirator. With his sources cut off, Tochar could not become more powerful than he already was. That still left the *Destructoids* to battle, and no weapon existed that could do so, not until and unless more large white crystals were found. At least by being there, maybe he could prevent Tochar from mounting one on a spacecraft and attacking elsewhere with it. As long as the *fiendal* was compelled to protect his settlement and life with the three weapons in his possession, Dagan reasoned, Tochar wouldn't attempt that daring feat.

He had hoped to work his way closer to Tochar by now, but the man had become leery since those strange incidents. He knew from Phaedrig that Koteas and Terin had been exposed with an unknown person's help, and the Thracians's destruction was carried out by an *I-GAF* team in an undetectable manner. *He* seemed to be getting nowhere on his mission, but somebody else was having splendid success.

Who and where was this sly person? How had he gathered his data about Syrkin and the Thracians? How had he inserted it into a computer network to which only certain people in power knew the entry code? If the secret agent—or whatever he was—destroyed the crystals, how had he done so when Kalfan scientists claimed that was impossible? Yet, if moonbeams weren't indestructible, neither was Tochar's defense system. Who—he wondered—possessed such a powerful secret, and why not share it or even sell it to his people and the Serians? If *Raz* Yakir had been approached with that crucial news or a sale offer, Yakir would—should—have told Phaedrig and *Autorie* Zeev. The honorable and sage Serian ruler knew an *I-GAF* agent had been assigned to the imperative mission, so surely Yakir would help defeat a mutual threat. If moonbeams weren't indestructible, Dagan reasoned, and that seemed a proven fact, why didn't the unknown factor blast Tochar's *Destructoids* into oblivion and render him helpless? It was frustrating to be faced by such an enigma, to be uncertain as to whether he had an ally in the shadows or another deadly problem to handle . . .

When his recovery time elapsed, Dagan rose from the firm surface of the *sleeper* and went to locate Starla to see what she thought about her *Thorin* session. He was told she had left Tochar's dwelling after she aroused and had returned to the *Liska*. Dagan went to his dwelling to await her arrival, hoping and assuming she would visit him soon.

"Is your chamber totally private?" Starla whispered in his ear.

Dagan fused their gazes as he replied, "Yes, I check it every *deega*. I'm familiar with all types of spying devices. Are you worried about something in particular? Are you afraid you revealed secrets during your drugged meeting with Tochar?"

Following her reply, Dagan gaped at her. "You did what?"

"The same thing you did during your first *Thorin* session. Since my wrist unit makes Tochar nervous, I didn't wear it. But I did have on another device that Cypher constructed for me in the shape of a disk on my belt. It transmitted my session to him and he recorded it."

After Starla walked to the *seata* and sat down, Dagan joined her. "So?" he hinted. "What did he ask and how did you respond?"

"Why don't I play the session for you?" she asked, having edited the tape to exclude anything she didn't want Dagan to learn, such as the query about rejecting Dagan if he turned against Tochar and her vow of complete loyalty.

He watched her take a thin instrument from a pouch suspended from her belt. "You brought it with you?" he asked in surprise. After she smiled and nodded, he scolded, "Do you realize how dangerous it could be to get caught with that disk?"

"I'm not foolish or reckless, my beloved. Cypher rigged the release switch to initiate a self-destruct sequence if not opened correctly."

"That was very clever of him, but what if Tochar had asked you about such a measure while you were ensnared by truth serum?"

"If he had, I suppose I wouldn't be here with you at this *preon.*"

"What happened to your promise not to endanger yourself?"

"Wouldn't it be far more perilous to not know I revealed a secret or I expressed a feeling Tochar didn't like or trust?"

"I can't refute your point, but be careful if you take such chance again." As Dagan listened to the tape, her answers concerning him pleased him, but Tochar's asking those questions evoked annoyance. "He seems greatly interested in our personal relationship." He saw her nod agreement as he listened to the remainder of her encounter. With the drugging hazard removed, it was time to pull Starla closer to him and away from the *fiendal.* "It's good he didn't ask if you trust him fully, because I don't think you do; and neither do I. This is the first time I've distrusted a leader, and that doesn't trek well with me, especially when you're also involved with him."

His admission delighted her and evoked her to reveal, "What relieved me was when he interrupted my reply about Moig's death and leapt to his next query: if I knew of any man he couldn't trust. I'm certain I would have told him what I suspected about Moig's death and other things."

"What do you mean? There's no mystery about it, is there?"

"I think he killed Moig because there was no way to treat him on Noy, and Tochar couldn't allow Moig to be taken to a place where Moig might reveal his secrets." Starla revealed Tochar had engaged in a private conversation with the doctor and, later, that they told her Moig had died during examination. "The timing was suspicious to me, and I saw an *Airosyringe* mark on Moig's arm when he was carried past me by Enforcers."

"Why didn't you tell me this sooner? This darkens Tochar's image and tells me he's more untrustworthy and dangerous than I imagined."

"I kept quiet because it was a horrible suspicion I didn't want to believe. I told myself the infusion could have been medicine, but I wasn't convinced. I also feared you would reveal it during another *Thorin* test, and, after those incidents, I was positive we were in for a second one."

"What I thought you were going to tell me was that Tochar suspected Moig of being the one behind his troubles, so he had Moig disposed of in a clever way. Are you sure it was a Serian patrol that attacked you and Moig?"

"Yes, because Tochar needs those drugs. If he wanted to get rid of Moig or me for any reason, he would have used another way and time. If somebody is creating problems for Tochar, I doubt it's one of his best friends. If I were Tochar, the one I would watch closely is Palesa; she's Thracian like Koteas and Terin were, though their planets have long been restrained adversaries. Palesa is in the best position to learn Tochar's secrets, and she has access to a means of sending messages from Noy."

Dagan wondered if Palesa could be the unknown factor in the enigma; yet, it seemed unlikely, since Palesa was in a position to kill Tochar and claim his possessions. "Thank the stars he didn't ask if there was any woman he shouldn't trust or you might have mentioned your doubts of Palesa and vexed him." *He certainly asked me about possible enemies from both sexes.*

"I wouldn't have mentioned her because Palesa is neither male nor female to me; I refer to Palesa as a 'her' and 'she' because she plays a female's role in public; but she's *Binixe,* from a race of hermaphrodites."

"I know; I've met several in the past. I recognized the

marks on her neck when her hair moved aside. Tochar's choice of that type of lover explains why he hasn't pursued a beautiful and authentic female like you."

Starla smiled and said, "He wouldn't stand a _flick_ with me. Seriously, we should stay alert and watch each other's back while we earn as much profit as possible until we can leave. Departure any time soon would be suspicious or unacceptable to him. We mustn't forget he has powerful contacts in other galaxies he can use against us; no doubt he would alert the Serian, Kalfan, and _I-GAF_ patrols to our locations; or he'd send a unit of Enforcers after us. If I left, you would be endangered, now that he knows about our relationship. If we both left, he would consider us treacherous and threatening. We don't want to end up like Moig or others who've crossed ways with him. The safest and wisest thing for us to do is to appear loyal to him, to show respect, and to have patience."

Dagan was thrilled to have Starla opening up to him, proving her trust in him and love for him. But a few of her revelations alarmed him. He realized that if Tochar had asked her some of the same questions the _fiendal_ had asked him, Starla would've exposed the perilous thoughts and feelings she just related to him. It worried Dagan that he might be the cause of Starla changing her mind and emotions about Tochar, as they could get her slain. "You're right, my love; we have to concentrate on survival during raids and while we're living here. But in the event Tochar does turn against either or both of us, do everything you can to escape Noy. I promise I'll find a way to escape and join you, so don't worry about me or try to reach me; believe me, Starla, I'm an expert in that area, so don't endanger yourself trying to rescue or warn me. Cloak and fly to Karteal and wait for me there." He gave her the coordinates for the location he had in mind as an emergency rendezvous point.

As soon as she had recorded them in her wrist device,

Starla asked, "What if you don't come within an acceptable time frame?"

"Whatever happens, love, don't ever return to Noy for any reason. If I haven't joined you within two *malees,* begin a new and safe life without me. But," he added, pressing his fingers to her lips to silence her protest, "in case I'm delayed, leave a message about where you're heading beneath the rock shaped like a *winger;* you'll find it without any trouble."

"I don't want to talk or think about such a disturbing occurrence. Did you record your session with Tochar? Can you play it for me?"

"I did, but I've already destroyed the tape," he was compelled to lie, the taste of the deception foul in his mouth. "I didn't say anything harmful to us because he didn't ask any questions that required such responses. In fact, he asked me the almost identical things he asked you. It's a good thing the words *loyalty* and *trust* have different meanings in my mind and he used *loyalty* or I would have been in deep trouble with him, or if we had had this talk before I was put under. We don't want to give him any reason to use that serum on us again, not with the way we feel. Agreed?"

"Absolutely, or we'll become space debris." As she nestled against his chest and he stroked her hair, Starla wondered if Tochar had asked him any questions about Yana and, if so, what his replies had been. It was time for Yana to make an appearance to Radu and others, which she would do tomorrow. For tonight, all she wanted was to make love to Dagan. She lifted her head and gazed at him. "I love you and want you," she murmured.

Dagan leaned forward and fastened his mouth to hers. Between kisses, he said, "I love you and want you, Starla, so much it almost scares me." He swept aside her bangs and kissed her forehead. "I'm convinced we were destined to meet and bond."

"I hope so, Dagan," she said, clinging to him.

"I know so." *But I'm unconvinced fickled fate will be as kind to us.* He carried her to his *sleeper* where he made tender love to her.

The following afternoon in her Yana form, Starla visited with Radu at the Skull's Den. During their talk, she hinted she might be taking a short trip with a "new and close friend," but she would return soon. She hoped that excuse would conceal her impending absence with the other space pirates, a trek which would take longer than the recent ones.

Between sips, the sexy blond with blue eyes murmured, "Sometimes it's difficult to keep to myself for long periods, but I don't want to evoke trouble with any of those in the settlement by showing myself too frequently. I shouldn't be here much longer than another *malee* or two, so I'll continue to be patient and reclusive. At least I'm learning a great deal from the computer programs that keep me company."

"I think your actions are wise for such a beautiful woman; men often do crazy things when they are tempted by one such as you, Yana. I shall miss you after your departure, but Tochara isn't the right place for you."

"I know, Radu, and I appreciate all you've done for me."

"It is easy to be kind to a gentle and lovely creature."

"Thank you, my friend."

They chatted another few minutes before she returned to Yana's dwelling and transported to her ship from that location.

Starla and Dagan ate at the Skull's Den before they retired to his chamber to make passionate love before the next day's departure. They lay on his *sleeper,* kissing and caressing, savoring their close contact, and dreading the imminent *wegs*-long denial looming ahead of them.

Starla's arms encircled the virile Kalfan's waist, her palms flattened against his broad and sleek back. Her nipples were erect and there was a constant tensing in her lower region. Her fingers slid into the fullness of his ebony hair; she liked the way the thick mane buried and tickled them. She was hot and tingly from head to feet. She relished his cool and supple bare skin next to hers.

Dagan's right hand sensuously traversed her torso and caused her to quiver. He ached to bury himself inside her, but he did not want to rush this event as it would be their last one for a long time. His mouth wandered down the enticing column of her throat at a *yema*'s crawl, brushed over her collarbone, and climbed a beckoning mound. His tongue swirled around the taut peak as his hand massaged its firm base. He gingerly teethed the nub to heighten her arousal, and coaxed soft moans of pleasure from her. He attached his mouth to a nipple and as he suckled wildly, he heard Starla gasp. He thrilled to giving her such exquisite delight.

When he trailed his fingers over her rib cage, across her abdomen, and toward the place between her thighs, she tingled in suspenseful anticipation. She was willing and eager to give her all to him. She sighed in bliss as his fingers entered her. She parted her thighs to allow him the space and freedom to do as he pleased, as it greatly pleased her.

Dagan's kisses were deep and hungry as he enflamed her with his skilled fingers. He savored how she murmured and wiggled and stroked his back. His tongue played with hers and he nibbled at her lips.

Fervent and scorching needs consumed Starla and Dagan. They kissed and fondled each other as they yielded to the glorious torment of wanting each other so intensely they would risk their lives and careers to steal such overpowering moments together. Desires had smoldered since their last fervid union; now, they were encouraged, stoked, and enticed to ignite into a roaring wildfire which neither could nor wanted to douse.

Starla felt the sleek strands of his ebony hair as she twirled them around her fingers and inhaled his masculine scent. She looked into his blue gaze, then admired his perfect features. She relished his kisses and caresses which were deliberate, seductive, and dazing. Her arms looped around his neck and drew his mouth closer and tighter to hers. There was not a spot on her that did not burn or quiver with longing and elation. She was nestled in his strong embrace as her fingers wandered over him for as far as she could reach. She cherished this man with all of her heart and soul, and surrendered fully to his tender conquest. There was a quickening in her lower abdomen and a sweet tension in her loins. His forefinger slipped within her, delving, thrusting, moistening, exhilarating her as his thumb remained at work on the throbbing nub until it seemingly exploded. He continued until every rhythmic spasm of ecstasy assailed her very core. She moaned, thrashed, and drew every drop of splendor from that experience.

Starla's lips brushed kisses over his neck, ears, and face. Her wits were devoured by love and desire for him, a yearning to pleasure him. She grasped his straining erection and massaged the shaft, causing him to groan and writhe in enjoyment as she titillated his body and tried to also daze his senses.

Dagan's mouth captured a still-damp nipple which he kissed, teethed, and brought to full attention. His achings were intense; he was feverish to cool his scorching eagerness within her. But first, he wanted to stimulate her to wildness again.

Starla savored the magic of his tongue and hands. A blast of searing heat stormed her, one so potent and demanding and swift that it astonished her coming so close to her previous release. "Take me, my love," she coaxed.

Dagan moved atop her, the force of his weight controlled as he settled himself in place. His mouth melded with hers as he slid the tip of his organ past her seductive portal, then paused a moment to draw a needed breath for renewed restraint. When he had obtained it, he thrust further until he was fully encased within her.

Starla's legs encircled his muscled thighs and locked him in that position. Together they undulated as one. He entered and half withdrew countless times with her coaxing him onward to greater swiftness, depth, and strength.

Starla felt no shame or restraint. A flood of suspenseful rapture washed over her, one so powerful that she could deny him nothing he wanted from her. She matched his pace and pattern, clinging to him, almost plundering his mouth, refusing to let him withdraw completely or for any span of time.

Dagan's ravenous appetite for her increased. Sometimes he kissed her slow and tender; sometimes fast, ardent, and firm. His passions soared and the sensations were magnificent as he delved into her receptive body. He labored with love and tenderness until he knew she was ready to seek the next level of gratification. He was glad he knew how to enflame and how to sate her. He wanted every encounter to be as special and satisfying for her as it was for him. He wanted to share such unions many times in the future, and he wanted her at his side forever, and somehow he must accomplish that personal goal. He realized when she was on the brink of release as she writhed beneath him, her kisses deepened, and her breathing quickened. He drove with speed and purpose to carry her over the last boundary into a glorious sector she hadn't visited before.

Starla clung to Dagan and collected the many sensations which flooded her quivering body. She had believed the experience would be enjoyable, but it was *magnificent*. Unless her wits and instincts had been destroyed, it was obvious she had won the man of her heart. She belonged to Dagan Latu in every way except one: legal bonding, a marital state which might never occur. But she would love and desire this galactic-hopping rogue until her soul lived among the stars in *Kahala*.

Dagan moaned and tensed as his climactic moment arrived. A landslide of pleasure carried him away as he found intoxicating release. He cherished every thrust and spasm to the fullest, and the woman who provided them. His mouth and hands continued to send sweet and receptive messages to her; this time, they were ones of satisfaction, joy, and serenity. His heart brimmed with love and jubilation; his mind preened with pride; his spirit soared with victory. Starla was his of her own free will, he told himself, at least until his mission was finalized. But she would remain his forever if he could find a way to extricate her from her past recklessness. "I love you, Starla Vedris. I've never known such pleasure and peace of mind."

She saw his tender gaze and was convinced he spoke the truth, evoking mixed emotions. Her fingers traced his sensual lips as she said, "I love you, too, Dagan; I always will, no matter our fates."

Many *deegas* passed before Starla and Dagan found themselves waiting in the *Adika*'s teleportation room to carry out their next moonbeam raid.

She glanced at the authentic-looking *Seki* emblem on the dark-green space ranger jumpsuit. "I presume these uniforms and insignia mean we're attacking somewhere in Kalfa. We—" Starla halted and shrieked, *"Pralu.* Dagan, we're under attack! That was a photon blast! Let's get to the bridge and save ourselves." She raced out the door with him behind her and yelling for her to be careful.

After they joined the Icarians, they found a panicked Sach piloting the ship while an injured Auken handled the weapon's controls with one hand.

While trying to evade enemy fire and escape the larger and slower vessel, the less than superb pilot shouted, "It was a trap! We veered off when she lacked the proper signal, but she came after us and fired on us!"

That told Starla and Dagan they had decloaked to send some type of signal to their target, and hadn't received the desired response.

A worried Auken glanced up. "Glad you came; I haven't had time to summon you since things went wrong. Starla, take over as pilot and get us out of here; at least get an obstacle between us and them; our force shield and cloaking device aren't functioning."

As she took the captain's seat from Sach, Starla sent a furtive signal to Cypher in the concealed *Liska* which indicated he was not to interfere in the grim situation unless she requested help or a rescue. Her darting gaze rapidly scanned the ship's instruments and monitors as her keen mind plotted an escape course and assessed the extent of their current peril.

With the skilled female at the helm and putting distance between the *Adika* and the transporter, Auken continued. "Dagan, see what you can do about the problems with my force shield and cloaker. Sach will help you repair them while I operate the weapons. We have speed and agility and a superior pilot on our side while you're getting the ship back to normal."

"I'm heading for that astroid belt twenty *preons* away," Starla revealed. "It's dangerous to challenge one, but it might be our only chance for escape and survival with our deflectors down. Since you're hurt and your reactions might be delayed or restricted, Dagan should be in charge of our defense until we're out of their range. With luck, they won't follow us into that hurtling maze. Sach can be checking out our problems while we head for our destination; then Dagan can join him after we reach it." After Auken nodded agreement to her suggestions, Starla advised, "Dagan, fire only if absolutely necessary. With our shield and cloaker malfunctioning, any drain on our power source could overload it and shut down our engine or life-support unit. Besides, if we strike them with a blast, that will only provoke them into pursuing us at all costs, especially if those are *Sekis* or *I-GAF*ers."

"She's right," Auken concurred. "Defend but don't attack." He looked at his second best friend and said, "Get started on those repairs, Sach; Dagan will join you soon. I'll watch the monitors for them."

No one spoke again in an attempt to prevent distracting Starla from her evasive course of action as she closed the distance to her target. With Dagan and Auken's helpful warnings, she dodged all incoming blasts with maneuvers that elated her teammates and astonished her pursuers.

Dagan was glad his lover's defense suggestion sounded logical so he wouldn't have to fire on the other ship. He was relieved that even though their survivals were in jeopardy, she had tried to avoid having life-taking charges added to their records as they had agreed. That told him she loved him and wanted a future with him. If it came down to a fierce battle, could he, Dagan mused, *should* he destroy the other ship and crew to save their lives and to protect his crucial mission? He hoped he didn't have to confront that awesome dilemma, nor endure her capture. He realized there was another possible peril: he recognized the location as being near the planet of Orr in his world's galaxy; if *Sekis* or *I-GAF* agents weren't in current pursuit, those forces could be soon if their persistent opponents summoned help while the *Adika* was vulnerable and their retreat was hindered. He dared not look at or speak to his cherished love, as he could cause either or both of them to lose focus on their critical tasks. His hands itched to take charge of the controls, but he couldn't do a better job than she was doing, though it would keep him from feeling so helpless.

Starla's anxiety and suspense mounted by the *preon* as she struggled to concentrate on getting them to safety. She must avoid exposure of herself and her mission, and certainly prevent the deaths of whomever was assailing them. The traveling expanse of scattered space debris and irregular-shaped bodies which ranged from a few to several hundred *migs* in diameter loomed ahead of them, but she was afraid the next photon blast would disable the ship before they could reach cover. If that happened, Dagan would be captured and. . . . *Stay alert, Bree! You have to get yourself and your beloved out of this perilous trap!*

Thirteen

At last, the *Adika* reached the asteroid field before the other vessel could overtake it. Starla murmured to the others, "If Cypher-T were here, he would get us through this belt without a problem and he could handle our repairs with haste and skill. But I'm glad he isn't here and won't be entering this perilous region because it could interfere with his circuits and damage him; I'm glad he's at Noy and I hope he's replacing the water in my ship's system in case we need the *Liska* for our next raid." She concluded the intelligent android would grasp her clues and not follow the *Adika;* she was certain he would understand she wanted him to return to the Free-Zone.

Starla guided the ship into the belt, then positioned it behind and kept pace with an asymmetrical body for a while. She observed the other objects moving around them, eluding them as necessary. Within *preons,* it was obvious the Kalfans didn't enter the hazardous location, at least not at the same penetration point. She glanced at the golden-haired male whose black gaze was locked on the forward screen and said, "Auken, it should be safe for Dagan to initiate our repairs. You and I can monitor the sensors."

Auken agreed, and Dagan left the bridge for the engineering section.

"How's your hand?" Starla asked the scowling Icarian. "Do you need to go bind it for comfort?" He shook his head, and she asked, "What happened back there?"

"I was taking my seat after I . . . stood to optically scan the transporter when she fired on us. The unexpected jolt knocked me down and I twisted my wrist; that's why Sach took over as pilot until you arrived."

"Why did they attack? Were you given the wrong code word or signal?"

"They fired the *preon* we decloaked to check her out. I wasn't given a chance to communicate with them, and they didn't issue a warning."

Starla knew he didn't have to stand to look out the viewer screen, so Auken had needed to be near the *transascreen*—perhaps with the strange black box still laying nearby—to check for that signal Moig had mentioned to her before she placed him in an ill-fated coma. With luck, Starla hoped, Cypher had picked up the frequency when he recorded the incident for evidence. Since the raid had been foiled, she wondered if that meant Syrkin had exposed himself, been removed, and hadn't been able to alert Tochar or Auken to trouble before his downfall. "Did you say anything to them after they fired on us?" she asked. "Do you know who's aboard that ship?"

"I used the watchword we were given; it must have been changed because it didn't halt their attack, and they never identified themselves."

"That's strange," she murmured, keeping an eye on a big asteroid as she began to weave her way through the in-motion maze.

"More than strange if you ask me. Don't worry; Tochar will find out what happened and make certain it doesn't occur again."

"If we get out of this trap alive," she muttered with a frown as she evaded collision with another large asteroid. She guessed their pursuers were *Sekis* and doubted those space rangers would give up the chase this soon. She tried to surmise their opponent's strategy so she could outwit it. She didn't want Dagan captured along with Auken and Sach as that wouldn't give her the time or opportunity to explain the truth to him as she struggled to convince those officers of her identity and mission. Until she proved herself, she would be locked away like one of the *villites* on this craft.

The passage of time seemed contradictory: snailish, yet swift. Starla perceived the heightening of Auken's tension and suspected he was afraid, a condition which the alien must have found annoying. She also was apprehensive, but neither summoned aid from their busy teammates and waited in silence as they watched for hazards.

Dagan finally communicated with Auken to relate he was checking on several solenoids, triaxial connectors, transducers, multiplexer interface adapter, and two inverters. He had replaced a couple of damaged parts, bypassed a module he didn't have a replacement for, and repaired another component. "I'm re-engaging the deflector shield now," he announced, "but she has a weak spot in section three, so keep that side away from the enemy if they return. Most of the sensors and scanners are back to normal. The indicators seem to be functioning correctly, but I can't be certain without the right kind of flow meter; there's one on Tochar's ship I can use after we return to base. I'll replace these substitutes I've rigged and the other damaged parts from those we got from Sion if Tochar hasn't sold them during our absence. Sach has sealed those two small ruptures, and pressure in all compartments has stabilized. We're still working on the cloaker; the interface coupling is fused solid; I'm trying to reroute it around that segment."

"I know you're doing your best, Dagan," Starla urged, "but we need it functioning fast so they can't detect our exit point and intercept us when we come out of this belt. We can't stay in here much longer; the field is getting very tight and crowded and navigation is becoming difficult. At least with the force shield up, we can bounce the smallest ones off our hull if necessary, but the large bodies are increasing in number and in velocity."

Dagan wished he could say something comforting and intimate to her, but that was unwise. He responded on the internal com-system, "If this idea works, I'll have it repaired in about ten to twenty *preons*. Don't worry, Starla, you can do it, you're one of the best pilots I've seen. I'll hurry."

"Why don't we halt and wait here for him to finish, conserve our power?" Sach asked Auken. "If those Kalfans are trying to get ahead of us and lay another trap, we don't want to zoom right into their snare."

"We can't, Sach," Starla replied. "Natural drift would crash us into one of the big asteroids, or pull us into that radiation belt to our right and knock out instrumentation. We have to keep going slowly and dodging these obstacles. If it gets worse, I'll have to turn around and keep pace with the original entry point; but we shouldn't exit without that cloaker. If there were *Sekis* or *parsec jumpers* aboard that vessel, by now, they could have an entire unit laying in wait for us along both perimeters. I can't get an accurate reading for other lifeforms with so much interference from this debris."

More time passed, and Starla noticed that Auken was showing signs of extreme tension. She knew why: she had been compelled to retreat along their previous course to escape the increase of asteroids; and he feared the Kalfans knew that action would be mandatory and would be waiting ahead to seize them.

"What's that?" she asked, motioning to the apparatus near him.

"Something personal of mine," Auken replied, and put it away.

So, she mused, still not trusted completely. . . .

Dagan and Sach arrived on the bridge, and the ebony-haired male said, "Engage her and see if she responds; we've done all we can. If she fails, we'll have to make a run for it."

"Hope for the best, my friends," Starla murmured as she

pressed the button. She smiled and whooped with joy. "She seems to work. Let's get out of here and put some distance between us and this quadrant."

"My suggestion exactly before that device realizes Sach and I tricked her and she gets angry and quits on us for spite," Dagan jested with a broad grin to help calm everyone's tension. "With that said, I'll hush so I won't distract our superior pilot."

As soon as the ship cleared the asteroid field, Starla cloaked them and went to starlight speed. As she performed those tasks, Auken, Sach, and Dagan scanned their monitors and sensors for the presence of other ships, but found none. Even so, each of them knew that another cloaked vessel could be lurking nearby; for that reason, she kept the *Adika* obscured until they were far away from their thwarted raid.

"Those were some excellent maneuvers, Starla. We're lucky to have you," Auken complimented her as he relaxed.

"Thank you, my friend. I'm going to decloak soon so I won't put stress on Dagan's repairs in case the device is needed later."

"Sounds like a smart precaution to me," the band leader replied.

Dagan looked at his weary lover and offered, "Why don't I take over for a while, Starla? You must be tense and sore from all the strain and pressure back there. I'm sure you can use a break."

"That would be appreciated, Dagan." She sent him a glowing smile and mouthed she loved him as they exchanged places. She knew he couldn't respond in like kind because he was facing the others, but he did give her arm a gentle squeeze as he assisted her to her feet. Once more they had survived near-death, Starla mused, but more perils loomed before them, and the possibility of eternal and agonizing separation.

* * *

Three *deegas* later, Starla and Sach were summoned from their quarters and told a medical wares ship was within their reach for a raid.

"If we take her cargo back to Tochar," Auken reasoned, "this trek won't be a total waste of time and supplies."

And it will help appease that fiendal's *fury.* Starla's mind reasoned.

"Medical products and drugs sell for high prices in secluded ports," Auken continued. "She should be a simple challenge with little risk."

"What if she's a trap?" Sach wondered. "Been put between us and the boundary to tempt us to take her to avoid going back emptyhanded?"

"What do you think, Starla?" the team leader questioned.

"Sach could be right; it would be a cunning tactic." She pretended to concur, in case the medical goods were in desperate need somewhere.

"What do you think, Dagan?" Auken queried the last member.

"I say we slip into our *Seki* uniforms and lay claim to her haul," the Kalfan agent answered; he would explain his clever reason to Starla later.

Auken grinned and said, "Dagan's right; we take her load."

After everyone was deceptively attired as space rangers, the raid was carried out without a problem, and a valuable cargo was taken aboard the *Adika*.

When the group reached Noy, it was late at night, so they did not meet with their leader or unload their cargo. Instead, Sach, Dagan, and Starla took a shuttle to the landing grid while Auken remained aboard his "injured" ship to sleep there. A fatigued Sach bid the couple farewell and headed for a nightspot to enjoy several drinks before retiring to his abode.

Starla decided, much as she loved and craved Dagan, she needed to concentrate on her mission and duty tonight, not on him. "I don't think you should come to my ship and I shouldn't go to your chamber tonight," she said, then searched her mind for a plausible excuse. "I'm certain Tochar is furious about our failure and will be looking for somebody to blame for our recent trouble. We not only didn't get those crystals he wanted, but we almost fell into a lethal trap. I suspect his Kalfan contact failed him; since we were assaulted, he might have been exposed and captured; if that's the reason, Tochar will be reality-impaired and furious. It could look suspicious for two of his newest team members to be so close so fast, despite our admissions during those *Thorin* tests. I know we haven't been alone for *wegs,* Dagan, but we don't want to take any risks of displeasing him. I doubt that medical haul will assuage him when it's moonbeams he wants badly. We should let him settle down tomorrow, then get together the following *deega.* Do you concur?"

Dagan, who needed to send and receive a report from Phaedrig, was compelled to respond, "Yes, I think that's wise. For all we know, he could be watching us this very moment and wondering if we're plotting against him. We should hug and kiss and go our separate ways tonight."

Starla decided to ask him tomorrow why he agreed with, actually coaxed Auken, to raid that medical ship, as she did not want to get into that offensive matter at this late *hora.* She smiled, shared an embrace and kiss with him, whispered she loved him, and headed for her shuttle. She heard Dagan leave in a landrover which had been left there by someone.

After reaching her ship, Starla found Cypher ready to pass along a message from Supreme Commander Thaine Sanger. She listened with relief and interest as the android told her that Syrkin had exposed himself while attaching a signaling device to the crystal shipment and had been arrested. "That explains why the evil traitor couldn't give the cue to Auken," Starla reasoned. "He was placing his world and many others in terrible jeopardy for selfish reasons. I wouldn't have been surprised if Tochar had destroyed him after Syrkin was no longer useful to him. Tochar wouldn't allow an equal to work with him later; those are the kinds of men who eventually become rivals and threats and assassinators. Wouldn't it be marvelous, my friend, if we could create a breach between Tochar and his Serian contact, make them believe they can't trust each other? But that's impossible without knowing the man's identity, and I don't know how we can obtain it, not yet anyway. Somehow, I must get closer to Tochar, Sach, and Auken; then, perhaps one of them will let that crucial name slip."

"Do not increase your mission velocity; haste or impatience evokes dangerous mistakes," Cypher advised. "We are making steady progress; our accomplishments are many and important. I understand your desires to defeat Tochar and to return home as quickly as possible, but do not rush your task and imperil it. The feat you performed in the asteroid belt will elicit praise and admiration in the *villites*. It is possible that episode will achieve a bonding goal and the rewards which accompany one." Cypher explained how he analyzed she was in no danger from the Kalfans when he saw their vessel depart in the opposite direction to continue to their destination. "I assessed the damage to the *Adika* and concluded it was not beyond the capabilities of Dagan Latu and Sach to repair or bypass them. Our instruments detected the signal Auken sent to the other vessel, the one Moig revealed to us. I recorded the frequency and incident as evidence. Following my return to Noy, I had our water system flushed and refilled; it has been decontaminated and sterilized for your consumption."

"Have you filed a report to Thaine?" Starla asked.

"Negative. In the event he made a verbal response, I did not think it was intelligent for him to learn I left you behind in possible peril. The disk is ready for you to complete the data; then I will send it to our superior."

"You're the best teammate I could have, Cypher. I'll add my news in a *preon*. Anything else happen during our separation?"

"On the preceding *deega,* I used a holographic image of Yana to dupe Radu and others with him into believing Yana was in the settlement while Starla was absent. All illusions were carried out at a distance to which the aliens could not approach her image and discover my tricks."

"You're so clever, my friend," Starla complimented the android. "No one should suspect Yana and Starla are the same person. We need to keep her around until we're certain we won't have a special use for her." She took a deep breath and said, "I'll finish that report so you can send it to Thaine. By the time I finish my cleansing and having a refreshment, if he intends to respond, he can do so before I take to my *sleeper.* I'm exhausted."

On the planet's surface, Dagan awaited a reply from Dauld Phaedrig concerning the communication he had sent out earlier. While he sipped a drink and lazed on the *seata,* he let his troubled mind drift to Starla. He wished he could be with the ravishing *spaceki* tonight, but realized he must put duty and this pivotal assignment above his personal desires for one *deega.* He had to discover what was going on; if mission matters were heating up and perils were increasing, Starla could be in danger and time with her could be shortening faster than he knew. He could not surmise why Phaedrig had allowed shots to be fired on them with him aboard, and he was angry and alarmed because Starla could have been injured or killed.

When the encrypted message came through from his superior in a code only *I-GAF* members knew, the skilled agent learned about Syrkin's fate. It was clear to him that the unknown factor's lead had been accurate again; yet, Phaedrig still had no idea who or where that source was. In regard to why an attack had occurred against the *Adika* with him aboard, the answer was that the *Seki* superior from the capital planet in Kalfa had put several of his rangers aboard after Syrkin's exposure and arrest.

Phaedrig's symbols deciphered to explain how he couldn't order the *Sekis* to cancel counterstrike plans because doing so would reveal there was an *I-GAF* agent in Tochar's band. Their orders were to disable and capture but not kill, so the *spacekis* could be interrogated before punishment: if an assault was hazardous, the rangers were to break off their pursuit and safeguard the crystals to their destination. "No more clues received from anonymous informant. No further data located on Starla Verdris."

Dagan wished he could recall his rash comments about Starla's piloting skills and prowess; that she would make a good agent; that she didn't believe in life-taking and resisted doing excess damage; that from how he saw it, she was into something over her head and didn't know how to get out; that he was certain Tocher wouldn't let her go alive; and how she had endured a hard life and made mistakes, but was a good person inside.

Phaedrig had cautioned if he was "getting too involved with one of your targets, Curran, don't forget she's a wanted *villite,* one of Tochar's band."

Dagan sent a short reply. "I haven't forgotten and I won't."

The following morning, Auken took Starla to a site where they were to place the cargo they had collected earlier from his ship. They had been assigned to unload and store their recent haul while Dagan and Sach worked on Auken's craft using parts stolen during the raid on the Sion space station. While aboard the *Adika,* the band leader had related to Starla and Dagan he had told Tochar how they had saved the team and his ship during the ill-fated trek. Auken had grinned and hinted they shouldn't be surprised if Tochar rewarded them for their courage and prowess. Starla and Dagan hadn't been given an opportunity to speak privately, but each was cognizant they had plans to meet that night in his abode.

At the cavern's entrance, too narrow for a landrover to drive through, Auken stood beside two vehicles and recorded the items and drugs before Starla carried them into a storage cave. The natural corridor used to reach the correct chamber was long and twisted. It was illuminated by hanging lanterns, a light source which was predated long before her parents' births, but a necessary one in this primitive location. It prevented her from taking a wrong passageway along the winding course, since there were many paths and recesses in the dark red grotto's interior.

As she worked, Starla wondered why Tochar had not commanded some of his Enforcers to assist them in order to lessen their time and labor. These weren't, she reasoned, the type of products the leader needed to keep a secret; and the site—one of several—was always under guard. Perhaps, she mused, there were items amassed in other cavities that the *fiendal* didn't want his hirelings to see. While alone, she whispered for Cypher to take a coordinates reading so she could return later to investigate that idea.

As she approached the cavern's opening to get another load, Starla heard Tochar's voice and halted before rounding the last bend, hoping to learn something vital. She signaled Cypher to go on alert and to record the conversation. She kept out of sight and eavesdropped as the *villite* leader told someone—perhaps Auken, but she didn't think so from his tone—about Syrkin's loss in Kalfa. When Tochar spoke about the thwarted moonbeam raid and boasted of how his special team had eluded Kalfan rangers, she knew his companion was not the other Icarian. She heard him brag about his loyal *spaceki* team which cunningly had substituted a raid for medical supplies so they wouldn't return to him empty-handed.

"Our accomplice on Ulux contacted me to relate the ill-timed news that Serian mines and shipments have been put under heavy guard by *Raz* Yakir's order," Tochar said, "so no crystal raids are possible any time soon. Unless, his thrall on Kian finds a way around that precaution. In the event that does not occur, my friend, I am considering a plan to mount the smallest *Destructoid* from atop my dwelling to my ship so my team can strike at will. That would leave me with my two largest ones for protection. If Dagan Latu—one of my recent hirelings and best men—cannot do that kind of work, I will get my special team to abduct a scientist from Seri who can."

Starla was horrified by that news and prayed her beloved would not be an accessory to such evil. She wished she knew who was with Tochar, but she dared not peek around the rocky corner and risk being seen. The other person hadn't spoken, but no one ever interrupted Tochar and the *fiendal* was still speaking.

"I cannot wait any longer for a big white crystal to be found and another *Destructoid* to be built so I can recover my losses," Tochar continued. "If we are going to get control of Trilabs and make use of its products, we must have one of those weapons to penetrate Darkar's force shield and complex structures. With Trilabs and the moonbeams in our possession, we will have great wealth and power, more than we can imagine or ever use. These are serious and pressing matters, my friend, but we will discuss them later. Go and look over the items stored inside to see if there is anything you want or need. I will join you soon in the lighted chamber. Starla Vedris is inside and will guide you around. Do not allow certain lust for her to show, my friend, she must not be offended; she is my best pilot and an elite member of my special team."

Before the man could respond or react to Tochar's suggestion, Starla hurried down the winding passageway to the chamber she had just left to pretend she was stacking containers. She did not want to be caught near the entrance and be suspected of spying, and she was eager to discover the identity of the stranger. As she made those preparations, she whispered them to the ever-vigilant android aboard her orbiting ship, then awaited a new adversary's arrival and exposure.

"Starla Vedris, Tochar sent me to—"

As she turned from her faked task, her startled gaze widened as much as the Maffeian's did as his shock sliced off the remainder of his sentence. Starla felt as if the blood drained from her face, her entire body, as she confronted Acharius, son of *Avatar* Faeroe, son of the planetary leader of Caguas in her Galaxy, a man near her age who knew and desired her.

"What in *Gehenna* are you doing here, Bree-Kayah?" he exclaimed.

Starla mutely cursed the traitor before her who was jeopardizing her mission, who surreptitiously had aligned himself with the forces of evil and darkness. As he gaped at her in shock, it gave her time to think rapidly about what to do. She wondered if she should slay him and try to bluff it out with Tochar; or let the *nefariant* live, escape fast, and admit defeat. In order to safeguard her mission, could she, Starla mused, kill the son of a Maffeian *Avatar,* a man whose father was a respected leader and a close friend of her parents? If she didn't eliminate him, sparing Acharius's life could cost innumerable ones on the planets in the United Federation of Galaxies, and her own after he exposed her to Tochar.

"Great *Gehenna,* you're on a secret assignment! Aren't you?" Reality returned to her opponent and the grim truth settled in on him. He didn't give her time to answer before he shouted into the rocky corridor behind him, "Tochar, come quick! We have a spy!"

Starla leapt aside as Acharius drew his laser weapon and fired at her, the beam zinging off the wall behind her and scattering debris as it did so. Cypher sent a vibratory warning signal via her wrist device that more danger was approaching. At the same time, she heard Tochar and Auken racing toward them and yelling questions.

As Acharius steadied his weapon to fire again, Starla knew decision time was running out.

Fourteen

Due to the past mysterious incidents, team members had been told to wear their weapons at all times. That was advantageous for Starla, unfortunate for her crazed assailant. She was given no choice except to draw her weapon and fire in self-defense, as Acharius never entreated or demanded her surrender. She lacked time to reason with him, to try to persuade him not to unmask her. It was clear to her that the reality-impaired man was trying to eliminate the only witness who could bind him to Tochar. Her dexterous fingers worked the weapon's settings in resolved haste, and she fired a lethal and accurate beam into his evil heart which sent his jolted body tumbling backward to the ground. She signaled Cypher to delay any attempt to transport her out of jeopardy, as she hoped she could salvage the situation with the threat of exposure removed.

Tochar and Auken reached the astonishing scene. Auken went down on one knee to check the man for signs of life and found none; he looked at Tochar and shook his head, then eyed Starla in confusion.

Tochar stared at her and demanded, "Why did you kill Acharius?"

Starla lowered the laser weapon to her side instead of holstering it, and left a finger on the trigger. She remained where she was, keeping a safe distance between them and feigning an expression of dismay. "Before I came here, I robbed him during a stop at Caguas in Maffei. He recognized me and attacked like he was zoned out. Look at the wall behind me; he fired at me twice, and his weapon wasn't set on stun. The damage and sound of his blasts revealed his intent to kill me. I was only trying to defend myself. I must have pressed the wrong button when I panicked and drew my weapon. Things happened fast and wild. I hope he wasn't a close friend. If so, I'm sorry about his loss." She noticed how cold and piercing Tochar's gaze and tone were when he replied to her desperate fabrications.

"Somehow I think there is a good reason why Acharius tried to kill you, Starla, and it had nothing to do with a simple theft. Acharius would have found that coincidence amusing, even sexually arousing. You are much too highly skilled and in control of your prowess to slay anyone by error or to panic in any situation. If he was a threat, you would have stunned him and allowed me to handle the matter. I heard what he shouted, so I think you silenced him for a good reason, one you should tell me."

Starla feigned dismay at his accusation. "I can't believe you would call me a liar and threaten me. Haven't I proven my fealty to you countless times and in countless ways? Perhaps he mistook me for someone else. I gave him no reason to react as he did. When I'm on a raid, Tochar, I'm on full alert; my guard was lowered during this unfortunate accident since I felt safe in here. Have you forgotten the troubles we've had, those so-called 'mysterious' incidents? The way he suddenly appeared and attacked me, he could have been an enemy, a saboteur. Your suspicions trouble and hurt me deeply. I can tell you intend to punish me or perhaps even terminate me without just cause, based on the rantings of a reality-impaired man. I have done nothing to deserve such wicked treatment and disloyalty, and I will not endure them. I shall leave your settlement and hire this very *deega*. I will be a great loss to you, my previous leader, for no one has been a better or truer raider for you than I have, including your best friends. I shall return to work for myself, since you think I can't be trusted." *Let's see if you apologize and beg me to stay. . . .*

"What if she's telling the truth, Tochar?" Auken reasoned. "She's never given me a reason to mistrust her. She's been an excellent teammate."

"We both heard what Acharius shouted about having a spy in here," Tochar insisted. "That is something I have suspected for many *wegs* since those incidents."

"It may not be Starla, and maybe Acharius did zone out for a *preon*."

Tochar kept his dark and chilly gaze on the woman before him. "Perhaps you are right, Auken, but I am skeptical. She will have to find a way to convince me I should take her word over that of Acharius. I shall have a long and serious talk with Starla in private. Take her to my—"

Starla glared at him and shouted, "You are not worthy of my fealty and you will not torture me for an absurd reason!" She darted into the nearest corridor, ignored shouts for her to halt, and vanished into engulfing darkness. She knew she didn't have much time before Tochar summoned Enforcers and they used lanterns to search for her. She didn't dare to imagine what the vicious *fiendal* would do to her if she was caught. Not even Dagan with all his elite prowess or claims of love could save her from such an enormous and powerful force. *Dagan, my love . . .*

Stop it, Bree, and focus on saving your skin! He's lost to you. She prayed no *Skalds* were lurking nearby, since the cannibalistic mutants were compelled to avoid the sun and favored caves. Her hands found the wall and guided her deeper into the location until she felt it was safe to stop and be rescued. "Cypher, lock on to my coordinates and get me out of here!" she commanded her loyal android. "Be ready to cloak the ship as soon as I'm aboard, then change her location fast."

* * *

Starla paced the bridge deck of her cloaked spacecraft, still tense from a close call with death and the gloomy destruction of her mission. Before she contacted her superior with the bad news, she had to settle down and clear her wits. "I don't understand how a man with his bloodline and status could have turned out so wicked," she mumbled. "Many times he tried to be my companion for private evenings. Many times we've been at the same special functions, even sat together at a few of them. I know his parents; he knows mine; our parents are friends. I'm certain Acharius would have pursued me as a legal mate if I had allowed or coaxed him to do so, but he did not appeal to me in that way."

She halted her aimless movements and asked Cypher, "How could he attempt to slay me like that when he has vowed love for me? My rejection of him was never done in a cold or cruel manner, and he seemed to understand and accept the fact my feelings did not match his."

"My data on human behavior and emotions—in particular, those of *villites*—suggests Acharius panicked and reacted from fear, humiliation, a survival instinct. I deduce his love was not pure, strong, self-sacrificing."

Starla did not want to discuss that emotion, since she had misused and betrayed the one man she claimed to love. She worried about Dagan's safety and survival in light of their intimate relationship, a fact of which Tochar was aware. Would Dagan, she fretted, be imperiled by her actions? If Tochar used *Thorin* on him again, at least the *fiendal* would learn Dagan had no idea about her having another identity or committing treachery. She dared not warn her beloved on the *Adika,* as there was no way he could escape the craft, and contacting him would make him appear to be her accomplice in whatever Tochar suspected her of doing. She would find a way to check on Dagan tomorrow after things settled down on the surface, and, if his life was in jeopardy, she would find a way to rescue him.

Before she changed the subject, she said to Cypher, "Your logic is accurate, as always. When Tochar challenged me after I eliminated Acharius, I reasoned it was reckless for me to stay and attempt to convince him of my false story. Since Acharius was from Maffei, Tochar might have thought to send out my image to someone there who would recognize me, so I couldn't permit myself to be the *fiendal*'s captive if he made that discovery. As long as he enters my image and voice into the network files, only data about Starla Vedris will be accessed and he'll remain ignorant of who I am. With that override command Thaine inserted in all databases, any information about Bree-Kayah Saar will be prevented from being retrieved. I'm vulnerable to exposure only if he shows or sends my image to someone who knows me. I can't return to the surface as Starla, but I don't want Tochar getting too nervous and taking precautions which could hinder the work of the next agent they send to defeat him. With luck, I will have convinced Tochar of my fealty and will prevent him from running another check on me. Auken believed me, so maybe he can convince Tochar I escaped out of anger and a fear of being unable to prove my innocence. It isn't my fault our mission was annihilated; I couldn't have foreseen Acharius's intrusion." In frustration, she slapped her thigh with her palm. "Blast him, Cypher! He's ruined everything we've worked for; we're useless now."

"Have you forgotten about your transmutation identity?" the android asked. "There are things Yana can do and facts she can gather. We can follow the pirates, observe their raids, and record them for evidence."

Starla grasped his metallic hand covered in realistic synthetic flesh. "You're right, Cypher. Our goal is too important for us to give up without first trying other tactics. We must not fail ourselves, our ranks, and our superior." She didn't tell him she also hated to leave Dagan, whose life might be imperiled and who might vanish forever if he left

Tochar's hire to avoid being slain by the *fiendal,* but she suspected the android guessed her additional motive. "I have an ample supply of phials from Yakir, so I can return to the surface as Yana and spy on them. Since Tochar should assume Starla is long gone, and the colony is crowded and busy, and Yana is already known there, no one should pay much attention to her."

She smiled at Cypher and said, "Thanks, my friend, for clearing my head and giving me comfort. After I refresh myself, I will contact Thaine."

Back in her quarters, Starla wondered again if there was a chance she could persuade Dagan Latu to join her side and cause; she pondered if she could trust him if he agreed, and what to do if he attempted to capture her. If she confessed to being both Starla or Yana, would bruised pride and ego cause him to feel as if she had made a fool of him and provoke him to react badly? Did Dagan possess that unpredictable and perilous code of honor and loyalty toward an employer like most of his kind did? By returning to him, even as Yana, she could obtain information about Tochar's actions. In her heart, she knew he was trustworthy, but she would confide in him only if she was given proof she was right.

On the planet's surface, Dagan entered Tochar's dwelling and asked why he had been summoned—almost by force—from his work on Auken's ship. "Sach acted strange when he brought me here. Is there a problem?" He took the *seata* Tochar gestured to and observed the man's odd behavior. He hoped he had not fallen under suspicion for an unknown reason. That dilemma seemed unlikely to him, yet, his gut instinct and keen perceptions warned him that a solar storm was brewing. He feigned an expression of curiosity and calm, but was on alert.

"My response to your question is yes, if—as I do—you consider the treachery of Starla Vedris a problem."

Dagan was taken by surprise and did not conceal his reaction. He stared at Tochar for a few moments and realized the man was serious. His love was being called . . . His heart pounded and his insides twisted in dread. "What are you talking about? There must be some grave misunderstanding. Starla is as loyal to you as the rest of us are."

"I hope that is only a figure of speech, Dagan, since she has revealed herself to be my enemy."

"Your . . . enemy? How can that be? What happened this morning to evoke such an astonishing accusation?"

Tochar related in detail the incident that took place in the cave two *horas* ago. "Despite an intensified quest for her which is still in progress, Starla has managed to elude my men and vanish completely."

Dagan was stunned and alarmed by all Tochar told him of Acharius's accusation of Starla and the shocking incidents that had ensued subsequently. Tochar did reveal how Auken had argued briefly in her favor, until she "proved to him she was guilty."

"Are you positive she's done something wrong?" Dagan asked. "If so, what treacheries did she commit?"

"She looked and behaved culpable before she fled my investigation."

"What if she was telling you the truth like Auken said? If she was convinced you doubted her and intended to harm her, maybe she got scared and panicked. She's only a female, a very young one at that, and alone. I can't imagine her being daring or foolish enough to spy on you. She never acted like she was observing us or stealing information. It sounds incredible that she could have fooled all of us and for so long."

"She did, Dagan, I am certain of it."

The Kalfan knew that an unknown factor was working against Tochar, but his beloved Starla? "How? Why? For whom? What could she have learned and how could she pass on your secrets to anybody?"

"I do not know, but I will after she is captured. You know Starla's skills. Do you think she could make such a blatant mistake as to slay a man by error or in panic? Neither do I," Tochar replied for him. "I know you two became close, so it is time for you to choose between us. Do you know who she was working for or where she would seek a hiding place, on Noy or on another planet?"

"This is a total mystery to me, Tochar; I have no ideas about her guilt or her whereabouts. She never gave me any reason to doubt or suspect her of being anything other than the woman I . . . believed her to be." Dagan made an intentional pause and implied the words he had omitted: loved and trusted, feelings known to the *fiendal* and cognizant a denial of them would cast doubts on him. "My mind's in a daze. It's incredible," he murmured again. He wondered who and what Starla could be: an agent for an alien galactic force who feared the man's increasing power, a hireling for a rival who wanted to seize the man's possessions or one for a disloyal partner, or an innocent ensnared by Tochar's suspicions. How could she have duped a lover and a skilled *I-GAF*er with such ease, if guilty? If not, why had she fled and to what location? Had Tochar harmed her and this was only a cunning ruse to cover his dark deed? If so, Dagan vowed he would punish the *fiendal*. As if he had been analyzing her and the matter, he said, "If what you say is right, we all misjudged her and she's one of the cleverest people alive."

"I never doubted Starla's courage, daring, or prowess; that is why she was working for me. No one has ever deceived me as she has, so her punishment must be severe as an example to others who might be tempted to do the same. I have ordered my contacts to watch for her in Kalfa and Seri in case she reached her ship, fled, and goes to either galaxy. I have given orders to kill her on sight before she

meets with her accomplice. If she is found here, she will
be thrown to the *Skalds*. My Enforcers are guarding my
defense sites, storage caves, and dwelling in the event she
tries to destroy any of them. I am certain she is responsible
for those mysterious incidents, but I do not know yet how
she accomplished it all. My men are searching for her in
the settlement and surrounding area; all chambers in the
cave have already been examined. Her image has been
placed on papers and hung in numerous locations. Anyone
caught hiding or helping her will endure her same fate. I
know you have strong feelings for her, Dagan, but I cannot
permit her to endanger us by divulging the secrets she gathered while working for me."

"Those measures sound harsh and hasty, and I can't help
but hope she isn't guilty; but if she is a betrayer to us, you
have no choice."

"Trust me, Dagan, she is a traitor. Are you going to look
for her?"

Dagan forced out a frown and shook his head. "I'm sure
your men can find her if she's still in Tochara or on Noy.
I'm still in shock; I need a few strong drinks at the Skull's
Den while I let this grim reality settle in. If you or your
contacts elsewhere get your hands on her, I think she should
be questioned before she's terminated. In your position, I'd
want to know who hired her and why, and I'd make certain
she wasn't replaced." *Convince him to keep her alive, Curran, until you or other agents can rescue or arrest her.* "I'll
be more than happy to question her for you. Within five
preons, I'll have answers for you, for me, too. If she duped
and used me and made a fool of me, she'll regret that error.
Blast it all! I should have known better than to mix work
and pleasure. This is the first time I've been blinded like
this, and it won't happen again."

Tochar mused on Dagan's suggestion. "Perhaps you are
right about interrogating her before her death; I will consider it. I hope you will understand why I must speak with

you using *Thorin*. You and Starla were very close, so I have
to make certain you are still loyal."

Dagan eyed him for a *preon* as if vexed, which would be
a normal reaction. "I'm being honest with you; but if that's
how it has to be in this difficult situation, let's get it over
with so I can visit the drinker soon."

Dagan was not surprised by the questions he was asked
during his *Thorin* test. The Kalfan used his immunity to
the truth serum and his cunning to convince Tochar of his
allegedly conflicting emotions. He revealed how he didn't
want to believe the accusations were true, though he admitted they must be because Tochar wouldn't be so positive if he didn't have proof on which to base them. He
related his anger at Starla for using him as a cover for
her own selfish desires, for enticing him to fall in love
with her if she detested men like him and wanted to destroy him along with Tochar. He admitted to being humiliated and furious for not seeing through her ruse; if
she had loved him and wanted to protect him, she would
have confided in him, warned him of peril if she was
exposed. He spoke about how she knew he could be in-
criminated by her actions and slain but she hadn't cared.
He said he might harm her if saw her again, though he
didn't lean toward harming anyone, to which his Dagan
Latu reputation attested. He said he shouldn't have weakened toward a female; he should have held to his opinion
that women were for pleasure, nothing more. The next
time he was in need of sex, he would use Yana or one
of the Pleasure Givers at the Skull's Den, but he wouldn't
become emotionally involved with another woman and
would try to forget the deceitful creature whose treachery
was gnawing at him and evoking an unfamiliar hunger for
cruel revenge.

When Tochar asked him if he knew anything about her

plans against him or who she really was, he responded, "No." And when the leader asked him to speculate on those two areas, Dagan said, "Nothing comes to mind. This seems inconceivable; it's baffling."

Tochar asked him if he had any questions, and he answered, "I want to know who Starla is and who she works for. I want to know why she betrayed Tochar and how she passed multiple *Thorin* tests if she was lying." To which he heard Tochar mutter, "So do I."

Dagan continued as if talking to his lost lover, "Why did you betray me, Starla? How could you make love to me, then endanger me like this? Did you really love me? Was I expendable to you? Why did you do this?"

Dagan was relieved when Tochar halted his lists of queries before he asked again, "Do you believe she is guilty of Tochar's accusations?"

"I'm not sure; I'm too confused to think straight. I guess she wouldn't have run if she didn't have something to hide. If she's innocent, why didn't she stay and ask me to help her prove herself to Tochar?"

"If Tochar cannot give you proof she is guilty, what then?"

"He's my leader. I have to accept his word and agree to his precaution. Dagan Latu is always loyal to the man who hires him."

"Do you love and desire Starla Vedris above everything else?"

"No, there are limits to what a man can do for his woman, unless he is a weakling or a fool. He must not dishonor himself or break his word or crawl on his knees to please her or to win her or even to protect her."

After Tochar completed the draining session, Dagan supposedly recovered on the oblong table before heading for the Skull's Den to appease his woes with strong drink.

* * *

Aboard the *Liska,* Starla contacted Thaine with the grim news about her exposure and how it had occurred. She related how she would remain on the case as Yana and revealed facts about Acharius's treachery and death. She observed Thaine's shock as he listened to the recording of the conversation outside the cave between the two men and the events inside involving her. It was obvious how concerned Thaine was about a Maffeian being an accomplice to Tochar's evil, and the discovery that the *fiendal* had his wicked eye on Trilabs on the planetoid of Darkar.

"At least we now know his Serian contact habitates on the capital planet of Ulux, and that traitor has a helper on the mining planet of Kian; perhaps those will be useful clues to *Raz* Yakir. You must warn him to put his scientists under guard to prevent their abductions." She then voiced an important question to Thaine: "Why did Yakir add new security to the mines and shipments without telling me?"

"I was to relate that news when we communicated after your return from Kalfa. *Raz* Yakir made that decision after Syrkin's evil was laid bare. He reasoned, with both sources cut off, Tochar might become desperate and make mistakes or try to mount a weapon on his ship, which he has plans to do according to what you overheard. Yakir reasoned that during a transfer process, the weapon is vulnerable to destruction."

Starla's voice was firm with conviction. "Not with me exiled from his band and settlement; there's no way that Yana can get near any of those weapons." *But perhaps there is someone who can . . .* "Keep the news about Acharius's death and treason a secret for now. I don't want Tochar to realize it's been reported and suspect I did it. Also tell *Raz* Yakir to use a plausible explanation for placing guards on his scientists; advise him to trust no one with the truth, as his traitor could be a disloyal friend or someone high in his government. It will be useful to me and our cause if Tochar remains confused about who and what I am and whether or not I'm innocent of his suspicions about me."

"Two of Tochar's cohorts are dead, Bree, so you've done an excellent job. You also have destroyed all crystals from previous raids; be proud of your accomplishments, even if they are your last ones there. We need to unmask and terminate accomplice number three in Seri, and Tochar will be without a means to get his hands on more crystals while we seek his defeat."

"But Tochar still has three invincible weapons, Thaine. I don't know how I can get to them and eliminate them, but I'll try; then you can attack. And check out Dagan Latu for me again; see if there is anything in his record to indicate he can be coaxed to join our side. If I can achieve that goal, it will give us someone on the inside, someone who can get to at least one of those weapons during its mounting on Tochar's ship. Then, maybe he and I—with Cypher's help in teleportation—can find a way to eradicate the other two."

"Don't take any unnecessary risks, Bree, or trust Latu without proof."

"I won't. I'll work in Yana's form for as long as possible and keep you informed of my progress and discoveries."

"I'll report these developments and your new strategy to *Raz* Yakir as soon as possible. Now that Tochar is wary, be more alert than ever, Bree."

"I will, Thaine. Please tell my family I love them and miss them."

That same night in his abode on Noy, Dagan pondered the mystery surrounding Starla. If she wasn't who and what she claimed to be, how could he discover the truth? He recalled her mock salute on her ship during his visit there, remembered she had no fingerprints to expose her; he reflected on her astute mind and countless skills. If she was an agent or enemy hireling, how had she duped him so

easily? Or had he been too blinded by love for her to notice
the clues she dropped or the slips she made, if there were
any? Why, if she loved him as she vowed, hadn't she confided in him? If she was innocent and merely had panicked,
or if Tochar had harmed her as the *fiendal* had done to his
family *yings* ago, Dagan swore he would slay Tochar with
his bare hands. One of the reasons he had become an *I-GAF*
agent was to find a way to get to Tochar, but their paths
had not converged until this mission. Yet, he reasoned, if
Tochar had killed her, why was the *fiendal* so furious and
unsettled and eager to find her? He worried about Starla's
survival, but he couldn't desert his mission to go search for
her, and, though tempted, lacked the means to do so. He
just wished he knew if she were alive and safe somewhere.

If only there was a way, he mused, she could contact him
to explain her actions and to appease his fears. Suddenly
he realized there was: she had a ship with an android who
could transport her into and out of his chamber. *If* she had
the coordinates. Coming to him in that manner wouldn't be
any more hazardous to him than the predicament their relationship had placed him in. Maybe her love was false and
his usefulness was past. But he didn't want to think along
that tormenting line.

He had contacted his superior earlier and told Phaedrig
the incredible news. He had asked Phaedrig to investigate
the matter, to find her if possible, and to hold her for his
interrogation. Yet, when a response had come only *preons*
ago, it had revealed that only her Starla Vedris record was
retrieved when all data bases were accessed. That seemed
impossible unless she had told him and Tochar the truth . . .
He was relieved that Phaedrig had put his men on alert to
watch for her and her ship, especially at Karteal, but he
couldn't relax until the enigma was solved.

At least his identity and assignment were safe and he
would be sent on further raids where he might gather evidence to defeat the *nefariant*. He would concentrate on that,

as there was nothing he could do about Starla until she
reappeared. He hoped that she wasn't on Noy and within
Tochar's reach. If so, there was no way he or her side could
rescue her, not with him being outnumbered by *villites* and
not with those *Destructoids* preventing an attack by her
friends.

The next morning, Starla teleported to Yana's dwelling
and gave the place a more lived-in appearance in case she
had visitors while using that identity on a frequent basis.
Afterward, Yana strolled around in the busiest area of the
settlement and went to the Skull's Den to observe the continued search for Starla Vedris. She saw the old-time
"wanted posters" and heard Radu and others talking about
the threats against anyone who befriended her. She chatted
with the rotund alien from Mu so she would be familiar
with the alleged facts about her treachery and escape. She
hoped Dagan would arrive soon so she could witness how
he was reacting to the shocking news. She wanted to see
if Dagan would turn to Yana or another woman to ease his
anguish and to pretend to others he wasn't hurting deeply
from her betrayal.

When she was left alone with Radu for a short time, Yana
asked in a whisper, "How is Dagan taking such a terrible
situation?"

The speckle-faced alien with rippled forehead was aware
of the Asisan beauty's interest in Dagan and also knew Dagan had seemed to stop seeing Yana after he became close
with Starla. "He was in here last night, drinking heavily
and brooding. He sat alone in a corner for *horas*. I think
he is as confused by the incredible event as others are. I
have known Starla for *malees* and believed her to be trustworthy. Tochar has not revealed the charges against her, but
they must be serious for him to order her death."

She noted a gleam of concern in his gray eyes, one seemingly mixed with disbelief and affection, and his reaction touched her heart. "I wonder why Tochar does not want her captured and questioned. Papers hanging around the colony say she can be slain on sight, or stunned and captured."

"If I were Starla, I would prefer death to capture and torture. It is said that Tochar is strict and harsh where enemies are concerned." He leaned closer across the bar and warned, "Never provoke him to anger."

Yana nodded understanding. "I have seen Starla many times, but we have never spoken; yet, from watching her at a distance, I cannot imagine what horrid deeds she committed to so enrage her leader. It is known she was one of Tochar's special team members, one of his elite *spacekis*. Do you think Dagan would imperil himself to help her if she's captured?"

Radu shook his head. "Dagan Latu is not a fool. To an adventurer and rogue like him, survival and honor come first."

Yana daintily took a sip of her drink before she murmured, "I wonder if he would resent my approaching him to offer comfort and friendship. Perhaps he will trust no female after being shamed and hurt."

Radu grinned. "A ravishing and interesting woman like you is just what he needs to help him forget Starla."

Yana smiled as if that opinion pleased her and to imply she still found the Kalfan desirable. "Thank you, Radu; you give good advice, my friend. I am fortunate to know you during my stay on Noy." *Fortunate to have a source of information like you and a safe place to conduct observations.*

"How much longer will you be here?"

"Perhaps one *malee;* I doubt more than two. Matters are slowly resolving themselves at home, so I hope to return there soon. But I shall miss you after my departure, and I will not leave without saying farewell."

Radu smiled before he left her to serve several men who entered.

In her Yana guise, Starla felt safe and confident against discovery; and Cypher was on standby to rescue her at the first sign of peril. Yet, tension and remorse nibbled at her nerves as she planned her next move, the difficult task of confronting her lost lover without letting her true emotions show.

Dagan opened the door to his chamber, stared at the Asisan beauty standing there, and asked, "What are you doing here, Yana?"

"I wanted to make certain you aren't suffering too badly."

He noticed the look of empathy in her crystal-blue eyes and heard it in her voice, but he wasn't in the mood to talk with her or to accept such seemingly authentic kindness. For a wild moment he had hoped it was Starla in his chamber, but knew it was too dangerous for her to visit him. "Suffering over what?" he asked, irritable from lack of sleep and worry, and from unaccustomed libation of too much strong drink last night.

Yana studied his annoyed reaction at seeing her. She had refused to use the pheromone to weaken him, at least this time. "The betrayal and loss of Starla Vedris."

Dagan grabbed her arm, yanked her inside, and demanded, "What do you know about Starla and me?"

She ignored his firm grip on her arm, one with pale-blue skin in this form. She softened her startled blue gaze and in a gentle tone—a voice so different from Starla's—replied, "It isn't a secret, Dagan. Everyone has been warned not to give her help or to conceal her; anyone caught doing so will be terminated, thrown to the *Skalds* for food. Talk spread fast about her alleged perfidy and disappearance. I was visiting with Radu and heard plenty from him and others in the Skull's Den. I'm sorry she hurt you."

Dagan caught the use of her word "alleged" and wondered why she had used it, but didn't ask. "I'm not in torment, Yana; I've survived worse incidents. It isn't fatal to lose one's relationship partner. I'll find another woman when I'm ready for diversion or sexual gratification."

"You don't have to lie to me, Dagan; you loved her; you told me so."

Dagan narrowed his gaze and asked in a gruff tone, "Did someone send you here to examine me or to give me comfort?"

"No, I came because I am concerned about you. This incident is strange, and many are whispering about it. Those who knew her are . . . mystified and dismayed by what sounds like . . . an incomprehensible occurrence. Our paths have not crossed, but her reputation and my sightings of her do not match what this situation implies."

Dagan was intrigued by her pauses and word choices, and amazed by her revelations. "That's dangerous talk, Yana, if it's reported to Tochar."

"I know, but I thought you should know how others feel. I do not believe you are the kind of man who would imperil me for telling you. What will you do if she comes to you for help?"

Dagan backed Yana against the wall and pinned her voluptuous body there with his. "I don't want to discuss Starla Vedris with you or anyone; not ever, understand? She was beautiful and satisfying, but she duped us; she wasn't for real, and I detest pretenders and despise being used. If we ever meet again, she'll be sorry she pulled me into her little scheme. If she expected to turn Tochar and others against me and get me killed, she failed, because he trusts me completely, and is right to do so. I don't want to hear anything else about your suspicions or those of anyone else or I'll be forced to report them to Tochar." *Tell the fiendal that, if he's the one who sent you!*

"I'm sorry if I've angered or offended you, Dagan; that was not my intention. I can help you forget her, if you'll allow me to do so. I swear to you I am a loyal friend."

Dagan released her and stepped backward. "Thanks for the generous and kind offer, Yana, but I'm not in the mood for this kind of talk right now. Please leave before I say or do something I'll regret."

"May I return in a few *deegas* to visit with you? As friends, if that's all you want. You helped me in a time of trouble, so I would like to help you."

Dagan reasoned he might need Yana as a cover against being implicated as Starla's accomplice or as a source of information, so he replied, "You can come see me again, but give me a few *deegas* alone."

She sent him a glowing smile and nodded. At least he hadn't turned to the alluring creature yet, and he did give her the impression he was hurting inside. Twinges of guilt chewed at her and desire blazed within her as she returned to Yana's dwelling.

That same evening, Dagan was warned by a message from Phaedrig that somebody in Seri and in Maffei had retrieved data from Dagan Latu's file by accessing the official network using an untraceable frequency and the correct password again, which meant the encroachers were in positions of power. His superior had been alerted by the cue Phaedrig had inserted to call his attention to any time an undercover *I-GAF* agent was checked out, but the procedures were carried out and terminated too fast for him to reach a terminal to determine their origins. Phaedrig was concerned about the intruders' motives and Dagan's safety. He asked Dagan if he should be extracted via a fake trading vessel or if he wanted to stay and bluff it out; the resolute agent said he would complete his assignment.

Dagan wondered if one check was done by Tochar's accomplice in Seri and the second by another contact in Maffei. Tochar had asked during his *Thorin* test if he knew Acharius from Caguas, so Dagan had asked Phaedrig to run a surreptitious probe on the Maffeian. It was possible that Acharius and/or Tochar had an additional conspirator in that same galaxy. Since he had been subjected to truth serum again, he was surprised they would remain suspicious of him, though he'd had an intimate and close connection to Starla. Perhaps they were simply making certain he was loyal before drawing him deeper into their band.

Perhaps Starla was an agent of some type or the hireling of a rival. He was aware her ship had cloaking ability but she couldn't linger nearby for very long without supplies and surely wouldn't be so reckless as to make an appearance to get them. But if she had lingered, he mused, would she come to him? If so, what would her story be? If she had deluded Tochar several times, she was immune to *Thorin.* . . . Then his speculations took a wild turn: What if the same was true of Yana? What if Starla and Yana were confederates? That would explain why Yana had backed away from him without causing trouble and why Yana seemingly had defended Starla to him. . . . Or perhaps the two women were working for the same person without each other's awareness. That would be a cunning and unsuspected ruse: two females assigned to defeat Tochar.

"Who, where, and what are you, Starla?" he murmured. "And you, Yana, there's no info available on you. Perhaps I should draw you closer, my seductive Asisan, and see what I can extract from you."

Cypher summoned Starla to her ship that night to communicate with *Raz* Yakir, galactic ruler of Seri, the man who had initiated this mission, one of two men who had selected her for this critical and perilous task, the man who had gifted her with the transmutation ability and chemical.

Starla listened to his astonishing words, then asked, "What do you mean, there's another agent working on this assignment, one from *I-GAF?* Why wasn't I informed about such an important fact? Who is he?"

"I do not know who the *I-GAF* agent is," *Raz* Yakir's voice wavered not at all in indecision, "their identities and missions records are inaccessible to me, to everyone except members of that force. I do not know if it is a male or a female. I do not know if the agent has been in Tochar's band for a long time, or if one arrived after you did and joined it, or if one has yet to infiltrate it. I was away resting when Supreme Commander Sanger tried to contact me, and he could not reach me until I returned late this *deega*. When Thaine related what had occurred there, I knew I should reveal this fact to you. There is no reason for you to further endanger yourself, Bree-Kayah; return home and allow the *I-GAF* agent to handle the mission from henceforth."

"I don't want to quit and leave, sir," Starla said in an emotion-choked voice, "this mission is too crucial to both of our worlds. I can still observe and gather facts in my Yana disguise."

"Do so only if your life and safety are not imperiled. You have done a superior job for us so far and I do not want to see you harmed. I have great respect and affection for you and I trust you without question or hesitation."

"Thank you, sir, but why didn't you tell me about the other agent?"

"I had selected you and planned your mission before the ruler of Kalfa asked for an *I-GAF* agent to be assigned to defeating Tochar and recovering the stolen crystals and weapons. I know the *I-GAF* is in charge of solving intergalactic crimes and pursuing intergalactic *villites,* but I wanted someone working solely for me on this vital matter. It is obvious there is a traitor high in my rulership and I—with the help of my agent—must be the one to expose and punish him. I also believe there is a better chance of success if separate agents are on the job, and without each other's knowledge so they cannot influence each other's findings or jeopardize each other's role. I want a fast resolution to this problem because of the value, power, and danger of moonbeams in the wrong hands and to prevent a flood of them across the nearest galaxies."

Yakir took a deep breath before he continued. "I believe a second agent—mine—can gather clues their agent misses or ignores. After I was informed of the other agent's assignment, mine was already on the case. I feared if I extracted you when you were already in place and the *I-GAF* agent was either exposed or killed, all progress would be lost; and that despicable *fiendal* would be on alert to an investigation and would anticipate the agent's replacement and make it impossible. I chose you because I think a woman might make discoveries a man cannot, because a gentle female would attract less suspicion. And, my pride is involved, Bree-Kayah. I feel a loss of control in my own responsibilities if I allow an *I-GAF* agent to be in total charge when it is my world and rulership being attacked and weakened. My pride urges me to be the one to solve the crimes committed against Seri because the *villites* dared to steal from us and because one of my subjects has betrayed me and my people. I ask your forgiveness for withholding this secret from you."

"I understand your motives, sir, and I agree with them. Does Thaine know of this other agent's existence?"

"He was informed at the same time I was, but I requested he keep that news to himself and he obeyed. When we spoke earlier, I told him I would reveal the secret to you. I considered asking Dauld Phaedrig to let his agent contact Yana and allow you two to work together. That way he would know I have one there and will learn about our shapeshifting secret. Since we do not know the identities of all traitors but we do know they are men in elite positions, I fear what might happen to you if the wrong person intercepted my message to him and learned of Yana's existence and location. I am certain Commander Phaedrig will be annoyed with me for taking the action I have and for failing to inform him about it, but, after all, I am the ruler of Seri and it is my right, my duty. There is also the possibility that Commander Phaedrig will want you off the mission and away from Noy; he could order his agent to expose Yana to force you to leave and let *I-GAF* handle the case. What action do you think I should take, Bree-Kayah?"

"In my opinion, sir, we should keep Phaedrig unenlightened for the time being, and I should continue to work here as Yana. Perhaps I can uncover his agent's identity and decide if it would be productive for us to work as a team. I already suspect who the agent might be, but I will not approach him to join forces until I am certain. I will keep you and Thaine informed of my progress."

"That is acceptable to me, Bree-Kayah, and I will inform your superior of our decision. Be careful, and withdraw any time you feel your Yana identity has been imperiled. I also have great admiration and esteem for your parents and I do not want to be the cause of their daughter's death; even this monumental mission's success is not worth the cost of your life."

"I will be careful, sir, and thank you for confiding in me and for your kind words about me and my parents. Both spoke highly of you when I was approached about taking this assignment. Bree-Kayah Saar out."

Starla and Cypher discussed the ruler's revelations and her plans for the following *deega* before she returned to Yana's dwelling on Noy. She got little sleep that night as she speculated on the *I-GAF* agent's identity. She hoped and prayed it was Dagan Latu and that was how he had passed his *Thorin* tests, but that could be wishful thinking. Tomorrow she would test her wild theory, after she inspected the cave where she had slain Acharius and escaped Tochar's revenge. Surely by now, it had been searched and eliminated and deserted.

Fifteen

Cypher transported Starla to Yana's dwelling after a rapid examination of the cave where she found nothing unusual among the stolen items stored there. After shapeshifting into her Yana guise, she prepared herself for a momentous visit with Dagan Latu. She attired herself in a multicolored garment that ended just above her knees and bared her shoulders, arms, and chest. The skirt had a slight flare below her hips, a fitted waist, and full bodice. A stretchy band at the neckline and thin straps held the top in place. Her feet were clad in sandals with ties which overlapped several times before they were secured above her calves. The cosmetics she selected enhanced the shade of Yana's eyes and the pale-blue tint to Yana's flesh. Thick and wavy golden hair with a faint blue tinge flowed midway down her back. She splashed on a fragrant scent but avoided using the phero-mone, as there was no intent to dupe or entice Dagan on this occasion. She fastened the neck ring at the base of her throat, one of its "gems" a miniaturized transmitter to keep her in touch with the android in case of an emergency.

Starla gazed at her Asisan image and took a deep breath. She closed her eyes for a moment to pray her perceptions about Dagan were right, as that would put her lover within her reach, then contacted her android. "I'm ready, Cypher, and leaving for his chamber. Stay alert but do not interfere unless I signal you by saying, 'This is futile and I want to leave,' then beam me out without delay." She knew her longtime companion heard her order but could not respond since the neck unit was a one-way device. She checked the *lazette* strapped to her right thigh beneath the garment to make certain it was set on *stun,* not *terminate,* as she doubted she could slay the man she loved for any reason. If he failed to prove he was an *I-GAF* agent, she would not expose her true identity or Starla form, so eliminating him as a threat would be unnecessary.

Dagan stared at Yana in shock. "Why did you return this soon? I thought we agreed you would not come again for a few *deegas.*"

"I had to see you, Dagan. May I come inside for a few *preons?*"

"Why?" he persisted. He was cognizant—and suspicious—of the absence of her previous magical and irresistible allure, an unnatural weakness which still vexed him. Until he knew the truth about his lost love, he couldn't initiate even a casual affair with Yana to assure Tochar of his fealty. He hoped one wouldn't become necessary, and dreaded making that repulsive decision. He had never misused a female before during a mission, yet, he was certain Yana was somehow connected to this situation, and a great deal was at stake: the safety of the United Federation of Galaxies.

"I must speak with you in private; it is important, very important."

Dagan caught the urgency to her words, so he stepped back and allowed her to enter his chamber. He followed her to where she halted near the room's waist-high partition that separated the sitting and eating areas. He saw her lean against it, as if requiring the divider's support. "Well?"

"Does Starla know the truth about you?"

Dagan was baffled by the unexpected query, and realized

his reaction was evident to her. "I didn't tell her about us, but somebody else may have. Why is that important?"

"I didn't mean the truth about us; she knew that fact."

Dagan's dark-blue gaze widened in surprise, then narrowed. "You told her about our one encounter?" Was that why Starla hadn't trusted him and confided in him, he wondered, or returned to make certain Tochar hadn't slain him, because she doubted his love and commitment to her?

"No, she told me after it happened."

His alert heightened. "But you said you two weren't acquainted."

"I thought it best not to reveal we are, given the danger of that fact. I wouldn't want to induce Tochar to investigate and shadow me."

"Why is that, Yana? Do you have something hazardous to conceal?"

"I have my reasons which I will explain later."

"Have you seen or spoken to Starla since this trouble began?"

"She disappeared from everyone's sight following that cave incident."

Dagan realized Yana had chosen her words with care, a response he deduced was a lie. "What else did Starla tell you? When?"

"The same *deega* you discarded me, she asked me to leave you alone because she loves you and had created a special bond with you."

"Starla told you she's in love with me?"

"Yes, and I believed her."

"Her treachery and connection to me could have gotten me killed, but she didn't bother to confide in me or even warn me of my imminent peril, so she has a strange way of proving that love."

"Just as you failed to prove your trust and love to her by withholding the truth about yourself and why you really came to Noy."

Dagan tensed. "What 'truth' are you referring to, Yana?"

"That you're an *I-GAF* agent working to defeat Tochar and his band; that you're immune to *Thorin* and that's how you duped him during tests."

"Where did you get such a reality-impaired idea like that?" Dagan sneered. "Who sent you here on such a ridiculous quest?"

"You can trust me completely, Dagan, or whatever your name is. If you wish to exchange facts on this matter, you must prove yourself to me."

"What are you trying to pull, Yana? I'm no *I-GAF* agent, nor a *Seki*."

She fused her confident gaze to his cynical one. "Yes, Dagan Latu, you are. Before I tell you everything I've learned about Tochar, you must prove your identity to me, prove my positive assessment of you is correct."

"What do you mean?"

She lifted his right hand and said, "Show me your *I-GAF* badge and I can tell you facts which will help you carry out your mission. Perhaps we can work together to defeat Tochar, unless you prefer to work alone."

"I work for Tochar, so why would I want to crush him?"

"Because he is evil and he must not obtain more moonbeams. With your help, perhaps we can shatter the white crystals in his *Destructoids* as I did with the others his *spacekis* stole during raids," she revealed to coax out the admission she needed. She knew she was exposing more than she had intended for Yana to relate this soon, but she felt he would have halted her probe by now if she was wrong about him.

Dagan took a few steps away from her, propped himself on the *seata*'s back, and stared at her. "Who are you, Yana? What are you? Why did you really come here with this preposterous accusation?"

"First, earn my trust by confirming my theory is accurate. I have already told you more than is safe if I am mistaken about you. I can proceed no further until you verify your identity."

Could Yana, he mused, be the unknown factor instead of Starla, as he had concluded this morning? "First," he countered in a sarcastic tone, "prove I should trust you by telling me how you seduced me so easily."

Without hesitation, she said, "With a spray which is a mixture of a heady aphrodisiacal fragrance and the ancient Kalfan mating pheromone. I know your species does not physically produce it anymore but your males are still susceptible to it, and it is sold and used in mating problem cases."

Dagan frowned. "So, it was a trick as I suspected. You're lucky I don't strangle you for using me like a sex slave. I'll warn you now, woman, don't try it again. Now, tell me why did you select me to ensnare?"

"Because you aren't like the others, riffraff of the Cosmos; and I needed help, a means of obtaining information about Tochar and his raids, possible protection if exposed. And I also found you irresistible."

Dagan ignored her last sentence and focused on her others. "You didn't learn anything useful from me, so you wasted your time and charms."

"No time spent with you was wasted; I enjoy you and your company." She noted his tense expression. "Relax, I'm not here to seduce you; that facet of our relationship is over by your insistence."

Despite her words, Dagan saw a gleam of desire in her blue gaze. "If I am an *I-GAF* agent, why did you wait until now to ask me to work with you?"

"I learned only *horas* ago there is an *I-GAF* agent on assignment here and surmised it is you; that is why I returned to speak with you. If I'm wrong, and I pray I am not, I'll have to slay you," she warned as she aimed the *lazette* at his heart. "Now that I have confided in you, I can't allow you to endanger me and my mission."

Dagan eyed the weapon and the way she held it, which told him she knew how to use it. But would she? The impassive expression in her blue eyes did not answer for him. He scolded himself for underestimating her prowess and placing himself at a disadvantage. "Why do you think it's me?"

"For many reasons, most of them impossible to explain, gut instinct I suppose. As a skilled and seasoned agent, you know we depend upon our intuition and perceptions as much as our training and experiences. Well, do we have a bargain? Do we make a profitable exchange? Do we work together, or separately if you prefer, to destroy Tochar?"

"You still didn't tell me who and what you are, and what you know about Starla. Is she alive and unharmed?" He had so many questions to ask her. "Did Tochar tell the truth about her betraying him and what exactly did she do to provoke him? Does she work with you or for the same person? Where is she? Who and what is she?"

She was elated by his concern over Starla's fate. "I promise to reveal everything about me and all I know after I make certain you are what I hope and believe you are. My lips are sealed until you do."

"Didn't you overlook one enormous hazard?" he asked with a chuckle. "Computer, do not open the exit door except by my voice command, seal all windows, and respond to requests made only in my voice. If I don't cancel those orders within one *hora,* shut down the environmental control system." He focused a challenging gaze on Yana and said, "Now, you'll answer my questions. If you shoot me, you can't get out of here alive."

Yana holstered her *lazette* and laughed softly. "Shall we see who runs out of air and relents first? I'm not afraid of you or of death, Dagan; if I must sacrifice my life in the line of duty and for such a crucial goal, I will do so. There's nothing you can do or say to extract the truth from me until I see your badge, and I know how that procedure works so

I can't be fooled. If you doubt my words and determination, let's sit down and wait until we can't breathe and you comprehend I am serious."

She finally had him convinced. "Yes, Yana. I know you're serious."

"Now that I'm your captive and I can't leave without your permission, what harm could it do to reveal the truth about yourself? Unless you release me, who could I tell about you?"

"How do I know you're trustworthy, despite what you've revealed?"

"You certainly can't ask Koteas, Terin, or Syrkin. Phaedrig couldn't tell you who I was when you checked on me; that was sneaky stealing my fingerprints and voice pattern, though they failed to be useful. You also checked on Starla, and I know what you learned about her. I wonder what Tochar would do if he discovered how you passed his *Thorin* tests. *I-GAF* agents are protected against truth serum by *Rendelar.* That's how you deceived him about yourself. I also have had the *Rendelar* procedure, so neither you nor Tochar nor Phaedrig can extract anything from me, not even with torture. The only way you'll receive answers to your queries is by being worthy of them. Since I am your prisoner, you have nothing to lose by confiding in me, but there is much you can gain by trusting me."

Little by little, comprehension dawned on him. "So, you're the one who fed those clues into our computer network. How did you obtain our secret entry code and gather those facts? How did you carry out those incidents with the crystals?"

Joy and relief flooded her as he half admitted to her supposition. "Soon, I'll tell you everything you want to know. The insignia, Dagan," she reminded him. When he remained silent and watchful, she added, "In case you think you can trick or frighten me, you're mistaken. I don't need you to release me from your chamber." With speed and nimble fingers, the weapon was in her hand once more, aimed at him. "This *lazette* is powered by a moonbeam that can cut through any material, including your walls."

"So, you tricked me again."

"I hoped thinking I was your captive would relax you into complying. I don't like deceiving you, Dagan, but you're being stubborn. Can't you see I'm telling you the truth? Use those keen wits of yours! This matter is grave, more important than either of our lives. Please relent."

Dagan studied her for a moment before he pulled a disk from his belt and held it over his right hand. His pressed the top surface to release the needed chemical. He set the disk aside and used his left forefinger to spread a clear liquid from knuckles to wrist and from thumb to outside edge. He watched Yana's gaze remain fastened to his flesh as the symbol seemed to materialize as if by magic. He was confused and surprised when tears misted her blue eyes and an expression of delight claimed her face. He lifted his fist and held it before his chin. "Satisfied?" he asked as he watched her stare at the authoritative emblem he'd exposed.

Her softened gaze traveled from his hand to his blue eyes. "So, I was right about you all along; you are a good and trustworthy man."

"Am I?" Dagan retorted as he used a second chemical to conceal his badge. "If you trust me, turn over that *lazette* and tell me everything."

She saw his gaze widen in astonishment when she held the weapon out to him, smiled, and asked, "Can I wet my throat first? Now that I've seen your *I-GAF* mark"—she said for Cypher's benefit—"we have a long talk ahead of us." When an astounded Dagan didn't take the proffered weapon, she set it down on the counter as she fetched a drink. "Want anything?"

"The truth will be nice," he quipped, flopping on the *seata.*

"Perhaps you should sit down before I shock you," she advised as she sipped the liquid from one of Yakir's phials with her back to him.

"I am seated. I want to hear every detail. Get to talking, woman."

"Just keep silent and watch for a few *preons,* then you'll understand." She observed Dagan as he gaped at her during her transmutation into Starla Vedris. Twice during the metamorphic process, he blinked his eyes and shook his head as if he doubted his sanity. Afterward, she said, "My real name is Bree-Kayah Saar. I was assigned by Supreme Commander Thaine Sanger of Maffei Star Fleet and *Raz* Yakir of Seri to defeat Tochar and the traitors in Kalfa and Seri and to destroy his crystals and weapons." She halted for a while to allow that shocking information to be absorbed.

Dagan's gaze roamed her flushed face and he looked into her pleading green eyes. She was alive and safe; she was an agent, not a real *villite.* She was within close proximity, but he could not reach out to her yet, much as he yearned to do so. She was . . . Yana. She had duped him . . . He needed time to clear his wits, to get answers, to ascertain her feelings about him. The name which sounded like "Zar" was familiar to him, as were those of Sanger and Yakir. "Are you related to Varian and Jana Saar?"

"I am their youngest daughter, a Star Fleet officer, a member of our elite and secret squad. Cypher-T is my longtime partner. You could not access Bree-Kayah's file because the network computers were commanded to respond with my Starla Vedris identity. No record exists on Yana, and her voice print does not match mine. I have no fingerprints to expose me."

"How can you shapeshift into a woman so different from your real self?"

"Yakir provided me with the chemical for transformation;

it lasts for twelve *horas* unless I use the antidote to return me to my form sooner. This is my true appearance," she told him as he studied her brown hair and green eyes and less voluptuous figure. "My image and voice pattern were programmed to respond only to queries about Starla Verdris in all data bases to prevent Tochar or his contacts from discovering who I am; at this time, all files on Bree-Kayah Saar are protected against retrieval by a special command cue. We didn't know a Maffeian traitor was working with him and would imperil me. After I reported my exposure to Thaine and Yakir and told them I would remain on the mission as Yana, Yakir told me an *I-GAF* agent had infiltrated Tochar's band, but he didn't know his chosen name or description. I took a chance—I hoped and prayed—it was you."

"You're Maffeian; that's how Acharius recognized you."

"When Acharius saw me in the cave, he must have panicked because he tried to kill me. I dealt with him the only way left open to me. I tried to bluff it out with Tochar so I could save my mission, but he didn't believe my explanation." She related the cave episode in detail and how Acharius knew her. "I wanted to disable Acharius, rather than slay him, but my weapon didn't have a setting to induce a coma to keep him silent about me."

"Is that what you did to Moig?"

"I did induce a coma after I questioned him with *Thorin;* that's how I learned about Syrkin and other things. But Tochar murdered him; I have the tape aboard my ship to prove it. Cypher-T logs everything I witness and he follows us on most of our treks to observe and record those crimes."

"Since you didn't know who I was until last night, how did I fit into your plans? Why did you tempt me and use me as two different women?"

"I tried to ignore and resist you, Dagan, but you made that impossible by pursuing and tempting me. I'm sorry I was forced to deceive you; I wanted to confide in you, but

I feared I was blinded by my feelings for you and couldn't make an accurate evaluation of you. How could I trust you when you kept passing Tochar's *Thorin* tests and you evoked raids on Sion and that medical supply ship and convinced me you were a *villite?* You also took me by surprise; I never expected to encounter a complication like you and I didn't know how to deal with that unfamiliar predicament; this was the first time I've allowed my emotions to sway me during a mission. After I got to know you, I was hoping to lure you away from your criminal life so we could share that future you offered. As Yana, I was appraising your true nature and character. I suppose, since you're an *I-GAF* agent on assignment, you were probably just using Starla to get close to Tochar and the others."

He smiled and shook his head. "You also caught me off-guard and I was wary about confiding in you, but I didn't lie to you about my feelings."

"You didn't?" she asked, afraid to trust her hearing.

"I was enduring the same agonizing dilemma you were because you were convincing as a *spaceki,* but I couldn't resist you. I kept trying to coax you away from Tochar and Noy so you'd be safe from harm and incrimination. Do you truly love me, Starla?"

"Yes, Dagan; with all my heart and soul. I was hoping there was some way I could save you so we could be together later, but I feared I couldn't entice Dagan Latu away from what I believed you were."

Dagan pulled her into his arms as he said, "I was right to pursue and tempt you because you are the perfect match for me. I love you with all my heart and soul, and we will have a future together after this mission is over."

Their tender gazes locked and communicated their feelings as they exchanged smiles and savored the wonder of their new relationship. Their eyes sparkled as if reflecting rays of moonbeams. They knew their fates and hearts were entwined.

Dagan secured her in a cherished embrace, as if needing to convince himself Starla was alive and within his arms. His heart surged with love and relief. He brushed kisses over her forehead, the scent of her clean brown hair entering his nostrils. His lips traversed her exquisite cheekbones, the length of her slender nose, and the curve of her chin. He used a cleanly shaved jawline to nuzzle her face, savoring the texture of her skin. He looked into her green eyes whose gaze was filled with undeniable emotions which matched his own potent ones. More talk could come later; for now, all he wanted to do was to hold her, to kiss her, to feel her heart beating next to his, to give thanks to the Supreme Being for the radical change in their destinies. *She's not out of your reach* kept racing through his head at lightning speed. Despite knowing that was true, he almost feared to believe it, as if accepting that reality would cause it to vanish.

"You can't imagine how scared I was about coming here to expose the truth to you. I don't know what I would have done if I'd been wrong about you." She laughed and jested, "I would have been forced to take you captive, transport you to my ship, and hold you prisoner there. Naturally you would have been compelled to relent to my every whim." Her eyes brightened with radiant passion.

He cupped her face between his hands and noted the seductive gleam in her merry gaze. His responsive body flamed with desire. "With you as my captor, I would have made an excellent and obedient love slave."

"Would have made?" she echoed and nibbled on his cleft chin.

Dagan lifted her right hand and placed suckling kisses on each fingertip. He pressed its back to his lips for it to be covered; then swirled his tongue in her palm. His mouth trekked over her wrist, along her arm, past her shoulder, up her neck, and teased at her earlobe.

Starla swayed against him and coaxed him to continue

his sensuous course of action. Her fingers grazed his broad shoulders, the cords in his neck, and the bulges in his arms. His skin was cool to her touch, soft and supple flesh encased by a rock-hard and strong frame. She closed her eyes and let her senses absorb every enthralling facet of him. She meshed her lips to his and clung to him.

Many times Dagan's tongue delved her mouth and savored her honeyed taste. His loins throbbed with an intense need to join with hers, but he didn't want to rush this heady reunion. His shaky hands untangled the tie at her waist and removed the one-piece garment and cast it aside. They wriggled down her panties, exposing her every charm to his adoring gaze. He took off her sandals, then stood before her. He paused only a moment to allow her to peel off his stretchy shirt before he brought their bare torsos into staggering contact. His mouth dropped kisses on her neck as it journeyed to one creamy breast to nibble there teasingly until his mouth fastened to the point and suckled it to taut attention.

Starla's hands roved his neck and stroked his black hair. Her insides quivered with anticipation and her body warmed with pleasure. She craved every sensation he evoked and enjoyed every emotion she experienced. She adored everything about him. Her senses were alive, yet, dazed. She was delighted, yet, tormented. *Pralu,* she loved him!

"If we don't lie down soon, Dagan, I'm going to melt into the floor," she gasped. "My legs are so weak and shaky I can hardly stand."

He chuckled and said, "I'm glad I'm not the only one who feels that way."

Dagan halted his loving siege to remove the rest of his garments and to relocate them to the *sleeper.* His provocative hand inched down her body and teased over her sleek thighs with sweeping and tantalizing strokes. He summoned everything he knew about lovemaking to give her supreme gratification. His mouth and hands explored her, evoking another hunger as soon as he fed the previous one.

Her stomach grew taut as his hands sought and found her secret haven and blissfully invaded it. She burned and yearned, using words and movements to plead for his deft caresses to continue. She reveled in the way his hands and lips made her feel wild and greedy. She relaxed and tensed simultaneously. His searing kisses and artful caresses sent all remnants of distracting reality fleeing. His adroit hand was clever and persistent as it pervaded her delicate folds, pulsing nub, and moist receptacle. Her hand captured his rigid manhood and stroked it imaginatively from tip to base. The friction created enticed him to groan and squirm in need.

At her fervid encouragement, Dagan positioned himself between her thighs and entered her with one vital thrust. She was more beautiful than *Kimon,* the mythical Goddess of Love and Beauty. Her skin was as soft as *majee,* an expensive and luxurious material. Her taste was sweeter than *corvie,* an exotic and rare fruit. How he loved her!

Starla kneaded his firm buttocks. She lapped her ankles over his calves and held him in a snug grip. That marvelous tension was building within her womanhood. Sheer rapture washed over her from head to feet and she felt weightless in space, almost spinning out of control. Never had she loved anyone more than this man. Never had she wanted anything more than she wanted this magnificent Kalfan. She surrendered totally to him and to the splendor of their new beginning, the sealing of their bond.

As her hands roved the rippling muscles of his back and he penetrated her over and over, she played havoc with his control, boldly and seductively threatening to steal it. As he entered her, she moved to receive him. As he retreated, she moaned at his loss and her uplifted hips quested for him. He was driven wild by the way her tongue danced with his and she rubbed her bosom against his chest, her nipples as hot as two tiny suns scorching his flesh. "Starla, my love, you're driving me wild," he warned in fiery delight, "shoving me dangerously close to the edge. *Kahala,* this is amazing."

Starla moaned and thrashed as she climbed the beckoning spiral upward. "Take me, Dagan, my beloved, now," she begged.

He increased his lunging pace to a gentle savageness, his need and love for her so great and her responses so urgent he could barely restrain his ardor and prevent his release. "I love you, Starla. You're mine; at last you're truly mine, and I belong only to you."

His words and actions sent Starla falling over the crest of victory. Her cry of release was muffled by his mouth as she raided that delicious recess for countless kisses as ecstasy burst into full bloom.

Dagan's body shuddered from the force of a gigantic climax just as hers was ebbing. He labored with loving tenderness and waning stamina until their spasms ceased and they were slaked. Afterward, he could hardly catch his breath, and he noticed hers, too, was labored. He gazed into her flushed and damp face and saw wet strands of hair clinging to her forehead. He realized it was more than the glow of sated passion or the results of feverish exertions assailing them. The chamber was stuffy, oppressive, sultry. He was relieved they hadn't lost consciousness before he noticed the problem and resolved it. "Computer, reactivate the environmental control functions; bring them to normal as fast as possible. Sorry, my love," he said to Starla, "but in the excitement, I forgot about my previous order for the computer to shut them down in an *hora* unless I canceled it."

They took gulps of fresh and revitalizing air as it was sent flowing into the room. They relaxed as their bodies cooled and they reveled in the serene aftermath of the lofty experience.

"*Pralu,* Dagan, I thought you had shown me all of your skills but I was wrong. Your prowess is unlimited." She nestled against him in supreme contentment.

Their ardent lovemaking had surpassed all other encounters, and they knew it was because there were no secrets or hesitations or fears this time, only total surrender and complete trust. Their faith in each other was complete. Soon, they would make plans. For now, they relaxed and savored their commitment, and napped peacefully. They were blissfully unaware of what was happening beyond his chamber.

Sixteen

The next morning, the slumbering couple was awakened by a communication from their joint target.

The Kalfan left the cozy embrace of his lover with reluctance to respond to a signal from the *telecom*. He sat down and, to conceal the lower half of his naked body, slid the *seata* forward until his waist touched the table holding the unit, then pressed the initiation button. "Latu here."

"I wanted to know how you are doing this *deega*."

"Fine, I'm with Yana," he said, and grinned roguishly at the *fiendal* whose image he viewed on the two-way visual system. Dagan knew his hair was mussed, his chest was bare, and his eyes revealed he'd just awakened; his condition would evoke an advantageous assumption on the part of the *villite* leader. The Icarian would presume he had mentioned the female's presence to prevent Tochar from talking about Starla in Yana's presence and hopefully would presume that if he truly loved Starla and was aching over her betrayal, he would not be having sex with another female this soon. "Do you need me to dress and carry out a task?" he asked.

"That is unnecessary. Relax and enjoy yourself until tomorrow."

"Thanks, but if you need me for anything, I'll come immediately."

"Everything is under control, Dagan, so do not worry."

"Have you resolved your annoying problem?" Dagan asked, deciding it would be suspicious if he didn't make a

query about Starla and thinking himself clever to dupe Tochar by the way he worded it for alleged privacy.

"No, but I expect it to be eradicated soon. My men are
working on it. I will inform you when that matter has been
handled. Tochar out."

"Latu out." He pressed the termination button and chuckled.

"What is amusing?" Starla asked. "He's trying to hunt
me down to slay me. Are you eager to be rid of me so
soon?" she jested.

Dagan joined her on the *sleeper* and cuddled her in his
embrace. "Never will I tire of you, my love, and Tochar
will never find you or harm you. Perhaps I forgot to tell
you," he said amidst nibbles on her neck, "I am possessive
and protective of my most precious treasure."

Starla laughed at the ticklish sensations. "You did, my
handsome space pirate, but I'm happy to hear it belatedly;
and so am I."

He rolled to his back, took a deep breath, and let it out
slowly. "I'm the luckiest and happiest man alive now that
I have you."

Starla laid her head on his chest and listened to his heart
beat faster as she said, "And I am the luckiest and happiest
woman alive to have you."

Dagan stroked her tousled hair and basked in the splendor
of their love for a while. Later, he said, "We have a long
and serious talk ahead of us, so why don't I get us some
food from Radu before we begin? I have nothing here to
prepare and, yes, I know how to survive under primitive
conditions. We missed our evening meal and I'm ravenous.
How about you?"

"Almost famished with hunger, and this time not for
you," she ceased.

"After we eat and talk, my ravishing treat, I'll see what
I can do about your lagging appetite in that area."

"Sounds perfect to me. Now, perhaps we should habitate

in Yana's dwelling where Cypher-T can send us food from my *servo* unit. That way we won't have to starve or go out for food."

"What I want is for you to remain aboard your cloaked ship and out of harm's reach, but," he added when she started to protest, "we'll discuss that later. I'll return soon." He left her side, took a quick shower, dressed, and left his chamber.

Starla retrieved her neck ring and spoke close to the center *gem* with a transmitter inside. "I was right, Cypher; he is a man worthy of trust and worthy of loving. I'll contact you when I am ready to transport to the ship to make my report to Thaine. First, Dagan and I must talk about us and our mission; we have much to learn about each other and many plans to make. Prepare him a disguised device for communicating with us aboard the *Liska* when we are separated; he must have a way to request a rescue from us if peril strikes. I love him and need him, my friend, so help me protect him, which will also safeguard our mission. Starla out."

Energized by glorious love and victory and stimulated by suspenseful anticipation about teaming up with Dagan to defeat the *UFG*'s worst enemy, Starla left the *sleeper* to bathe in a primitive shower which used running water and a bar of soap, unlike the automated cleansing unit aboard her ship and everywhere in her advanced world. She used an extra toothbrush and paste from a tube to refresh her mouth since she lacked a bottle of self-cleansing liquid. After she dried off, she donned her garments and neck ring and brushed her hair. She touched the pouch suspended from her belt to make certain she had another phial of transmutation chemical if needed. She decided she should contact Cypher and tell him to transport a container down with extra clothes, grooming aides, and another set of phials—the shapeshifting agent and its counteragent. But she didn't have time to carry out that task because Dagan returned with their food, and they sat down to eat.

After they finished their meal and when Dagan asked Starla to tell him everything about her, she knew it was unnecessary to explain that the Maffei Galaxy was comprised of thirteen planets and numerous planetoids and was ruled by a Supreme Council of three men: their ruler—the *Kadim*—and two other members, men who were all-powerful and who made their laws. An Alliance Assembly of sixteen men—the Supreme Council and thirteen *Avatars,* planetary leaders—carried out those laws. On each planet, several *Zartiffs* governed appointed regions. Their highest form of military was Star Fleet, based on the capital planet of Rigel, and accountable to the Assembly, as were the ground units in the Alliance Force. The Elite Squad, a unit of specialists of which she was a member, answered only to the Supreme Council and worked under the leadership of Thaine Sanger, who also was in command of Star Fleet. The majority of their most powerful weapons, drugs, and chemicals were creations of and produced by Trilabs, an inaccessible complex on the planetoid of Darkar which orbited Caguas: one of the prizes Tochar craved. Those were facts he already knew as an *I-GAF* agent, powerful men who roamed the five allied galaxies.

Just as she knew, the Kalfa Galaxy consisted of ten planets and many planetoids; Gavas was their capital and Orr possessed moonbeam mines. Their galactic ruler was the *Autorie;* their space force was a unit of rangers called *Sekis.* As with her world, Kalfa had planetary and regional leaders.

"Tell me everything about yourself, my love," Dagan stressed with great interest as he settled himself on the *seata* to listen and observe.

"My name is Bree-Kayah Saar and I'm often called Bree by my family and close friends. As I've told you before,

I'm twenty-two *yings* old. I'm sixty-nine *hapaxs* tall and I weigh one-thirty *pedis*. You can see that my hair is brown and my eyes are green. I'm the youngest child of Varian and Jana Saar; both are retired and live on our family's private planetoid Altair which orbits Rigel. I have a twin brother and sister, forty-eight *yings* old." She laughed and said, "I was a late and most unexpected baby, so it was a good thing Maffei no longer practiced birth and population control, as it once did."

She returned to where she left off before her humorous inclusions, "Galen is on the Supreme Council and is mated to Rayna who helps my sister run the research labs on Altair; they have three children, a boy and twin girls. My sister is bonded to Jason; he's in charge of Star Base Security on Rigel; he's a full-blooded Earthling like my mother. Amaya is a retired Elite Squad member; they have two children—twins. My mother is a renowned scientist; she's retired but still dabbles in research. She's a wonderful, strong, generous, beautiful woman who's done many important things for our world, including saving our people when a lethal alien virus attacked there before my birth. So has my father," Starla admitted without boasting.

Dagan saw her eyes glow with love, pride, and respect and her stirring words caused him to miss and grieve over his lost parents and siblings.

"Father was a Star Fleet commander with his own starship for many *yings*. Later, he served as the Supreme Commander of Star Fleet, the Alliance Force, and Elite Squad—and was an ex-member of that unit. He saved our world several times from intergalactic threats before the Tri-Galaxy or United Federation of Galaxies were created. He is a unique and special man. I am proud to be his daughter and to follow in his footsteps."

As she sipped a drink, Dagan remarked, "Your great-grandfather was a past *Kadim,* a legendary ruler. I have read and heard much about him. I am curious: How did your parents meet, since she is from the distant Milky Way Galaxy and we have no contact with them?"

Starla knew well the story of how her mother had been captured from her planet and brought to Maffei long ago to become a *charl,* a captive mate for reproductive purposes when most Maffeian females were sterile, a practice her parents helped eliminate. Her parents had fallen in love at first sight, but her father had been unable to bond with Jana Greyson for many reasons. That part of their story could remain withheld until after Dagan got to know them, so it would not affect his opinion of her father, a man entrapped by a cruel destiny which was altered later. "After my mother came to Maffei, she was tricked into uniting with Ryker Triloni, my father's half-brother, grandson of the past ruler of the Androas Galaxy, and a matchless genius in science. After his accidental death, she inherited Trilabs; she felt it was too powerful and important for one person to own and control so she turned it over to our government and bonded with my father. My father was and is her only love; they taught me what true love is and that is why I waited for the right man to enter my life."

After she smiled and kissed his cheek, she continued. "My superior is Supreme Commander Thaine Sanger; he's also my brother's best friend since childhood, as were our fathers since their childhood and while serving in Star Fleet together. I went through training fast because my family had taught me so much before I entered the academy. After I scored high in all areas, I was assigned to the Elite Squad. I've been a member for two *yings* and carried out several missions. Since the Squad works in secret and my face wasn't known outside our galaxy, *Raz* Yakir and Thaine selected me for this mission; they assumed a female agent would be less suspicious than a male. *Raz* Yakir is the one who supplied the transmutation phials, my Starla Vedris record, and my means of making contact with Tochar. The crew of that pursuit craft were advanced androids that were programmed to look, act, and talk as if they were humans so Tochar would believe I possessed a dark heart and violent nature like him and his men."

She explained how she contacted her superior and the Serian ruler via an untraceable frequency, how she obtained needed data from network computers from them, how Yakir surreptitiously entered the clues and facts she gathered, and how she had received Cypher. She revealed Yakir's motives for sending her and for not telling Phaedrig about her presence. She told him that Acharius was the son of the *Avatar* of Caguas and how they knew each other. "I hope my parents, friends, and his family understand and forgive me for what I was forced to do to protect our galaxy and others."

He grasped her hand and gave it a comforting and gentle squeeze. "I'm certain they will, Starla; or I should say, Bree-Kayah."

"We should not use each other's real names in private or we could make a slip when Dagan and Yana are in public. Now, tell me everything about you, my beloved. What is your real name?"

"I agree we should stick to Dagan and Yana at all times, but it's Curran Thaiter. I was born, reared and trained on the capital planet of Gavas in Kalfa. I'm twenty-eight *yings* old. I'm seventy-five *hapaxs* tall and weigh two-twenty *pedis*. My hair is the shade of the sun and my eyes are aqua." He watched her try to imagine how he looked in his natural colorings.

He found her study and expression so arousing, he hurried on with his revelations before he was compelled to halt and make love to her. "My family was slain during a crime *yings* ago, but I'll relate that bitter story after I complete my history. I was a *Seki* for many *yings* before I was asked to join *I-GAF.* I use many disguises and identities during my assignments, but when I'm not on a particular mission, I live, work, and appear as Dagan Latu to keep that identity well established for other missions. Dauld Phaedrig is my superior and I answer only to him."

He wasn't sure of how much she knew about *I-GAF,* so he skimmed over that subject to enlighten or refresh her. "Agents work alone, in small teams, or in large units according to the crime we're solving. We can go anywhere in the *UFG* and no one can interfere with our methods; we cannot be questioned, reprimanded, or punished for them. Our assignments are requested by rulers or planetary leaders, but how we resolve the trouble is up to us. It's rare for an agent to have contact with rulers or leaders during an assignment. Phaedrig selects the agent or team to carry out a mission, and no agent has been disloyal, disobedient, or been terminated for a crime or incompetence. If one goes bad, he will be hunted and eradicated by *I-GAF* alone. When an agent retires, crucial facts about *I-GAF* are erased from his memory. Although *Rendelar* prevents susceptibility to truth serum, elderly men with weakened bodies might not be able to resist revealing secrets during a torture session. As you know, *Rendelar* and *Thorin* are creations of Ryker Triloni and their formulas are known only by Trilabs. As with all Trilabs formulas, any attempt to analyze them results in initiating a self-destruct sequence; he was indeed a rare genius. The chemicals and dyes used for our tattoos have similar self-destruct tags in them."

He turned his body sideways to face her as he continued, and she did the same to listen. "Phaedrig has access to all known computer networks and he inserts the data needed for mission identities. There is one system which cannot be breached by anyone except Phaedrig and *I-GAF* agents; that is the one which contains our personnel and assignment records, so they will be safeguarded against traitor encroachment. All other networks have a cue inserted which alerts Phaedrig when one of his agents is investigated, but Yakir was too clever and fast to be traced when he checked on me. As to how Syrkin and Yakir's traitors retrieved data on us, both are in positions of power, knowledge, and trust. We carry no credentials to be found, and our hand insignias are made visible only by us when needed." He related the description of *I-GAF* headquarters and told her it was on a barren planetoid in Kalfa, but did not disclose its location.

"Back to my family," he said with a grimace. "I was on a mission three *yings* ago when *villites* faked a chemical hazard in the area where my family lived on Gavas. Inhabitants were to gather their most valuable possessions and flee in supplied crafts, since they couldn't return home until the contamination was cleared away. During the evacuation procedure, *spacekis* attacked two of the rescue vessels carrying the wealthiest and most prominent citizens; everyone aboard was murdered, including my family and many of my friends. That vicious *nefariant* took away my parents, my sister and her family, and my two brothers and one's family; they killed young and old, male and female, by blowing up the vessels after they robbed them. When the *villites* proved to be elusive, I resigned as a *Seki* to work full-time to use my wits, skills, and energy to track down those responsible: Tochar and his band. The *fiendal* thought he had eliminated all witnesses, but he failed to notice a surveillance monitor at the boarding point; that's why he's so adamant about their destruction during our raids."

"Tochar and his band murdered your family and others . . ." she repeated in horror. "He's worse than I imagined. You must hate him terribly."

He nodded. "I was able to capture or terminate all of them except for Tochar, Auken, Sach, and Moig; but their faces and names were seared into my memory. For a strange reason, they always managed to evade me. I suspected my closest superior was involved in the *fiendal*'s good luck; that explained why the case was impeded, why clues I gathered were lost or ignored or dismissed, and why I was ordered to abandon my 'futile obsession' and was shifted to another investigation, which compelled me to resign to work on my own. My prowess and persistence seized the attention of *I-GAF* and that's why I was asked to join the Force. I accepted because I needed distraction from my losses and I needed to have stimulating adventures and challenges to keep me going and to sharpen my wits and skills. I also believed it would get me within range of Tochar. My appearance was changed to conceal my identity and Curran Thaiter was reported slain. Phaedrig inserted a fake record about Dagan Latu, and I created a reputation for him as an adventurer, *bijoni,* and dashing rogue who barely eluded arrest numerous time for shady incidents. Dagan is said to live for pleasure, money, and excitement, and is fiercely loyal to his leader. Perhaps you'll understand my suspicions about my past *Seki* superior when I tell you it was Syrkin." He noted her reaction and said, "That's right, the same Syrkin involved in this mission. He was probably Tochar's accomplice for *yings*. At least he's been dealt with by now and is off my mental list. When this trouble came up, Phaedrig assigned me, even knowing my past connections to the *fiendals* and my hunger for revenge, for justice. He was confident I wouldn't allow my personal feelings to sway my judgment and behavior, and I couldn't be recognized as Curran."

This time, she gave his hand a comforting squeeze. "That's terrible, Dagan. We'll find a way to punish them for slaying your family and to prevent them from doing more evil."

"We'll do our best, my love. Now tell me, how did you destroy those stolen crystals? That is what you told me while you were Yana, right?"

She nodded, then explained what she had done and why that same procedure would not work against the *Destructoids,* how getting near them was impossible, lethal for one person to attempt. She listened as he related the reason for suggesting the raid at Sion, for coaxing Auken to attack the medical supply vessel, and for repairing Tochar's ship: tricks to evoke trust in him and to lure Tochar off Noy and into a trap. She revealed everything she had learned and all she had done since starting her assignment. Dagan told her what he planned to report to Phaedrig about her: the truth.

"He'll be angry with *Raz* Yakir, Thaine, and me for our secrecy."

"Miffed for a while perhaps, but he's intelligent, and victory is what matters, so he'll understand and forgive their little deception."

"Will he resist Yana helping you defeat Tochar?" she asked. "Will he order me to leave? If he does, do I have to obey him?"

"How can he resist after all you've accomplished and with the skills you possess? You're as qualified on this matter as I am, more so, since you're the one who's gathered all the useful facts and thwarted Tochar in many ways. But if he did order you to leave, you would be forced to obey."

"Forced?" she echoed in astonishment. "How so?"

"By insisting your superior recall you, and Sanger would comply."

"I'm not deserting you in the face of danger. If they attempt to order me away, I will resign and they'll have no authority over my actions."

"Even a private citizen must submit to *I-GAF* requests and commands. Phaedrig would have your *Kadim* summon you home; and since your ruler is no longer a family member, he would honor Phaedrig's request."

"But my brother is on the Supreme Council; Galen would help me."

"Would you risk dishonoring yourself, the Saars, your superior, and your ruler for selfish reasons? If I'm left alone, I'll be fine; I promise."

"I know you're highly skilled and experienced, Dagan, but Tochar is evil incarnate; he's invincible at this point; you would be trapped here without me and my ship to supply an emergency escape if needed, and I can provide safe communications and other things you might require in your task. If you're . . . slain, this mission would be defeated instead of Tochar. At least Yana would be here to take over, to perhaps help another agent infiltrate his band. How is that being selfish?"

"Your reasoning is superior, my love, and I will repeat it to Phaedrig. I doubt he will ask you to leave. As for me, I wish you would depart, but I'm certain I could not convince you to do so." He chuckled as he stood. "We have been doing so much talking, we need to wet our throats," he said, as he entered the other area to pour them another drink.

Starla watched him with an adoring gaze. She was elated by the realization that her lover was the kind of man she could introduce to her family and friends with pride. He deserved their respect, admiration, and acceptance. There was no problem with him being a Kalfan, a race compatible in the biological and physiological areas, and comparable in appearances. It would not matter to them that her social status was higher than his, or that his authoritative rank was higher than hers. Though her family's wealth was enormous and her bloodline's achievements were almost matchless and legendary in the *UFG*, that would not make a difference to her or to her family or to a confident male like Curran Thaiter.

After he joined her on the *seata*, she told him that since his family was dead, the Saars would become his family in all ways. "The only two things that will concern them are if you love me and are worthy of me; both are true, pirate of my heart. We'll have a wonderful future as mates; we can work together, or retire and do something new and different."

"We'll make our choices and plans later, after we defeat Tochar and get away from this awful place."

"What if we can't defeat him since he has those *Destructoids?*" The thought preyed on her mind.

"We'll find a way to eliminate him and those weapons. We have your ship for communications and escape if necessary, and Cypher for assistance and protection. With the three of us teamed up, how can we fail?"

"We'll make mission plans later; you'll be leaving soon with Auken and Sach and we'll be separated for a long time. Cypher and I will shadow you while cloaked to protect you and record evidence. Cypher will make you a disk to wear on your belt so we can hear everything said and you can request help if needed. At least I'll be able to hear your voice and be there if needed. Right now, I want you and need you to fill my storage bays for a long haul since you'll be unable to supply me with daily nourishment."

At that stimulating hint, flames of desire leapt through Dagan's body and flickered brightly in his eyes. As Starla pressed close to him, it was as if he could detect a tangible matching blaze of fiery passion within her. He wanted, needed, and loved her so much that his potent emotions almost stole his breath. He willingly followed her to the *sleeper* and paused beside it. He didn't assist when she undressed first him, then stripped off her own garments. He was enspelled by the way her mouth made several sensuous and erotic treks over his face and chest. Soon, her questing and experienced fingers and mouth had him squirming and moaning in exquisite delight as she tantalized, pleasured, and sated him in one way, only to reheat and cool him again in another.

Dagan had not realized he could become aroused and slaked so many times in one afternoon; he was enchanted by her provocative and generous actions. He pulled her body into place atop his so he could kiss her and reward her in like kind for the *hora* of rapture. His fingers kneaded her soft but firm buttocks. His mouth drifted down her neck, nibbled at her collarbone, and fastened to one of the smoldering peaks which dangled down and enticed him to capture it.

Starla was elated to be in his arms. Bliss filled her as he heightened her hungers. She pushed aside thoughts and worries about the perils looming before them; all she wanted to know and feel was the glorious splendor of this occasion and this man. Musky scents teased at her nostrils, increasing her eagerness to have him. She was rolled to her back to give him freedom to roam her body from end to end, and to explore every beckoning region between those two locations. Pleasured into a near mindless state, she thrashed upon the firm surface beneath her as he drove her wild with anticipation, then gave her sweet release.

Dagan received sublime pleasure at each passionate encounter and was slaked thoroughly; yet, he couldn't get enough of her and always wanted, craved, more. His feelings and needs went beyond sexual ones; he loved her with all his heart and being, and she filled his life in so many areas. She was unique, magical; she was his.

Starla writhed and moaned as his titillating tongue caused colorful lights to dance before her closed eyes as ecstasy shook her to her core. She could not imagine her life without him, on and off a *sleeper*. He stirred her blood and wits and emotions. When he entered her welcoming body, her legs enclosed his hips and held him clamped against her. His kisses were pervasive, delicious, fervent.

Dagan relished the way she imprisoned him within her arms and legs, her mouth feverishly working upon his. When she reached the brink of release, he thrust rapidly to help push her over that precipice. Moments after she arched her back and moaned in glorious fulfillment his body erupted in a molten frenzy that resulted in glorious appeasement.

With sweet victory obtained, they cuddled and kissed, serene and exhausted. Yet, each was worried about the other's safety and survival. Within reach was the one person who fulfilled their yearnings and destiny. Beyond this cozy chamber was the one threat which could tear them apart forever, which could create chaos across the Universe.

Dagan feared she wasn't safe without him or with him, as Tochar's unknown sources could track her down wherever she went and slay her. The *fiendal* he wanted to defeat was responsible for the deaths of his family and for many other innocents and, if he wasn't cautious and smarter, that evil force could take from him his newfound love and joy. How could he protect her if she remained at his side, he fretted, even as Yana? Yet, where could he hide her from Tochar, who might have another contact in Kalfa and/or Maffei? What would he have to say and/or do to force her to leave him if matters worsened when she was determined to stay?

Starla's troubled thoughts journeyed along a similar course: if Tochar discovered who and what Dagan was, her love would be tortured and killed. If she didn't stay nearby, she and Cypher could not protect him, could not help him carry out this vital mission. She wished there were no such things as Tochar, moonbeams, and perilous missions; but all three existed.

For the remainder of that *deega,* they talked, made love twice, ate a late meal, and fell asleep nestled together.

The following morning, Dagan was summoned by Tochar to do a task for him with Auken and Sach, saying only one *deega* was required and he would return to Yana's side by dusk. Before he left his chamber, he insisted she shapeshift into Yana and remain there during his absence. He observed the transformation in amazement, and was relieved the process was not painful. As he embraced her and brushed his lips over hers, he murmured, "I feel deceitful kissing and hugging Yana, though it is you within her. This is a strange experience and it near dazes my wits."

She laughed as she viewed his playful expression and jested, "Perhaps I should welcome you back tonight with this sexy body. Yana is more endowed than I am," she said, as she rubbed her breasts against him. "With this magical secret, you can have two eager women as your love slaves."

Dagan chuckled. "I only have enough stamina to sate one women, as my prized treasure is most demanding and greedy."

"Your mating appetite will increase greatly if I splash on that irresistible scent," she murmured in a seductive tone.

"As beautiful as you are as Yana, I love Starla. She tempts, arouses, and sates me as no other female could. She is the one who captured my heart and enflames my body. Now, if I don't leave fast, I might be compelled to overlook this image and be late meeting the others."

Yana watched her lover leave and stepped backward for the door to close. Earlier she had shared a long and sensuous shower with Dagan and dressed when he did. She reminded herself she needed to signal Cypher to teleport certain items to her, including a meal so she would not have to leave his chamber. She started to retrieve her neck ring from the privacy room where she'd left it last night so sounds of their passionate lovemaking would not singe the android's "ears," though she had forgotten about its presence earlier when passion stole their wits in the bathing cubicle.

When the exterior door swished open, she halted and turned expecting to see her beloved returning to retrieve a forgotten item, but saw instead two of Tochar's Enforcers entering. She tensed in alarm. "What do you want here? Dagan has left."

"Tochar wishes to speak with you," one said. "Come with us."

Yana stared at the black-clad men. "I do not understand. I—"

A low-energy beam stunned Yana into silence and darkness.

When she awakened, she was strapped to the oblong

table in the testing room at Tochar's dwelling and the *fiendal* was leaning over her imprisoned body. Without the transmitter in her neck ring, she could not alert Cypher to her peril, and—with it hanging in the bath chamber—he was ignorant of all aspects of her abduction. She hoped Tochar did not keep her there for more than ten *horas,* as surely that was the span of time remaining in her transmutation scheduled . . .

Tochar stroked her hair and said, "Do not worry or be afraid, Yana; I only want to ask you a few questions; then I will release you."

"What questions do you wish to ask?" She watched Tochar place an *Airosyringe* to her arm and eject *Thorin* into her body. "What was that?"

"A harmless serum to entice you to speak only the truth."

She was prepared with a persuasive story, one records in Asisa would confirm if checked. Still, Yana must appear greatly distressed to dupe him. "You have no right to do this; my secrets are mine alone."

"This settlement belongs to me, Yana, so I have that right. Relax and let the serum take effect and this will be over soon. If you lie or resist, the pain will be excruciating, so please be honest and compliant."

"Does Dagan know you are doing this to me?"

"I will enlighten him at the proper time. Now, relax and sleep."

As she pretended to surrender to the *Thorin,* she fumed over her capture. She had forgotten to ask Dagan to enter her voice in the computer system so she could order the door sealed during his absence. It was apparent the Enforcers had gotten an entry card from Radu, who owned the rental abodes. She surmised that Dagan had been lured away so Tochar could ensnare and interrogate Yana. Considering what her lover had revealed to her about this *fiendal,* she knew his evil far exceeded her previous beliefs. She could not imagine what the cruel and perverted Icarian might do to the ravishing Yana while she was supposedly unconscious or how she could prevent anything in her helpless condition.

Seventeen

"Can you hear me, Yana?" Tochar asked later.

"Yes, I hear you." When he parted her lids to check her
eyes, she forced them to de-focus and appear glazed. She
felt the heat of a flush on her cheeks, this time from tension
instead of a chemical aide. With luck and training, she
hoped she could dupe the *fiendal* again. She knew, if he
ever got his hands on Trilabs, he would have access to *Rendelar* and to the only chemical which could penetrate its
power to resist *Thorin*. She must not let that happen or her
world and others would be in grave peril, and no *UFG* ruler
or agent would be able to prevent mental probings. If Tochar
got control of Trilabs, no secret would be safe from his
discovery; but as long as he didn't attack Darkar's defenses
with a *Destructoid,* it was invincible.

"Will you answer my questions with total honesty?"

"Yes," she murmured in a softened and slowed tone.

"Why do you spend time with Dagan Latu?"

"I love him and desire him. He is handsome, virile, fun—"

"That is sufficient. Does Dagan love you?"

"I do not think so."

"Who does Dagan love and desire?"

Be careful and clever, Bree. "I believe it is Starla Vedris."

"How does Dagan feel about Starla's treachery?"

"She betrayed and hurt him. She crushed his pride. She
humiliated him. He is angry. He would not forgive her if

she returned. He does not understand why she defied To-char. He—"

"Did Dagan tell you those things?"

"No, but I sensed them and made conclusions from his slips and expressions. He does not talk about her; it makes him angry."

"Would Dagan help Starla elude Tochar if she returned to him?"

"I do not think so; he is loyal to Tochar and angry with her. He speaks highly of his leader. He is a man of honor."

"Why did Dagan turn to you so soon after Starla deserted him?"

"I think it is to appease his pain, to shove her from his heart and thoughts, for sex, for companionship, for—" She was pleased he interrupted her after she had given enough reasons to satisfy him.

"Has Dagan ever done or said anything to make you suspect he would betray Tochar in any circumstance?"

"No."

"Why were you afraid for me to question you?"

"I have secrets to protect. My life is in jeopardy."

"What secrets? Tell me who you are and why you are here."

"I am Mayoleesee Bargivi of Crepal in the Asisa Galaxy. I was reported missing and am presumed dead. The mate of my sister tried to slay me, so she would inherit our family's wealth, power, and status which belongs to me by birthright. I came to Tochara to hide until he is slain. I hired a *bijoni* to kill him, but he surrounded himself with guards and cannot be reached at this time. Until he is dead and his threat no longer exists, I cannot return home. I am certain he has hired men to search for me and slay me, but they will not look on Noy; they would believe it is too distant and primitive and I would have no way to get here."

"How did you travel to Noy?"

"I disguised myself and paid a trader to bring me here;

then I killed him so he could not reveal my location for payment."

She was barraged with questions. "How did you meet Dagan and why did you couple with him? Where do you habitate? Who are your friends? How do you spend your time?"

She related how and when Yana met Dagan, that he and Radu were her only friends in the settlement, how Yana allegedly spent her time, and the location of the unit she rented from Radu. "When I met Dagan Latu, I believed he was a man who could protect me if danger approached. I seduced him to draw him close to me, but he met Starla Vedris and discarded me. I realized I loved him, so I pursued him again when I heard she was in trouble and missing. I am taking advantage of his anguish and loss. If he comes to love me, I will ask him to return to Crepal with me and become my mate. I will offer him wealth, power, status, and safety."

"Will Dagan accept your generous and enticing offer?"

"I do not think so; he is proud; he is an adventurer, a loner. He does not love me and would not desire to become my mate."

"But you still intend to ask him?"

"Yes, it will give him comfort and restore his pride to know he is so highly desired and loved by another woman." She heard Tochar chuckle at those romantic notions which he must consider silly.

"Do you know Starla Vedris?"

"Only by sight and reputation. I observed her a few times when she was at the Skull's Den or walking in the settlement. I heard her speaking with Radu and others there. We have never talked or been introduced."

"Rest while I decide if I have more questions to ask."

She heard him leave, and prayed he would believe her tale and release her soon. If not, she was in deep trouble when she transformed before his piercing black eyes or

when he returned and found Starla Vedris strapped to the
table. Dagan also would be imperiled by that incredible discovery. Perhaps, she reasoned, Tochar had gone to seek veri-
fication of Yana's claims; she knew he would receive it, as
the real Asisan beauty had been found injured and abandoned recently on a barren planetoid in the Serian Galaxy.
Mayoleesee had revealed her heart-gripping story to *Raz*
Yakir before she died, and Yakir had told no one about the
woman so he could make use of her tragic tale, and hoped
that wasn't insensitive of him.

As the *horas* passed, Yana knew that Tochar was aware
the *Thorin* had worn off long before this time. She couldn't
imagine why the *fiendal* didn't return to check on her while
he awaited a response to his query. It was strange that the
reply was taking this long, if indeed it was. Surely, she
fretted, Yakir had not confided the truth about Yana to the
wrong person, to Tochar's accomplice!

She wondered if Dagan had returned to his chamber and
found her missing. Even so, her beloved would think she
had gone to her ship or to Yana's dwelling to retrieve something, and there was no way he could communicate with
the *Liska,* not yet. And Cypher, if his program allowed it,
he must be worried about not hearing from her by now.
Then there was Thaine and Yakir, who had not received a
report from her since she started her task as Yana; they
must be concerned. The dark reality was that Tochar could
get rid of her and no one would know what had happened
to her.

At last, the door opened and two men entered the room:
Tochar and Dagan. The Kalfan approached the table and
released her. With his back to the *fiendal,* Dagan gave her
a wink to indicate everything was all right. For their target's
ears, he said, "I'm sorry if this matter upset you, Yana, but
Tochar thought it was imperative to check you out since

you're so close to me and I'm so close to him. You did fine, so we can leave now."

She caught his hints and played along with his ruse. "I was captive here for a long time, so I was frightened. I feared I might be sold to my enemy after my identity and problem were discovered."

"Do not worry, Yana, your secrets are safe with us," Tochar added. "Dagan will make certain no one and nothing harms you during your visit. If anyone threatens you, contact me or any of my Enforcers for help."

"Thank you; that is very kind and generous," she murmured as she glanced at the now smiling Tochar.

"Dagan is a friend, so I must assist and protect those close to him."

"Thanks, Tochar," the Kalfan said. "I appreciate it."

After they exchanged farewells, Dagan and Yana left the lofty location via the *trans-to*. While walking to their transportation unit, he whispered a warning for her to be cautious with her words in case a listening device was planted in the vehicle, as he knew one was concealed in the lifter.

"Affirmative," she whispered a reply. After they were seated in the landrover, she cuddled against Dagan's side, certain Tochar was watching them; the potent and evil gaze upon her surely must be his. For the *fiendal*'s ears, as she was positive he was listening to them, too, she said, "I was terrified when Tochar's men invaded your chamber and abducted me only a few *preons* after your departure. It is fortunate for me I was dressed, for they did not ask permission to enter. They stunned me with an energy, beam and, when I awoke, I was imprisoned to that table. I do not know what he asked me. Did he reveal my answers to you?"

"Yes, he told me who you are and why you're hiding here."

"Now that you know the truth, does it anger or disappoint you?"

"Of course not, Yana, but you should have confided in

me. I can't help you and protect you if I don't know the truth."

"I'm sorry; I realize how strongly you must detest lies and tricks. I wanted to trust you, but I feared for my survival, and you turned from me for a while. I will be totally honest with you from this *deega* forth."

"Excellent, because I don't want contact with another deceitful woman. It's obvious that I picked the wrong female when I leaned toward Starla instead of you; she fooled all of us, but forget about her; I will. If you don't mind, I'll continue to call you Yana. Your real name is long and hard to pronounce, and it could imperil you if overheard by the wrong ears."

"That is fine with me, and your precaution is wise. Thank you."

"And you don't have to worry about Tochar endangering you. He knows we're close, so he wouldn't sell you to your enemy. He's a good leader and he wants his men to be happy and satisfied."

"Do I give you joy and appeasement?"

"Of course you do, woman. Any man would be lucky to have you."

"It pleases me to hear those words. I would do anything for you."

"Thanks, Yana."

They kept quiet during the brief remainder of their ride.

As they entered Dagan's chamber, he gestured for caution until he checked the place for security with a concealed detection device. To mask their silence, he said, "After you refresh yourself, pour us a drink so we can relax before our meal."

When he was certain it was safe to speak and behave freely, Dagan seized his lover almost roughly in his distress over her close call with exposure and death. He covered her face and mouth with kisses and embraced her with relief, joy, and love. "What if you had transmuted back into

Starla while he was holding you captive or what if *Thorin* had an adverse effect on that shapeshifting chemical? I could have lost you, woman."

She clasped his handsome face between her hands and fused their gazes. "It was scary, but I'm fine; I have three *horas* to go before I alter."

"What if he had asked us to stay and eat with him or he had probed you longer? That was too close; we can't allow it to happen again. I love you and need you, Starla, so I beg you to remove yourself from this peril."

"What do you mean?"

"You have to leave Tochara, tonight."

"No," she protested. "You would be alone, vulnerable."

"I'm in greater peril with you here because I worry about you and that's distracting. Besides, Tochar will become suspicious if I start acting crazy about Yana so soon after losing Starla, and I might do so because I know it is you beneath her facade. You must stay where you're safe except when and if Yana has to make an appearance to continue our ruse. I have to concentrate on our enemy or I could endanger both of us and prolong this mission."

"I understand your dilemma, so I'll stay on the ship if you insist, but I'm not leaving orbit when you might need to escape fast."

He covered her mouth with his and kissed her tenderly, the compromise acceptable. "Now, tell me what happened this morning."

"First, let me speak to Cypher and assuage his concerns about me."

Yana fetched her neck ring from the privacy room and contacted the android. She told him she would be returning to the ship later tonight and would update him on the events that had occurred. She told him to send down the communication device he had constructed for Dagan and another set of phials in case she needed them before her return.

After Cypher complied with her requests and she showed

Dagan how the device worked, she completed her revelations.

Then, Dagan related his arrival at Tochar's and the shocking discovery he had made about Yana being there. "It was a struggle to conceal my panic and fear, but I told him it was fine with me to test you; however, he could have asked me to bring you in for questioning. He said it was done in secret so you wouldn't be alerted to his plans and attempt an escape if you had anything to hide. He said he needed to check you out for both our sakes and safety, but I'm certain he was concerned only about his. He played the recording of your session, and you were excellent, my love."

"Thanks." She disclosed that most of her tale about Mayoleesee was true. "I'm sure he checked it out and that's why he believed me and released me. Did he ask you how you felt about Yana?"

Dagan nodded. "I think I convinced him my only interest in you is hot, wild sex; I joked I was getting as much pleasure from you as I could before my next trek, but had absolutely no interest in leaving with you or becoming your mate. He appeared to be satisfied with my answers."

"That's wonderful. Where did you go with Auken and Sach?"

"Into the wasteland to meet a *spaceki*'s shuttle. It was a man named Koi from the Ceyxan galaxy. He had a load of stolen high-tech computer chips and memory boards to sell to Tochar. We delivered the payment, collected the cargo, and stored it in that cave where you had trouble."

"If we decide to take that haul off Tochar's hands, I have the caverns coordinates recorded in my ship's computer system."

"I don't think that's a wise idea at this time. Tochar placed a heavy guard on all of his caves and the two defense sites. We can't risk getting caught around or inside any of them. He even had us install battery-operated motion detectors which will sound an alarm if intruders encroached. I know how to bypass and disarm the sensors, but that would look suspicious since only Tochar, Auken, Sach, me, and the Enforcers know about them."

"You're right; it is too dangerous. We'll let him keep them for now."

Dagan chuckled at her humorous words. "That's very kind of you," he jested. "I'm sure Tochar will be appreciative of your generosity."

"What's next for us to do?"

"Tochar said the team might be leaving in two *deegas* for a raid, but he didn't reveal the target or destination. He said he'd know by tomorrow. That means we'll be parted soon for a long time."

Her gaze locked with his, and she missed him already. "I need to feel you next to me. Life can end without warning if we aren't careful. Make love to me, Dagan, before I have to leave you."

"I feel the same way; I need for our bodies to be united as one. First, would you change into yourself?" he coaxed. "I need to fuse with Starla before you must leave my side."

She smiled and nodded, then sipped from the appropriate phial. She watched him as he observed her transformation. He still was as amazed as she was about the astonishing procedure and their vast dissimilarities. She grasped his hand, and they walked to the *sleeper* where they undressed and lay down, safe in the secured chamber.

As he ravished her earlobe, he murmured, "I love you more than I can say with words or show you with actions, more than you can imagine, more than I ever thought possible, more than my own life and successes."

"The same is true for how I feel about you, Dagan, my only love."

With separation looming before them, they were compelled to make profound and earnest love. Even so, their feelings ran deeper and stronger than mere physical desire. They bonded on every level: emotional, carnal, and spiritual. They knew, if anything went wrong, this could be their last time to make love. Yet, even if everything went right, it would be *wegs* before they were together like this again, long and tormenting and lonely *wegs*.

Starla's fingertips brushed over Dagan's tanned face with its expression of intense concern and fervent longing for her. She inhaled his manly scent and stroked the raised muscles on his chest and arms. She moved her hands over his shoulders. His physique was splendid and virile, and she opened herself to absorb pure and raw and magical sensations, the kinds only Dagan could evoke from her.

Dagan gave carefree abandonment to his hands, lips, and tongue as the magnitude of his hungers increased and he strove to heighten Starla's. Her brown hair was spread around her shoulders and his fingers toyed in those lustrous locks. He savored the silky texture of her bare skin, her creamy throat. His breathing became erratic as his eagerness escalated. He enjoyed kindling her to a combustible point and fanning those flames into a roaring blaze that licked magnificently over her luscious body. His mischievous and playful tongue darted around the protruding nubs of her creamy breasts and flicked them into greater rigidity. His hand roved past her navel and into the dark patch between her parted thighs.

Starla urged him to penetrate her with forceful, deep thrusts. She pressed on his firm and undulating buttocks to coax him to encase himself completely within her sweltering body.

He lifted his head and gazed into her green eyes, glowing with the same feelings that raced through his mind and body. He leaned forward and sealed their mouths once more. This woman had brought his deceased heart to life again. She had retrieved and given him a peace he had lost long ago. She was the one he wanted for his mate, to be the mother of his children. He knew he would sacrifice his life to save hers if such a grim occasion arose, and she would do the same for him. Yes, his joyful heart sang, they were as perfectly matched as identical twins.

Starla knew it would never have been this way with Antarus Hoy or any other male in existence. This man—Curran Thaiter—was the one she had waited and searched and longed for since coming of age as a woman. He was her destiny, her spiritual half. He was the owner of her heart.

They labored as one until they achieved the ultimate joyful culmination.

Each knew she would have to leave his side, arms, and chamber soon; but they nestled together for a while to savor the golden aftermath of the magnificent experience, their last one until it was safe to meet again; and both prayed that moment would come.

After Starla returned to the *Liska,* she related everything to Cypher that had taken place since she left her ship two *deegas* ago. She reported to Thaine, who would pass along the information to *Raz* Yakir. Thaine was delighted she was safe, was remaining aboard her cloaked ship, and was teaming up with the *I-GAF* agent. Thaine passed along words from her family, and she gave him messages for her parents and siblings. She told her superior she would contact him again when she had something new to relate, which she hoped would be soon.

Before she left the bridge to retire for the night, she smiled at her android and said, "I love Dagan so much, Cypher, and I don't want to lose him. Please help me protect him from harm."

"I will guard him as I guard you, Bree-Kayah. I will remain on alert and be prepared to rescue him from any peril that arises. I will record all he hears and sees via the unit you gave to him."

Starla was surprised she blushed and hesitated when she asked, "Did you record anything . . . private that happened between us?"

"My analysis of those situations indicated you would not want me to do so. Intimate meetings with him are not part of our mission's evidence."

She laughed and quipped, "You get smarter every *deega,* my friend. I shall sleep now, but awaken me if anything out of the ordinary happens."

On the evening after Starla's return to her ship, Dagan was summoned to Tochar's dwelling to be told he would leave at midmorning the next *deega* with Auken and Sach aboard the *Adika.* For the first time since he joined Tochar's band, he was informed of their target and destination: the planet Ulux in Seri for a load of moonbeams in his accomplice's possession.

As Starla and Cypher listened to and recorded the meeting via the disguised disk on his belt which was programed at a frequency which the *fiendal*'s security system could not detect, they heard Dagan say he wasn't in the mood to visit with Yana before his departure as she was getting clingy and he'd been feasting on her for two *deegas,* so he was exhausted and sated. Starla knew that was a hint for her to keep away from him tonight, which turned out to be a smart precaution.

Not long after Dagan returned to his chamber, he left again. She heard him order a meal from Radu, speak to others, enter the men's privacy cubicle, then contact her. She listened to his rush of words.

"I have to talk fast, Starla. I'm in the reliever at the Skull's Den. My place isn't secure; Tochar is testing me for loyalty following his disclosure. You heard what he told me: we leave at midmorning for Ulux to pick up crystals from his partner there. Don't come down as Yana because I can't remove the listening device in my chamber and he would hear everything we said and did. I've already given him an excuse for avoiding you. If I'm not seen with anyone and since my chamber is monitored, if anything goes wrong, he'll know I didn't betray him. Send a report to Phaedrig, but tell him not to take any action at Ulux; Cypher has the code to use. Follow me in your ship and record any evidence you hear. I love you. Take no risks."

She realized that before she shadowed his trek, she had to establish a plausible explanation to cover Yana's absence in case Tochar checked on her while Dagan was gone. She waited until her beloved left the Skull's Den before she entered it as Yana, as she had overheard something useful to her. As she sipped a drink, she told the owner she wanted and needed to shop for things unavailable in the settlement and to seek a diversion to alleviate boredom and stress, but she required safe passage. Radu unknowingly provided the means for her to carry out her subterfuge; he persuaded a close and trusted friend—J'Ali—to give Yana a ride to another planet to which the alien was headed tomorrow, the news she had overheard between the Ceyxans as Dagan awaited his meal. By a stroke of good luck or the intervention by a Divine Hand, that location—thanks to planetary alignments this time of *ying*—was in the same direction as Ulux, almost positioned between the two points of departure and final destination. She put her strategy into motion by smiling and accepting the "kindness" of J'Ali.

Afterward, she went to visit the near incompetent doctor who had been exiled from his world for performing illegal procedures on patients. She told the man she needed something for a headache, which he provided for a small payment for a friend of Radu and Dagan. The real reason she had gone to his office was to obtain its coordinates so she could make another visit during the night to retrieve two crucial items to aid her ruse.

* * *

The following morning, she entered the Ceyxan trader's vessel as Yana, confined herself to her assigned quarters, and watched them leave orbit with the knowledge Cypher was following in her cloaked ship.

Her plan was to deboard J'Ali's vessel on the other planet, find a private spot, and have Cypher teleport her to the *Liska*. That necessary precaution would place her only *horas* behind Dagan, a span which her faster craft could vanquish in a hurry. She deduced, if they could unmask the last traitor during this trek, that would leave only the *Destructoids* —an awesome task—to deal with after their return to Noy.

Suspense and anticipation surged through her as she reflected on a daring ruse which, if it worked, could resolve that one remaining obstacle and terminate its threat, leaving Tochara vulnerable to attack and defeat. She had put *Raz* Yakir on standby for assistance, as he concurred with her "clever" and astounding idea.

Now, she reasoned, all she had to do was protect Yana from discovery while on the Ceyxan's vessel, rejoin Cypher soon, catch up with Dagan, and attempt her daring ploy—a scheme she had been unable to share with him since it entered her mind. Despite her cunning, there remained one problem to resolve: she must find a way to enlighten Dagan without exposing either of them. That was where *Raz* Yakir's sly but hazardous suggestion would come in handy, if it succeeded; yet, it didn't stand a chance if one or the other of them couldn't discover the identity of either the traitor on Ulux or his confederate on Kian. Yakir was working on both of those angles, and hopefully, they would be given the facts they needed.

Yana settled herself against the *seata* and went over the entangled episodes many times to examine them for oversights and to work out the details. She hoped and prayed no threat would strike the Ceyxan *villite*'s vessel while she was aboard, as *Raz* Yakir could not order Serian patrols from their path without it appearing suspicious to his traitor.

Eighteen

While en route to Ulux on the *Liska,* Starla and Cypher monitored an enlightening conversation between Dagan and the two Icarians:

"Is the identity of our contact confidential?" Dagan asked. "Will I be going with you two or staying aboard the ship?"

Auken laughed before saying, "We'll all go to meet with him after we dock at the space port and shuttle to the surface. You're one of us now, Dagan; Tochar trusts you completely. We'll be meeting with Iverk."

"Iverk?" Dagan echoed. "I'm not up to date with officials' names, so, I don't know who he is."

Starla's voice reflected her love and pride as she said to Cypher, "He's so cunning, to pretend to be uninformed about Seri's leaders and politics so Auken will clarify and incriminate Iverk on our record."

"He's the Serian *Ysolte,* Head-of-Defense, third in their rulership line," Auken enlightened Dagan. "He's powerful, wealthy, trusted, and clever. He visited the mine on Kian recently and had his hireling there give him a tour of the place; that's how he got the moonbeams we're going after."

"But I thought Tochar said the mines had tight security," Dagan said.

"They do; that's why Eick couldn't smuggle them out for him. Eick concealed a stash in one of the chambers. Iverk wore his official garment on the tour, a long and flowing robe. He concealed the crystals in a pouch secured around his waist. Naturally," Auken added between chuckles, "security wouldn't dare search or question their *Ysolte*."

"You're right; Iverk is sly and brave; still, he risked a lot to take them. Any chance there's one of those big white ones among them? Tochar could use another one for a *Destructoid* aboard his ship or yours."

"No, but it wouldn't do him any good in any case without the weapon. Iverk told him no more had been constructed."

Starla and Cypher knew that wasn't accurate, as *Raz* Yakir had one made covertly and it was awaiting a power source: a large clear moonbeam. She was elated that the ruler had kept his word about secrecy, even with the man who was only two steps below him in the line of rulership.

"How are we supposed to fly in and out of there alive?" Dagan asked. "What if our images are checked and we're exposed and attacked; worse, trapped on Ulux? Do we have an escape plan if one's needed?"

"Don't worry, Dagan, we won't be caught, or even halted for a *preon*. Iverk is Head-of-Defense, so he deleted our records from their files. He gave us the correct passwords, and told us what kind of convincing papers to forge. For this visit, we go in as legitimate traders."

Starla remarked to Cypher as the crew of the *Adika* chatted about unimportant topics, *"Raz* Yakir will be distressed to learn the traitor's identity. We must contact him with that vital information, thanks to my clever Dagan. After we reach orbit in another *weg,* I'll teleport to meet with him and put his idea in motion; with the betrayer's name, Yakir's ruse is possible. It's a tricky ploy, and I'm leery about attempting it."

"Raz Yakir would not allow you to use that tactic if he was not certain it would succeed," Cypher assured. "Do not be afraid or doubtful, Bree-Kayah. I will monitor your moves and be prepared to extract you at the first sign of peril."

"And Dagan, keep a close watch on him for his safety. It's strange and contradictory that Tochar—if he truly trusts Dagan now—would have a listening device planted in his chamber, then allow Auken to expose such a valuable fact. We must be on alert for tricks, Cypher, but do not intrude on any situation until you are certain my life or Dagan's is in imminent danger. We're close to victory, so I don't want anything to impede it."

Starla was elated she had reached this point in her plan without any trouble. If Tochar had checked on Yana since her departure, he should be convinced Yana was on another planet, taken there by one of Radu's trusted friends. Cypher had retrieved her where J'Ali dropped her off, and they had caught up with the *Adika* without problems. When the time came to return to Noy, if their impending plan failed and if she couldn't find a similar ride back, Yakir would arrange for a disguised craft to transport Yana to the settlement to try another tactic.

She looked at the android. "We must contact *Raz* Yakir and give him the bad and good news so he can finalize his part of our first cunning ruse." She looked uncertain, and turned to her android for encouragement. "Do you think it will succeed, Cypher? The hazards are many."

"If the episode is timed accurately and no unknown factors arise, it cannot fail," he said with supreme confidence. "It is doubtful your next image and actions will evoke suspicions. It is believed that Yana is far away, and Starla is either dead or in hiding. We heard Auken reveal to Dagan that Tochar has been unable to retrieve any information about Starla's fate or location."

"That's true, but the *fiendal* is deceitful, a most untrustworthy leader to all hirelings except his two close friends. I believe Tochar doubts my guilt but would never admit he made an error. He entrapped himself by overreacting to the cave incident. Now he needs to slay me to prevent exposing his mistake, which he assumes others will view as a weakness."

"Your reasoning and conclusions are logical."

"Thanks, Cypher. Now, you can signal *Raz* Yakir for me."

As she spoke with the Serian ruler, Starla made a shocking discovery.

"Do not teleport down as yourself," Yakir warned her. "Someone has tampered with Starla's criminal record; perilous false acts were added to it, along with an order she is to be terminated on sight. If I delete the record or command, it will arouse the suspicion of my traitor. Come to me as Yana; that will be safe if you are seen, which I will try to prevent."

"The name of your traitor is Iverk, the *Ysolte,*" Starla revealed. "His hireling is a miner named Eick." She went on to relate everything Auken had told Dagan. She had anticipated the long silence that ensued her probably painful disclosure. She kept quiet as she gave Yakir the time he needed to digest that grim fact.

"I am astounded by his treachery; yet, he is one of three I suspected and am having observed by my covert Cyborg unit. None of those men know they are being watched, as those units are highly advanced and have the ability to shapeshift at will; that prevents the same image from making too many appearances in close proximity to its target."

"I stole the blood sample you require and removed Starla's from Noy so it could not be used to learn her identity," Starla related. "It is fortunate blood was taken from our enemies and stored for emergencies in that primitive location."

"Excellent; I will have my research team standing by to make cunning use of it. After you arrive, we will discuss our plans and finalize them. Rest and relax, Bree-Kayah; I will have everything prepared before we meet."

Cypher recorded the coordinates Yakir gave to him and

a rendezvous time was set for one *hora* after they reached orbit in a *weg*.

While Starla prepared herself to teleport down as Yana, she reminisced on the quick and tender messages Dagan had sent to her along his journey when he was alone. His voice and words had warmed her body and elated her heart. She wished she could have responded, but the device was a one-way transmitter. Still, he knew she had heard him or that Cypher would receive and relay his messages. She was eager to see her beloved again; and it would be soon, astonishingly sooner than he expected.

Later as she stood on the sensor pad, Cypher told her to be careful before he transported her into the presence of Yakir in his private chamber.

Starla—in her Yana form—and Yakir exchanged smiles as the ruler stepped forward to greet her, his eyes glowing with undeniable affection.

"It is good to see you again, Bree-Kayah Saar, safe and alive. I gave my word to your parents that I would protect you during your loan to me. You have done a superior job and I am forever grateful to you. I was certain of all your splendid qualities, but they have proved even greater than I imagined. I was wise to select you for this mission."

"Thank you, sir; your remarks are generous and appreciated. Here is the blood sample we need," she said, passing the valuable tube to him.

Yakir handled the item as the prized treasure it was. He walked to an alcove where a statue sat on a high pedestal. He pressed a concealed button and a door opened. He handed the sample to a man and issued his orders.

As he did so, she observed him. As always, the tall and slender man with a gentle brown gaze evoked her respect and admiration. His braincase was large and hairless; a deep indention traveled from his forehead to his nape, separating the two cranial hemispheres. Yet, no bulging veins or bumps were visible on his smooth pale-green flesh. His nose was thin; his eyes, round; and his mouth, small with narrow lips. Perhaps, she mused, the sizes and shapes of his bold features made his skull appear bigger than it was, particularly when added to his great height and slim build. Even so, she did not find the alien's appearance to be frightening or repulsive. On the contrary, Yakir possessed a calm expression and genial aura. He was extremely intelligent, educated to the highest degree. Almost everyone who met or heard of him held the cordial and wise ruler in high esteem.

After the door was sealed, Yakir said to her, "Come and sit while we talk. We have much to do and swift action to take before the *villites* reach Iverk and complete their task and elude us. They will dock at our space port within two *horas* and reach the surface one *hora* later, so our schedule is limited. It is fortuitous your ship is faster and you arrived before them."

She watched Yakir turn to guide her to a comfortable sitting area, and she followed him. The elderly man—clad in a flowing black robe with gold braid trim and a gold Serian emblem to the left of his heart—moved slowly but gracefully, regally, across the enormous and beautiful room.

After they were seated facing each other, Yakir smiled at her. "Later," the aged and venerable ruler said, "you must tell me all you have seen, done, and learned. Reports—of a necessity—have been swift and to the point; I am eager to hear the details of your many successes. First, we have important work to do. Are you ready to put our clever ideas into motion?"

Her heart raced, but she replied, "Yes, *Raz* Yakir, I am ready, though I must confess I am nervous about the amazing angle you suggested; still, I believe it can be done with your help."

Yakir smiled, a mischievous twinkle in his brown eyes. "I have no doubt you can achieve our goal. You have proven yourself to be smarter and braver than our enemies. We will not be interrupted unless there is an emergency. If one occurs, you will hide in my secret chamber."

She laughed and quipped, "It would be difficult to explain Yana's presence and how she came to be in here." She turned serious. "Although Iverk is occupied elsewhere, we would not want someone to mention Yana's strange visit to him."

"If our strategy is successful, Iverk will not be in a position to contact that evil *nefariant* and betray me and our people again. One of my cyborgs captured and hid the miner who aided Iverk's treachery; he is the one we will use to expose and snare our wicked *Ysolte*. Eick revealed the truth to me while in the grip of *Thorin,* so I possess the facts you need to trick Iverk, you will hear and learn them soon. Eick's blood was drawn and the transmutation chemical for your first trick has been prepared. Another cyborg is watching Iverk and will alert me the *preon* he meets with the *villites;* their images are programed into his memory for recognition. You—"

"He does know that Dagan Latu isn't to be harmed, correct? I'm sorry I interrupted you, sir," she gave a hasty apology for her impolite action. "I have told you about our love and bond and our decision to become mates, so I fear for his safety and survival since he is unaware of our risky scheme."

Yakir smiled and comforted her. "I understand your feelings and concerns. Do not worry or fear; the *I-GAF* agent will not be harmed. After their captures, you and Dagan will return to Noy to defeat Tochar in the manner you suggested. Auken and Sach will accompany you and do your bidding. There was sufficient time after you related your ruse to me for Trilabs to supply the drugs you require for it, and for my scientists to create your other needs. Now, we must go over every detail of our two deceptions to make certain nothing has become entangled or been omitted. I will explain my idea on how to enlighten Dagan without exposing you two."

Starla listened in awe, then they hurriedly discussed the two daring ploys that could eradicate Tochar and his threat within a few *wegs,* if nothing went wrong. She knew that perfect timing was imperative, so was Dagan's rapid and unquestioning trust and obedience. She hoped and prayed her beloved would believe her and cooperate instantly when she appeared before him in an unfamiliar guise, that of an enemy, a male whom he might suspect was only trying to trick and expose him.

"Eick! Why did you come here?" Iverk demanded, then yanked his hireling inside, glanced around the exterior, and closed the door. The tall Serian towered over the shorter alien from another planet.

In the transmuted form of Eick, she said in a rush in Eick's voice, "Iverk, we have a complication and somebody's going to catch *Karlee!* The Security Force at the mine is acting strange, asking many questions." She saw anger mingle with worry in Iverk's round gaze. The thin lips of his small mouth almost vanished as he tightened them. Anxiety was flowing through his body, as veins along the pale-green covering on his semi-divided braincase enlarged and protruded.

"What kind of questions? What did you tell them?"

Eick glanced at the three men and asked, "Can we talk here?"

"Yes, tell me everything; these are trusted friends. What is wrong?"

"They said there should be more crystals, hinted some are missing, but I don't see how they could know how many and what colors we found. They questioned everybody several times, asking the same things over and over. They strip-searched us and examined the mine twice, even used a device to see inside us to make sure we hadn't swallowed any to smuggle them out. They've been acting suspicious ever since your visit when I gave you those crystals to sneak out." She noticed that disclosure alarmed him; the size of his round eyes increased and their shade darkened, veins on his cranium pulsed rapidly, and he straightened to his full height and stiffened.

Eick gave a dramatic shiver. "I could feel them watching me and I heard them whispering about using truth serum. I took my leave when it was time and came here. I made sure I wasn't followed. I can't return. I need the payments you've been holding for me; you have to get me somewhere safe to hide, maybe to Karteal or Maffei. Find somebody to alter my hair to blond and my eyes to aqua. Since I'm not Uluxan like you, I can be disguised. I'll change my name, maybe to Galen or Raimi. But I don't want to escape on no weapon's transporter and have one of them androids with silver eyes monitoring me. I want to go some place warm and pretty; I'm tired of dark caves; they're dangerous. You said if I helped you steal those crystals and put them signal boxes on the transport vessels, you would protect me and pay me good. I thought we had a future together, but things have changed. I don't want no *I-GAF*er or no elite squader chasing me down. I don't want to be put in no coma or put down forever. It's over, Iverk; our plans have changed. This new one has to work for all our sakes."

"Calm yourself, Eick; you can go with my friends when they leave soon. They will take you to the haven where they live. You can find work there until it is safe for you to come back and return to Kian."

"Not me, never. Find somebody else to help you steal moonbeams."

"Do not worry, Eick, I will protect you and help you. Auken," Iverk said as he faced the Icarian, "I want you to take good care of Eick for me. His loyalty and assistance deserve a reward and sanctuary from your leader."

"I'll take Eick where he needs to go," the *spaceki* said.

The disguised Starla perceived the unspoken message that passed between the two *villites:* Eick was to be taken away and disposed of en route to Noy. As Eick, she pretended to be duped and thanked Iverk and Auken, and hoped Dagan was intrigued by the many clues she was dropping for him.

"Sit down, Eick," Iverk said, "and relax while I finish speaking with my friends before they must depart. A long journey awaits you soon."

Eick took a seat, then leapt up and asked, "Can I have a drink? Do you have any *mumfresia;* it's my favorite?"

"Yes, the refreshments are there," Iverk replied, motioning to a bar.

"Anybody else want one?" *Eick* asked. "How about you, space rogue?" she added as she neared the place where her lover was standing.

The others said no, but Dagan requested a container of water. He wondered why the miner kept using words spoken between him and Starla, and wondered if the man was sending him clues about something. Perhaps Eick's mind had been programed by chemicals or the exposed man had been coerced into helping them ensnare Iverk. Yet, he reasoned, why wasn't the talk that had been taking place and being recorded by Cypher revealing enough to provide sufficient evidence? Why was Eick there?

Eick/Starla poured the two liquids and handed one to Dagan. "Look at my back," she mouthed to the baffled Kalfan, then presented it to him. She pressed a button on her belt which made a message appear, one hidden from the others' view by her position. She prayed her lover would believe what he saw. After she allowed him time to read it, she concealed it and gulped down the drink, a small one. "I'll have another," she murmured and went to get it, surreptitiously passing a special weapon to Dagan as she did so. She filled the container, went to her seat again, and sipped it.

Dagan held the weapon out of sight as he studied the situation. The astonishing message had said: *I'm Bree/Starla/Yana. Shapeshifted. Have a plan. Help me capture them. Trust me, love. Cypher-T on alert.* He glanced at the miner nearby as he took a swallow. Was it possible, he mused, that was his beloved Bree-Kayah in Eick's form? He remembered how different Yana was from Starla. But, Eick was a male! Even so, only his cherished woman could know the things just revealed to him and related the clues "Eick" had spoken earlier. What strategy did Starla and Yakir have in mind? How could he credibly explain the captures of Iverk, Auken, Sach, and Eick and his sole escape when he reached Noy, when only by returning could he get close enough to Tochar to defeat him? He concluded that Starla and Yakir must have come up with another way to destroy Tochar and his awesome weapons; surely they would not jeopardize the crucial mission when victory was at long last within reach. He hoped they were right, because after they took action, it could not be changed. He bided his time as he awaited an attack signal from . . . "Eick."

Iverk handed Auken the container of moonbeams and said, "Without Eick's help in the mine, we cannot get more until I find a replacement. Tell Tochar not to worry, I will find another helper soon. Eick, it is time to leave. Go with Auken and the others. Here is your payment."

Eick took the bag and thanked Iverk, who nodded his large head. As the traitor and Icarians clasped wrists in a farewell gesture, she retrieved her special weapon, pressed it against Sach's back, and stunned him with haste. She was elated when Dagan did the same to Auken without delay.

As both golden-haired men sank to the floor, Iverk gaped at the miner and Kalfan. "What are you two doing? This is treachery. Tochar will hunt you down and slay you both. These are his friends and crystals. There is no place in the universe you can hide from him. You have slain yourselves."

"Tochar will be defeated and powerless soon," *Eick* said,

"as you are defeated and powerless on this *deega,* Iverk, Traitor to Seri and the *UFG."*

Iverk looked at their weapons, then their faces. "Your brains have been destroyed, just as your bodies will be when Tochar finds you."

Eick walked to the door and opened it; *Raz* Yakir and four cyborgs were standing there. She watched the regal man approach Iverk and stare at him for a moment before shaking his head in revulsion.

When Iverk started accusing "Eick" and Dagan of breaking into his chamber and threatening his life, Yakir lifted his hand and said, "Silence! I know what you have done. The evidence of your greed and treason is recorded and it is undeniable. You are the first traitor Seri has known in over two hundred *yings.* You will die for your betrayal and dishonor."

"Your intelligence has left you, Yakir. I am the *Ysolte!* You cannot take me prisoner and terminate me. Our people will not allow such an evil deed."

Without raising his voice, Yakir refuted, "I am *Raz;* I am The Law. Your own mouth has sealed your dark fate. The incriminating words you spoke in your chamber to the *villites* who lay at your feet and the confession of Eick will be played for the High Council. No Serian will argue in your defense or protest your termination after the dark truth is heard. Have you no shame and remorse for endangering your people, endangering all who live in the United Federation of Galaxies, and perhaps those beyond it? You knew the powers of the moonbeams and crystaline weapons; yet, you gave or sold them to Tochar. That is unforgivable, high treason. You must die."

"No, Yakir, *you* must die!" Iverk shouted in a madness born of defeat and desperation as he drew a weapon and fired a lethal beam at the ruler.

Starla sensed the crazed man's reaction and flung herself

in Eick's form between the two Serians as Dagan simultaneously sent a laser blast into Iverk's chest.

The witnesses stood stunned in place for a few moments as two lifeless bodies collapsed to the floor.

Nineteen

Starla gazed at the cyborg who had shoved *Eick* aside and taken the direct hit from Iverk's deadly blast; she realized the unit had saved her life, just as—from instinct and training—she had attempted to save Yakir's. She assumed the cyborg's advanced sensors and programming had allowed it to scan Iverk's physiological functions, to analyze their meanings, to deduce the man's impending response, and to react to the threat much faster than she was able to do. As she had staggered backward, Dagan had seized her arm and prevented a fall. She pressed herself against him, forgetting her strange image at the time.

Dagan embraced her and held her tightly for a *preon,* relieved and overjoyed he had not lost her forever. He leaned back his head, gazed into "Eick's" eyes, and suddenly began chuckling. "Great stars, this is weird to be hugging and about to kiss a man. It is you, isn't it, my love?"

Eick laughed and said, "It's me, Dagan, Bree-Kayah. I'm glad you believed that message and aided me, but we didn't anticipate Iverk's death."

Dagan looked at the ruler and said, "Nor did I, sir. I wasn't close enough to use this stunner Starla passed to me, and Auken ordered me and Sach to set our weapons on the highest level to be ready for trouble. It was the only way I could disable him when he became reality-impaired."

"Do not worry, you did the right thing. Iverk sealed his own fate."

Dagan's gaze went from Yakir to *Eick*. "What's going on, Starla? Won't this obstruct our mission? How will I explain their losses to Tochar?" he queried, motioning to the unconscious Icarians and the Serian's body.

"That will not be necessary," Yakir replied for her. "Sach and Auken will be returning to Noy with you."

Dagan stared at the smiling ruler in confusion. "I don't understand. How is that possible? They won't turn against Tochar." His gaze brightened as he asked, "You're sending replacements transmuted into their forms?"

"No, they will go with you and do your bidding. We will discuss our next ruse in my chamber after this matter is tended." To the other cyborgs, he said, "Take the two prisoners to the holding room and Iverk's body to the cremation unit. Make certain no one sees them." He turned to Dagan and *Eick*. "Come, we have much to prepare and do. After your departures, I will reveal Iverk's treason and assassination attempt to the High Council, but it will not be announced publicly until after Tochar's defeat."

Later in the *Raz*'s chamber, *Eick* swallowed the reversal chemical to return to Starla's form.

As she did so, then changed clothes in an anteroom, Yakir explained to Dagan the reason for using that tactic. "We obtained a sample of Eick's blood after he was seized; it is necessary to have a person's body code before he can be reproduced by another. Every race and person have their own unique colorings, features, and traits. Another chemical is added to complete a particular person's current image. That is how Bree-Kayah became Yana and Eick, using their blood codes and appearances. Perhaps she has already told you the tragic tale of Mayoleesee Bargivi of Asisa."

After Dagan nodded, Yakir disclosed, "That same method

is how you will trick and capture Tochar; you will appear to
him as Iverk to lure him into your trap. Auken and Sach will
be programmed by a mind-controlling drug from Trilabs to
assist you. After all three are your prisoners, you will enter
the defense sites and destroy the crystaline weapons; then
the cloaked force standing by will attack the settlement. All
villites will be caught for punishment. Other inhabitants will
be ordered to evacuate before all colonies on Noy are razed.
It will no longer be a haven for *nefariants.* Our assault in
the Free-Zone will be justified because those who hide there
invaded our sectors and provoked it. We have a right to protect our citizens and their possessions. Surely no other galaxy
will protest our action."

"Even if they do, it will be too late to prevent it. But
how will I get a transmutation phial made without Tochar's
blood? Will your scientists be going with us and make it
there after he's apprehended?"

"Starla stole a sample before she left the settlement to
come here; the phial is ready for your use."

Dagan looked at her in amazement. "It's a good thing
Yana won't have to return and try to excuse her absence,
but how did you pull off that feat?"

She explained how she had handled Yana's absence in
case Yana's return had been necessary. "We couldn't attempt
this ruse before because I didn't know about the blood storage until recently, when Auken told us to place ours there
in case it was needed. Remember?" He nodded. "Also, I
needed to gather enough knowledge about Tochar to dupe
his men before he could be detained and substituted, if a
way could be found to remove him from sight before he
was replaced. Since I was never trusted with their secrets,
I couldn't be certain whether or not a password existed for
gaining entrance to the sites and for exposing an impostor.
That's also why I never tried to become one of his Enforcers. Before we depart, you will review tapes of Iverk to
help you play him convincingly. Auken and *Iverk* will lure

Tochar to the *Adika* where you and I will take him prisoner."

She said with a grin, "This time, it will be Tochar who is subjected to *Thorin*. If there is a code word, you will have it before you leave the ship. Cypher and I will confine them and monitor you while you go to the surface as Tochar to destroy the weapons. Then we can join the final battle or allow the force to handle it." She was delighted when Dagan praised her intelligent planning.

"Our mission would not be this close to victory without all you and Cypher have done, and with *Raz* Yakir's help," he added. "With success in reach and credited to you three, no one in the *UFG* or *I-GAF* could protest your secrecy and actions." He saw Starla and *Raz* Yakir smile in relief. "Will I use the same type of device Starla used to destroy the other crystals?" Dagan asked.

"Yes, just attach them near the crystals, set the timers, and put a safe distance between you and the explosions."

After all plans were made, Dagan remarked, "These are clever ideas and they should work."

"Using Iverk and Tochar's images were Bree-Kayah's suggestions," *Raz* Yakir revealed. "It was mine for her to use Eick's. I needed to have a recording of the dark bond between Eick and Iverk as evidence for the High Council. Our *Ysolte* was a leader of elite status; he was trusted, respected, admired. I am certain my accusations would have been believed, but having proof assures its acceptance by his friends and family."

"I think that's wise, sir," she concurred.

"So do I," Dagan agreed with them. "Sometimes it's hard to believe somebody you love and trust can betray you." The Kalfan related how Syrkin had once been his superior and friend until Tochar darkened his heart and gained control of his mind and actions.

Starla explained to Dagan that she hadn't related her

ideas to him earlier because they had been out of contact when the plans had occurred to her.

"I understand, and I'm glad you followed through with them. As I said, we're a perfect match, a perfect team; and my ego is intact."

"You and Bree-Kayah have done a superior job on this assignment; you have saved the United Federation of Galaxies and perhaps lives beyond it."

"First," Dagan reminded the elderly man, "we have to defeat Tochar and destroy those weapons."

"You will succeed; I am certain of that fact. When your final deed is done, there will be a ceremony here to reward you two with our highest commendations and with gifts of gratitude. A celebration will follow it. Your family, friends, and superiors will be invited."

"That's kind and generous of you, sir, but we only did our duties."

"No, Bree-Kayh Saar, you went far beyond your duties to achieve these glorious goals. I shall never forget how you offered your life to save mine. Your parents and family and people will be very proud of you."

Once more, she thanked the ruler for his heartwarming words.

"Now, you can rest and visit with each other tonight and tomorrow while the preparations are being made."

Starla snuggled into Dagan's tender embrace in the large and luxurious suite they had been supplied by Yakir, one guarded by a cyborg. They had feasted on a delicious meal, laughed, talked, relaxed, and soaked for an *hora* in a sunken bathing pool. The chamber's lighting was diffused, soft and lovely music filled their ears, heady fragrance wafted in the air, and dark reality was far away. It was as if this was the first time they could be themselves, could feel safe and be assured of privacy, and could concentrate only on each other.

While in the pool, they had kissed and caressed each other until they were compelled to make love in a feverish rush, urged to sate the desires which had smoldered during their long span of denial but were quickly fanned into urgent and blazing needs upon contact. Afterward, they had bathed, dried off, and moved to a spacious *sleeper.* They had talked and titillated each other for an *hora* until endless passions were rekindled.

As Dagan nibbled at her earlobe, he murmured, "No one will disturb us tonight and tomorrow, so many glorious *horas* alone." He lifted his head and locked their gazes as he added, "But I'm glad that cyborg is standing guard since Yakir can't erase your fake record until Tochar is apprehended, just in case he checks on Starla again. He shouldn't, but that *fiendal* is unpredictable and dangerous. I don't want anybody reading that false file, then seeing you and harming you by error."

Starla kissed his cleft chin and stroked his ebony hair. "Don't worry about me; I'm safe with you, my skilled parsec jumper."

"I hope so, but we aren't taking any risks; no showing this beautiful face and ravishing body outside this room or Yakir's meeting chamber."

"I promise to be careful and alert; you do the same."

"I will." Dagan drifted his fingertips over her bare skin. "Just out of curiosity, my love," he asked, "did you change completely into a man?"

Starla laughed merrily. "No, I was given only Eick's outward image. But," she added as she laughed again, "that would have been an interesting and enlightening experience." As he grinned, she slipped her fingers around his engorged manhood, moved her hand up and down its length, and said, "Then, I would know how this feels."

"Wonderful," he responded in a husky tone as she stimulated him.

"And how this feels," she added as her questing lips and tongue kissed and licked a path to his arousal and tantalized it wildly and skillfully.

"Rapturous and breathtaking," he said in a now-ragged tone as his body burned and his craving for appeasement increased at a rapid pace. He moaned and writhed as she enthralled and pleasured him. When he began to teeter on the brink of release, he controlled that reaction, rolled Starla to her back, and blissfully assailed her body. He took her to the pinnacle of ecstasy many times with his roving hands, lips, and tongue before she cascaded over its beckoning edge.

Dagan continued to stroke and kiss her, allowing that splendid and enchanting experience to mingle with the next.

He looked at her radiant expression and glowing eyes and said, "You're the most beautiful and utterly irresistible woman who's ever existed. I'm lucky you were unattached. I would have tried everything imaginable to win you away from him, even if I had to pursue you from one side of the Cosmos to the other. It's incredible I found someone so compatible and perfect for me. I can hardly wait until we are mates by law; then, you will be mine forever, Bree-Kayah Saar."

Starla's fingers swept aside a stray lock of black hair, then looked into his adoring blue eyes. "I am yours, Dagan, in every way except one, and that will be taken care of as soon as this mission is completed. I, too, would have done anything and everything to win you away from another woman, for I am greedy, selfish, and possessive when it comes to you. You stole my heart and wits with ease and speed, you cunning space pirate. I could never replace you if I lost you."

"You won't ever lose me, my love, never."

Their mouths meshed, their hands roamed, and their spirits soared into passion's realm. They made beautiful, imaginative love until they were sated, fatigued, and contented. Soon, they surrendered to peaceful slumber in each other's arms, to awaken the following morning to enjoy that *deega* and night in a similar manner.

Starla and Cypher left orbit around Ulux in the cloaked *Liska.* Dagan, Auken, Sach, and a cyborg guard departed in the *Adika.* Five ships of Serian patrol units followed close behind them, cloaked for secrecy. While en route, they would be joined by several *I-GAF* teams.

Dagan stored the transmutation phials in a safe place; he realized he was looking forward to the procedure and to the heady but dangerous adventure looming before them. The cyborg assigned to him was to guard the two prisoners and keep them drugged for their unknowing but willing participation. He was glad Starla would be staying out of the perilous action, as his concentration on the ruse would be better knowing she was out of harm's way, and *Yana's* presence at his side would be suspicious. At last, Tochar Galic would pay for his evil, including the murders of his family and friends, and would never be given another chance to imperil Starla. *Bree-Kayah,* he corrected, the name soft and lovely on his tongue and in his head, perfect for the woman he loved.

In a few *wegs,* if everything went as planned, he reminded himself, this mission would be over and a new life would begin for Curran Thaiter and Bree-Kayah Saar, as mates. He wished they were taking this trek together, but this wasn't the time to indulge themselves or to appear unprofessional to the other team members while en route to a crucial event. Soon, they would have plenty of time to stimulate and sate their endless desires. They could enjoy a daily existence together with no more secrets to guard, disguises to use, perils to confront and vanquish. At least they could communicate with each other during this journey, view images, and talk on occasion. But until they reached Noy, there was little to do.

Yet, Dagan couldn't dismiss a twinge of worry. He hoped nothing had been overlooked and no mistakes were made. But with Iverk's unplanned death, they didn't know if the Serian traitor was supposed to contact Tochar after their rendezvous, nor did Auken or Sach when interrogated with *Thorin.* Tochar's standard order was that during raiding treks, there was to be no communication between him and the pirate ship to prevent any advanced technology from detecting their signals and locating their positions. Yet, if Iverk had been told to contact him and did not, Tochar's suspicions could be aroused to a hazardous level; the *fiendal* had the means to blast the *Adika* and all other ships in their small fleet into oblivion. Even so, no weapon they possessed could match a *Destructoid* or be protected against its firepower. Or, Dagan worried, Tochar might refuse to come to the ship, even at Auken's and *Iverk's* urgings. Of course, *Iverk* could go to the *fiendal's* dwelling, but a nervous Tochar could have a unit of Enforcers with him or be heavily armed. If so, that would make the *fiendal's* capture difficult or impossible, and might create a situation where he—himself—was exposed. There was no way he knew everything the two *villites* had said to each other, since Iverk couldn't be interrogated. If Tochar caught him in a mistake, the game was over; and if Tochar had plenty of hirelings with him, death was a strong probability.

There was also the slim possibility that the shapeshifting chemical or process could fail. He certainly didn't want to remain as Iverk or Tochar for the rest of his life! There was also a possibility, even if he reached the defense sites, that the destruction devices wouldn't work. And there was a chance he might encounter someone who suspected he wasn't the leader and challenged him. No plan, the *I-GAF* officer reasoned, was totally foolproof, but he hoped and prayed the impending ones were.

Aboard the *Liska* a short distance away, Starla was experiencing similar fears and feelings. "He'll be walking into this danger all alone, Cypher; there's no way I can go with him as a backup in any form. If I had thought about it sooner, I could have transmuted into Auken. I want to be with him; I want to guard him, to help him."

"Do not be afraid, Bree-Kayah. He will succeed."

She laughed and said, "That sounds like human confidence to me. Have you inserted a human traits' chip I don't know about?" she teased.

"My programming has not been altered or upgraded since we began this mission. However, on future assignments, that would be a logical addition."

Starla did not tell the android this might be their last mission as a team, and she felt guilty about keeping that news from him. They had been together for a long time, and she would miss him if she retired. But, she and Dagan—no, *Curran*—might team up for a while until they were ready to settle down in one place and have a family. Sharing adventures and meeting challenges together sounded exciting and tempting to her. Perhaps Cypher would make an excellent protector and assistant for them . . .

"He likes you," she murmured almost unknowingly to her companion.

Cypher's silver visual sensors locked on her. "That does not compute."

"Sorry, my friend. Dagan likes you," she clarified. "You heard what he said about you in *Raz* Yakir's chamber about how important you are to this mission and its success. As I do, Cypher, Dagan views you as being alive, a friend, a teammate, a good and loyal companion."

The android analyzed her words, tone, and expressions.

He deduced all were sincere and complimentary. "If I were human, your praise and feelings would be moving to my emotions. It is beneficial he views me in that manner since you have become close to him. He is a superior teammate for you. His personality and presence are acceptable to me."

Starla laughed at his use of "acceptable." "I am delighted you find Dagan admissible and satisfactory for our tight unit," she teased. "I wouldn't want you two conflicting at every turn when he joins us permanently."

"Does he intend to resign from *I-GAF* and work with us?"

"Yes, and I hope you don't mind. Do you have any objections?"

"I am programmed to protect, obey, and assist you. My chips do not allow me to complain or defy your orders."

"But they allow you to have an opinion and to tell me if I am wrong."

"I do not locate a reason to disagree with your decision this time."

"That's all I needed to hear, Cypher. Thanks."

After orbit was obtained at Noy, the mind-controlled Auken contacted his leader in the settlement. "We've returned, Tochar, but we have a problem: Iverk is with us and he wants you to come talk with him."

Elsewhere on the *Adika,* Starla and the disguised Dagan listened to the conversation in progress via a transmission device on Auken. Another one embedded in Auken's ear allowed Dagan to pass messages to him which Auken relayed to his friend on the planet's surface. But they had anticipated most of Tochar's questions and reactions and had prepared Auken for them.

"Bring him to my dwelling," Tochar said in an annoyed tone.

"He refuses to leave the ship," Auken replied.

"Let me talk to him."

"He's locked himself in my quarters."

"What is wrong with him?" Tochar raged. "What happened on Ulux? Why is he here? This is foolish and rash."

"He's acting strange and secretive. He gave us the crystals, but he insisted on coming to Noy with us to speak privately with you."

"Put me through to him in your quarters." After Iverk's image appeared on his viewer screen, Tochar demanded, "Why are you here? This is reckless. You have probably exposed yourself. Come—"

In Iverk's voice and forcing the Serian's face to line with anger, he cut off the *fiendal.* "No, you come to me, Tochar. We have matters to settle. I will not be surrounded by your guards when we talk. I will await you here."

"He disconnected our signal," Tochar said to Auken. "Where is Dagan?"

"He's preparing the shuttle for our return later."

"Tell him to come after me so I can deal with Iverk."

"Dagan is making a minor repair on the shuttle's engine; it will not be ready for use for another *hora* or two, and Iverk is crazed. He's been acting this way during the entire voyage. Sach and I can't do anything with him. He won't tell us what's wrong, and we're afraid he might harm himself."

"You think I should come up now, not wait for the shuttle?"

"If you need Iverk back on Ulux, you should come settle him down. If there's trouble back there, you need to find out about it before he zones out completely. It would be faster and easier to teleport you here."

"You are right. Give me time to prepare myself. Tochar out."

* * *

Ten *preons* later, Tochar contacted Auken and said, "Lock on to my coordinates and bring me aboard."

"Sach, are you ready in the transporter room?" Auken asked.

"Entering the coordinates," Sach replied. "Transmission in progress."

After Tochar materialized on the sensor pad, his black gaze traveled from Auken to Sach to Dagan, who was standing behind Auken. "I thought you were working on the shuttle," he said to Dagan as he stepped forward.

"It's fine. Welcome aboard and into my trap, Tochar," Dagan sneered as he left the concealment of Auken's body, a weapon in his hand. He watched Tochar gape at him in confusion, which gradually altered to fury.

"What is the meaning of this treachery, Latu? Have you zoned out? Take him prisoner!" Tochar ordered his two friends.

Dagan chuckled when the two men remained frozen to their spots, having been ordered not to respond to any of the man's orders. "They can't help you; no one can help you. By the authority of *I-GAF,* I arrest you for the many crimes you have carried out and instigated."

Tochar gaped at the Kalfan, then at his fellow Icarians. "Are you two betraying me and siding with this fool? Explain your actions immediately!"

"Auken, Sach, return to your quarters and remain there," Dagan said. He saw Tochar's dark gaze widen as he witnessed his men's obedience.

"What is wrong with them? What did you pay my friends to trick and betray me?"

Dagan grinned. "Nothing. They'll be sent to a termination unit just like you will after I get rid of those *Destructoids.*"

The door swished open. Starla and the cyborg joined Dagan.

She smiled and said, "I see you have everything under control."

Tochar's gaze darkened, narrowed, and chilled. "You are both dead. My Enforcers will never allow either of you to get near my weapons. I suspected something was wrong. I told Palesa if I had not returned within the *hora,* to alert them to danger. If I am not freed immediately, she will have the weapon on my dwelling mounted to my ship and it will attack a different location on various planets until I am released."

Dagan laughed again and said, "Don't worry, *Tochar* will return to the surface very soon. He will be the one to destroy your weapons."

"You are reality-impaired! What deception are you trying to pull?"

"Before nightfall, your defenses will be destroyed and a large force of Serians and *I-GAF* agents will attack the settlement; it will be razed, as will the other *villite* havens on this planet. Cloaked ships are standing by to carry out the assault as soon as I give them a signal to begin."

"Where is Iverk? What has he told you?"

Dagan was surprised by Tochar's response to the stunning revelation, as if that bad news hadn't registered in his mind. "Dead; he was exposed and tried to assassinate *Raz* Yakir. That was me you spoke to earlier. I presume from your reaction and arrival that I impersonated Iverk perfectly."

"How could you pretend to be a Serian? That is impossible."

"Let's just say I used a little magic and cunning." Despite his claims, Tochar didn't look as if he believed him, but that didn't matter.

"What is wrong with Auken and Sach? They are not themselves"

"You're right. We control their minds and actions with drugs." Dagan saw panic and rage fill Tochar's gaze and stiffen his body. Obviously, grim reality was beginning to settle in on the ensnared *fiendal*.

"Why is Starla, here? Were you two working against me all the time?"

"Yes, separately at first; then we teamed up after you tried to kill her. She's also an agent, but not for *I-GAF;* that's all you need to know."

"How did you two pass my *Thorin* tests?" Tochar persisted.

"Let's just say we used another magical trick."

"Rendelar," Tochar guessed. "Soon, I would have controlled that and all other potent chemicals. I would have exposed and slain you both."

"If you could have gotten your evil hands on Trilabs; you can't."

"Who are you, Dagan? A blood lust for me gleams in your eyes."

"Curran Thaiter. I was a *Seki* when you attacked Gavas with that faked chemical hazard and killed my family and friends." He watched Tochar's gaze brighten as the evil man recognized that name from the past.

"Thaiter was the one pursuing us with a vengeance, but he is dead."

Dagan glanced down at his body and scoffed, "I don't think so. Do I look dead to you, my love?" he asked Starla.

Her adoring gaze roamed his full length. "Not to me, my beloved."

"What—"

"No more questions, Tochar! Not by you anyway. It's our turn to ask them, and you will tell us all we need to know."

"I will not tell you anything, Thaiter! If that is who you are."

"Oh, I think you will; you won't have any choice. Is the *Thorin* ready?" Dagan asked the cyborg who nodded. "Put him under now."

They watched Tochar try to back away from the cyborg's

approach. He was unable to break its strong grip on his arms which were pinned to his sides. The *fiendal* thrashed and squirmed and cursed them as he was injected with the truth serum.

"You will regret this treachery!" Tochar shouted at the smiling couple.

"The only thing that feels better than defeating you, Tochar, is finding and winning this unique woman for my mate. I should be a little grateful to you since you're the one who brought us together."

Starla knew how much Dagan was savoring this coming victory. At last, he had justice for his slain family and the threat to their worlds would be over soon, and their bonding ceremony awaited them.

They listened and watched as Tochar used his remaining span of awareness to curse and threaten them with vows of horrible revenge, to which Dagan chuckled. Then, Tochar's brief questioning began . . .

Starla stared at Dagan in the transmuted form of their enemy. She asked, "How do you feel?"

He lifted his brows and took a deep breath. "Strange. Shapeshifting is a wild experience. You can feel your flesh crawling and itching as it alters. Even your bones and muscles change. It's amazing, stimulating, but a little scary. That isn't my voice I'm hearing or my body I'm seeing." Though he had taken on Iverk's vastly different form for a short time, assuming Tochar's more similar one seemed just as incredible to him.

"You look and sound exactly like Tochar, my beloved. You'll dupe them. Soon, this mission will be finalized in a glorious victory. You have the password, so hurry before Palesa gets nervous and sounds an alarm."

"Tochar was probably deceiving us with that desperate

threat, but I won't take a chance he wasn't telling the truth. I'll see you soon, my love."

"If not, I'll be coming down after you," she warned in a playful tone. "Please watch your back since I won't be there to do it. I love you, Dagan."

"I'll be careful. I love you, woman. Now, send me down."

He stepped on the sensor pad and she teleported him to the _fiendal's_ abode. She returned to the bridge and sat down, a device in her grasp to overhear the events taking place below her position. The drugged Tochar, Auken, and Sach were being guarded by the cyborg in Auken's quarters on the _Adika._ Cypher was at the helm of her ship, also monitoring Dagan's progress. The mixed Serian and _I-GAF_ force was on alert, ready to take action upon Dagan's successful return. Starla contacted her android and said, "Be prepared to rescue my love if anything goes wrong since I may lack time to signal you if that becomes necessary."

"Affirmative," the android responded.

Dagan masked his tension as he entered his transmuted form's lofty dwelling and immediately faced his first challenge: duping the _fiendal's_ hermaphroditic lover. Although in public Palesa appeared to be and behaved as a woman—a ravishing creature with purple eyes, soft fair skin, and long red hair—she was _Binixe,_ a race of androgynes whose bodies possessed male and female sex organs and were self-reproductive. They were a mysterious and private people who rarely intermingled with outsiders, so he didn't know how or when or why Palesa had coupled with Tochar; that meant he couldn't allow her time to ensnare him with a mistake.

"What happened, Tochar? Where are the others? What is wrong?"

He was relieved he had overheard Tochar's endearments for her and made clever use of them. "Only a minor problem, my beauty. It will be handled soon. Go to the Skull's Den and wait for me to join you there."

Palesa looped her arms around his neck and pressed her sensual body to his. "First, we must finish what we started before you were summoned. I will quickly arouse your appetite again. Let me remove your—"

Tochar grasped her wrists and loosened her hold on him, smiling as he did so. "There is no time at the present to enjoy ourselves. I have guests coming. I will join you soon at Radu's after I speak to them."

"I will retire to my chamber and wait there, and we will go together."

He stroked her cheek as he asked in a mellow tone, "Why do you disobey me this *deega,* my beauty? I have important matters on my mind, things to be settled. A man is arriving soon and he does not wish to be seen by anyone; that includes you, my precious treat. Besides, he is delivering a special surprise for you," he tempted the epicene being.

"What is it? You must tell me or I shall be overexcited with curiosity."

He laughed and shook his head, golden hair swaying at his nape. "Do not spoil my pleasure by coaxing me to reveal it. You must leave now."

"If you insist, I will go, but join me soon or beckon my return. I will reward you in many wonderful ways for my surprise. I will—"

To silence her, he grasped her shoulders, turned her body toward the door, and said, "Go, quickly; my preparation time is limited. You can also surprise me later with those delicious treats."

Via the large *transascreen,* the transmuted Dagan watched the *Binixe* exit the *trans-to,* get into a landrover, and drive toward the settlement. He hurriedly located Zarafa and had Tochar's abused slave teleported to one of the Serian ships for her safety and survival, disclosing to the astonished woman she was being freed and sent home. He didn't have to worry about Tochar's two robots, as the automatons remained in an inactive mode until the *fiendal* needed them to perform tasks.

He said to Starla, whom he knew was listening, "Palesa and Zarafa are gone. I'm going to plant the first device. I'll seal the door when I leave so no one can enter before the explosion."

After the device was in place and the timer was activated, *Tochar* took a landrover to the first defense structure. He gained entry with ease and speed using the password supplied by Auken and verified by the *spaceki* leader. He chatted with two men on duty while he surreptitiously planted the second device and started its timer. Afterward, he did the same with the third device at the second defense site. At both locations, he ordered the guards to lock the structures and to check out the area for a possible intruder; he doubted their lives would be spared when the detonations occurred, but that could not be helped. Taking any other action or assuming any other command would have been suspicious, even for their leader.

He rode to Yana's dwelling and entered it. "Starla, I'm ready to return. Everything is done here. Lock on to me and bring me aboard."

Starla was prepared to comply and did so. The moment he stepped from the sensor pad, she flung herself into his arms and said, "You're safe now, my beloved. Transmute to yourself so I can cover your face with kisses. We have fifteen *preons* until the blasts."

He cupped her face with his hands and fused their gazes. "I know you're a highly skilled and experienced officer, my love, but please remain aboard during the remainder of the action. There are a lot of *villites* down there who will fight their best to escape, and I don't want you injured."

It felt strange to be staring into Tochar's black eyes but speaking to Dagan. "Do you have to go? Can't the others battle and capture them?"

"I'm an *I-GAF* officer, love, and this was my assignment so it's my duty to assist the others. You've taken more than your share of risks during this joint mission, and most of the accomplishments belong to you, so please stay here where you'll be safe. I'll be distracted with you in harm's path. It took me twenty-eight *yings* to find you; I don't want to lose you now."

"What if you need my help as a backup?"

"I'll be fine, so don't worry about me. Besides, my friend Cypher will be monitoring and protecting me."

She knew he had faith in her prowess and his concern was born only from love for her. She smiled and relented to his request.

"Thanks, my love," he said in relief and kissed her. "Now, I have to transmute. I don't want to go down there looking like this."

As soon as Dagan was himself again, they embraced and kissed; this time, their mouths meshed in a long and tender one. Arm in arm, they observed the three massive explosions on the viewer screen.

"Let's hope the devices worked and those *Destructoids* are gone."

"I'm sure they did, love. Well," he said, as he hugged her, "it's time for me to leave." Dagan told the large force of men to prepare to start the action in ten *preons,* which would allow the dust and debris to settle. He checked his weapons, kissed her again, and teleported to another ship to join a unit of agents who were awaiting his arrival before departure.

"Stay safe, my beloved, and return to my side," Starla murmured to herself. She held a listening device close to her ear to catch every word Dagan spoke, her heart pounding in apprehension as he again faced peril.

Starla decided she would teleport to her ship to observe the action with Cypher. She had the cyborg and prisoners sent to a Serian vessel for detainment there. She set the *Adika*'s automatic pilot so it would circle Noy until its fuel was spent and its orbit decayed, if it wasn't confiscated for use by one of the other forces. If not, it would burn up upon entry into the planet's atmosphere. She gathered her things and left the craft—one in which she had spent many *deegas* as an alleged *spaceki*—for the last time.

"How is the mission progressing?" she asked Cypher as she took a seat near him on the *Liska*'s bridge and locked her gaze to the monitor.

"Dagan and the combined forces just shuttled or teleported to the planet's surface; the final battle has been initiated. The colony's inhabitants are fleeing in many directions. Some are going into hiding. Some are taking shuttles to their ships. Many are fighting or preparing to do so."

"Sheer chaos is taking place, I believe. Those blasts must have terrified most of them, but I'm certain everyone realizes what happened. It must be clear to them the defense sites are destroyed; so is Tochar's dwelling. Perhaps they will assume he has been slain and they are helpless. With the advanced weapons we have and the skills of our combined force, the *villites* are sure to lose, but still they fight and attempt to escape."

"Even surrender will not ensure life for some of the *vil-*

lites. Many have committed crimes which warrant t͏
tion."

"And confinement to one of those barbaric penal colͦ
isn't an enticement to evoke their surrenders," she add͏
"We're lucky we were born into good families and sitͧ
ations. I wouldn't want to be a real member of Tochar's
band this *deega.*"

If it were possible, Cypher would have chuckled in
amusement at her second sentence. Even so, he grasped her
meaning and slip. It somehow pleased him to realize she
thought of him as a person.

"Look," she said, "they're rounding up groups of people
in several locations and scanning their records device to see
who to apprehend. Those with criminal files are being taken
aboard one of the vessels. Others are being sent into the
Skull's Den and other structures to await evacuation. Dagan
said he would make certain Radu was given a chance to
leave, unless the Ceyxan has charges against him which are
unknown to us. I wonder what they will do with Palesa,"
she murmured, recalling how the *Binixe* had tried to seduce
her beloved, though Palesa had thought it was her lover.

"The *I-GAF* agents will decide the androgyne's fate."

"Look there, Cypher," Starla said again, pointing to another screen. "Some of Tochar's Enforcers are taking refuge
in the caves. Since I don't see any of our men in that area,
I'll inform Dagan of their hiding places."

Starla contacted him with that information, but did the
task in a hurry to prevent distracting him longer than was
necessary. Any time a *villite* tried to sneak up on or lay a
trap for Dagan, Cypher warned the Kalfan and exposed the
nefariant's location, giving Dagan an advantage and a safeguard. Their advanced sensors and communication abilities
also allowed Cypher to send Dagan warnings for others who
were fighting near him.

She saw a few of their men go down from lethal blasts,
though her side was using stun-only settings for captures

errogations. Their bodies were collected by fellow
s and teleported to their ships. Injured men also were
eved and treated aboard their vessels. She watched as
ne of the *villites* surrendered after their weapon's power
as depleted. She saw visitors or noncriminal inhabitants
turn themselves over to the assault team so they wouldn't
be slain by mistake or accident.

She grasped why those who knew Dagan Latu as one of
Tochar's men were not seeking help from him and were
attacking him: he had changed into *I-GAF* attire and made
his hand insignia visible! *"Pralu,* Cypher, look at Dagan!
I just realized he's using his uniform and badge. I was so
worried and distracted by his jeopardy, I didn't notice until
now." Her gaze roamed his striking image; he was so handsome, authoritative, confident in that dark-blue garment and
while displaying his imposing emblem.

"It was a logical measure for self-defense."

Starla smiled and added, "And for intimidation. Even
brave *villites* fear the awesome power and elite prowess of
parsec jumpers. Isn't he magnificent, Cypher? My family
and friends will love and respect him as much as I do. I
can hardly wait for them to meet him. Mother, Amaya, and
Rayna will be delighted to learn I'll have a mate soon. Such
glorious *deegas* and exciting adventures await us, my friend.
We three will become the most requested team for certain
assignments. We'll travel the galaxies together until we're
ready to settle in one place and have children."

Cypher analyzed her remarks and emotions and deduced
no response was required or expected. Yet, oddly and illogi-
cally, he found her words to have a pleasing effect upon
him. Perhaps, he reasoned, his emotions chip had begun to
function better or he had gathered more data to assist his
comprehension of certain human feelings and situations. He
was amazed and confused that he *liked* and *was stimulated*
by plans she had expressed.

Starla sat on the edge of her seat. With the use of laser

instruments that were powered by moonbeams, no s.
was impenetrable to her side. She observed and wai.
suspense as the confrontation continued until darkness
clouds partially obstructed her view. Night also compel.
the combined forces to cease their assault until morning
She listened as secure areas were set up for the Serians and
I-GAF agents so they could take shifts guarding, resting,
eating, and sleeping. She was amused when Dagan turned
off his transmitter so she wouldn't overhear the men talking
and joking, since he remained below with them.

"I shall eat, enter the cleansing unit, and sleep for a
while, Cypher," she told her trusted android. "Summon me
if I'm needed or peril strikes at my beloved." She doubted
she would slumber well, but she wanted to be rested for
what lay ahead of her.

Upon arising early the next morning, Starla dressed and
hurried to the bridge. "Anything happening?" she inquired.
"Is Dagan all right?"

"The one you love is safe from injury and death; he
sleeps at this time. *Villites* are still being located and apprehended by our forces. Many have been taken aboard the
other vessels. Some ships have been permitted to depart;
many who are not wanted for crimes were allowed to go
with those leaving. Others are to be transported to new locations by the Serians."

She sat down and listened as the evacuation order was
issued and the news was announced that the colony would
be razed. Anyone in hiding was warned the event would
take place in two *deegas,* allowing them time to surrender
or depart. It was revealed that all other colonies on Noy
would face the same fate, so it was foolish to take refuge
in one of them.

"I wonder what the *Skalds* will eat after everyone is

she mused aloud, the strange thought flashing across ...ind like a comet.

...hey will find nourishment on plants and animals or ...y will die," Cypher answered.

"We certainly don't want to rescue and relocate flesh-eating mutants. It's best and safest for others if they're left here to their natural fates."

"That is logical. They live, but they have the minds and traits of wild beasts. They must not be placed around other humans and endanger them."

"Good morning, my love," a mellow voice came over the transmitter.

"Good morning to you, Dagan," she responded, his sound warming her from head to feet. "When will you be joining us?"

"We have a few more pockets of *villites* to clean out, then I'll be coming aboard. I have to show our team where Tochar's caves are located so the stolen goods can be recovered. As soon as our reports are filed, we'll leave for Ulux. The rest of the team can finish up here and at the other settlements; they're smaller and less inhabited, so it won't take long. At least Noy won't be used as a stronghold or haven for more *villites* again. *I-GAF*ers are taking charge of Tochar, Auken, Sach, his Enforcers, and a few others. The Serian patrols will take command of the other debris; they'll turn them over to whatever galaxy they're wanted in the most."

"That's wonderful news. What about Radu and Palesa?"

"A Ceyxan trader gave them a ride to Mu where he's from. He was grateful to be spared, but I don't know what either one plans to do later. They were warned to keep away from *villites* in the future or risk trouble."

"I hope Radu heeds those words; I liked him. He didn't seem to be the kind of person to live and work among such nefarious beings."

"He stopped by a few *yings* ago with a friend and won

the Skull's Den in a *resi* game; that's why he stayed, (
what he told us. Sorry, but I have to suspend transmission,
I'm needed for those tasks I mentioned earlier. I know," he
said with a chuckle, "I'll be careful and I'll see you soon.
What could possibly happen to me with you and Cypher
on guard? By the way, good morning to you, Cypher. Take
good care of Starla for me. Dagan out."

"Affirmative. Cypher out."

Starla grinned and said, "See, I told you he likes you."

"When my emotions chip is functioning at full capacity,
I will like him, too," the android told an amused Starla.

As the *Liska* left orbit with Cypher in control of the
bridge, Dagan said to Starla in her quarters, "I just finished
filing my last report with Phaedrig and turning in my resignation. As I told you, *I-GAF* agents must be single to
prevent distractions. He said he hated to lose me, but he
understands my decision and sends his congratulations and
best wishes. He'll be on Ulux, so you can meet him there
and I'm sure you'll like him. Phaedrig's planning to send
the Thracians news about the crimes and fates of Koteas
and Terin, and give them a slight warning about their acceptance and use of men like Tochar and the perils of dealing with them. After the Thracians learn how powerful the
UFG is, which will be obvious from Tochar's stunning defeat, perhaps they'll join our Federation. The more galaxies
that are included, the fewer to cause us problems later."

"That seems to be a wise precaution to me."

"I agree. I told him Tochar doesn't have any other accomplices, according to what he related during our brief
questioning. I suppose with Iverk dead, we'll never know
why he joined forces with Tochar. Phaedrig plans to question Tochar further to learn how and when he met Syrkin,
Iverk, and Acharius and how he persuaded them to turn
traitor to their people. It's helpful to learn *villite*'s motiva-

...ons for use in future missions. After their final interrogations, Tochar and Syrkin will be terminated for their many crimes."

"They knew the laws when they broke them, so punishment shouldn't come as a surprise to any of them. This mission has been so long and hard and often frightening that it's amazing it's over. We shouldn't ever face this kind of threat again, because *Raz* Yakir told me that all white and green crystals which are found in the future will be destroyed upon their discoveries, and no weapons will be made from them again. Only moonbeams with good traits will be saved: you probably know red ones are useful in heating and lighting; yellow provide many medical purposes; and blue are excellent for superior surgical lasers. As Cypher said, it would be terrible to seal the mines forever, to destroy the good with the bad."

"He's right, as usual. Now, we have two things left to do, my love."

She nestled into his embrace and asked, "What are they?"

"First, we must attend the ceremony and celebration on Ulux, where I'll meet your family and get their approval. Second and most important, we must bond as mates and begin our new life and work together."

She gave him a hug as she replied, "I adore both of those ideas, particularly the last one. But you do not need my parents' approval, though you shall receive it, I'm certain. They'll love, respect, and accept you as I do."

"Still, I want to speak with them before we bond. They're legendary and prestigious figures across the entire *UFG* and I'm eager to meet them. It will be an honor to join your family; mine would be pleased and proud if they were alive to share in this happy event. Did you know that *I-GAF* agents study many of your father's past tactics for use in our missions?"

Starla realized he left the topic of his lost loved ones in

a hurry, probably to avoid dampening their joy on occasion. Yet, she knew he would relate his complete soon, just as she knew he came from a family as wond as hers. Since his had been wealthy and prominent and volved in Kalfa's government, he would not feel out of pla in her social rank. "No, I didn't," she answered his question, "but Father was and still is a man of superior intelligence, prowess, and statue. So is my mother, and my sister and brother. I'm not boasting, but their achievements are many and have been crucial to the survival of our people."

Dagan stroked her brown hair and smiled. "I've read Maffeian history so I know you're telling the truth. It's normal to be proud of them, and I want to hear more about your family during our trek to Ulux."

"It's late now and we're exhausted, so we'll contact them on rising to let them know the final battle has taken place and we're safe and on our way. We can speak to them for a while, but you'll learn more after you meet them." Yes, she decided, during their journey she would tell him many glorious tales about her family's intergalactic adventures and seemingly star-crossed romances; all had been players in dangerous games of perilous intrigue and had surrendered to irresistible passions. They had challenged and defeated many enemies and awesome forces, and each had almost lost their chosen one during near-fatal battles. She wanted him to get acquainted with her family and for him to form his own opinion before she revealed dark episodes which her parents and siblings had confronted, endured, and conquered long ago.

"I'm looking forward to getting to know each of them. My parents, sister, and two brothers would have been delighted by my choice of mates. I never imagined I would be the son to carry on the Thaiter bloodline. We'll have a splendid time creating our own family after we retire from trekking around the Universe. Have you told Cypher he'll be our teammate until we settle down in Maffei?"

 and he actually sounded and appeared to be
  ⸱. I'm beginning to wonder if we aren't rubbing off
   ⸱n; he talks and acts like a human more every *deega*."
   inclined her head toward him, changing the subject as
  ⸱e asked, "Tell me, my beloved, was it difficult to spurn
  ⸱alesa's cravings for you?" she jested.

Dagan chuckled and nestled her closer. "For a while
there, I was afraid I couldn't get away from her grasping
arms and lewd intentions."

"You did a superb job; she never suspected you for a
moment. Of course," Starla said with a merry laugh, "I
would have teleported down immediately if she had refused
to stop tempting my property."

Dagan rolled to his side and nibbled on her ear. "Possessive, are you?"

"When it comes to you, my dashing space rogue, I am.
I adore your name, and I can hardly wait to see you as you
truly are. Though I must confess, Cypher used one of our
computer programs to display your image with sun-kissed
hair and aqua eyes and the facial changes you mentioned.
I should tell you, Curran Thaiter is far more handsome and
appealing than Dagan Latu, which I never believed was possible for any man."

He warmed as her gaze roamed his face and her fingers
trailed over his bare chest. "Thank you, my love. As soon
as we reach Ulux, you can see for yourself if your assumption is correct. *Raz* Yakir said he would have a skilled medical team ready to restore me to myself. The procedure is
quick and painless, especially with those new moonbeam
laser scalpels. When I meet your family, it will be as Curran
Thaiter. As for you," he murmured as he kissed her nose,
"I much prefer Starla's image to Yana's." He chuckled. "I
wonder how long it will require before Curran and Bree-
Kayah roll off our tongues as easily as Dagan and Starla
do now."

"I'm sure we'll make many slips since we've used those

names for so long, but we have all the time we'l. correct them. Right now, what we need is this," sh. mured as she kissed him and caressed his virile body, . next to hers, their flesh in sensuous and stirring conta.

Dagan sealed their mouths in a series of long, slow, a. deep kisses which quickly merged into intense, needy one. as their mutual desires heightened. His questing hands ventured over her responsive body, titillating and pleasuring.

Starla did the same, stimulating and enticing him ever upward on that intoxicating spiral to ecstasy. Dagan had been right all along: they were a perfect match in every way. She kissed his lips and murmured, "I love you with all my heart and soul and we shall be so happy together."

He gazed into her glowing green eyes and radiant expression and his heart overflowed with wonderful and potent emotions. "Yes, we will, Bree, for I love you with all my heart and soul."

Soon, their pleading bodies were joined in a blissful union and their spirits soared the heavens. The hearts and lives of Curran Thaiter and Bree-Kayah Saar—third child of Maffeian Varian Saar and Jana Greyson Saar of Earth—had been bound forever by generous destiny, just as those of Galen and Rayna, and Amaya and Jason had been forged long ago. Evil had been defeated, and now peace ruled the Federation.

As the *Liska* journeyed through the vast reaches of space with Cypher at the helm and recent perils left far behind, Bree-Kayah and Curran made rapturous love in a splendid setting which was ashimmer with starlight, moonbeams, and ever-present magic.

Two Hearts joined by Fate, Aliens no more;
Light conquered Darkness; Fiery passions soar.
On wings of Splendor, these lovers wished to ride;
Trekking through a Universe so perilous and wide.
Evil has settled; Treachery has fled;
Peace and Love now rule in their stead.
Moonbeams and Magic, though wondrous they be;
A glorious Destiny awaited child number three.
But children are born to a legendary Saar line;
I wonder what adventures those heirs will find . . .

Author's Note

It was a thrilling challenge to create Book IV in the
"Moondust" Series, a sequel that would stand on its own
for those of you who haven't read the first three sagas. I
am deeply grateful for the letters so many of you sent to
me and to my publisher requesting its continuation. I origi-
nally planned only three books in the series, but after writing number three, Starla and Dagan leapt into my head and
heart and begged me to let them share their romance and
adventures with you. Naturally I was hooked immediately
and helpless to resist their pleas.

If you missed sagas I-III, they are available from Pinna-
cle/Zebra Books through your local bookstore, or by ordering
them from the publisher.

In book #1, *Moondust And Madness,* Commander Varian
Saar (Zar) of Maffei abducts Earthling research scientist
Jana Greyson to take her to his galaxy as a captive mate,
as most of the Maffeian females were rendered sterile years
ago by an enemy's treachery. Jana finds herself a pawn in
an intergalactic struggle with foes determined to destroy
Varian and to conquer his world. Jana seeks her new fate
and freedom with the alien starship commander whose
looks, fame, power, status, wealth, and prowess are enormous; and his secrets are many and hazardous. Yet, under
their law and from enemy threats, Jana is out of Varian's
reach. Or is she . . .

In book #2, *Stardust And Shadow,* an injured Jana, after
winning Varian's love and acceptance, believes she went to
sleep in his arms and aboard his vessel, a bright future in

r them. But she awakens on Darkar—weakened and
. from a near-lethal illness—to find herself with
an's treacherous half brother, legally bound forever to
ker Triloni, a scientific genius, owner of Trilabs, one of
e most powerful and invincible forces in existence. Worse,
Varian is about to wed another woman, Jana's arch-rival and
the bitter enemy who had placed her in Ryker's clutches.
She is forced to accept the truth that she loved and trusted
the wrong brother. But Ryker seems to be changing for the
better and he promises to save Earth from certain doom, as
he possesses the only weapons and knowledge that could
do so. Yet, there is a price she must pay for his aid: she
must surrender willingly to him and produce him an heir
to his holdings and to the rulership of the Androas Galaxy,
for which Ryker is next in line. As the Tri-Galaxy heads
for war, Ryker pursues her heart and commitment with a
sincerity she cannot deny.

In book #3, *Starlight And Splendor,* twenty-five years
have passed since Ryker's death and the marriage between
Jana and Varian, who are still very much in love and savoring blissful passions. Now, their twins face perils and
bittersweet romances. Galen seeks his destiny in the arms
of a beautiful and deceitful seductress who might be his
doom and a destroyer of his world. During what was to be
a short visit to Earth with the Sangers to study her mother's
world, Amaya's wits, courage, and skills are tested to the
fullest when she meets an irresistible but forbidden Earthling and is taken captive by evil scientists. All Saars join
forces to battle their worst enemy and to thwart certain destruction of their world when an alien virus—one without
a cure that spreads and kills rapidly and against which the
Maffeians have no immunity—is unleashed on their planets,
along with vicious criminals who wreak havoc on all planets
before they mysteriously vanish until their next attack,
strangely forewarned by an unknown traitor. Three romances and many adventures are entwined in this story as

the Saars battle for their world's survival and to win the hearts of those they love.

Many of you have requested more books in this series, several even pleaded for me to write as many sagas as there are in my nine-book Gray Eagle/Alisha "Ecstasy" Series. If you want to read more stories about the Saars, let the publisher of Pinnacle Books know, as the decision is theirs.

If you would like to receive a Janelle Taylor Newsletter, a complete list with cover pictures and plot descriptions of my thirty-three novels, and a bookmark, send a self-addressed stamped envelope (long size best) to:

Janelle Taylor Newsletter
P.O. Box 211646
Martinez, Georgia 30917-1646

Reading is fun and educational, so do it often! Until next time . . .

More praise for
A Perfect Crime

"Francie Cullingwood . . . is believable both as a sophisticated art expert and as an unhappily married woman caught up in the thrill of an affair. Her callow lover, his emotionally delicate wife, and their young daughter are also real enough to be your neighbors. The tricky work, though, has gone into the bad guys—Francie's egomaniacal husband, Roger, and the ex-con named Whitey he recruits to do his killing. Despite the madness of their actions, they remain human-scale monsters."
—*The New York Times Book Review*

"[*A Perfect Crime*] confirms Peter Abrahams's talent—as displayed in *The Fan*—for turning a single character's obsession and revenge into a peg onto which to hang a plot. It contains tight, seamless storytelling that begs to be turned into a screenplay."
—*Chicago Tribune*

"Abrahams has crafted a thoroughly absorbing novel of the decline and fall of a modern marriage—in which murder replaces divorce. The characters ring true, the suspense keeps the pages turning, and the ending is a shocker. *A Perfect Crime* is a perfect thriller."
—LISA SCOTTOLINE
Edgar Award–winning author of
Rough Justice and *Legal Tender*

*Please turn the page
for more reviews. . . .*

By Peter Abrahams:

THE FURY OF RACHEL MONETTE
TONGUES OF FIRE
RED MESSAGE
HARD RAIN
PRESSURE DROP
REVOLUTION #9
THE FAN
LIGHTS OUT
A PERFECT CRIME*

Published by Ballantine Books

A PERFECT CRIME

Peter Abrahams

BALLANTINE BOOKS • NEW YORK

A Ballantine Book
Published by The Ballantine Publishing Group
Copyright © 1998 by Pas de Deux Corporation
Excerpt from *Crying Wolf* copyright © 2000 by Pas de Deux Corporation.

All rights reserved under International and Pan-American Copyright Conventions. Published in the United States by The Ballantine Publishing Group, a division of Random House, Inc., New York, and simultaneously in Canada by Random House of Canada Limited, Toronto.

Ballantine and colophon are registered trademarks of Random House, Inc.

Grateful acknowledgment is made to Creeping Death Music for permission to reprint an excerpt from the lyrics of "Master of Puppets" written by Lars Ulrich, James Hetfield, Kirk Hammett, and Cliff Burton. Lyrics reprinted by permission of Creeping Death Music.

www.randomhouse.com/BB/

Library of Congress Catalog Card Number: 99-90124

ISBN 0-345-42680-0

Manufactured in the United States of America

First Hardcover Edition: October 1998
First Mass Market Edition: September 1999

10 9 8 7 6 5 4 3 2 1

THIS BOOK IS DEDICATED
TO ALAN COHEN.

Many thanks to Ron Lawton for his information on chain-saw sculpture, to Peter Borland and Judith Curr for their excellent editorial advice, and to my wonderfully supportive agent, Molly Friedrich.

The scarlet letter was her
passport into regions where
other women dared not tread.

—Nathaniel Hawthorne

1

Thursday, the best day of the week—the day of all days that Francie was predisposed to say yes. But here in the artist's studio, with its view of the Dorchester gas tank superimposed on the harbor beyond, she couldn't bring herself to do it. The problem was she hated the paintings. The medium was ink, the tool airbrush, the style photorealist, the subject slack-faced people in art galleries viewing installations; the installations, when she looked more closely, were neon messages fenced in with blood-tipped barbed wire, messages that though tiny could be read, when she looked more closely still. Francie, her nose almost touching the canvases, read them dutifully: *name that tune; do you swear to tell the truth?; we will have these moments to remember.*

"World within world," she said, a neutral phrase that might be taken optimistically.

"I'm sorry?" said the artist, following her nervously around the studio.

Francie smiled at him—gaunt, hollow-eyed, twitchy, unkempt—Raskolnikov on amphetamines. She'd seen paintings of slack-faced people looking at paintings; she'd seen neon messages; she'd seen barbed wire, blood-tipped, pink, red-white-and-blue; seen art feeding on itself with an appetite that grew sharper every day.

"Anything else you'd like to show me?" she said.

"Anything else?" said the artist. "I'm not sure exactly what you . . ."

Francie kept her smile in place; artists lived uneasy lives. "Other work," she explained, as gently as she could.

But not gently enough. He flung out his arm in a dramatic sweep. "This is my work."

Francie nodded. Some of her colleagues would now say "I love it" and let him learn the bad news in a letter from the foundation, but Francie couldn't. Silence followed, long and uncomfortable. Time slowed down, much too soon. On Thursdays, Francie wanted time to behave as it might in some Einsteinian thought experiment, hurrying by until dark, then almost coming to a stop. The artist gazed at his shoes, red canvas basketball sneakers, paint-spattered. Francie gazed at them, too. *Do you swear to tell the truth?* Even bad art could get to you, or at least to her. She saw something from the corner of her eye—a small unframed canvas, leaning against the jamb of a doorless closet, went closer, to end the shoe-gazing if nothing else.

"What's this?" An oil painting of a plinth, cracked, crumbling, classical, bearing a bunch of grapes, wine-dark, overripe, even rotting. And in the middle ground, not hidden, not flaunted, simply there, was a lovely figure of a girl on a skateboard, all poise, balance, speed.

"That?" said the painter. "That's from years ago."

"Tell me about it."

"What's to tell? It was a dead end."

"You didn't do any more like it?" Francie knelt, turned the painting around, read the writing on the back: *oh garden, my garden.*

"By the dozen," said the artist. "But I painted over them whenever I needed canvas."

Francie kept herself from glancing at the busy pieces on the wall.

"That's the last one, in fact. Why do you ask?"

"It has a kind of . . ." Something. It had that something she was always looking for, so hard to put in words. To sound professional, Francie said, ". . . resonance."

"It does?"

"In my opinion."

"No one liked them at the time."

"Maybe I'm just a sucker for overripe fruit," Francie said, although she already knew it wasn't that. It was the girl. "Caravaggio, and all that," she explained.

"Caravaggio?"

"You know," she said, her heart sinking.

"A kind of grape?"

"He said that? A kind of grape?" Nora, having finished her lunch—a very late lunch, eaten on their feet at a coffee place in the North End—helped herself to Francie's. "Soon the past will be completely forgotten."

"And life can begin," said Francie.

Nora paused in midbite. "You feeling okay?"

"Why do you ask?"

"How's Jolly Roger these days?"

"Why do you ask?"

Nora laughed, choked slightly, wiped her mouth. "Can you play for me tonight?"

Nora meant tennis: they belonged to the same club, had played together since eighth grade. "Not on Th— no," Francie said.

"I hate to cancel on her."

"Who?"

"Anne? Anita? New member. Shy little *frau*, but she has a nice game. You should meet her."

"Not tonight."

"You said that. What's tonight?"

"Work," Francie said, not without a twinge inside. "And you?"

"Got a date. He called me this morning."

"For tonight? And you said yes?"

"He already knows I've been married twice—do I have to simper like a virgin for the rest of my life?"

"Who's the lucky guy?"

"Bernie something."

Francie picked up the check—Nora's settlement from marriage one had gone the other way the second time— and got her car from the parking garage. She turned on the radio, found Ned, drove out of the city.

"And we're back. I'm Ned Demarco, the program is *Intimately Yours*, our beat marriage, love, family in this increasingly complex world. It's Thursday, and as our regular listeners know, Thursday is our free-form day, open-forum time, no studio guests, no set topics. We talk about what you out there want to talk about. Welcome to the program, Marlene from Watertown."

"Dr. Demarco?"

"Ned, please."

"Ned. Hi. I really enjoy your show."

"Thank you, Marlene. What's on your mind?"

"First, can I ask you something?"

"Shoot."

"That voice of yours. Do they do anything to, like, enhance it?"

Ned laughed. "Lucy, in the control room: Doing anything to enhance my voice?" He laughed again, easy and natural. More relaxed with every show, Francie thought. "Lucy says she's doing all that science possibly can. Anything else, Marlene?"

"It's about my husband, I guess." The woman paused.

"Go on."

"He—he's a wonderful father, an excellent provider. Even helps out around the house."

"Sounds ideal."

"I know. Which is why I feel so guilty for saying this, even having it in my mind."

"Having what in your mind, Marlene?"

She took a breath, deep and troubled, audible down her phone line, over the air, through the speakers in Francie's car. "Lately I've been daydreaming a lot about this boy I went with back in high school. And nightdreaming. I'm talking about all the time, Dr.—Ned. And my question is, Would there be any harm in looking him up?"

Ned paused. Francie could feel him thinking. She drove into a tunnel and lost him before the answer came.

The city dwindled in her rearview mirror until there was nothing left but the tops of the two big towers that gave downtown its distinctive look, intruding on a cold, silvery sky. Francie crossed the New Hampshire line, drove north on roads of less and less importance, entered the wilderness beyond the last bed-and-breakfast, and came to Brenda's gate at dusk. She got out of the car, unlocked the gate, drove through, leaving the gate closed but unlocked, as she always did. The rutted track, thick with dead leaves, led up over a hill, then down through rocky meadows to the river. Most of the light had drained from the sky, but the river held on to what was left, in odd blurred streaks of red, orange, and gold: like an autumnal Turner seen through a fingerprint-smeared lens. Francie stopped in front of the little stone jetty, where two dinghies—red *Prosciutto* and green *Melone*— were fastened to the lee side. Climbing into one, she discovered the cause of the odd blurring—a skin of ice lay on the river. So soon? She rowed out to the island, oar blades slicing through the fiery glaze, sheared ice scratching against her bows.

Brenda's island, two or three hundred feet across the river, almost halfway, was a fat oval with flattened ends, no bigger than an acre. It had a floating dock, five huge elms, isolated from disease, thick brush that hadn't been cleared in years, and a flagstone path leading up to the cottage. Francie unlocked the door and went inside, closing the door and leaving it unlocked, as she always did.

The cottage: pine-floored, pine-walled; all that old, deep-polished wood made it almost a living thing, like a fairy-tale tree house. There was a south-facing kitchen, looking down the river; an L-shaped dining and living room facing the far shore; and upstairs two square bedrooms, each with a brass bed, one unmade, the other covered with pillows and a down comforter. A perfect little cottage that had been in Brenda's family for more than a hundred years; but Brenda, Francie's former college roommate, was the last survivor, and she lived in Rome. She'd asked Francie to keep an eye on it for her, using it whenever she wanted, and Francie had agreed, long before anything ulterior came along.

Francie switched on the generator, lit the woodstove, poured herself a glass of red wine, sat at the kitchen table, and watched night swallow everything—riverbanks, river, floating dock, great bare elms—leaving only the stars above, like holes pierced through to some luminous beyond. The skateboard painting—*oh garden, my garden*—drifted into her mind. Could she properly buy it for herself if the price was right? The artist would probably be glad of the money, but a sale to the foundation would do more for his career. Francie debated with herself for a while. The answer was no.

She threw another log into the stove, refilled her glass,

checked her watch. The first feeling of anxiety, like a thumb pressing the inside of her breastbone, awoke within her. Perhaps some music. She was running Brenda's CD collection through her mind when the door swung open and Ned walked in.

"Sorry I'm late," he said.

"You scared me."

"Me?" he said with surprise. He smiled at her; his face was ruddy from the cold, his black hair blown by the river breeze. The atmosphere in the cottage changed completely: the night lost its power, lost its grip on the cottage, withdrew. "You all right?" he said.

"Totally."

They faced each other in the kitchen of Brenda's cottage. The expression in Ned's eyes changed, dark eyes Francie had learned to read like barometers, meteorologist of his soul.

"You know what I love?" he said. "When you're waiting here, the only light for miles around, and I'm rowing across." He came closer, put his arms around her. Francie heard herself moan, a sound that happened by itself, in which she heard unambiguous longing. She didn't care if he heard it, too, couldn't have kept the sound inside in any case.

"I missed you," he said. His voice vibrated against her ear; and yes, what a voice it was.

"What did you tell Marlene?" Francie said, her face against his chest.

"Marlene?"

"Who wanted to get in touch with her old high school boyfriend."

"You caught the show?" He leaned back a little so he could watch her face. "What did you think?"

"You're getting better and better."

He shook his head. "Thanks, but it was flat from beginning to end—and just when this syndication thing is in the air."

In the silence that followed, Francie felt his mind going somewhere else. She repeated her question: "What did you tell her?"

He shrugged. "That she'd be playing with fire."

A little chill found the nape of Francie's neck, a draft, perhaps; it was an old dwelling, after all, with almost no insulation. The very next moment, Ned put his hand right on the spot, right on the chilly part, and rubbed gently. Then the voice, in her ear again: "But sometimes fire is irresistible."

Francie felt her nipples hardening, just from the words, just from the voice. *And life can begin.* They went upstairs, Francie first, Ned following, as they always did.

Brenda's cottage was their world. In truth, their world was even smaller than that. They spent no time in the living room, except to feed the stove, had the occasional drink in the kitchen, but not food—Ned never seemed to be hungry—and they both showered in the upstairs bathroom; other than that, their time together was spent in the made-up bedroom on the second floor. It was not much bigger than a prison cell, a prison cell where the sentence was never long enough.

There was no sound in the made-up bedroom, other than what they made themselves under the down comforter. Sometimes Ned moved very slowly; sometimes he just reached between her legs with no preliminaries, as he did now. It didn't make any difference: Francie, who had always responded slowly in sex, or not at all, responded to Ned no matter what he did. She started moaning again, and the moans turned to little cries, and rose in volume, so loud they could surely be heard outside—or so she thought, although that didn't matter either: they were alone on an island in the middle of the river, with no one to hear, and then she was coming, just from the touch of his fingertip.

After that, they moved together, not like dancing partners, or old familiar lovers, or any of those other similes, but more like a single organism rearranging its limbs. Their world shrank still more, smaller now than even the bedroom, down to the space under the comforter, a warm, humid, gentle world where the ancient connection between sex and love was at last clear, at least in Francie's mind. She stared into Ned's eyes, thought she saw into him to the very bottom, thought he was doing the same to her.

They came together—how Francie disliked the vocabulary that went with all this—could reach this supposed goal of lovers whenever they wished, and Ned settled down on her.

"It's different every time," he said after a minute or two.

"I was thinking the same thing."

They lay quiet. Francie pictured Ned rowing across in the darkness, herself in the cottage, both hearts beating in anticipation. "It's like 'Ode on a Grecian Urn,'" she said, "except the anticipation is met." He was silent. "At least in my case," she added, not wanting to speak for him. But Ned had fallen asleep, as he sometimes did. Because of the way he was lying on her, Francie couldn't see her watch; she would let him sleep for a little while. They breathed together, noses almost touching. In a way, this was best of all.

Sometime later, Francie heard a sound outside the window, a sound she couldn't identify at first, then realized was the beating of heavy wings. An owl, perhaps. There was at least one on the island; she'd watched it, flying by day, minutes before she saw Ned for the first time: August, only a few months earlier.

Francie sat on the floating dock, her feet in the river's flow. She spent an hour or so studying slides before putting them away and lying back, eyes closed to the sun. The slides lingered in her mind—images of cold-hearted children, alienating and unsettling—then faded. Francie was close to sleep when she felt a shadow pass over her body. She opened her eyes and saw, not a cloud over the sun, but an owl flying low, something white in its beak. The owl spread its wings, extended its talons, disappeared in the high branches of one of the elms. Turning back to the river, Francie caught sight of a kayak, gliding upstream.

A black kayak with a dark kayaker, paddling hard. As he drew closer, Francie saw he was shirtless, fit without being muscle-bound, hairy-chested, gleaming with sweat. He didn't see her at all: his eyes were blank and he seemed to be paddling with all his might, as though in a race. He flew by, into the east channel of the river, and vanished behind the island.

Francie lay back on the dock, closed her eyes. But now they didn't want to stay closed, and she didn't want to lie down. She rose, toed the end of the dock, dived into the river. The water was at its warmest, warmer than she liked. Francie swam a few strokes, then jackknifed her body as she'd been taught long ago at summer camp, and kicked easily down into the cold layers beneath.

Francie had always been good at holding her breath. She swam on and on close to the bottom, ridding herself of sun-induced lassitude before rising at last, clearheaded, to the surface. She broke through, took a deep breath—and saw that the kayak, having rounded the island, was now bearing straight down on her, only a few strokes away.

The kayaker was paddling as hard as ever, eyes still blank. Francie opened her mouth to yell something. At that moment he saw her. His body lost its coordination instantly; his blade caught a crab, splashing water at Francie's head. The splashed water was still in midair, a discrete body, when the kayak flipped over.

The paddle bobbed up and drifted beside the upside-down kayak, but Francie didn't see the man. She dived under the kayak, felt inside; he wasn't there. She peered down into the depths, saw nothing, came up. A second later, he burst through the surface, right beside her, gasping for breath, bleeding from a gash in his forehead.

"Are you all right?" she said.

He looked at her. "Unless you're planning to sue me."

Francie laughed. Their legs touched under the surface. He called her—at work—the next day. She hadn't been looking for love, had resigned herself to living the rest of her life without it, and perhaps for that reason had fallen all the harder.

Ned awoke. Francie knew he was awake right away, even though he hadn't moved at all. She was opening her mouth to tell him about *oh garden, my garden* when he stiffened.

"What time is it?" he said.

"I don't know."

He rolled over, checked his watch. "Oh, Christ." In seconds he was gone from the bed, gone from the room, and the shower was running. Francie got up, put on the robe she kept in Brenda's closet, went down to the kitchen, finished her glass of red wine. All at once, she was hungry. She let herself imagine going out with him, having dinner somewhere, feasting, then coming back, back to the little bedroom.

Ned came downstairs, knotting his tie. A beautiful tie—all his ties, his clothes, the way he wore his hair— beautiful.

"Hungry?" she said.

"Hungry?" he answered with surprise. "No. You?"

She shook her head.

He leaned over, kissed her forehead very lightly. "I'll call," he said.

She tilted her face up to his. He kissed her again, this time on the mouth, still very lightly. She licked his lips, tasted toothpaste. He straightened.

"Rowing back is another matter," he said.

Then he was gone, the door opening and closing softly. The draft reached Francie a few seconds later.

Driving fast toward the city, Ned realized how hungry he really was. Had he eaten at all since breakfast? He considered stopping somewhere along the way but kept going, one eye on the radar detector; he liked eating at home.

Ned switched on the radio, found their only affiliate, a weak AM station that replayed the shows at night. He heard himself say: "What do you mean by looking him up?" a little too sharply; he'd have to watch that.

"You know," said the woman—Marlene, or whatever her name was. "Finding out where he is. Giving him a call."

"To what end?"

"To what end?"

He should have gotten rid of her right there; he had so much to learn about the entertainment part. "For what purpose?"

"I guess to see what happens."

"Marlene?"

"Yes?"

"In your description of your husband's good points, I think—correct me if I'm mistaken—you omitted any mention of your sex life."

"I've tried, Ned. To make it more exciting. Nothing works."

"What have you tried?"

The car phone buzzed and Ned missed the woman's answer; he didn't recall it being interesting anyway, although he suspected the question was the kind the syndicators liked.

"Hello?" he said into the phone.

"Dad? Hi, it's me, Em."

"I recognized the voice."

"You think you're so funny. Where are you?"

"On my way."

"There's no dessert."

"What would you like?"

"Rocky road."

"Consider it done. Love you."

"Love you, too, Dad."

Ned stopped at a grocery store near his house, bought two pints of rocky road, a jar of chocolate sauce, almonds. At the cash register, he noticed some nice fresh flowers: irises, always a safe choice. He bought some for his wife.

2

His mind on those moans and cries that Francie made, Ned parked in the garage beside his house, sat for a few moments in the darkness. There had to be some evolutionary purpose for those female sounds, some reason important enough to outweigh the risk of attracting predators in the night. Did it have anything to do with the bonding of the couple, its positive consequences for the next generation? Ned rubbed the spot on his forehead, an inch above the right eyebrow where the headaches began, as one was beginning now, picked up the grocery bag, went into the house.

Em was at the kitchen table in her pajamas, busy with her paint set. The next generation. "Guess what this is going to be."

"The solar system."

She nodded. "Guess how many moons Saturn has."

"A lot. Ten, maybe."

"Eighteen. Which one's the biggest?"

"That's a tough one. Triton?"

"Triton, Dad? Triton belongs to Neptune. I'll give you one more chance."

"Rocky road?"

"You're not funny."

Ned scooped ice cream into two bowls—three scoops in his, he was so hungry—spooned out chocolate sauce,

14

sprinkled on almonds. He raised his first spoonful. "Here's looking at you, kid."

Em rolled her eyes. "Why do old people always fall for that stupid movie?"

"Old people?" He took a bite and almost winced at the pain; ice cream was the fuel his headache had been waiting for.

Anne came into the room, carrying an empty laundry basket. "You're late tonight."

"It's Thursday, Mom," said Em, before he had to reply. "When Dad stays late to plan next week's shows."

"I forgot," said Anne.

Ned turned to her. "You look tired."

"I'm all right. How was the show?"

Did she never listen to it? "Not bad." He reached into the grocery bag, handed her the irises.

"These are lovely," said Anne. "What's the occasion?"

"No occasion."

"For God's sake, Mom," said Em, "where's your sense of romance?"

Ned flossed his teeth, brushed them, took two ibuprofen and a Nembutal, and went to bed. His brain shut down, compartment by compartment, until finally there was nothing but the headache between him and sleep. Then it was gone, and he sank into a dream. A cottage dream: he was lying in the red boat but somehow looking out the window of the little bedroom; Francie reached around him, ran her fingers, those soft, beautifully shaped fingers, up the front of his thigh, higher. He was hard at once, groaned, rolled over, reached for her, almost said, "Francie." But it was Anne; his hands had known right away, had saved him. The dream broke up in fading pieces, the image of the red boat last of all.

She fondled him. It was nice, familiar, homey. But

Anne coming on to him? This was unusual. He tried
to remember the last time—her birthday? his?—but
couldn't. As though reading his mind, she said, "I do
have a sense of romance, you know."

That got to him. "I know." The words thickened in his
throat; he almost confessed everything, right there. But
he mastered himself, said no more; she misinterpreted
the catch in his voice, taking it for lust; slipped him inside
herself without ceremony; moved her hips in lithe
comma-shaped motions, efficient and pleasing; ended in
a silent shudder, like an express elevator reaching the
top floor.

She lay on his shoulder. "Was that good?" she said.

"Of course."

And after a minute or two: "Did you come?"

"What do you think?" He squeezed her arm.

She said nothing. Not long after, she rolled over and
went to sleep. The compartments in Ned's brain reopened. The headache returned. His eyes stayed open.

Francie showered, dressed, made the bed, went downstairs. She washed her wineglass, corked the wine, turned
off the generator. Then she stood unmoving in the darkness. The silence was complete, Brenda's cottage under a
spell, as it so often was.

Francie opened the door, letting in the river sounds,
then closed and locked it behind her. Brenda's key hung
anonymously on her key chain, one of many. The moon
had risen and in its light she saw mist along the bank,
rising with the temperature; the ice had melted away.
Francie climbed into the dinghy, cast off, rowed across
the west channel to the stone jetty, reflected moons bob-
bing in her wake. She tied up, redid Ned's knot—he'd
taken *Prosciutto*, as always—substituting two half hitches
for his series of lubberly grannies, and glanced back at

the cottage: a geometric shadow under the free-form shadows of the elms. The owl rose into the sky, its white wings flashing like a semaphore in the night.

She drove to the gate, got out, locked it, went on. For five or ten minutes she was alone with dark woods rising on either side, shutting out the sky. Then headlights of another car appeared. That broke the spell; she stepped on the gas like any other exhausted commuter hurrying home, although she wasn't tired at all.

The house—on Beacon Hill, but heavily mortgaged and in need of sandblasting and a new roof—was dark, except for the light in the basement office, a big, private space that would have made a perfect bedroom for a teenager, if one had ever come along. Francie let herself in, turned on the lights, checked the messages, checked the mail, opened the fridge, found she was no longer hungry, drank a glass of water. Then she went downstairs, through the laundry room, and stopped outside the closed office door.

"Roger?" she said. No reply. Was he sleeping on his couch? Francie thought she heard the tapping of computer keys but wasn't sure. She went upstairs, got into bed, and was almost asleep herself when *oh garden, my garden* took shape in her mind, with those rotten grapes and that skateboarding girl. A teenager, of course. She tried to stop herself from going on in that direction but failed, as she always did. To come into the house, to see a skateboard lying in the front hall and a backpack slung over the banister, to hear strange music rising up from that basement room. Think about something else, Francie.

Em. She thought of Em. Em would soon be a teenager, although Francie wasn't sure of her exact age, didn't know her birthday. Ned almost never talked about her, never at all unless Francie asked, and of course Francie

had never seen her, not even a picture. From the absent
picture of Em back to *oh garden, my garden* wasn't a big
jump, and from there to an idea: what a present the
painting would make for Ned! Was there any way of
giving it to him? In some ways they were like spies, governed by the rules of their trade. She was never to call
him, he called her, and only on her direct office line; no
letters, faxes, E-mail; they met only at the cottage. Preserving his marriage was the reason, and Em was the
reason for that. Francie understood. She could keep a
secret, in the sense of not telling another person—and
in any case had no desire to shout her love from the
rooftops—but she hated the spycraft.

Still, presents were a gray area; he did bring her
flowers once in a while when he came to the cottage.
Always irises, probably because she had made such a
fuss about them the first time. She didn't particularly like
irises, although it didn't matter much. They had usually
wilted by the next time she saw them, the following
Thursday. Francie fell asleep, turning over schemes for
getting *oh garden, my garden* into Ned's hands.

Roger knew she was there, outside the door. He glanced
at the time on the upper-right-hand corner of the screen:
12:02 A.M. Was it gratitude she expected for working
these late hours? He was the one who had paid for the
M.F.A., those summers at I Tatti, the accumulation of all
that useless knowledge she had found a use for. He went
back to his résumé.

Exeter, first in his class. Harvard, summa in economics,
captain in tennis. Twenty-three years with Thorvald
Securities, beginning as an analyst, ending as senior VP,
number three man. Number three on the chart, but the
brains behind everything, as everyone knew—everyone
with any integrity. "Wow is all I can say," as the counselor

at Execumatch had told him at their first meeting. "Let me guess—you got sixteen hundred on your SATs."

"Correct."

"And in the old days yet, before they started monkeying with the numbers."

"Old days?"

"Sure. Now you can make mistakes and still be perfect. Is that indicative or what? But this"—tapping the résumé—"this is the real deal."

Then why was he still looking for something suitable a year later?

Roger loosened his tie, closed his résumé, clicked his way onto the Web, logged on to the Puzzle Club.

>*MODERATOR: Welcome, Roger.*

Roger made no reply; he never said anything on the Web. The next day's *Times of London* crossword was up, and beside it in the Puzzletalk section some live-time discussion was taking place. Roger checked the time— 12:31—and began the puzzle. One down: a six-letter word for disorder. He typed in *ataxia*. Two down: seven letters, pugilist—*bruiser*. Three down: nine letters, to cut an X—*decussate*. So one across must be *abduct*, and four down . . . he tapped away at the keys, completing the puzzle at exactly 12:42. Not his best.

Roger scanned the discussion in progress.

>*MODERATOR: But what do you mean, Flyboy, by a quote perfect crime????*
>*FLYBOY: One they cant finger you for it, of course.*
>*MR.BUD: Finger you? Sounds like a bad EdGRobinson flick.*
>*REB: No such animal. But perfect crimewise you cant*

*be anywhere near the scene, not w/DNA and all that shit.
Flake of dandruff falls off your head, you fry.*

*>MODERATOR: So you get someone to do it for you, is
that it?*

*>FLYBOY: Right = and they get busted for some other
caper and rat you out rotb.*

>MR.BUD: You are a bad movie Flyboy.

>MODERATOR: rotb????

>FLYBOY: right off the bat.

>MR.BUD: Jesus.

*>REB: But he's right. A perfect crime = it's got to be ab-
solutely unconnected = like someone in China pushed a
button. Click. You're dead.*

*>FLYBOY: Or a penny drops off the Empire State
Building. Goes right through your skull to the sidewalk.*

*>MODERATOR: A penny drops off the Empire State
Building????*

Roger left the Puzzle Club, switched off the screen, removed his tie and shoes, lay down on the couch, pulling a
blanket over himself. He laughed aloud. The vulgarity, the
ignorance displayed on the Web for everyone to see: had
they no self-awareness at all? He closed his eyes, called
up the image of his completed *Times of London* puzzle,
word for word, perfect, done. Ataxia: that was the problem
with the world these days. Perhaps he could slip it in
during his breakfast interview.

A window table at the Ritz.

"Roger?"

"Sandy?"

"You haven't changed a bit."

Roger made himself say, "Neither have you."

"That's a crock," said Sandy, sitting down. Roger
hated that expression, hated when men patted their

paunches and said "What do you call this?" as Sandy was doing now, especially since he didn't have much of one. The waiter poured coffee; Roger left his alone, afraid that his hand would shake.

"Still playing?" asked Sandy. Sandy had been number two on the tennis team, thrashed by Roger in challenge matches every spring. Now he ran the third-biggest venture capital firm in New England.

"Infrequently," said Roger. Perhaps he should ask Sandy whether *he* still played, but that might lead to some sort of loathsome rematch twenty-five years after the fact, so he reached for his coffee cup and said nothing. The cup clattered against the saucer; he put it down.

"Can't remember the last time I had a racquet in my hand," Sandy said. "Fact is, we've taken up rock climbing, the whole bunch of us."

"Rock climbing?"

"You should try it, Roger. It's a great family activity."

Roger had nothing to say to that. He tore his brioche into little pieces.

"How's Francie, by the way?"

"You know my wife?"

"Slightly. She gave a talk a few months ago on this new sculpture we've got in the lobby. I don't pretend to understand the sculpture, but your wife had us all eating out of her hand."

"Did she?"

"That combination of looks and brains, if I can say so without being politically incorrect . . . but I don't have to tell you, do I, you lucky devil?"

Roger picked up his butter knife, dipped it into a bowl of raspberry jam, spread some on a scrap of brioche, trailing a glutinous spill on the white tablecloth. Sandy gazed at the red stain for a moment, then said, "I hear there've been changes at Thorvald."

"Yes." How to explain it to Sandy? Sandy wasn't very bright; Roger retained a memory of him frowning over some tome in the Widener Library. No doubt best to say something vague and diplomatic, and move on. Roger wiped the edges of his mouth with the napkin and readied something vague and diplomatic. But the words that issued were: "They were very stupid."

Sandy sat back. "In what way?"

"Isn't it obvious? They were such idiots, they—" He smothered the end of the sentence: *fired me*.

"They what, Roger?" Sandy asked.

It occurred to Roger that in the past year Sandy might have begun doing business with Thorvald, have his own sources inside. "It's not important," he said. *What's important is giving me a job, if you're not too dim-witted to see how much I can help you.*

Sandy sipped his coffee in silence. Did Sandy resent him for those weekly drubbings, so long ago? Was it possible he didn't understand that there'd been nothing personal, that it was simply how the game was played? This was a negotiation to be handled with care.

"Sandy?"

"Yes, Roger?"

"I could use a job, goddamn it." Not what he'd meant to say at all, but Sandy was one of those pluggers—a baseliner, as he recalled, with no imagination—and pluggers exasperated him.

And now Sandy was giving him a long look, as though he were sizing *him* up, which was ridiculous due to the disparity in their intellects. "I wish I could help, Roger, but we've got nothing for someone of your level."

That was a lie. Roger knew they were looking or he wouldn't have set this up. But too tactless to say; Roger substituted: "You know how many times I've heard that?" His orange juice spilled, perhaps because of a convulsive jerk of his forearm; he wasn't sure.

After the waiter was done mopping, Sandy said, "None of my business, Roger, and please don't take this the wrong way, but have you ever considered early retirement? I know that Thorvald gave—that Thorvald usually does the right thing with their packages, and with Francie doing so well, maybe—"

"What's she got to do with this?"

"I just thought—"

"Do you know how much she grossed last year? Fifty grand. Barely enough to cover her hairdresser. Besides, I'm too young—"

"We're the same age, Roger. I stopped thinking of myself as young quite some time ago. The promising stage can't last forever, by definition."

Roger felt his face go hot, as though reddening, although surely no change was visible. He composed himself and said, "I wasn't aware that stage had occurred at all, in your case."

Sandy called for the check soon after. Roger snatched it from the waiter's hand and paid himself. Sandy met someone he knew on the way down the stairs, stopped to talk. Roger went out alone. On the street, he realized he had forgotten to leave a tip. So what? He had the feeling—strange, since he had been going there since boyhood—that he would never eat at the Ritz again.

Roger bought a bottle of Scotch in a shop where they called him *sir*, although not today—there was a new clerk who could barely speak English—and took a taxi home. The driver had the radio on.

"What's on tap, Ned?"

"Thanks, Ron. Male infertility is the topic today on

Intimately Yours. *In the studio we'll have one of the foremost—"*

"Mind turning that off?" Roger said.

"Pliss?" said the driver.

"Radio," said Roger. "Off."

The driver turned it off.

In his basement office, Roger drank Scotch on the rocks and played Jeopardy! on his computer. The first European to reach the site of what is now Montreal. The economic unit of Senegal. The largest moon of Neptune. Who was Cartier, what is the C.F.A. franc, what is Triton? All too easy. He tried to get into his old computer at Thorvald but couldn't pass the firewall.

He refilled his glass, had another look at his résumé. Too bad, he thought, that IQs weren't standard CV material. Why shouldn't they be? What better measure? He rose, opened a file drawer, dug through press clippings, photographs, ribbons, trophies, down to a yellowed envelope at the bottom, addressed to Mr. and Mrs. Cullingwood. He read the letter inside.

Enclosed please find the results of your son Roger's Stanford-Binet test, administered last month. Roger's intelligence quotient, or IQ, as measured by the test, was 181. This places him in the 99th percentile of all those taking the test. It may interest you to know that there are several schools in our area with first-grade programs for gifted children which may be appropriate for Roger. Please do not hesitate to contact us for further information.

Roger read the letter again, and once more, before putting it away. He topped off his glass, logged on to the Puzzle Club. The *Times of London* crossword hadn't appeared yet, but there were others, including *Le Monde*. That one took him almost an hour—his French was rusty. When he had finished all the puzzles, he gazed at the on-line discussion that had been scrolling by the whole time.

>MODERATOR: *How did we get onto capital punishment????*

>BOOBOO: *The Sheppard Case. What they based the fugitive on.*

>RIMSKY: *Yeah, yeah. But how about it when it works the other way = coldblooded killers on parole?*

>MODERATOR: *I don't think that happens very often, do you????*

>RIMSKY: *Let me tell you something I'm a corrections officer down here in Fla.*

>BOOBOO: *So?*

>RIMSKY: *So I know what I'm talking about when it comes to coldblooded k's.*

>BOOBOO: *:)*

>RIMSKY: *:) yourself. Ever heard of Whitey Truax, for example?*

>MODERATOR: *????*

>FAUSTO: *What's this got to do with the $ of apples?*

>MODERATOR: *Let Rimsky tell his story. Rimsky = what's w/Whitey Truax?*

Roger followed the discussion until footsteps overhead made him take his eyes from the screen. Francie. He was surprised to see night beyond the little window high in the basement wall.

And the bottle almost empty, although he was sober, completely. Sandy's worst moment had been his salivating over Francie. There had been lust in his eyes, beyond a doubt. What a complete—what did the Jews say?

Putz. That was it. He didn't even want to work for—with—a putz like Sandy.

But something about that lustful look, Francie, Jews, and the word *putz* itself—a lubricious mix—gave Roger a sudden urge to sleep upstairs tonight, something he hadn't done since . . . he couldn't remember. Donning his crimson robe, he poured what remained of the Scotch into his glass and a second one, and carried them upstairs.

"Francie?" he called. "Is that you, dear?"

3

His first day in the halfway house, Whitey Truax went looking for whores. This was nothing he had planned: no one planning would have considered it, since the job they'd found Whitey—spearing trash on the I-95 median—ended at five, and he had to sign back in at six.

Just before dawn, the DPW pickup began dropping off the crew one at a time, stringing them out a few miles apart. Whitey was last. Riding alone in the back, he saw the sun coming up between two high-rises, and started trembling. He'd been facing west for seventeen years, or maybe it was just the morning chill.

The pickup pulled over on the north side of exit 42, Delray Beach, and Whitey climbed down. Then it drove away, and there he was on dewy green grass, a free and unsupervised man. He shrugged on his reflective vest, stuffed the tightly folded orange trash bags in his pocket, stabbed a Mars bar wrapper with his steel-tipped pole.

Stab, stab, stab: Whitey was full of energy. By four, he had filled a dozen bags, all they'd given him, and worked his way almost down to exit 41. With nothing more to do, he stood leaning on his pole, sweat slowly drying, and watched the cars go by, most of the models unfamiliar. Was this a bad way to make a living? Too hot—he'd never liked the heat—but otherwise not bad at all. No watching your back, no taking shit: cake.

27

Rush hour now, and traffic was stop-and-go. A woman in a convertible looked at him, not twenty feet away. She had a ponytail, damp at the end, and wore a bikini top—must be coming from the beach, thought Whitey; but he wasn't really thinking, just staring at her tits, heavy, round, mesmerizing. The combination of visual overload and complete tactile deprivation made him start trembling again, just a little. He opened his mouth to say something to her, but the only word he could think of was *fuck*, and he knew that wouldn't work. Traffic lurched ahead and she was gone, leaving him with the memory of those big tits. Her shoulders had been heavy, too; in retrospect, it was possible she was fat, even grossly so, but this realization barely surfaced in Whitey's mind. Retrospection wasn't one of his strengths.

Instead his mind wandered, not very far, to those sounds women made when they got excited. He'd heard them in movies. No X-rated stuff allowed inside, of course, but even in normal movies women made those sounds. Melanie Griffith, and who was that other one he liked? Whitey could see her face clearly, mouth open, but he was still fishing for the name when he felt something stir against his ankle. He jumped back—he was very quick—thought *snake*, thrust the steel tip at the reptilian head, right through, pinning it wriggling to the ground. Hadn't lost his quick, not one little bit.

As it turned out, the creature was not a snake, not a reptile at all, but a bullfrog. Too late to do anything about that. Whitey watched it die, blood trickling into a crown pattern over its eyes, wriggling becoming sporadic, those pop eyes growing dim. Whitey felt bad, but not too bad: the frog's own damn fault, after all, for making him panic. Whitey panicked sometimes, especially if he was surprised. That was simply the way he was—didn't make him weak or anything. But the syndrome—word he remembered from the testimony, so long ago—combined with his quickness, could lead to trouble, as he knew well.

Which was why he had to stay calm. He took a few deep breaths to settle down, placed his foot on the bull-frog's back, withdrew the steel tip. The bullfrog hopped up on its hind legs.

"Jesus fucking Christ," Whitey said, and let him have it again. The frog lay still after that, facedown, legs spread flat on the ground. That was when the possibility of whores arose in Whitey's mind, whores that very day.

A DPW truck picked him up a few minutes later, left him outside the depot at five.

"Hey, you."

Whitey, walking off, stopped and turned.

"Where you think you're goin' with that?"

Whitey thought fast. "No place."

"No place is right. Equipment stays here."

Whitey came forward, tossed the steel-tipped pole onto the truck bed. "No harm intended."

The guy just looked at him.

A bus drove up, number 62. He checked the social worker's handwritten instructions: his bus; it stopped a block from the halfway house. But Whitey didn't get on. Instead he set off toward a neon-lit intersection he could see in the distance, the kind of intersection where there might be liquor stores, bars, women. Whitey felt in his pocket. He had thirty bucks, plus four hundred and some in the bank account the social worker had helped him open the night before.

What would thirty bucks buy? A Pepsi, for starters. They hadn't had Pepsi inside, just Coke, and Pepsi was Whitey's drink. He went into the first convenience store he saw. "Wow," he said to himself, or maybe out loud. There was so much stuff. He went to the cooler at the back and found the Pepsi. They'd changed the design on the can. He liked the old one better. Had they fooled around with the taste as well? He remembered hearing something about that.

Whitey took a six-pack, went to the front of the store, laid it on the counter next to a cigar display. "With you in a sec," said a voice a few aisles away.

Whitey eyed the cigars. Weren't cigars in these days? He'd never smoked a cigar, not once in his whole goddamned life. Whitey glanced around. There was a video camera, but it hung loose from the ceiling, all askew. Whitey boosted the biggest cigar in the box, slipping it up his sleeve in the familiar motion of a man patting his hair in place.

The clerk appeared. "Anything else?" he said.

"Matches," said Whitey.

"Matches are free."

Whitey took two packs. "Thanks a bunch."

He walked another block toward the neon intersection, stopped, cracked open a Pepsi, tilted it up to his mouth. Christ, it was good, even better than he remembered. He swallowed half of it, then lit the cigar, filling his mouth with a thick ball of hot, wonderful smoke, slowly letting it out, curling through his lips. He was alive. Standing outside an electronics store—a banner on the window read: ARE YOU READY FOR HIGH DEFINITION?— Whitey sipped his Pepsi and puffed his cigar. A gorgeous weatherwoman on a big-screen TV was pointing at flashing thunderclaps on a map of some European country, France, maybe, or Germany. European weather: this was the big time. Whitey watched transfixed until he happened to notice the price sticker on the TV. And that was the sale price. He walked away.

Cigar in his mouth, the remaining five cans of Pepsi dangling from the empty plastic ring, Whitey reached the intersection. Liquor stores, yes. Bars, yes. Women, no.

He went into Angie's Alligator Lounge and sat at the empty bar.

"What can I get you?" said the bartender.

Alcohol was out: halfway house rules. "What've you got?" said Whitey.

"What have I *got*?"

"Beer," said Whitey, first word that came to mind. "Narragansett." That had been his beer.

"Narragansett?"

"Bud, then."

The bartender served him a Bud. "Buck and a half."

Whitey gave him two bills, waved away the change, just waved it away with his cigar, very cool.

"I'll level with you," Whitey said. He waited for the bartender to say something or change the expression on his face. When none of that happened, he continued, "The truth is I been away for a while."

The bartender nodded. "Narragansett is kind of a collector's item."

"And a little company would be nice, you know? Someone to talk to," he added, but the bartender had already picked up the phone. He spoke into it quietly for a few moments, not looking at Whitey once, hung up. Less than a minute later, a woman walked through the front door, sat down beside Whitey; the bartender found something to do among the bottles. Whitey laughed, more like a giggle that he modulated at the end.

"What's funny?" said the woman.

Whitey took a hit off the cigar. "Inside you get shit," he said. "Out in the world all you got to do is ask." He turned to her. She was stunning. He could smell her. That was stunning, too. What sounds would she make, coming and coming? His mouth dried up.

She was watching him, squinting just a little, possibly

from the cigar smoke, or maybe she'd forgotten her glasses. "You're the one wanted a date, right?"

Whitey swallowed. "A date," he said, liking the sound of that. "Yeah."

"You wanna finish your beer first?"

"Beer's a no-no."

She rose. He went with her to the back of the lounge and out a back door. "We're leaving?" Whitey said.

"Know what a liquor license costs?"

She led him into an alley, around a corner, and into a hotel. The sign said HOTEL, but there was no lobby, just a beefy guy behind bulletproof glass, his head on a desk. The woman went by it, up a flight of stairs—oh, following her ass up the stairs, that was something—into a room with a bed and a sink in it and nothing else.

"Mind washing off?" said the woman, nodding to the sink. "Can't be too careful these days." She was still stunning, despite the harsh strip lighting in the room. Her pimples or whatever they were didn't bother him at all, and he was used to that kind of lighting.

Whitey washed off. When he turned to her, she was sitting on the bed, yawning. " 'Scuse me," she said. "Okay. Suck is twenty-five, fuck is forty, suck and fuck fifty."

Whitey didn't know what to say, couldn't have spoken anyway, his mouth being so dry. He tried some calculations. Suck and fuck was clearly a deal, but fuck alone was what he wanted—to be deep inside her, to make her make those Melanie Griffith sounds—and all he had was thirty dollars, minus what he'd paid for the beer and the Pepsi. Christ! He couldn't even afford suck.

"But since you look like a nice guy," she said, breaking the silence, "I could maybe do you a little discount."

Whitey tried to say something, could not, put all his money, even the change, on the bed. She stared at it. He leaned over her, smoothed out the crumpled bills.

"Oh, hell," she said, scooping it all into her sparkle-covered purse, "let's not ... what's the word? Starts with *D*."

Whitey didn't know. He just knew that he was going to get laid after all. The knowledge turned on a kind of buzzing inside him, a buzzing he hadn't heard for a long time, not since—but best not to think about that. He put his arms around the woman and pulled her close, knocking her head awkwardly against his belt buckle.

"Easy," she said. "Take your pants off."

But Whitey didn't have time for that; he made do with just pulling them down below his knees. Meanwhile the woman lay back on the bed, hiked up her skirt, pulled off her panties, and he saw that other sex, the lips and hair, all real, right there, as the buzzing grew louder. She stuffed the panties down the side of her boot. Whitey fell on her, shoved himself inside.

Not quite inside, perhaps against her thigh. She reached down between them, took his penis in her hand—"Dicker," she said, "that's the word I was looking for"—and guided him in.

"Oh, God," Whitey said, "oh my God." He thrust himself in and out, almost drowning in the buzz, about to come any second, when suddenly he remembered Melanie Griffith. Slow down, big guy, slow down, he told himself. He had to hear those female sounds. He slid his hand down her stomach, into the wetness, found her clit, or something, and started thrumming it back and forth, fast as he could.

"Knock it off," said the woman.

Whitey froze. His hard-on went droopy inside her, just like that. The buzzing stopped. In the silence he heard some little animal behind the wall. The woman made a hitching motion with her hips.

"You stupid bitch," Whitey said.

"Huh?"

Everything was going sour, like the last time. Where were the smart women? His needs were simple and this one was supposed to be a professional, for God's sake. It made Whitey so angry, he hit her, not hard, only the back of his hand against her pimply face.

Whitey realized almost right away that he had to make it up to her. "Okay, so we both made mistakes," he said. "Don't mean we can't—" But she writhed around under him and jabbed at a button on the wall that he hadn't noticed. "What's that about?" said Whitey. "Look, we were getting along pretty good there for a while. No reason we—"

The door burst open. All fucked up, like the last time, but things that hadn't happened before were happening now, like this beefy guy coming in with the baseball bat. But the panic inside Whitey was the same: a screaming gusher from deep in his chest, boiling up and spraying red in his brain. It took away visual continuity, leaving Whitey with a few strobe-lit impressions: the beefy guy going down, the bat now in his own hands, blood here and there, *are you ready for high definition?* And then he was out the door and in the street.

Whitey returned to the halfway house at 6:05, signed the clipboard. "Sorry I'm late," he said. "Got off at the wrong stop."

"Everyone does, first day," said the social worker. "But don't make it a habit."

"I brought you a Pepsi."

"That was thoughtful of you, Whitey. I've been going through your file. Seems you were quite the stickman up north."

Silence. "Stickman?"

"Isn't that the term? Hockey player. I don't really know the game."

"That was a long time ago."

"What I'm getting at, we're big on recreation here at New Horizons. Physical activity helps to take the edge off, if you know what I mean. Ever considered maybe getting into jogging, for instance?"

"I'll think about it," Whitey said.

"That's all we ask."

4

Francie, in her bedroom, stripped off the heavy brown wrapping paper and had a good look at *oh garden, my garden*—the best kind of look, alone, private. She'd bought it on her way home from the office for $950, unable to resist, now that it was for Ned. The artist hadn't cared at all whether the buyer was Francie or the foundation. His only request had been for payment in cash. Francie hadn't anticipated that, but on reflection it suited her fine. Standing at the foot of her bed, with the painting propped up on the pillows, she liked it more than ever.

There was a knock at the door. She almost said "Who is it?" but who else could it have been?

"Dear? Are you awake?"

Francie slid the painting under the bed, kicked the wrapping paper in after. "What is it?" she said, thinking, *dear?*

"Can I come in? Into the matrimonial chamber?"

"It's not locked, Roger."

The door opened. Roger came in, wearing a Harvard-crested robe over his shirt and tie and carrying two tumblers. "You're in your nightie."

"I'm going to bed."

He sat down on the end of it, held out a tumbler. She

noticed that his feet were bare; legs under the robe, bare, too. "Care for a drink?"

"Thank you, Roger," she said, laying it on the dresser. "But I'm a little tired."

He gave her a long look, as though he was trying to communicate some emotion. She had no idea what it could be. "Is something the matter?" she said.

He laughed, that single bark he'd been using for laughter the past year or so. "We haven't played tennis in some time, have we, Francie?"

"No." *He* hadn't played in years. But they'd met on a tennis court: Francie, on her college team; Roger, a few years out of Harvard, helping the coach after work. Francie was a good player, if not in Roger's class, but good enough so there were boxes of mixed-doubles trophies somewhere in the house. Had he come to set up a match? She almost laughed herself but lost the impulse when she saw him staring at her thighs.

Roger licked his lips. "I understand you know Sandy Cronin."

"We've met."

"I had breakfast with him today."

"How did it go?"

"Quite well." Roger took a sip from his glass, a sip that became a long drink. Silence. Then: "Do you know the word *putz*?"

"Yiddish for *prick*."

His eyes glazed at the word, or maybe the word coming from her mouth. What was going on? He touched her hand. "Let's go to bed."

That would have been her last guess. The perfect reply, the honest reply, came to her immediately: *I'm a one-man woman, Roger. I don't sleep around.*

"Is something funny?" Roger said. His hand was still

touching hers, not holding it, just touching the back. An odd gesture—not friendly, not warm, not erotic.

"No."

"Sit down, Francie."

"Why?"

"Is that a lot to ask?"

She sat down. His hand covered hers, stroked slowly up her arm: a hard, horny hand, like that of a manual laborer, which Roger was not.

"Have you been drinking?" she said.

"That's not a very nice suggestion," said Roger. "And inaccurate. I'm feeling uxorious, if you must know."

His hand reached her shoulder, jerked quickly down, took possession of her breast. Francie recoiled, but he hung on to her nipple, manipulating it in various ways, as though hoping to stumble on some combination that would change her mood, like a safecracker fiddling with a lock.

"Roger, for God's sake." She tried to push him away. He fell on her—was much bigger and stronger—and as he did she noticed for the first time that although there wasn't a single white hair on his head, his nostrils were full of them. His Harvard robe fell open, his penis pressed against her, and at that moment—unbidden, ill-timed, insane—the image of Ned's penis appeared in her mind.

Roger's, almost a schematic in contrast, butted against her rigid body.

"Stop it now," she said. And then his mouth was on hers, his tongue probing. This wasn't him at all. She twisted her head, tried to roll away, but Roger got his hand under her ass, pulled her close, forcing his penis against her. At the same time, she felt his finger moving behind her.

"What the hell are you doing?"

"Spicing up our marriage. You are my wife."

"You're sick." Francie struck out at him, barely aware of what she was doing.

He stopped moving, stopped pressing, raised himself. Four scratches ran across his cheek, blood welling in the deepest. Their eyes met. Roger's eyes: but behind them could have been anybody, and the face was the face of a man who resembled Roger. It reddened under her gaze; at the same time, his penis dwindled, as though all the blood had drained to his head. He got off her, rose, straightened his robe; his tie remained perfectly knotted. He went to the door, opened it, turned.

"You may fool other people, *dear,* but you don't fool me. Never have. And now you're a dried-up cunt as well, no matter what anyone else thinks." He went out, closing the door softly, never touching the wound she had made.

Francie didn't start crying until she was in the shower, hot as she could stand, scrubbing and scrubbing, bathroom door locked. Crying: from not being able to stop, to realizing it wasn't doing any good, to stopping. Getting out of the shower, she saw her wretched face, fogged in the mirror, and turned away. She dried herself, brushed her teeth, brushed her hair, but stopped abruptly in midstroke: *no matter what anyone else thinks.* What did that mean? She thought back, searching for some mistake in her spycraft, found none. Then who was *anyone else*? Sandy Cronin? Was his behavior tonight some form of sexual competition? With a noncompetitor, of course, and still he had lost. Clear in her mind theoretically, the disconnection between sex and rape had now been demonstrated as well.

Francie put on a fresh nightie—flannel, to her ankles—and went to bed, curled up in a ball. She tried to keep her mind from doing anything, but failed. It went right to her most vulnerable spot. Why wouldn't it, after what had just happened on the bed, and with the skateboarding girl underneath?

Francie's most vulnerable spot, in three acts. Act one: the months of frequent, if not passionate—how could it be passionate when it was regulated by doctors, ovulation calendars, thermometers?—fucking that had preceded the discovery that it was Roger's fault. Not fault, but contained in his body: low sperm count, and what sperm there were, deformed. Act two: sex in a petri dish, forcing the coupling of her eggs with the best of the deformed sperm—also a failure. Act three: a conversation repeated many times in different words, but first held as they left the doctor's office for the last time. Francie: *I guess that leaves us with adoption.* Roger: *What would be the point of that?*

That same act three might have done double duty as the beginning of the last act of their marriage as well, a long, attenuated denouement with this twist of Roger's job loss at the end, and a second twist after that, if you counted Ned. Roger's question—*What would be the point of that?*—had illuminated some long-concealed but essential difference between them, masked by Roger's early dominance: his intelligence, education, worldliness, and his good manners, which she'd perhaps mistaken for kindness. Would a child have made it all better? Francie didn't know; she just knew she had wanted one, wanted one still. Roger, in the end, had wanted to pass on his genes.

Francie thought again of Em: how she would like to meet her, even see her from a distance. Her mind moved on to Ned and quite abruptly, like a heat-seeking detector, to that earlier inappropriate mental image of his penis. Magnificent, like those on a Grecian urn—or were they too mannered? The comparison was probably to some simpler art, more robust, more iconic, even primitive: the Sumerians, perhaps; a Babylonian stone carving, for example.

My God, she thought suddenly. *How can I be thinking of sex?* But she was. Ned drove everything else out of her mind; he was deep inside her, and not even there. After a while, her body unfolded, her hand came up under the flannel nightie, and she found herself as ready as she'd ever been. What was this all about? The power of love, she decided, strong enough to keep Ned with her all the time, Roger reduced to nothing. A calming thought, but the glowing numbers on her clock kept changing, and still she didn't sleep. She picked up the phone and called the only person she could call at that hour.

"Hello?" said a sleepy-sounding man.

"Bernie?" Francie said.

"Yeah?"

"What's your last name, Bernie?"

"Zymanzki, with two Z's. Do I know you?"

"Put Nora on."

Rustling sounds, fumbling, a grunt. And Nora: "Francie?"

"Yup."

"What's wrong?"

"Tell me about divorce."

"I'm a big believer; you know that. I believe in it more than I believe in marriage."

"And in my case?"

"Unless I'm missing something, it's long overdue. Stop it, Bernie."

Nora paused for a moment, long enough for Francie to supply the missing piece. She remained silent.

"Francie?" said Nora. "Are you crying?"

"Why do you ask?"

Pause. "I've got a court on Tuesday, sugar, five-thirty. We'll talk."

* * *

Francie lay awake all night, got up at dawn. She dressed, packed her briefcase, went downstairs to Roger's door. She knocked. No answer. She opened the door. The room was dark, except for the glow of the computer screen. Roger sat before it, his back to her.

"Roger?"

No reply. No sound but the tapping of his fingers on the keys.

"It's time to talk about divorce."

No reply. The tapping didn't stop. Perhaps he bent a little closer to the screen. Francie closed the door and left.

Roger stopped typing, leaving twenty-nine across—hell, in ideal form—blank. He went upstairs, into her bedroom—their bedroom—suddenly felt dizzy, sat on the bed. As the dizziness passed, Roger noticed torn wrapping paper sticking out from underneath the bed, investigated, found a painting. He studied it for a few moments—an amateurish effort—and put it back.

Divorce: unthinkable. Loss of job, breakup of marriage, what a hideous cliché. And he'd devoted most of his adult life to Francie, was certainly responsible for that polish of hers that so impressed the Sandy Cronins of the world. Plus they'd done so much together—at that very moment, he remembered a gorgeous running topspin lob she'd made to win a key point in the Lower Cape mixed-doubles championship ten, perhaps fifteen, years before. Those legs of hers, like a dancer's, and she was still beautiful, in some ways more than ever, as the Sandy Cronins pointed out. The bastards envied him. Corollary: she was an object to be proud of. Perhaps they'd hit a bad patch, but didn't every marriage? As soon as he landed a suitable job, everything would be all right. Until then, that fifty grand she brought in was essential. No, divorce was out of the question. He would be ready with an apology the moment she got home. He could swallow his pride, up to a point, even though denied his marital rights. And perhaps there'd been something wanting in his approach last night, probably due to rustiness. That, too, could be fixed.

What kind of flowers did she like? He thought of calling one of her friends to find out, but he didn't really know her friends. Except Nora, whom he didn't like, and Brenda. Where was Brenda? London? Paris? Rome? All easily reached by phone. He found Francie's address book in her kitchen desk.

Brenda. Rome. He dialed the number, heard a female voice: *"Questa è la segretària telefònica di . . ."* Roger had no Italian and wasn't aware that he'd reached an answering machine until he heard the beep. He hung up without speaking.

Tulips? Petunias? Gladioli? Probably not gladioli—weren't they associated with funerals? Roger's mind leaped to another thought: what if something happened to Francie? The fifty grand would be gone, and while he had life insurance, she did not. Who was that insurance peddler—Tod? Tad?

Roger put on a suit and tie and went out to hunt for flowers. It was snowing, fluffy snow that quickly spread a thick carpet on the sidewalk. Roger's ankles were cold; he glanced down, saw he was still in his slippers. He stepped back inside, put on his L.L. Bean boots, decided to try Brenda again. God was in the details: the flowers had to be right.

"Pronto," said a voice, again female, but not the answering machine. He felt a change in the way his luck was running.

"Brenda?"

"*Sì?*"

"This is Roger Cullingwood."

"Roger?" Pause. Then: "Is Francie all right?"

"Very much so. I'm having a little dinner for her tonight, in fact."

"I can't possibly make it on this kind of notice, Roger."

He laughed and heard the echo of the laugh in the line—a strange barking sound, surely distorted by the Italian phone system. "I know that. The problem is I can't remember her favorite flower."

"And you called me in Rome? Aren't you sweet. Lilies, of course."

"Lilies. Thanks very much." He was about to say good-bye when she asked, "How's the cottage, by the way?"

"Cottage?"

"You know—Francie looks in from time to time. I hope."

"I wasn't aware."

"On the Merrimack. In it, rather."

"In it?"

"I've got another call, Roger. My love to Francie."

When Francie came home from work, there were lilies on the hall table and in the kitchen, lobsters steaming in the pot, champagne on ice. The dining room, unused for at least a year, maybe longer, was lit with candles, the table set with the Sèvres that had belonged to Roger's grandmother.

"My apologies, Francie," said Roger. "I don't know what got into me. I was drunk, as you said, but that's not an excuse. I'm deeply sorry."

Francie was speechless. She hadn't even expected to find him upstairs.

"No need to say anything." He sat her down, filled her glass. The scratches on his face were invisible. Francie saw he'd covered them with face powder, probably from her drawer, since it was too dark for his complexion. "Recognize this champagne?" he asked.

Laurent Perrier Rosé: they'd drunk it to celebrate the end of the hiking trip he'd taken her on in the Cevennes, following the route of Robert Louis Stevenson. That had been years ago, not long before the petri-dish phase. Francie was amazed that he would remember, amazed by the candles, the lilies. It was all perfect, and unreal, like a Cary Grant movie; and pathetic, which Cary Grant never was. That—the pathetic part—and the secret fact of Ned, undermined the righteousness of her anger.

He cracked a claw. "Remember that summer, Francie?"

"Of course." She saw that he was without a tie, almost the first time she'd seen him that way since he'd been fired.

"We had fun, didn't we?"

"Yes."

"You're not eating. I didn't overcook it, did I?"

"It's just right." She took one bite, could barely get it down.

"That's better," he said, beaming. "Here's to France. And Italy, too, for that matter."

They drank to France and Italy. "What's this all about, Roger?"

"Just dinner," he said. "No agenda. A quiet marital dinner."

"Did you hear some news today?"

"News? What sort of news?"

"About work."

Roger kept smiling, but his eyes no longer participated. "Everything's going to be just fine."

"What did you hear?"

"Nothing definite. But I'm optimistic."

He went back to the hiking trip, bringing up details she was sure he would have forgotten: the shepherd with the steel teeth, the one-eyed dog that had followed them for days, the blue-black cherries they'd picked off a tree, eating until they could eat no more, cherry juice dripping off their chins. All true. But what had become of that Roger, and how responsible was she? Too late to go back—or even think about it—but would there be dinners like this in some future with Ned, candlelight in his eyes, melted butter on his fingers, time?

"And now for dessert," Roger said.

"None for me."

He came in with a pecan pie, her favorite. "Just try it," he said.

Again one bite. Had she ever tasted better? But still she could hardly swallow.

"I went heavy on the butter and added a little maple syrup," Roger said.

"You baked this yourself?"

He nodded.

"But you don't bake."

"I followed the recipe in one of your books. It's really not that complicated, is it?"

He tilted back his head, waiting for an answer. The candlelight illuminated the patch of face powder and the white hairs in his nose. All at once, Francie felt she was about to vomit. She pushed back her chair.

"If you've got work to do or something, don't let me keep you," Roger said. "I'll clean up." He swirled the champagne in his glass, forcefully, into a tiny pink-and-golden maelstrom. "And Francie? About this divorce business—could you give it some thought?"

"I'll give it some thought."

"That's all I ask." He raised his glass to her, champagne slopping over the side.

5

Nora had a 5:30 court, but Francie got stuck in traffic and arrived ten minutes late. Nora was already in the bubble, hitting with the assistant pro against a woman Francie didn't know. Nora hadn't said anything about doubles, Francie preferred singles—and weren't they supposed to have a talk? Francie changed and hurried onto the court, stripping the cover off her racquet, apologizing. The women met her at the net.

"It turned into doubles," Nora said. "Why don't you play with Anne? Anne Franklin, Francie Cullingwood. Francie, Anne."

They shook hands. Anne was pretty, slim, fine-complected, and didn't quite look Francie in the eye: no doubt the shy *hausfrau* Nora had mentioned. "I've heard such good things about you," Anne said.

"Who's been talking?"

Anne blinked. "Why, Nora."

"Don't believe a word she says," Francie said. "What side do you like?"

"Forehand," Anne said. "But if that's your side, I could . . ."

"Not a problem," Francie said, going to the backhand, swinging her racquet lightly, trying to make her arm feel long. She always played better if her arm felt long.

48

"Hit a few, Francie?" called Nora from the other side of the net.

"Serve 'em up," Francie said, not wanting to delay the game any more.

The assistant pro went to the net and Nora got ready to serve. "Better stay back on the first one," said Anne.´ I have trouble with her serve."

"Tell me about it," said Francie, backing to the baseline.

Nora boomed in her big serve, the jamming one that spun nastily into the returner's hands. To Francie's surprise, Anne stepped away—fast and light on her feet—and chipped a low forehand crosscourt. If Nora had a weakness it was getting down for the low volley; she could do no more than float Anne's return back down the middle, two or three feet above the net, and Francie, closing, put it easily away.

"Beautiful volley," said Anne.

"Your setup," Francie said.

Nora's next serve kicked out wide on Francie's backhand. Francie didn't quite get around on it and the assistant pro picked off her return, angling it at Anne's feet from point-blank range. Somehow Anne dug it out, bunting it down the alley for a clean winner.

"Partner," said Francie.

They broke Nora at love, something Francie didn't remember seeing before, won the first set 6–2. Neither did Francie remember the last time she'd played with a doubles partner whose game so nicely fit her own, Anne's speed and steadiness matching her power and shot-making.

"What've you guys been smoking?" asked Nora on the changeover.

They toweled off, drank water, changed sides. "New in town?" said Francie as she and Anne walked toward the baseline.

"No," Anne said. "Just getting back into the game now

that my kid's a little older. I didn't realize how much I'd missed it."

"Boy or girl?" said Francie.

"Girl."

"What's her name?"

"Emilia."

"Pretty."

"And what about your kids?" said Anne.

"Don't have any," Francie replied, handing her the balls. "Your serve."

Francie didn't play as well in the second set, but Anne played even better, and the assistant pro, frustrated, lost her cool a little and started blasting the ball with all her might, usually out. Six–one.

"Thanks for putting up with me," said Anne as they went to the net to shake hands.

"Putting up with you?" said Francie. "I was on your back the whole second set." She tapped Anne's behind with her racquet. "Nice playing."

After, they sat in the bar, Francie, Nora, Anne. The club had a new microbrew on tap. Nora ordered a pitcher. Francie signed the chit. "You like microbrews, Anne?" Nora asked, filling their glasses.

"I'm not sure I've ever tried one."

"Live a little," said Nora. She raised her glass. "Here's to fuzzy balls."

The bartender, used to Nora, didn't even turn, but Anne's face, still a little pink from tennis, went pinker. She took a tiny sip, said, "It's very good," put down her glass.

"While on that subject," said Nora, downing half of hers, "I may be getting married this spring. Or next week."

"Congratulations," Anne said.

"She's just being funny," Francie said.

"Not true. Bernie wants to marry me."

"Did you ever get his last name?"

"Does it matter? I'm not going to use it anyway."

"I kept my maiden name," Anne said. "My parents weren't too happy about it."

"Maiden name," said Nora. "Can you believe an expression like that? If you ever started really thinking about things, you'd want to shoot everybody." She refilled her glass. "With the exception of Bernie. He's kind, sweet, and gentle. He does have that toenail thing, though."

"Fungus?" said Francie.

"Whatever it is turns their nails all hard and yellow." Nora went to the bathroom.

Anne, still pink, turned to Francie. "Nora mentioned your husband was quite a tennis player."

"He was," Francie said. "And yours?"

"He doesn't play. I—I've tried to get him interested, but he has no free time."

"What does he do?"

"He's a psychologist." Anne took another sip of beer, bigger than the first, as though fortifying herself. "Can I ask you something?"

"Sure."

"I hope it's not too pushy."

"We'll never know at this rate."

Anne went pinker still, and Francie felt a little ashamed of herself. "Are you and Nora playing in the tournament?"

"What tournament?"

"The club doubles championship."

"We don't play together anymore. Not in tournaments."

"But you won it a bunch of times—I saw in the trophy case."

"We finally decided to preserve the friendship instead."

"I know you're joking. You're both so supportive on the court."

"Not of each other. The last tournament we played they called the police." Anne's eyes widened. "Now I am joking," Francie said; how delicate this woman was. "What's on your mind?"

"First," said Anne, "I'd better confess I don't usually play as well as I did tonight. Not nearly."

"And second?"

"I wondered if you'd like to be my partner in the tournament."

"How could I say no?"

Nora was back, Anne gone. "She's not as fragile as she makes out," Nora said. "See the way she went right at me with that overhead in the second set?"

"She probably assumed you'd be moving to cover the empty court."

"Is that your way of saying I'm fat?"

"No. 'You're fat' is my way of saying you're fat."

"So you're not saying it?"

"My meaning is clear."

"Because even supposing I'd put on three or four or fifteen pounds—did you notice how hard I'm hitting the ball?"

"You've always hit hard."

"Not like this. I'm going to write an article for *Tennis Magazine*—'Eat Your Way to Power.' Just a little beefy hip rotation and pow—F equals MA."

"You're working on the M?"

"That's what's revolutionary about it."

Nora ordered more beer; Francie signed. "Ready to talk about Roger?" Nora said.

"As I'll ever be."

"Does he have that toenail thing, by the way?"

"You'll have to ask him."

"Meaning you don't know?"

Francie said nothing.

"Meaning you're not occupying the same bed? Of

course. And that would be your Byzantine way of telling me. How long has this been the case?"

"Some time."

"That would be months."

"Many."

Nora shook her head. "One month is my limit when it comes to abstinence—must be tied to the cycles of the moon, something tidal. After that, I need life support." She studied Francie's face, quite openly. "Can't be good for you, either," she said. "Someone like Anne, that's different—modest sex drive at best."

"How would you know something like that? Maybe she's in bed with her husband as we speak."

"Ironing his shirts is more like it," Nora said. "Can I ask you a personal question?"

"No."

"When was the last time you had an orgasm? In the company of another human being, that is."

"What difference does it make when I had an orgasm? Nuns—"

"You're not a nun. Answer the question."

The true answer was last Thursday, and not only one. Francie came very close to saying just that: her lips parted, the tip of her tongue curved up to form the *L* of "last," and after that the whole tale—cottage, kayak, little bedroom—would come spilling out. Francie clamped her mouth shut, held it all inside; she could keep a secret.

"What?" said Nora. "What?"

Francie tried to think of some breezy diversion, some bridge to another subject, but nothing came to mind. Nora's eyes narrowed. "This divorce can't come too soon."

"I don't know about that," said Francie.

"Why not?"

"Maybe if he had a job again, Nora, but right now it wouldn't be fair."

"Fair? You said fair?"

"Yes."

"Then maybe it's time to consider a boyfriend."

"And that would be fair?" Francie asked—very close to the first question she would have asked if the real story had come spilling out.

"You're asking me if cheating on Roger would be fair?"

"If you want to put it that way."

"That's the way people put it." Nora thought, drank more beer, thought again. "Got anyone in mind?" she said.

"No," said Francie, feeling Nora's gaze and not even trying to meet it.

A long silence followed. Nora poured the rest of the beer, looking at Francie from the corner of her eye. "Did I ever tell you about my grandmother?" she said.

"Rose? I knew her."

"But did I ever mention the time I called her number, six months after she died?"

"Why?"

"Because there was something I'd meant to tell her." Nora rose. "Good luck, kiddo."

"Good luck?"

"With Anne," said Nora. "In the tournament."

Francie went home. The phone was ringing. She picked it up.

"Francie? Anne Franklin. Hope it's not too late. They just called me with the draw—we play Friday at four-thirty, if that's all right."

"Fine."

"And I was thinking maybe we could set up a practice match before that."

"Sure."

"I've got a court Thursday at six."

"Thursday's out," Francie said.

"I'm sorry—that's the only time they had."

"We'll just have to wing it," Francie said.

Francie went to bed but couldn't sleep. She kept thinking of Nora's grandmother, kept hearing the chill in Nora's voice when she wished her luck. That was unbearable: candor, as they said, was the soul of friendship, and she had let Nora down. There would have to be at least one change in Ned's rules.

6

Thursday. Francie spent the day in her office, preparing a report (negative) for the acquisitions committee. ". . . menstrual performance, coupled with an installation consisting of outsize Tupperware (e.g., casserole dish—10 ft. diameter) suspended from a . . ." She found she'd already typed that sentence, not once but twice, as a quick scroll through the text revealed. She couldn't concentrate at all. This often happened on Thursdays, but this Thursday more than ever.

The phone rang. Francie reached for it with dread. Once before Ned had called to cancel, at about this same time. But it wasn't Ned.

"Francie? Tad Wagner here."

"Yes?" She'd heard the name but couldn't place it.

"Your insurance agent—classmate of Roger's."

"Oh, yes."

"How're you doing?"

"Fine, thanks."

"So I understand. I saw a nice article in the *Globe*."

"That was really about the foundation. I wasn't even supposed—"

"I'm impressed. But the reason I'm calling—now that this career of yours is taking off, have you given any thought to a term policy in your own name?"

"A term policy?"

"That's the instrument I'd recommend in your case."

"Are you talking about life insurance?"

"That's my forte." He pronounced it correctly—at least Harvard gave you that.

"I have no dependents, Tad."

Pause. "What about Roger? Word is he's . . ."

What about Roger? Roger had supported her for years. And if they did end in divorce, she could change the beneficiary: *to Em*. "How much does it cost?"

Tad described different options. Francie settled on a term policy for $500,000 with Roger as beneficiary and hung up. Tad must have been desperate for business: that *Globe* article was six months old.

Ten to four. Enough. She saved and printed her report. Then she wrote *To Ned, with all my love, Francie* on a plain sheet of paper. She stared at the words. They seemed alive on the page.

Francie folded the paper, put it in an envelope, taped it to the rewrapped painting leaning against her desk. She'd never written Ned a note before—written communication was out—but this was special. He could destroy the note if he wished. The pleasure of writing it had been exquisite: it made their relationship real. Francie packed her briefcase, picked up the painting, took the elevator down to the garage.

She drove out of the city under a low and fast-darkening sky, planning what she would say about Nora. It was just a question of making him see how close they were, how trustworthy Nora was. Francie was sure he would understand. Her heart grew light and buoyant—she could feel it, high in her chest, like a bird about to fly. She felt as happy as she'd ever been, at least as an adult, until just across the New Hampshire line, when the car phone buzzed. She realized immediately that she'd forgotten to send the goddamn report upstairs to the acquisitions committee.

"Hello?" she said.

But it wasn't the committee. First a faint background voice, female, said, "Three minutes to air," and then Ned came on. "Hello," he said.

"Ned."

"Hi." He never spoke her name on the phone. There was a pause, and in it Francie thought: *Say you'll be a little late.* He said, "I'm sorry, but I can't make it today."

"Oh."

"Two minutes to air."

"Really sorry. Something's come up; I'll explain later."

"Something bad?"

"Nothing bad, but I've got to go."

"Bye, then."

"I'll call."

Too late to go back to the office, and Francie didn't want to go home. She kept driving, wishing she hadn't said *Bye, then* like that. Something coming up had to mean something involving Em—a parent-teacher meeting, a dance recital. Em came first. Em was the reason Ned couldn't get divorced; Em was the reason for secrecy. Francie understood that, accepted it. If she had a child, she would be the same . . . Francie didn't finish the thought. A competing one had risen in her mind, obtrusive: *If I had a child, I would never take the risk, not for anyone.* She shoved this second thought away, back down into her unconscious or wherever it had sprung from. She didn't have a child: she couldn't know. And how unfair to Ned. He loved her, he loved Em. Did that make him bad?

Francie was almost at Brenda's gate before she remembered the show. Switching on the radio, she caught

Ned in midsentence, the signal weak and scratchy with static but audible: ". . . pain will ever go away? Maybe not—that's the truth of it. But it will change into something else, something more manageable. Time may not be a healer, but at least it turns wounds into scars, if you see what I mean."

"I think I do, Ned." The woman was crying. "Thank you."

"Rico from Brighton. Welcome to *Intimately Yours*."

"Hey. Great show. Can we switch to something different for a second?"

"Thursday, Rico. Anything goes."

"I'd like to talk about the Big A."

"The Big A?"

"The A-word, Ned."

"Adultery?"

"You got it."

"And what's your angle?"

"The scientific angle."

"Which is?"

"You know," said Rico. "Nature's law. It's in a man's best interest to get his genes out there as much as possible and it's in a woman's best interest to have a man around to help with the kids. I mean, that's a contradiction, right?"

"And the implication?"

"That it's not about morality. You do what you gotta do."

There was a long pause, full of static. Then Ned said, "Why don't we throw that out to the listeners—the Big A, a question of—"

Francie lost him completely. Night had fallen now. Her headlights glinted on Brenda's gate. She unlocked it, drove through and up the hill. At the top, she tried the radio again, and Ned came in clearly. ". . . reduce this to a bunch of genes? Let's take another call."

All at once, Francie had a crazy idea. She had a phone, it was a call-in show, she knew the number. Why not call him? He'd never said not to call the show. Free-form Thursday. She picked up the phone and dialed; no chance of getting through anyway.

"*Intimately Yours,*" said a voice. "Who's this?"

"Iris," said Francie. "On a car phone."

"And what did you want to talk about?"

"Genes."

"Mind turning off your radio? You're next."

Francie waited, her heart beating its Thursday beat again. What was the saying? Hide a tree in the forest. Did it apply to what she was doing? Maybe not. Maybe this wasn't such a good—

"You're on."

Ned spoke, right in her ear, but with a tone he never used with her: "Iris on her car phone, welcome to the show. What's on your mind, Iris?"

Maybe not a good idea.

"Iris? You there?"

Francie said, "I just want to tell you how much I like your show. Thursdays especially."

Silence. It seemed endless. Then the line went dead. She turned the radio back on, felt herself blushing like a schoolgirl.

". . . lost Iris. Let's take another call." Ned, his voice pitched higher than she'd ever heard it. Not a good idea, not well executed, not funny. Francie pounded her hand on the steering wheel.

Early retirement: an infuriating suggestion. On the computer in his basement office, Roger opened the file containing his résumé and made a single change, adding

IQ—181 (Stanford-Binet) on the line below the date of his birth. He printed the résumé, read it over. The new entry didn't look bad, no worse than a long list of specious awards, for example. Quite professional. He prepared a mailing list of potential employers for the revised résumé.

After that, Roger logged on to the Puzzle Club, started the *Times of London* crossword. Where was he? Hell, in ideal form: that would be *dystopia*. Seven across, six letters: ugni, sylvaner. He typed in *grapes*. Ten down, nine letters: loss. Roger paused, sat for a few moments, then went up to Francie's bedroom; their bedroom. He bent, looked under the bed. The painting of the grapes and the skateboarding girl was gone.

Roger grew aware of Francie's clock radio, broadcasting to an empty room; she was like that, leaving on lights, running the tap the whole time she brushed her teeth. "Genes or no genes, Ned," a woman on a phone line was saying, "it'll always be cheating in my book."

"Sounds like the first line of a country hit," said a studio voice, gentle and sympathetic: the kind of male tone suddenly common in broadcasting, a tone Roger hated.

"Let's take another caller," the man said as Roger moved to shut him off. "Who have we got? Iris on her car phone, welcome to the show. What's on your mind, Iris?"

A long pause. Roger was unfamiliar with Francie's clock radio; he fumbled for the switch, found the volume instead, turning it louder.

"Iris? You there?"

"I just want to tell you how much I like your show," a woman said. "Thursdays especially."

Roger froze. Time seemed to freeze with him. The radio went silent, until at last the smooth-voiced man cleared his throat and said, "Oops, looks like we lost Iris. Let's take another call."

"Hi, Ned. Can we get off this adultery thing for a minute? I'm having a problem with my—"

Roger turned off the radio, stood motionless by the bed.

Francie. Beyond doubt. What had become of her, calling any talk show at all, to say nothing of a smarmy, prurient one like that? To let herself be used by them, like one of those pathetic big-haired women on television? He left the room, closed the door, stopped. And why would she call herself Iris?

Car phone. What was the number of Francie's car phone? Roger didn't know, had never called it. He went downstairs to the kitchen desk where Francie kept all the household accounts. He found the latest cellular phone bill, noted her number, and dialed it, leafing through the bill as he waited for a ring.

"The cellular phone customer you have called is not available at this time," said a recording.

Roger wondered where she was.

Francie drove down to the stone jetty, printing fresh tire tracks in unbroken snow. The snow should have warned her of what lay ahead, but not until her head-lights shone on the river, white instead of black, did she realize it was frozen. She got out of the car, stepped onto the jetty, looked down into the dinghies: five or six inches of snow on their floorboards, caught in the ice.

Francie gazed across at the island, the tops of the elms white against the night sky. She hadn't anticipated this; a New England girl, and she hadn't foreseen winter, the changes it would bring for Ned and her. Now she saw them very clearly—motel rooms, dark parking places, furtiveness. Her mind recoiled, and Ned's would, too. Without the cottage, they had a relationship entirely mental, like some Victorian exercise in frustration. How long could that last?

Francie walked to the end of the jetty, sat down. Her feet took charge, lowering themselves to the ice. Then she was standing. Nothing cracked, nothing split; the ice felt thick and solid. She went back to her car for the painting, then moved out onto the ice, one step after another.

Francie walked across the river. She wore leather city boots, not even calf-high, but high enough. The snow on the river was only an inch or two deep, the rest blown away by the wind. This was easy—good traction, and no rowing, no tying up—with Brenda's wintry island more beautiful than ever. A moonless, starless sky, but she could see her way easily; the snow brightened the night. A shadow stirred in the elm tops, rose high above. The owl. Francie paused to watch, lost it in the darkness, took another step. The next moment she was plunging to the bottom.

Down she went in complete blackness, icy water bubbling around her, so cold it made her gasp, swallow, gag. Her foot touched something: the bottom? She pushed off, a panicked, reflexive kick, and frantically kicked toward the surface—or what she hoped was the surface, because she could see nothing but bubbles, silver on the outside, black within. But the surface didn't come. Was she moving at all? So heavy: she struggled with her coat, freed herself from it, tried to get rid of her boots, could not. She kicked, wheeled her arms, felt pressure building in her chest like an inflating balloon, and always the never-ending shock of cold. Her head struck something hard and she sank.

As Francie sank, she had a strange thought, not her kind of thought at all. She wasn't religious, certainly didn't believe in any kind of quid pro quo, deal-making God. But still, the thought came—*If you let me live, I'll never see Ned again*—as though she were guilty, and this the punishment.

Francie kicked again, once, twice, the bubble about to burst from her chest. Her head had struck something hard: the underside of the ice? She raised her hands in protection, and her fingers reached into night air. Francie broke through the surface, choking, retching, but alive. She floundered in a pool of black water, no wider than the top of a well.

Francie commanded her hands: on the ice. They obeyed. Pull. They pulled, but the ice broke off. Francie tried again, and again, and again, hands, face, body numb, teeth chattering at an impossible speed, breaking off chunks of ice, breaking, breaking. She heard a terrible cry, her cry, and then the ice held for her. She flopped onto it, drew herself up, inches at a time, to her chest, her waist, and out.

Some shivering mechanism now controlled her body. She staggered across the ice, onto the jetty, into her car. The keys? In her coat: gone. But then she saw them glinting in the ignition, left by mistake. What was happening to her? She turned the key, switched on the heater, full-blast. The engine was still warm. It had been only a few minutes. She clung, shaking, to the steering wheel, and remembered *oh garden, my garden*: gone, too.

It was after midnight when Francie got home. From his basement office, Roger heard her footsteps overhead. He waited an hour by the clock and went upstairs.

Francie's boots were on the mat by the front door. They looked wet. Roger went closer. They were wet. He picked one up. Soaked, inside and out, and it was too cold for rain. Had she gone for a walk on the beach, strayed too close to the surf? He sniffed: no salty smell, but to be sure he gave the leather a lick of his tongue as well. Freshwater, then, and at least a foot deep. Freshwater: ponds, lakes, rivers. He gazed up the stairs, thinking.

Roger put the boot down, aligned the pair neatly. He went into the kitchen. Francie's purse lay on the table. He looked through it: wallet, with driver's license, credit cards, forty-two dollars; zinc lozenges, tissues, vitamin C, a key ring. Key ring. Not like her. She always left her keys in the ignition when she parked in the garage, no matter what he said.

There were seven keys on the ring: car key; two house keys, front and back; a key to her locker at the tennis club—he had had one just like it—a small key that would be for luggage; and two he couldn't identify. These two he removed from the ring and laid on the table.

Roger went to Francie's kitchen desk, found paper and a pencil. He placed the keys on the paper and traced their patterns. Then he pocketed the paper, put the keys back on the ring, left the purse the way he'd found it, went downstairs to his basement room. The crossword waited, unfinished. One down, nine letters: loss. That would be *ruination*.

7

"**G**ood show this afternoon, Ned," said Kira Chang, vice president of Total Entertainment Syndication, raising her glass. "Here's to *Intimately Yours*."

Sitting at the table in Ned's dining room, they drank to the show: Anne, at the far end; Trevor, Ned's producer, on her right; Lucy, the director, next to him; Ned at the end; Kira Chang on his right; Trevor's assistant next to her. Ned didn't like the wine at all, wished that Anne could have done a little better. And he wished she could have done better with the whole dinner, despite the late notice.

Ned had called at 3:30, and Anne had said, "I wasn't planning any dinner at all—isn't it Thursday?"

For a moment he found himself holding his breath. "Meaning what?" he said.

"Thursday, Ned. When you stay late to plan the shows."

"Yes. Normally. But Kira Chang's in town."

"Who's she?"

"I told you. Sweetheart. The syndicator."

"I thought that was next week."

"The meeting's next week, but she happened to be in town today and she dropped in. Trevor says it's a good sign, so we should take advantage of it."

"I'll do my best," Anne said.

Her best: the oyster stew, the lemon chicken with snow peas, the tiramisu from Lippo's. And this maroon-colored wine, possibly Romanian—he couldn't read the fine print on the label.

"Delicious, Anne," said Kira Chang. "And I hear you're quite a tennis player, too."

Anne smiled nervously. The light in the dining room was a little too strong; it made her look washed out, or was that just the effect of Kira's presence?

Trevor refilled his glass—not for the first time—and said, "One thing we've never discussed, Kira, is the name of the show. What do you think of it?"

Kira looked at Trevor across the table. "There's only one answer to questions like that—I'll let you know after we poll the audience."

"To see what *it* thinks, you mean?"

"That's right."

"Isn't that leading by following?"

Kira smiled at him. "This isn't art, Trevor. It isn't even politics. It's just entertainment."

"Total entertainment," said Ned.

Kira laughed. "Bingo."

She left soon after. Ned walked her out to the waiting taxi. A cold wind blew down the street, ruffling her glossy hair. She turned to him.

"Thanks for dinner," she said. "And don't forget to thank Anne again for me. I hope I didn't upset your routine."

"Not at all," Ned said. Their eyes met. He said what was on his mind. "Did you really like the show today?"

"Not much," Kira replied. "But that's what I like, right there. The way you asked that question. You're good with women, Ned. That's your strength. And it goes a long way in this business."

"But the show?"

"Too early to say. I hope you understand that when we green-light something like this we often bring in our own people on the production side."

"The show was Trevor's idea in the first place."

"The cast-iron sincerity in your tone—that's part of the appeal, for sure," she said, opening the door of the taxi. "But the metaphor to keep in mind, if you want to make it big in broadcasting, in anything, is the multistage rocket."

"Meaning the booster falls away?"

"Good night," she said, closing the door. The taxi drove off.

"Did it go all right?" Anne asked when they were in bed.

"Fine."

"What a relief. She made me so uncomfortable."

"How?"

"She's so poised, so . . . everything I'm not."

"Don't be ridiculous," Ned said. The booster falls away: that meant ruthlessness, and he wasn't the ruthless type. He rolled over and tried to sleep; the headache awoke over his right eye, unfolding like a flower.

"Francie?"

Francie opened her eyes. Roger was standing by the bed, looking down at her. A jolt of adrenaline rushed through her, washing away decaying fragments of terrible dreams.

"Hope I didn't scare you," he said with a smile. "Not going in today?"

Francie started to speak, but her mouth was too dry, her throat, her whole body, hurting. She tried again. "What time is it?"

"Nine-thirty. You slept through the alarm."

Francie glanced at the clock radio.

"I shut it off," Roger said. "How can you bear that station?" He smiled again. "Coffee?"

"You've made coffee?"

"Should be just about done." He reached out as though to pat her knee under the covers, thought better of it, went out. Francie sat up, saw her damp clothes lying in the corner. She rose, aching in every muscle, kicked the clothes under the bed, got back in just as Roger returned with a tray: buttered toast, marmalade, steaming coffee.

"You should stay home," he said. "You don't look at all well."

"I'm fine."

Roger pulled up a chair, watched her sip the coffee. "Working late last night?" he said.

"Yes."

He nodded. "I hope you're appreciated," he said. "Some *especially* important project, is it?"

"I don't know what you mean by especially important. The acquisitions committee meets next week—it's always a busy time."

"Seen anything you like recently?"

"What do you mean?"

"Objets d'art. What else could I be referring to?"

"Nothing." But it had been years since he had discussed her work. "I'm recommending a few pieces."

"Such as?"

"There's a photographer in Providence. She does old people under streetlights, in black-and-white. Mostly black."

"Any paintings?"

"No paintings," Francie said.

* * *

Roger dressed warmly: turtleneck, chamois shirt, thick corduroy pants, ski hat, Gore-Tex gloves, his L.L. Bean boots. He went into the garage, opened Francie's car, looked in the glove box, found a wrinkled envelope with a map drawn on it jammed at the back, as he'd been sure he would—he knew her, and nothing she did could change that. *Directions to B.'s*, she'd written in her neat hand. He studied the map for a minute or so, replaced it. Then, putting a shovel in the back of his car, he drove to a hardware store. The clerk made keys from the two patterns. Roger filled his tank and headed west, out of the city. His car had four-wheel drive and good tires, but the sky was low and dark and snow was in the forecast. He switched on his headlights and set the cruise control prudently to fifty-five.

Snow was falling by the time Roger stopped in front of Brenda's gate—marked *wrought-iron g.* on the map, as he recalled—falling, but falling hard enough to have obliterated any trace of tread marks? Roger's eyes followed the track that rose up the hill beyond the gate, white, smooth, unbroken. He had his first moment of doubt.

The gate was padlocked. Roger got out of his car, took out the two keys. The first one worked. He drove through, his wheels spinning slightly as he came to the top of the hill, and cautiously down the other side, foot on the brake the whole way.

He parked by a stone jetty, covered in snow, and looked out at the island in the river. Snow, clean and pure, lay deep on everything: the trees, the roof of the cottage, the river. Roger remembered going out in the Adirondack woods as a boy to cut down a Christmas tree with his father's man, as they called him, Len; how Len had pretended to chop off his own foot, having brought along a Baggie of ketchup to complete the illusion: red stains in the snow, Len laughing his toothless laugh, a drop of mucus quivering from the tip of his hairy nose. Roger's father had fired Len that very day for putting such a scare into the boy.

Roger stepped onto the jetty, saw no sign of tracks across the river. Doubt again. Was he seeing ketchup and thinking blood? He gazed down onto two dinghies, filled with snow. It was falling harder now, the flakes bigger. Roger reached into the nearest dinghy, picked up an oar, and jabbed it on the river ice. Solid. He lowered himself onto the river and started across, testing the ice with the oar at every step.

Roger walked onto the island, past the giant elms, also reminding him of his boyhood, up to the front door of the cottage. Snow on the porch, snow on the glider, even a little mound of it clinging to the upper hemisphere of the doorknob. Doubt. He took out the remaining key. It worked. Roger went inside.

He closed the door, took off his boots, took off his gloves. Kitchen: a wine bottle on the table, half full. Roger reached for it, stopped. *Flake of dandruff falls off your head, you fry.* Strange, how the mind worked. He put on the gloves, drew the cork, tilted the bottle to his lips, not quite touching, and tasted the wine. Still good, although not much of a wine. He stuck the cork back in, left the bottle in the same spot on the table.

Roger opened the refrigerator, empty, and the cupboards: dishes, glasses, the expected. He went into the living room, ran his eyes over the books, mounted the stairs. He glanced into a bedroom with a bare mattress on the bed, moved into the bathroom: bar of soap and a bottle of shampoo in the shower. He picked up the shampoo with his gloved hand. Principessa was the brand,

and the writing on the bottle was Italian. A towel hung over the rail; he could see it was dry.

Roger went into the last room, another bedroom, this one made up. He checked the closet: two life jackets and a terry-cloth robe on the rail, something silver glinting on the high shelf at the back. He reached for it, a box, a silvery slippery box that he almost dropped. Lancôme face powder: would have been messy. He put it back. Then he knelt, peered under the bed, saw dustballs. He pulled back the duvet, checked under the pillows, stared at the sheets. White sheets, spotless. He bent over the center of the bed until his nose was almost touching the bottom sheet and sniffed. He smelled nothing.

Ketchup, instead of blood. Had he built a huge construction on a foundation of nothing? Then, straightening, Roger saw brown-tipped flowers in a glass vase by the window, dying but not dead. Irises? Yes, but even if they were, what then? Nothing certain. A foundation of very little. If he had made one mistake in his life, in his work, it was letting his brilliance speed him along too quickly. *Homo sapiens* was a jealous species.

Roger smoothed the duvet, went downstairs. He stood in the kitchen for some time, watching the snow fall. Then he put on his boots and went out, making sure the door was locked behind him.

Roger walked back across the river, poking ahead automatically with the oar, his brain rearranging the few pieces—irises, wine, wet boots, call-in show—and projecting the shapes of missing ones that might not even exist. He almost didn't notice the bump in all the white smoothness of the river, a protrusion like driftwood covered in snow.

Bending over it, Roger dusted off the snow. Underneath he saw not driftwood but a brown-paper-wrapped package, frozen stiff. He got his hands on it, pulled; the package didn't budge. Clearing away more snow with the blade of the oar, he saw that the package, tilted at a forty-five-degree angle, was stuck in the ice.

Roger went to his car, returned with the shovel, chipped away carefully. After a few minutes, the package came free. Then he was down on his hands and knees, tearing at the frozen paper.

A painting. One half blurred and damaged, all murky brown and green. But the other half showed a crumbling plinth, a few dangling red grapes, the front wheels of a skateboard.

The wind began to blow at the wrapping paper. Roger scrambled around, gathering it up. He came upon a white envelope, threw off his gloves, ripped it open. Inside a note: *To Ned, with all my love, Francie.*

Roger stood in the middle of the river, snow falling harder, wind whipping icy flakes at him from different directions. His mind was the same—a turmoil of thoughts, racing by too fast for even him to examine. *Must clear, must clear, must clear,* he thought, and with great effort he forced his brain to stop, his mind to go blank. He stood panting, his head empty, feeling nothing, not cold, snow, wind.

And into this calm, a meditational calm, although he'd always despised the idea of meditation, came a first brief thought, or rather, memory. *A perfect crime: it's got to be absolutely unconnected—a penny drops off the Empire State Building, goes right through your skull.*

8

Roger drove back to the city, still at a prudent fifty-five, but his mind was racing. He was used to the speed of his mind, had known it to run far ahead of him before, but never in this supercharged way. His whole body was shaking slightly, like a shell that could barely contain the forces within. *Hold on to one thought,* he instructed it, or at most a single train of thought. He settled on one right away, a simple syllogism. Major premise: F tries to make a fool of R. Minor premise: R is not a fool and will not bear it. Conclusion: question mark.

Not quite a question mark, because he knew that some action was required. She had come into their house—his house, his ancestral house—with another man's sperm inside her, perhaps many, many times. Another man's sperm: a vulgar, dirty, contemptuous betrayal, almost slimy, like a plot development in one of those movies about alien beings in human shape. Another man's sperm—what a primitive fixation she had with the substance, on reflection—inside her, and she talking and smiling away at him. Smile and be a villain, Francie. There was no fixing anything now, no going back. And what was society's answer? No-fault divorce. If this were Sicily, or Iran, countless other places, he could now—what? *Kill her with impunity.* A crime of passion, almost expected. Divorce implied nothing more than absence of affection, lack of feeling. Therefore divorce did not apply. He felt. He felt the opposite of everything husband should feel for wife. She was his enemy, had proved him wrong in one of the basic decisions of life, whom to marry. What action was appropriate? Question mark.

Not quite a question mark. Deep in his mind, did he not already know the answer must be related to that penny dropping off the Empire State Building? *Yes.* The conclusion awaited, long before the thinking was done. But slow: this was not Sicily or Iran. America, land that had deteriorated so much as he grew older, had failed him so badly. Slow: there would be many steps along the way, down and down toward that coppery glint. And every step must be a careful step, all planning, all preparation thought and rethought.

For example, on the front seat beside him sat the damaged painting and Francie's note. *To Ned, with all my love, Francie.* His mind writhed away from the words. *Get back on track, one thought, one thought.* The painting, the note. Too risky to hide them in the house and he no longer had an office. Was there any other space over which he held exclusive control? The answer came at once, probably because of the morning's business with the keys: his locker at the tennis club.

Step one, then. There were two kinds of lockers at the club: full-size metal ones in the locker room, and half-size wooden ones lining the thickly carpeted hall that led to the courts. Because of his dislike for showering at the club, Roger had taken a locker in the hall. He walked to it now, the painting wrapped in the scraps of brown paper he'd salvaged, note tucked inside, and unlocked the door with his key. Inside he found equipment he'd forgotten about—racquets, cans of balls, tennis shoes, towels. No room for the painting. He put the painting down, the brown paper unfurling, glanced around, saw no one, took everything out of the locker, picked up the painting, rewrapped it imperfectly, one corner protruding, and was just placing it inside when a female voice spoke right behind him. "Roger?"

He slammed the door shut, wheeled around, saw a big woman in a purple warm-up suit, a pair of racquets slung over her shoulder. "Oh. Nora." Not very smooth, perhaps, possibly lacking in friendliness, so he added, "Hello. Nice to see you."

"Likewise. I didn't know you were playing again."

"Playing again?" How to handle this situation? He looked at her: only Nora, after all, a jock, not very bright; he'd never understood what Francie saw in her. "Thinking about it, in any case," he said. "Come to reintroduce myself to the gear. Shake hands with my racquet." A witticism—shaking hands with the racquet was the age-old introduction to the forehand grip. He laughed.

Nora didn't. Her brow, in no way noble, or even intelligent, wrinkled. *Must I explain the goddamned joke?* Roger was thinking, when three women came down the hall on their way to the courts, talking woman-talk. "Say hi to Francie," Nora said, joining them.

"Will do," said Roger with a smile, turning the key in his locker, then trying the handle twice to make sure it was locked.

Driving home, Roger fought the urge to stamp down on the gas, to smash the cars around him. *On track, stay on track, use your brain.* He used it to think about crime.

Roger knew that people sometimes got away with crime, but did any of them *necessarily* do so? Or did they simply rely, tacitly or explicitly, on sloppy police work, nonexistent police work, luck? He considered luck. A person could be taken on a cruise ship, for example, invited for a glass of champagne on a deserted stern deck at night, pushed over the rail. It might work, but was it teleologically guaranteed to do so? Of course not. Someone might be sitting in the shadows, obscured by a lifeboat, and witness the whole thing. Or the falling person might cry out, attract a quick glance through a porthole or from someone on a lower deck, leading to alarms, searchlights, rubber boats crisscrossing the wake. The person might even fall unnoticed but then happen on a piece of driftwood, cling to it until dawn, be rescued by a fishing boat. Therefore the cruise ship scenario, attractive because no body and therefore no evidence is found, required luck, would not succeed of necessity, was far from perfect.

Calmer now, Roger was in no way downcast by the negative result of this speculation. Quite the opposite, if anything, for all at once he was hungry and thirsty, his appetite keener than it had been for a long time. He pulled into a suburban steakhouse, the kind of place he would never enter—wagon wheel by the door, cowboy pictures on the wall—and ordered a big steak and a double Scotch on the rocks. What was this strange feeling bubbling up inside him, strange but not quite forgotten? He put a name to it: enthusiasm. And in the next moment he realized with a shock—ironic, unsettling, but finally pleasant—that he had found a job at last.

"I'll have another," he said to the waitress.

"Another drink, sir?"

"Another of everything."

"Including the garlic bread?"

"*Pourquoi pas?*"

"I'm sorry?"

"Yes, garlic bread by all means."

Accidents, he thought, chewing his food with relish, trying to keep pace with his mind. Tampering with brakes, with steering rods, with ovens, with furnaces, with ski bindings all required technical knowledge; all carried the risk that evidence of tampering might remain. And if tampering was suspected, the first suspect would be the spouse.

Roger removed the round paper napkin from under his glass, wrote on it:

poison—no—expertise, traces
contract killer—no—in his power
arson (house)—no—evidence—accelerant
infection (injection?) with some disease—

"Care for anything else, sir?"

Roger slid his hand over the napkin. "Just the check."

The waitress went off. Roger raised his hand slightly to peek at the napkin, like a poker player checking his hole card. The disease idea. Pro: like an accident, it provided a credible noncriminal explanation for death. Con: it required expertise, a disease not readily contagious yet fast-acting and certain. *No,* he wrote beside it, but reluctantly. He paid his bill, went into the bathroom, tore up the napkin, flushed the shreds down the toilet, got in his car, started home. He had gone a few blocks when he made a sudden U-turn and sped back to the restaurant. What if some scrap of the napkin was still floating in the toilet bowl? He hurried inside—"anything the matter, sir?" said the waitress—strode into the bathroom, peered into the toilet. Nothing but water; he flushed it again anyway, just to be safe.

"Francie?" he called, entering the house on Beacon Hill; their house, under the laws of the Commonwealth, but his by moral right, since he had inherited it from his grandparents. No answer. He went into the kitchen, saw her purse still on the table and a stack of mail, some opened, on the desk. He riffled through it, found a letter from Tad Wagner: *Please find a copy of your coverage statement. Once again, thanks so much, and if I can be . . .*

Roger checked the coverage statement. Amount: $500,000. Beneficiary: himself. Yes, he had found a job, and it came with a suitable performance bonus. Had his mind somehow known about Francie even then when he'd first thought of Tad and arranged to run into him on the street? A reunion that had led to a drink, talk of Francie's success, proud exhibition of the *Globe* clipping—but no explicit discussion of her possible insurance needs, unnecessary with the Tads of the world. The human mind had unplumbed powers, his especially. He heard Francie moving about upstairs, left the desk the way he'd found it.

Roger was putting cookies on a tray when Francie came into the room: the sight of her. Her face, once such an appealing mix of elements—bright eyes, strong features, soft skin—was nothing but a mask. How clearly he saw that now. Despite all the thinking he had done that day, despite the need for long and careful preparation, despite that glinting coppery goal sometime in the future, he wanted to beat her head in, then and there. "Care for a cookie?" he said, offering the tray.

"No thanks," she said.

"Feeling better?"

"Yes."

She was wearing a coat: an old one, he noticed, unworn for a year or two. "Going somewhere?"

"Didn't I tell you? I'm playing in the tournament."

"Mixed?" he asked.

"Women's doubles, Roger," said Francie, taking her purse and moving toward the door that led down to the garage.

"Good luck, then." She went out. He waited until he

felt the vibration of the opening garage door under his
feet before calling, "Don't forget to bend your fucking
knees."

"God, what fun," said Anne. Still sweating slightly, they
sat at a corner table of the tennis club bar, overlooking the
courts. Seven–five, two–six, seven–five: they'd knocked the
number one seeds out of the tournament. "That backhand
down the line you hit at five all ad out—unbelievable. I
wouldn't have the guts to try that, not in a million years."

Francie just smiled.

"And then your two best serves of the night, right
after. Bang bang. I could have kissed you." Beer came,
and water, lots of water. Pink with exertion and victory,
Anne talked on and on, reliving the match, her words
sometimes tripping over themselves. Francie hadn't seen
her like this, suspected it didn't happen often. She wondered about Anne's husband.

Anne paused for breath, took a big drink of water.
"Was it Jimmy Connors who said that tennis is better
than sex?"

"Maybe his tennis," Francie said. "Not ours."

Anne glanced at her, and in that glance Francie saw
her realizing she'd been talking too much, at least in
terms of some inner code. Her mood changed, the blood
draining from her face, leaving her pale. Her eyes took
on an inward look: something was on her mind, something unrelated to tennis. She tried some beer, started to
speak, stopped, and finally said, "Can I ask you something, Francie? I hate to be too personal, but the truth is I
find you so easy to be with—like someone I've known
for a long time."

"Ask away," said Francie.

Anne said, "Are you a good cook?"

"That's the question?"

Anne nodded.

"I have two surefire appetizers, two surefire entrées, one dessert," said Francie. "The rest is silence."

Anne smiled, an admiring smile that made Francie a little uncomfortable. "I thought my lemon chicken was surefire, too," she said, "but I guess I was wrong." The inward look again. Francie waited. "Does your husband ever bring people home for dinner at the last minute?" Anne asked.

"He's actually been doing the cooking lately," Francie said.

"Aren't you lucky."

Anne added something else that Francie didn't catch. She was thinking of their own dining room, and the happy sounds that used to fill it. At one time she and Roger had entertained a lot, then less, and since the loss of his job, not at all. Plotted on a graph, she wondered, would those dinners track the health of their marriage? Down, down, down, with upturns here and there: a stunted marriage, like a tree growing in the face of an impossible wind.

"Thursday of all days," Anne was saying, "when he usually works late. It was going to be a McDonald's night, and then boom. So I threw together the lemon chicken, but they hardly touched it. And I suppose the wine wasn't very good either, although that didn't stop them from drinking plenty of it. I'd read an article on Romanian wine, goddamn it." Was Francie imagining it, or had Anne's eyes filled with tears? Tears, yes: and Anne saw that she saw, and tried to explain. "He cares so much about his career. The least I can do is put a decent meal on the table."

Francie could imagine Nora at this point, saying, *Your husband sounds like a jerk.* She toned that down. "I don't see the connection. And if he's any good at his job, a failed lemon chicken won't make any difference."

"You think? He's so ambitious."

"I do. Lighten up, for God's sake."

Anne's eyes cleared. "I'm sure you're right," she said. "You're so clearheaded, Francie, so in control."

Francie, suddenly picturing herself under the ice at Brenda's cottage, her breath escaping in silver-and-black bubbles, said nothing.

"Can I ask you a favor?" Anne said.

"But first do me one," Francie said. "Stop asking if you can ask and just ask."

Anne laughed. "With pleasure." She reached across the table, touched Francie's hand. "Give me one of those surefire recipes of yours."

Francie took the paper napkin from under her glass and wrote:

Francie's Roast Lamb, serves 8
7 cloves garlic, 1 halved, rest chopped
2 pounds baking potatoes, peeled and . . .

She came to the end, added the reminder to keep the gratin warm while waiting to carve the lamb, handed the napkin to Anne. "Enjoy."

"Oh, I'm sure I will," said Anne. "The very next time we have company." Her face brightened with an idea. "Maybe you and your husband would like to join us?"

"That sounds nice," Francie said.

9

Anne, having checked her watch and said "Oh my God, the sitter," left in a hurry; Francie sat alone at the corner table in the bar. Looking down on court three beneath her window, she watched the second seeds playing their match. They were good, but nothing like the pair she and Anne had just beaten, nothing like the pair she and Anne had so quickly become. Francie couldn't remember playing this well at any time in her life. How was it possible, with so much on her mind? Her near-drowning, her stupid on-air phone call, the loss of *oh garden, my garden*, Roger's attempted seduction, to put the kindest light on it, and his subsequent attentiveness, just as disturbing. Some of it had to do with Anne, of course—they fit together so well—but was the rest simply chance? Or was it one of those Faustian bargains, her life falling apart while her tennis got better and better? She wanted no part of that. Tennis was her game, but just a game. In any case, her life wasn't falling apart—not with Ned in it, no matter what happened. Francie paid her bill, went downstairs to her car, started for home.

Roger sat before his computer. The Puzzle Club was up, but he was not really attending. In fact, he was staring through the words on the screen, into a translucent beyond, his mind working out the possibilities of planting a bomb in an Israeli consulate, having first ensured that a visiting art consultant would be inside at just the right moment. A wretched idea, he concluded: messy, inelegant, leaking evidence, guaranteed to provide a full-scale investigation, and he knew nothing of bombs, bomb-making, bomb-planting. He leaned his head against the screen and thought, *What am I doing?* The computer hummed quietly against his brain.

Perhaps he was wrong about everything. All his evidence was circumstantial. Even her note and the call to the radio show could be logically explained: maybe she had developed one of those fan manias for a celebrity, maybe it was all taking place in her head, maybe she and the smooth-talking poseur had not even met. Did that sound like Francie? No. But there was a basic instability to her character—indeed, in the character of every woman he had ever known—so nothing could be ruled out. For his own peace of mind, if nothing else, he required eye-witness evidence. For example, was she really playing in the tennis tournament, or was that a lie to cover her presence somewhere else?

Roger pulled into the parking lot of the tennis club just in time to see Francie come out the door and walk to her car. She was wearing a warm-up suit and tennis shoes, didn't look his way, and probably wouldn't have noticed him if she had. He could see in his headlights that she was lost in thought, no doubt had fumbled away a close match, probably choking on a big point. No matter: she hadn't lied about the tournament. She drove past him, out of the parking lot, turned north, toward Storrow Drive and home. He followed. Once inside, he would offer her a drink, perhaps make a fire, if there was any wood in the storage room. From there he knew he could find some subtle way of bringing the conversation around to call-in shows. He needed hard evidence.

Francie's car phone buzzed. She answered.

"Are you on speaker?" Ned. He had never called her on the car phone before.

"No."

"Are you alone?"

"Yes. What—"

He interrupted. "What's that sound?"

"I don't hear anything." She checked her rearview mirror: two rows of double headlights winding back toward the western suburbs.

Silence.

"I'm at the place," he said.

"The cottage?"

"Don't say that. It's a cellular call, for God's sake." Pause. "Can you make it?"

"Tonight?"

"Tonight. I'm here tonight."

"Is something wrong?"

"Just can you make it."

"Yes, but—"

"Good." Click.

"—the ice." But the ice. Would he try to cross before she arrived? No. Not having the key to Brenda's, he would wait in the warmth of his car. But what if he didn't? Francie didn't know Ned's cell phone number; the rules made it unnecessary. She tried information— unlisted.

Francie exited at Mass. Ave., crossed the Charles, drove north. But what if he didn't wait in the warmth of his car? Was she willing to let him die to follow the spy-craft rules? No. She called information, asked for Ned

Demarco in Dedham—she didn't know the street—
found the home number, too, was unlisted. She stepped
on the gas. Some time passed before she realized Ned
wasn't in danger: she'd locked Brenda's wrought-iron
gate and he had no key to that either, couldn't drive
down to the river. But she stepped on the gas anyway.

Francie drove north into winter. The roads were bare
but lined with snowbanks that rose higher and higher as
she crossed into New Hampshire, the tree branches sagging lower and lower, weighted down with white. Had
there ever been this much snow so soon? Behind her the
long tail of headlights, like a wake of yellow phosphorus,
slowly dwindled down to one lone pair. Not long before
she turned onto the last and most minor of the roads that
led to Brenda's, it, too, disappeared.

Is something wrong?

Just can you make it.

Francie came to Brenda's gate—and found it wide
open. Had she left it unlocked last night in her distress?
What other explanation was there? She looked once
more in her rearview mirror, saw nothing but bright
moonlight shining on a black-and-white wilderness: deep,
crisp, even, but ahead of its time. She drove through.

Ned's car, an all-wheel sedan, had cut two well-defined
tracks in the snow. Francie followed them down to the
jetty, found the car. But Ned wasn't in it, and the inside of
the windshield was already frosting over with the freezing
breath he had left behind. In the moonlight—the dazzling
moonlight of a full moon in a clear sky over clean snow—
she saw footprints leading across the white river. She followed them.

Reasoning that where he had gone, she was safe to go,
that the river had had one more day to freeze, that she
had to see him, Francie walked across the river and

didn't think once of the night before. She reached the other side, still in Ned's footprints, their inch-deep walls black-shaded in the moonlight, took the path under the elms to the dark cottage—at least she hadn't left it open, too—and climbed the stairs to the porch.

Ned stepped out of the shadows. She jumped. "What the hell were you thinking?" he said.

Francie put her hand to her breast. "The call?"

"Yes, of course, the call." He came closer, his face strange in the stark light: much older, its future lines blackened by the night. "How could you do something so—so flippant?"

"It was meant to be funny."

"Funny?"

"And a private message as well."

Ned's voice rose, lost its beautiful timbre. "Message? What message?"

"Ned—I'm sorry."

"Me, too, believe me, since I'm the one at risk. But what was this message that was so important? Tell me now. You have my full attention."

He was even closer now, in her space, as if they hadn't been lovers, and a droplet of his spit—tiny, insignificant, barely felt—landed on her cheek. Unintentional, he wasn't even aware it had happened, but all at once Francie remembered the deal she'd made under the ice with the god she didn't believe in, and she felt her whole body stiffening, and words came out of her mouth unedited, unconsidered, but from deep within: "Maybe we'd better call this off."

"What did you say?" He stepped back, as though struck by a sudden gust.

Francie didn't repeat it; she just watched his eyes, dark and still.

Ned spoke again, his voice nearer its usual range. "I didn't mean to get into something unpleasant, Francie. I just wanted an explanation."

She shook her head. "I'm starting to see what I should have seen already. This is too much for you, Ned—it's making you unhappy."

He stared at her. His eyes changed, grew damp, reflected the moonlight. "What are you saying?"

"You don't need this."

"You're telling me my needs?"

"I think I know you, Ned."

"Do you?" The dampness spilled over his lower eyelids, onto his face. She had never seen Ned cry, had never seen any man cry, except at funerals and in the movies. "You can be goddamn arrogant sometimes," he said, his voice quiet and thick. "You think I don't know what you're really saying?"

"What am I really saying?"

"And now you're going to toy with me, too. You're really saying this is making *you* unhappy, *you* don't need *me*."

"Please, Ned. No psych one-oh-one."

His face crumpled. "When did you stop loving me?" Ned pushed past her, hurried down the stairs, down the path toward the river. Somewhere behind the house a clump of snow fell from a tree and landed with a thump. Ned stumbled on snow-covered rock, kept going. Francie went after him.

He didn't walk back across the river to the jetty but straight out into midstream, in the direction he'd come paddling from in his kayak the very first time. Francie caught up to him out in the middle of the river, in the middle of all that whiteness, as bright as day on some planet where the skies were always black.

She touched his shoulder. He stopped at once. "It's dangerous," she said. "Come back."

He turned, stood before her, hands at his sides, moonlit tears streaming down his face. "When? Just tell me that. When did you stop?"

"Never," Francie replied, and put her arms around him.

"Oh, Francie," he said, taking a deep breath, letting it out slowly, a white cloud—the only one—rising in the night. He nuzzled against her, leaned on her—she felt his weight. "Do you know how rare this is?" he said. "Wouldn't there be something wrong with two people who could just throw it away? We'd be . . . diminished."

Francie held him tight. Ice cracked, but far away.

"You do love me?" he said.

"Yes." He was right: she'd never felt this for any human being, knew she never would again. Now she was crying, too.

They walked back to the island. Francie unlocked the cottage. They went upstairs to the little bedroom, to the world under the down comforter. They lay still for a long time, holding each other. A long, healing time to get back to their places in the relationship; Francie, at least, couldn't find her old place, but the new one was not far from it, and maybe better. The lying-still phase came to an end.

After, Francie said, "There will have to be some changes."

"I know."

"I have to be able to call you. Somewhere, sometime."

"All right. I'll figure something out."

"And there's someone I have to tell. I won't say it's you, if you don't want, but I have to tell."

"Who?"

"My best friend. She already knows, anyway."

Ned's body tensed beside her. "How does she know?"

"Nora knows me. She hasn't said anything, but she knows."

"Nora?"

"You'd like her."

Pause. When it came, his response was a surprise. "Maybe I'll meet her someday. After ... after Em's grown up."

He had never before held out the promise of a better future. Francie lay beside him, savoring the implication of his words. "I'm going to get a divorce," she said.

Another silence, longer than the last. "Maybe not right away, Francie," he said.

"Why not? It's no pressure on you."

"I know that. But aren't there ever times you feel you're in a very delicate situation, where everything is poised just so?"

"I'm not sure," Francie said, and it occurred to her that in some ways he had more feminine intuition than she had. If there was an emotional IQ test, Ned would probably come out on top, the same way Roger did intellectually.

"You must have felt that sometime in your life," Ned said. "When the slightest disturbance, even of something that doesn't seem related at first, upsets everything."

Francie immediately pictured deformed sperm under a microscope. "I won't do anything right away."

"Or without telling me?"

"Or without telling you."

He kissed her. "Now you're thinking."

She laughed. He did, too. "You're a bastard," she said. "You know that?"

"All men are bastards," he said.

"Some more than others."

"Then there's hope for me?"

"Yes," she told him.

He switched on the bedside lamp, checked his watch. "Oh my God," he said. "The sitter." He started to get up, turned to her. In the yellow light of the lamp, his face was its youthful self again. "Maybe I can get out here on non-Thursdays once in a while," he said.

"That would be nice."

"And it might help if I had a key. It's cold out there."

"I'll get you one," Francie said. "Wimp." She smacked his bare butt as he got out of bed.

There was a toolshed behind the cottage. Roger had found an ax inside. He held it now in his gloved hands, staring up at the light in the window, through which had come sounds Francie had never made for him. It was easy to muse on perfect crimes and abstract killers when evidence was circumstantial. It wasn't easy now when evidence was hard. Why not simply crash his way inside, charge up to that lighted room, start swing swing swinging this goddamned ax? His blood rushed through his body at the thought, his muscles tensed, his teeth ground together. He took a step toward the door, and a few more. A bird—owl—glided down from the sky and settled on the roof. Great horned, *Bubo virginianus*. Roger halted.

Why not? Because of after. Would the ax-swinging feel good enough to render him content to spend the rest of his life in jail? For that would surely happen, given the shambles there would be inside the cottage, the pools of DNA, the two cars parked by the jetty, the obvious suspect with no alibi.

Roger returned the ax to the shed, crossed the river a few hundred yards upstream, retracing the route that kept his footprints out of sight, made his way to the wrought-iron gate where he had left his car. From there, he could just make out the upstairs light in the cottage, dim and partially blocked by trees. He was glad of the sight: a guarantee that he had imagined nothing. The light went out as he watched.

10

*T*hink.

A penny drops from the Empire State Building. Someone in China pushes a button.

Think.

Think, Roger told himself, sitting in his basement office, of murder most antiseptic. He went over his list, now committed to memory. *Accidents—mechanical, household, while on vacation; poison; contract killer; arson; disease; bombing.* All wrong, for one reason or another. *Think.* All thinking boiled down to two procedures, rearranging the pieces on the board and inventing new ones. What were the pieces? Motive, means, opportunity; evidence, suspects, alibis. A complexity of permutation and combination, orbiting this central problem: if a wife is murdered, the husband is the first suspect and remains so until ruled out with certainty. That was what made murder disguised as something else—accident or disease, for example—so attractive. The murderer would be left with nothing to do but mourn, and he could do so without anxiety, no crime being suspected.

To mourn: Roger knew exactly what suit he would wear to the funeral, a black wool-and-cashmere blend from Brooks Brothers, bought years before. Did it still fit? He went to the closet, tried it on, checked himself in the mirror. Perfect. Still wearing the suit, he returned to the computer. Roger entered none of his thoughts on it, just felt better being near it when there was thinking to do.

A penny. A Chinese penny. Rearrange the pieces: husband, wife, lover, cottage, painting. Was he missing something? Yes: killer. Husband, wife, lover, cottage, painting, killer. Six pieces, four human, two objects. Deep in his brain, Roger felt a slight tectonic shift. These were promising numbers, might be made to work, and this was in all likelihood a fundamentally mathematical problem, as most problems were.

Item six: killer. Almost from the beginning, he had rejected the idea of a contract killer, automatically forcing item six, killer, into congruence with item one, husband. Had he been too hasty? At first he couldn't see why. A contract killer had power over the contractor. Before-the-fact power: what if the contract killer was also an informer, for example, or decided to become one in order to extricate himself from some past or pending legal difficulty the contractor knew nothing about? The contractor thus sets up himself. And after-the-fact power: supposing everything follows plan but sometime in the future the contract killer decides he wants more money or is arrested on some other charge, say another murder, and starts casting about desperately for a deal? The contractor is thus dealt.

But was this flaw so basic that the contract killer idea must be abandoned? The flaw, thought Roger, start by isolating the flaw. Trust, it was a matter of trust. The contract killer could not be trusted. But trust was a factor only in honest relationships. *Rearrange the pieces.* In a dishonest relationship, dishonest now from the contractor's point of view as well as the subcontractor's— yes, that was the proper term, subcontractor; getting the terms right was half the battle—trust was irrelevant. Deep in his brain, he felt a further shift.

What followed from that? His fingers shifted to the keyboard. The urge to make a list was overwhelming. Roger gave in to it, but with great care. No computer, of course, with its memories so hard to erase completely, possessed, like humans, of a kind of subconscious, but pencil and a single sheet of paper, torn from the pad so no impression could be left on the page beneath. Under the heading *Dealing with subcontractor*, he wrote:

> 1. *The contractor is Mr. X. In this scenario, the subcontractor does not know the contractor. Either he is (a) working for a middleman, (b) thinks he is working for someone else, or (c) does not know whom he is working for.*

A was out. It merely transferred the flaw of the subcontracting method to someone else. *B* was intriguing. Who could this someone else be? Supposing, as one had to, that the crime was "solved"; then the subcontractor would be arrested, and would eventually lead the police to the person he thought he was working for. This person, this false contractor, would therefore be required to have a plausible motive of his own, or the police would keep looking. *Rearrange the pieces.* Some artist, perhaps, some disappointed artist, one of those scruffy, half-mad types she so often dealt with, is finally rejected once too often? Why not? Roger foresaw procedural difficulties but couldn't see a mistake in the theory, so didn't rule out the artist at once.

Who else would have a motive? The lover's wife, if indeed he had one. Roger toyed with a wild idea of finding this wife, seducing her. What triumph that would be! But not to the purpose. The wife had a motive—enough. He disciplined his mind, running a line through *A*, circling *B*, and ran his eyes down to *C*.

C: does not know whom he is working for. That would mean the subcontractor never meets, talks to, or has written communication with the contractor; ideally does not even suspect the existence of the contractor. The implication: he believes that the crime originates in his own mind!

Oh, this was wonderful, to work so hard, to drive his mind through all these difficulties like an icebreaker. Ice. Roger thought at once of Brenda's cottage, and then of cubes floating in a tumbler of Scotch. Perhaps one little snort would help him think even better. He went upstairs to the kitchen, saw through the barred oval window on the landing that it was day.

And there at the table sipping coffee with a faraway look in her eye sat Francie, wearing a robe. Roger composed his face into friendly upturned patterns—that was essential from now on—and said, "Morning, Francie. Not working today? I thought you were feeling better."

"It's Saturday, Roger."

"So it is." He checked the clock: 9:45, perhaps too early for a drink. He poured himself a cup of coffee instead.

"But you look like you're going somewhere," Francie said.

"I do?"

"Somewhere dressy," she said. "Or a funeral."

Roger glanced down, saw with dismay that he was still wearing his black Brooks Brothers suit. And just as sloppily, he'd left his list on the desk in the basement office. Suppose she'd been in the laundry room, not the kitchen, and wandered in while he was upstairs? "The fact is," said Roger, "I was going to ask you out to lunch."

"With the godfather?"

He made himself laugh, that strange barking sound.

But how could it be a normal laugh when he had no desire to take her to lunch at all? And to think how recently he had tried to get into her bed! It suddenly hit him, after the fact, and perhaps harder for that reason, what her state of mind must have been that night. He laughed again, needing some outlet for the hot surge inside him, and said, "That's a good one, Francie—your reference being to the suit again, I take it."

Francie gave him an odd look. *Well, it might be odd, you slut, you whore.* He kept his eyes from veering toward the block of knives on the counter.

"Did you say something?" he said, vaguely aware that she had.

"I said I won't be able to make lunch today, but thanks."

"Otherwise engaged?"

"The tournament," Francie said. "Second round."

He had forgotten that she had indeed been at the tennis club last night, had not lied about that; he sensed gaps in his knowledge, gaps that might undermine his thinking, thinking being no substitute for research. "You won?"

Francie nodded.

"And celebrated long into the night?"

"If you call one whole beer a celebration," Francie said.

He could have killed her easily, right then. "Who's your partner?" he heard himself ask.

"You wouldn't know her."

He busied himself with cream and sugar, mastered his emotions. "Don't be so sure. I've traveled widely in tennis circles, in case you've forgotten."

"Her name's Anne Franklin."

"I knew Bud Franklin—played for Dartmouth. Is she married to Bud?"

"I haven't met her husband."

"Is he in real estate? Bud went into real estate?"

"I don't remember what he does. But it wasn't real estate."

C. Back downstairs, Roger had trouble bringing his mind to bear on the problem. How he regretted that night in her bedroom. How hobbled he was by his breeding, education, background. Any bricklayer or welder would have punched wifey in the mouth and raped her on the spot, restoring order. On the other hand, he suddenly thought, what if she was now the carrier of some disease? Maybe he'd been lucky after all.

C. He began to focus. *C: does not know whom he is working for.* Ah, yes. This concerned the subcontractor never communicating with the contractor, ideally not even suspecting his existence. The subcontractor believes the crime originates in his own mind. An elegant concept, but did it have any practical application?

How could there be no communication between contractor and subcontractor? Even a map sent in the mail, or an anonymous call from a phone booth, constituted communication and therefore carried risk. Roger spent an hour on this problem, by the clock, dwelling on hypnosis, confessionals, memory-altering drugs, and other fancies, without finding a viable way of hiding the contractor from the sub. Therefore he must abandon *C* or approach it from a different angle.

A different angle. What was the essence of the idea? Was it the noncommunication of contractor and sub? No. Another tectonic shift, this time a big one. No. The essence of the idea was the subcontractor's belief that the crime originated in his own mind.

Yes.

Roger gazed into the computer, seeing not what was on its screen, the Puzzle Club, but an image of Francie lying dead, the sub standing over her, the police bursting in. Caught in the act and with a guilty mind: nice.

Nice, but in the next instant, Roger had an idea so brilliant, so glittering that it took his breath away. Indeed, for a few moments he couldn't breathe, put his hand to his chest, felt his heart racing, thought he was about to die right there and then, at the worst possible moment, as if Columbus's heart had burst at the first sight of land.

Roger's heart did not burst. Its beat slowed, not quite to normal, but out of the danger zone, and he recovered his breath. Then, too excited to sit, he rose and paced back and forth in the basement office, contemplating his revelation. Francie lies dead, the sub standing over her, yes, but is it the police who come bursting in? No. It is the husband.

The husband: with no record of violence in his past, no criminal record of any kind. But even if he had such a record, would any prosecutor try him for what would happen next, any jury convict? No. The husband, in his rage, in his grief, in a red blackout, could take his vengeance with impunity. He would be a hero. And therefore, to bring C to its conclusion, whatever thoughts the subcontractor had about the arrangement did not matter in the end because he would not live to reveal them.

IQ 181, and possibly that had been an off day. Roger laughed at this joke, not a bark but long, gut-busting hilarity, tears rolling down his face.

The door opened: Francie, folded warm-up suit and other tennis clothes in her hands. He froze.

"Are you all right, Roger?" she said.

"Fine, fine," he said, animating his body. "Just ... something funny on the Internet."

"Like what?" Francie said, turning to the computer. Roger stepped between them—his list lay by the keyboard—but casually, he made sure of that.

"Oh, it's gone now, gone into space."

"What was it?"

"A . . . a play on words. About ataxia. The more ataxic the state the higher the taxes. That kind of thing."

"I don't get it. What's ataxia?"

"Just a word, Francie, just a word." He rocked back and forth, beaming down at her. "Maybe not that funny after all. Maybe I'm simply in a good mood."

She took another look at the computer, another at him, left the room. Soon after he heard the garage door open and close.

Theoretical phase complete. Now to find the sub. Roger thought right away of the man whose name had come up during the Puzzle Club discussion on capital punishment. He didn't remember all the details of the crime, and the story, related by Rimsky, the prison guard, had been garbled in the telling, interrupted by on-line idiots, and would now indeed have disappeared into space, but the name came to him at once. Perhaps it had lain deep in his mind the whole time, steadying his thoughts like a keel.

All problems were fundamentally mathematical, their solutions wonderfully satisfying: an incoherent sea of data reduced to a simple equation.

Chinese penny = Whitey Truax.

Roger held a match to his list and dropped the flaming paper in the wastebasket.

11

"**G**ot some pornos," said Rey, Whitey Truax's roommate at the New Horizons halfway house. He popped one into the VCR. They watched.

"Turn up the sound," said Whitey.

"The sound? Who gives a fuck about the sound?"

Whitey gave Rey a look. He didn't like Rey. He didn't much like Hispanics anyway, not the ones he'd met inside, and on top of that, what was Rey? A nobody: drunk driver, deadbeat dad, some punk thing like that. Inside, he wouldn't even have dared talk to Whitey. Here he had opinions.

But Rey turned up the sound without another word. They watched some more. "You think those women are real?" Whitey said.

"Real as it gets, Whitey," Rey said. "They're amateurs."

"What's that supposed to mean?"

"Says so right on the box—'Amateur Housewives, volume fifty-four.' " He flipped Whitey the box.

Real housewives having real sex, Whitey read. *You might see your neighbor.* He watched two amateur housewives entertaining some men by a swimming pool. "They've got tattoos on their tits," he said.

"So?"

"So since when do real housewives have tattoos on their tits?"

101

"Jesus, Whitey, where have *you* been?"

Of course that pissed Whitey off. He threw the first thing that came to hand—a Pepsi can, full—at Rey. Not playfully, like some frat boy: Whitey didn't have that gear. The Pepsi hit Rey in the face, bounced on the floor, sprayed all over. The door opened and the social worker looked in.

"Boys, what's going on?"

"Little spill," said Rey, dabbing blood on his sleeve. "I'll clean it up."

The social worker's gaze went to the TV. "Adult videos? 'Fraid not, boys—against regulations."

"Innocent mistake," said Whitey. "But seeing as you're here, maybe you could settle something for us."

"What's that?" said the social worker, his eyes on the screen.

"Rey claims those women are real. I say they're not."

"Real, Whitey?"

"He don't believe they're amateurs," said Rey, "even though it says right on the fucking box."

"Is it anything to be angry about, Rey? But I agree with you, there's no reason they couldn't be amateurs—think of how many home video cameras there are in this country."

Whitey was impressed. "Hadn't thought of that," he said. "Where would you run into one of these amateur housewives?"

"At home, of course," said the social worker with a laugh. Rey laughed, too, and finally Whitey as well.

But because of the memories the joke stirred up in Whitey, there was nothing funny about it. They kept him awake that night, those memories of cottage country.

Whitey and his ma lived in a trailer close to Little Joe Lake, although not close enough for a water view. Little

Joe wasn't a big lake—Whitey first swam across at the age of nine—but there were about two hundred cottages, most of them owned by city people who didn't seem to care that it was too small for speedboats and contained no fish worth the trouble. It was a good place to grow up: that's what the locals said. In summer Ma was busy cleaning the cottages. In winter they had the welfare checks. Ma watched TV and drank; Whitey went to school, played on the hockey team, but mostly skated by himself on the frozen lake, sometimes long into the night.

Despite a personal visit by his coach—Whitey had made third team, all-state as a sophomore—he dropped out of school the next autumn. Algebra, history, biology: he was almost nineteen and he'd had enough. That winter he skated on the lake, shot a few birds, got bored. One day, he broke into a cottage, not to take anything but just to see how the city people lived. He liked the way they lived; even more, he liked being inside their cottage—quiet, secret, powerful. He got the feeling that the cottage somehow knew he was there but of course couldn't do a damn thing about it.

Whitey broke into another cottage the next week. This time he took an electric guitar. He tried to teach himself how to play, but that didn't work, so he hocked it for forty bucks in a pawnshop across the Massachusetts line, where no one knew him. He bought a jug of wine, borrowed Ma's heap, took one of the cheerleaders to a spot he knew. But she had signed some nondrinking pledge at her church and wanted to do nothing but talk about the high school kids and the teams and all that shit he'd left behind. Just to snap her out of it, he almost brought her to one of the cottages with the idea of breaking in together, like Bonnie and Clyde. But he didn't—that would have destroyed the secret part; he tried to feel her up instead. She pushed him away; he pushed back, pushing her right out of the car, and drove off.

Whitey broke into cottages, two, three times a week. He was tidy: used a glass cutter to take out a windowpane, puttied it back in place when he was through. No one passing by—a state trooper patrolled once a month or so—would have suspected a thing. You had to go inside to see what was missing: TVs, microwaves, toasters, fireplace screens, golf clubs, cutlery, sleeping bags, tents, record players, scuba gear, crystal glasses, china figurines, rugs, paintings, barbecue grills, canoes, stone carvings, stuffed animals, chess sets, booze. No one knew. The city people didn't come to open up until Memorial Day weekend, at the earliest. With the profits, Whitey bought himself a used pickup, a gold chain, a leather jacket.

Long before Memorial Day—he still had plenty of time to make plans for when the city people did return—Whitey broke into a cottage he had previously ignored. A little cabin, old and run-down, alone on a tiny island at the far end of the lake, connected to the shore by a footbridge.

Snow was falling as Whitey walked across the footbridge, cold, hard flakes blown sideways by the wind; they stung his face in a way he didn't mind at all. Whitey circled the cabin, found a rickety door at the back, took out his glass cutter. But when he pressed it to the pane, the door swung open on its own—not the first unlocked cottage he'd found.

Whitey went inside. He still got that rush, right away, of being inside a living thing that knew but couldn't do shit about it. Besides, it was nice and warm in the cabin, and even quieter than usual, probably because of all the muffling snow.

Whitey moved into the kitchen. Not much there: toaster oven, coffeemaker, china bowl on the table, unopened bottle of gin on the counter. He checked the fridge, as he always did. Usually they were shut off and empty except for baking soda or moldy lemons, but sitting on the top shelf of this one was a cake. A chocolate cake with pink icing flowers, *Happy Anniversary Sue,* and a big pink *One.* He plucked a pink flower, popped it in his mouth, washed it down with a hit of gin. He liked gin.

Whitey went into the living room. Not much there either: brass fireplace set, framed Sacred Heart of Jesus on the mantel, cases full of books, useless to him. He mounted worn stairs to the floor above, looked in on a bedroom: a bed, unmade, more books. Nothing. Not even a TV. He was about to turn and go back down when a door opened inside the bedroom, a cloud of steam floated out, and then a woman—naked, except for the towel wrapped around her head. Her eyes opened wide, her hands went to her mouth, then her breasts. How satisfying was that? And there he was, in the leather jacket, with the gold chain around his neck and the glass cutter in his hand. Whitey knew right then that this was what the rush was all about; this was what he'd been waiting for.

"Hi, Sue," Whitey said. Christ, he was quick, putting it all together like that. He heard a sound like buzzing in his head.

"Truax," called a voice. "Phone."

Whitey sat up in bed. Sunlight in the room, Rey already gone. Morning, but he hadn't slept at all, and nothing but a doctor's note could get him off work—one of the parole conditions. He rose, went to the front hall, picked up the phone.

"Donald?"

"Ma."

"You're in the new place?"

"Yeah."

"How is it?"

"How is it?"

"Nice?"

"Yeah, Ma, nice."

"Well, it has to be a sight better than that other . . ."

In the pause that followed, Whitey heard a clicking sound that might have been her dentures. "Got to get to work, Ma."

"You got yourself a job?"

"Yeah."

"What kind of job?"

"For the municipality."

"My God, Donald. For the municipality?"

"Got to go, Ma."

"But, Donald—when are you coming home?"

"Home?"

"Course, I'm in a different place now. Had to, 'cause of . . . all the fuss."

"I know that."

"But there's plenty of room, for a visit, I'm talking about. And they say there's ice on the river already—I'm on the river, did I tell you? Knowing how much you like the skating—and besides, you haven't met Harry."

"Who's he?"

"My cat. He's the funniest little cat, Donald. Why, the other day—"

"Bye, Ma."

"Good to talk to—"

Whitey speared trash on the median, speared it angrily when he bothered to spear it at all. He was exhausted, robbed of a night's sleep by that dickhead Rey and that asshole social worker. And the fucking sun was hotter than ever. He'd been in Florida for three years now—cheaper for New Hampshire to farm him out for the last part of his sentence—but he hadn't got used to the heat. He saw another bullfrog and didn't even bother; he might have if it had tried something or even looked up at him, but the frog sat there doing nothing. Then a scrap of newspaper drifted by and came to rest against the steel tip of his pole. Glancing down, Whitey saw a baldness ad and above it a short article headlined HOTEL CLERK REMAINS IN COMA. Next to the article was one of those police artist sketches of a man: an ugly son of a bitch who didn't look like him at all, except for the hair. He stabbed the paper and buried it deep in his bright orange trash bag.

12

Wearing his black suit from Brooks Brothers, Roger took a little business trip to Lawton Center, New Hampshire, an old mill town where the mills were all boarded up and the river, a tributary of the Merrimack, flowed through unimpeded, clean and useless, as it had in the past. The river was frozen now. A vacant-eyed boy in a Bruins sweater rattled slapshots off the bridge support as Roger drove across. An ugly town—he didn't care for the countryside either, preferred the south of France to anywhere in New England, anywhere in the United States for that matter. Why not live there? Why not buy a *mas* in the Vaucluse or the Alpilles? No reason at all . . . after. He parked in front of the public library and went inside.

The library had microfilm volumes of the *Merrimack Eagle and Gazette* going back to 1817. Roger found the year he was looking for, spooled the roll onto the machine, slowly scrolled his way through the arrest, trial, and sentencing of Whitey Truax.

The first thing he liked was the photograph of Whitey, age nineteen. He had crudely cut hair, very pale, eyebrows paler still, eyelashes invisible, but dark, prominent eyes; and a strong chin, slightly too long. He looked confident, crafty, and stupid: a combination Roger couldn't have improved on if he'd invented the character.

But even better, almost startling, was the photograph of the victim, Sue Savard, accompanying her obituary. She looked like a cheap version of Francie. The resemblance amazed Roger. Staring closely at the woman's image, he could blend it into Francie's in his mind, the way the director in some art film Francie had dragged him to long ago had blended the faces of two actresses. At that moment, Roger realized that writing Francie's obituary would be his responsibility. He quickly sketched it out in his mind, doing a conscientious job, dwelling on her love of art, her contributions to the artistic community, mentioning her tennis in passing. Probably wise to read Nora the rough draft when the time came, in case she had any suggestions. And Brenda, too—no doubt Brenda had a soft spot for him after that business with the lilies.

Photographs: good and better, but best of all were the details of Whitey's crime. Rimsky's Puzzle Club account of the crime on Little Joe Lake, a few miles to the west, had been promising; the *Eagle and Gazette* delivered. Whitey had been arrested at his mother's place near the lake within an hour of the event. Sue's husband—and there was a sidebar about him that Roger scanned quickly: a rookie cop in Lawton, apparently, and he'd caused what the paper called a disturbance when they finally brought Whitey to the station in Nashua; but not material, and Roger factored it out—the husband, driving to his cottage to celebrate their anniversary that evening, and thus discoverer of the crime, had passed Whitey's pickup on the way out, and was able to give the police a good description. Whitey's first story was that he'd been passing by the cottage, seen an open door, and gone to investigate, like a good neighbor, so finding the body. When the police asked him why the Savards' toaster oven was in the bed of his pickup, Whitey admitted that he'd gone there to steal but had found the body, already dead. The police then turned to the cuts and scratches on Whitey's hands and face. Whitey should have asked for a lawyer at that point, or long before, but instead again changed his story, now claiming that the woman had attacked him in the course of the robbery, and he had struck out in fear, killing her unintentionally in self-defense. The medical examiner arrived soon after that with his preliminary report that there was evidence of rape, and other outrages not spelled out in the small-town paper. Mrs. Dorothy Truax—the whole discussion had taken place in her trailer—jumped up and shouted that Sue Savard was a well-known whore. Prompted by that cue in a direction his mother hadn't intended, Whitey then said that the woman shouldn't have been wandering around naked in the first place—he wasn't made of stone, after all. If only she hadn't threatened to sic the cops on him, no real harm would have been done. He signed a statement to that effect.

Faced with this confession, Whitey's public defender sent him to a psychiatrist in hope of manufacturing some sort of insanity defense. The psychiatrist did his best, testifying that Whitey's compulsive housebreaking was rooted in a desire to avenge himself for early childhood abuse by his mother, to recover the parts of his personality that had been lost, the form of the residential dwelling, with its narrow doorway leading to a mysterious interior, being essentially female. Further, when an actual female suddenly appeared, the modus of symbolic compensation was instantly destroyed, and Whitey, decompensating rapidly, descended into madness, the rape and murder being the result of an insanity that was necessarily temporary due to the uniqueness of the circumstances.

Whitey's peers on the jury were not persuaded. After a

two-hour deliberation, they found him guilty of murder in the first degree as charged. The judge, taking into account Whitey's age, handed out fifteen to thirty years, instead of a life sentence. There was a final photograph of Whitey climbing into a police van, a silly half smile on his face, as though he'd thought of something funny.

Roger switched off the machine, rewound the spool. It was a shabby little library, with no one inside but himself and the librarian at her desk. She was looking at him now and her lips were moving.

"I said, is there anything I can help you with, sir?"

"Perhaps the local phone book," Roger said.

She brought it to him: a smooth-skinned but gray-haired woman with fingerprint smudges on her glasses. "Looks like quite the winter we've got coming," she said.

"Does it?" said Roger. He glanced out the window, saw hard little snowflakes blowing by. The librarian withdrew.

The uniqueness of the circumstances. What were the circumstances? Cottage, break-in, unexpected presence of a woman. If Whitey's psychiatrist was right, that combination, given his background, had guaranteed the result. Roger inferred that if such a combination were to occur again, and Whitey were introduced into it, he would replay his role, unless he had changed in some fundamental way. And if the psychiatrist's explanation was wrong, Whitey still might come through, for other reasons that might yet be fashioned, especially with that amazing resemblance.

No use speculating. Roger opened the phone book to the *T*s, found one Truax: Dot, 97 Carp Road, Lawton Ferry. He found Lawton Ferry on a map, seven or eight miles to the east, on the Merrimack—not far downstream from Brenda's cottage. The details were still unclear, but somehow geography, too, was on his side.

* * *

Lawton Ferry wasn't one of those picturesque New England towns city people liked to visit; now, mostly hidden under the falling snow, it looked its best. Carp Road ran along a bluff on the west side of the river but took no pleasure in the view, the houses, small and worn, all lining the wrong side of the street. Number 97 was the last house, the smallest and most worn, a peeling box with a single duct-taped window facing the street. Roger drove slowly by, came to a chain-link fence at the end of the road, turned around. A dented minibus with writing on it—LITTLE WHITE CHURCH OF THE REDEEMER—came up the street and parked in front of 97.

The driver climbed out, slid open the passenger door, helped a thin old woman step down. She wore enormous square-shaped sunglasses, carried a white cane. The driver took her arm, led her around the minibus to the recently shoveled walk. There she shook herself free of him and tap-tapped to the front door by herself. The driver, annoyed, got back in the minibus, closed the door hard, made a three-point turn, and drove off while the woman still fumbled with keys.

She opened the door. A cat darted out. The woman disappeared inside.

Roger stayed where he was, parked by the chain-link fence, running the engine to keep warm. After a while, the door to 97 opened slightly and the woman, no longer wearing her sunglasses, stuck her head out. Roger switched off the engine. "Harry," called the woman, "Harry."

Roger could see the cat, foraging in an overturned trash can in her driveway, in plain view from the house. The cat stopped, swiveled its head toward her.

"Harry," she called again, "where are you, you naughty boy?" The cat didn't move. The woman closed the door. The cat crept back into the trash can.

Roger got out of his car, approached the old woman's house, stopped before the trash can, conscious of arriving at the border between theory and practice, between thought and action: his Rubicon. He crossed it without hesitation, saying, "Here, kitty." A fine beginning. The cat emerged at once, tail up. Roger bent down, held out his hand. The cat brushed its whiskers against his skin, laid back its ear. Roger picked it up and carried it, purring, to the house. Cats had always liked him.

He knocked at the door.

"Who is it?" called the woman.

"Missing a cat?" Roger called back.

The door opened. The woman peered out; that is, held her head in the attitude of peering. Her eyes, pale blue irises encircling glazed pupils, seemed to stare over his shoulder. "You've got Harry?" she said.

"If that's the little fellow's name," said Roger.

She put on her sunglasses. "Reason I have to ask, I can't see, not down the center. Just at the edges a little, if I turn my head like this." She turned her head. Roger covered his face, as though rubbing his brow. "And even then it's no good, all flickering, like when the picture tube is on the fritz. Come to Ma, you bad boy."

Roger put the cat in her arms; it resisted for a moment, digging its claws into the sleeve of his funeral jacket before letting go.

"Naughty boy," she said, stroking it. "God bless you, mister."

"Bless you, too, ma'am." And then his memory reached back to chapel at Exeter for something if not exactly apposite, then at least suggestive: "Better a neighbor that is near than a brother far off."

The woman went still, her head tilted up at him as though searching his face. "You're a Christian?" she said.

"Certainly," Roger said, "although I wouldn't impose my belief on anyone."

"No danger of that here," said the woman. "Jesus is my life."

"Mine as well."

She reached out with her free hand, touched his arm. "Maybe you'd like a cup of tea?"

"No need to go to any trouble," said Roger, looking beyond her to a photograph on the television: Whitey in hockey uniform. "Although I wouldn't mind a chance to wash my hands—Harry gave me a little inadvertent scratch."

"Oh, the bad, bad boy. Come right in. My name's Dorothy, by the way, Dorothy Truax. But you can call me Dot."

"Nice to meet you," said Roger, stepping inside but leaving his own name unspoken. He looked around the tiny room: couch, TV, icebox, hot plate, card table, two folding chairs, sink.

"Bathroom's just down the back," said the woman.

Roger took two steps down a dark corridor and into a bathroom full of unclean smells. He ran the water for a few moments and returned to what the woman no doubt called the parlor. She had plugged in a kettle, was hanging tea bags over the sides of two stained cups, moving with the confidence of a sighted person in her own home.

Water boiled. They sat—Roger at the table, Dot on the couch—drinking tea. Not drinking, in Roger's case. "This hits the spot," he said, reaching his cup toward the sink without rising and pouring the tea slowly and silently down the drain. "Who's the fine-looking hockey player?"

Dot rested her cup on the saucer in her lap. "That

would be my son Donald. But everyone called him Whitey practically from day one, no matter what I did."

"Who does he play for?"

"Oh, Donald doesn't play anymore. How could he? That picture's from before all the trouble."

"Trouble?"

"Which was really what drove me into the arms of Jesus, since it was all my fault, according to that wicked doctor. And he must of been right since I've gone blind, too, for my punishment."

"What wicked doctor was this?"

"The psychiatrist at Donald's trial. He said the most disgusting things. What he couldn't understand was that a boy needs discipline, firm discipline, especially after his father run off, and at such an early age."

"Discipline's essential when it comes to children."

"You're so right. You have kids yourself, Mr.—?"

"A houseful."

She raised her chin, an aggressive chin slightly too long, like her son's. "Then you know they sometimes need the buckle end of a belt to keep them in line, especially suggestible ones like Donald."

"Suggestible?"

"Easily led astray."

"For example?"

"For example? There are examples aplenty. Why else would he have served such a horrible long sentence?"

"You're saying he was manipulated?"

"By everyone, his whole life. Nothing easier than manipulating Donald—on account of he's basically a good person."

Roger, on the verge of asking again for an example of his straying, decided not to push it too hard. Easily led: that was good enough. "He's free now, I take it?" he said.

"If on parole is free. They've got him at the New Horizons House."

"Is that nearby?"

"Of course not. It's in Delray Beach. Just to make things worse they made him finish his time in the stinking heat down in Florida." Her hands squared off into bony little fists.

"What are his plans?" Roger said.

"Do you think he tells me? He never calls, and when I call him he's short with me, so short. Since he heard what that doctor said, things haven't been the same between us." Tears rolled down from under her sunglasses, glistened on her wrinkled face: an unpleasant sight. "Mr.— sir, being as how you're a good Christian, maybe you could see your way clear to helping me now."

"How?"

"Just by praying with me—saying a little prayer for Donald."

Without further warning, the woman fell to her knees on the dusty, threadbare carpet, held out her hands. Roger knelt in front of her, took her hands, ice-cold hands that seized his in a death grip.

"Dear Lord," said Roger, "please hear this prayer for our beloved Whitey—"

"Donald, if you don't mind," the woman interrupted.

"—for our beloved Donald, and help guide him in useful ways. Amen."

Dot toppled forward on him, sobbing. "Sweet, sweet Jesus, what a beautiful prayer." Her tears wet the side of Roger's face, ran down his neck; he cringed. "So perfect," said Dot, her mouth moving against his shoulder. " 'Guide him in useful ways.' That's all Donald needs, all he's needed his whole goddamn life." She clung to Roger. "You're a preacher, you must be. Praise the Lord." She raised her hands, felt his face with her fingertips. Roger flashed forward to a little scene of Dot Truax doing it again, only this time with him seated in a witness box and a jury watching. He glanced at her scrawny neck, doubtless easy to snap, but that wasn't him, wasn't smart.

"A preacher," the old woman breathed, fingertips still on his face. At the same time, Harry rubbed up against the side of his leg. Roger's skin crawled.

13

Francie, in her office, checked out slides of rain paintings submitted by a new artist. Not paintings of rain but paintings made by rain falling on fast-drying color fields of thick pigment. A gimmick perhaps, and making a statement that had been made many times, but the paintings themselves were strangely beautiful, especially the two deep, roiling blues, *Madagascar* and *Untitled 4;* they reminded her of the primeval soup that all earthly life was supposed to have come from. She was reaching for her loupe to take a better look when her phone rang.

"Hi." It was Ned. "What are you doing this second?"

"Looking at rain paintings." Her heart beat faster right away.

"I thought it would be something like that," he said. There was a silence. "I really just wanted to hear your voice."

The rain paintings, her office, her job, all shrank to insignificance.

"I'm at the studio, but I can't work at all today," Ned said. "Does that ever happen where you are?"

"Yes."

Another silence, thick with tension like that of desire, at least in her mind, and then: "I keep thinking about you—something you did once, in particular."

"What?"

118

He lowered his voice. "Something you did to me. We did together. At the cottage."

In his mind, too. Francie's heart beat faster still. "What was it?"

"You don't remember?"

"Stop teasing me."

He laughed. "Say you love me. Then I'll tell."

"You know I do."

"But say it."

"I love you," Francie said.

The door opened and Roger walked in. Francie felt the blood draining from her face as though a plug had popped out the bottom of her heart. Had he heard? For a moment, he stood very still at the door, his eyes on her— a very brief moment. Then he was raising his hand and fluttering his fingers in a delicate little greeting that wasn't him at all. At the same time, Ned was saying, "I dream about it sometimes. Don't you remember the first time you ever—"

"I'll have to get back to you on that," Francie said.

"Someone's there?" said Ned.

"As soon as I see the report," Francie said. Roger was walking around the office, examining things with interest. "Talk to you then."

"I hope they didn't—"

She hung up.

"Some big mover and shaker?" said Roger, sitting in one of the chairs opposite her desk.

"What?"

He nodded to the phone. "In the art world."

"No," said Francie. "What brings you here?"

"Can't hubby pay a visit to wifey's workplace?"

But why now? It had never happened before. She looked at him closely, trying and failing to penetrate the facetiousness, the big smile, to discover if he had indeed heard anything as he came in the door. All at once the lying, the subterfuge, and maybe most of all her talent for it, made her sick. She rose, almost stumbling, mumbled something about the bathroom, hurried out.

In the cubicle, Francie stood over the toilet for a few moments. Her nausea ebbed. She went to the sink, splashed cold water on her face. A pale face, she saw in the mirror, and the eyes troubled. Yes, she hated the lying, but she wanted love—was that too much to ask? And even if she didn't, it was too late. She was in love, close to the kind of love the poets wrote of, love that took away hunger, that focused the mind, waking and sleeping, on the loved one; a kind of love that turned out to be not just a literary conceit but real, after all.

Francie returned to her office. Roger was standing by the desk, talking on the phone. "Oh, here she is," he said. "Nice talking to you, too. I'm sure we will." He handed Francie the phone.

"Hello?" she said.

"Francie? Anne here. They want to reschedule our match for tomorrow, same time."

"No problem."

"Great," said Anne. "I think I just met your husband."

"You did."

"I didn't catch his name."

"Roger," said Francie, looking at him. He smiled.

"He sounds so nice."

"Remember Bob Fielding?" asked Roger, gazing out the window of Francie's office. "And you've got a view."

"No," said Francie.

"Sure you do. Used to be with Means, Odden. Now he's running his own place in Fort Lauderdale."

Francie had a vague memory of whiskey breath and air kisses that always managed to land. "Maybe I do."

"You must. Can't forget a character like Bob Fielding. The fact is, he's doing very well. And there just might be something appropriate for me down there."

"Have you talked to him?"

"I'm way ahead of you," Roger said. "My flight leaves in a couple hours, if you don't mind giving me a ride to the airport."

Francie drove him to the airport. He seemed happier these days, indeed almost happy; it had been years. She caught a glimpse of a civilized end: Roger working in Fort Lauderdale; she, in Boston—he would never expect her to leave her job; Em reaching the age where Ned would consider divorce.

Francie dropped Roger in front of the terminal. "Good luck," she called through the open window as he walked away, garment bag over his shoulder, briefcase in hand. An affecting figure, she thought at that moment, even brave, and she felt a sick little stab beneath her heart.

Roger turned. "Luck is not a factor," he said. A gust of wind caught the skirts of his open trench coat and raised them behind him like wings.

Roger's first flight—discounting babe-in-arms vacations to the Caribbean, London, Paris—his first conscious flight had been from Logan to Palm Beach at the age of six. Some of the excitement of that day, long worn away by the tedium and annoyance of countless flights since, returned to him now as he sat in a window seat and watched the earth recede. He ordered a Scotch, but just one, and came very close to talking to his neighbor.

A smooth beginning: landing on time in Miami, renting a car, meeting Bob Fielding in his dismal office. Bob hadn't heard Roger was no longer with Thorvald and asked *him* for a job, but no matter: this was all a play, a fiction designed for the day, if it ever came, when he could swear under oath and prove beyond a reasonable doubt that, yes, he had flown to Miami but, no, not for any illegal, to say nothing of deadly, purposes—only to feel out a former colleague about the possibility of a job, as Bob Fielding would attest. Bob Fielding: long forgotten, but still, a piece on the board, to be rearranged. IQ 181—on a bad day. Roger hurried down to his car and drove north to Delray Beach.

Fucking mosquitoes. They'd moved the highway crew west, onto 441, practically in the Everglades. Clouds of mosquitoes rose up whenever Whitey jabbed at the grass with his steel-tipped pole, whining around his head, tormenting him. Plus the heat and the humidity were too fucking much. He was tired of sweating that clammy sweat every time he moved, of the sun burning down on the back of his neck. And then there was the threat of AIDS. Rey said you couldn't get AIDS from a mosquito, but why not? Would you bite someone that had AIDS? No. Getting bit by a mosquito that had bitten an AIDS victim was the same thing. Ever seen the blood when you squish a mosquito? he'd asked Rey. Could be anybody's blood, the blood of some ninety-pound faggot junkie on his deathbed. Whitey swatted at one now, just after it got him right on the face, and examined the palm of his hand: crushed mosquito parts in a red smear. "Fuck," he called out aloud. "Fuck, fuck, fuck." There was no one to hear, the traffic being light, car windows all rolled up against the heat.

A Lexus went by, then a Benz and a Porsche. Whitey stabbed a scrap of aluminum foil, dropped it in the bright orange plastic bag. "Done much thinking about your future?" the social worker had asked the day before.

"Fuck," said Whitey. "Fuck, fuck, fuck." He was too busy spearing trash, swatting mosquitoes, and being angry about the future to notice the car pulling to the side of the road behind him. The opening and closing of the door didn't really register either—what was he trained to do? fuck all; society had completely failed him—and it was only when a voice, a male voice, educated and polite, said, "Excuse me, sir," that Whitey turned.

Sir? Whitey couldn't remember ever being called sir before, certainly not by anyone like this: a tall man, almost as tall as Whitey, with dark hair cut in a distinguished way like that black-and-white actor, the name didn't come to him, smooth skin, an expensive black suit. "Me?" said Whitey.

The man smiled. "Maybe you can help me," he said, producing a map. "I'm a little lost."

"Where you headed?" said Whitey as the man came closer, donning rimless glasses, unfolding the map. A banknote fell out, fluttered to the ground, where a sudden breeze caught it, rolled it over, threatened to carry it away. Without thinking, Whitey speared the bill, raised it up on the steel tip. "Dropped something," he said, and saw what it was: a one-hundred-dollar bill.

The man plucked it off the steel tip with thumb and index finger, said: "How the heck did that get there?"

Whitey thought, *Plenty more where that came from.* Sharp thinking, because the next second the man was returning the bill to his money clip—a money clip, not a mere wallet, and gold besides—and Whitey saw them, thick and green. Whitey took all that in from the corner of his eye, crafty, unnoticed.

"Thanks," said the man, tucking the money clip into his right front pocket; Whitey made sure to note the exact location, although he had no idea what he was going to do with the information. "Now, what I'm looking for," said the man, frowning at the map, "is Abner and Sallie's Alligator Farm. It's supposed to be around the junction of . . ." His voice trailed off.

A rich guy, maybe, but not very bright. Whitey could see the back of the sign for the turnoff to the alligator farm about two hundred yards away; the man had driven right past it. "The alligator farm?" said Whitey. "That's a bit tricky."

"I was afraid it would be," said the man.

Whitey paused, quickly scanning the man's face again, confirming his first impression: an innocent. "Tell you what," he said. "How about I just hop in with you, make it easy, like."

"I couldn't really ask that," said the man.

Whitey wasn't sure what that sentence meant. "Meaning I'll guide you there," he said.

The man laughed, a strange barking laugh that Whitey didn't get and forgot about almost at once. "That's very good of you," the man said, "but I couldn't take you away from your work."

"Not a problem," said Whitey, "long as I'm back at five."

The man checked his watch, a Rolex—Whitey had seen them in *Playboy*—and said, "I guarantee it. And I'll pay you for your time . . ."

"Yeah?"

". . . Mr. . . ."

"Whitey"—Christ, maybe having his real name out there wasn't such a good idea, especially if this guy ended up getting rolled, or something—"Reynoso." Rey's last name.

The man held out his hand. "Pleased to meet you, Mr. Reynoso. Everyone calls me Roger."

They shook hands, got in the car. A brown leather jacket, soft and luxurious, lay on the front seat. Whitey lifted it carefully and thought of the leather jacket he'd had long ago, leatherette, actually. "Here's your jacket."

"Not mine," said Roger, starting the car. "Belonged to my assistant—former assistant. Just toss it in the back."

Whitey tossed it in the back and said, "That way," and Roger drove back up the highway. A nice car, with sun-roof, CD player, cell phone. "Hang a right," said Whitey, and Roger—a cautious driver, Whitey saw, both hands on the wheel, back straight, eyes on the road—swung onto the turnoff. The road narrowed from two-lane blacktop to one, the blacktop turned to dirt, huge ferns and other growths Whitey didn't have names for closed in from above, and then they were at a barbed-wire gate on which hung a sign: WELCOME TO ABNER AND SALLIE'S ALLIGATOR FARM. OBSERVE ALL RULES.

"You certainly know your way around," said Roger. "Are you from this area, Mr. Reynoso?"

"Hey, call me Whitey," said Whitey. And: "No." Giving him that much, but not actually divulging where he was from, playing it close to the vest.

"Where are you from, if you don't mind my asking?"

"New . . ." Whitey was going to say New Mexico, then remembered something about the best lie being close to the truth, and thinking what the hell, said, "Hampshire. New Hampshire."

"No kidding," said Roger.

"You're from New Hampshire, too?"

"I have interests there," said Roger.

Interests—Whitey liked the sound of that, wanted to know more. "Interests?" he said.

But maybe that was too subtle, because Roger said, "And what brought you down here?"

"Well, Florida, you know," said Whitey.

"The climate?"

"Yeah, the climate," said Whitey, although he hated it.

"And the mosquitoes," he added, a remark that just popped out.

Roger laughed his strange laugh. "You've got a sense of humor, unlike . . ." He didn't finish the sentence, but somehow Whitey knew he was talking about the former assistant. The jacket must have been almost new: Whitey could smell the leather. "I like a sense of humor," Roger said.

"Me, too," said Whitey. He tried to remember a joke he'd heard about a rabbi, a dildo, and a parrot, but before he had it clear in his mind, an enormous woman with thighlike upper arms poking out of her tent dress came to the other side of the gate. Roger slid down the window.

"You all for the gator show?" she said.

"Yes," said Roger. Whitey thought for a moment about his job, but as long as he was at his post for the five o'clock pickup he was fine, and it was only three-thirty; besides, he'd never seen a gator show.

"Four bucks apiece, 'stead of five. On account of no rasslin' today."

"I beg your pardon?" said Roger.

"No gator rasslin'. My husband's the rassler, and he's with the lawyer right now." She leaned on the car; it rocked under her weight. "The environmentalists, they got a court order to stop the rasslin'. For 'protecting the health and safety' of the gators. Of the gators! Ever rassled a gator, mister?"

"No," said Roger, handing her money, his nose narrowing as though he were trying to cut off the sense of smell.

"Well, I sure as hell have—where you think I got this scar?—and I can tell you it ain't the gators need protectin'. Park it in the lot and stay on the people side of the fence."

She opened the gate. Roger drove into a dusty little

yard, parked beside the only other car, a rusted-out Chevy on blocks. A few feet beyond it stood four or five rusted rows of bleacher seats, and beyond that lay a ditch, filled with algae-crusted water and lily pads, and fenced in with ten-foot-high chain-link. Six alligators, five of them between eight and twelve feet long, the sixth a baby, lay motionless on the far bank.

Roger and Whitey sat in the bleachers, read the rules—*Positively No Feeding, Do Not Stick Fingers Thru Fence, No Teasing*—watched the gators. The sun was hot, the air full of small, sharp-edged flying things, the gators still. After only a minute or two, Whitey's shirt was sticking to his back; he noticed that Roger, in his black suit, didn't seem to be feeling the heat at all.

For no reason that Whitey could see, the baby gator suddenly rose up and made his way to the ditch. It stood at the edge, seemed to be looking at Whitey and Roger, the only spectators across the way, then slid into the water and disappeared.

"Cute little bugger," said Whitey.

Silence. Roger was staring at the water. Whitey was just about to say "cute little bugger" again when Roger turned to him. Whitey realized for the first time that there was something about Roger's gaze that made him reluctant to meet it; in fact, he couldn't. "You seem like a bright guy," Roger said. Whitey looked modest. "So let me ask your advice on something."

"Like what?"

"Maybe it's even happened to you."

"What has?" said Whitey, starting to lose the thread. A frog croaked nearby; Whitey spotted it, a big bullfrog, even bigger than the one he'd speared on I-95, sitting on a lily pad.

"Reducing it to the simplest possible terms," said Roger, "did anyone ever take something valuable from you?"

"Not that I can remember." But then Whitey thought of his freedom, and wasn't sure.

"You're a lucky man," said Roger. "But suppose someone did. What would you do?"

"Like what kind of thing?"

"Call it a work of art."

"Get it back, of course," said Whitey. "I'd go after the fucker and get it back."

"And which is more important?"

"Huh?"

"Of the two. Revenge or recovery of the object?"

Whitey felt Roger's gaze on his face, suddenly knew the word for what this was—networking, or maybe mentoring. In any case, he knew this was an important question. Revenge or recovery of the object: he tried to sort out the terms. The right answer, from his point of view, was to go after the fucker. Who gave a shit about art? On the other hand, maybe Roger was the type who did give a shit about art.

"That's a tough one," Whitey said, searching Roger's face for some clue. Their eyes met, and Whitey turned away, again unsettled by looking into Roger's eyes, and as he turned, he saw the baby gator surfacing in a patch of lily pads, weeds trailing off its snout. Eeny meeny minie moe, said Whitey to himself, eeny being revenge and meeny recovery. Recovery won.

"The art," said Whitey, and could see from Roger's nod, a satisfied nod, as though he'd expected Whitey to do well all along, that he'd guessed right. "Recovery of the art," Whitey said, "every goddamn time."

"My former assistant thought otherwise," Roger said.

"He did, huh?" said Whitey, shaking his head.

The baby gator glided over to the bullfrog's lily pad. A green blur, some splashing, and then the bullfrog's legs were dangling from the baby gator's mouth. The baby gator submerged.

"He is a cute little bugger," Roger said. "Awakens old, old memories."

"Oh yeah? Like what?"

"I wouldn't want to bore you," Roger said.

"Hey, you're not boring me, Rog, I swear."

Roger's face tightened, for no reason Whitey could see, as though he'd felt a sudden pain. He glanced at Whitey—again Whitey looked away—and went on. "I brought one like him home the first time I ever went to Florida, with my aunt. I was six years old."

"So you're not from here?" But Whitey knew that already from the way Roger said "ont," just like he did.

"Can you guess what happened?" Roger said, maybe not hearing the question.

"It escaped?"

"A good guess, Whitey, a very good guess. But no. My parents didn't let me keep it. They made me give it to the zoo."

"I know just how you feel," Whitey said. "Same thing happened to me with a weasel. Only it wasn't the zoo. My ma just made me let it go, back in the woods."

"Did she?"

"You don't know my ma—that's her through and through."

"This was in New Hampshire?"

Whitey saw no other course but to admit it. He nodded.

"You know your way around the woods up there?"

"Shit yeah, Rog. I grew up like that goddamn what's-his-name."

"Natty Bumppo?"

"Never heard of him. It'll come to me."

But nothing came. The baby gator appeared on the far

side of the ditch, climbed out, lay with his elders in the sun; no sign of the bullfrog. Roger said, "My former assistant didn't."

"Didn't what?" said Whitey, who was thinking of his own bullfrog, and the crown-shaped ring of blood on its bumpy green head.

"Didn't know his way around the woods."

"No, huh?" Whitey conceived a brilliant question: "What were his qualifications, anyway?"

"Not the right ones, evidently. Do you know that saying about law and sausages, Whitey?"

"Law and sausages?"

"You don't want to look too closely at how either of them is made. My work's a bit like that."

Law and sausages. Whitey didn't get it. Was Roger trying to tell him he was a tough guy or something—dangerous? Whitey couldn't see it. He, Whitey, was tough and dangerous—he thought of that stupid whore and her pimp with the baseball bat, and what had happened to them. Or was Roger trying to tell him that the assistant had to be tough and dangerous? Or maybe—

Roger checked his watch, his Rolex, stood up. "Better get you back to your post," he said. "Wouldn't want to put your job in jeopardy, would we?"

"Well, the thing is—" said Whitey, but Roger was already walking away and didn't seem to hear.

Roger pulled over at the side of 441. He turned to Whitey, who'd been smelling the leather coat in the backseat, again gave him that look that seemed to see deep inside. "I said I'd pay you for your time." And there was a one-hundred-dollar bill—not the same one, because there was no hole—held out for him. He was thinking all kinds of things to say, like it's too much, and I didn't really earn it, but while he was in the middle of thinking them, he grabbed it.

Roger smiled.

Whitey opened the door, started to get out. But how could he let this go without at least trying? What was there to lose? "This assistant thing," he said, "are you looking for a replacement?"

Roger raised his eyebrows in surprise. "I hadn't really thought about it yet." He seemed to be thinking about it now, staring into the distance. "I'd need someone more discreet this time," he said. "Discretion is the sine qua non in this business."

That threw Whitey, and he licked his lips a couple of times before saying, "You never said what the business is exactly."

"I thought I had," said Roger, sounding disappointed in him for the first time. "It's the recovery of valuable objects."

"Such as what?"

"Paintings, shall we say."

"Like that someone's stolen?"

"Precisely like that."

The DPW truck came into view, shimmering on the horizon.

Now or never. "I want the job," Whitey said.

"Do you—"

"Swear to God."

"—know the meaning of discretion, Whitey?"

"It means no questions and keep your fuckin' mouth shut."

Roger nodded. He scribbled a number on his alligator farm ticket stub. "Call me tomorrow. We'll set up an interview."

Whitey stuffed the ticket stub and the money in his

pocket, got out of the car. A job interview: he'd never had one. This was the big time.

The DPW truck dropped Whitey at the depot. He caught the number 62 bus, reached the stop a block from New Horizons at five to six. He was almost out the rear door, had one foot on the pavement, when he saw the cop car parked up the street. Did that mean anything? No. But he said, "Oops," like he'd almost gotten off at the wrong stop, and stepped back on the bus. The driver, watching in his mirror, muttered something Whitey couldn't hear.

The bus drove on, picked up speed, approached New Horizons. Whitey saw a cop on the sidewalk, talking to the social worker. As the bus drew closer, Whitey saw that the cop was showing something to the social worker, a piece of paper. And as the bus went right by, within a few feet of them, Whitey saw what it was: the artist's composite, with nothing right except the fucking hair. Whitey stayed on the bus.

Roger was sleeping the deepest sleep he'd had in a long time when the phone rang. He fumbled for it in the darkness of the strange room, answered.

"Rog? It's me, Whitey Tru—Whitey Reynoso. I'm calling like you said."

"But it's four in the morning."

"Kind of anxious to get started, is all."

Was he drunk? Stoned? Planning some scheme of his own? Was this not going to work, after all?

"Rog? You still there?"

"Yes."

"So maybe you could come and pick me up."

"Where are you?"

"On 441, of course. Where you picked me up before."

Was he armed? Alone? His voice was full of impending surprise. "Very well," said Roger.

His motel room had a kitchenette. Roger took the biggest knife from the drawer, hid it under the seat of his rented car, drove out to 441. Could he kill Whitey? Certainly. There was a deep, violent well of hatred in him, as he was sure there was in most people; he'd known it since boyhood. It made war possible, and perhaps all human civilization. The only problem was scheduling: Whitey wasn't supposed to die yet.

Roger came to the spot where he'd found Whitey, saw a lone man in the headlights, slowed down, slow enough to bring any overeager accomplices out of the bushes, slow enough to see that Whitey was holding some sort of bundle, slow enough to hear him cry, "Hey, it's me," as Roger went by.

A few hundred yards beyond, Roger made a U-turn and drove back. He stopped the car, one hand on the knife. Whitey came out of the shadows, opened the passenger door, got in. His eyes were bright. "Hi, Rog. Had me concerned there for a minute. Here. I brought you something."

Roger inched the knife out from under the seat. Whitey laid the bundle between them: something wrapped in a denim jacket. "Open it, why don't you?"

With his free hand, Roger opened the jacket—and there was the baby gator, its mouth fastened shut with packing tape. Roger felt Whitey's gaze on him, waiting for his reaction.

"You've done well, Whitey, very well."

Whitey laughed with delight. "Feisty little bugger, that gator, let me tell you."

"Not an alligator, actually," Roger said. "It's a crocodile—you can tell from the angulation of the jaw."

"Whatever. Tore my jacket to shreds. My only jacket."

Roger silently counted three and said, "You can have the one in back."

"Cool," said Whitey, donning the leather jacket right away. It felt great. The gator watched with its slitty yellow eyes.

14

"**A**ny hints?" asked Anne, eyeing their opponents across the net as the players took their serves before the top-bracket semifinal of the club championships.

Francie checked them out: two wiry women wearing elbow braces and knee pads. She thought she recognized the taller one from her college days; she'd played for Brown, or possibly UConn—a distant memory, no more than a fragment, but unpleasant.

"How was your overhead in the warm-up?"

"I didn't make a single one," said Anne with alarm. "You think they're going to lob us?"

"To death," said Francie.

Francie was right. The wiry women, tireless, unsmiling, grim, fed them—Anne particularly, as they saw her game begin to fall apart—junk, chips, dinks, lobs; they served conventional, Australian, from the I, even both back for a point or two; and they called the lines very close. First set: 6–2, the 2 coming on Francie's serve.

On the changeover, while the wiry women iced their elbows and knees, Anne turned her flushed face to Francie and said in a low voice, "I'm so sorry. They're hitting every ball to me and I'm playing like shit."

Francie put her hand on Anne's knee, felt it trembling. "First of all," she said, "it's only tennis. Second, it's not over." She leaned forward, spoke in Anne's ear. "This set we're going to do a little lobbing of our own."

"Will that work?" Anne asked. Francie saw the blue disk of her eye in profile, inches away: still, waiting for the response.

"At least those fucking knees of theirs are going to ache tonight," she said. The blue disk brightened, bulged slightly; Anne laughed.

She laughed, but her game did not come back, at least not right away. Her lobs were short, and the wiry women proved adept at putting them away, one of them grunting an annoying little "Ho!" on every overhead. Francie and Anne fell behind 1–3, 1–4.

Anne's serve. "This isn't working," she said as Francie handed her the balls.

"Any other ideas?" said Francie.

"No," Anne replied, her face pinker than ever. Francie watched a vein throbbing in her forehead. She wanted to say *forget whatever's fucking up your mind and just play.* Instead she glanced across the net, saw the opposition waiting restlessly on the other side, eager to get on with the demolition.

"Go with your second serve," she told Anne.

"What good will that do? They're clobbering my first."

"Probably none, but try it."

Anne tried it. The wiry women, fooled by the change of pace, netted the first two returns. On the next two, they were ready and hit aggressive crosscourt shots, but Francie poached on both and put them away, the second drilling a padded knee and drawing an angry glare— unintentional, on Francie's part, but somewhere in her heart, she said *yes.* 2–4.

Anne's lobs grew stronger and deeper in the next game, forcing the wiry women to scramble in the back-court for the first time in the match. Now Francie and

Anne were making the easy putaways. 3–4. Francie's serve. Four all. Francie and Anne then broke serve again, but Anne, serving for the set, double-faulted twice. Both sides held after that and they went to a tiebreak.

A long tiebreak, full of jittery errors on both sides, kept alive by an outrageous out call on the far baseline that brought a surprisingly furious look to Anne's face. 7–7. "Can you believe that call? It was in by a foot."

"Anne?"

"Yes?"

"Just win this point."

Their eyes met. Francie thought she saw through the doubtful outer person to a stronger one inside. Anne nodded.

Next serve to Francie, a spinner into the body. She hit a weak return, picked off at the net, angled at Anne's feet. But Anne made one of her miraculously quick reflexive shots, catching the ball on her racket, deflecting a soft lob, her best of the match, over outstretched racquets on the other side, landing indisputably within the lines for a winner.

"Beautiful," said Francie, suddenly filled with the feeling—rare for her, but the greatest pleasure the game had to give—that she could do anything she liked with the ball.

She took two of them from Anne, put one in her pocket, bounced the other a few times, tossed it up, bent her knees. The ball reached the top of its arc and seemed to pause. With all the time in the world, Francie hit it in the bottom right quadrant as hard as she could: an ace down the middle.

"Oh, yes, Francie."

Match tied at one set apiece.

But it was really over, probably decided somewhere in the middle of the second set, perhaps at the moment

Francie volleyed the ball off that padded knee. Francie and Anne began playing better and better; the wiry women, their soft game beaten, had no fallback. In what seemed like a few minutes, Francie and Anne went up 5–0, 40–15 in the third set.

Anne serving at match point. To the backhand. One last lob, a good one, over Francie's head. She went back to take it, calling, "Got it."

Anne came across behind her: "Mine."

"Got it."

"Mine."

They were both in midswing when Francie ran her over. A cry of pain from Anne; their racquets collided— but somehow struck the ball, which arced toward the net, ticked off the tape, and dropped untouched on the other side. Game, set, match.

Anne lay on the court, face ashen, lips blue. She sat up, tried to rise, could not. Francie knelt beside her. "What hurts?"

"Ankle. What if I can't go on?"

"Don't have to. We won."

"That went over?"

"Yup."

Anne made a fist, almost pumped it.

Francie sat on the court, gently removed Anne's shoe, rolled off her sock, and supporting the weight of Anne's leg in her lap, examined the ankle.

Shadows loomed over them. "Did you hear a cracking sound?" said one of the wiry women, not quite hiding her satisfaction.

"More like a little rip," Anne said.

Francie looked at the wiry women pursing their lips. "Nice match," she said, reached up to shake hands, and asked them to send someone from the desk. They went away. Anne was gazing up at her. "You'll be okay by Saturday," Francie said.

"You think?"

"I've done that ripping number a hundred times. We're going to win this goddamn tournament."

Color began returning to Anne's face.

But it was her right ankle, and she couldn't drive. Francie and the desk attendant helped her out to the parking lot, and Francie drove her home in Anne's car.

"I hate to inconvenience you like this," Anne said. "My husband will drive you back the minute he gets home."

"No trouble," Francie said. "Got anything to drink? Beating a pair like that's worth a celebration."

"I never thought we could. You were so cool out there, Francie."

"I like to compete," Francie said. True, but not the kind of remark she'd normally make, possible now only with the endorphins flowing through her brain.

"And you were serving so hard—just like Nora."

"That turns out not to be a compliment," Francie said. She explained Nora's Newtonian theory of big hips and hard hitting.

Anne laughed and said, "You know you've got a great body."

"I most certainly do not."

"Come on—men on the other courts are always looking at you. That's never happened to me in my whole life."

Anne lived in Dedham, a small Federal house with a big lawn, not far from the green. Leaning on Francie, she limped up the shoveled walk, unlocked the door. They moved into a little hall, with cut flowers—irises—in a vase beside the mail and a stack of audiotapes. "I'll get ice," Francie said, seeing the kitchen straight ahead.

A bright kitchen, with three places set on the table and a note stuck to the fridge: *Anne—I'll handle dance pickup. Back at 8.* A note probably written early that morning; Anne's husband would be tired, in no mood for more driving. Francie checked her watch: twenty minutes to. She opened the freezer, found an ice pack under a container of rocky road ice cream, took it to the living room.

Anne sat in a corduroy-covered chair, her leg up on a footstool. The ankle was more swollen now, but Francie had seen worse. She laid the ice pack on it.

"You're an angel," said Anne.

"Does it hurt?"

"No. There's some wine in the cabinet over the sink, but I don't think it's very good."

"Let's save it for Saturday night," said Francie, picking up the phone.

"What are you doing?"

"Calling a cab."

"Please don't," said Anne, glancing out into the darkness. "They'll be home any minute."

Francie started dialing.

"Please. I feel guilty enough already."

Francie paused for a moment, then gave in. She hung up the phone, poured Romanian wine for both of them, sat on the couch.

"To victory," said Anne.

They drank a toast to victory.

Paintings hung on Anne's walls, all but one framed reproductions, of no interest to Francie. The one original, partly obscured by a desk lamp, was a still life of a bowl of grapes. She thought at once of *oh garden, my garden.* This painting had none of its resonance, but the technical skill of the artist was as high, perhaps higher: the grapes glistened, as though they'd just been washed.

"I like that painting," Francie said.

"You do?"

"Who's the artist?"

"Well," said Anne, "the fact is, me. Although I wouldn't say artist."

Francie rose, took a closer look at the painting, liked it even more. *A.F.* was painted in a bottom corner, almost too small to read. "Tell me more," she said.

"Like what?"

"Where you learned to paint. What other stuff you've done. Et cetera."

"I can't say I ever really learned. And I haven't done anything in years, Francie."

"How come?"

Anne shrugged. "Family life." Her gaze turned inward. "And I guess I got discouraged." She brightened. "But are you really telling me you like it?"

"I am."

"That means a lot. The truth is I'm so jealous of you. I'd kill for a job like yours, Francie."

"I'm not an artist," Francie said.

"Neither am I."

"Don't be so sure. I'd like to see more."

Anne thought. "They're all packed away in the basement," she said. "Except one I did of my husband, just after we got married. My last real effort, now that I think of it."

"Where is it?"

"In the bedroom. You can go up. First door on your right."

Francie went into the hall, climbed the stairs, entered the first room on the right. A bedroom, with a king-size bed, and over it, in oil, the head of a dark-eyed young man, all greens and browns, edged in white. Not as good as the grapes in technique, but it resonated more— whether because of Anne's artistry or the subject's resemblance to Ned, Francie didn't know. An astounding likeness, not photographic, but in affect, and perhaps all the more powerful for that reason. It froze Francie on the spot, there at the foot of Anne's bed. She stared at the painting, unaware of time, unaware of anything until a car door slammed, close by.

Francie hurried downstairs, through the hall, into the living room. Anne looked up with a smile. "Find it okay?"

"Yes. Anne—"

"And what did you think? I've never been that happy with it, but it's Em's favorite for some reason."

"Em?"

"Emilia. My husband started calling her Em, and it stuck."

Francie heard the front door open.

"Speak of the devil," Anne said.

15

A nightmare that began with cute domestic touches. "Honey, I'm home," called Ned in a parody of a sitcom-daddy voice. Not someone who sounded like him, but Ned: beyond doubt.

And a girlish voice responded, "Dad. Don't be such a dork."

Francie, motionless in Anne's living room, her motion-lessness that of the dreamer desperate to flee the night-mare but suddenly paralyzed in every muscle, heard the words, heard Ned's voice, and Emilia's, Em's—Em, Em, Em, a warning often sounded, completely missed—heard their voices strangely distorted, as though all sounds but the highest treble and deepest bass had been eliminated. Visual distortion came, too. Colors—the walls, the rug, Anne's face—veered toward yellow.

"In here," Anne called back, her eyes brightening. She glanced at Francie with the expectant look of someone about to introduce people certain to like each other, about to bring two positive components of her life together. Francie felt blood rushing to her throat, her cheeks; she blushed like the kind of schoolgirl she'd never been.

Footsteps in the hall. All her senses, all her thoughts in turmoil, Francie glimpsed her face in the mirror over the fireplace. She looked normal, even composed. No trace of a blush, no discomfort, completely cool. How was that possible? She should have beheld an image of terror and shame. Then Ned walked into the room, his daughter, Emilia, Em—with his dark eyes, his erect posture—at his side. He saw Francie, stopped dead, went white: horrified. Horrified for all to see.

Anne saw. "It's not as bad as it looks, Ned," she said. "Just a sprain. Please don't worry. And the great thing, the important thing, is we won the match."

"The match?" Ned said.

"We're in the finals! Ned, this is Francie, my new tennis partner. Francie, my husband, Ned."

Their eyes met. Ned tried to hide what was going on within, but he couldn't do that from Francie. She saw horror—his first thought must have been that Anne knew all, the second perhaps that Francie had had some kind of breakdown and come to confess—give way to confusion. Neither moved to close the space between them, to shake hands. Francie spoke first. "Hello," she said, not coming near the right note, unable to remember how to say hello to someone for the first time.

"Nice to meet you," he said, also hitting it wrong, and adding a faltering little smile that was off target as well.

Francie, aware of Anne's glowing face, almost a caricature of enthusiasm, tried to think of something to say. She met people all the time, always knew what came after *hello* and *nice to meet you*. But this time nothing did. There was no light remark, no easy meaningless flow. The room and everyone in it grew yellower and yellower, and the urge to bolt from it grew as well, almost overwhelming her. At the same time an inane phrase— *nice to meet you, too*—readied itself in her mind. But *nice to meet you, too* was playacting, a lie. She didn't want to say it, not unless she absolutely had to, didn't want to smile and be a villain; she just wanted to get out. The silence went on and on. Surely Anne, so sensitive to atmosphere, would notice, would feel the awkwardness.

"Well, then," Ned said. "I guess congratulations are in order. As long as you're not really hurt. Sweetheart."

"I'm fine," Anne said, somehow missing not only the silence, the awkwardness, but also the fact that while Ned was speaking to her, while he was saying *sweetheart*, his eyes were still on Francie. "Never better, in fact. Winning a match like that—and it was all thanks to Francie—is just so . . ." Words failed her. "How would you put it, Francie?"

All eyes moved to her. Her tennis self took over, rescuing her. "We haven't won anything yet," she said automatically.

"You see, Ned?" said Anne with delight. "That's my partner, right there. Just like Vince Lombardi."

"Thanks," Francie said, and Anne started laughing at the way she said it, but she was the only one.

"Who's Vince Lombardi?" Em said.

The question was directed at Ned. He licked his lips and quoted: " 'Winning isn't everything, it's the only thing.' "

"Puke," said Em, glancing at Francie to see if she really thought like that. Francie caught the glance—this was a child she could like; at the same time, she was aware of the proud paternal smile that flickered briefly on Ned's face, despite everything. *Em came first.* Again Francie glimpsed herself in the mirror and was stunned to find a smile on her face, too.

"Not that I'm suggesting she resembles Vince Lombardi in any other way," Anne was saying. "Quite the opposite, as you can plainly see. In fact, the men on the other courts are always—"

"I've really got to get going, Anne," Francie interrupted, her voice much too loud, or so she thought.

"But Ned just arrived," Anne replied. "You've hardly had a chance to meet. At least finish your drink first. And why don't you have one, too, Ned? Even if it is that Romanian stuff."

"I'm not really—"

"Come on, Ned. You wouldn't want Francie to think you're a wine snob."

Ned's mouth opened. Francie knew what was on his mind: *Francie knows better.* He said nothing, went into the kitchen. Em moved closer to her mother, gazed down at her ankle. Francie had already seen the Ned in Em; now she saw Anne in Em's graceful stance. "How did you win playing on that?" Em said.

"Your mom's tough." The words popped out of Francie's mouth unbidden. Now her subconscious was defending Anne, shoring her up. Not hard to understand why, like the guilty parent who buys her child an ice cream cone an hour after the spanking. Her next thought was conscious, and she kept it to herself: *she'd better be.*

Em was looking at her in surprise.

"She knows that's not true," Anne said.

Ned returned with an empty glass. "What's not true?" he said, an overflow of anxiety in every syllable. Surely Anne heard it, too.

But she did not. "That I'm tough," she explained, handing the bottle to Francie. "Mind filling Ned's glass?"

That forced them into proximity. Ned held out his glass. Their eyes met briefly; his filled with pain, then went blank. Francie poured. Their hands, so familiar with each other, almost touched and even at that moment seemed right together, like perfect lovers in miniature, at least to Francie. The two hands right, and everything else wrong.

"Thank you," he said. And: "Cheers." He wasn't good at this, but she was worse.

"Cheers." She made herself say it, too.

They drank. Francie tasted nothing, wasn't even conscious of the wetness.

"It happened on the last point," Anne was telling Em. "Two–six, seven–six, six–love."

"So you didn't choke?" Em said.

"Em!" said Ned.

"But Mom always chokes in the big matches. She says so herself."

"Couldn't this time," Anne said. "Francie doesn't know the meaning of the word."

"Oh, but I do."

"Don't listen to her, Ned. She's very modest. Why, I didn't even know about her job till just the other day, a job I'd die for."

Another silence.

"Oh?" said Ned at last.

"Tell Ned about your job, Francie."

"It's nothing, really."

"Nothing! Francie buys all the art for the Lothian Foundation."

"Oh?" said Ned.

"Is that all?" said Anne. " 'Oh?' Men, every time—right, Francie?"

"It's not a big deal," Francie said. "In fact, there's a committee, and—"

"Mom's an artist," said Em.

"I know," Francie said. They all turned to the still life behind the desk lamp. Grapes. And here was the girl, in the room, as though she'd stepped out of *oh garden, my garden*: a wild card.

"You should see the one she did of Dad—it's much better. I'll get it."

"I—"

But it was too late. Em was flying up the stairs. They

watched the long Day-Glo laces of her sneakers flap out of sight.

"She can be a bit wild sometimes," Anne said.

"She seems like a great kid," said Francie.

"She is," said Ned, his voice suddenly thick. Anne shot him a glance. He cleared his throat, drank from his glass, perhaps a bigger drink than he'd planned, because a red trickle escaped from one corner of his mouth, ran diagonally down his chin. He didn't notice, but Anne did. "Ned," she said in a half whisper, and mimed a cleaning-up motion, another domestic detail—a wifely detail—that made Francie writhe inside.

"Excuse me," Ned said, wiping his chin.

And then Em was back with the portrait.

"Really, Em," said Anne, "I don't think Francie—"

"It's all right," said Francie. She gazed at the painting. So did Ned and Anne, while Em gazed at them. Francie's eye couldn't help seeing things. Ned's sensuality, for example, one of his most obvious characteristics, was completely missing. And perhaps because of the immobility of the pose, and the way his body almost filled the canvas, like Henry VIII in Holbein's portrait, Anne's Ned appeared more powerful than in life, even dangerous. She'd missed him, not entirely, but by a lot, yet somehow the resemblance was still astounding.

"Well?" said Em.

"I like it very much," Francie said.

"Think it's worth anything?"

"Em!" This time they said it together, husband and wife.

"Is it for sale?" Francie said.

"Of course not," Ned said. Too quick, too emphatic— and Francie knew at once that he was afraid she might do something crazy, like make an offer, the way she'd called *Intimately Yours*. Anne noticed: Francie caught her giving

Ned a look; he caught it, too. "I wouldn't want to part with it, is all," Ned said. "But it's not my call."

Anne smiled at him. He smiled back, another faltering smile, even more false than the first, but Anne appeared to miss that.

"You like it 'cause it makes you look cool, right, Dad?" said Em.

"Right. Cool, that's me." He tousled her hair. She made a face. Anne laughed.

Francie set her glass down on an end table, not softly.

"Yikes," said Anne. "We're keeping you."

"Not at all," said Francie. Em was staring at her.

"Mind giving Francie a lift, Ned?"

"A lift?"

"To the tennis club—her car's there."

"Not necessary," Francie said. "A cab will be fine."

"I wouldn't hear of it," Anne said.

"No, really," Francie said, and reached for the phone. Anne covered the receiver with her hand. Their fingers touched.

"You know where it is, Ned?" Anne said. He nodded. "And we're out of milk, if you get a chance."

"Thanks for the drink," Francie said, moving toward the door.

"Thank you," said Anne. "For driving me home, for being so kind, for everything." She started to get up.

"Don't," Francie said.

But Anne did, hardly wincing at all. "See? It feels better already." She leaned forward, kissed Francie on the cheek. "We're going to win this thing."

Em gave her mother another surprised look. Ned held the door. Francie walked out: a cold night, cold everywhere, except the spot that Anne's lips had touched. That burned.

"And to celebrate we'll get together for dinner," Anne called after her. "The four of us."

They drove in silence, down the block, around the corner, both staring straight ahead.

"The four of us?" Ned said, speaking quietly, as though there were still some risk of being overheard.

"You and her," said Francie. "Me and Roger."

"God."

Francie sat up straight, hands folded in her lap. What was there to say? She felt Ned's eyes on her.

"It's so incredible," he said. "It almost makes you believe there's some God. Or anti-God."

Francie said nothing.

They rounded another corner. Farther now from home, Ned's voice rose to conversational level. "I thought I was going to have a heart attack," he said.

"It was horrible." Francie knew that the full horror of it wouldn't be apparent for a long time: a series of little revelatory bombshells awaited her.

Ned licked his lips. "I know. But . . ."

"But what?"

"But looking at it rationally, what does it change, really?"

She gazed at him. "I beg your pardon?"

He shrugged. "This just adds the visual component to what you already knew. I have a wife. That wasn't a secret. Now you've seen her. It could be worse."

"How?"

"Suppose she'd been your sister, for example."

Her stomach turned.

"Things like that happen, Francie."

"Not to me."

Ned's hand left the wheel, perhaps on its way to

touching her, paused, and went back. "We fell in love," he said. "That's a fact, and nothing changes it."

"You're wrong."

Ned pulled into the parking lot at the tennis club. Lights glowed in the windows of nearby houses, sparks flew from a chimney and vanished in the night sky. He faced her. "Are you saying you don't love me anymore?"

Francie didn't speak.

"Because if that's the case, I want to hear it."

She remained silent. She thought she saw tears in his eyes, but then a cloud covered the moon and they were gone. "I love you," he said. "More than ever."

"What do you mean, more than ever?"

"The way you were tonight. With Em. With Anne, even. You bring out the best in her."

"Stop it."

"And in me. It's true. You were the only adult in the room. I adore you. I'll do anything you want, leave Anne, anything."

"Don't you see that's impossible now?"

"Why? Why is it impossible?"

There were two reasons. First, what would be left of him, after? Second, she couldn't allow it, not now, not knowing Anne—and the girl. Francie gave Ned the second reason.

She watched him absorb it, saw his pain, also saw how young he looked, and more beautiful than ever. Yes, there was no question: he was beautiful. Beauty in pain was something to which she reacted strongly, especially when it was visible to the eye. "Then that leaves us right where we are, doesn't it?" he said. "Why can't we just go on like this?"

Francie laid her hand on his knee. "You're a sweet man," she said. "But . . ." For a moment, there was a lump in her throat and she couldn't get the sentence out. But only for a moment. ". . . where we are is intolerable now," Francie said.

"What are you saying?"

"It's over, Ned."

"You don't mean that."

"I do."

His lip quivered. Then he mastered himself and said, "Tell me you don't love me."

She said nothing.

He covered her hand, still on his knee, with his: two hands that still went together perfectly. "Until you can say that, nothing's over."

"Then—" began Francie when the car phone buzzed.

"Shit," said Ned.

It buzzed again. "Answer it," said Francie, thinking that Anne might have fallen, might have reinjured her ankle.

Ned put the phone to his ear, said, "Hello?"

But it was on speaker, and the car filled with a woman's voice, not Anne's. "Ned? Hi. Kira."

"Kira?"

"The same."

"I'm very sorry," Ned said. "I don't have those figures yet. I'll call you in the morning."

Pause. "Okeydoke." Click.

Ned put the phone down. "Syndication," he said, rubbing his forehead as though struck with a sudden ache. "Go on, Francie."

She withdrew her hand and said, "Let's just leave it like this: we can't see each other anymore."

"You know that won't work."

"It has to."

"Please, Francie." He leaned toward her, put his arms around her, brought his face to hers. She leaned back, forced herself to lean back, because it was unnatural, like rejecting herself.

"It won't work—you already know that in your heart," Ned said. "How could someone like you ever throw this away?"

"How couldn't—"

Someone tapped at her window. Francie pushed Ned away, hard enough so his back hit the door, then twisted around, saw Nora peering through the fogged glass, racquet bag over her shoulder, steam rising off her hair, still wet from the shower.

"To be continued," Ned said softly.

16

"I heard all about it," Nora said as the windows of Ned's car slid down. "Way to fire, kiddo. How's Anne?"

"It's just a sprain," Francie said.

"She going to be ready to play for the hardware?"

"She says so." Francie opened the door. She turned to Ned, found she couldn't quite look at him. "Thanks for the lift," she said, again attempting to find the tone she'd use with a new acquaintance, again getting it wrong.

"The pleasure was mine," he said, not even trying: more than that, making a deliberately careless reply, one she didn't like at all. And then, could that possibly have been his hand she felt, brushing the back of her thigh as she got out of the car?

Francie glanced at Nora—what had she seen? what had she heard?—but Nora's eyes weren't on her. "Hi, Ned," she was saying. "How's it going?"

He peered at her. "Nora, right?"

"Got it in one. Legal Seafood, at Chestnut Hill—you and Anne were ahead of us in line."

"I remember."

"Finally caught your show the other day," Nora continued, talking past Francie, turning on the charm, in fact. With her profile view of Nora's face, Francie could see her doing it. "Blended families, I think it was," Nora said. "Are those callers for real?"

"Paid-up members of Equity, each and every one," Ned replied. Nora laughed, was still laughing when Ned said, "Good night, ladies." His eyes lingered for a moment on Francie, then turned orange under the sodium arc lights as he drove out of the parking lot. They watched him swing into traffic and accelerate away, tires spinning on a patch of ice.

"What do you think of pretty boy?" Nora said.

"Pretty boy?"

"Come on. He's gorgeous. Gorgeous, smart, sexy—and funny, too."

"Grow up," Francie said.

"Testosterone versus estrogen—what could be more grown-up than that? No holds barred. On the other hand, he's married, and I soon will be. Bernie wants me in white—can you believe it?"

"Why not?"

"Why not?" Nora said, and gave Francie a look at a bad moment, the very moment the first of those bombshells she'd anticipated was going off in Francie's brain: *Someone like Anne, that's different—modest sex drive at best.* What were the implications of that now?

Nora's eyes narrowed; then she went on: "Maybe you're right. Some marriages—I'll take that a little farther—most marriages baffle me. Why should mine be any different?"

Francie hadn't followed, was aware that a question had been asked, no more. She nodded.

"What does that mean?"

Francie didn't answer. She had meant to tell Nora about Ned, the constant omission of this fact of her life putting too great a strain on their friendship, but how was that possible now? Nora knew Anne—and more, much more, had speculated about Anne's sex drive, found Ned attractive: how horribly tangled every little aspect of this was—and would thus be put in the intolerable situation of having to lie for Francie, an adulteress once removed. Impossible. Impossible and unnecessary, since it was over. She had just seen Ned for the last time. That was that. The resolved and the unresolved, all in a box. It just had to be closed and put away: a tidy, persuasive image, like slicing through the Gordian knot. But the back of her thigh still tingled in the place he'd touched it, if in fact he'd touched it at all.

"Are you saying that Anne and Ned make sense to you, for example?" Nora asked. "As a couple, I mean."

Francie whipped around to face her. "Who the fuck does?" she said.

Nora stared at her. "What's wrong?"

"Nothing."

"Bullshit. You're a thousand miles away, and when you're not, you're mean as a snake. And you look like you've seen a ghost. I'll take that farther, too—you look like shit, if you want the truth, which isn't your style at all. Something's wrong, very wrong. Fess up."

Francie took a deep breath. At that moment, she remembered the conversation on the ice: *There's someone I have to tell. I won't say it's you, if you don't want, but I have to tell.* Had she mentioned Nora's name? Yes. Had Ned therefore assumed that Nora already knew? How else to explain his reply when she'd thanked him for the ride? *The pleasure was mine.* Was it a sort of inside joke, inviting Nora in on the secret? If so, why now, when he'd always been so careful? Did the burden of the secret sometimes grow so intolerable that the truth had to burst out, even be flaunted? That could be dangerous—could have been, Francie corrected herself, because it was all going in a box, resolved and unresolved.

"Go on," Nora said. "Spill it."

"There's nothing to say."

Nora nodded. "Okay, pal." She swung away and walked off toward her car. Francie wanted to call out to her, *Nora, Nora,* and just let whatever happened after that happen. But she didn't. She hadn't done any damage yet, not to Anne or Em, and that was the way it had to be.

Francie went home. The answering machine was beeping in the living room. She switched on lights, listened to the message. "This is Roger," said Roger. He hated speaking to machines—she heard it in his voice. "Things are . . . promising. Vis-à-vis Bob Fielding. I'll be here for another day or two. No need to pick me up." Long pause. "And good luck. I'm referring to the tournament. If you're still alive." Another pause. "In it, that is. Good-bye."

Francie saw the future: Roger in some condo in Fort Lauderdale, she staying here. Just a few hours ago that would have seemed if not ideal then much better than what she had. But now there would be no Ned to complete the imperfect picture. Even if he did leave Anne, no Ned. She told herself that a few times, then went upstairs, stripped off her warm-ups and her tennis clothes, lowered herself into a hot bath. No Ned. But what if he did leave Anne, and then some time went by—how long? six months? a year? more?—and after that he called her? Was that okay? No. Why not? She was trying to answer that question when the phone rang. Francie picked it up, expecting Roger.

"How's Saturday night?" Not Roger, but Anne.

"Saturday night?"

"After the match. For our little foursome. I thought we could try Huîtres—am I saying it right? Ned loves seafood."

"Are you sure you're going to be able to play?"

"I'm on my feet right now! No pain. Maybe it's all

mental, like they say. Your confidence is rubbing off on me. That's what Ned thinks."

"He said that?" Francie said, wishing she could have phrased it as "Does he?" or just kept her mouth shut.

"No, but it's what he thinks. I can tell. So how about it?"

Never. "Roger's out of town right now. I'll have to get back to you."

"Okay. But I'll go ahead and make the reservations. I hear it's a pretty hot place."

It had been hot, as Francie recalled, the year before; then cursed herself for the thought. "Sounds nice," she said. "Take care of that ankle."

"I told you. No pain. We could go out there and whip 'em right now, you and me."

Call waiting sounded. "I've got another call," Francie said.

"Then bye. And thanks again."

Francie pressed the button. "Think if this were France," said Ned. "Or Scandinavia."

Her mouth went dry. "Where are you?" she said, thinking Anne might walk in on him any second.

"Back in the car," Ned said. "I forgot the goddamn milk. Serendipitous because it gives me a chance to call you."

But he'd never called her at home before. "What are you doing, Ned?"

"What I should have been doing from the start. As I would have done, I hope, in France or Scandinavia."

"What are you talking about?"

"You've been there. You know, better than I, how the Europeans handle this kind of . . . situation. There's no either/or. We could be open, semiopen at least, like Mitterrand, and no one would think twice. And above all, no guilt. That's the part I'm cutting out—the horrible guilt, the headaches. Is love something to feel guilty about, Francie? They understand these things in Europe."

"Would Anne?"

"Why not, under those circumstances?"

"Here in America, Ned. Would Anne?"

Silence.

"Would Em?"

Silence.

Would Roger? she asked herself, the most worldly of the three, certainly the one with the most experience of Europe. *Possibly,* she told herself. But they weren't Europeans; they lived not in a land of complaisance but of either/or. "Then that answers that," Francie said, "doesn't it?"

"You're letting guilt run your life," Ned said. "And there's nothing to feel guilty about—you've got to see that."

"I don't. There is—and there could be a lot more. That's what we've got to prevent."

"Then just tell me you don't love me."

She couldn't.

"And even if you did"—his voice broke—"even if you did say it, even if you meant it, I wouldn't give up. I'd make you love me again."

Francie covered the mouthpiece with her hand. She didn't want him to hear her crying.

"Francie? Are you still there? Francie?"

"Yes."

"I thought you'd hung up. Don't hang up."

"I'm not."

"I should have called you at home long before this. I can't tell you how many times I've wanted to—I memorized your number, even though I never used it. I've been so fucking careful, I almost forgot what this is all about."

Francie covered the mouthpiece again.

"Francie? Are you still there?"

She mastered herself. "I've got to go."

"Why? Is he there?"

"No."

Pause. "Where is he?"

"Out of town."

"Then why do you have to go?"

"I just do. And Ned?"

"What is it, angel?"

His first term of endearment. "Don't call me that. And don't call here anymore. Not here, not at the office, nowhere."

"You don't mean that, Francie. You couldn't. I'm not some stranger. I know you."

She hung up. It rang again, almost immediately. Had he not only memorized her number but entered it in his speed dialer? How did that reconcile with his spycraft? Suddenly she saw him in a new light, knew what must have been happening inside his head for months, months of struggling against his own spycraft, fighting the urge to call, the urge to see her, the urge to live with her. Francie saw him in a new light, but she let it ring.

After it stopped, she got out of the bath, dried herself. There she was in the mirror again: nothing normal or composed about her now.

She put on her nightie, went down to the kitchen, brewed tea. Found herself brewing tea, more accurately, although she seldom drank it, didn't like it. Brewing tea and thinking of Mackie, a Scottish baby-sitter hired by her parents when she'd been small. Mackie drank tea from morning to night, following a strict ritual, a ritual Francie followed now. Mackie: her red arthritic fingers wrapped around a china cup, her pale eyes squinting through the steam, her opinions. Mackie had many opinions—about Catholics: hypocrites; dogs: diseased;

men: nasty—opinions that had given Francie nightmares
and gotten Mackie fired. But the warm cup felt good now
in Francie's hand, and so did the hot tea inside her. *Men
are nasty, dear; don't you ever be trusting them. But
Mackie, what about Daddy? Now that's a sharp question,
isn't it, dear? Some, not I, don't you know, but some, might
even say the kind of question a Jewish lawyer would be
asking, not a sweet-tempered lass such as yourself.*

There was a knock at the front door, perhaps one in a
series only half heard. Roger? Home on some earlier
flight, with sudden news, good or bad? Francie went to
the door, put her eye to the peephole. Not Roger, but
Ned. Ned with flowers in his hand, irises, fucking irises
of course. She leaned her head against the door. He
knocked again.

Francie opened up.

He smiled. "I like your nightie," he said. "It's so
chaste."

Francie, forcing herself not to glance furtively past
him at the neighbors' windows like some cartoonish
sloven that Grosz might have painted, said, "What do
you want, Ned?"

"Aren't you going to invite me in?"

"Go deliver the milk." Francie closed the door in
his face.

But she didn't go away, just stood there. He knocked
again. Francie didn't move. He spoke, quietly, but she
heard. "That wasn't nice, about the milk," he said.

Francie just stood there, just stood there for as long as
she could, and then opened the door. Ned walked in.

He closed the door behind him. "Brought you some
flowers," he said, holding them out.

"I don't like irises."

"You don't?"

"Not particularly."

It wasn't so much the crestfallen look on his face per se, but that of all possible emotional reactions to the situation they were in, it had dominated, that did something to Francie. He was mortified that he'd been giving her irises all this time and hadn't known. There, standing in her front hall, the flowers now dangling uselessly at his side, he looked . . . adorable: a horrible girlish adjective, a horrible girlish trap, but there was no other way to put it.

She took him in her arms, could not stop herself.

"That feels good," he said in her ear. "I was afraid it might never happen again."

"This is the last time," Francie said, but she didn't let go.

"Don't say that." The tip of his tongue stroked her earlobe. The feeling triggered some force in her body, in her mind, irresistible. "Let's go upstairs," he said.

"No," she said, pushing him away, or trying to, or at least sending her hands a message that he should be pushed away. But he stayed where he was, his breath in her ear, his arms around her, their bodies close, feeling together the presence of another world, not far away. "We can't," she said. "Anne."

"There's no help for that."

"Don't be stupid."

"No, Francie. This happened. It's happening. You might as well try to . . . to . . ." He couldn't think of an analogy. "We're not machines," he said, finding another image, "with an off switch."

"But Anne," Francie said.

"I'll get a divorce."

"No."

"Then she can't know, that's all. She can never know."

"No."

"That's the best we can do. No one gets hurt."

No one gets hurt. Was it possible? Francie didn't know. But how could it go on, now that she knew Anne, played tennis with her, had started to become a friend, knew her daughter? It couldn't. There was no future for her and Ned. But tonight? Just one night? No one would get hurt tonight.

She turned toward the stairs. He followed her up, his hand trailing down her back like a charging device.

Having caught an afternoon flight from Lauderdale, having found Francie not at home, and having left a clever little bit of misdirection on the answering machine just because it felt like the kind of nifty move he would be making from here on in, Roger lay dozing on the couch in his basement room. The phone woke him. He ignored it, preferring to let his mind return to what it had been dwelling on during the plane ride, the details of the post-Francie stage of his life. At first, he'd imagined living alone, staying in the house, soldiering on. But why rule out female companionship? He thought of Brenda, Francie's friend in Rome, thought of how she'd sounded on the phone. He remembered how attractive she was—rich, too, which was important because even with the insurance settlement he would never be able to see to the needs of a woman even more high-maintenance than Francie. Brenda: wasn't there some story of a party she'd once been at where Pavarotti and Sutherland had sung Beatles songs around an upright piano? He could see himself building a life out of things like that. What was the name of that tailor's shop near the Trevi fountain where he'd had that gray suit made, the one with the subtle navy flecks? He could picture the facade perfectly, but the name eluded him, was still eluding him when he thought he heard a voice upstairs—not a voice, but two voices, female and male.

Roger removed his shoes, left his basement room, crept up the stairs in stocking feet. The door to the kitchen

hung open a few inches, admitting a yellow wedge of
light. He hovered in the darkness, listening. He heard a
man say something about divorce. A man with the sick-
ening voice of a pleaser: radio boy. Then Francie said
something he didn't catch. And Roger wanted to hear,
wanted to hear everything. He stuck his head in the
kitchen, saw no one, nipped around the corner into the
unlit back hall, and from there along the corridor, also
unlit, that led to the front of the house. He hung in the
shadows beside the stairs leading to the second floor.
And there they were, in a foul embrace.

Whitey, I need you now.

Francie said, "No."

Radio boy said, "That's the best we can do. No one
gets hurt."

They were still for a few moments; then Francie
turned, turned so that she was looking right at Roger,
right at him, and he thought, *Now you're dead.* But her
eyes were wet and he was in the darkness, and she didn't
see him. Up the stairs she went—what had she meant by
no?—and radio boy followed, up and out of sight, but
not before Roger got his first good look at him, the
image predictable. Roger listened to their withdrawing
footsteps with all the concentration at his command, but
it wasn't necessary. He knew where they were going: into
her bedroom, their bedroom, in fact, their marital bedroom. After a few minutes, he went up, too, silent as a big
cat in his stocking feet.

The marital door was closed and no light leaked out
from under. But Roger didn't have to see; he heard the
sounds of their lust, those cries of Francie's that she'd
never made for him, and the passionate noise of radio
boy, and bullshit words of love. Simple death was too
good for her. But if he was honest with himself, Roger
had known as soon as he had researched the Sue Savard

case that there was nothing simple about the kind of death that Whitey handed out, hadn't been anything simple then, and after all those cooped-up years would be even less simple now. Fair enough. After tonight, he wouldn't feel bad about it anymore, would cast off any future guilt. She was violating him in every way; it was a form of rape. This was a rape crisis and there was nothing to feel guilty about. His conscience was clear.

And what of radio boy? He was in the marital bed, raping him, too. Roger thought again of searching out some weapon, knife or poker, then bursting in to bludgeon and stab. Again he asked himself, would any jury convict him? And again the answer: in this rotting, leveled-out, lazy-minded country, yes, any jury could. No matter. He had Whitey. How complicated would it be to troll radio boy in Whitey's path? Complicated, perhaps, he conceded when no immediate solution presented itself, but he'd been born to solve puzzles. This was his métier. The stakes were higher, that was all. He was coming into his own.

On the other side of the door, Francie made some vulgar sound of culmination. *Come, bitch.* Roger imagined her in an open coffin at the funeral home, her face expressionless.

17

"**W**here were you?" Anne said.

She was sitting at the kitchen table, foot resting on a chair, ice pack on her ankle. Ned set the milk down in front of her, a half gallon of nonfat and a pint of 2 percent for her coffee, the cartons still cold although they'd been sitting in the car for almost two hours; it was a cold night. "I had a flat," he said. But two hours!

"A flat?"

"A flat tire."

"But you know how to change a flat, Ned."

"The spare was flat, too. And all the gas stations around were those self-service-only kind. I had to walk for miles."

"Oh, I'm sorry."

"Don't be. Just one of those things."

"I was starting to worry."

"About what?"

"That you'd had an accident or something."

"I'm fine."

Anne took off the ice pack, set it on the table. As she leaned forward, an idea came to her; he saw it coming in her eyes. "Why didn't you call AAA?" she asked.

The unexpected. "Are we still members?"

"I think so. Doesn't the fee show up on the Visa?"

"Damn. I forgot all about it."

166

"Or I could have come and got you."

"Not with that ankle." *Wasn't that the whole point of all this, that you couldn't drive, for Christ's sake?*

"You're sweet," Anne said. She held out her hand. He helped her up. "It's late," she said. "Let's go to bed." She led him from the room. They were in the doorway, almost out, when she stopped and said, "The milk." Ned turned back, picked up the cartons, took them to the fridge. Em had posted a new watercolor on the door: two big women, almost filling the frame, holding up a golden trophy. It gleamed. The quivering Keith Haring lines radiating from it showed that. At the bottom was written, *Go for it, Mom and Francie!*

Anne saw him looking at it. "Isn't she great?"

"She's got real talent, in my opinion."

Anne looked puzzled. "What do you mean?"

"I've always loved her art. You know that."

Anne laughed. "I meant Francie," she explained.

"Oh."

"What did you think of her?"

He shrugged, and thought at once of Judas. "She seemed nice enough," he said.

"She's more than that. She's so . . . together. They live on Beacon Hill."

How disappointing she could be. He nodded.

"I haven't met her husband yet, but we will after the match. We're going out to dinner, the four of us."

That had slipped his mind. Unable to counteract it, he said nothing.

"That's all right, isn't it?"

"Oh, sure."

They went upstairs. Anne used the bathroom first, went to bed, kissing her fingers and pressing them to his lips as they passed in the doorway, blushing only a little. Ned showered, flossed and brushed his teeth, stimulated his gums with the rubber-tipped brass stick, sprayed deodorant under his arms, took as much time as he could, then followed. The bedside light was off. He quietly got in at his side, lay down near the edge, his back to her, hoping she was asleep by now.

But she was not. He knew that, knew her, knew even before her hand lightly stroked the side of his ass, moved around to his stomach, down. At the same time, he felt her nipples pressing into his back, importunate.

Her nipples were hard, but he was not. It took an uncharacteristic amount of effort to make him so; finally she did it with her mouth. That was unusual, too. Then she slid on top of him, cocked her hips over him, settled down with him inside her.

"Your ankle," he said.

"Hush."

Anne started moving. Did uncharacteristic events come in threes, like plane crashes? This time they did. He began to go softer, softer and softer by stages—like a goddamned flat tire—with each grinding of her hips. Not a development that lent itself to secrecy, and Anne soon felt the change. She arched back, fondled his balls, and when that didn't work reached farther, got a fingertip between his buttocks: an insinuating first. What had she been reading? But it did no good. Nothing did, nothing could, not with the image of Em's triumphant trophy-raising painting so fresh in his mind. Anne and Francie, going for it. His penis slipped out of her and nestled down at its base. DNF, wasn't that what they said in horse racing? Did not finish.

"Sorry," he said.

"It's all right."

But it had never happened before. If there was a God, one of the old-fashioned, narrow-minded, judgmental sort, he would now of course be in the process of sabotaging his erectile capacity for life. But Ned didn't believe in any god like that and, worse, was also psychologist enough to know that such sabotage could be easily accomplished by, and against, the self.

Anne rolled off him, lay on her back. He knew those sensitive eyes of hers were open, staring into the darkness. Had she been close to an orgasm? Yes, of course, and what modern husband could leave her there? Not him. Ned crept down in the bed, began running his tongue down her stomach, lightly and teasingly, he hoped.

"Don't," she said, and turned away from him, drawing her knees toward her chest.

Lightly, teasingly: all wrong. This wasn't about seducing her, for Christ's sake; the job was to make her come. He should have been direct: licked her like it was the last night on earth, the way he'd just been doing to Francie. He'd been false, pro forma, more like a bad date than a husband, and Anne didn't miss things like that.

Time passed. Ned heard a siren far away, the furnace firing up in the basement, Anne's breathing, growing steady and even. He closed his eyes, but sleep wouldn't be fooled that easily.

Another siren; the furnace switched off; and Anne spoke. Startling him: so sure he'd been that she was asleep.

"Did Kira Chang get hold of you?"

"What?"

"You know. Kira Chang. From syndication, or whatever it is. She called while you were taking Francie back to the tennis club. I gave her the cell phone number."

"Thanks. She did." Silence, the kind that had to be filled. "Some minor screwup—I'll take care of it in the morning."

The furnace switched back on, ran for a while, went silent. Anne was silent, too. The headache started behind

Ned's right eye, where it always did, but this time spread deeper than ever before. Deeper and sharper. *What the fuck am I doing?* he thought. *What the fuck am I doing?*

"Ned?" Anne said quietly, and then a little louder, "Ned?"

He was asleep.

Anne slipped out of bed. Having gone to bed naked in preparation for sex with Ned, she put on the long sweatshirt she usually slept in and went downstairs. She didn't turn on any lights, didn't need them, knew her own house. Through the kitchen, through the door that led to the garage, a single-car garage where Ned's car, the later model, had precedence over hers. Anne switched on the garage light, and there was his car. She walked around it, saw just that: his car. All the tires seemed the same, none noticeably flat. What was she looking for? She didn't know.

Anne opened the driver's-side door, popped the trunk, where the spare was. She looked inside, saw his roof rack, kayak paddle, a bag of rock salt, a bouquet of flowers—irises, still fresh. The spare lay under the floor mat. She unsnapped the snaps, rolled it back. On top lay the tools—jack, crank, lug wrench—all still sealed in factory plastic. Beneath the tools she found the instructions, also sealed in plastic, and under them was the spare. It had never touched pavement: the manufacturer's label was still stuck to the treads. That didn't mean it wasn't flat, or hadn't been flat earlier that night. Anne moved to lift it off but couldn't. It was bolted in place. The bolt had to be loosened first, and the wrench had never been used. So no one had ever removed the tire to try it out.

Anne ran her hand over the spare, prodded it, punched it softly with her fist. It seemed as rounded and firm as the others, but she really couldn't tell. She stood over the trunk, gazing down inside, gazing at the roof rack, the kayak paddle, the rock salt, the irises, the tools, the spare. Anne had never been good at solving puzzles, had hated math, didn't like crosswords, was always nervous when people started playing games like Botticelli. She knew what she was seeing had to add up to something, but she couldn't make it happen. Then she noticed a road map wedged between the spare tire and the wheel well. She tugged it out.

A road map of New Hampshire. So? She unfolded it. Just a New Hampshire road map, territory very familiar to her. She ran her eye over some of the spots—Tuckerman's Ravine, Franconia Notch, Wildcat, Waterville Valley, Lake Winnipesaukee. Some time passed before she spotted the little red X on a tiny island in the middle of the Merrimack River.

A red X. Meaning? Anne had no idea. But her next thought gave it some: Kira Chang. She closed the trunk, leaving the irises to die.

18

A pretty girl got on the bus in Bridgeport, just after dawn. The only empty seat was on the aisle beside Whitey, so she took that, might have taken it anyway, he thought, catching the way she checked out his leather jacket from the corner of her eye. It was a cool jacket, no doubt about that, the coolest article of clothing he'd ever owned. He'd also bought himself a pair of cowboy boots from his first week's salary, made in Korea, but very cool as well, black with silver stitching and thick heels that must have made him at least six-four. And he still had two hundred dollars and change left over, plus what remained of his gate money. *Yeah, babe,* he thought, giving her another look, *check me out.*

A pretty girl, but kind of cheap-looking: spiky hair, lots of earrings, and—as she shrugged herself out of her coat—a little snake tattoo coiling up from her cleavage. Whitey got hard right away. There was a bathroom at the back of the bus. Was it possible to get her behind that door and fuck her brains out? Things like that happened. He remembered that exact scene from one of Rey's videos, except it took place on a plane, not a bus. The girl on the plane had made the first move, dangling her long red fingernails in the guy's lap.

This girl didn't do that. Neither did she have long red fingernails; hers were unpainted and bitten to the quick.

Whitey made himself interesting by staring out the window for a while, like a guy having deep thoughts, then sat back and glanced at her as if noticing her for the first time, and if she happened to glance back and see how built he was under the leather jacket or even better the bulge in his pants, they'd be on their way. But she didn't.

"Where you headed?" he said at last.

"Providence."

He nodded. "Rhode Island," he said. Nothing else came to mind. A few miles went by. "Just passing through?" he said.

"I'm sorry?"

"Providence. Just passing through?"

"I go to Brown."

Brown—what the hell was that? He thought back, all the way back to his high school days on the ice.

"The college?" he said.

"I'm sorry?"

"Brown. The college."

"Yes."

Now they were getting somewhere. He noticed that her neck wasn't completely clean. Necks—where had he heard that if you squeezed a woman's neck while she was coming she had a better orgasm? Why not just say to her: Hey, ever hear about this neck thing? And then they'd be in the bathroom at the back of the bus, trying it out. He licked his lips a couple of times, getting ready to say it.

The girl took out a book, some kind of art book. She opened it to a picture, one of those pictures any kid could do, just a bunch of rectangles, and stared at it. He squinted at the title, *Entrance to Green*. There wasn't even any green in it, for Christ's sake. She took out a pencil and wrote in the margin, *Anuszkiewicz: geometric recession counterbalanced by tonal shift—cool → warm*. His hard-on went away.

She studied the art book the rest of the way, gazing at one bullshit picture after another. Whitey stole sidelong peeks at the coiled snake rising and falling in its soft, springy lair as she breathed. Only as the bus was pulling into Providence station did Whitey get an idea. *It's the recovery of stolen objects. Paintings, for example.* Why hadn't he thought of that earlier? The girl gathered her things and started up the aisle. "I'm in the art business myself," he called after her. She didn't seem to hear. He thought of the steel-tipped pole he'd left behind, and that snake, rising and falling on her breast.

Whitey got off the bus in Boston. He'd been there once before to play in a tournament at the Garden, but all he remembered was eating oysters, the first and only time he'd ever tasted them, horrible slimy things that were supposed to make you horny but hadn't; he'd puked in the locker room that evening, and they'd lost to one of the big Catholic schools, the way they always did. So he had to ask some loser on the street, "Hey. Where's the Garden?"

"Ain't no more Garden, pal. Where you been? It's the Fleet."

"Huh?"

"Fleet Center, now. But the same location. What you do, you—"

"The Public Garden," said Whitey, realizing his mistake. The man looked at him funny but gave him the directions. The Garden, gone. For a few blocks that pissed Whitey off, more than pissed him off, reminding him of the big percentage they'd cut out of his life. But after a while he began to see the bright side. If Gardens could come and go, then anything was possible, and that included a big score.

Whitey followed the directions, soon found himself

walking on a street lined with fancy shops, their windows full of Christmas displays. He saw a leather jacket, a lot like his, went closer: identical to his, right down to those little V-shaped upturns on the chest seams. He checked the name of the shop—Newbury Leather—then took off his own jacket to examine the label. It had been cut out. He stood there wondering about that until he felt the cold, noticed that snow was falling. He hadn't seen snow since they'd sent him down south. Whitey gazed straight up into the sky. From that angle the snowflakes were black against the cloud cover. He'd grown up in snow and never seen that effect before. Change was possible. He was changing, getting smarter. Black snow was an interesting idea, for example, the kind of interesting idea someone in the art business might have, someone like him. *Someone like me, you bitch,* he thought to himself, meaning the girl on the bus. He crossed a street and entered the Public Garden.

Roger was waiting under the statue of George Washington, just as he'd said he'd be. Snow clung to the brim of George Washington's bronze hat, and to Roger's hat, too, a black fedora, or some other hat with a name. Roger even looked a little like Washington, except he was smiling. He held out his hand, gloved in black suede. Whitey shook it, squeezing harder than normal because his own hand was bare, *so it was a bit of an insult,* like Roger was a prince and he was a peon or something.

"Ever play any tennis, Whitey?"

"Tennis?"

"You'd have been good."

Whitey wasn't sure how to take that: tennis was for fags. "Well, here I am," he said.

"I never doubted you." Roger handed him an envelope. "A week's salary, plus an advance I hope you'll find suitable."

Whitey took it. Was he supposed to open the envelope and count the money? Only an asshole would take money without counting it. But the envelope stopped him, although he didn't know why. Whitey stuck it unopened in his pocket.

"Familiar with the city, Whitey?"

"Yeah."

"Then why don't you take the day to get situated? Saturdays are difficult for me, this one especially."

"Okay," said Whitey, who would have bet anything it was Friday.

"Come here tomorrow, same time. If it's convenient. I may have something for you by then."

Something? Convenient? Whitey was a little lost, but he said, "Sure, I can make it."

Roger's smile faded. "Tomorrow, then," he said, and walked away.

Whitey watched him go. Roger followed the path around a frozen pond and headed across the park. He wore a long black coat that matched his hat and gloves, looked rich, untouchable; and was almost out of sight, obscured by distant trees and thickening snowfall, when Whitey's mind finally processed what his eyes had seen at once: Roger had been wearing slippers, plaid ones lined with sheepskin. What did that mean? That Roger couldn't be trusted? Whitey ripped open the envelope, found ten fifties. What had Roger called it? An advance? What did that mean? Five Cs for something he didn't even understand: that bought a lot of trust. But slippers? Whitey tapped the bills against his palm: slippers. And then he thought of the cut-out label from the leather jacket and realized this had to be Roger's neighborhood—he was close to home. And where would that be, exactly? Whitey went after him.

Roger came to a street that bordered the park, crossed

it. Whitey closed the distance between them until he could distinguish the red of Roger's slippers. Too close, probably. If Roger glanced back he would certainly recognize him. But Roger didn't glance back. Whitey knew why: because he was a prince and Whitey was who he was. Roger kept to a steady pace, up a hill lined with big brick houses, all with fancy grillwork, fancy doors, fancy knockers. He turned left on a street that mounted still higher, stopped at a door, took out his keys, opened it, and went inside. Whitey walked past, noted the number and street name, kept going.

He'd accomplished something; what, he wasn't sure, but it gave him a good feeling. He walked to the top of the hill, down the other side—stepping carefully, because his cowboy boots were slippery on the snowy bricks—found a bar at the bottom. Money in his pocket and a day to kill. Whitey went inside and ordered breakfast: a draft and a large fries. Same again. Then another draft. He was free, and feeling good.

The bar began to fill up. Someone next to him ordered oysters. Whitey eyed them, glistening on crushed ice, felt a little funny. He started thinking about Sue Savard. Strange, how the mind worked: he hadn't thought about her in years, would have supposed he'd completely forgotten what she looked like, but now that he was back up north, back up north and free, he could picture her, especially her eyes the moment he'd gotten himself inside her. The truth was that he'd never had sex like the sex he'd had with Sue Savard. And he hadn't meant to hurt her at all—that business with the glass cutter had been mostly just to tickle her, give her a little added pleasure. Women had an enormous capacity for pleasure, according to Rey, and his amateur housewife videos proved it; real housewives, even the social worker said so, real housewives with video cameras. Someone—a mustached man with

thick lips—slurped down one of those oysters. Whitey
paid his bill and left.

Money in his pocket. A day to kill. Whitey returned to
the bus station, got on the bus to Nashua, took a taxi to
Lawton Ferry, 97 Carp Road.

A dump, as he knew it would be. He knocked on the
door five or six times, called, "Ma," then walked around
the side, peering in the windows. He saw dirty dishes,
dirty clothes, pictures of Jesus, but no one was home.
Fine. He didn't really want to see her anyway. What he
wanted was the pickup.

He found it in the rotting barn behind the house. His
old pickup, but painted white now, with LITTLE WHITE
CHURCH OF THE REDEEMER stenciled on the side. That, and
the fact she'd never mentioned it, pissed him off, so much
that he started kicking with his new cowboy boot,
kicking a hole right through the wall of the barn. What
gave her the right to do that? He calmed down when he
realized that if the pickup hadn't been used he'd never
have gotten it started after all these years. Besides, he'd
soon be able to afford something much better. Whitey
opened the door, saw a cat curled up inside. He yanked it
out, found the keys under the seat, fired up his old car.

Whitey drove east to Little Joe Lake, took the rutted
road that led to the far end. Nothing had changed, or if it
had, the snow was hiding all the signs, but everything
seemed strange. He had changed: he was bigger, stronger,
smarter, and that made all the difference.

Whitey parked by the footbridge to the little cabin on
the island. He sat there for a long time. Square one, and
he was back. If only Sue Savard was inside now, everything would be different. This bigger, stronger, smarter
him would make sure of that, would know how to stop
the screaming in some harmless way.

Not that it had been his fault, all that screaming. Why hadn't she realized what it would lead to? Why hadn't she been able to stop it herself, to keep her own goddamn mouth shut and not force him to do it for her? Her fault, but still Whitey was filled with regret—he'd blown his chance with Sue Savard, the sexiest woman he'd ever known. What would Sue Savard have been like now?

19

"Hello. Is Francie there?"

"No."

"Well ... I ... This is Anne Franklin. Her tennis partner? We spoke once before."

"Yes."

"We—did Francie mention the dinner plans?"

"Dinner plans?"

"We were thinking of going out to dinner after the match."

Silence.

"The finals, tonight. Didn't Francie mention it?"

"I've been out of town."

"Oh. I was just calling to confirm the time: seven-thirty at Huîtres. I booked a table for four in nonsmoking, if that's all right with you."

"Four?"

"Ned's coming, too."

"Ned?"

"My—my husband."

Silence.

"I'm not sure I caught his name."

"Ned. Ned Demarco. Francie's never mentioned him either?"

"Perhaps I've been inattentive."

* * *

Roger's mind ran through its gears, each one more powerful than the last, spinning, whirring, so fast that he had to pace, the excess mental energy escaping into his body. *The lover's wife, if she existed:* at one stage, a hypothetical and false contractor in a superseded plan for Francie, but now that she did exist, he felt . . . confusion, so strange for him. Fact: Francie was sleeping with the husband of her tennis partner. He found that harder to believe than the adultery itself. It reduced her to the basest commonality, like one of those illiterates on a TV tell-all show, a walking mockery of his taste. Was it possible for him to have misread her so grossly? Or—or was this something different, something more sophisticated: could it be possible, for example, that this tennis partner, this Anne, knew of the affair and accepted it? Roger's mind was already at the next stop, waiting with a disgusting image of Francie in bed with the two of them, and before he could digest that, was preparing another, even worse, with four participants. He felt a responding pulse in his groin. No! Were they animals, beasts, mere rutting things? Not him. He stopped pacing, poured water; it trembled in the glass, like an earthquake warning. He drank, tried to calm himself. *It's all right, Roger,* he thought, quashing all images. *The lover's wife is just another piece on the board, part of the problem, and all problems are fundamentally mathematical. Permutations and combinations.*

The door opened and Francie walked in, snow in her hair, her appearance revealing nothing at all of what he now knew hid within. "Hello, Roger." She glanced around. "Were you on the phone?"

"No." But had he said *permutations and combinations* aloud? The air in the room felt disturbed, as though the last ripples of a sound wave hadn't quite flattened away.

She took off her coat, her old coat—*where's the new*

coat, Francie?—and hung it over the back of a chair. "When did you get back?" she said.

"Moments ago."

"How was the trip?"

"Didn't you get my message?" Enjoyable, asking that. *Dance on my string, Francie.*

"Yes, but it didn't say much."

Enough to do the job. "Cautious optimism, then—how does that sound?"

"Fine." She was watching him, waiting for details, waiting for . . . for some suggestion that he might be moving to Fort Lauderdale, of course! What better moment to spring a surprise:

"Your tennis partner called. She's invited us to dinner tonight."

Oh, Francie was very good, showing almost no reaction at all. "Don't worry," she said. "I'll cancel."

"Why would you want to do that?"

"I know how you hate those things."

"Not at all. In fact, I've already accepted."

"You want to go?"

"Why not? She sounds . . . charming, and she is your tennis partner. You must be a nice fit."

"A nice fit?"

"On the court. You're in the finals, after all."

"Anne's a good player."

He poured another glass of water, started for the door that led to his basement room, stopped with his hand on the knob. "Her husband's coming, too," he said. "I didn't quite catch his name." He paused, his back to her. "Fred, is it?"

"Ned."

That surprised him. He'd expected something craven: "I'm not sure" or "Ned, I believe." Surprised him and infuriated him. He went downstairs without another word.

* * *

Roger sat by the glassed-in window in the spectators' gallery off the bar, overlooking court one. On the court, the umpire was already in her chair, and the players were warming up their serves. He studied them one by one. First, the opposition: a stocky woman with an uncoordinated service motion, each component slightly mistimed, and a thinner one with better form but little power. Then he turned to Francie and her partner: Francie had improved her serve since he'd last seen her play, years before; she'd perfected her slide step, now got her legs nicely under the ball, hit it hard. And her partner, Anne: a delicate-looking woman, she reminded him of a Vassar girl he'd dated long ago, his only serious girlfriend before Francie. Anne had the best form of all, but she wasn't putting a single serve in the court. He leaned forward, trying to figure out why, at the same time hearing the gallery—there was room for fifteen or twenty people, no more—fill around him, hearing Francie's name mentioned more than once. He should have been prepared, but was not, for that smooth voice.

"This seat taken?"

He turned to face radio boy. "No."

"Thanks." Radio boy sat down beside him. He held up crossed fingers. "My wife's playing for all the marbles."

"So is mine," said Roger.

Radio boy looked down at the court. "Which one is she?"

Roger pointed her out.

"Oh, Francie," said radio boy. "I met her the other night—when Anne twisted her ankle." He held out his hand. "Ned Demarco."

Smooth, smoother even than Francie. Roger had no choice but to shake his hand, hand that had been all over his wife. "Roger Cullingwood."

"Nice to meet you, Roger. Let's hope we bring them a little luck."

Roger smiled, a smile that spread and spread, almost culminating in that laughing bark. But he held it in and said, "There's no luck in tennis."

"Heads," said Francie. The coin spun in the air, bounced on the court. The umpire bent over it.

"Tails," she said.

Francie and Anne touched racquets, moved back to return serve, Anne in the deuce court, Francie in the ad. "How's the ankle?" Francie said.

"I feel fine."

But she didn't look fine: her face was colorless, except for the mauve depressions under her eyes, and the eyes themselves couldn't meet Francie's gaze.

"Hungry?" said Francie.

"No."

"Me either," said Francie. She glanced up into the gallery, saw Roger and Ned side by side, talking. Even though she hadn't been able to derail Anne's dinner plans, had prepared herself for the possibility that they might sit together, she wasn't prepared. She swung her racquet a few times, tried to make her arm feel long. "Let's work up a fucking appetite," she said.

Anne smiled, a smile barely there, quickly gone. *Was she about to burst into tears? What the hell was going on? Tennis, Francie. Just watch the ball.*

The server tucked one ball under her skirt, held up the other—"Play well," Francie said—and served. Not a hard serve, not deep in the box, on Anne's forehand. By now Francie had seen Anne do many good things with a serve like that—the crosscourt chip, the lob into the corner, the down-the-line putaway. She had never seen her jerk it ten feet wide, never seen her hit with such a tight, awkward motion. A little spot of color appeared on Anne's cheek.

"Sorry," she said, not for the last time.

"Not a problem," Francie said, also not for the last time.

When the match ended an hour and fifteen minutes later, the red spot had spread all over Anne's face, down her neck, vanishing beneath her collar. But Francie had stopped seeing that bright redness, stopped hearing the "sorry's," stopped saying encouraging little things, stopped noticing Anne's double faults, unforced errors, mishits, blocked all that right out. Blocked out everything in her life as well—Ned, Roger, the cottage. She just played, forgot her life and played as she had never played before: winning her serve at love in almost every game, hitting winners from all over the court, making shots she seldom even attempted, topspin lobs from both sides, inside-out forehands, backhand overheads. Everything went in. At the same time she learned that Vince Lombardi had been wrong, that winning wasn't the only thing, or everything—it was nothing. All that mattered was hitting that ball on the goddamn nose, again and again and again; pounding, booming shots that never came back. The sound of the ball off her racquet was frightening. They lost 4–6, 4–6.

The umpire handed out trophies, big ones for the winners, little ones for Francie and Anne. The winners stayed on the court to have their pictures taken. Anne, her face now draining of blood and as blank as a shell-shocked soldier's, went into the locker room, Francie behind her.

A fancy locker room, with whirlpool, sauna, steam, all deserted on a Saturday night. Francie started to lay her hand on Anne's shoulder, held back. What to say? All she could think of was "Jacuzzi?"

"In a minute," said Anne, not looking back at her. Anne turned down the row that led to her locker; Francie moved on to hers.

She sat on a stool without stirring for a minute or two, the muscles in her legs tingling, a human version of the hum of idling machines. She felt great. What other potentials were locked up in her? The potential for love had already been freed by Ned, and others still inside probably had to do with the children she'd never had and never would. She felt less great.

Francie stripped off her clothes, opened her locker, put on the faded maillot hanging inside. The whirlpool was at the back of the locker room, near the showers. She switched on the timer, got in, closed her eyes, and had a crazy idea almost at once: Why not just take off for somewhere far away, by herself? The Atlas Mountains, Prague, Mombasa. She'd driven through the Atlas Mountains years ago with Brenda, stoned on kif—that many years ago—remembered robed Berber children holding up chunks of amethyst by the roadside, stunted magicians performing their purple tricks. Why couldn't—

Francie opened her eyes. Had she heard something over the sound of the bubbles? She twisted the timer down to zero, listened, heard it again, then got out of the whirlpool and followed the sounds to Anne's locker.

Anne was sitting on a stool, her back to Francie. She was wrapped in a towel, her head in her hands, her shoulders shaking.

"Anne?"

No reply, just her sobbing, full-throated and ragged. Francie moved around in front of her. "Anne. Please. It's only tennis."

Anne looked up, tears streaming down her splotchy face, snot, too: misery undisguised. "It's not the tennis,

Francie. I—" The sobbing took over. Her towel slipped, exposing her breasts, but she didn't notice. Francie couldn't help noticing, even at that moment couldn't help comparing them to her own: the two pairs of breasts in Ned's life.

"Please, Anne." Francie touched her shoulder. "Everything's all right."

At her touch, Anne fell forward, grabbed Francie around the waist, clung to her, her wet face against Francie's wet bathing suit. "Help me, Francie."

"With what? What's wrong?"

And then Anne's face was tilted up at her, imploring, and Anne, fighting the sobbing demon inside her for control of her own voice, got the words out. "It's N—it's Ned. I . . . I think he's having an a-a-affair."

Francie, stroking the back of Anne's head, went still. The towel had fallen to the floor, and Anne, naked, was holding on to Francie harder than ever, her crying eyes locked on Francie's, desperate, pleading. "Oh, God," Francie said, doing all she could not to cry herself. "I'm so sorry."

At that moment, with them in each other's arms, Francie saw Nora standing wide-eyed at the end of the row of lockers. Francie shifted her own eyes once in the direction she wanted Nora to go. Nora went.

Anne made a sound, partly smothered by Francie's breast, somewhere between laughing and crying. "Don't you be upset, Francie. It's not your fault. You're the best thing that's happened to me in a long time. She's"— the laughing component vanished—"she's just so much prettier than me, and so much smarter. I guess he couldn't resist."

Francie stepped back, freeing herself from Anne's grasp. "Who are you talking about?"

Something—the new distance between them, the change in Francie's tone—made Anne grow aware of her naked-ness. She reached for the towel, rewrapped herself, rose un-steadily to her feet. "No one you know, Francie. It's terrible of me to inflict this on you, especially after that exhibition out there."

"Fuck that," Francie said. "Who?"

"Her name's Kira Chang. She's high up in some big media outfit in L.A. She even had dinner in my house. Can you believe it?"

"Are you sure?"

"Sure?"

"That it's happening. That he's . . . doing this."

"I haven't walked in on them or anything, if that's what you mean."

"Then how do you know?"

"I just do." She shivered like a baby after a long cry.

"But based on what?"

"Little things, but a wife always knows deep down, doesn't she?"

"What little things?"

"Like the other night, the night he drove you back here. He didn't come home for hours and he had some feeble story about a flat tire. I know he was with her."

"How?"

"She called him. It must have been about the arrange-ments. She's that brazen."

Brazen. Francie flinched at the word; did Anne not see? "But how can you be sure?" Francie said. "What's your evidence?"

Anne stopped mopping her face with a corner of the towel, stared at Francie. "You think I'm stupid."

"You know better. Why do you even say things like that?"

"It's your tone. I haven't heard you like this before, so impatient."

Francie took a deep breath. Anne had the right story but the wrong name; that meant she really knew nothing, not with certainty, and it had to stay that way. What Francie was seeing now wouldn't compare with what would happen to Anne if she ever learned the truth. "I just don't want you jumping to any false conclusions," Francie said. "How do you know he didn't have a flat tire, for example?"

"I checked the spare. He said he hadn't been able to use it because it was flat, too, but in fact he hadn't even unbolted it to look."

"Does he have a pressure gauge?"

"Pressure gauge?"

"One of those little sticks to put on the valve. That's all you need to check pressure—the tire can stay where it is."

"I don't know."

"That's what I mean about jumping to conclusions."

"Do you think I should ask him?"

"Why not?"

"I'm not good at that kind of thing."

"Then—then just look in his car."

"That's a good idea. You're so smart, Francie." She stared at her feet. "God—what I've put you through tonight."

"It's still early."

Anne looked up, started laughing, laughter that threatened several times to turn to tears, but did not. "You're the best, Francie," she said, and embraced her again, kissing her on the cheek. "Don't be mad at me."

"Let's just hope he has that pressure gauge," Francie said, hating herself for it, but it was just the kind of pragmatic remark she would have made if Kira Chang really were a suspect, and she had to stay in character, Anne's tennis partner and newfound friend.

"Oh, Francie. Do you think he does? I love him so much." Her eyes filled with tears, but not tears of misery this time; she had hope, was starting to believe in her marriage again. "I even have these fantasies of us getting old together, going for long walks in the woods, that kind of thing. Do you?"

"Do I what?"

"Have fantasies like that."

"Everybody has fantasies."

Anne bit her lip. "Francie?"

"Yes?"

"If you had to bet on the pressure gauge?"

"It'll be there," Francie said.

Quick, Francie. Shower, dress, dirty things in the gym bag, out, out ahead of Anne. Francie hurried up to the bar. A few people actually applauded as she came in. Francie hardly heard. She scanned the room for Ned, found him—drinking Scotch with Roger. She went to their table. They both rose, something she couldn't recall either of them doing separately, ever.

"Very well played, Francie," Roger said.

"Just incredible," Ned said. "If only—"

"Thanks," said Francie, interrupting whatever was coming after that. "I'm thirsty."

They sat down. The waiter appeared. Francie ordered water and a beer. Anne would be there any moment. She had to get Ned alone, but how? Both men were looking at her, both a little flushed, both on the point of making some remark as soon as the waiter left. "Damn it," she said, kicking Ned under the table, "I forgot something. Excuse me." She got up, left the bar, went down to the lobby, borrowed a pen and a piece of paper at the desk, drank from the fountain, did this and that, looked busy. Where was Ned? Didn't he get it?

Ned walked into the lobby, saw her. By now she was at the bulletin board, pretending to scan it. He stood beside her. "You didn't have to kick me so hard," he said, eyes on the bulletin board.

"Is there a pressure gauge in your car?"

A pause, but very brief. Francie was sure she felt him reeling inside. "What does she know?" he said, almost too low to hear.

"She doesn't *know* anything. She thinks you're having an affair with Kira Chang."

Francie glanced at him. His eyes were closed and there was a V-shaped groove on the right side of his brow. He opened his eyes, turned to her. "What are we going to do?"

Get on the next plane to Marrakech, she thought, *you and me.* She said, "Do you have a pressure gauge, yes or no?"

"No."

"Give me your keys."

He glanced around, handed her the keys.

"What did you tell him?" Francie said.

"That I was going to the bathroom."

"Then go."

Ned headed for the locker room. Francie hurried back upstairs to the bar, thinking fast. She had come in Roger's car, Anne in Ned's. Roger would have a pressure gauge; she seldom went in his car, had never actually seen his pressure gauge, but she knew him.

Roger was writing something on a napkin as she approached the table. He smiled. "I was getting lonely all by myself." He folded the napkin, pocketed it.

"I can't find my hairbrush," Francie said, the kind of female inanity he wouldn't question. "I must have left it in your car, if you'll give me the keys."

"Your hair looks fine to me."

"Thanks," she said, holding out her hand. He gave her the keys.

Downstairs, across the lobby, out. The two cars were parked side by side under the full glow of a sodium arc light. Francie unlocked Roger's, flipped open the glove box, riffled through the contents: manual, warranty, maps, calculator, touch-up paint; pressure gauge. She grabbed it, locked the car, unlocked Ned's car, opened his glove box. The contents burst out, cascaded to the floor: CDs, tapes, floppy disks, bills, letters, receipts, crayon drawings, crayons, elastics, tokens, and M&M's, which in turn came spilling out of their box in a second flood. Francie scooped everything up, crammed it all back in the glove box, jammed in the pressure gauge, and was just about to lock up when she noticed the front door of the club starting to open. She tossed Ned's keys on the seat, banged the door shut with her foot, leaned against Roger's car.

They came across the lot, Anne in the middle, Roger and Ned on either side, their faces orange under the light. She handed Roger his keys. "Find that hairbrush?" he said.

"No."

"I think I've got one," Anne said, waiting for Ned to unlock his car.

"It's open," Ned said, getting in.

"You're a trusting soul," said Roger, unlocking his car.

Anne got in, opened the glove box. Everything exploded back out again, into her lap. "Yikes," she said, starting to sort through it. "I thought I had a hair—"

Francie saw Anne's hand closing on something, saw her raise it up into the light for a better look: the pressure gauge. She gave Francie a quick smile, private and conspiratorial, through the window.

20

"I hope this doesn't offend anyone," said Ned, dispensing with his elegant little fork and slurping the oyster right off the shell. "The only way to eat them," he said, patting his mouth with a napkin. He'd ordered a dozen, the others—Francie, Anne, Roger—half a dozen each.

"Not at all," said Roger. "Boldness is all when it comes to certain of the appetites."

"I'm sorry?" said Ned, pausing, the next oyster halfway to his mouth.

"You know that old saw," Roger said, tasting the Montrachet he'd ordered and nodding to the waiter. " 'He was a bold man that first eat an oyster.' "

Francie could see from the look on his face that Ned didn't know. "Swift, isn't it?" she said. "And since the bold man probably wasn't bold enough to venture into the kitchen, his wife must have tried it first."

Laughter. Roger raised his glass to her. Ned's eyes lingered on her face; didn't he realize those eyes were too obviously appreciative, even loving, if you knew them? Next his foot would be touching hers under the table; she drew her feet under the chair and said, "The bread, please." Ned passed it to her, his hand moving a little quicker than Roger's.

The waiter filled their glasses. Anne drank half of hers

in one gulp. "Swift," she said. "Do you know the *Marriage Service from His Chamber Window*?"

No one did.

She drank some more. " 'Under this window in stormy weather / I marry this man and woman together; / Let none but Him who rules the thunder / Put this man and woman asunder.' "

Silence.

"How times change," Roger said.

Anne looked across the table at him. "Beautiful, isn't it? I wanted it read at our wedding."

Roger refilled her glass.

"This is wonderful wine, Roger," Anne said. She glanced at Ned. "I'll know something to order from now on."

"If we win the lottery," Ned said. Roger's eyes swept over him; Francie thought Ned's dark face darkened some more.

Roger turned to Anne. "But?" he said.

She put down her glass. "But?"

Roger smiled. "But Swift didn't make the grade?"

Anne glanced again at Ned.

"It wasn't raining on our wedding day, for one thing," Ned said. "And we were indoors."

Roger topped off Ned's glass. "Where was this?"

"Our wedding? In Cleveland."

"Ah," said Roger.

"We're both from Cleveland," Anne said.

"I've never actually been there," Roger said, sipping his wine. "Have you, Francie?"

"Yes," she said, stupidly adding, "it's very nice."

"I'm sure it is," Roger said. "And what brought the two of you here?"

"Ned did postdoc work at B.U. We liked it so much, we stayed."

"Your field, Ned, if it's not rude to ask?"

"Psychology."

"You teach at B.U.?"

"I have. Now I'm in private practice."

"Don't be so modest, Ned," Anne said. "He's also on the radio five days a week."

"Really?" said Roger. "In what capacity?"

"Ned has his own show."

"Psychology instruction?"

"More like advice," Anne said. "It's called *Intimately Yours*. *Boston Magazine*'s doing a piece next month."

"Dear Abby of the air?" said Roger.

"I wouldn't put it that way," Ned said.

"My apologies."

"None necessary. I just try to help the callers think things through on their own."

"From what perspective?"

"I'm not sure I follow."

Roger shrugged. "The usual suspects. Freud? Jung? Adler? Frankl?"

"All and none. I take what I need from what's out there. I've found that sticking to dogma usually makes things worse."

Roger looked thoughtful. "Taking what you need," he said. "Sounds interesting. I'll be sure to listen in."

"WBRU," said Anne. "Ninety-two point nine."

The waiter returned and started clearing the first course. "And what do you do, Roger?" Ned asked.

"Nothing as sexy as that," he said. "I raise private investment capital. Very drab."

"What's the name of your company?"

"That," said Roger, "I'm not at liberty to say at this moment." Then he winked at Ned; Francie had never seen him wink before, would almost have thought him incapable of it.

"Finished, sir?" the waiter asked Ned, seeing he'd left three oysters uneaten.

"Yes."

"Can't let those go to waste," said Roger, lifting one off Ned's plate. "Mind if I emulate you?" he asked, and ate it off the shell; his lips glistened. "You're so right," he said. "There's no other way."

"Excuse me," Francie said, and went to the bathroom.

Her face in the mirror: still looking normal. How was it possible, with Roger at his very worst? With what she was doing to Anne? And Ned—why was he asking questions he knew the answers to? Yet there was her face. Normal. Why wasn't it an ultrasound of what was happening inside, like Anne's? She splashed cold water on it anyway.

Anne came in, talked to her in the mirror. "Isn't this fun?" she said. "You never told me Roger was so smart."

Anne went into the single cubicle, and then came the tinkling sound of her urine flowing into the bowl. "And so distinguished-looking," she continued unselfconsciously, as though they were sisters. "Can I ask you something personal?"

"Sure," Francie said, and in the mirror her expression changed. It was the eyes: they grew alert, like an animal's, even those of a dangerous one.

"Why didn't you and Roger have children?"

Finally, something that made her face change. It crumpled.

"Francie? Have I said something wrong?"

"No." Face still crumpled, but voice even. "We wanted them but it was a physical impossibility."

"I'm sorry."

"Nothing to be sorry about. It happens all the time. We got over it."

Francie heard her tear off a strip of toilet paper. "Em was so impressed with you."

"It was mutual," Francie said. Her face began to smooth itself out.

"Really? You liked her?"

"Who wouldn't?"

Anne came out of the cubicle. "What nice soaps," she said, and washed her hands. Their gazes met in the mirror. "Do you have any sisters, Francie?"

"No."

"Neither do I. I always wanted one."

Francie handed her one of the plush little towels folded on the granite sink top.

"Are you mad at me?" Anne said.

"Why would I be mad at you?"

"The way I played. Will you ever forgive me?"

"I don't think like that."

"Oh, I know you don't, Francie. You're like a lion— that's how *I* think of *you*—strong, proud, loyal."

"Stop it."

"If only you'd told me about that"—Anne lowered her voice—"pressure gauge"—and raised it—"earlier, we would have won that goddamn match."

"Next year," Francie said, although she knew she couldn't bear a whole year of dinners like this, ski weekends, double-dating, conspiracy.

Anne grinned. "Is that a promise?"

"Francie's promised we're going to try again next year," Anne said.

"I'll put it on my calendar," Roger said before calling for another bottle of Montrachet.

He went to the bathroom between the entrée and dessert, as Francie knew he would. She'd been his wife for a long time, was familiar with his bladder capacity.

"How awful would it be if I stole one of those soaps?" Anne said.

"Which one?" Francie asked.

"Guess."

"The oatmeal."

"She knows me so well, Ned." And to Francie: "Do you think it would be all right?"

"I'm sure they budget for it," Francie said.

So Anne went, too. And then they were alone.

Their eyes met. "You never told me what a shit he is," Ned said.

"Didn't I?"

"No. Why the hell did you marry him? Or is that out of bounds?"

"You can ask me anything," Francie said. "He was different then."

"No one changes that much."

"And maybe I misjudged him. He seemed so . . . original to me then."

"Original? He's a throwback, Francie."

"It's not that simple," she said. She didn't like the way Ned was looking at her, as though her stock had fallen in his eyes because of the company she kept. "And please, don't bring out your tool bag. It's been a long, slow decline, maybe worse since he lost his job, which you knew about, if I'm not mistaken."

"I was just making conversation."

"Were you?"

"No." He smiled, a rueful, boyish smile, and looked . . . adorable, even at a time like that. Francie reached out with her foot, felt for his, found it.

"A long, slow decline," she said. "I didn't realize the extent of it, until . . ."

"Until what?"

"Till you came in your kayak."

Ned's eyes changed. She knew what he was going to say before he said it, was already thinking the same thing. "I want you," he said.

They looked at each other in a way they shouldn't have, not in a public place.

"Monday night," he said. "At the cottage."

"Monday?"

"There's no show—they're broadcasting the Pops Christmas concert."

Francie thought, *We can't*. But she didn't say it.

"Six-thirty?" he said.

Francie thought, *No*. Ned's foot pressed against hers; that little touch, through shoe leather and so far from erogenous zones, nevertheless sent a wave of sensation through her so powerful, it almost made her gasp. She couldn't get that *no* out, began having counterthoughts like *how can one more time hurt?* and *if I'm saying good-bye it should be in person*, and then Roger was back, and Ned's foot was gone.

"So," said Roger, picking his napkin off the chair and replacing it in his lap as he sat down, "what's the plan?"

"The plan?" said Francie.

"Just coffee? Or perhaps something sweet."

Francie had coffee, Roger and Ned cognac, Anne a cake called death by chocolate.

"This is incredible," Anne said, "but I can't possibly finish it. Anybody want some?"

No one did.

The bill came. Roger took it from the waiter's hand.

"Wait a minute," Ned said. "Let's split it, at least."

"Sharesies?" said Roger. "After you win that lottery. No, this is my treat. Mine and Francie's, that is. It's been a pleasure."

"But Roger, it was my idea," said Anne.

"And a very good one. We'll do it again soon."

* * *

Outside a cold wind was blowing. Anne and Francie stood hunched inside their coats while the men went to the parking garage across the street.

"Do you think it's true what they say about oysters, Francie?"

"No."

Anne was quiet for a moment. "Then maybe it's the wine."

"What is?"

"If it's not the oysters."

Francie was silent.

"Having an effect on me. If you know what I mean." Anne looked at Francie sideways. "Can I ask you something?"

"I'm going to kill you," Francie said.

Anne laughed. "Sorry. And sorry for saying sorry. But it's kind of . . . intimate."

"Ask away."

"In a marriage," Anne said, "after you've been together for some time, if you see what I'm getting at. What do you do to keep him—to keep things stimulating?"

Francie felt sick.

"I don't mean you personally. What does one do? I read in *Cosmo*—on *Cosmo*, actually—that some men like dirty talk. In bed, I mean, during . . ."

"I don't think it's a matter of tricks," Francie said, realizing the truth of it as she spoke.

"Then what is it?"

"Enthusiasm." That had been missing from her bed—hers and Roger's in the days they shared it—if not from the start, then certainly since their procreative fiasco.

Anne nodded; Francie could see she was making a mental note.

The two cars drove out of the parking garage, stopped

in front of Huîtres. "Good night," Francie said. And she thought, *Good-bye. Have the fucking strength to make it good-bye, good-bye to you both.*

"Night, Francie," said Anne, getting into Ned's car. She smiled over the top of the door. "Enthusiasm—I should have known."

Francie went to bed alone. She lay awake for a long time, staring at the ceiling. Then she got up, found sleeping pills in the back of the medicine cabinet, left over from the bouts of sleeplessness that followed the last artificial insemination. She took two, returned to bed, waited for them to act, which at last they did.

Anne went to bed with Ned. They lay in the darkness.

"How were your oysters?" she asked.

"Fine."

"Mine, too. Better than that."

"That's good."

"I've decided I love oysters." She moved closer to him, not quite touching. Enthusiasm, but perhaps *Cosmo* was right, too. Why not come out with all guns blasting, as Francie would? She put her mouth to his ear, breathed into it. His whole body tensed gratifyingly, giving her the courage to go on. In a low voice she said, "I love your cock, Ned. I want to . . . do things to it." She reached down his body.

He stopped her hand. "I'm sorry, Anne. I have a splitting headache."

She froze. "That's supposed to be my line," she said, the kind of witty remark Francie might make. But she couldn't keep it up; all the air went out of her, and then her mind started dragging her down a long spiral, down and down while Ned fell asleep.

A long spiral, all the way back to the pressure gauge.

Anne got out of bed, left the bedroom, walked down the hall. She heard Em make a noise in her sleep, paused outside her door. Em rolled over in her bed, then lay quiet. Anne moved on, downstairs, through the door that led from the kitchen to the garage. Yes, he had a pressure gauge, but did that mean he had used it? No. But perhaps she would be able to tell whether that little rubber thing, the protector, the guard, whatever they called it, had ever been unscrewed from the valve. Might there not be greasy fingerprints on it, or stripped threads inside? She opened Ned's trunk, examined the rubber valve guard on the spare. No fingerprints. She unscrewed it. It stuck just a little before giving way, as though this were the first turning, but she didn't know enough about the subject to make that judgment. She peered inside, could see nothing wrong with the threads. Proving? Nothing. He did have that pressure gauge, he did get headaches sometimes, and over the years she had been less and less sexual with him: it was probably her own fault. Why had she been like that? She didn't know. Perhaps she would work up the nerve to discuss it with Francie.

Anne was about to close the trunk, to go back to bed, to try the enthusiasm gambit again, perhaps the next morning or tomorrow night, when she noticed that the map that had been jammed into the wheel well against the spare was no longer there; and the irises: gone, too. Anne searched the trunk, the glove box, under the seats, behind the visors, but she didn't find them.

She stood in the garage, thinking, getting nowhere, and her gaze fell on the trash barrels, lined up along the wall. She began with the nearest one. It held two green plastic bags. She took out the first, unknotted the red ties, dug through, found nothing but recent garbage. Then she removed the second bag, was starting to open it as well, when she noticed the irises, crushed at the bottom of the barrel. The map of New Hampshire with the red X in the middle of the Merrimack River lay under them.

Picking his napkin off the chair and replacing it in his lap as he sat down! Roger lay on the couch in his basement HQ, his mind racing much too fast for sleep. Weren't they aware that the proper place to leave a napkin while away from the table was to the left of the forks, folded in half, and that only a boor would leave it on his chair? Evidently not: it was symptomatic, emblematic, of the contrast between them and him. Picking the napkin off the chair, replacing it carefully on his lap, because why? Because under it was this little digital recorder, not much bigger than a credit card—birthday gift from Francie, he recalled, so he could record business ideas while in the car—spinning silently away. He rewound it and listened again, editing out background noise—laughter, cutlery clattering on china, chair legs scraping the floor—transcribing it black-and-white in his mind.

N: *You never told me what a shit he is.*

F: *Didn't I?*

N: *No. Why the hell did you marry him? Or is that out of bounds?*

F: *You can ask me anything. He was different then.*

N: *No one changes that much.*

F: *And maybe I misjudged him. He seemed so ... original to me then.*

N: *Original? He's a throwback, Francie.*

F: *It's not that simple. And please, don't bring out your tool bag. It's been a long, slow decline, maybe worse since he lost his job, which you knew about, if I'm not mistaken.*

N: *I was just making conversation.*

F: *Were you?*

N: *No.*

F: *A long, slow decline. I didn't realize the extent of it, until . . .*

N: *Until what?*

F: *Till you came in your kayak.*

N: *I want you.*

PAUSE: laughter, cutlery on china, scraping chairs.

N (cont'd): *Monday night. At the cottage.*

F: *Monday?*

N: *There's no show—they're broadcasting the Pops Christmas concert. Six-thirty?*

LONG PAUSE: more laughter, cutlery, scraping.

R: *So. What's the plan?*

21

Late Saturday afternoon, the sky glowing orange through the grillwork of bare black trees—oak, maple, poplar—around Little Joe Lake. Riding in his own car, a ten-year-old Bronco with 124,000 miles on the odometer—many of the taxpayers knew Saturday was his day off, and wouldn't care to see him swanning around at their expense in the cruiser with CHIEF on the side—Joe Savard followed the lane that ran up the east side of the lake. With snow on the ground he preferred the Bronco anyway, at least until the town came through with new tires for the cruiser. His request had been tabled till the April meeting, along with the school textbooks, the cable TV contract, and the landfill amendment. And of course the streetlight question, he added to himself, nosing over to the side to let a white pickup go by; the streetlight question, a hopeless perennial, like mud in the spring. The driver raised his hand in thanks, perhaps flashing the peace sign, although with the pickup's windows so dirty, Savard couldn't be sure. The body, too, although not so dirty he couldn't read the words on the side panel: LITTLE WHITE CHURCH OF THE REDEEMER. Savard pulled back into the lane and kept going.

At one time, there'd been many Savards in the area and they'd owned the whole lake. It was probably named after a Savard: in a box somewhere lay a family Bible signed by generations of them, and they seemed to have restricted themselves to three male names, Joseph, Lucien, and Hiram; so he could have done worse. Now he was the last one, and all he owned was the single cabin built on what wasn't much more than a big rock a few yards from shore at the north end, reached by the lop-sided little footbridge that might not last another winter. That rock being the last of the land, him being the last of the people: probably the reason he hadn't sold the cabin back when he should have, after Sue.

Not that he'd done much reasoning during that period. He'd just left the cabin unattended for a few years, unwilling to see it or even think about it. But after his second marriage, he'd started renting the cabin out in summer, hoping to raise extra cash for some of the little things his second wife seemed to like. Later came the divorce, another good time for selling out. But it was around that time that he'd discovered his hobby, and now he drove out to the cabin almost every day off.

Savard parked at the end of the turnout that led from the lake road to the footbridge. Lifting his chain saw off the passenger seat, he stepped down and noticed that someone else had parked there, not long before. He could tell from the way the tires had pressed four deep prints in the snow after tracking in from the south, as he had—old tires with hardly any tread left at all. He followed their route with his eyes, backing out, returning to the south, through the long shadows of the trees on the snow, snow turning red-black in the dying light.

The footbridge creaked once or twice as Savard walked across. He wasn't especially tall—six feet if he stood his straightest—but he had the broad and power-ful family build. Many Savards had anchored the Dart-mouth line, going back to the early years of football, although not him—he'd gone to Vietnam instead. Not by choice; he just hadn't been able to get the kind of math scores Dartmouth required. Algebra 1, geometry, algebra 2: a maze he'd wandered through in high school without finding his way, despite never missing class, sitting in the front row, staying after for extra help, puzzling over the homework problems every night, but too often failing to solve for x. SAT math score: 470. He still remembered that goddamned number, probably the only number that had ever been solid in his mind. Four seventy led to war; war led to law enforcement, which became a profession after Sue. End of story. The truth, which had come to him years later the way truths did in his case, if at all, was that he hadn't liked school anyway, except for sports, and would probably have disliked Dartmouth, too.

Savard opened the cabin door, went inside. It was no longer the kind of cabin anyone would want to rent. Savard had gutted it, sledgehammering all the partitions on both floors—some emotions had got loose that day, the room where it had happened, all the rooms, were now gone—ripping out the second floor itself as well, down to the structural beams. He'd left one toilet, one sink, both unusable now with the water turned off and the pipes drained for winter. The rest was space, high and open, mostly shadows at this hour, except for the red glare on the lakeside windows, a color reflected dully on the unpolished surfaces of the bears.

Savard still thought of them as bears because that was what he'd been after at the start, life-size bears carved—if cutting with a chain saw could be called carving—from the biggest cedar trunks he could find, dead standing and naturally dried when he could get it. After the divorce, those days off had gotten a little too long, and he'd gone to work once a week for a woodlot across the Maine line, not far from Kezar Falls. The work was hard; he'd been handy with a chain saw since boyhood; he got to wander around in the woods; they paid him: a good job. One evening, while he was walking back toward the logging road and his ride out, a big bear had reared up at him through the trees. He did what you were supposed to do, which was nothing. He wasn't afraid, not with that chain saw in his hands—the noise alone would do the trick. The bear didn't move either, as if following the same guidelines, and after watching for a minute or so, Savard realized it wasn't a bear, but a tall tree stump that looked like a bear.

Savard went closer, circled the stump, then without thinking, pulled the cord and raised his saw—a heavy Black & Decker four-footer—and gave it a little more definition between the head and shoulder. Almost too much: he went at the snout with more finesse, narrowing it, then rounded off that big muscle pad behind the neck. He stepped back for a better look—terrible.

But he'd gotten the bug, and the next Saturday he drove home with ten foot of cedar, most of it sticking out the back of the Bronco. White cedar, specifically: he'd always liked the soft, sunny glow hiding under its sappy skin. Savard had floated his log across the water to the cabin, dragged it up to the door with the ATV he'd had then—one of those little things he'd thought would please his second wife; she'd ridden it once—and humped it through the door.

The carving had taken a year. By the end of that time he'd settled on the right tool—an electric Stihl 14, only four pounds or so, delicate enough for eyes, claws, nostrils—and had learned the most important lesson: to let the wood guide the saw. His first bear was man-size and stood by itself on its hind legs, but he didn't fool himself into thinking it was anything but crude. There was just one good thing about bear number one: it had that poker face that makes bears so dangerous. Savard brought back a new tree trunk the next week to see if the poker face had been an accident.

Savard didn't finish bear number two, if finishing meant carving a complete bear down to the ground; in fact, he never attempted another complete bear. He'd gotten the second bear's poker face almost right away— this one was even more ambiguous, if that was the word—and was sawing his slow way down to the chest when he lost focus. As he worked, he began to find himself watching not the side of the chain where the bear was emerging, but the other side, the tree side. For no reason, he decided to make bear number two half-bear, half-tree. There was a . . . relationship between the bear and the tree, a complicated one, not especially pleasing to either of them, if that made any sense. It took Savard four months to reach that point with the second bear. Bear three began the next Saturday.

By now Savard had lost track of the number of bears he'd carved with his chain saw. Many had ended up in the woodstove, making floor space for new bears. Not that anyone looking at the recent ones would have identified them as bears. Savard was interested in only two things now: the struggle, if you could call it that, between the bear and the tree, and the pokeriness, if that was a word, of the face, even though there no longer was anything re-sembling a face. Struggle and pokeriness, his termi-nology for what he was doing with the bears. It didn't have to make sense because he never discussed it with anyone. No one else ever came inside the cabin; no one else had ever seen them.

Savard lit the woodstove, dragged the floor lamp—the only piece of furniture in the place—into position, switched it on. He surveyed his latest bear, a big one be-cause the trunk was big: old, slow-growth cedar, with thin-spaced rings and a grain that felt like satin. His latest bear—a massive, twisting shape, almost too massive to be able to twist, but it did—locked in combat with some force in the wood. He knew the force was real, having felt it through the saw. Strapping on his Kevlar-lined chaps—he'd had over thirty stitches in his legs by now, didn't want more—he filed the teeth and rakers in the chain as sharp as he could get them, put on his headphones. In the beginning he'd kept his ears uncovered, lost in the sound—much quieter than a gas-powered saw, but still whining and buzzing nastily as metal turned wood to dust. Later, noticing that his hearing wasn't as sharp as it had been, he'd worn protection. Now he preferred music, Django Reinhardt specifically. That was the way he worked: Paris singing in his ears—he'd never been to Paris, never been anywhere, really, except Vietnam, but Paris must have been something like Django's music, if it wasn't still—Paris singing in his ears, the saw throbbing in his hands, sawdust shooting through the yellow pool of lamplight, swirling past the blazing windows that faced the setting sun.

Joe Savard worked all night. When dawn came, and the east side windows lit up, first milky, then butter-colored, he saw what he had seen so many times before, that he'd only made things worse. Still, as in all those other times, he felt good just the same. Hard to explain. A feeling kids get when they stand in a doorway pressing their arms against the jambs, then quickly step free, arms levitating by themselves, as though weightless; a feeling like that, but all over.

A good feeling, followed by ravenous hunger. Savard closed up and drove to Lavinia's, a diner he liked a few miles up 101. Black coffee, bacon and scrambled eggs, side of hash browns. While he waited for his order he asked for a phone book. He found a listing for the Little White Church of the Redeemer in Lawton Ferry, on the eastern border of his territory.

Food came. He ate it all, almost ordered the same again; would have, even a year or two ago. But he was up to 220, and that was the limit.

"How about a blueberry muffin, Joe?" asked Lavinia. "Baked personally in the oven of yours truly."

No refusal possible. He ate the muffin, but without honey, even though he was very fond of honey.

"I like appetite in a man," Lavinia said, clearing his plate, refilling his cup.

"Sure you do," Savard said. "You own a restaurant."

She gave him a look, a complicated one that he didn't meet for more than a second. He had no desire to get closer to Lavinia. Not true: he had a strong desire to get closer to Lavinia, but only once or twice, and that wasn't for him.

Savard drank up, paid his bill, leaving a bigger tip than usual, and was halfway out the door when he paused, then went back inside and picked up the pay phone. He dialed the Little White Church of the Redeemer.

"You have reached the house of God. No one is here to take your call right now."

Savard left a message after the tone.

22

"**A**h, right on the dot," said Roger, standing beneath the statue of George Washington, Sunday at ten. "Punctuality is the courtesy of kings."

"It is?" said Whitey, red-eyed, yellow-faced, blue-lipped, rumpled, as though he'd spent the night drinking and then slept, or passed out, in his car. But he didn't have a car, and where had he slept, come to think of it? An unknown factor, quite certainly inconsequent; still, it was a relief to remember that Whitey wouldn't be around much longer.

"Just an expression," Roger explained, at the same time calculating with some precision the time remaining to Whitey—thirty-three hours, at most, thirty-two and a half, at least. A romantic concept, in a way: hadn't innumerable potboilers been based on the conceit of a character given only a short, fixed time to live? Although not, Roger thought, a character like this. He found himself smiling at Whitey.

"Never heard of it," Whitey said. Not a conventionally likable character, but a character nonetheless, in his silly leather jacket and pointy cowboy boots, beyond vulgar.

"No matter. How about some coffee?"

"Now you're talkin'," said Whitey.

They walked out of the Public Garden, waited for the light to change. Just as it did, Roger caught sight of a large, well-dressed family coming out of the Ritz across the street: an unmatronly mother with upswept blond hair, two tall young adults, some teenagers, one smaller child, and then the father. Something familiar about the father, and in that instant, Roger said, "Go."

"Huh?" said Whitey.

There were people in front of them, blocking at least their lower selves from view. Roger ground his heel on the toe of Whitey's cowboy boot. "Fast. Be back in one hour."

"What the fuck?"

But then the light changed and Roger had no choice but to step off the curb and start across the street, couldn't look back to see whether Whitey was following instructions, or tagging after him and thus aborting his plans, possibly forever. Roger's path intersected that of the monstrously teeming haut-bourgeois family, and in its rear guard the father—Sandy Cronin—spotted him and said, "Hello, Roger."

But therefore, if spotting now, hadn't spotted him earlier, as he waited for the light. "Sandy. Well, well. And all the little ducklings. Merry Christmas."

"And to you, Roger. You and Francie both."

"Thank you, Sandy. I'll make a note to pass it on."

Roger walked on, across the street, along the sidewalk, to the awning of the Ritz, and there, passing behind a top-hatted doorman, he glanced back. The Cronins were well inside the park now; the little one had tossed a chunk of ice at one of the bigger ones, and they all seemed to be laughing. Sandy himself, in his camel-hair coat, was patting a snowball into shape. What kind of justice was this, that a mediocrity like Sandy could so prolifically pass on his mediocre genes, while he, Roger, had been denied? Beyond justice, for justice was merely a human construct, after all, what kind of science was it?

How could nature select Cronins over Cullingwoods, unless the degradation of the species was the goal? In his mind's eye he saw again that ineradicable microscopic image of deformed sperm—his—twitching spastically in the petri dish. Ineradicable, yes, but also ineradicable was his suspicion that somehow, in some way yet unknown, it was Francie's fault: Francie, with her babbling of adoption, missing the whole point.

Roger noticed that the Cronins were gone. Noticed, too, that there was no sign of Whitey. The Cronins hadn't seen Whitey—more important, had not seen the two of them together. The plan remained viable, but it had been a near thing. Roger recalled chaos theory, how a butterfly fluttering its wings in the wrong patch of sky could destroy the world. No amount of planning could permanently overcome the inexorability of the natural forces. But all he required was thirty-three hours, to keep those butterflies at bay for thirty-three hours.

Whitey wandered around for a while, at one point sensing he was close to the old Garden, but failing to see any sign of it or its replacement. He did find a bar in the shadow of an overpass and, gloveless, hatless, feeling the cold through his leather jacket—not as warm as he'd expected—went inside. Had a beer. Two. Three. And a shot. He didn't like being stepped on. What was the word? Literally. He'd been stepped on, literally. Why did he have to put up with that shit? He was a free man.

Whitey, pissed, looked around the bar, hoping for some customer who might rub him the wrong way. But he was almost alone, the only other drinkers being a few old drunks with disgusting faces. Stepped on, literally. He knew why, too, had figured it out immediately: Roger hadn't wanted to be seen with him, not by his buddy in the camel-hair coat. A buddy of some kind, no question:

screened by the statue of George Washington, Whitey had watched them gabbing in the middle of the street. Roger couldn't have been ashamed to be seen with him, or why would he have offered the assistant's job in the first place? A legitimate assistant, and therefore someone who should be introduced to camel-hair-coated buddies crossing the street. Instead he'd been stepped on. Why? Whitey couldn't figure that out.

He checked his watch, had one more shot to ward off the cold, laid a fifty on the bar. A fifty: that made him think. Just days back in the world, not the halfway house world but the real one, and already making good money. And it wasn't like Roger was some kind of dangerous dude—he was in the art business, for Christ's sake— while Whitey had known many genuinely dangerous dudes, had spent almost half his life with them. Roger: not dangerous, a well-paying employer—but maybe not to be trusted either, not completely. That was all, Whitey told himself. Just be smart. He left the bar feeling much better.

"You're a bit late, Whitey."

Back under George Washington, temperature falling, refreezing the snow below snowball-making range, condensing the breath that rose from Roger's mouth with his words.

"Got a little lost," Whitey said, playing it smart.

Roger looked at him for a moment, thinking. For the first time it occurred to Whitey that his boss might not be the brightest. Talked fancy sometimes, but that didn't make him bright.

"Thought that was your point," Whitey went on, "for me to get a little lost." That was pretty funny, and he laughed at his own joke.

Roger did not laugh, clearly didn't get it; for sure, not

the brightest. He licked his lips, his tongue bright red in contrast to the cold chalk color of his face and lips. "Remember how we spoke of discretion, Whitey? How important it is in this business?"

"Yeah."

"And I'm sure you realize that competition is a factor in all businesses."

"Like McDonald's and Burger King."

"So you won't be taken aback to learn that I have competitors, too."

"In the art recovery business?" Whitey said. Just to nail it down, that that was the business.

Roger smiled. "Sharp today, Whitey, are you not?"

At least Roger had the brains to see that. Whitey shrugged. "No more than usual." Roger's smile broadened. Whitey wondered whether this was too soon to ask for a raise.

"That's why I hired you," Roger said. "But wouldn't it be foolish to show every card to the competition?"

"That guy on the street's a competitor?"

"He thinks so."

"And I'm one of the cards?"

Roger put his gloved hand on Whitey's shoulder. "You're my ace in the hole."

Roger's car was parked nearby.

"What tunes have you got?" said Whitey as they drove along the expressway in light traffic.

"None."

"With a CD player like that?"

Roger said nothing. Whitey flipped on the radio.

"—Ned Demarco, reminding you we won't be in our usual time slot tomorrow, but please tune in for the annual Christmas—"

Roger jabbed at the control buttons. Metallica came on, "The Shortest Straw," one of Whitey's favorites. "That's more like it," he said, glancing at Roger with surprise; he wouldn't have taken him for a metal fan. Roger stared straight ahead.

They got on 93, followed it northwest through the suburbs, toward New Hampshire. After a while Roger turned down the radio and said, "Can you take care of yourself, Whitey?"

"Take care of myself?"

"This business has rough edges sometimes."

"The art business?"

"Any business where big money's involved."

"Big money?"

Roger glanced at him. "I may have an assignment for you, Whitey. Its successful execution would most probably lead to a substantial escalation in your salary."

Execution? Escalation? Whitey kept mum, playing it safe.

After a period of silence, except for the radio—White Zombie doing "Warp Asylum," another favorite—Roger said, "A raise, Whitey. Of sizable proportions."

"Big, you mean?"

"I do."

How big was big? Whatever it was, he deserved it, was worth every penny. Watching the scenery go by, very cool, very something else he couldn't remember the word for, started with "non," Whitey said, "What's this, like, assignment?"

"We'll get to that, but first—are you hungry?"

"Nope."

"Thirsty?"

"No."

"Need to use the bathroom?"

"Soon."

Roger nodded. "After that we'll talk."

Pit stop. Roger gassed up, Whitey took a long piss, picked up some Reese's on the way out, a little hungry after all. Back on the highway, Roger switched off the radio.

"Listening, Whitey?"

"Why wouldn't I be?"

"I'm going to describe a painting to you."

"Shoot."

"It's called *oh garden, my garden.*"

"About hockey?"

Roger's eyes shifted toward him. "Why would you think that?"

"No reason." Except for Boston Garden, now gone. It made a kind of sense, didn't it? But maybe not the kind he could get across to Roger. They'd faced Xaverian the only time he'd skated on Garden ice, and Whitey had scored their only goal, before being ejected in the third period for spearing.

". . . grapes," Roger was saying, "and in the background, or more accurately the middle ground, a girl on a skateboard. Can you visualize it so far?"

What was this? Grapes? Skateboard? Girl? "What's she wearing?" Whitey said.

Roger paused, and again Whitey reflected that he might be a little slow. What the girl wore would have been the first thing he himself would have noticed. "I'm not certain," Roger said. "Perhaps a tunic of some sort."

Tunic? What the hell was he talking about? At that moment it was clear to Whitey that Roger was a little out of touch, and he made a decision, then and there: he was working for Roger, yes, would follow orders, but—would use his own . . . discretion! Discretion. Wasn't that what

Roger was always going on about, the importance of discretion in this business? Everything was coming together.

"Tunic," Whitey said. "Gotcha. Anything else?"

Another pause to think. Jesus, discretion and plenty of it. "You're sure you've got it so far?" Roger asked.

"Yeah. I mean, what's to get?"

"The name of the painting, for example."

"My garden."

"Oh garden, my garden," Roger corrected.

"Whatever."

Silence descended for some miles. The Merrimack appeared, frozen but snowless, the color of the low clouds overhead. Whitey occupied his mind with the lyrics of Metallica's "Harvester of Sorrow," those he could remember. He ate the last of the Reese's. No Reese's on the inside, for some reason; he realized how much he'd missed them.

They crossed to the west bank of the river, left it behind. Roger spoke at last. "Do you know the word *provenance*, Whitey?"

"Providence?" said Whitey, thinking of the girl on the bus, the snake between her breasts, her breasts themselves.

"Provenance," Roger said, a little slower.

"Sort of."

"No matter," said Roger. "It's a technical term, specific to our business. The reference is to the chain of ownership of a given work, establishing authenticity, you see. In the case of *oh garden, my garden*, the chain has been broken."

"Yeah?" said Whitey. He pictured a thick gold chain, the kind pimps wore. A diner came into view. It had a red neon sign—Lavinia's—and an old Bronco parked out front. "Still haven't had that coffee," Whitey said.

"Perhaps on the way back," Roger said. "I'd like to beat the weather."

Whitey glanced up at the sky. "No snow till tomorrow," he said.

But it made no difference. Roger passed the diner by, took a back road, then another, came to a gate in the middle of nowhere. He got out, unlocked the gate, then drove on, crunching snow on a track thawed and refrozen, up a long hill. He stopped at the crest. Below lay the river, frozen but snow-blown clear by the wind, with an island in the middle and a single cottage on it, sheltered by trees. A stone jetty jutted from the near bank, two dinghies tethered to it, caught in the ice. Roger sat there in silence, waiting for—what? Whitey didn't know.

At last Roger made a sound, a kind of laugh, maybe. "Ever been married, Whitey?"

"Nope."

"Not unwise, in the final end. But without marriage, we'd be out of business."

"We would?"

"The dissolution of marriage leads to conflict when it comes to the ownership of material objects. Take our little painting, for example. Its rightful owner is our client, a woman who lives in Rome." Roger nodded toward the island in the river. "Whereas this little retreat now belongs to her former husband. Not enough for him, apparently— he made off with the painting, too, sometime in the past, oh, few weeks, say. According to information we've developed, he intends to secrete it away in the cottage. Do you see where this is headed?"

"Sure," Whitey said, opening the door. "Won't take five minutes."

Roger grabbed Whitey's arm, held on to it hard; Whitey didn't like that at all. "Intends, Whitey. I said intends."

"What the fuck does that mean?" Whitey said, shaking free of Roger's grip.

For one moment, Whitey saw a strange look in Roger's eyes, as though he was about to take a shot at him or something. Cold wind blew in the open door. Roger covered his eyes with his hand, rubbed them hard, and the look was gone. "My apologies, Whitey. This business can be . . . intense at times. Perhaps it's led me to be unclear somehow. What I'm saying is that the painting in question is not at present in the cottage. Not now, at this moment."

"No?"

"No."

Whitey closed the door.

"But it will be there tomorrow," Roger continued, "if we can rely on our information."

"Coming from where?"

"I beg your pardon?"

"This information," Whitey said, "where's it coming from?"

Roger stared at him for a moment, then smiled and answered, "Rome."

"Good enough," Whitey said. "Then tomorrow I go in and get it."

"You're way ahead of me, aren't you?"

"Well . . ."

"Yes, you go in, but not until night, at six-fifteen precisely."

" 'Cause of the darkness, right?"

"Partly. And partly because that's the earliest the painting will be there in an unguarded state."

"It's coming in a Brinks truck?" Whitey asked. Yes, he was sharp, couldn't remember ever being sharper.

"Nothing like that—this is just a domestic dispute. But why court acrimony?"

That made sense—Whitey wanted nothing to do with guards or courts. "You're telling me," he said.

"We're agreed, then. You go in at six-fifteen, not a moment before, not a moment after. And this is very important, Whitey: you arrive by taxi."

"Taxi?"

"Available at the bus station in Nashua. Have the driver drop you at the gate—and get a receipt."

"What for?"

"Reimbursement, of course."

Meaning? Whitey wasn't quite sure. "But what about the driver?" he asked.

"What about him?"

"Making me in a lineup or something."

"Lineup! What an imagination you've got, Whitey. This can never become a legal matter. The painting belongs to the woman in Rome. The ex-husband has no standing to pursue it. Any law enforcement agency would laugh him off, I assure you."

Silence.

"Understood?" Roger said.

Was it? A lot of blah-blah but basically it came down to six-fifteen, taxi, painting. "It's not complicated," Whitey said.

"You may have a real future in this business," Roger told him.

Whitey grunted.

"Once beyond the gate," Roger went on, "you cross the river and enter the cottage." He handed Whitey a key. "Don't turn on any lights. You'll need a flash. Save the receipt. Upstairs are two bedrooms. The one on the right is not made up. The painting will be hidden somewhere inside it. I'll be told the location at exactly six-thirty. There's a phone on the bedside table and I'll call from the car and tell you where it is. Then you simply collect it, recross the river, and return here, where we are now. I'll be waiting. Any questions?"

It was a snap; Whitey grasped the whole scenario, even the parts he hadn't been told. "The woman—she's going to call you from Rome, right?"

"No putting anything past you."

"And the place used to belong to her—that's how come you have the key."

"Another bull's-eye." Roger punched him softly on the shoulder. "And one more thing."

"What's that?"

"She doesn't want the frame."

"How come?"

"How come?" Roger drew a deep breath. "I believe it was chosen by the mother-in-law."

"I get it."

"And since she doesn't want the frame," Roger continued, "you'll have to cut the painting out."

"With what?"

"Something sharp," Roger said.

Whitey knew what was coming, beat Roger to the punch. "Save the receipt?" he said.

Roger shook his head in admiration.

23

"Sleep well?" Roger said.

Monday morning. Francie, who hadn't slept at all, came downstairs to the kitchen and found Roger standing at the stove, glancing up from a cookbook to smile at her over his reading glasses, doing something with eggs.

"Yes, thanks," Francie said, trying and failing to recall any previous time he'd done something with eggs.

"Good," said Roger, "good, good. Take a pew—chow'll be down in a jiff."

Take a pew? Chow? Jiff? Francie took another look at him, saw exhilaration in the flush on his face, in the sprightliness of his movements. "More news about the job?" Francie said.

He paused, steel whisk poised above the blue gas flames. "Job?" he said.

"In Fort Lauderdale."

"Oh, that. Promising, as I believe I mentioned. More and more promising all the time."

There was one place set at the table. He gestured to it with the whisk.

"Aren't you eating?" Francie said.

"I already have. Up betimes."

Francie sat down, although she wasn't hungry at all. Roger bustled over with a plate of eggs and toast. He watched her, beaming, as she tasted the eggs.

"Delicious," she said. They were. Why was this talent emerging now, after so many years spent anywhere but the kitchen? "You can cook, Roger."

"Much like a chemistry experiment," he said. "And you never know when it might prove useful."

Lauderdale: that was his way of telling her it was going to happen, that he'd soon be cooking for himself in some one-bedroom condo on a waterway, that what was left of their marriage would fade to a civilized end. But it was too late for her and Ned. She had proved to herself that she could cheat—the word people used, as Nora said, no point avoiding it—proved she could make a mockery of Swift's *Marriage Service from His Chamber Window*, but she couldn't do it with Anne's husband. A long, confused night of thought and counterthought had boiled down to that: not with Anne's husband. She was surer of that than anything she'd been sure of in her life. All that remained was telling him so in person, at the cottage in—she checked her watch—a little more than ten hours.

Roger went to the cupboard, returned with a jar of Dundee's. "Last of the marmalade," he said, spooning some—too much—onto the edge of her plate. "You might as well finish it off." Then he poured coffee for both of them and sat across the table. Francie managed two forkfuls of eggs and half a slice of toast; her body had its priorities, wanted no food until she had done the right thing.

"Ever been to the Empire State Building, Francie?" Roger asked.

"With my father, when I was ten. Why?"

"Or China?"

"You know I have—on the NEA trip. What are you getting at?"

"Getting at? Nothing, really. Maybe we should do more traveling, that's all. Think of all there is to do and see, had we but world enough and time, et cetera."

Francie sipped her coffee. It, too, was excellent, better than hers.

"Possibly with another couple," Roger went on.

She put down her cup.

"Anne and Ned, for example," he continued. "A pleasant evening, didn't you think? Although I can't say much for the restaurant."

Francie said nothing.

Roger tilted his cup to his face, revealing those white nose hairs—it hadn't been her imagination—then set the cup carefully down in the saucer, as though the object were to make no clinking of porcelain on porcelain. "Does he play tennis?"

"Who?"

"Who? Ned, of course. Ned Demarco." He watched her. "You're not ill, are you?"

"I don't know if he plays."

"No? I thought Anne might have mentioned it."

"Not to my knowledge."

"Because if he does, I might pick up the old racquet again myself. How does a week of mixed doubles in the Algarve sound? Or possibly Sardinia."

"I didn't think we were in the financial position for that sort of thing."

Roger's eyes left hers. He picked up the empty marmalade jar. "Perhaps not at this moment," he said, carrying it to the sink.

Francie rose. "I'd better get going." She paused at the door that led down to the garage. "I may be late tonight."

Roger opened the cabinet under the sink. "As you wish," he said, and dropped the jar in the trash.

A dark day, the clouds so low and thick that the streetlamps of the city remained lit for the morning commute, and headlights glowed from every car. Dark, too, in Francie's office, where the phone was ringing as she came in the door. She picked it up.

"Francie?"

"Nora."

"Thought you might call yesterday," Nora said. "Maybe to explain that teary little scene in the locker room."

"Anne was upset, that's all. About losing."

"And what about you, babycakes?"

"Me?"

"Were you upset about losing, too?"

"I don't like to lose. You know that."

"But I've never seen you look like that about it," Nora said. "I've never seen you look like that about anything."

The words marshaled themselves in Francie's mind: *I've got something to tell you, Nora.* But she didn't voice them, couldn't, not without making Nora her accomplice, or risking the loss of Nora's friendship, or damaging Anne. Those were the three possibilities, none acceptable, the worst being damaging Anne, and therefore Em as well. Francie hadn't done any damage yet, had to keep things that way for only a matter of hours more, had to put everything, resolved and unresolved, in a box and close it forever. So instead of *I've got something to tell you, Nora,* she replied, "There's always a first time."

"And you do what you have to do, what goes around comes around, you get what you pay for. Are we going to talk in clichés from now on?"

"You and I?" Francie said. But she saw it was possible, a possibility her mind squirmed from.

"You and I. Something's wrong, very wrong, and you're not telling me."

"Nothing's wrong."

"Bullshit," Nora said. "Bullshit, bullshit, bullshit. Not

only is something wrong, but it's something you can't handle by yourself."

Francie didn't dare speak, knowing that nothing she said could be right.

"Tell you what," said Nora, sounding a little more gentle, as gentle as Francie had ever heard her, in fact, although most people would have called her tone crisp, "I'll meet you somewhere after work. How's five-thirty?"

"I can't."

"Why? It's not Thursday."

"What do you mean, not Thursday?"

"For months now you haven't been available on Thursdays. I'm clumsy and slow, Francie, but I get there."

Francie almost spilled everything on the spot. What was left to spill? But she thought, *No damage yet,* and found a way out. "Now who's the bullshitter, Nora? There's nothing slow and clumsy about you, as you know. And this Thursday's fine. I'll meet you then."

A long pause, followed by: "You're too smart for me. See you then, babycakes."

"Bye."

"B—oh my God, I've got it. Anne's sick, isn't she?"

Francie held on to the phone.

"Or—or you are." Francie heard a strange new note in Nora's voice, almost frantic. "Is that what those Thursdays are about, Francie, some kind of treatment?"

"I'm not sick," Francie said, but thought, *Is there something wrong with me, after all?*

"It's Anne, then."

"No."

"You don't have cancer?"

"No."

"Neither does she?"

"No."

Nora laughed with relief. "So it can't be that bad, can it? Whatever it is."

Francie was silent.

"See you on Thursday, then," Nora said. "How about Huîtres?"

"Somewhere else," Francie said. "I'll call you."

Francie left the lights off in her office. The world outside the windows grew darker. She did no work, just thought about what was to come. She would get to the cottage first, of course, as she always did, but would leave the woodstove unlit, wait for him in the kitchen with her coat on. Then, when he came in, she would stand and say, *It's over, Ned. Because of Anne it's over.* After that, whatever he said or tried to do, she would stick to that point: because of Anne. That was what couldn't be rationalized, argued away, compromised. *Just stick to it,* Francie told herself, *and stay out of the square little bedroom upstairs, whatever happens.*

But the thought of that little bedroom . . . her mind returned to it over and over—the brass bed, the comforter, what happened beneath. By three-thirty Francie had had enough: enough waiting, thinking, sitting still. She left the office, got her car from the parking garage, headed for New Hampshire.

The first snowflakes fell as Francie crossed the state line, tiny ones, laceless and hard. She barely noticed them, was too busy trying to cap all the memories her mind boiled with—black kayaks, those dark eyes, his skin; too busy clinging to her mantra: *It's over, because of Anne it's over.* She was going to be early, earlier than she had ever been. Perhaps she would light the woodstove after all, wait for him beside it. Nothing wrong with lighting the woodstove, was there? It wasn't necessary to sit in the cold, to fabricate symbolic expressions of her coming internal state. Everything could be normal tonight and she could still do her duty, as long as she didn't go up to the little bedroom. Then, out of nowhere, her mind offered up an image that would keep her out of that bedroom. The image: Anne's face, but the giant face of a two-stories-tall Anne, like a character in a children's book, watching through the bedroom window from the outside. There was nothing scary about Anne's face, but this image scared Francie just the same. She tried to blot it out and found it wouldn't go away.

Snow fell harder as Francie drove north, isolating her in a twilit cocoon, a strange cocoon that felt not the least protective. She was too preoccupied to notice the snow much, but she was very aware of the unprotected part.

24

At six-fifteen, precisely. Roger had been clear about the timing, clear about everything, going over and over the details until Whitey tuned out completely. He already had it all down pat in his mind anyway: the taxi, the receipts, the call from Rome, the hidden painting, the necessity for a cutting tool, a sharp one. Piece of cake. The only problem was Roger. Two things. First, it was now evident to Whitey that he was smarter than Roger. Second, after that toe-stepping bullshit, Roger couldn't be trusted, not completely. Whitey kept juggling those two things in his mind. Not too bright, not too reliable. Not too bright, so maybe his plan could be improved. Not too reliable, so Whitey would have to make any improvements on his own. He didn't grasp all that at once, but by the time his eyes opened Monday morning—Whitey waking slumped in the cab of his pickup in the parking lot of some suburban mall where he'd spent the night, running the engine for five or ten minutes every hour or so to keep warm—he had most of it.

Whitey checked his watch: not even six, still dark, just over twelve hours to go. He climbed down out of the pickup, pissed against somebody's tire, considered Roger's plan. For one thing, he didn't like the taxi part. He'd ridden taxis three or four times in his life and hadn't been comfortable, not with that meter ticking away. And, despite Roger's reassurance, why drag a witness into the picture, especially when he had the pickup? Funny, too, the pickup with REDEEMER now written on the side. Didn't people redeem things from pawnshops, things like paintings? Whitey tried to tie it together into some sort of joke, and almost did. All that thinking before he even finished his piss! His mind was sharp today, speeding as fast as it ever had, maybe faster. He had barely zipped up and returned to the cab before he had another thought, connected to the pawnshop idea—and Christ! to get this picture of how his own mind was working, making connections, redeemer and pawnshop—how amazing was that?

The pawnshop connection was this: How much was the garden painting worth? *My garden,* or *oh my garden,* or whatever the hell it was. Roger had never said anything about its value, just that it was part of a divorce dispute. But would anyone fight over something worthless? No. So the question was: How much? Whitey turned the key and goosed the engine a couple times, *vroom-vroom.* How much? A word almost came to mind, a word they used in war movies when some guy, usually the toughest, was sent ahead to check things out. The toughest guy, who just nodded and did whatever it took. Whitey put the pickup in gear and drove out of the mall parking lot.

He made a few stops along the way. First, a pizza place for breakfast: deep dish with everything and an extra-large Pepsi. Second, and by now he was almost in New Hampshire, a hardware store for his supplies: a flashlight, batteries, and something sharp. He was still searching for the right sort of sharp something when a clerk approached.

"What are you lookin' to cut?" asked the clerk.

Canvas. Painting canvas. But what was painting canvas,

exactly? Whitey wasn't sure. "Like cardboard," he said. "Heavy-duty cardboard."

"Heavy-duty cardboard," said the clerk, moving toward a bin. "This here should do you."

"What is it?"

"Box cutter."

"Does it come any bigger?"

"There's this one."

"I'll take it. And I need the receipt."

Third, a stripper's bar for lunch. Whitey sat by himself at the back, had a beer, a Polish sausage, another beer. That Polish sausage was something, squirting in his mouth with all those spices. They didn't serve food like that inside. The reminder of what he'd missed out on pissed him off a little and he ordered another beer—just the one, since he was on the job—plus a shot of bar whiskey, even though he could now afford better.

The place was packed: smoke, noise, suits and ties, hairy hands stuffing money into garter belts. Red garter belts, because it was Christmas, and some of the girls wore Santa Claus hats as well, but that was all. He watched them jiggle around, rub themselves against brass poles, bend over. He got a hard-on, all right, but it didn't last. The problem—and he could figure it out easily the way his mind was working today—was he could see right through everything. It was all a fake: those huge, hard tits, the way their hands went down and almost started going to work on themselves, but not quite, how they opened those lipstick mouths as though feeling pleasure while their eyes flickered here and there. They were pros and what he wanted were amateurs— amateur housewives, like the women in Rey's video. He wanted to show one of those amateur housewives what he could do, to make her make those sounds for real. Women, amateur women, were helpless when they were making those sounds, and the dick was the tool that did it. Sue Savard should have given him the chance. There was a body, a real amateur body. Whitey got hard again recalling it, ordered another beer—and a shot. This really was the last; when the glasses were empty and the hard-on was gone, he paid his bill and went outside.

Snow falling, just as he'd told Roger it would, falling hard, cleaning everything up, whitening the world. He'd always liked snow, now wondered for the first time—what a day he was having, mentally, and it had barely begun!—whether it had anything to do with his name. They'd called him Whitey because of his hair, of course, not because he liked snow, but maybe he liked the snow so much because of the name; identified with it, he thought, remembering a word the prison shrink used all the time. And right after remembering that word, he remembered another: *reconnoiter,* what the toughest guy did in the war movies. He wiped his windshield clear with the sleeve of his leather jacket, got in the pickup, drove on. Time to reconnoiter.

Whitey came in sight of the Merrimack a couple hours ahead of schedule. That was one variation from the plan. No taxi was a second. And now came a third: Whitey didn't cross the river, over to the side with the gate, the lane through the sloping meadow, the jetty, those frozen-in dinghies. He had his reasons. What sense did that six-fifteen precisely shit make when it would be dark long before then—soon, in fact? And what had Roger said about a Brinks truck? Wouldn't be too smooth to run into that on the way in, would it? But the biggest reason was that Roger had stepped on his toe. No excuse for that, no forgiveness. He was a free man now, and much more, an administrative assistant, a professional. He had rights. And what he had in mind wouldn't be difficult. He knew his way around these woods. Whitey recalled that Roger had asked him about that at the gator farm, almost in those same words: *Know your way around the woods up there?* Probably figured Whitey for this job at that very moment; maybe Roger was a little smarter than he'd thought. But not in Whitey's league, especially not on a day like today. Following back roads on the east side of the river, Whitey sped north, fishtailing around the curves. He knew the woods, and he was one hell of a driver.

Snow fell harder. The plows gave up on the back roads and the traffic dwindled to nothing, except for Whitey in his pickup. When the time came, he didn't even pull to the side to put on the chains, just stopped in the middle of the road and got them out of the truck bed. So quiet with the snow all around like cotton, he could hear his own pulse. He climbed back in the cab, switched on the radio, but couldn't find the metal station they'd picked up in Roger's car. The station had been playing Metallica, but not "Master of Puppets," his all-time favorite Metallica song. He felt like hearing it now: *Master of puppets I'm pulling your strings, twisting your mind and smashing your dreams.* Pure poetry, but Whitey couldn't find the station and kept going in silence.

He spotted the island from the top of a rise. It looked different from this side of the river, wilder because the cottage was almost hidden from sight by those big trees and everything whiter even than yesterday, snow coating not just the branches and the roof but the trunks themselves, and the sides of the cottage. Whitey found a lookout two or three hundred yards farther on, drove to the end of it, his chains crunching on the unpacked snow. From this angle, on the edge of a steep incline leading down to the river, he had a view of the upstream end of the island, and beyond it the long sloping meadow on the other side. He saw no sign of a Brinks truck, or anything else; nothing moved except the snow, angling down now as the wind began to rise. Whitey turned up the heat.

He watched the island, the unlit windows of the cottage, the smokeless air above the chimney. What were the details of the garden painting? Nothing to do with hockey, he recalled, but something about a girl in a miniskirt. Eating grapes, was that it? Sounded kind of interesting, just on its own, but the question, the big question, as Whitey saw it now, remained: How much?

Snow. Supposing, Whitey thought, you were a Brinks truck driver, and you knew snow was on the way. Wouldn't you try to beat the weather, make your delivery earlier, in the morning, say? Sure as shit you would. Meaning the painting was already there, and any tracks left on the lane through the meadow were wiped out, as was the lane itself. Whitey checked his watch: 4:15, precisely. Precisely, you fucker. Roger would be waiting for him at the gate in a little more than two hours. Meanwhile snow was falling harder and harder, and now darkness was falling, too. Someone planning to cross the river would be smart to do it soon, while he could still see where he was going. There was no one around to see *him* in this storm, so the argument about waiting for darkness didn't stand up anymore. Brinks truck, cover of darkness—no longer factors. Was there another reason for him not to go now? Whitey couldn't think of one; at the same time, he could feel the key Roger had given him, an ordinary brass key, inside his pocket, waiting there against his thigh, pressing on his skin. Paintings could be worth millions. Millions: wouldn't that be something? A garage full of cars—Benz, Porsche, the biggest goddamn pickup on the market—plus any woman he wanted. He could advertise for them, for Christ's sake, and they'd come running with their tongues hanging out.

Whitey clipped the flashlight to his belt and opened

the door. All these reasons, all this back-and-forth, all this thinking, but it came down to one thing: he couldn't wait to get inside. Back in action. Yes! He climbed out of the pickup, locked the door—no one around, but you never knew—and looked around for the easiest route down to the river, the easiest route down, but more important, the easiest route back up. Roger could sit by the gate on the other side all night if he wanted. Meanwhile, he'd be on his way to—to somewhere—with a million-dollar painting in his truck. The idea of it made Whitey laugh to himself a couple of times. He stopped laughing when he realized he'd almost forgotten the box cutter. Whitey unlocked the door and took it off the seat.

Whitey started down, slipping and sliding on the snowy bank in his cowboy boots, grabbing at branches for support with one hand, holding the box cutter in the other, but never in danger of falling. He did know his way around the woods, and he'd always had great balance, had been up on skates at the age of two. As he walked across the river, plodded, really, sinking to the knees with every step, snow getting inside his boots but not bothering him at all, he felt for the first time the full force of his freedom. He was a giant, could do anything—reach the island in a single bound, rip one of those trees right out of the earth, smash the cottage to bits with it. The song came to him again and he sang it as he went, the wind driving thick snowflakes right into his mouth. *Master of puppets I'm pulling your strings, twisting your mind and smashing your dreams.*

Whitey walked onto the island. Moving under the shelter of those big trees, he heard a sharp hooting high above, glanced up, saw an owl making shivering motions, shaking the snow off its feathers. It stopped shivering as he watched, stared down at him with yellow eyes.

Whitey stepped up to the porch through smooth, untrodden snow. He brushed more of it off the little round window set in the front door, put his face to the glass: a shadowy kitchen, everything gray except the half-full bottle of red wine on the table. No sound, no movement, no armed guards. Whitey took out the brass key, tried to put it into the lock. It wouldn't go. He had a horrible moment, even began to hear that panicky buzz. Had Roger lied to him? But why? And worse, was it some kind of setup? He glanced around, saw no one, just snow swirling through the trees. Then, probably because his mind was working so well today, he solved the problem just like that, solved the problem by sticking the key in his mouth. Whitey gave it a good lick, tried again. The warm wet key slid right in. He turned it, opened the door, went inside. A little avalanche tumbled in after him; he closed the door as well as he could, without actually bothering to bend down and get rid of all the snow now packed in against the riser.

Whitey looked around: a pine-smelling cottage, all polished and clean, the kind that belonged to rich people from the city. He picked up the bottle of wine. Chateau something: French. What had he had a shot of at Sue Savard's? Gin. He pulled the cork with his teeth, took a hit. He'd only drunk wine once or twice, so long ago he didn't remember the taste, just that he hadn't liked it. He didn't like it now. Maybe he'd get used to it. Rich people, the kind who owned million-dollar paintings, drank wine. He moved through the dining room, more quiet and careful than in the old days, around the corner to the living room, found the stairs. They rose up into darkness. *Don't turn on any lights. You'll need a flash.* Whitey unclipped his flashlight, switched it on, started up. Outside the owl hooted. The sound sent a jolt through Whitey, but not a sharp one, not sharp enough to set off the panicky buzz, although he did tighten his grip on the box cutter.

Upstairs are two bedrooms. Whitey shone his light into each, one made up, one not. That was where things got a little complicated. The painting was hidden in one of them, but which? Roger hadn't made that clear, as usual. Whitey went into the made-up bedroom, facing the side of the river with the jetty and the dinghies, now completely buried under the snow, and the sloping meadow, featureless in the failing light. From this spot, he'd easily see any headlights, Roger's, for example. He checked his watch, found he couldn't read it without the flash. Four-fifty-one. Plenty of time.

But which room? Fucking Roger. Whitey went into the one that wasn't made up because searching it would be easier. He saw a closet, a chest of drawers, a bed. He opened the closet. There was a shelf at the top. He reached up, ran his hand along it, found nothing but dust. Empty wire hangers hung on the rail. On the floor lay a single pair of shoes: women's shoes. Whitey picked them up, soft leather shoes, deep red in color. He shone his light inside one, read *Fratelli Rossetti, Roma*. He held it to his nose, sniffed deeply, smelled several smells he couldn't identify, and knew he wanted a woman, bad. An amateur housewife woman, yes, but of the special kind who would wear shoes like this. Once he had the painting, he could have a woman like that, more than one. A woman with Sue Savard's body, but—what was the word?—a classier face. To get a blow job from a woman with a classy face: wouldn't that be something?

Where was he? Right. Looking for the painting, the garden painting with the girl in the miniskirt, sucking on grapes. Not in the closet. He tried the chest of drawers, opening the bottom one first because he'd seen the technique used years before by burglars in an episode of *Miami Vice*; on the cell block, of course. There was nothing in the drawer but a magazine called *Bellissima*, with a beautiful woman on the cover. Whitey leafed through it and found nothing interesting; women, all right, but modeling clothes and makeup instead of fucking, sucking, and begging for it up the ass. Besides, the writing was in another language.

Whitey opened the next drawer, leaving the bottom one open as well. That was the point: you could work faster if you didn't have to take the time to close one drawer to get to the next one. On the other hand, leaving the drawers open meant that the break-in would be discovered by the first person who entered the house. Had Roger said anything about covering his traces? Whitey couldn't remember. But why not cover them? He closed the next drawer from the bottom, closed the bottom one, reopened the one above. There was nothing inside.

And nothing in any of the others. Whitey paused, drumming his fingers on the wood. Where would he hide the painting? Under the chest? Down on his hands and knees he peered under the chest and, while he was there, turned and swept the beam of his flash under the bed. Nada. He got up, raised the bare mattress, saw nothing but bare springs. Quiet and careful, but not fun, like all those other break-ins long ago, grabbing all those toasters and TVs. This was a drag, and pissed him off. His gaze fell on the mattress. Was it in there? He slashed at the mattress with the box cutter. It sliced through the covering with surprising ease, exposing the stuffing. Whitey tore it out by the fistful until he was sure the painting wasn't inside. No painting, but a big fucking mess. That answered the question of whether he should cover his tracks. No way was he about to pack all that shit inside by flashlight and do whatever else—he couldn't begin to even imagine the steps involved—he'd have to do to make everything look normal.

So, no painting, and it was 5:13. What next? He remembered the other bedroom.

Whitey crossed the hall and entered it. His light glinted on the window, a mirror, a vase full of dead flowers. Same kind of room as the other one, but all made up, meaning more work. Work made him thirsty, and maybe that wine hadn't been as bad as he'd first thought. Whitey went downstairs and downed the bottle.

Back in the made-up bedroom, feeling better, Whitey got busy. By now he had a system—systems were the sign of an administrative assistant, a professional man, an operative like him. He began with the closet. Two life jackets hung on the rail, and a terry-cloth robe. Whitey sniffed the robe and smelled something faint, faint but nice. Then he pointed the beam along the shelf, a high shelf, higher than the one in the other room. Something at the back caught his eye. A box, round and silvery. Jewelry? Whitey stuck the box cutter between his teeth and reached up for it. A slippery box: as he drew it toward the front of the shelf, it slipped from his grasp, started to fall. He grabbed at it, missed, and the box fell to the floor, bouncing off his head on the way down. The next thing Whitey knew there was powder all over the place and he was sneezing—perfumed powder on his jacket, up his nose, sticking to his face. He patted his hair, checked his hand under the light: sticky pink powder, now on his palm and fingers, too.

What the fuck? Whitey thought. He found the silvery box in a corner of the room, examined it under the light: Lancôme, he read, and more writing in another language. He threw the box at the wall, hard. On the follow-through, the flash in his other hand shone up in his face and he saw himself in the mirror, the box cutter between his teeth and his hair, pink. He snatched the box cutter from his mouth, said, "What the fuck?" aloud.

Whitey went to the mirror, brushed at his hair, couldn't get rid of the powder, stinking faggot powder all over himself. He checked his watch—pink powder on it, too: 5:22. He had time. Time for what? Face it. There was no fucking painting. The storm had kept the Brinks truck away, would keep Roger away, too. Nothing left to do but haul his ass out of there, back across the river, back to the pickup. But first a shower. He wasn't going anywhere covered in pink.

Whitey went into the hall between the bedrooms, left into the bathroom, jabbed his beam here and there: toilet, sink with a toothbrush and toothpaste in a wall cup, towel on a hook, shower. He turned on the hot tap, not expecting hot, since the tank would be switched off for the winter. Whitey didn't care, since cold didn't bother him, but it was nice when hot started flowing anyway; if not hot, at least warm. He laid the box cutter and his watch on the rim of the sink, positioned the flashlight on the toilet tank so it pointed at the shower, then stripped off his clothes and stepped under the water.

"Ah." It felt good. Whitey realized he had a little alcohol hum going in his body, the way you sometimes realize that in showers. He wasn't drunk or hammered or anything, just humming. *Master of puppets I'm pulling your strings, twisting your mind and smashing your dreams.*

Shampoo, there on the little tile shelf. He held it to the light: Principessa, and more foreign writing. Christ, it was like he'd left the country or something, gone far away. He squeezed a big dollop on his palm, started scrubbing his hair. Scrub, scrub. He worked his way down, reached his dick, first just cleaning it, then thinking, what the hell, he had time, when the water went cold, just like that. Whitey turned off the tap and got out of the shower, the flash spotlighting his neglected dick, already down to semi-hard. He reached for the towel, hanging on the hook, and went still.

A footstep. He'd heard a footstep, downstairs. Whitey had a funny thought, a thought that scared him, awoke the panicky buzz: the last time Sue Savard had been in the shower and this time it was him. So what Whitey-thing was down below?

25

The box cutter lay on the rim of the sink. In the spreading cone of light from the flash, Whitey could see the blade glinting there in easy reach, but could he pick the thing up cleanly, without first knocking it into the basin or on the floor, or making some other noise? He wrapped the towel around himself, extended his right hand toward the sink, saw how it shook; that had to be the booze, couldn't be fear—he was as tough as they come. Whitey took a few deep, silent breaths to sober up. He heard the wind outside—it had risen to a howl while he was in the shower—but he didn't hear another footstep. Maybe he'd imagined it, maybe it was nothing but the old roof beams creaking in the storm. Yeah, the beams for sure, or possibly—

He heard another footstep, a footstep beyond any doubt, and snatched up the box cutter without making a sound, quick as a snake. The next moment, not even aware of having done it, Whitey had the flash in his other hand, switched off. Total darkness, black as black could be, his friend. He waited, motionless, listening for more footsteps, hearing none. An idea came to him: maybe the Brinks truck had turned up after all, not early, but late, because of the snow. Made more sense. If so, they would be coming up the stairs any second to hide the painting in one of the bedrooms. All he had to do was stay where

245

he was, silent and still—and hope that the Brinks men just did their job and hit the road, hope that none of them had to take a piss. Then, with any luck, he could still grab the painting and get out before Roger arrived. This was going to work!

It was all in the timing. What time was it? Where was his watch? He'd just seen it. He remembered: on the rim of the sink—a digital watch he'd stolen on the cell block, but a cheap one without a glow button. That meant he would have to switch on the flash to read it. Too risky. Thank Christ his mind was working so well today. Whitey stepped back into the shower. He set the flashlight carefully down, freeing his hand to silently draw the curtain, one of those curtains that was not quite transparent, not quite opaque. The air in the shower stall quickly lost its warmth, but Whitey didn't care—he'd never minded the cold, was sweating anyway.

The sound of the storm rose higher. Listening only for footsteps, Whitey was slow to hear the change in tone, a low rumble that mixed in like a bass line. Then the wind slackened for a moment, and he heard the new component clearly, felt it through the icy tiles of the shower: something motorized down below, electrical—a generator. Of course there'd be a generator out here on an island in the middle of the—

A thin strip of light shone through the crack under the bathroom door. Fucking Jesus. They'd turned on the lights, and darkness was his friend. Brinks guards carried guns, didn't they? How many could he take out, how fast? Some, for sure: he could do things when that buzz was buzzing in his brain, and it was buzzing. Everything depended on how many there were—if they opened the door at all. He almost wanted them to now, to pay for making him sweat like this.

Footsteps on the stairs, slow, very slow, but coming up.

Whitey heard some good news in those footsteps: First, there was only one set of them, only one person, although that didn't mean there weren't others waiting downstairs. And second, that one person had a light tread, so probably wasn't very big, certainly not as big as Whitey. He kept his eyes on the glowing crack under the door.

The footsteps, light, almost soundless, as though the guard was wearing tennis shoes, reached the landing and paused. Whitey could almost feel the guard going over his instructions. The footsteps receded into the bedroom that wasn't made up, and Whitey remembered the way he'd left it, mattress stuffing all over the floor. Before he had time to figure out what could come of that, there was a faint click—light switch going on—and another pause, longer than the first. Whitey waited for a call downstairs for help, a voice talking into a cell phone, a police whistle, something, but nothing happened. No movement at all, meaning the guard wasn't hiding the painting. Then the footsteps returned to the landing, paused again, continued into the other bedroom, where Whitey had had the powder accident.

Another click, another pause. Whitey heard a sniffing sound. Then came a few of those light footsteps, followed by another pause, and then a soft grunt, almost too soft to hear. A grunt: the kind you make when you're reaching for something, or—or bending down, like maybe to slide something under a bed! Whitey had astonished himself. His mind had never been like this, not even close. *All right,* he thought, *job done, split. Then my job: scoop up the painting, out the door, across the river, into a future full of money.* Whitey pictured his getaway clearly, at fast-forward speed.

But having hidden the painting, the guard didn't seem in a hurry to leave. Whitey heard the metallic clicking of wire hangers on the closet rail. Then came another one of those sniffing sounds. More footsteps. After that, a faint creaking, the kind bedsprings make. *For fuck sake,* Whitey thought, *don't take a goddamn nap.* But he knew he might do the same thing if he had a job like that. He was toying with the idea of silently slipping into the bedroom while the guard slept and whipping the painting right out from under him, when the bedsprings creaked again; another sniff, like the guy was smelling something— oh, Christ, that goddamn powder—and then more footsteps. Footsteps getting louder, coming closer. *Don't you start with me,* Whitey thought. Buzz buzz. *Get out of my fucking life.*

But that didn't happen. There was another pause. Whitey saw two black breaks in the lit crack under the bathroom door, breaks that would be made by two feet standing just outside. An armed guard on the other side of the door, and all Whitey had was a stupid little warehouse tool. His hand tightened around it.

Whitey heard another metallic sound: the doorknob turning. He retreated to the back of the shower; from there he couldn't see the crack under the door, hoped that meant the guard couldn't see him either. He heard the door open, heard the click of the switch, and the bathroom filled with light, blinding him. Even as it did, even as he blinked furiously and shaded his eyes, he remembered his clothes, all over the floor.

Sniff, sniff. Whitey, his eyes adjusting to the light, heard that sniffing, didn't move. A footstep, another, and another. Whitey clung to the box cutter: he wasn't going back to prison, no matter what. One more footstep, and then the guard was right in front of him, but turned toward the sink, his image blurred by the shower curtain. Not a big guard at all, holding something in his hand. A gun? No. More like—dead flowers, the dead flowers from the vase in the made-up bedroom.

No gun at all, as far as Whitey could see. In fact, the guard didn't seem to be wearing a uniform, but a long coat instead. The guard's other hand moved, picked up something from the sink—Whitey's watch. Slowly the guard's head came up, from the watch to the mirror over the sink. And in that mirror, through the translucent shower curtain but clear enough, Whitey got his first look at the face of the guard: not a guard, certainly not a Whitey-thing, not even a man. A woman. The relief was indescribable. He flung the curtain aside.

The woman spun around, dropping the watch, dropping the flowers, putting her hands to her mouth, making a lovely frightened little noise in her throat.

Whitey smiled. "Nothing to apologize about," he said, holding up his hand, the empty one. Totally in control, master of the situation. Master reminded him of masturbate—was there a connection between the two words?—and of what he'd been about to do before the water turned cold. No longer necessary. "Nothing at all," he said. "I know you've got a job to do."

She backed up as far as she could before the sink stopped her. "Job?" she said. Whitey liked her voice, an educated voice, classy. He saw that the woman was just that: classy. This was no pocket-change whore like that pockmarked hag in Florida. This woman had snow melting in her hair, soft skin, innocent eyes. She was pure, amateur, perfect. She was the one. The buzzing rose and rose inside him.

"The painting, and whatnot," Whitey explained, not sure his voice was at the right volume, with the buzzing so loud.

Painting—the word got her attention; he could see that in her eyes, and what eyes, unlike any female eyes that had ever looked at him. And she was looking at him, no doubt about it.

Looking right at him, so why pussyfoot? Why beat around the bush? Whitey almost laughed aloud at his own wit. Almost, but he had to be cool. Cool as he could be, he hit her with his best shot: "How about us two we go back into that bedroom and see what we can see?"

The woman's eyes, still on him, shifted a little, gazed down, came to the glass cutter in his hand. He had forgotten to hide it behind his back, and anyway it was a box cutter. Glass cutter was the last time, not that it—

And then she was gone, just like that. Whitey had never seen a woman move so fast. He moved, too, out of the shower, out of the bathroom, onto the landing in time to see something he hardly believed, the woman leaping right from the top, taking the entire staircase in the air, hitting the ground floor with a loud squeak of her tennis shoes, her body contracting into a ball to absorb the force of the fall, staying on her feet. By that time, Whitey was halfway down himself, saw her darting off toward the living room, following the L to the dining room, kitchen, the door. He chased her, making storm-like howls of his own as he remembered his mother chasing him around the yard, her belt buckle whistling past his ear, beside himself with the tremendous charge of it all. But the woman—what a body she must have under that coat!—was fast, really fast, almost as fast as he was. He didn't catch her until she reached the door, forced to slow down to jerk it open. She actually had it halfway open, was on the point of disappearing into the storm on those quick feet, when Whitey sprang right over the kitchen table, flew across the room, and caught her a good one with his shoulder.

A real good one. The woman bounced off the door-jamb, back into the room, sprawled facedown on the floor. Whitey caught his breath, picked himself up, walked over to her. She was already up on her hands and knees. He bent over, got one hand in her hair—beautiful hair, so soft and clean, he'd never felt anything like it—raised her head, held the box cutter to her throat.

"This is going to be something else," he told her.

But then somehow she was rolling out of his grasp, leaving him with a handful of hair and a sharp pain, high up the inside of his leg: the bitch had tried to kick him in the balls. He tripped her up; she fell again, knocking the table over; he leaped on top of her—leaped right into the path of the wine bottle, already in her hand, arcing at his head. The bottle caught him right in the face, smashing against his nose, broken glass digging deep long tracks down his cheeks. He saw nothing but red, but at least she was under him; he could feel her wriggling. Whitey got hold of her somewhere, he didn't even know where, but it didn't last: wriggle, wriggle and she was out from under, rolling again, getting away. He slashed out blindly with the cutter, a last, desperate try, and felt the blade slice home, dig deep in flesh. At the same moment, he heard a loud pop—her Achilles, you lucky bastard—and a cry of pain. Lucky, lucky bastard, because she was down again, crawling toward the door, yes, but her running days were over. Whitey crawled after her, through a red haze, jabbing with the cutter. The woman swung round, still had a piece of the bottle, got him again, got him in the face again! He was fighting a fucking woman for his life. Whitey went crazy. Slash slash slash with the cutter. And some more.

Silence.

Not quite silence, Whitey realized after a while. There was a dripping sound, drip drip. He got to his knees, found the towel he'd been wearing, wiped blood from his eyes, picked shards of glass from his face, wiped more blood. The woman lay still, what was left of her. He wanted to kill her even though she was dead.

Time passed. Drip drip. Whitey gripped some piece of overturned furniture, pulled himself to his feet. He gazed around, reeled a little, made his slow way back around the L, through the dining room, living room, then even more slowly up the stairs. He went into the bathroom, sat on the toilet, put on clothes, took a breather, put on the rest of them. His watch was frozen at 5:33. He dropped it in the wastebasket.

Whitey went into the made-up bedroom, lowered himself to the floor, hands on the bed to support his weight. He checked under the bed: no painting. *Garden,* or whatever it was. No painting at all. He knelt there breathing for a while, then got up, went downstairs, back along the L, past the woman, out the door.

Still snowing. Whitey felt cold at once, much colder than he'd ever been. He walked as far as he could, two hundred feet or so, and sat down to rest with his back against one of those big trees.

While he rested, Whitey noticed that he'd left the lights on in the cottage. Was that smart? He tried to think— painting, divorce, Brinks truck, *six-fifteen precisely*—and got nowhere. Nothing added up. Didn't matter anyway: maybe he had the strength to get back across the river; he didn't have the strength to go back inside and close things down first. Where was that box cutter, by the way?

And other things. Whitey was trying so hard to think of other things he might have left behind that he almost didn't notice a flash of headlights on the east side of the river, where the pickup was. A flash in a snow-filled sky, and then gone: his imagination again? What was this imagination all of a sudden? Then the pain started: no imagining that.

Whitey thought about getting up, almost did once or

twice. That woman: he didn't understand her at all, had never dreamed there could be a woman like that. She'd ruined him. *Master of puppets I'm pulling your strings, twisting your mind and smashing your dreams.* Whitey didn't sing the words aloud, just mouthed them. That was a good thing because sometime later a figure came out of the shadows behind the house.

A tall figure, certainly a man this time, almost as tall as Whitey. He carried something in his hand and bent low as he went by the dining-room windows so he wouldn't be seen from inside. A cunning kind of guy—Whitey could tell right away. The cunning guy crept around to the door. The porch light gleamed on what he had in his hand: an ax. The cunning guy slowly straightened, peeped quickly in through the round window. The next moment he whirled around and scanned the darkness. The porch light shone clear on his face: Roger. He was looking in Whitey's direction but would never see him, not through all that falling snow, not in that darkness. Darkness was Whitey's friend.

Raising the ax, Roger pushed the door open and went inside. Whitey forgot about his weakness and pain, stood up at once. He headed for home. High above, the owl hooted, or it might have been something new in the storm.

26

Snow, handled by Roger's car with ease, but as he drove up the eastern side of the river—despite and because of what he'd told Whitey, Roger had no intention of crossing to the gate side until it was all over and time to call in the local constabulary—he began to think he'd had enough of northern winters, perhaps enough of America itself. Rome: mild in winter, homogeneous in culture, and how long would it take to learn the language? Two or three months? An expensive city, of course, but with the insurance settlement, plus whatever he retained from the sale of the house—and the market was improving at last—supplemented by his pension and Francie's, there would be enough to meet his modest needs. *Roma aeterna, Roma invicta.* Latin had been one of his strongest subjects; therefore, he could assume that the vocabulary was already in place. Call it six weeks to moderate fluency, two months at most.

A necessary result of the execution of his plan, of course, would be some sort of contact with Brenda. She would probably attend the funeral; indeed, it would be his obligation to inform her of it. No doubt she would feel some sort of misplaced responsibility, given the involvement of her cottage. A drama easily foreseen: hand-wringing, if onlys, et cetera. He would absolve her.

Thus they would have roles to play with each other, right from the start, his infinitely sympathetic. Simpatico.

Roger came to the lookout he had chosen, a treeless ledge on a rise almost opposite Brenda's island, but on the east side of the river. It wasn't a question of distrusting Whitey, but more that concepts like trust couldn't fairly be applied to someone like him. Whitey responded to stimuli, a frog in a laboratory, and although Roger had done all that could be done to predetermine the stimuli Whitey was about to encounter, he could not, because of randomness, unpredictability, chaos theory, account for them all. Better, then, if the frog expects the scientist to approach from the left, to approach from the right.

Roger checked the time—5:40. On schedule, despite the snow, everything still according to plan. He used the singular for convenience, but to be accurate there were three plans: the plan as it was understood by Whitey, the plan as it would be executed by the participants, the master plan laid out in Roger's mind like lines of programming language or a sequence of DNA. DNA, that was it—and Whitey not a frog, but a gene of the most mutable type, capable of warping whole chromosomes, of growing into a monster. A monster under Roger's command: deployed in the unused bedroom, searching for a painting that wasn't there—although it existed, would be disposed of in the denouement, when Roger resigned from the tennis club and cleaned out his locker, perfect reason to be there with a plastic garbage bag. Funny—creative, really—this use he'd made of the painting, like Picasso making a bull from bicycle parts. But a minor detail. Major detail: the monster trapped as Francie and her oyster boy came up the stairs. Would it happen right then, Whitey making some little mistake that gave away his presence, leading to panic, his and theirs? Or would they get safely to their little nest, begin doing the things they did, with Francie crying out her petty pleasures, and Whitey listening and listening until he could hear no more, bear no more; he would want some, too, lots and lots.

And all the time, Roger would be waiting in the woodshed at the back, arriving not after Whitey but before; not waiting at the gate, as Whitey expected, but coming inside, to react with horror.

"Whitey, what have you done?"

And Whitey makes his stupid reply.

And Roger, saving the day, commands, "We've got to get this cleaned up. Come quick."

They run together, a team, to the woodshed, where the props stand ready.

"Hand me that mop, Whitey, in there." Prop one.

Whitey reaches down, baring his neck for the ax. Prop two.

Lines of programming language.

How quiet it would be after that, a tranquil interlude for arranging bodies, adjusting evidence, driving over the river bridge, around to the gate, parking his car beside the others, dialing 911, waiting to tell his story. A story slightly different from the one he'd first outlined, changes necessitated by the addition of the lover—horrible oleaginous word, quite appropriate in this case—to the dramatis personae. A story that now went like this: *A Christmas Eve surprise party, Officer, for Ned's wife—she was so upset over that tennis match. The three of us were meeting here tonight to put up the decorations, with the idea of having everything ready when we brought her here on the twenty-fourth. A surprise, you see, to show how we all care, to cheer her up. But when I arrived, a little late, what with the snow and all, I found . . . [breaks down, composes self] And he saw me, Officer, and I—I pan-*

icked. I ran and ran. He chased me, caught me by the woodshed. We struggled, I remember falling, grabbing the ax; it's all a jumble after that.

All a jumble, but beautifully organized, planned like a mini-Creation: Roger even had a bag of red decorations in the car. *Merry Christmas, Noel, Joy to the World.* Prop three.

Roger pulled off the road, parked in the lookout—and saw another car parked nearby. A pickup truck, actually, but so covered by the blown snow, it was hard to tell. Abandoned, perhaps, possibly for the duration of the storm, possibly forever. Putting on his hat and gloves, zipping up his parka, taking the decorations and his twelve-inch, heavy-duty flashlight from L.L. Bean, Roger got out of the car, locked it, started down toward the river, hunched against the wind. In its perfect, triple-helix form, the plan wound so beautifully in his mind that he almost didn't notice, almost didn't process an obvious sight in the middle of the river: lights shining on Brenda's island.

Lights? Lights on the island? Hadn't he been clear about the flash? Should he have supplied Whitey with one? No. He wanted Whitey to buy it himself, wanted the receipts for everything—taxi, flash, weapon—found on Whitey's body: the master plan. Roger tore off a glove, read his watch: 5:49. Lights at 5:49? There were to be no lights at any time, and Whitey wasn't to be inside until 6:15. Six-fifteen precisely, with Francie and lover arriving at 6:30. It was a two-bladed plan, timing and psychology snipping together like scissors. Timing had been the easy part. So why lights? Why lights at 5:49?

Roger hurried across the river, or tried to, but the snow was deep and light, and he sank to his waterproof, insulated-to-minus-forty-degree boot tops with every step. By the time he reached the island—lights glowing in every window of the cottage—he was breathing heavily.

Roger's mind fired possible explanations at him: Francie and lover had arrived early, or one or the other; Whitey had arrived early, gone inside because of the storm, forgotten about the lights; someone else— repairman, tramp, Brenda!—was inside; a surge in the wires had activated some automatic timer. And other explanations waited like bullets in an ammunition belt, but by now he was at the woodshed, reaching in, grabbing the ax, moving swiftly toward the cottage.

Swiftly, but not without thought. Smarter than ever in a crisis, or potential crisis, as he corrected himself, Roger remembered to crouch low as he went by the windows, staying out of sight from within. He heard nothing from inside: no voices, no music, no movement. The electric surge–automatic timer explanation rose higher on the list. A simple matter to switch it off, restore darkness, hide as planned by the woodshed, continue as before, everything on schedule. He climbed onto the porch— and saw that the door wasn't quite closed.

Almost, but not quite: snow packed in against the riser. Therefore? Roger straightened out of his crouch, peered through the window. And saw disorder, all a jumble, all a scramble, red, red, red, but—

The deed was done.

Deed done, deed done, deed done; there she was, laid out facedown beside the overturned table, in tennis shoes, one white, one red, and her hair a new color, red, red, red. From idea to reality, from conception to birth: his plan had borne fruit. But—

No Whitey. No Whitey to close the circle with, to write the last line of code, to make it perfect.

Roger whirled around, whirling with his body as his mind was already whirling inside, stared into the night, into the storm, saw nothing but night and storm. Red, so much red: she'd struggled, fought, perhaps hurt Whitey— even, oh what luck that would be!—killed him. Was it possible? Could he still be inside, dead or dying? What a simple revision that would be; in a second or two an amended plan took shape in Roger's mind, complete. He shouldered the door open and went in, the ax in his hands.

Silence. Red in streaks, in drips, in pools; the cottage a shambles, the overused word never more fitting. Roger found a roll of paper towels on the counter, dried off the soles of his boots, mopped the damp tracks he'd already made, stuffed the paper towel in his pocket for later disposal—*flake of dandruff falls off your head, you fry*— and followed the red trail.

Dining room, living room: no Whitey. On the staircase: no Whitey. In the unused bedroom: cupboard drawers pulled out, mattress stuffing all over the floor, no Whitey in the closet, no Whitey under the bed. In the love-nest bedroom: red handprints on the duvet, a red row of penny-sized drops, almost perfectly straight, on the floor by the side of the bed, pink dust or powder here and there, perfumed air, no Whitey in the closet, no Whitey under the bed.

Roger tried the bathroom last: no Whitey curled up dying on the floor; a flashlight, not a body, in the shower. But someone had taken a shower—condensation still clung to the margins of the mirror. What else? More red: the tiles, the toilet, the sink; more perfumed powder—he realized the whole cottage was redolent of feminine scent; and a watch, Whitey's watch—Roger recognized it—in the wastebasket. He picked it out with his gloved hand. It had stopped at 5:33. He checked his own watch:

6:15. *Six-fifteen precisely.* What had happened? Theories readied themselves in his mind, but what good were they? The deed was only half done and Whitey was on the loose. Roger saw himself in the mirror, eyes enormous, deep V-shaped notch between them, ax in one hand, Whitey's watch in the other. He dropped the watch back in the wastebasket, started downstairs.

Down the stairs, through the living room, dining room, careful to avoid contamination with the red, mind working, working. Suppose—suppose the lover was on his way even now, due in twelve minutes? Suppose Whitey was lying out in the snow somewhere? Crawling toward the gate, perhaps, in hope of finding Roger. Ergo, what? Roger had no idea. No idea. That scared him. It wasn't a matter of cognition, knowing that he was in a dangerous situation. It was a matter of feeling fear. Had he ever felt fear before? Not like this.

Roger went into the kitchen, his body trembling now. He stared out the window, holding tight to the ax handle. Never this afraid, but never had he failed to sort his way through suppositions, premises major and minor; never had he failed to think. What had gone wrong? Francie and Whitey had both arrived early, but why? Who had been first? And then? And then? His mind, powered by those 181 IQ points, came up with nothing but question marks. All problems were fundamentally mathematical, yes, but in this case there were too many unknowns. The chaos butterfly had fluttered its wings. Clutching the ax in both hands, Roger plummeted down and down into depths of fear he hadn't imagined.

But that was nothing. Nothing, because the next moment, something caught his eye—a movement reflected in the glass. He whirled around, whirled again as he had whirled at the front door, again with his brain whirling inside: whirled around in time to see her raise her bloody head off the floor, see her turn toward him, see her look him right in the eye.

But not Francie. It was Anne.

27

Paralysis.

Roger knew paralysis for the first time in his life. He couldn't move, couldn't speak, couldn't even think: paralysis physical and mental, paralysis complete. All he could do was accept sensory input—not process it, not analyze, syllogize, parse, deconstruct, induce, deduce, subdivide, ramify—merely accept. The worst part was that during this period of paralysis, however long it lasted, and of that he wasn't sure, his eyes were locked on Anne's, the whole long time.

And hers on him.

As he watched, the intensity of light in Anne's eyes slowly changed, as though someone were adjusting the dimmer, turning it down. But not all the way. At one point, the dimming halted, and Anne opened her mouth and formed a word. No sound came out, but the word was clear: *Help*.

Roger didn't move. He had his reasons, knew them without thinking, since he couldn't think, a priori. First, this inexplicable paralysis. Second, he had no qualifications to provide help of the kind required. Third, he doubted it was in his interest. Of that he couldn't be sure, not with so much data missing, but if forced to make an unsupported mental leap, he would have had to conclude that the survival of Anne would be of no help to him. So: help, no. He just couldn't.

Roger didn't tell her that, didn't say *no*, because he couldn't speak, but perhaps she understood anyway. The dimming control inside her began to turn again, down, down, down to nothing this time. Her head dropped to the floor—no, not dropped, she lowered it delicately, or since she couldn't have had the strength for that, it was lowered delicately, as though by some unseen, protective force. Impossible, of course, the existence of such a force, for reasons too manifold to list.

With that, with her eyes no longer locked on his, her eyes still open, eyes in every manner but the essential, and therefore no longer eyes at all, Roger's paralysis lifted. His mind cried out at once for data, starved for it, writhing around inside him for the lack of it. Whitey and Anne: it made no sense. How would Anne ever have known about this place? Why would she have come here? Was it conceivable that she'd been conducting an investigation much like his, but from the other side? Roger didn't know. He needed data. Still, he couldn't quite ignore a feeling, not of satisfaction, because of the miscarriage of his plan, but of a related wistfulness, bittersweet, based on the realization that he had come so close. So close: some bug in the programming had upset the timing; some other factor, probably uncontrollable, was responsible for the presence of the wrong woman.

Enough. A digression, although at the speed his mind worked it probably lasted less than a second, and therefore cost him nothing. Data. Start with the time: 6:30. Six-thirty! Was it possible that Francie and her boy were still on their way, might walk in at any moment? Roger hurried to the door, stuck his head out, saw nothing but snow, falling straighter now, and less heavily; heard nothing but the wind in the trees, lower in tone. But, yes, it was possible. Roger glanced around the kitchen. Could he somehow clean up, hide the body, hide every trace? Probably not. Was it in his interest? Why would it be? It wasn't even in his interest to turn off the lights, in case the following question lay waiting for him in the future, in a courtroom, for example: *Who turned out the lights?* No. Simply get out and get out fast. And if they were coming? Roger didn't know. Then he thought: what if Whitey was even at this moment crawling to the gate? Simultaneously—it could still happen! Not as planned, but in essence. If only he could be lucky just once in this goddamned life. Roger took the ax and went outside.

He made his way across the river to the western bank, toiled up the snowed-in lane through the meadow. Snow fell, but lighter now, and the wind was dying. Wouldn't Whitey's tracks still be visible if he'd gone this way? Roger shone his light back and forth across the meadow, saw snow unmarred all around.

He reached the gate: locked. Beyond it sat one car, covered in snow but a minivan from the shape—not Francie's car, as he would have known at a glance had he come from this side, but Anne's. Could Whitey be curled up behind it, or possibly inside? Roger unlocked the gate, walked around the car. No Whitey. But inside? More than unlikely, almost impossible. But if Whitey was inside, then at least he could control the damage by simply finishing him off right there. It meant leaving evidence because he would first have to brush snow off the window. Decision: Roger stood by Anne's minivan, following long and complex ramifications through his mind. Then he brushed a swath of snow from the windshield and shone his light inside. No Whitey: just an open road map on the front passenger seat and a shopping bag from F.A.O. Schwarz in back. Were children involved? Roger didn't recall. He scooped up some snow, tossed it on the bare glass. It wouldn't cling for some reason, though he tried and tried. No matter. The falling snow would do the work, as it would cover his own tracks, tracks he saw clearly in the beam of his flash. He relocked the gate and started back to the island, failing to notice until he was almost there that the snowfall had stopped.

No snow, therefore tracks, L.L. Bean tracks, therefore—what? Process, process, process, Roger instructed his mind. But instead of processing, his mind writhed. "How much fucking data do you need?" he said aloud, perhaps shouted. Nothing came, not a wisp of an idea. This had never happened before. His mind had always risen eagerly to any challenge. Now challenge had become torment. No Whitey, no more snow, Anne dead, the cottage all red inside. Therefore? Nothing. No response. "Think," he said, and smacked his forehead with the palm of his hand, hard.

Nothing.

Roger walked back across the river and onto the island, avoiding the circle of light around the cottage. He leaned against a tree in the shadows, waiting for an answer. Perhaps a mind as powerful as his had powers that couldn't be completely understood and so couldn't be completely commanded, like some supercomputer approaching the realm of artificial intelligence. A calming thought. Roger relaxed slightly, shone the light on his watch: 7:00. Would they be coming now? No. They had a hot thing going, but not so hot they'd venture out on a night like this, with the prospect of so many clement nights lying ahead. Therefore—and just as Roger felt his mind come to life at last, felt it really readying itself to think—he realized he had seen not only his watch in the flashlight's beam but something else as well. He switched it back on, swept it across the snow, saw dark stains on white.

Little stains, like ink drops on blotting paper, but these, he saw as he knelt in the snow, were red, not blue. They'd melted down into shallow pits, the red congealing now, still slightly wet. He took off his glove to make sure of that, touched the red with a fingertip, felt the wetness. After that he plunged his hand into clean snow, rubbed, rubbed, rubbed it off. At the same time his mind was spooling out lines of programming.

Subject: damage control. Datum: Whitey bleeding, perhaps to death. Task: to make sure he did so. Then came a mental leap, too swift to follow exactly, although he half caught images flying by: pattern of blood drops, unmarred snow by the gate, the snow-covered pickup parked at the lookout. Knowledge.

The next moment, Roger was on his way back across to the east side of the river, ax in hand, properly gripped near the head, blade down. Yes: Whitey curled up dying in a parked car; Roger had picked the wrong vehicle, that was all. He reached the east bank, scrambled up the ridge, grasping at tree branches, up over the top, onto the lookout. The pickup was gone.

And the hood of his own car had been brushed off, to identify it, of course. Therefore: Whitey and he weren't . . . a team anymore. Roger darted around the car, checking the tires—unslashed. The only sign of Whitey's mental state was the smashed-in rear window. Not good enough, Whitey. Roger unlocked the car, got in. Where would a Whitey-type go in these circumstances? The answer came at once: home to Mama. Not good enough either, Whitey. Roger started his car, backed out of the lookout.

In the headlights, snow was falling again, falling hard. His tracks, the brushed windshield of Anne's car, any other evidence left behind—all would be gone forever in a matter of minutes. This was a tidying-up operation, and nature was helping. The murder of Anne would be a perfect crime, just not the perfect crime he'd had in mind. Roger considered Columbus, bold discoverer of what he hadn't been looking for. That was one similarity they shared. But Columbus's greatest accomplishment had been in crossing that uncrossed ocean for the first time. After that the voyage was easy. The lesson: as long as he emerged tonight immaculate, he could deal with Francie at his convenience, like Columbus on a later trip, or Cortés, Pizarro, Balboa. At the same time, he felt an inner stirring, deep in his brain, in the heart of its very core, that some route toward his original goal still existed, a route involving Whitey. If he could make contact with it, draw it to the surface, examine for feasibility and refine for deployment, all before finding Whitey, then he might have to prolong Whitey's life, or prolong it even more, to be accurate, since Whitey had already exceeded his allotment by almost an hour. Otherwise he would merely tidy up, as planned. This was more like it: he was doing what he did best, what he'd perhaps been born to do—ordering disorder. As he turned south on the lane, Whitey's treadmarks not quite filled in with snow, Roger caught a glimpse in his rearview mirror of the cottage glowing on Brenda's island. He prepared his reaction to news of the tragedy.

Drip drip. Lawton Ferry, 97 Carp Road. A dump. Whitey knocked on the door. Why would he ever think this was home? He'd never even been inside. He knocked again. *Come on, you stupid bitch.*

"Who is it?" A high, shaky voice, but hers: Whitey knew that at once from the way it grated on him.

"Open the fuckin' door."

Pause. "Oh my God."

Click. The door opened. A thin old woman, bent and ugly, stood there gazing up in his direction, the centers of her eyes milky where they should have been black. "Oh, Donald," she said. "You've come home at last." She held out her arms.

"Are you nuts?" Whitey pushed past her, went inside, glanced around. A dump, and a stinking one.

She closed the door, followed him, sliding along crab-wise, her head at a funny angle.

"What the hell are you doing?" he said.

"This is only how I can see just a teeny little. Around the edges like. Don't work for TV at all, but I can't say I miss it. Have you any idea the kind of filth—" She stopped, her face averted, but maybe seeing him semiclear from that angle. "Oh, Donald, has something happened?"

"Why would you say a stupid thing like that?"

"But you're bleeding. Aren't you? Aren't you bleeding, Donald?"

"That matters to you? Acting like you never seen blood before?"

"What do you mean?" she said. He started down the hall to the back of the house. She twisted her head frantically, trying to get him in her field of vision. "It's all the fault of that ungodly psychiatrist. I hope he burns in Hell for a thousand years."

"Shut up, Ma," Whitey said. "Where's the sewing stuff?"

She started to cry: same old cry, like fucked-up crows. He went back into the front room.

"What the hell's the matter with you?"

She wiped her eyes, her snotty face, on the back of her hand. "You said *Ma*, Donald."

"So?"

"It's been a long time."

"You're out of your mind, you know that? Now, where's the sewing stuff?"

"Sewing stuff?"

"I don't have time for this. The sewing stuff, in that basket thing."

"My sewing basket? The wicker one handed down from Granny Nesbit?"

"Just tell me where."

"But, Donald, I don't sew anymore. Haven't for years. I can't see the TV, never mind for sewing. I'm having eye difficulties, or haven't you been listening?"

Whitey wanted to smack her, smack and smack and smack, but he was too weak, hurt too much, and it wouldn't get him the sewing stuff any quicker, if at all. So he just took her by the wrist, and squeezed a little, family style. "I don't want you to sew. I'll sew. Just get me the basket."

"But what's torn, Donald? I knew you were hurt, just knew it."

"No one's hurt. A little fender bender is all."

"A fender bender? Cross your heart?"

"Every time."

She disappeared in her bedroom, returned with the sewing basket. "What's there to drink?" said Whitey, taking it.

"Tea, of course," she said, "and some Pepsi."

"I mean a drink."

"Like alcohol?"

"Yeah. Alcohol."

"But you always liked Pepsi."

"I want a fucking drink, for Christ sake."

"None of that here, Donald, not since I joined up with the Redeemer Church. Have I mentioned them? And I really wish you could see fit not to take the Lord's name in vain."

He was already in the bathroom at the end of the hall, closing and locking the door. A stinking little bathroom. He turned on the light, looked at himself in the mirror. Blood, and plenty of it. *Someone was going to pay.*

Whitey found gauze and a roll of tape in the cabinet, also a bottle labeled Vicodin. Wasn't that one of Rey's favorites? He swallowed the three or four remaining tablets, took off his jacket and shirt, began to bandage himself. A long slash across his gut, a puncture in his chest that he picked a sliver of long green glass from— and that reddened the bandages almost right away— others. But they'd heal, no problem. The worst was under his chin, where a big flap hung down like a goddamn bullfrog tongue, dripping red in fat round plops: no bandaging that.

As Whitey opened the sewing basket, he remembered the bullfrog he'd speared through the head down on the I-95 median. Now, what the hell was that supposed to mean? Like God was watching from up in the clouds or something? He'd done nothing wrong on the median— thought it was a snake, remember? He'd killed the wrong thing, was all. And out on the river just now, he'd been put in an impossible situation, done what he'd had to. When the going gets tough, the tough get going—

"What's that, Donald?"

"Get the fuck away." He listened for her retreating footsteps, heard them.

—and he was as tough as they come. He found a satin thing, cushion or whatever it was, full of needles, selected the thinnest, threaded it with beige thread, to blend with his skin, tied a knot in the end, got to work. Whitey had seen it done before, between periods in his last season. A skate blade had sliced his forearm, right above the glove, and the beery-breathed doc who came to all the games had sewn him up in the dressing room. Whitey stitched the chin flap back into place, hissing from time to time, but getting it done, making himself whole again; he was no fucking bullfrog.

He put his shirt and jacket back on, went into the kitchen. She was standing in the middle of the room, squeezing her hands together.

"Where's that Pepsi?" he said.

"In the fridge, Donald. Are you all right?"

Whitey popped the can open, sat at the rickety table, drank. It hit the spot. He liked Pepsi.

She came closer, hovered. "A bit to eat, maybe?"

He wouldn't have minded, except for the smell. "What stinks in here?" he said.

She sniffed. "I don't smell anything."

"What's the matter with you? It's like a goddamn shithouse."

She sniffed again. "Maybe it's the Kitty Litter. I'm not strong enough to carry it out anymore. And Donald? You know the awful part? Harry's gone."

"Who's he?"

"The cat."

Gone as far as the barn. Maybe he'd tell her, maybe not.

"I must have mentioned our marvelous cat," she was saying. "On the phone, wasn't it, at that New Horizons place? And now you won't be meeting him. Isn't that the way? He disappeared the day that man came to visit. Vanished."

"What man?"

"A sort of preacher man, but not with the Redeemers. He said a prayer for you."

"Huh?"

"A beautiful prayer—*please hear this prayer for our beloved Donald*—I made him change it from Whitey, such a silly nickname—*and help guide him in useful ways*."

"Are you making this up?"

"No, Donald, that's what he said. The most beautiful prayer I've heard in my entire life. How could I forget?"

"Guide him in useful ways—is that what he said?"

"Don't shout, Donald. My hearing's perfectly fine. It's the vision that—"

"When did this happen?"

"Oh, some time ago."

Smack, smack, smack, but only in his mind, even though he was feeling a little better now, what with Vicodin and Pepsi. No smacking Ma. "Where was I?" he said.

"Where were you?"

"Yeah. When this visit happened."

"Why, down there at the New Horizons establishment, naturally. And I wanted so much for you to meet Harry. He was the smartest little—"

"What did he look like?"

"Gingerbread, I guess you'd say, although—"

"The man, asshole—what did he look like?"

Her forehead got all cross, the way it used to: kind of funny now, with her eyes like that, and no belt buckles possible. "Look like?" she said. "I'm afflicted with vision problems, or can't you get it through your thick skull?"

Not that funny. Smack. He did it then, but who wouldn't have? And it felt good; why hadn't he done it long ago? He picked her up off the floor, sat her at the table. "What I'm trying to find out, Ma—I know you like when I call you Ma—is would you know him if you heard him again?"

Ma repositioned her dentures, gave him one of her

hateful looks, but not so hateful now with no eye power behind it, and said, "Honor thy father and mother."

"Accidents happen. Would you know him if you heard him again, yes or no?"

"You could try saying please."

"If I do you won't like it."

One of the best things he ever said. It silenced her. At last she hung her head—oh, why hadn't he done it long, long ago?—and said, "I'd know him."

" 'Cause why?"

"He talked fancy." She sniffled.

"Fancy?"

"You know."

"I don't."

"Fancy. Like with Harry. Harry has these long claws. The gentlest possible cat, but long claws. And this preacher man said they gave him an *inadvertent scratch. Inadvertent,* Donald. Now, who on God's earth talks like that?"

Whitey knew the answer to that; he didn't know what or why, but he knew who. He was nobody's fucking bullfrog, nobody's . . . puppet. Did Roger really think of himself as the master? Whitey would see about that.

First things first. It took him no time to find his mother's purse, pocket what was in it, walk out the door without another word, a six-pack of Pepsi in his hand.

Lawton Ferry, 97 Carp Road. No pickup: an unpromising deficiency, but not definitive, and because not definitive, Roger took the ax with him when he left his car and went to the door.

He knocked.

"Donald? Is that you?"

"A friend of his."

Pause. "I know your voice."

"I'm your friend, too."

Pause. How slow people were. "But how could you be Donald's friend? You don't know him."

Slow, and they didn't even get there. "I prayed for him. Doesn't that make me his friend?"

"I don't know." Pause. "Harry disappeared the day you came."

"But he's right here, by the trash can."

"You don't mean it."

"As I live and breathe."

Pause. "Are you sure it's him?"

Roger described the animal as he remembered it.

"Merciful God—it's Harry!"

"Why don't I bring him in?"

"I'd be obliged."

"Here, kitty," said Roger into the night. "Kitty, kitty, kitty."

The door opened. The woman had a split lip, far too insignificant to account for all the blood Roger saw—on the kitchen table, the counter, the refrigerator, down the hall to the back.

"Have you got him?" said the woman, her sightless eyes gazing up at him. He didn't like seeing sightless eyes again so soon, therefore was a little gruff perhaps when he said, "He's absconded once more."

"I don't understand," the woman said. "Harry," she called, leaning outside, "Harry."

Roger went past her into the house. He followed blood down to the bathroom; formed meaning from gauze, tape, needle, thread; returned to the kitchen; saw the open purse, a hideous object made of shiny green plastic; made meaning of it, too.

"Harry, Harry."

"It's useless," he said. "Close the door. Snow's coming in."

"But he'll freeze."

"Harry? He's a survivor."

"Do you really think so?"

"Without question. Nine lives, and all that related folklore."

She closed the door, came inside. "You're right. Harry's a survivor."

"Then shall we agree not to worry about him? The pertinent question is—what are we going to do about Whitey?"

"Donald."

"Donald."

"Good question." She moved to the table, sat down, closed her eyes. A tear or two escaped her almost lashless slits. "He wasn't the nicest boy to his mother, not tonight, not anytime. And after all the sacrifices I made." She gazed up at Roger, unseeing. "Do you know what I've done for him?"

"What you could, I'm sure. Now our job is to help him, don't you agree?"

"But how?"

"You must think."

"Should we say another prayer?"

"In a minute. But first, we should establish where he's gone."

"He didn't tell me."

Roger laid the ax silently on the table. "Perhaps he let slip some clue."

"Clue? You talk like a cop." She turned her head sideways, trying to catch a glimpse of him. "What's your name, anyway?"

"Harry."

"But that's the cat's name."

"No matter. What matters is where your son has gone."

"No need to raise your voice. That's the same thing I said to him. Now I suppose you'll smack me, too."

"What a suggestion. All I'm saying is that surely even someone of your—surely you can appreciate that in order to help him, I have to know where he is."

"He didn't say. Maybe back to New Horizons."

"It's a thought."

"You know about New Horizons?"

Her face tilted up in inquiry. This, as Roger had suspected for some time, was an impossible situation. Simply put, oversimply perhaps, this woman was negative. She knew all of the bad and none of the good: a potential witness of the most damaging kind.

"Useless now, dangerous in future."

"What's that?"

"Did I say something?" Roger rose.

"It sounded like a prayer, the beginning of prayer. Like the next line is *oh Lord, hear my humble call.*"

"Yes," he said. "Why not?"

"We're going to pray for Donald?"

"Let us kneel."

They knelt.

"Maybe that's a good omen," she said, "you having the same name as Harry."

"There are no omens," said Roger.

Still, how odd, his idle thought at their previous encounter of the ease of snapping her neck. And now here they were. Data: her memory of his voice, the timing of his visits, her knowledge of his awareness of New Horizons—those were his rationale; her split lip, Whitey's bloodstains, the psychiatrist's testimony establishing motive—those were his protection. Anything else? Oh, yes, the gloves, still on his hands, rendering him immaculate. His gloved hands: he raised them.

She lifted her head in unseeing synchrony, waiting for his prayerful words, exposing her scrawny neck. Roger performed the logical act, but it wasn't as easy as he'd anticipated, in the doing.

28

Francie tucked her car in behind a plow and stayed there, creeping along through the rolling country on the west side of the river at twenty miles an hour. In the darkness of late afternoon, she could see nothing but the back of the plow, lit in a way not at all comforting, more like an alien spaceship with monstrous creatures hidden inside. An alien spaceship leading her on to her wretched task: Francie tried rehearsing the little speech for Ned in her mind. It sounded pitiful; aloud, would be even worse.

At the intersection of the lane that led to Brenda's gate, the plow continued north and Francie turned east, out of its shelter. Any local could earn extra money by clearing the roads, and someone had done a quick job on the lane, perhaps an hour or two before. Blowing wind and fresh snow were undoing it almost as quickly, but the lane was still drivable, and Francie was halfway to the gate when her car phone buzzed.

"Hello?"

"Francie?" It was Ned.

"Yes."

"Are you on the way already?"

"I am."

"I hope you haven't gone too far."

"I just left," she said, lying because she sensed what was coming, didn't want to waste emotion, his or hers, on what would now be a side issue.

"Still in the city?"

"Yes."

"That's a relief," Ned said. "Because I'm not going to be able to make it. Something's come up, and I just can't."

"Something about Anne?"

"No, no. Nothing like that. Work related. I'll explain later."

"It doesn't matter," Francie began, and prepared to blurt out the whole thing, get it over with. Why had she cared about the *setting* in the first place? Why had she wanted to pretty it up? Doing it, getting it done, was all that counted. "It doesn't matter, Ned," she repeated, "because—"

"You're too good to me," Ned interrupted, then lowered his voice, as though there was a risk of being overheard. "But it does matter. It matters to me. I'm really sorry, Francie. And I wish I could say it won't happen again, but you know I can't even promise that. Oh, how I wish—" His voice caught, the way it did sometimes, a hint of the emotions underneath that always stopped her in her tracks but that she couldn't allow to stop her now. "I can promise I'll make it up to you somehow," he went on.

"No, Ned, it doesn't—"

"But right now I've really got to go—I'm already running late. Call you tomorrow. I'm sorry, Francie."

"Just—"

Click.

Why go on? That was the first thought to rise out of Francie's confusion. She had no desire to be in the cottage alone and stepped on the brake, too abruptly. Her car fishtailed in momentum-gathering swings, then whipped around and glided backward, weightless and out of control, but slower and slower, straight up the lane toward Brenda's gate. Francie did nothing to stop it, felt no fear, just waited for the out-of-control period to end. It was easy to see this spinout, this loss of control, as a metaphor, and Francie did, even as it happened: a metaphor of her and Ned in toto, and even of their coming denouement as well, now slipping away from her. She had to tell him, had to tell him now, would have no peace until she did.

Gravity reasserted itself; the car came to a soft padded halt halfway up the hill. Francie still had the phone in her hand. But where was he? Not at work, because *Intimately Yours* had been bumped by the Pops Christmas concert. And calling him at home was out, because Anne might answer, and saving her from all this was the whole point. Anne, that two-stories-tall Anne of the fairy tale, was the only one who mattered now, had become the master, in some funny way. Francie's car was pointed back toward home, the engine still running. She gave it gas, rolled down Brenda's lane, and realized at that moment that she would never see the cottage again.

A self-pitying thought she attacked immediately: too fucking bad. Was there a right to be happy, if that insipid word was the word? She'd been happy with Ned, happier than ever in her adult life, but she'd been sucking the happiness out of someone else's universe. There was no right to that. A clear decision, and once made the hard part was done: in her mind if not yet in life, she and Ned were over, finished. Telling him was all that remained. Anne would never know. Period. No harm done, and nothing to cry about.

Francie reminded herself of that last part several times as she turned left on the highway, headed home, was so deep in her own thoughts that she didn't notice she'd drifted across the center line until the headlights of an oncoming car were almost upon her. Francie swerved, once more losing her grip on the road; the other driver, also across the center line, swerved, too. They missed each other by inches, Francie continuing south, the other car—a minivan—going north, much too fast. As her wheels gained traction, Francie had a crazy thought: what if they'd collided, what if she'd been killed at that moment, with Ned still untold? A tidy ending for everyone, all loose ends forever unknown. She slowed to thirty miles an hour and kept the speedometer there until she reached the interstate. Anna Karenina, Emma Bovary— exemplars from a superseded age, a darker one for women, and not for her.

"Chief Savard?"

"Speaking."

"John More, returning your call."

Savard, just back in the office after clearing a pileup out at the Route 139 three-way stop—invariable pileup site whenever it snowed—thought he recognized the voice but couldn't recall the name. His caller sensed that before he had to admit it out loud.

"Reverend More, of the Little White Church of the Redeemer."

The pickup. A minor matter, especially on a night like this, but he had the reverend on the phone. "It's about your pickup."

"My pickup?"

"The church's, I guess it is. I happened to see it over near my place on Little Joe Lake and . . ." And he'd been curious, as he would have been about any vehicle parked there. Curiosity gave him no legal right to ask any questions, so he didn't.

"Is this about the taillight on the minibus? It's going into the shop on Friday. I really hope you're not planning to issue a ticket. They were booked solid."

"This isn't about the minibus, Reverend. It's about the pickup."

"We don't own a pickup."

"A white one, with the name of the church on the side panel."

"Oh," said the reverend. "That doesn't belong to us in an official sense. It's registered to a parishioner. We do use it from time to time, for dump runs and such."

"The dump's closed on Sunday."

"As well it should be." There was a silence. "Was there some question you had, sir?"

"That's when I saw your pickup," Savard said. "Yesterday. Sunday."

"Impossible. We only use it in the summer, and never on Sundays, of course. It isn't even insured right now—we renew the policy in May."

"I thought you said it belonged to a parishioner."

"And so it does. But since she can't drive it herself and has been generous enough to provide it, we handle the insurance and registration."

"Why can't she drive it herself?"

"The poor woman's legally blind."

"Well, someone was driving it."

"I don't see how that could be. It's shut up in the barn behind her house." The reverend paused. "Oh my goodness—you're not suggesting that someone stole it?"

"I'm not suggesting anything."

"Would it be asking too much for you to drive out and have a look?"

"Can't do it tonight, Reverend, not with the storm. But give me the address."

"Ninety-seven Carp Road, Lawton Ferry."

"And the name of this woman?"

"Perhaps you should mention me first when you call on her. Not that she's in any way lacking as a citizen. She's quite an independent sort, that's all—lives alone with her cat, remarkably self-reliant."

"I'll do that," Savard said, opening his notebook, taking out his pen. "What's her name?"

"Truax," said the reverend. He spelled it.

Savard didn't write; his pen was still, poised above the unblemished page.

"Mrs. Dorothy Truax," the reverend continued, "but everyone calls her Dot. God bless."

The snow had stopped by the time Savard parked in front of 97 Carp Road, and the air had stilled, but the temperature was falling fast, as it often did after a storm. The moisture in his nostrils froze before he reached the front door.

Savard knocked. No answer. The house was dark, but why would a blind woman and a cat need lights? He kept knocking, kept getting no answer. "Mrs. Truax," he called, loudly in case her hearing was going, too. "Mrs. Truax." Speaking the name did something to him, something unpleasant. That made him knock harder, but it didn't bring a response.

Savard went back to the cruiser for his lantern, shone it on the barn. The doors were unlocked but closed, and would be kept that way for a while by a snowdrift two or three feet high. Savard walked around the barn, found a hole in the wood, down at kicking level. He knelt, shone light through it, saw lots of rusted junk in the barn, but no pickup. Savard was just starting to rise when something twitched in the darkness. He reached for his gun—a first in his career, despite many provocations much stronger than a stirring in a shadowy barn—and a cat leaped out of the hole in the wall, flowed out of it, really, and landed soundlessly at his feet. The cat faced him, registered his presence, ran across the snow to the house, scratched at the front door.

Savard waited by the barn. He remembered the woman from the trial, everything about her, could picture her perfectly as she was then; remembered, too, the psychiatrist's testimony. Nothing would have surprised him less than seeing the door open, glimpsing a bony hand usher in the cat. But that didn't happen. The door remained closed, with the cat outside.

Savard arced his beam over the house, noticed the peeling paint, the duct tape on the lone front window. He considered peering through it, had taken a first step in that direction, when his radiophone buzzed.

He took it out of his pocket. "Savard."

"Hi, Chief." Carbonneau—all the others called him Joe. "Got a call from a snowmobiler, out on the river." Savard heard shuffling paper, waited for whatever it was Carbonneau had misplaced. He was long past the stage of being amazed that snowmobilers would be out on a night like this, prepared to hear that one or more had fallen through, even though the ice was six or seven inches thick by now. No matter how cold it was, there were always soft spots in the river, as one or two snowmobilers learned every year. "Had the name somewhere here, Chief," Carbonneau said.

"Are we going to need Rescue?" Savard said. "Dive team?"

"Oh, it's nothing like that," Carbonneau said. "I don't think. This guy was on the river, out by Pinney Point."

"The lookout?"

"Yeah. Not our side . . . but now that you mention it, Chief, what about that island?"

"With the cottage?" Savard said. He hadn't mentioned anything, only thought it; Carbonneau was far from perfect, but there were advantages in having worked together for a long time.

"Yeah. Whose side is that on?"

"I don't know," Savard said. "What's up?"

"This guy—I'll have the name in a minute—saw lights on in the cottage. All lit up like a Christmas tree."

"So?"

"That's what I said. It's Christmas, right? The thing is, this guy goes out on the river every winter, year after year, like. And he's never seen lights on in there, not once."

"Sounds like kids." Cottage break-ins weren't common on Savard's side of the river, at least not ones committed by local boys; local boys knew that Savard was strict about cottage break-ins—he'd dealt summarily with one or two cases in his early years, and that had been enough.

"That's what I thought," said Carbonneau. "Maybe still out there, Chief."

"Send Berry," Savard said.

"Berry's back down at the three-way. More bumper cars. And Lisa called in sick."

So it was him. Savard turned from the darkened house, walked down to the street. As he got in the cruiser, the cat made a screeching sound that ended on a high, keening note. A cold night, but cats could take care of themselves; this one would find its way back to the barn, wait for Dot Truax there. Savard put the cruiser in gear and headed for the river.

* * *

Francie slept a troubled sleep, caught in one of those partially controllable dreams where the real and the fantastic were all mixed up. Outside, the city was quiet, except for the rumble of the plows she half heard, muted by sleep, muffled by snow. In her dream, she wrestled with a problem: *oh garden, my garden* was back under her bed, the bed she was sleeping in, and she had to get rid of it at once, but what explanation would she give to Anne, two-stories-tall Anne, watching through the window? She had to come up with some scheme to make Anne go away, but what?

The phone started ringing. Maybe that would work, maybe Anne would answer it, giving her time to grab the painting and run from the room. But Anne couldn't be distracted that easily; the phone rang and rang until finally Francie reached out of her dream and answered it.

"Francie?"

"Brenda?" The glowing red numbers on the bedside alarm read 4:37. Perhaps Brenda had made some mistake with the time difference.

"Oh, Francie, thank God you're there."

"What's wrong?"

"Thank God it's you. I was going out of my mind. Something awful's happened. At the cottage."

"At the cottage?"

"There's been a murder, a horrible killing, Francie. Some policeman, the chief, I think, just called me—my number's on the tax roll, of course. And I thought it might be you. An unidentified woman, he said. They must have assumed it was me, I guess. A local-type policeman, he wasn't very clear. Are you sure you're all right, Francie?"

"Yes. You're positive he—"

"Wait—I've got another call."

Francie, on her feet beside the bed, phone clutched in both hands, waited. *You're positive he said a woman?* That was the question she'd begun. What if Ned had gone to the cottage anyway, had changed his mind, changed his schedule because he hadn't believed she was still in the city, had felt guilty in consequence, or had simply worried about her out there in the storm? What if it was Ned?

"Francie? Sorry. It was—"

"Are they sure it was a woman, Brenda?"

"Yes. That was the policeman again. They've made an identification. It's some poor woman from Dedham."

"Dedham?"

"Yes. I have no idea what she was doing there—her name wasn't familiar to me at all. Franklin, I think he said. Anne Franklin."

On the edge of frenzy, mental and physical, she tried the number, Anne and Ned's number, in Dedham, almost incapable of hitting the right buttons. Busy. She tried again and again and again. Busy, busy, busy. She snapped on lights, ran down to the kitchen, threw open the door to the basement—more light, more light—ran down those stairs, too, burst into Roger's room.

Roger: not sleeping on his couch but sitting in front of the computer, face silvery in its light, bent over a sheet of paper covered with a pattern of connected boxes, pen moving rapidly. He swung around, startled, as she came in.

"Oh, Roger, something terrible's happened."

"What would that be?" he said, rising, pocketing the sheet of paper.

"Anne. She's been killed, Roger. Murdered."

Francie went to him, almost staggering, clung to him, began to shake. She buried her face in his chest. He patted her back.

29

In the kitchen, Francie tried the Dedham number, over and over, getting a busy signal every time. Murdered. In the cottage? Had there been an arrest? How? When? Why? Brenda had told her almost nothing. She called Rome, heard Brenda in Italian: *"Questa è la segretària telefònica di . . ."* She left a message, ran upstairs, threw on some clothes. When she came back down, Roger was waiting in his crimson robe with a package wrapped in foil.

"What's this?" she said.

"I made tuna sandwiches. Isn't it customary to bring food?"

"Are you coming?" she said.

He spread his arms, like great red wings. "It wouldn't be right," he said. "My relationship was peripheral."

But he walked her down to the garage. Their cars sat side by side, both in pools of wintertime snowmelt. Francie saw that his rear window was shattered.

"Oh, that," said Roger, although she hadn't said anything. "Some smash-and-grabber, it would seem, but nothing was taken. The alarm must have scared him off." He handed her the sandwiches. "Don't forget to offer my condolences."

* * *

Francie drove west on Storrow. Not yet dawn, but in-coming commuters were already on the road, a yellow stream of headlights paralleling the dark one of the Charles. Their world was no longer hers. Murder: all those questions and many others roiled in her mind, in-cluding the one she most wanted to avoid—what had Anne been doing at the cottage in the first place? Wasn't there only one thing she could have been doing? And didn't that mean she must have found out about what went on in that cottage? But how? Had Ned confessed? *Something's come up,* he'd said. She'd asked, *Something about Anne?* And he'd said, *Nothing like that. Work related.* Therefore? Francie had no idea. And murder? Francie was lost.

She parked in front of the house in Dedham. The downstairs lights were on, silhouetting the stocky form of a snowman in the front lawn, a ski pole over one shoulder like a sentry's rifle. Francie walked up the path, unshoveled but packed down by many footsteps going in both directions. Worse than lost, Francie, because at that moment, standing at the door with its Christmas wreath, she had the most unworthy thought of her whole life: Perhaps there would now be some future for her and Ned after all. Even with Anne's wreath hanging there, Francie had that thought. What was she made of? She knocked on the door.

"Who is it?" said a woman almost at once, as though she'd been waiting by the door. Francie didn't recognize her voice.

"Francie Cullingwood," she said, and added, "a friend of the family."

The door opened. A gray-haired woman in a quilted housecoat stared out at Francie with big dark eyes: Ned's eyes. The woman didn't have to tell Francie who she was.

"I'm Ned's mother. You've heard?"

"Yes."

The dark eyes gazed past her, into the sky, graying in the east. She shivered. "Come in."

Francie went into the little hall. Everything looked the same: a stack of mail on the table, a few audiotapes, irises in a vase. Francie glanced sideways into the living room, ahead into the kitchen.

"Ned's gone," the woman said, as though reading her mind, and Francie thought, *Does she know?* Francie saw no sign of any such knowledge in the woman's face, and besides, she hadn't seemed to recognize her name. "The police came down from New Hampshire," Ned's mother went on, "and took him to do ... what needed to be done."

They went into the kitchen. "Tea?" said Ned's mother. "Or maybe coffee? I suppose you'd call it morning."

"Nothing for me."

"I'll have tea," the woman said, going to the stove. "Keep moving." She had trouble with the switches. "Why anyone would need such an elaborate oven I have no idea." Gas ignited with a pop, settled down to a steady blue flame.

Francie tried to remember what Ned had said about his mother, recalled nothing. He almost never spoke of family life; she thought of the Chinese walls dividing different departments of Wall Street law firms in the interest of preserving the appearance of something or other. But didn't his mother live in Cleveland? Weren't they all from Cleveland?

"How did you get here so fast?" Francie said.

The woman paused, tea bag dangling in her hand. "I don't follow you."

"I thought you lived in Cleveland."

"True. I flew in yesterday, to spend the holidays."

He hadn't mentioned that either.

"Holidays," Ned's mother said, coming to the table,

cup clattering on the saucer. "Can you imagine?" Their eyes met and Francie sensed that this was the moment for tears, but none came. Big dark eyes, just like Ned's on the surface, but much drier underneath.

"It's a good thing you're here, Mrs. Demarco," Francie said.

The woman shrugged that aside. "There's nothing good," she said. "And it's Mrs. Blanchard, actually. I remarried." She sat down, sipped her tea; Francie remained standing. "What was your connection again?" said Mrs. Blanchard. "To the family, I mean."

Francie hadn't said. "Anne and I . . ." Tears were on the way now, but hers; she stopped them, cut them off completely and at once, went on. "We were tennis partners."

"Oh, yes, the tennis," said Mrs. Blanchard. Tea slopped out of her cup, splashed on the table, dripped off the edge, stained her housecoat. She didn't appear to notice. "As a friend of hers," she said, "can you give me any idea what in God's name she was doing—"

The phone rang. Mrs. Blanchard crossed the room and grabbed it off the wall before it could ring again.

"Yes? Are you all right, dear? What's hap—no, nothing." Her eyes shifted to Francie, sponging up the spilled tea. "There's a visitor, that's all." She covered the mouthpiece, spoke to Francie. "What was your name again?"

Francie repeated it. The woman talked into the phone, raised her eyebrows, held it out for Francie. "It's Ned," she said. "He wants to speak with you."

Francie took the phone. "Ned. Ned. I—" Mrs. Blanchard sat at the table, back to Francie, head still, still and alert. "I don't know what to say."

"Don't say anything, Francie," he said.

"Oh, but Ned, it's so—"

"Don't say anything to anybody," he went on, and she realized she'd misinterpreted him; he hadn't been referring to the uselessness of words at a time like this. "And don't say *Ned* like that, not to anybody," he continued. "You sometimes look in at the cottage as a favor to your friend, that's an unavoidable fact, no hiding it, but nothing more, nothing about me, nothing about you and me." Francie had never heard his voice like this, low and pressing, the words coming fast. "Do you understand?" he said.

"Not really." She turned her back, hunched over, spoke softly and right into the phone so Mrs. Blanchard couldn't hear. "I don't see how it makes—"

"Is my mother there? Nearby, I mean?"

"Yes."

"Then shut up, for Christ's sake. She misses nothing." Francie heard a coin dropping into a pay phone. "But you're wrong about what you were going to say, Francie. It does make a difference. Just think about it."

"How?"

"Goddamn it. Why are you doing this? Don't you care about me at all, Francie?"

She did, much more and without a doubt, but the thought of replying to the question at that moment sickened her. And she still didn't understand what difference it made now if their relationship was known; also knew that she wasn't going to find out, not with Ned's mother in the room. She changed her tone for him, tried to approximate the tone she'd have used if she really had been nothing more than Anne's tennis friend, but had no idea what that would sound like either. "Do they—do they know what happened?"

A pause, a long one. Then came a sob, thick and ragged. "She was slaughtered, Francie. Slaughtered. That's what happened."

Click.

Francie put down the phone. Mrs. Blanchard was on her feet. "He didn't want to speak to me?"

"He had to go."

Ned's mother gave her a close look. She might have been about to say something, but at that moment Em walked into the room in her pajamas.

"Morning, Grandma," she said, and then noticed Francie. "Oh, hi."

"Hi," said Francie.

Em brushed her hair out of her eyes. "Getting ready for another tournament?"

"No."

The girl hit the button on the countertop TV, reached up in the cupboard for cereal and a bowl, put them on the table. On the screen, a commercial for pain relievers ended and two newscasters appeared at a desk. Francie was right beside the TV; she switched it off. Em and her grandmother both turned to her, understanding registering on the woman's face, surprise on Em's. Francie, unable to invent any explanation for her conduct, said nothing. She went to the fridge, opened it, said, "Two percent or nonfat, Em?"

"Two percent," said Em, glancing at the dark screen of the TV.

Francie poured milk in her bowl. "How about some strawberries on top?" She'd seen them in the fridge.

"Sure."

Francie took a handful of strawberries from their carton, washed them in the sink. Not a good idea, strawberries, because a strawberry couldn't remain a simple strawberry, of course, but had to be red, ripe and full of life. Francie put them on a plate, set it before Em.

"Thanks," said the girl, popping one in her mouth and placing the others one at a time among the cornflakes in a star-shaped pattern. She raised her head. "Mom up yet?"

Francie and Ned's mother looked at each other; neither answered.

"Hey," said Em. "What's up, Grandma?"

"Maybe you'd better go," Ned's mother said to Francie.

"I'd like to help."

"That won't be necessary," said Ned's mother. "Most considerate of you, but it's a family matter."

Francie turned to Em, but what could she say? Em's mouth opened, strawberry-red inside.

Francie didn't put up a fight; she left, now a coward on top of everything. She was outside on the walk, almost to her car, when she heard Em's wail: piercing, unmitigated, unbearable—catastrophe beyond repair.

And she'd forgotten to leave the sandwiches, somehow still in her hand. She realized she'd loved Anne. It wasn't too strong a word.

30

Back in her own house, Francie found a stranger talking to Roger in the living room. "Here she is now," said Roger as Francie came in. The stranger rose, a big, broadly built man with a broad face; he reminded her of the blacksmith in the background of a Dutch genre painting she could picture but not identify at that moment.

"Francie, this is Mr. Savage, chief of police in Lawton Center," said Roger. "Mr. Savage, my wife."

"Pleased to meet you," said the chief, speaking to Roger although his eyes were on Francie. "And it's Savard. Joe Savard."

"My apologies," said Roger. "Will you be needing me any longer?"

"No," said Savard. "Thanks for your help."

"Think nothing of it," said Roger. He came to Francie, took both her hands in his, said, "Oh, Francie. It's dreadful, just dreadful." Then he left, pausing to pick a few dead leaves from the base of a plant as he went out.

"Please sit down," Francie said. Savard sat on the window seat, back to the morning outside, darkened by thick, low clouds; Francie couldn't sit, but leaned on the arm of a chair by the fireplace, about three steps away. "What happened to Anne?"

"She was murdered sometime last night, Mrs.

Cullingwood, in the cottage owned by your friend—" He leafed through his notebook.

"Brenda."

He found the page. "It says here Countess Vasari."

"She's not a real countess," Francie said, an unconsidered remark that made her sound like a pompous fool, exactly the opposite of her intent.

Savard looked up from his notebook. "What's the difference?"

A good question. What had she meant? That Brenda was back to being plain Brenda Kelly again; that she didn't want this man to form a false impression of her, Francie, because of some improbably and temporarily titled friend. "Nothing. I didn't mean to interrupt."

"There's not much to interrupt at this stage. The lab guys are still at the scene and we haven't got a suspect." Savard closed the notebook, laid it on his knee. His hand was big, thickened by some sort of hard work, but not ugly. "I'm hoping for some help from you," he said.

"Anything," Francie said.

He nodded. "Your friend says she hasn't been to her place for two or three years—she couldn't remember exactly—and that you kept an eye on it for her."

"That's true."

"How often did you go up there?"

"A few times a month in summer. Sometimes more."

"And in winter?"

"Almost never."

"When was the last time?"

A Friday. The day after she'd fallen through the ice. Ned had called her for the first time on her car phone, had been waiting there, surprising her on the darkened porch with his fury over her call to the radio show. She made the calculations in her head—it took longer than it should have because she kept remembering him out on the river: *Wouldn't there be something wrong with two people who could just throw it away?*—and gave Savard the date.

He wrote it down. "Did you notice anything unusual when you were there?"

"No."

"No sign of a break-in, or an attempted one?"

"No."

"Nothing missing or out of place?"

"No."

"Anything spilled, knocked over, broken?"

"No."

There was a pause. Francie had a cast stone figure by Jean Arp on the bookcase—Roger's wedding present to her, not a big or important one, but Arp nevertheless—and the policeman's eyes were on it: whether taking it in or thinking about something else, she couldn't tell.

His gaze swung back to her. "I assume you have a key to the cottage?"

"Two," Francie said. "One for the gate, one for the door."

"Have you ever lost them?"

"No."

"Given them to someone else?"

"No."

"Had copies made?"

"No." Although Ned had asked for one, she now recalled: *Might help if I had a key. It's cold out there.* But she'd never gotten around to doing it: everything had fallen apart first.

"You know of no other person with access to the cottage, then?"

"No."

"Would you mind showing them to me?"

"Showing what to you?"

"The keys, Mrs. Cullingwood."

They were in her car in the garage, hanging from the ignition. When she came back with them, Savard was standing by the bookcase, bent over the Arp, his hands behind his back. Francie almost said, *You can touch it if you want.*

But did not. Instead she said, "Here they are," and handed him the keys.

Savard glanced at them, handed them back. Standing next to him by the bookcase, Francie sensed his physical strength. Not that he made himself look big or puffed out his chest—he slouched a little, if anything. Neither was he dressed in clothes designed to show off his physique—he wore a baggy gray suit, a little shiny at the elbows. But she sensed it, all the same.

"So Anne Franklin didn't have keys to the cottage."

"No."

"Did she know your friend Brenda?"

"No."

He nodded to himself. It suddenly hit Francie that this man, or an assistant, had probably asked Ned these same questions already, hours before, that he might be searching for discrepancies as well as facts. She was considering the implications of that, and how they fit with Ned's instructions—*nothing about you and me*—when Savard said, "How long has she known about it, then?"

Francie felt a strange rush of blood to her face and neck, as though she were going scarlet; couldn't have been, of course, not with her complexion. "It?" she said.

"The cottage."

"I don't understand."

"Its existence and location," Savard said. "When did you first tell her about it?"

Discrepancies: awareness that he might be searching

for them was no help without knowing what he'd heard already from Ned. She stuck to the truth. "I never did."

"So she made no mention to you of going up there?"

"We never discussed the cottage."

Savard opened his notebook, read to himself. Francie, reading upside down, saw lines of neat handwriting too small to make out, culminating in a circled notation writ larger at the bottom of the page: *FC—nexus?* That scared her for many reasons, not the least of which was the presence of a word like that in the notebook of a man who looked like this. She realized she had no idea what was coming next.

"I wonder, then," he said, closing the notebook, "how she found out about the cottage."

"So do I," Francie said.

"And what she was doing up there."

Francie said nothing, was sure she knew the horrible answer to that question, lacked only the steps in between. Was silence the same as a lie? In some cases, like this one, yes.

"When was the last time you saw her?"

"Saturday night. We went to dinner, the four of us, after tennis."

"How was she?"

"In what way?"

"Her mood."

Francie thought of the scene in the locker room. "A little upset, at first."

"Any idea why?"

"We'd just lost the match." Was a partial truth the same as a lie? Ditto.

"Is that enough to upset a grown woman?"

"Ever play competitive sports, Mr. Savard? It was the club championship."

Savard gave her a quick look; for a moment she

thought he was about to smile, but he didn't. "Who else knows about the cottage?"

"You mean that Brenda has it? Lots of people."

"And were any of them acquainted with Anne, to your knowledge?"

Besides Ned, there was only Nora. Francie gave Savard her name and number. Why not? Nora knew Brenda, so he would have found her eventually.

Savard wrote Nora's name and number in his notebook and said, "Then there's your husband."

"What about him?"

"I assume he knew about the cottage as well."

Had Roger known? Francie had never told him: at first, for no particular reason other than the kind of marriage it had become—he wouldn't even have expected to hear a detail like that—and later because of Ned. She gave Savard a careful answer: "Roger didn't know Anne—they met for the first time on Saturday night."

His eyes went to the sculpture, were still on it when he said, "What was Anne like, Mrs. Cullingwood?"

"She . . ." Francie got a grip on her emotions; if she was going to get through this, whatever *this* was and whatever *getting through it* meant, she would have to keep them well capped. "She was wonderful, Mr. Savard."

He gave her a sharp glance. "Do you want to sit down?" he said. "A glass of water?"

"I'm fine. Anne was . . . good. There was no meanness in her, if you're thinking about enemies, or something like that. She was good." Francie, realizing she had raised her voice, lowered it, went on: "She was talented, she was loving."

"In what way talented?"

"She was a fine tennis player, for one thing. And a very good painter."

"Painter?" he said.

"Yes."

"Do you mean an artist? The kind you evaluate in your job?"

How did he know about her job? Roger, of course. "I didn't evaluate Anne. She was my friend."

"I'm just making sure I understood what you meant by painting, that's all," Savard said. "The fact that she painted could be important."

"Why?"

"Let's sit down."

"I told you I'm fine."

"Whatever you say," Savard said, but he returned to the window seat. Francie followed, leaned again on the armchair, feeling manipulated in some way. "It doesn't surprise me to learn she was an athlete, Mrs. Cullingwood."

"Why not?"

"There's evidence of a tremendous struggle last night."

Francie felt faint, might have fallen had it not been for the chair; had he foreseen that? Savard's image began to dissolve, almost did, then slowly returned to normal, as though some director had changed his mind about ending a scene. Savard was watching her closely.

"Go on," she said, her fingers digging into the fabric of the chair.

He folded his massive hands in his lap, a gesture that seemed ceremonial to her, even religious. "Before she died, she managed to write a word on the floor. Very small. She must have changed her position slightly after that, because it was covered by her arm and we didn't see it at first. The word she wrote was *painting*."

"Painting?"

"Yes. Do you have any idea what she could have meant by that?"

"No."

"But you must know something about her work—in order to have made the judgment that she was good."

"I've seen some of her paintings."

"Do any stand out in your mind?"

That was easy: the portrait of Ned. But *nothing about you and me*. "No one more than another," Francie said.

"Do you know of any painting she might have been working on recently?"

"No."

"Or something she wanted to try in the future?"

"No," Francie said. "Do you think she meant to . . . to tell us who killed her?"

"Perhaps not the actual attacker."

"The actual attacker? I don't understand."

Savard unfolded his hands, rubbed them together slowly. "How would you characterize her marriage, Mrs. Cullingwood?"

"In what way?"

"Were they happy together?"

"I rarely saw them together."

"Meaning you saw them separately?"

He was so quick; didn't look like he would be, but was. "Meaning I didn't see them together enough to form an opinion about something like that," Francie said as calmly as she could.

"Did Anne ever say anything that led you to believe they had problems?"

Yes, in the locker room. "No," Francie said. A lie: total, direct, inescapable.

"How would you describe her self-confidence?"

"That's a strange question."

"There's not much to go on, Mrs. Cullingwood, as I mentioned. Getting a picture of her in my head will help."

"Self-confidence. It's not easy to know something like that about a person."

"I disagree," Savard said. "In my experience, it's one of the first things you notice."

They looked at each other. He was right, of course. Quick, and there was more to him than that. "Not as high as it should have been," Francie said.

"On a scale of ten," Savard said.

"Isn't that a rather brutal method for measuring something as abstract as self-confidence?" Francie said.

"No," Savard replied. "Brutal was what happened to her in your friend's cottage."

It finally hit her. "What did she use to write with—the word *painting*?"

"I think you've figured that out."

Francie didn't speak; for a moment she couldn't even breathe.

Savard rose, came closer. "I need your help," he said. "And so does she, if you accept that rationale."

"Three," Francie told him. "The answer to your question is three."

"Any reason a woman of such qualities would have a self-confidence level like that?"

"I don't know."

"You must have thought about it."

"Why do you say that?"

He opened his mouth, said, "You're," then stopped. "I'll withdraw the question." A beeper went off. Savard took it from his pocket, read something on its screen, put it and his notebook away. He moved toward the door, then stopped and turned. "Sometimes women unhappy in their marriages have affairs," he said.

Francie again felt the upsurge of blood in her neck and face.

"If she was," Savard continued, "what's to be gained by hiding that now?"

"What are you saying?"

"When a wife is murdered, we always check the husband first, Mrs. Cullingwood."

"I thought you said there was no suspect."

"I misspoke. We have no evidence pointing to a specific suspect. But Mr. Demarco has no alibi for last night."

"No alibi?"

"No convincing explanation of his whereabouts during the period when his wife was killed." He handed her a card. "Call if you can help."

He went into the hall; Francie followed. "But there was a struggle, you said."

"I did."

"Then wouldn't there be signs of that on the attacker?"

"There would. On the actual attacker."

Savard opened the door. Roger was outside, sprinkling a handful of salt crystals on the walk. He looked up. "Safety first, Chief," he said.

"You're so right," Savard said. "I meant to ask if you've ever been to Brenda's cottage, Mr. Cullingwood."

"Never. The fact is, I'd forgotten all about it, if I ever knew in the first place. Did you ever mention it, Francie?"

"I don't think so."

Roger spread his hands. "It was Francie's baby, Chief."

Savard glanced back at Francie, then got in his car, not an official police cruiser but an old Bronco, and drove away. Francie and Roger looked at each other. "Close the door, Francie," he said. "You're letting in all the cold."

Roger went inside a few minutes later. He didn't see Francie in the kitchen, the hall, the living room. He walked over to the plant in the corner, a dieffenbachia.

Pausing to pick a few dead leaves from the base of it as he went out! Who could compete with brilliance of that magnitude? He plucked the digital recorder that Francie had given him from behind the stem and dropped it in his pocket.

31

Francie had no distance from what she was doing, no inner watchfulness, no control. This life after Anne, or at least in the first few hours after Anne, had all the intensity of loving Ned, an inverse intensity that now served to heighten pain, not pleasure. From her bedroom, Francie dialed Ned's number, heard his mother's voice on the machine: "You have reached the Demarco residence. Please leave a message at the tone."

She had to see him. Francie hung up, realizing as she did that he might not be home yet—might still be in New Hampshire, or on his way back. Had to see him. On his way back: she was thinking car keys, coat, Dedham, was turning from the phone—had to see him—when it rang. She snatched it up.

"Francie, is it true?" Nora, not Ned.

"About Anne, you mean?"

"What else would I mean?"

"It's true."

"Oh, God. What happened?"

"They don't know."

"But she was murdered?"

"Yes."

"At Brenda's place?"

"Yes."

"What was she doing up there?"

307

"They don't know."

Pause. "I'm coming over."

"Not now, Nora. I'm on my way out."

"Where?"

"Please." Had to see him. "There are things I have to do."

"Like what, Francie? What's going on?"

"I'll call you later."

"But—"

Francie hung up.

She drove back to Dedham under a sky that was one low sagging cloud from horizon to horizon. Ned's garage door was open, no cars inside. Francie parked on the street and waited.

The house was quiet, the curtains drawn. Francie stared at it for a while, then at the snowman with the ski pole over one shoulder. She noticed that he wore a name tag, frozen into his chest, with writing on it too distant to see. After a minute or two, she had to get out of the car, walk up the path, read it: *Mr. Snowman, VP Xmas Productions.* Anne humor. Francie dug the tag free with her fingernails, put it in her pocket, went back to the car. She had pulled it out three times for another look when Ned drove up at last. He wheeled into the driveway, braked in front of the garage, hurried toward his front door. Had he not noticed her?

Francie jumped out of the car. "Ned."

His head snapped around. He saw her, began to speak, stopped himself, glanced back at the house, then came toward her, cutting directly through the knee-deep snow in the yard, ice balls clinging to the tassels on his loafers.

Then he was on the sidewalk, and she got a good look at his face. Had to see him. But what had become of her beautiful man? This blue-lipped gray face, red around the eyes, had all his features but was not him, and the eyes themselves, fugitive, blinking, burrowing things, were not him either. Francie wanted to wrap him in her arms, somehow make him better, settled for holding out her hand.

After a moment or two, he took it and then held on tight. "Oh, Francie, it hurts so much."

Francie, determined not to cry, to hold it all in, almost did.

"I'll never ever be the same," he said. His voice had changed, too, lost its richness and musicality, now did no more than deliver the words. "And what about Em? Tell me that? What about Em? I'm going to have to go in there now and tell her . . . tell her."

"She knows."

"She knows?"

"Your mother told her."

He dug a knuckle into his forehead above the right eye, hard. "Are you sure?"

"I was here."

"You were?"

"Don't you remember? We talked on the phone."

He squeezed his eyes shut, opened them. "What is happening to me?"

She stroked his hand. He withdrew it, looked back at his house. "But you can't come here, Francie. People will suspect."

"Suspect what?"

"About us, of course."

"What difference does it make now?" Francie said. Over his shoulder she saw a curtain part, Ned's mother peer out. Their eyes met. The curtain closed.

"How can you say that? It makes all the difference. I don't want Em to ever know, ever to think that everything wasn't . . . wasn't just the way it seemed."

That made no sense to Francie, not anymore, but the intensity of her reaction surprised her. "Is that what your life's going to be from now on?" she said. "Preserving some past that never was?"

Ned's arm twitched. For a moment Francie almost imagined he was going to hit her. An unworthy thought, beneath them both, contemptible—until she happened to glance down and catch his hand uncurling from a fist. But a fist could mean tension, not violence, and she knew there was no violence in Ned, had never seen the slightest sign, so he couldn't possibly have been involved in Anne's death, no matter what this man Savard suspected. Francie could barely allow her mind to articulate the thought. Could she have known him that little? No. Savard was far off course. She didn't believe it, not for a second.

Ned took a deep breath. "You're tough, Francie. That's one of the things that . . . attracted me to you. But your timing's not always on."

"What do you mean?"

He came a little closer, lowered his voice. "What do I mean? What's the matter with you? How can you say what you just said about my marriage? My wife is dead. Where are your feelings?"

"Where are my feelings?" Francie, who had never struck a human being in her life, did it now. Her scarlet handprint took shape on his washed-out face. She walked away.

He followed. "Wait, Francie. I take that back. I'm not myself. Please."

He touched her shoulder; she halted. Even at a moment like this, his touch sent that familiar, irresistible feeling down her back. The man for her; it was inescapable. She swung around and asked him, "Where were you last night?"

He seemed to jerk back, almost as if she'd hit him again. "What kind of question is that?"

"Savard's question."

"You've talked to him?"

"He came to the house."

"What did he want?"

"To know what I thought of your marriage."

"My God. What did you tell him?"

The mark she'd made on him was already fading, but it sickened her to see it. "Don't worry about me, Ned."

"I don't understand."

"I won't let you down."

Ned's eyes met hers at last. "Oh, I know that, Francie. I wish I could hold you now, so much."

"So do I." She wanted to kiss that redness on his cheek, dared not. Was there somewhere they could go? Was that an evil thought? What was she made of?

"But it doesn't really answer my question," Ned said. "What exactly did you tell him?"

"That I didn't know enough to comment on your marriage."

"And nothing about us?" he said.

"Nothing."

"Perfect," he said. "Perfect as always. I'm sure that'll take care of it."

"It won't, Ned, because Savard thinks she was the one having an affair."

"That Anne was?"

Francie nodded.

"And I followed her out there?"

"Or paid someone to do it."

He laughed, a strange, barking laugh, almost like Roger's but lower in tone. "That's idiotic."

"Then why not tell him where you were last night?"

"Please, Francie, not the third degree."

"You think this is the third degree? Why can't you tell him? You said on the phone that it was work related. Is there a patient confidentiality issue, or something like that?"

"Something like that. Please don't ask me more."

"I won't," Francie said. "But he will."

"He's just a small-town cop, nothing to be concerned about."

"You think so?"

"Yes."

"He's trying to find out how she—how Anne knew about the cottage."

"I have no idea."

"Maybe not how. But we can both guess why she went out there."

"She didn't know anything. There has to be some other explanation."

"Like what?"

He had no answer.

"It must have come from you, Ned."

"Impossible. You know how careful I've been."

Had he? Careful maybe about the cottage, but not careful the one night at her house, the night of the milk run and the invented flat tire, the night he discovered she didn't like irises. Francie, remembering the pressure gauge, turned to Ned's car in the driveway.

"What are you looking at?" Ned said.

"Maybe she found something in your trunk."

"Like what?" But he was already moving toward the car. Francie went with him. He opened the trunk: roof rack, rock salt, kayak paddle; and under the floor mat, tools and the spare. "What's there to find?" said Ned, just as an old Bronco pulled into the driveway. Ned and Francie wheeled around, backs to the open trunk.

Savard got out of the Bronco, carrying a shiny metal

box. He nodded to Francie, spoke to Ned. "I'd like to see your wife's paintings, if you don't mind."

"Her paintings?"

"Mrs. Cullingwood hasn't explained?"

"No," said Francie. "I have not."

"It's kind of pressing," Savard said to Ned, "or I wouldn't be bothering you like this. We found something after you and I talked last night." He told Ned what Anne had written on the floor of Brenda's cottage.

He didn't seem to understand, his eyes, those new eyes, going to Francie, back to Savard. "I haven't even seen my daughter yet," he said.

"I won't come inside," Savard said. "You could bring them out here, if there aren't too many."

"Her paintings?"

"I'll help, if you want," Francie said.

"I'll do it myself." Ned went into the house.

Savard gazed into the open trunk, then at Francie. "Did Anne ever ask you to buy one of her paintings for your foundation?"

"Why do you ask?"

"Just wondering whether you ever turned her down."

"The answer is no to both."

"You must do that a lot—turn people down."

"It's part of the job."

"Do you tell them the truth?"

She met his gaze: surprising eyes, almost unguarded, almost as though interested in the answer for its own sake. "Enough of it, Mr. Savard," Francie said.

Ned came into the garage from the house with some paintings, went back for more, leaving the door open. Francie heard Em crying in another room, heard him talking to her, his voice closer to normal, comforting, sweet; Francie knew the effort that must have taken. He came back with more paintings, arranged them all in a row of seven leaning against the wall.

Anne's paintings: the still life with grapes, another still life with fish and wine, two seascapes, a desert landscape, an abstract with deep blue spirals, a self-portrait. Francie wanted them to be great, was already toying with a fantasy of Anne's posthumous fame, and her its engineer. But they were not great; the still life with grapes was the best, and even it was not as good as she'd first thought, flawed in ways she hadn't seen before; she argued with herself that the fault lay with the harsh strip lighting in the garage, and lost.

"That them all?" Savard said.

"Yes," said Ned.

But Francie knew it wasn't. Where was his own portrait, the one that hung over the bed in the master bedroom? Francie didn't look at Ned, or at Savard, kept her eyes on a slightly fussy cactus in the desert landscape. How could he have missed his own portrait? She thought of Dorian Gray.

Savard examined the paintings one by one, spending ten or fifteen seconds on each. Francie had watched many people look at paintings, their levels of concentration ranging from superficial to profound. Savard's was of the latter, but she had no idea what he was seeing. "Are there any works in progress?" he said.

"No."

"Did she have a studio somewhere?"

"No."

"So this is it?"

"Yes."

Savard studied the self-portrait: a younger Anne in a black turtleneck, holding a paintbrush, a dull gold band almost invisible on her ring finger.

"Will you be needing me any longer?" Ned said.

Savard took his eyes off the self-portrait. "Just one more thing," he said, and opened the little metal box, an evidence kit, Francie realized—she'd seen them on TV. At the bottom lay a road map of New Hampshire, folded open to a panel of the southern part of the state. She saw a small red X on the Merrimack River. "Have you seen this before?" Savard said.

Ned shrugged. "A road map. Is it important?"

"That remains to be seen."

Ned reached for the map. Savard jerked the box out of his reach. "Haven't dusted it yet." He checked to see if they understood. "For fingerprints," he explained. "We'll also check for fibers—try to match car interiors, floor mats, that kind of thing. But does it look familiar, Mr. Demarco, at first blush?"

Ned gazed down into the box. Savard turned to Francie, seemed suddenly to notice her presence. "I'm sorry, Mrs. Cullingwood. Didn't mean to keep you so long."

A dismissal. Polite, almost deferential, but a dismissal. Why? And why now and not before? Francie had no choice. She tried to establish the proper distance in her tone. "If there's anything I can do, Ned."

"Thanks, Francie." He did it better.

Francie got in her car and drove away. In her rearview mirror, she saw Ned and Savard talking in the driveway, or more accurately, Ned talking and Savard listening, very still.

Roger took his car to an auto glass shop and had a new window installed. On the way home, he stopped at the newsstand of the Ritz, found mention of Anne, but none of Mrs. Truax, none of Whitey. He parked in his garage, closed the door, carried the ax inside, and tucked it behind the woodpile in the storage room off his basement

HQ, woodpile left over from the evenings when they'd had fires. Then he went upstairs and poured himself a Scotch, drank it looking down on the street from the living room window.

Whitey was *(A)* dead in the woods, perhaps not to be found until spring, or *(B)* alive and somewhere out there. *A* would be lovely, but he had to plan for *B*. Roger tried to quantify the threat represented by Whitey, in the event he fell into the hands of the police. Not, based on the evidence on his digital recorder, that the police were much to worry about: a dumb cop confused in predictable ways. Roger had already dealt quickly with the puzzle of lover boy's reluctance to explain his whereabouts. The answer was obvious: he and Francie had met somewhere else. Perhaps determining where might be useful.

But not exigent. Exigent was identifying the points of vulnerability represented by Whitey. A leather jacket with no label. A small sum of money in untraceable bills. A story of alligators and a disputed painting. A name: Roger. Not much, but neither was it nothing, especially the name. Roger sensed a complex equation that could only be balanced by the death of Whitey. But the problem was deeper than that, much deeper, because the perfect solution, perfect in that it rendered him blameless, even sympathetic in some eyes, had involved tying two deaths together in an invulnerable little package, and how could he do that now? That meant—my God!— that in order to be rid of Whitey, to be rid of him and blameless of that ridding, he would have to design another, completely separate, perfect crime! Roger foresaw a horrifying string of perfectly unincriminating homicides stretching on and on into a never-ending future, horrifying in the vastness of its numerology, in the demonic intertwining of its permutations and combinations. What kind of a life was that? He had a dreadful premonition—no, not premonition, no such thing—that the truly perfect part of a perfect crime might be the inevitable, wired-in-from-the-inception, inclusion of its own punishment: the perpetrator being the true target from the start. But, no, that was sophistry of the most unscientific and moralistic kind, and in this case outrageous—he was not the one in the wrong. But what a thought, Whiteys row on row, all in need of being put down with all their fingers pointing elsewhere. Chaos. Chaos leading to madness, even in a being possessed of a thousand brains like his. Oh, *A* would be lovely.

"Please, *A*," he said aloud, as Francie came walking up the street. In a well-ordered world, in a world that meant something, Whitey would be lying frozen solid under a dark tree, but since this was what Roger had been given for a world, he had to plan for *B*.

And there was Francie, so alive, alive at least in the sense a cow lives, unaware of the concept of slaughterhouse. So lucky, and she didn't even know it! But what was this? As she came closer, Roger saw that she was crying; not making a sound or anything like that—her mouth was closed—but tears were streaming down her face. Why?

And then facets rotated slightly in his mind, and he thought, *Of course! She blames herself, the whore.* He took a little satisfaction from that, but there was more—he could feel it coming, coming: a tremendous improvisation. Nothing mystical about improvisation, nothing more than normal, logical thought process, simply speeded-up exponentially, like subatomic particles in an accelerator. His brain had an accelerator mode, and now it offered up an improvisation based on the theme of Francie's despondency and guilt over— could he push it that far? yes!—over engineering the

murder of her tennis pal, an improvisation that would
end on the final triumphant note of her suicide.

There was even a coda, written for a potential re-
appearance by Whitey: a few simple notes that tied
Whitey, the instrument, to Francie, the mastermind.
What credibility would a convicted killer like Whitey
have, faced with the awesome probative impact of her
suicide? And how tidy. The name Roger, for example?
Why wouldn't Whitey have heard the name of the
mastermind's husband, poor cuckold?

Maybe there was a God, after all.

Francie came up the brick walkway. Roger stepped
back from the window. What kind of suicide would she
choose, what method would be character-appropriate?
An important question. Were there any asps in the house?
Roger laughed aloud. What a brilliant joke! Francie
would have loved it.

32

Savard walked into the station just before three that afternoon. "He cracked."

"Yeah?" said Carbonneau, looking up from his chair at the duty desk.

Something was wrong; Savard knew that right away, but not what. "Cracked in the sense that he coughed up his alibi, anyway. And it checks out."

The next question should have been: *What's his alibi?* Instead, Carbonneau said, "Well, uh, maybe not surprising."

Savard didn't get that at all. Something was wrong: too crowded, for starters—Berry, Lisa, Ducharme, Morris, Feeney, more. The whole department in the room, every shift.

"This a mutiny?" Savard said.

"Oh, no, Chief," said Carbonneau, but he didn't seem to want to go on.

"Then what?" said Savard, starting to smile; a birthday or something like that he was supposed to remember but hadn't.

"Those prints," said Carbonneau, and glanced around for help that didn't come. "Prints we lifted off that bedspread."

"Duvet," said Lisa. "Goose-down duvet."

Carbonneau gave her a look; that wasn't the kind of help he'd had in mind. "The lab got a match." He bit the inside of

his lip. Berry was doing it, too, biting the inside of *his* goddamn lip.

"And what?" said Savard. "They were mine? What's
going on?"

Their heads all swung around to Lisa, sitting at her desk
with the coffee cup full of candy canes. She looked at Savard,
almost in the eye. "They were Whitey Truax's," she said.

The name did something physical to him, sent a cold
wave down his shoulders and back, heated up his face at the
same time. He sat down in someone's chair, heard a voice
saying, "You all right, Joe?"

"Yeah." Then, still in the grip of these weird physical
sensations, he realized the mistake he'd made; the realization sent a pulse of adrenaline through him, made him
normal again. He got up fast. "Let's go."

"Where?" someone said, but not Lisa; the best shot in
the department, she was already unlocking the gun rack,
taking her .303 off the wall.

They drove to Lawton Ferry in three cars, eighty miles
an hour, lights flashing, sirens wailing, the whole performance. For once, all that sound and fury suited Savard's
mood, calmed him down, if anything. Beside him, Lisa
buckled on her vest.

"I called down to Florida," she said. "You knew he was
part of that rent-a-con thing?"

"Yeah."

"He got parole early November, went missing from the
halfway house after Thanksgiving. The asshole couldn't
even give me the exact date. But he's wanted down there
on an assault charge that could go up to something else if
the victim succumbs. That's what he said. The asshole, I'm
talking about. Succumbs. A social worker."

"They never sent us anything?"

"Nope."

He'd always known Whitey would be free someday, had even wondered at one time what he'd do if he saw him on the street. But as the years went by, he'd thought less and less about Whitey, and after hearing of the transfer to Florida, almost nothing. Hadn't forgotten him, more a case of reclassifying him as one of those bad accidents that can happen to people. Now, with Anne Franklin at the medical examiner's, it was all fresh again, and personal.

They pulled up at 97 Carp Road, jumped out, took aim, summoned Whitey on the bullhorn. Nothing, of course. Savard walked up to the duct-taped front window and did what he'd been about to do the night before: looked through.

"Goddamn it," he said. No one's stupidity bothered him like his own. He strode to the front door and broke it down. They went into the lousy little place and stood around the body of Mrs. Truax. The cat came in the open doorway and rubbed itself against Lisa's leg.

Whitey drank the last can of Pepsi, tossed it out the window. Late afternoon, deep in the woods on an old lumber road, maybe into Maine, running the engine from time to time to keep warm. The cold had never bothered him before, but it did now. Last can of Pepsi, and the gas—down to what? A quarter of a tank, although he could see space between the quarter line and the needle, a hair below. But call it a quarter. And on the radio, zip. Nothing but static—proving how deep in the woods he was.

What else? He felt like shit, hurt all over, chest and face especially. And that face in the mirror: nasty. Hungry, too, and nothing to eat. He counted his money: $542. Not bad—had he ever had more in his pocket?— but he couldn't figure out how to make it help him.

Whitey saw his breath, smelled it, too. When was the last time he'd had pickles? He thought of the stripper bar where he'd had lunch before ... whatever had gone down went down. Those silicone tits or whatever they were—was that the same stuff they made computer brains out of?—seemed a lot more appealing now, out here in the cold. Too fucking cold. He switched on the engine again, cranked the heat up full blast, lay down on the bench seat. From there he could gaze up at the trees, all bare and spiky, pressing down from high above. He didn't like that at all, and closed his eyes.

When Whitey woke up, it was dark and the needle on the lit-up dash was down, way down, almost on empty, dropping closer and closer as he watched. Not that empty meant empty—he knew his car. Then the warning light went on. He switched off the engine. Metal popped for a minute or two, and by then it was getting cold again, much too cold already. A man, even a man like him, could freeze solid in the woods on this sort of night. Without gas in the tank, he would die. He turned on the light, counted his money again. Five forty-two: piss. Seventeen years and that was what he had to show for it. Made him mad.

And millions, or at least a million, had been in reach. He remembered how it felt to be a giant, capable of ripping trees out of the ground. He didn't feel like that now. *Master of puppets I'm pulling your strings.* Those words meant something, contained some message for his ears alone, but he didn't know what. And then there was the girl in the miniskirt, sucking on grapes. Sounded good. Worth a million or more, meaning it was painted by a famous artist, such as Picasso, or others, who didn't come to mind at that moment. Had Roger ever mentioned the name of the artist? No. Just one more of his fuckups. Whitey went over the fuckups—no Brinks truck, no

painting, no mention of a woman who would try to kill
him. No mention either that Roger would park on the
wrong side of the river, would be lurking around the cottage with an ax. What had Roger been planning to do
with that ax? Whitey knew the answer to that, had seen it
on Roger's face under the porch light, had smashed in
the window of Roger's car because of it, but still it made
no sense. Did Roger blame him in some way for the
fuckups? Whitey wasn't able to think his way through
that one. Could have been killed, twice, and didn't even
know why. Someone owed him an explanation. And
what about benefits, like his medical expenses, and
danger pay? He realized that everything had changed
the moment Roger stepped on his toe. Why hadn't he
done something then and there? He dwelled for a while
on the memory of what had happened to an inmate
down in Florida who'd just brushed against him in the
chow line, spilling Whitey's pudding. This was a democ-
racy. No special treatment for anyone. So what did Roger
deserve now?

But he was cold, hungry, weak, deep in the woods: all
on the bad side. Was there anything on the good side,
anything going for him? Only the fact that he knew
where Roger lived. And the night. Night was his friend.
Whitey fired up his truck.

He nosed his way back out of the deep woods, out of
the darkness, silence, long shadows, the chains taking
him safely to the first plowed country road. A plowed
road, but no sign of life, nothing but whiteness outside
and the red of the warning light in the cab. By the time he
saw the glow of the first crummy village, the needle had
sunk far below the empty mark, almost the width of his
baby finger. The engine stuttered once, twice, and died—
just as he rolled up to a one-pump station at the cross-
roads. He got the feeling it was meant to be.

A kid appeared.

"Fill it," Whitey said.

The kid didn't move for a moment, staring at Whitey's face in the glare of the pump lights.

"Hockey game," Whitey said.

The kid nodded. "Sell Band-Aids inside."

Whitey went in, bought Band-Aids, sandwiches, candy bars, a shake, said, "Hockey game," to the woman at the cash before she could even ask; he was coming back.

"You guys," she said.

He was in Maine, all right, could tell by the way they talked. He got back in the pickup, stuck the Band-Aids over his stitches, tried a chicken sandwich. That hurt too much to eat, so he just downed the shake—had to keep his strength up for what lay ahead—and headed south.

Night is my friend. Sounded like a line from a song, a good one, a Metallica song. Whitey tried to think of what could come next. *End* rhymed with *friend*, but what went in between? He couldn't get from *friend* to *end*, soon gave up, tried the radio instead. Now a few stations came in, but unsteady and playing shit. He switched it off.

Whitey stopped in the last town before the turnpike, filled up again, bought two quarts of chocolate milk, drank them in the 7-Eleven parking lot, felt better right away. He worked his way through a candy bar, taking little bites, chewing carefully, then started on the chicken sandwich: yes, getting stronger—he was something else. A bus pulled in, BOSTON in the destination box, and a woman stepped down, followed by the driver. The driver went into the store; the woman got into a waiting pickup, almost as old as Whitey's, put her arms around the man behind the wheel, and gave him a big kiss. Then she saw Whitey watching and sat back in her seat; they drove away.

Whitey hit the radio button again. Plenty of stations now. He turned the dial, heard bits of this and that:

oldies, folk, jazz, commercials, "—nald 'Whitey' Truax,"
"down to minus twent—"

His name? Had he heard his name on the radio? He
twisted his way back up the dial, failed to find the station,
or if he did, it was playing music now. His name on the
radio? He thought ahead to the turnpike with its toll-
booths, its speed traps; and his truck, all white with that
REDEEMER shit on the side.

And got out fast. He walked across the parking lot to
the bus, waited outside the closed door. After a minute
or two, the driver came out of the 7-Eleven, scratching at
instant tickets. "One," Whitey said to him, getting out his
money.

"All the way?"

"Huh?"

The driver gave him a look, took in the Band-Aids and
his fucking hair. "Boston," he said. "End of the line."

"Yeah," said Whitey.

Whitey sat at the back, the only passenger at first, one
of only a few by the end. It was warm on the bus, and with
the winter night gliding by outside and what he'd been
through, Whitey should have fallen asleep right away.
But he couldn't sleep, not with the flashing blue lights he
saw from time to time, not with his name out there on the
radio, not with things so uneven between him and Roger.
He was back on a bus, didn't even have his truck—would
never have it again. Would never have it again: he
stopped thinking about the future right there, at least of
any future beyond evening things up with Roger. What
did he have? The night, and knowing where Roger lived.
What did he need? A hat for one thing, to hide the hair
he saw glowing back at him from his window at the back
of the bus.

He bought one at the pushcart stand in South Station,

red wool with *Holy Cross* written on the front. In the bathroom, he pulled it low over his ears and forehead, turned up the collar of his leather jacket, hunched down inside. He checked himself in the mirror: could have been anybody. Anybody nasty. Whitey walked out into the city.

And lost the night right away. The sky seemed to brighten almost at once, as though everything was speeding up, black rushing to turn blue, a cloudless icy blue with a cold wind whipping through the downtown streets and pain on the faces of all the well-dressed people walking fast to wherever. No one looked at anybody. Whitey walked fast, too, tall in his cowboy boots, trim in his leather jacket, anonymous in his wool hat. Daytime, but safe for now.

He was hungry, craved doughnuts, soft and sweet, hot chocolate, coffee with lots of sugar, but passed by every restaurant; couldn't go in, not with his name out there on the radio. He came to the statue of George Washington; an icicle hung from the end of his saber. A saber would make a decent weapon, much better than what he had, which was nothing.

Whitey went through the Public Garden, following the path around the frozen pond. He crossed a street, climbed the hill past all the big brick houses with their fancy grillwork, doors, knockers, turned left on another street, climbed higher. And there he was, standing outside Roger's door, a tall and massive door, black with gold numbers and fixtures. He noticed that Christmas wreaths hung from the doors of the neighboring houses but not from Roger's. That didn't help him with the next step. What was it? Whitey didn't know.

The mailman was coming up the street, red envelopes in his hand. No way he could just stay there, waiting outside the door. Whitey kept going, rounded the next corner, came to an alley. An alley, he realized, that backed against Roger's house, where Roger might keep his car, for example. Whitey walked down the alley.

He didn't see Roger's car in the alley, no cars at all, just garage doors lining both sides. No numbers on them either: how was he supposed to know which garage was Roger's? He thought for a while, wondered about going back around to the street, counting the houses on the block, or maybe trying to identify them by their rooftops, then coming back and—

A garage door slid up, three or four garages down the alley from where he stood, on the right. A car backed out. The rear wheels hadn't even appeared before Whitey recognized Roger's four-by-four, the window replaced already. All neat and tidy. Whitey ducked behind a trash barrel.

Over the top of the barrel, he watched the car emerge, caught the profile of a woman in the passenger seat, and Roger beyond her at the wheel, checking his mirrors. The front wheels angled out, the car backed toward him a few feet, then straightened and drove forward, off down the alley.

Safe.

But the woman! Had he ever seen a woman like that? Yes, as a matter of fact, but he couldn't think who at the moment. Could she possibly be Roger's? What a thought. Then it hit him: she was a grown-up version of Sue Savard, but oh so much better. A perfect Sue Savard, the way Sue Savard would have looked with an actress playing her. Whitey was so knocked out, so distracted by these unusual thoughts, that he almost didn't notice the garage door sliding back down, almost didn't realize that Roger had triggered some sort of remote control from his car, almost didn't grasp the significance of it all. He charged out from behind the trash can, flew toward that closing door, skidded the last few yards across icy bricks, jammed the toe of his cowboy boot—fucking toe stepped on by Roger—under it just in time. Yes: he was in; and got that old, old feeling.

33

"Not a cloud in the sky," said Roger, driving west on Storrow, hands at the proper ten-minutes-to-two position on the wheel. "My suit satisfactory?"

Had he ever asked her opinion of what he wore? Not that Francie remembered. She glanced at the suit: black wool, perhaps blended with cashmere, probably from Brooks Brothers. "It's fine," she said, recalling that they'd discussed this particular suit once before, her mind about to zero in on the occasion when he did it for her.

"Doesn't make me resemble a luncheon companion of the godfather?"

"What are you getting at?"

"Why, nothing. Quite a funny joke you made about this suit, that's all. Perhaps I'm just fully appreciating it now." He smiled at her. "You always had that sense of humor, Francie, come what may."

His teeth shone, his shave was close, skin smooth, color high. He might have just returned from a spa weekend. She decided to leave him.

Decided at that moment, regardless of Roger's situation, of whether the Lauderdale job came through, or whether the timing suited Ned. She would start searching for an apartment tomorrow—perhaps moving into a hotel for now. Why spend another night in the house? He

could have the house, keep whatever he wanted; there'd
be no trouble from her.

A decision that had nothing to do with Ned. But what
about him? She had planned to end their relationship
the night Anne died. Would she have been able to do it?
Had it ended anyway? If so, if Anne's death should have
ended it, her own will having failed, what was the
reason? Was there a reason, precise and definable, more
than lace-curtain niceties? Yes. She felt that reason in
her throat, a hard lump of guilt that wouldn't go away. To
put it as baldly as she could, to lacerate herself with it,
she had been fucking Ned and it had killed his wife. But
even punishment like that didn't make the guilt go away.
And worse, that new apartment of hers—she could already picture Ned knocking on the door. What was
wrong with her?

"Something troubling you, Francie?" They'd stopped
at a traffic light and Roger's eyes were on her. "You seem
preoccupied."

"We're on our way to a funeral, Roger."

"Yes," he said, as the light turned green, "it's emotional, I know."

They parked outside the church, five or six spaces behind a hearse and a black limo. The wind blew out of the
west, driving snow off the ground, spinning it in various
shapes. "I thought you had a warmer coat," Roger said,
taking Francie's arm as they walked down the sidewalk,
the wind in their faces.

"I'm not cold," she said, and was starting to pull her
arm away when a car door opened in front of them and
Savard got out. He hadn't shaved closely, hadn't shaved
at all, and his color was bad.

"A quick word with you, Mrs. Cullingwood?" he said.
"If you'll step into the car for a moment."

Francie saw Nora climbing the steps of the church. "About what?" she said.

"The investigation."

"Will you be needing me, too?" said Roger.

Savard shook his head. "This is only for those with some connection to the cottage."

"Of course," Roger said. "I'll save you a place, Francie."

Francie sat in the back of Savard's car, not the old Bronco this time but a police cruiser; a worn heel from someone's shoe lay upside down on the floor mat, rusted cobbler's nails showing. Savard got in beside her, opened a manila envelope, took out some photographs. "Have you ever seen this man?"

She examined a police photograph, full face and profile, with numbers at the bottom. "No," Francie said.

"Take your time."

She did, and gave him the same answer.

"Have you ever heard the name Whitey Truax? Or Donald Truax?"

"No."

"Anne never mentioned that name?"

"No. Is that him?"

"Yes."

"What's his connection to Anne?"

"Probably none," Savard said. "I'm almost certain they met for the first time late Monday afternoon."

"I don't understand."

"He broke into your friend's cottage. Your other friend was there. He killed her. He's done it before—is on parole at this moment, in fact."

"For killing someone?"

"Yes."

"A woman?"

"Yes."

"Did she have some connection to Anne?"

"No." Savard was staring at the photograph. There was a silence, a strange one; she had the crazy notion that he was about to start crying. He did not, of course, but looked up at her with dry eyes and said, "There's no connection at all."

"How do you know it was him this time?"

"Normally I ask the questions." Their eyes met. Did he expect her to apologize for asking questions? She remained silent. "But yours are good," he said at last. "The answer is he left his prints all over the place. He also killed his mother a little while later, down in Lawton Ferry."

"Why? I don't understand any of this."

Savard put the photographs back in the envelope. "I'll fax you the testimony of the psychiatrist from his trial, if you're interested. Thanks for your time, Mrs. Cullingwood."

Francie reached for the door handle, understanding one little part. "This means that all those questions you asked me before . . ."

"What questions?"

"The ones that seemed to be leading to . . ."

"The husband?"

"Yes."

"Are irrelevant now," Savard said. "They were before we had the prints, actually." Pause. "It turned out that Mr. Demarco—or is it doctor—"

"I'm not sure which he prefers."

Another pause. "—had an explanation for his whereabouts."

"I'm not surprised," Francie said, a loyal remark, almost wifely.

"Why is that?"

"He has a private practice, as well as the radio show."

"So?"

"It must raise issues of patient confidentiality."

"Not this alibi," Savard said.

"Not this alibi?" Francie said. "What do you mean?"

Someone rapped at the window of the car. A man in a clerical collar stood outside. Francie opened the door so he could talk to Savard, but it wasn't Savard he wanted.

"Francie Cullingwood?"

"Yes?"

"I wonder if you could help us this morning."

"How?"

"The deceased had a longtime tennis partner from Cleveland." He frowned at a sheet of paper. "I'm not sure which one of these it is. In any case, it was thought that representatives of various aspects of her life might speak briefly at the ceremony. Tennis being one, you see. The problem is that the woman, the tennis partner, is snowed-in in Cleveland. It's been suggested that you might be able to find a few words."

"Ask Nora."

"Ms. Levin? She was the one who gave me your name."

Impossible, out of the question, never. Francie, searching for some polite way to tell the reverend, felt Savard's eyes on her back, on the back of her head, specifically. Impossible, out of the question, never—but how could she say no?

"I'll do it," Francie said, and got out of the car. Savard got out, too, opened the driver's-side door, gave her a little nod over the roof.

Francie sat beside Roger in a pew five or six rows from the front. Roger leaned into her ear. "What was your little colloquium about?"

"I'll tell you later."

Ned, Em, Ned's mother, and a gray-haired man sat in the first row; all Francie could see were the backs of their heads and Ned's arm around Em's shoulder: the family.

Do you have any sisters, Francie? Neither do I. I always wanted one. She saw Nora, across the aisle; a few tennis players she knew; forty or fifty other people she didn't know; the reverend, whom she stopped listening to as soon as she realized he'd never met Anne; and the coffin, a fine-grained blond wood coffin, not ornate. After a minute or two, she was looking at nothing, and withdrew into plans for her little speech.

Right away she thought of Swift's *Marriage Service from His Chamber Window: Let none but Him who rules the thunder.* She remembered exactly how Anne had looked reciting it at Huîtres, her face flushed from wine, tennis, emotion. *Wonderful wine, Roger. I'll know something to order from now on.* From Swift it was a quick jump to *Gulliver's Travels*, from there to the Brobdingnagians, and there she was, up against two-stories-tall Anne, watching through the windows.

Are you mad at me?

Why would I be mad at you?

The way I played. Will you ever forgive me?

And: *You're like a lion—strong, proud, loyal.* Francie sat in the pew, hearing nothing, but no longer seeing nothing; she was staring at the coffin, couldn't take her eyes off it. She almost didn't feel Roger poking her arm, then jerked her head up and saw the reverend beckoning her from behind the lectern.

The next thing Francie knew she was the one standing behind it, overlooking the coffin, the eyes of the mourners all on her. *I have no right to be here, less right than anyone.* That was the truth, the honest beginning, but whom would it serve? Watching eyes and waiting faces. No impatience. They, all of them, had time in common. Faces: the gray-haired man's, same cheekbones, same chin, Anne's father; Em's, the face of the girl on the skateboard—and Francie suddenly understood what made *oh garden, my garden* work, the tension between the carefree girl and those tumescent grapes, just beginning to rot; Ned's, almost as white as the reverend's collar, except for two spots growing redder on his cheeks. And there was Savard standing at the back. She suddenly wanted to cry out: *Let none but Him who rules the thunder.* But did not, had nothing prepared; remembered Savard's little nod, started talking.

"I played the best tennis of my life with Anne. It's just a game, I know. But that's what Anne was like. She brought out the best in everyone. There was something about her, I don't know what it was, not to put in words. But I'm going to be thinking about it for a long time. About her. Even in death she'll still have that power, you see. To bring out the best, at least in me, I hope to God."

And what voice was this? Hers, of course, but strange in her ear—unmodulated, unmediated, undirected. Her inner voice. Had she ever heard it aloud before? Yes, once before: out on the ice with Ned, when she'd told him, "Maybe we'd better call this off."

Was there more to say? Just one thing, and Francie said it: "I'm going to miss her."

Then she was sitting beside Roger again, not knowing quite how she got there, left with three memories: Em crying; Nora squeezing her hand from her seat by the aisle; another little nod from Savard at the back, perhaps nodding to himself, not meant for her at all.

"Well done," said Roger.

At the graveyard: fewer people, a hole in the frozen ground, more talk. All familiar: she was in the art business, knew something of funerals. Coffin lowered, symbolic shovelful of dirt thrown in, ancient wordless method for getting the message across, and it did, sounding a wintry rattle on the coffin lid that made Francie flinch.

She didn't believe in an afterlife, or God, although she'd just hoped to him in her little speech. And once before, made a deal with him, this time under the ice—a deal on which she'd reneged. Francie felt the cold then, through and through. The wind caught someone's hat, blew it between two gravestones and out of sight.

Ned, Em, and the two grandparents were standing at the gate as Francie and Roger went out. "Thank you both for coming," Ned said.

"So sorry," Roger said.

Anne's father stepped forward, took Francie's hand. "That was so beautiful, what you said. And true— everything about her, going back to when she was a little girl, came into focus for me when you spoke." His eyes filled with tears, but he blinked them away; Francie sensed some inner strength in him that hadn't been passed on. "Will you be coming to the house?"

"Grandpa and I are going to decorate the tree," Em said; she held tight to his hand. "It looks so bare." Or maybe it had been passed on after all, just skipping a generation.

"I . . ." Francie looked at Ned, saw that notch in his forehead above the right eye.

"Yes," he said. "Please do. Some people are stopping in." He turned to his mother. "You called the caterer, didn't you, Mom?"

She nodded. "But don't expect anything elaborate."

"Be that as it may," Roger said, "Francie and I wouldn't dream of intruding at a time like this."

"It wouldn't be an intrusion, would it, Ned?" said Anne's father.

"You could help with the tree," Em said.

Roger smiled down at her. "Perhaps some other—"

"I'd be honored," Francie said. "Why don't you take the car home, Roger? I'll be back later."

Their eyes met; his were cloudy, as though film were whizzing by at high speed, just beneath the surface. "As you wish," he said. "But don't be too too late."

The caterers had laid out a buffet in Ned's dining room: salads, cold cuts, a bar. There were people Francie didn't know, from the radio show, the B.U. psychology department, Cleveland. She poured herself a glass of red wine because she couldn't think of a convincing reason not to, and she needed it, and went into the living room.

The corduroy chair was gone, and in its place stood the tree, Anne's father looping a string of lights around it, Em cross-legged on the floor with a cardboard box of ornaments wrapped in tissue. Francie sat beside her.

"Mom," Em began, choked on the word, went on, "made most of these herself."

Francie wanted to comfort her in some way, to stroke her head, but it wasn't her place. She unwrapped an ornament. "She was a glassblower, too?"

"Oh, yes," said Anne's father. "She learned at summer camp. They said she had a knack for it."

Francie examined the decorations: delicate translucent balls, red, green, gold, and a few of all three colors at once, that changed from one to another as she turned them in her hand; tiny bells with tiny glass clappers that rang with tiny crystal peals; stained-glass saints with alien medieval faces but relaxed, modern poses; oddities, the opposites of gargoyles, she supposed—a dog with a pagoda-roof head, a bicycle with Marlon Brando faces for wheels, a smile made of two glass snakes, one red, one green, and white Chiclets; and a Tower of Pisa, with a robed figure on top. Galileo, but studying him closely, Francie saw that he held not metal balls but a bottle of champagne and a stemmed glass, perfectly formed but no more than a quarter of an inch tall. "These are great," she said.

"Do you think so?" Em said, watching her carefully; so was Anne's father, from a footstool on the other side of the tree.

"Oh, yes." Better than her paintings, much, much better; of another order entirely. "Are there more?"

"Just the angel," Em said. "It lights up from inside."

But it wasn't in the box.

"Maybe it's still in the closet," Em said. "I couldn't reach the top shelf."

"I'll get it," Francie said, rising. "What closet?"

"Upstairs," said Em, "on the left." She gazed down at a glass elephant in her hand, playing its saxophone trunk.

Francie climbed the stairs, opened the first door on her left. Something wrapped in red tissue lay on the top shelf. She took it down, removed the tissue, saw a shining black angel with spun-glass wings and a face that reminded her of Miles Davis. Anne, in death, kept growing in her mind.

Turning to go downstairs, Francie saw the closed door of the master bedroom. Inside hung the portrait of Ned, unless he'd taken it down. She went closer. Why hadn't Ned shown his portrait to Savard? Perhaps he simply hadn't wanted to bother taking it off the wall, carrying it down. Francie knocked on the door. No response. She opened it slightly, looked in. The room was unoccupied and the portrait hung in its place. Francie went in.

Standing at the foot of the bed, she studied the painting, saw what she had seen before—the resemblance, unaccountable in strictly photographic terms, the powerful, dominating pose, the surprising absence of sensuality—but nothing more, nothing that would explain any reluctance to have it examined. Then it struck her that something might be written on the back, some title or dedication. She laid the glass angel on the covers, walked around the bed, leaned over, got her hands on the frame—and heard a moan.

Ned's moan. Francie whirled around, eyes on the closed bathroom door, heard him again. He was there, a few steps away, in quiet agony. Francie took those steps, not to say anything, not to put any pressure on him, just to hold him, to let him know she was there. She knocked quietly on the door.

Silence. Then he said, "Em? Is that you? I'll be down in a minute."

Francie heard agony in his tone, yes, but something else as well, something urgent and furtive that made her try the door. Locked. So she stooped, stooped to a lower level, to look through the keyhole in the old period door in Anne's old period house. Ned was there, but not alone, and she'd misinterpreted the sound she'd heard. Francie's eyes, expert eyes, trained for grasping detail and composition, took it all in, understood for her what her reeling mind could not: the half-clothed embrace, the glossy-haired woman, Chinese-American, leaning back on the sink, Ned curved over her, their faces turned toward the door in listening attitudes. Then Ned's gaze fell toward the keyhole, fastened on it, and slowly went through changes that ended in horror.

"Francie?" Ned said. "Francie?" Through the keyhole, she saw him push himself away from the woman. "Oh my God, Francie, no."

What happened next? Francie didn't know, only knew she was somehow bolting down the stairs, free-falling, not even in contact with them, the glass angel in her hand. There was Em, still on the floor, going through the ornaments.

"Here you are, sweetheart," Francie said, and gave her

the angel. Then came a pause, in which neither of them seemed to breathe, and Francie took the liberty of touching Em's head; her hand did so, really, and she didn't stop it.

Then she was in the hall, getting her coat, walking out of the house, leaving. Walking fast, fast, fast. She could tell how cold it must have been from the hard bright snow on the ground and the icy sky and the whining wind, but she didn't feel it at all. She was burning up. Walking, walking, walking: Francie walked and walked, but couldn't escape the burning, and finally there was nowhere to go but home.

34

What a house Roger had! Whitey explored it from
top to bottom. He'd been inside the cottages of the rich,
the second homes, but never seen anything like this. The
furniture, the rugs, the stuff! Even this sculpture or whatever it was on the bookcase in the living room, made of
some material he'd never seen, maybe a rare stone or
mineral, so smooth. What was it worth? Whitey picked
up the sculpture—heavy, but not as heavy as it looked,
maybe not so valuable after all—turned it in his hands: a
strange, curved thing that reminded him of tits from one
angle, ass from another. At that moment a phone rang,
nearby and loud, startling him. He dropped the goddamn thing; it fell on the gleaming hardwood floor, just
missing the edge of the thick carpet, and smashed in
pieces. The noise was shattering; in the midst of it, he
heard a voice, spun around, saw no one.

"Francie? Nora. I was going to swing by and ride out
with you. Guess you've already left. See you there. God, I
hate funerals, this one especially." Beep.

Beep. Just an answering machine. Whitey told himself
to stay cool. He said it out loud. "Stay cool." Cool like ice,
like snow. He glanced down at the remains of the sculpture. The cool thing, the smart thing, would be to leave no
trace, right? In case some illegal act was going to happen,
ay. He went into the kitchen—what a kitchen! like there

341

was a restaurant on the other side of the door—found broom and dustpan, swept up the mess, dumped it into a trash bin under the sink. Cool.

Beep. He jumped. The fucking thing had beeped again. Whitey returned to the living room, stared at the red light blinking on the phone. He wasn't sure which button turned it off; maybe better, cooler, to forget about it, leave no trace. But what about the jumpiness? He went to the cabinet beside the tall plant in the corner, a waist-high cabinet with a silver tray on top bearing bottles—Scotch, vodka, gin, all fancy brands. He tried the vodka, not that he liked vodka particularly, but because they said it had no smell: leave no trace. He was getting very smart, and it went down nice like that, surprisingly nice, warm from the bottle. Beep. He took another, just a tich, as Ma used to say back in her drinking days, before this religious shit. Didn't matter—he had no plans to see her again.

What were his plans, anyway? Exactly, like?

Mulling that question, Whitey opened the cabinet, just to have something to do while he thought. There were photograph albums inside. He leafed through one, saw Roger, a much younger Roger, in tennis whites, his arm around a beautiful woman, the woman he'd seen in his car, the super–Sue Savard. She wore a little tennis skirt. What a body! What was her name? He'd just heard it on the answering machine. Francie. He searched the albums for more pictures of Francie, preferably nude, but there was nothing like that. Roger and Francie smiling on a chairlift, Roger saying something to Francie on a sailboat, Roger reading a menu at an outdoor café, Francie staring into the camera.

Beep.

Most of the pictures were dated underneath, none

more recent than ten years ago. The last album, the most recent, petered out in the middle with two last pictures: Roger, Francie, and a big woman, standing on a tennis court, the two women laughing, Roger watching them; and Francie and another woman, both in bathing suits, sitting on a floating dock. They both had nice bodies, Francie's better—bigger tits, for starters—but the bathing suits weren't as revealing as some, and Whitey was about to close the book, when he realized there was something odd about that last picture. He studied it carefully, especially the wooden house behind the trees in the background, and then he recognized it— the cottage out on the island in the middle of the river. What did this mean? It had to mean something. Whitey didn't know. He peeled the photograph off the page and stuck it in his pocket.

Beep.

Whitey helped himself to another tich of vodka, more than a tich. It had to mean something. He went into the kitchen and opened the fridge, looking for chocolate milk. There was none, but he found a jar of peanut butter, scooped some out with his fingers, ate it. He wandered to the desk in the little alcove, glanced at the mail on top, opened a drawer, saw a twenty-dollar bill, pocketed that, too. Under it lay a newsletter from some tennis club. CULLINGWOOD-FRANKLIN TO VIE FOR DOUBLES CROWN, he read, a headline followed by a brief article summarizing tennis matches, and two photographs, one of Francie, the other of . . . could it be? Yes. How could he forget that face, face of the woman who'd tried to kill him? Meaning? Meaning that there were—what was the word? Connections. Had to mean something. What? Whitey couldn't take the next step, but the buzzing had already started, deep inside his head.

Beep.

Tich.

He didn't feel his strongest, because of what she'd done to him, and that might be bad. He ate more peanut butter from the jar to give him strength. What next? What next? There was still the basement. He found the stairs and went down.

Nice and dark, the only light coming from narrow windows at the top of the wall, at street level. He could see well enough, was in a laundry room: washer, dryer, clothes hanging on a line. Bra and panties, for instance, which he felt as he went by. He opened a door, entered a large room, darker than the first; here the street-level windows were covered with black paper, and the only light came from a glowing computer screen. Computer, printer, desk, file cabinets: an office, Roger's home office, where he worked late into the night, making all his money. Maybe he took little naps on that couch with the sleeping bag on top, or maybe that woman of his, Francie, sometimes came down for a quick one.

Beep. Very faint now, but he heard it; his senses were keen. That would explain in some way why darkness was his friend, but in what way, exactly, he didn't know.

Whitey sat at the desk, looked at the computer screen. On one side was a crossword puzzle. He checked two or three clues, had no idea. On the other side of the screen he saw a heading—Puzzletalk—and under it lines of print scrolled slowly by, a conversation of some sort. Was this one of those chat rooms, where, according to Rey, at least, you could pick up girls or download porn? He scanned it quickly, saw it had nothing to do with sex, but—what was this? *Rimsky?* His eyes flashed up to the top, catching a line as it disappeared from view.

criminals?

>*BOOBOO: Oh, please, not capital punishment again!!!*

>*FLYBOY: Yeah, we know how you like to fry 'em up on a daily basis down there in Fla. but give it a REST.*

>*RIMSKY: This is why Rome fell. The barbarian's inside your walls and you don't even know it.*

>*BOOBOO: ???*

>*RIMSKY: Member that guy I was telling you about? Whitey Truax?*

>*BOOBOO: ???*

>*FLYBOY: Who gives a?*

>*MODERATOR: I remember.*

>*RIMSKY: First chance he got he jumped parole killed two more people, one of them his mother. Not a deterrent, kiddies?????*

The buzzing grew louder. Whitey tried to read on, but the words had stopped scrolling; the response, if any, was off the screen, and he didn't know how to make it appear. *One of them his mother?* Impossible—he'd hardly even tapped her; picked her up, dusted her off. She'd been fine when he left. Rimsky had it wrong. And he could prove it, prove the asshole wrong, just by calling her on the phone.

Whitey picked up Roger's phone and dialed her number. It was answered on the first ring.

"Sergeant Berry," said a man.

Whitey snapped the phone back in its cradle.

Beep.

Buzz, buzz. And Rimsky. What was he doing on Roger's computer? Whitey remembered Rimsky: a guard on his cell block, a shit disturber, which was what they called the ones who made a little extra effort during the cavity searches. And now here he was on Roger's

computer. *Member that guy I was telling you about?*
When? Telling who? Rimsky, on Roger's computer. Connections. Connections all over the place, past and present.
Yes: past and present, an expression he'd heard before,
and now understood a little better. One thing for sure, it
was all about—yes! talk about connections—masters
and puppets, and the goddamn thing was, the thing that
made him want to puke up all that vodka and peanut
butter—and he almost did—the goddamn thing was—

Whitey heard something over the buzzing, a mecha-
nized, metallic rumble. The garage door. He rose, listening
hard. A car door closed beyond the far wall. They were
home, home from the . . . funeral. And he knew whose
funeral it must have been. Connections. His mind was
making them like never before. But what did it add up
to? What was the complete picture? He needed time to
think, but—

Footsteps: hard shoes on the cement floor of the
laundry room, coming his way. He looked around wildly—
no, not wildly, stay cool, stay cool—and saw another
door, at the end of the row of filing cabinets. He hurried
across the room, but quiet, quiet and cool, opened the
door: a small room, cold and musty, with a single street-
level window, not blacked-out but very dirty, and shadowy
objects inside. Trunks, beach umbrellas, a woodpile. Beep.
Whitey went in, closed the door silently, knelt behind
the woodpile. An earthen floor: common in basements
where he came from, but strange to find in a house like
this. And there was something hard under his knee. He
reached down, freed it, picked it up—an ax.

"Joe Savard of the Lawton police calling for Nora
Levin. Missed you at Anne Franklin's funeral today,
would like to talk. Please get back to me at one of the following numbers."

* * *

Roger entered HQ, glanced at the computer screen. *Times of London* puzzle up—one across, strengthening, eight letters: *roborant*, no doubt—saw some illiterate conversation taking place, switched off the machine. *Think,* he commanded, and the marvelous brain responded without hesitation.

Two problems: Francie and Whitey, once conjoined in an elegant solution, now separating fast like particles that had failed to collide. Of the two, Whitey presented by far the more unknowns, variables, intangibles, unless he was frozen solid in the woods, and that would be lucky, and he, Roger, had always had rotten luck.

So, Francie, less unknown, less variable, less intangible, first. Soon she would be home, despondent. Funeral day: the atmosphere would never be better for the ending he had improvised, but the details had to be right, had to be in character, had to be her. Would she leave a note? No, not her style at all. No note. That made it easier. And what of the method itself? Suitable, fitting, Francie. Nothing messy, nothing violent, nothing brilliant. He heard a faraway beep. The answering machine. He ignored it: wouldn't be for him.

Where was he? Nothing messy, nothing violent, nothing brilliant—something feminine, something that would make her weeping friends agree, *Yes, that was Francie, all the way.*

The problem having been properly framed, the answer came at once: gas. Gas, of course. Gas was feminine. Gas was her.

What gas? CO.

CO. Roger pictured the molecule in his mind, a simple thing, not particularly attractive but sturdy, like a reliable peasant. CO—odorless, colorless, plentiful. And so simple, like one of those schoolboy science projects that never failed: insert subject in garage, close doors, run fossil-fuel-burning internal combustion engine, wait outside.

The details, the adjustments: his brain sketched those in without any active direction from him. Difficult to persuade or trick the subject into inserting herself into the garage for the requisite time, of course, but neither was it necessary, the only necessity being that her body be found there. Much easier to perform the operation elsewhere— her bedroom, say, while she slept—and then transfer the end result to the garage when convenient. After that, the performer of the operation had merely to open the bedroom windows for an hour or two, and then the garage doors as well, perhaps screaming a desperate plea into the alley—would a trashman come running?—those procedures to be followed by the frantic call to 911, punctuated with a cough or two. Perfect, perfect, perfect. Oh, to have a brain like this, to never know boredom.

Beep.

Gas, generated in garage, required in second-floor bedroom. How was gas transported? By pipeline, of course. At one stage of his life he'd done rather well in pipeline stocks; was it his fault that Thorvald had bungled the timing when he'd finally persuaded them to jump in with both feet? His mind stuck for a moment, stuttering on Thorvald, and he had to give it a little push, to remind it of the coming insurance settlement, sale of the house, the art—the Arp alone worth a tidy sum—and then Rome, or some other rosy future.

His mind got back to work. Pipeline. A garden hose was a pipeline, connectable to the gas outlet, in this case an automobile tailpipe, with tape, duct or electrical, both of which were available on the premises. How many feet of hose were required, from garage, upstairs to kitchen, around corner, up stairs, down hall, under bedroom door? One hundred? One hundred and twenty? Also available on the premises: several garden hoses, mutually attachable, were kept in the garage. Correction: not in the garage but closer at hand, in the storage room directly adjacent to HQ.

To begin: inspection of equipment. Roger opened the door to the storage room, went in, found three garden hoses coiled on one another in front of the woodpile. He paused for a moment, sniffed the musty air. What was that smell? Peanut butter? Impossible—no peanut butter in the storage room. He carried the hoses out and closed the door.

Roger inspected the hoses for punctures or tears, found none, screwed them together. Next? Fossil fuel supply. He went into the garage, checked the gauge on Francie's car—hers, not his; he would never make an error as fundamental as that—found it three-quarters full. Much more than enough. Next? Her bedroom windows. It was a cold night; they would be closed. Next? There was no next. That was it: a simple plan. The complicated part, the part that would ultimately be more persuasive than any forensics, was the psychology—in this case female psychology, believable in every detail. Despondency, despair, guilt, suicide: like train cars barreling down the track. No more thinking to be done. To pass the time, Roger sat at the computer and took a virtual tour of Rome, refreshing his memory.

35

Francie walked all the way home, the wind at her back most of the time, arriving just after four under a rapidly darkening sky. She was no longer burning up, was probably cold, although she didn't feel it, numb inside and out. She'd been through everything, now knew Ned's alibi and why he was reluctant to use it, knew all but the where of it; knew, too, something of how it felt to be in Anne's position, with another woman, unseen, exerting force on her life like some orbiting body composed of dark matter. A powerful force that shook, unsettled, reduced: could reduce her to the state of Anne sobbing on her stool in the locker room, fallen completely apart. But Francie hadn't earned the right to be in that state, was the other woman, not the wife—in this case not even that, but the other other woman—and so any falling apart would be ridiculous, absurd, pretentious. And shameful: a feeling with which she was filled to the brim already. So although her mind was ready to start writhing with the kinds of questions that must have tormented Anne—had he really been working on such-and-such a night? how had they met, how had it begun? what did he tell her in bed? what did they do? the same things? different things? the same things better?—she couldn't allow it. Among other reasons, she owed Anne some dignity.

Francie went in the front door, stood in the hall. The house was dark, as always at this time of day in winter. She heard the refrigerator door close, heard the beep of the answering machine, crossed the shadowy living room to the flashing red light, pressed the button.

"Francie? Nora. I was going to swing by and ride out with you. Guess you've already left. See you there. God, I hate funerals, this one especially."

Francie reset the machine, stopped the beeping. She didn't call Nora, wasn't ready for that. What should she tell her? Everything? Why not? Was there any reason to go on keeping Ned's secrets? No. She thought of Savard— he had heard Ned's alibi, knew that secret, but hadn't told her. Ned's second secret: did its burden, too, sometimes grow intolerable, demand to be flaunted? Francie's memory readied the image seen through a keyhole. She closed her inner eye to it, or tried to, and returned to Savard. There was no reason he should have told her— he probably operated on a need-to-know basis, and in this case had decided she didn't fit the category. But then she remembered the little nod he'd given her, twice.

Francie went upstairs, through her bedroom, into the bathroom, drew a deep bath, stripped off her funeral clothes, lay in the tub. If there was no reason to keep Ned's secrets, there was no reason not to tell Nora. Oh, she didn't want to do that. How could she and Nora ever be the same? But were they the same now? Not really. It was a sham. So Nora had to be told. Tomorrow, not today: she needed breathing room.

There was a knock at the door.

"Francie? Is that you in there?"

"Who else would it be, Roger?"

"Of course, of course. Just being pleasant. There's dinner, whenever you're ready."

"I'm not hungry."

"One must eat, Francie dear."

Francie went downstairs in her robe.

"In here," Roger called from the dining room.

She entered the dining room. He'd set two places at one end of the table. Candles, the good silver, his grandmother's Sèvres. "Champagne, Roger?"

"Why not? Life does go on. Here we are, the proof." He filled two glasses, clinked them together in a toast, handed one to her. He drank, peered at her over his glass. "You look despondent, Francie."

"I'm all right."

"You'll feel much better after a little something." She sat down. "Isn't that what Winnie-the-Pooh used to say? A little something. Remember when the Latin translation came out? *Winnie-Ille-Pu.* Cute idea, wasn't it?"

"I don't remember, actually." But how she would have loved reading *Winnie-the-Pooh* to some child of her own. She took her first sip of the champagne, tasted nothing but the alcohol, downed half the glass in one swallow.

Roger raised the lid of a serving dish, revealing two plump and perfect omelettes. "An omelette sort of evening, don't you think?" he said, serving her.

Francie emptied her glass, refilled it. She began to feel, not better, simply less.

"*Bon appétit,*" said Roger, cutting a good-sized bite from his omelette. He looked up. "How do they say it in Italian?"

"The same. *Buon appetito.*"

"That's what I like about you, Francie. That flair." He chewed his omelette, patted the corners of his mouth with a napkin. "How do you like it?"

Francie tried some. "I can't believe how good you are at this."

"Pshaw," he said, waving off the compliment, an awkward gesture that overturned his glass, which knocked down hers as well. "Shit," he said, rising abruptly, sopping up champagne with his napkin. He took the glasses, both broken, to the kitchen, returned with sponges, new glasses, another bottle. "Oh, well," he said, filling the glasses from the first bottle, uncorking the second, "accidents happen, do they not?"

Francie drank, refilled her glass from what was left in the first bottle.

Roger returned to his omelette, wielding knife and fork, silver clinking on china. "How went the tree-trimming?"

"What you'd expect."

"And Ned? It is Ned, isn't it—name never anchored itself in my mind, for some reason. How is he taking it?"

Francie rose, too abruptly, and something silver clanged to the floor. "I'm sorry, Roger, I'm very tired. The dinner's very good, and it was . . . kind of you to prepare it, but I'm going to bed."

"I understand completely. Why don't you take the bottle with you?"

"Thanks. I think I will."

"Good night, then. Sleep well."

Francie went upstairs, taking the bottle and her glass, closed her door, got into bed, drank a glassful and then another. She put the glass on the bedside table and turned off the light.

Francie closed her eyes. *No tears, just sleep, go numb.* But first her mind tormented her with a parade of images: Ned in his kayak, Em on a skateboard, Anne at the net; Kira Chang. They faded when they'd had enough, and her last thoughts were of Roger: how nice he'd been, even considerate. She thought of going downstairs, inviting him up to lie with her. Would there be comfort in that, an omelette sort of thing? But no. And apartment hunting still began tomorrow.

"Mr. Savard? Nora Levin, returning your call."

"Thank you. I've got a few questions about the murder of Anne Franklin."

"I thought you had a suspect."

"We do. But I'm still puzzled about what she was doing at that cottage, and wondered if you had any ideas."

Pause. "No."

"Were you aware that she made an attempt to leave some clue about the murderer?"

"No."

"She wrote the word *painting* on the floor of the cottage. Does that mean anything to you?"

"I know she painted."

"I've checked all her paintings. I don't think that's what she meant. Is there some other painting she may have been referring to, a valuable one, perhaps?"

Silence.

"She wrote the word in her own blood, by the way," Savard added. *"Painting."*

He heard the woman inhale. "I have one thought," she said. "But I'm not even sure what I saw, let alone whether it's relevant."

Roger finished eating, left the rest of his champagne untouched, cleared the table. He scraped the leavings into the garbage disposal, loaded the dishwasher, except for the champagne flutes and the Sèvres, which he washed by hand, turned the machine on, using the energy-saver switch. He dried the glasses and the china, put them back in their cupboards, returned to the dining room and blew out the candles. Then he sat at the kitchen table and did nothing. The house was silent.

An hour later, by the clock, he rose, removed his shoes, went upstairs. He put his ear to Francie's door, listened, heard nothing. Francie had come through beautifully tonight, looking the part to perfection. *Despondent, officer, if I had to put it in a word. I tried to cheer her up, but . . .* Roger went into the guest bathroom at the end of the hall, returned with a towel, left it lying by the door. Then he started down to his basement HQ, where the pipeline project awaited.

First, like a surgeon, gloves. Then into the garage, the windowless garage, invisible. Roger stuck one end of the three linked garden hoses into the tailpipe of Francie's car. He secured the connection with duct tape, triple-wrapping the tape two or three feet along the hose, making it absolutely leakproof. He paused. Would used duct tape, found in the trash, say, constitute evidence, dangerous to him in any way? Probably not, but he made a note to ball up the remains afterward and melt them away on the stove, just to be safe. The hoses he would disconnect, recoil, put back in the storage room until spring. Anything else? No. He opened the door to Francie's car. Her key was in the ignition, where she always left it when parked in the garage, despite his every admonition. Taking hold of the key between gloved forefinger and thumb, Roger turned it, started the engine. He held the open end of the hose close to his face and felt a warm little breeze.

Then, out of the garage, up the stairs, uncoiling the hose, his mind making silent chortles as he went. First floor, through the kitchen, around into the first-floor hall, up the stairs, into the second-floor hall. He switched

off the lights and walked softly to her door. About five or
six feet of hose left: perfect.

Nora and Savard stood before the half-size wooden
lockers in the corridor leading to the indoor courts at the
tennis club.

"This one," Nora said.

"I'd need a warrant."

"And what if I did it?"

"That would be a crime."

"Arrest me," Nora said. She kicked in the locker.

Roger listened at the door again. Silence. *Are you
sleeping, are you sleeping?* Of course she was. Lethe,
refuge of the guilty feminine mind. Now came the tricky
part, the only tricky part, really. With the end of the hose
in his left hand, he took the doorknob in his right and
turned it slowly, very slowly, very silently, as far as it
would go. Then, holding it there, he knelt and pushed the
door open an inch, very slowly, very silently. He laid
the end of the hose on the rug inside the bedroom, closed
the door back over it, flattening the plastic only negli-
gibly. Then, door closed, the turning back of the knob,
very slowly, very silently. Done. Still kneeling, Roger
rolled the towel he'd left there—to be laundered later
in the unlikely event it retained gas residue—into a long
sausage and aligned it firmly in the strip under the door.
Done and done! Roger knelt in front of Francie's door
for five full minutes, by his watch, and heard not a sound,
not a whisper of a sound, from the other side. He rose at
the end of the fifth minute precisely. How did they say
"the end" in Italy? Oh, Roger: perfect, perfect, perfect.

And then the light went on.

"I get it," Whitey said.

Roger spun around. Whitey! There was Whitey filling

the hall, crude stitches in his face, an ax in his hands. Any other relevant details? *No.* How did he get into the house, for instance? Roger's brain turned on him: *not relevant, not relevant, not relevant. Let me think.*

"I get it now," Whitey said.

Think.

But how, with that look in Whitey's eyes?

Think.

"Get ready to have your dreams twisted," Whitey said. Or some such gibberish. "You couldn't possibly 'get it,' Whitey."

"You must think I'm pretty dumb." Whitey took a step toward him.

"Not at all, not at all," Roger said, and what presence of mind, to keep his voice down like that. "You misunderstand me. The point, the salient point, Whitey, is that"—*Yes! Brilliant! Back in control!*—"we're both victims here."

"I'm nobody's victim," Whitey said, and took another step.

"Not victims in the sense you mean. I'm speaking metaphorically, if you will. The background is rather complex, but try to focus on the idea that everything can still work, surprisingly smoothly, even, if you—if we—keep our wits about us. The first step would be to switch that light back off."

Whitey did not. Neither did the look in his eyes disappear; in fact, it grew madder. "You set me up," he said.

"Oh, so that's it," said Roger. "Nothing could be further from the truth. But before I explain, I must ask you to keep your voice down."

Whitey did not. "There was no painting in the first place," he said.

"Certainly there was. I had it in my own hands at one stage in the proceedings." *Think. What is the goal? To get that ax, to drive it through Whitey's skull.* "What you must understand, what you've got to take on board, as it were, is that we've both been manipulated by a third party. Why don't we put down that implement, so out of place in a domestic setting like this, and go downstairs for a quiet discussion?" *Drive it through Whitey's skull, and then through Francie's, aborting the CO procedure.* An improvisation of an improvisation that could still work—his brain was already sketching in the adjustments.

Whitey's hands tightened on the handle; Roger saw the tendons pop out. "No one manipulates me," he said.

"Am I not aware of that?" *Adjust, adjust.* "And because of that attribute, so prominent in your character, this is going to be your lucky day."

"How's that?"

"Because the opportunity has arisen for taking revenge on your manipulator. Putative manipulator," Roger amended, to forestall another touchy reaction.

Whitey took another step, was now no more than six feet away. "You killed Ma," he said.

Perhaps *revenge* had been too potent a word, perhaps he'd introduced it too abruptly into the mix, too unadorned. But a daring counter presented itself; no time for even his brain to think it through to the end, but the feeling surrounding it was the feeling that always accompanied his best ideas. "I did it for you, Whitey."

Whitey, who appeared to be on the verge of taking another step, paused. "For me?"

Got him! "We're partners, Whitey. I'm on your side."

"What do you mean you did it for me?"

"I'm familiar with the psychiatrist's testimony, Whitey. I know she's responsible for the . . . perturbations in your past."

"Perturbations? Are you accusing me of fucking my own mother?"

"No, no, no. Perturbations, Whitey." How to explain it? *Think, think.* Whitey took another step. "Ups and downs," Roger said, perhaps too explosively, perhaps too loud. "Ups and downs."

Whitey halted. "You killed her because of that?"

"If I've gone too far, forgive me, Whitey. It was with the best intentions. And what kind of a life did she have, anyway? The crux of the matter is that we're partners. Share and share alike. If you've spent any time in this house, you know a certain amount of wealth is represented. Why, the Arp alone is worth its weight in gold."

"What's an arp?"

"What a character you are," Roger said. "He was a famous sculptor, and I've got a rare piece of his, down on the bookcase in the living room. For your next birthday, shall we say? Why don't we go down and take a peek at it?"

"Fuck that," Whitey said. And that look in his eye, the one Roger didn't like, which had faded a bit, intensified. Unaccountable.

"I hope I haven't offended you, Whitey. As your partner, the last thing I'd want to do is violate your amour propre in any way."

Whitey made a little flicking gesture with the blade of the ax, as though warding off insects, came closer, close enough for Roger to see the tiny drops of pus seeping through his stitches. "Killed her and set me up for that, too."

"No, no, no. Didn't you hear what I just said?" *Heard, but not understood. Yes, dumb, a dumb animal, almost preverbal. How to put it in his vernacular, to accord him the respect his like always craved? What is the right vulgarism? Something bodily, no doubt. How about:* "I wouldn't step on your toes, Whitey. Not for anything."

The expression in Whitey's eyes worsened dramatically,

became animal, in fact, and Roger's mind flashed a quick memory of the eyes of a wolverine he'd cornered in the boathouse at the Adirondack camp as a boy. "But you did step on my toe, you son of a bitch," Whitey said, and raised the ax.

Not getting through, not getting through. Roger's brain was frantically pursuing various strategies, spinning with permutations and combinations, scattering scraps and tailings of this or that scenario in the mental air—*think, moron, think*—when the door opened at his back.

Francie peered out, blinking in the light. "What's all the noise, Roger?" she said. "And I smell something odd."

"Impossible," Roger said. "It's completely odorless."

Francie's eyes adjusted to the light. She saw the second man, recognized him at once from the police photograph—Whitey something. His eyes, awful eyes, locked on hers. She looked to Roger. "What's going on?"

"Improvise," Roger said, more like a mumble, as if to himself.

"What are you talking about?"

"The chaos butterfly," Roger replied.

"I don't understand you."

Roger snapped his fingers. "But I understand you," he said, "only too well." He pointed at her, his eyes every bit as awful as Whitey's but in a different way. "There's your manipulator, Whitey, at long last. This is your big chance. The only chance you'll ever have. I can't dumb it down any more than that. Don't blow it."

Odorless? Manipulator? Butterflies? What was he saying? Francie opened her mouth to speak, but Whitey spoke first.

"I won't blow it," he said. "But she'll keep."

"No," Roger said, "that's specious reasoning, if we can even dignify it with the term. You can't possibly—"

"Shut the fuck up," Whitey said, and swung the ax like a baseball bat—Roger's eyes incredulous—swung it so hard Francie heard it whistle in the air, right through Roger's neck, the blade sinking deep into the wall. Then came a horror of spouting blood and screams, hers and Whitey's, and in that time of horror and nothing else, with the ax stuck in the wall, Francie had her chance, too, her only chance, to get away, but she froze.

The screaming stopped. Whitey jerked the ax out of the wall. He stared at her. "You're just like her," he said, "but way better."

Francie closed the robe at her throat. Was he talking about Anne? Anne's killer, talking to her like this? She shook, but felt nothing but fury. It washed away everything else—horror, fear, grief, confusion.

"Never," she said.

"What do you mean, never? I haven't even said anything yet." He came toward her, still holding the ax, but in one hand now and low, the blade dripping.

"Never," Francie said, and heard for the second time that day the sound of her inner voice, her true voice.

"You got that wrong," Whitey said, still coming. "Like right now is when, while we got this buzz buzz happening. It's going to be incredible. Master's away and puppet plays. Fuckin' poetry."

His free hand flashed out, very quick, got hold of Francie's robe. "Don't you touch me," she said, and kicked him in the groin with every bit of strength she had. He doubled up, blocking the hall. She kicked him again, not as accurately, and got both hands on the ax, yanked it, but not free. He held on. They wrestled for it. And fell, rolling down the bloody hall, coming to the top of the stairs with him on top, the ax handle caught between them. Whitey wedged his forearm into her throat.

So heavy. So strong.

"Going to be even better now," Whitey said. "I like all the smells." He arched his back, pulled at the ax handle, forced it slowly up between their bodies, the blade slicing through Francie's robe. He gazed down at her, his face a foot away. "I'm going to come in holes you don't even have yet."

Every hair on her body stood on end. *Never.* Francie got a hand free, tore at his face, tore and tore and tore, ripping out the stitches, redoing all Anne had done, and more. Whitey screamed, jerked aside. Francie scrambled out from under him, grabbed the ax, rose, and was starting to swing it when he charged up from under her, inside the arc, caught her in the stomach with his shoulder, and she went down with him on top again, and again they were rolling, but this time down the stairs, Francie, Whitey, the ax, rolling, tangling together in—what was it? A garden hose. Francie got her hand on the hose, whipped a length of it around Whitey's neck as they fell, tried to jam it between the banisters, tried to break his neck, but he punched her, full in the face and very hard, and she let go.

Then they were on the floor in the hall, and Whitey was up first, both lips split wide, baring all his teeth. Bleeding all over, but up first, and with the ax, while she was still down—and everything had gone snowy, like bad reception.

"Nice try," Whitey said, looming over her. He raised the ax.

The hose: wrapped around his ankles. Francie rolled aside, but so slowly, as the ax came down, and pulled, but so weakly, on the hose. Whitey lost his balance, almost fell, but didn't. Francie heard the thunk of the blade sinking deep, felt no new pain. Whitey went still.

"You stupid bitch," he said.

Francie, on the floor, saw his leg, inches away, and the ax, buried deep in his thigh, and high up.

"Thought you could trip me?" he said. "With my sense of balance?"

He pulled the ax out, stood over her, started his backswing—but blood came gushing from his leg. Francie could hear the flow. He gazed down at what was happening, went white. He toppled over soon after. Francie lay on the floor as the warm pool grew around her.

Splintering sounds at the front door. Francie sat up. The door cracked open. Savard burst in, and others. They said, "Oh, God," and things like that.

He knelt beside her.

"Sorry I'm so goddamn slow," he said. "You all right?"

"No."

He took a long look at Whitey.

"Why are you looking like that?"

"I don't mean to be looking like anything." He turned to her, the savage expression still on his face. "I owe you," he said.

Francie started crying.

"Don't cry."

But she couldn't stop. She cried and cried. "Is it all right, Anne? Is it all right?"

He picked her up and carried her outside. Flashing lights everywhere. "Oh, Anne." But she said the name softly now, and soon got hold of herself.

"I can walk."

"You're sure?" He watched her carefully, his face softened now, close to hers.

"Yes."

He put her gently down. Nora ran up from a squad car, took Francie in her arms. "It wasn't your fault."

"Whose was it?"

"Not yours, sugar, not yours."

Would she ever be able to talk herself into that?

Someone in the house said, "Open the windows."

36

Francie didn't hear from Savard until the spring, a few days after Nora's wedding; she thought she knew why he'd waited. "Read about it in the *Globe*," he said. "Were you there?"

"Of course."

"Nice time?"

"Very."

"I'm not married, myself."

There was a silence.

"Ice is breaking up," Savard said at last.

"You called to tell me that?"

"Not really. I wondered if you were interested in bears."

"I know nothing about them."

"Good. Maybe you'd come up here and take a look at something for me."

Francie went. Savard met her in Lawton Center, shook her hand. His was big and warm, full of latent strength but reserved at the same time, if she could read that much in a handshake. "You're aware of this supposed resemblance to my former wife?" he said, his gaze on Francie's face.

"Yes."

"I don't see it at all."

He drove her in the Bronco out to his cabin on Little Joe Lake. The radio was on.

"—and we're delighted to welcome a new station to the *Intimately Yours* network today, KPLA in Los Angeles. My name's—"

Savard switched it off. With Em in the house: that was the part Francie still hadn't been able to understand. At that moment, the same moment she realized Savard must have had the radio on for a purpose, she remembered something Anne had said, just before asking for a surefire recipe: *He cares so much about his career.* Maybe in the end Em had come second, not first. The burning-up feeling, which had accompanied every thought of Ned since that last day in his house, was absent for the first time.

Savard parked by the shore of the lake. It was a clear, windless day, the blue sky reflecting dully off the still-frozen perimeter, brightly off the open water beyond. They got out of the car, approached the little footbridge. Francie stopped. "I'm a poor picker of men," she said.

Savard started to reply, held it inside.

"Go ahead," Francie said.

"One out of three ain't bad."

Francie laughed, her natural reaction, and she let it happen. They walked across the bridge to the cabin, where Savard paused and added, "If I'm not being presumptuous."

Their eyes met. "Let's see these bears of yours," Francie said.

Savard nodded. "But I want your true opinion."

"Everyone says that."

"They do?"

"But no one means it."

Savard went a little pale. He unlocked the door. "After you."

Francie walked into the cabin and looked around for what seemed to Savard an unendurably long time.

"So?" he said. "Good or bad?"

Don't miss Peter Abrahams's next thriller,
CRYING WOLF,
coming from Ballantine Books in March 2000.

For Nat, a shining all-American boy with blue-collar roots, acceptance to New England's exclusive Inverness College seems like the opportunity of a lifetime. Then he meets Grace and Izzie Zorn, twin sisters who, although biologically identical, are utterly different. Thrown off by the irresistible attraction of this astonishing pair, Nat's moral compass starts to fail him. Together they discover a long-forgotten tunnel beneath the school's campus, where an innocent game will take a horrifying turn.

. . . Nothing bad was supposed to happen. They were only crying wolf. Who knew the wolf would be real?

PETER ABRAHAMS
CRYING WOLF

For a sneak preview, please read on . . .

"'*Beyond Good and Evil*'—part one," said Professor Uzig. Philosophy 322 met in the small domed room at the top of Goodrich Hall, one floor above the professor's office. Windows all around and lots of wood—mahogany molding, wide-plank pine floor, oval cherrywood table, and sitting at it Professor Uzig, Nat, Grace, Izzie, and four other freshmen, only one of whom, the top student in his English class the previous semester, Nat knew. "Who wants to go first?"

Everyone looked at everyone. No one spoke. Outside, Nat saw a crow fly by, and beyond it a black plume of smoke rose from somewhere in the lower town, an area he'd not yet set foot in. The flats, they called it, probably where the security officer, and all the hardware clerks, maintenance people, gardeners, secretaries, receptionists, lived. He looked back across the table, found Izzie gazing at him. Grace, too. They both gave him a little nod, the same nod exactly, and at exactly the same instant. And despite the fact that he had barely had time to get through the reading once, finding it by far the hardest text he'd ever come across, despite his certainty that he didn't understand it well, or possibly at all, a thought came to him, and he uttered it aloud: "Does the very fact that most people think something make it automatically wrong?"

Silence.

The crow, or another one, cawed nearby.

Then the bright girl from English 103 said, "Yeah. What is

all that rising above the common herd stuff about? Sounds kind of elitist to me."

Grace snorted.

Izzie said, "Maybe he is elitist, but there's something almost . . . sweet about him at the same time."

And someone else said: "Sweet? Nietzsche? He was a syphilitic, dangerous bastard."

And they were off.

They talked about the fatalism of the weak-willed, the charm of the refutable idea, and how living things must vent their strength; about the will to power, Wagner, the Nazis and Hitler, and how the true and selfless may be inextricably linked, possibly identical to, the false and appetitive; they talked about the pressure of the herd and the courage of the original thinker; they talked about Friedrich Nietzsche. Professor Uzig hardly spoke, just sat in his captain's chair—none of the other chairs had arms—still and neat in his white shirt, navy tie, charcoal-gray tweed jacket, but dominated completely by the intensity of his concentration. Nat could feel him listening, feel him judging, and was sure the others could, too. But what judgments he was coming to remained unknown, with one exception. A bearded student wearing a tie-dyed shirt asked when they would be getting to Kurt Cobain, and Professor Uzig replied, "What's the point of developing powerful analytical tools if all you're going to do is waste them on popular culture?"

The bearded student said, "But I thought . . ." and looked around for help. None came.

Just the same, Nat began to see the connection between Nietzsche and Kurt Cobain, not only Kurt Cobain, but so much of modern life, began to understand what Professor Uzig had been saying about Nietzsche's influence down on Aubrey Cay. For example, hadn't he read something in part one about how even the laws of physics might be subjective? He was searching for the quotation, leafing quickly through his copy of *Beyond Good and Evil*, when he heard Professor Uzig saying, "Until tomorrow, then."

The chapel bell tolled. Class was over. Ninety minutes, go

like that. The sound of the bell, by now so familiar, seemed strange for a moment.

A foot pressed his under the table. He looked across at Izzie, writing in her datebook, her golden-brown hair hanging over the page: dyed hair, he knew that now. His mind, already racing, began racing in another direction.

Grace, sitting beside Izzie, caught his eye. "I'm hungry," she said.

The three of them ate in the lounge at the student union: yogurt for Izzie, chocolate cake for Grace, an apple for Nat, unable to afford much eating off the meal plan. He noticed the empty space where the high-definition TV had been, told them about Wags and the theft of the two TVs.

"Were you scared?"

"A ponytail?"

"He just disappeared?"

Nat took them down to the basement corridor in Plessey Hall. He showed them the padlocked doors to the storage lockers and the maintenance room, and the only unlocked door, the one to the janitor's closet.

Grace opened it. They regarded the brooms, mops, buckets, cleansers.

"Wags did the same thing the year he was at Choate," Izzie said.

"What same thing?" said Nat.

"The breakdown thing. Drugs."

Grace was inside the closet now, rummaging around. Without looking, Izzie reached out and took Nat's hand.

"Drugs?" he said. "I never saw him with any drugs."

"The damage was done."

Inside the closet, Grace said, "I've had an original thought."

"Don't scare me," Izzie said.

Grace laughed, turned sideways—Izzie letting go his hand he instant before—raised one foot high like a trained Thai oxer, and kicked the back wall of the closet with a force that tartled Nat. The top half of the wall fell out in one solid panel, ropping into darkness on the other side.

They crowded into the closet, peered through the opening. Beyond lay a narrow unlit tunnel, narrow but tall enough to stand in, with one large-diameter pipe and several smaller ones receding into the shadows and finally disappearing into complete blackness.

"This looks like fun," Grace said.

"Uh-oh," said Izzie.

CRYING WOLF
by Peter Abrahams
Published by Ballantine Books.
Available in hardcover in March 2000.